# A TALE OF FOUR PLANETS

A Tale of Four Planets
Book Two: The Rejected Counsel of Oomb

A Novel by David Taylor

ISBN: 978-1-62137-997-3 (softcover)
ISBN: 978-1-62137-998-0 (ebook)
Library of Congress Number on file with publisher.

Published 2017 by Virtualbookworm.com Publishing Inc., P.O. Box 9949, College Station, TX 77842, US. 

# BOOK TWO:

# THE REJECTED COUNSEL OF OOMB

a novel by David Taylor

"I believe that unarmed truth and unconditional love will have the final word in reality."
-Dr. Martin Luther King, Jr.

dedicated to my family

# Contents

# Philly No-Zone, 2062

"In other news, the American Union Space Agency reports the Smoke and Mirrors is only hours out from its destination, nearly seven light-years away. The world-famous, out-of-this-world-famous spaceship is returning to the planet, Oomb. Oomb, of course, is the name given by its ancestors, the same as our ancestors named our planet Earth. It's the fourth of eight planets in the Callaway X Centra solar system.

"Terraforming engineers have joined the Smoke and Mirrors crew for this historic second mission. They will be conducting what government officials are terming immigration feasibility studies. Those engineers, together with select others, will actually set up camp, down on the planet's surface. They are bringing along crops for harvesting, including soybean and tomatoes. They want to learn how well Earth plants and themselves as Earth animals can adapt to the local ecology, and how well the local ecology can adapt to Earth plants and Earth animals. They will especially want to gauge the impact on the resident intelligent species, the Oombians. The Oombians look like trees, but they can walk and fly, and they play a game called 'oof,' remarkably similar to golf. As well, the Oombians demonstrate extraordinary telepathic abilities.

"The Smoke and Mirrors's second mission will also take our brave astronauts back to the planet Fafama in solar system Alpha Centauri C, a mere five light-years away from Earth. Fafama, of course, is where we made the first direct contact with an extraterrestrial intelligence, after we received messages from there which welcomed our communication.

"Captain Helena Taylor made all kinds of news

heading up the first humanned mission outside our solar system. This mission almost ended in disaster, after the starship's calamitous encounter with an ice comet. On the second mission, we can expect Taylor and her crew will be making lots more news. But as you saw here first in an exclusive WVAU WOW-team report, her daughter is garnering some headlines of her own, with a different sort of frontier exploration. Yesterday, I caught up with Shelly Taylor in the Philadelphia quarantine zone, the so-called No-Zone, where she explained a little of *her* mission. For the full half-hour interview, please join us tonight at 11:30. But right now, here are some excerpts."

"...Are we going to get to see your Mom dancing with one of the tree persons on Oomb?"

"Actually, I think my Dad might steal the spotlight. He's a golf fanatic, and is looking forward to trying their game that's like golf. I think they call it 'oof.'"

"How *did* your father feel about watching his wife 'bust a move' with an extraterrestrial political leader on Fafama?"...

..."What are you expecting to accomplish in the Philadelphia quarantine zone?"

"The Philadelphia zone is one of the oldest, along with portions of NewYork City, Baltimore and Miami. As I'm sure many people already know, the first quarantines were quarantines in their original sense. Um, they were supposed to protect the larger population from dangerous infectious disease, stem its spread. And they were supposed to be temporary. What we were dealing with was a bacterium similar to typhoid fever. It got incubated in the streets transformed into Venetian-style canals by the rising waters from global warming. But with that other epidemic of rising gang violence,-"

"Ms. Taylor, we don't want to minimize the salience

of your history lesson. Maybe we'll have time to return to that. But if you could just tell us, in a few words, what you're hoping to accomplish...?"...

..."Flamboyo Sanchez, here, is one of many heroes of the Philly No-Zone. He's one of several reasons it should go back to being the Philly Yes-Zone."

"Mr. Sanchez, thank you for joining us for this interview."

"Ms. Taylor asked. How could I refuse?"

"Ms. Taylor has placed a lot of weight on your shoulders, hasn't she?, terming you a hero?"

"I'm no hero. All I do is organize young people to get some exercise and help with the trash cleanup."

"Flamboyo is as modest as he is handsome, Joyce. He led the recruitment of other adults for a neighborhood watch group. They call themselves Eyes On The Prize. Thanks to their efforts, thousands of boys and girls can safely run, skip, and hop, plus remove garbage off the sidewalks. Without neighborhood watch protection, those children couldn't even go from one street corner to the next without putting their lives at risk."

Dr. Morel Engeling left off from reading the transcript crawl on the TV screen mounted above an abundance of liquor and wine bottles. In its place, he stared down Flamboyo. Flamboyo was seated beside him at the bar. Seething contempt laced Engeling's amusement, as he uttered in his faintest voice, "So, Captain Taylor's self-congratulating savior of the no-zones is virtually leading you around on a leash with her condescending flattery...leading you around," Engeling bared his teeth in a snarly hiss, "because how could you refuse her slightest request?"

"I would have thought someone of your perceptiveness would have seen more easily through my act than that delusional-" Flamboyo spat out the crassest possible swear word with most sincere bitterness. It didn't matter to him, that Shelly might have taken deep offense. He was certain many other privileged viewers of the just-aired news segment would also have taken deep offense...far more offense than they likely ever took to the conditions children as much as adults had to endure in the no-zone. By comparison, to what did mere foul cussing amount? Partly, Flamboyo's bitterness was about that. And partly it was about Shelly's boyfriend in the picture meaning unbearable disappointment. That was, were Flamboyo to ever allow her flattery to get to him to any significant extent...as though it hadn't already.

Dr. Engeling nodded knowingly with his persistently piercing stare. For Flamboyo, it gave the man's grin an unsettling likeness to a bare human skull's visage. "Curse to your satisfaction, Señor Sanchez. But, speaking of delusional, don't delude yourself. Don't think you're at all persuading me this Shelly Taylor woman means nothing to you. Something about men who try to project virility through their utterance of words they know wound the sensibilities of others. It's how utterly insecure they really are. Like they aren't sure, beyond carelessly offending others who shouldn't be so easily offended, that they have much to substantially offer. In short, I find myself questioning the wisdom of having reached out to you in particular. More mistakes like this, and I'm going to get myself resurrected."

"Who the- Look, man..." Flamboyo's head careened about wildly, as he abruptly changed course from cussing anew.

Engeling knew how easily he could have mocked Flamboyo Sanchez, simply by expressing wonder over how Flamboyo didn't get whiplash.

"They are words. Words." Flamboyo couldn't help grinning self-consciously.

"So, I'm putting my fate in the hands of a rudderless politician who worries way too much over what other people might think. Even in my case where you couldn't offend me if you tried."

Flamboyo shook his head tentatively, then with certain fury. It was as much to shake himself out of drawing his gun to blow off Engeling's head as anything else. "Man, you have no idea who you're dealing with." Flamboyo's head-shaking slowed. He was back to a controlled simmer. "With a tug on my earlobe, man, that's all it would have taken. I could have had you pumped full of lead for your welcome to the no-zone!"

"Look." Engeling opened his arms expansively to go with his conciliatory, backing-off tone of voice. "What I'm saying is, this Good Samaritan routine of yours, giving those children false hope, it might have worked. It might have intoxicated the authorities under-the-table-careless of your comings and goings, more's the better for my plans. Or conversely, dealing with me might trick your less-naive associates into allowing you to safely continue with your most cherished mission after all, where those wretched kids' false hope is matched by your own. Either way, you have to understand that once you allowed the space hero's daughter into your scheme, you put a bull's-eye on your back. And for my purposes, that negates you as an asset. Tug on your earlobe to have me picked off now if you must."

Flamboyo's grin stretched from ear to ear, like his grandfather Roberto's used to. "So you don't know shit about who you're dealing with, man! That's right! Shit!" *Think what you want about my foul language*. "But you're about to find out."

"I'm about to find out." Morel nodded mocking disbelief. But next thing he knew, another guy in the tavern threw back his chair as he lurched to his feet and shouted Flamboyo's way, "Hey?! Saint Sanchez?! Makes no f-n' difference what your f-n' game is! It ends here!!"

Flamboyo Sanchez dove under the small circular table and bar stool, pulling Engeling with him. Simultaneously, the man who feigned his rage was directed at "Saint Sanchez" whipped out a pistol from his tattered sweater, and he started firing.

When Flamboyo popped up from under the table to shoot back, he made it appear he was lashing out wildly. Engeling and any other witnesses were supposed to believe Flamboyo sprayed bullets everywhere in the hope one of them would find its mark. But Flamboyo took care his retaliation came close, without in fact hitting his most trusted associate who started the gun fight. Wood splinters burst like fireworks from table and chairs both, all around Flamboyo's feigned target. Said feigned target was likewise careful not to wound Flamboyo as he easily, fatally could have.

No matter their mutual effort. The bartender shot a projectile the size of a sewing needle out of his shirt sleeve. The trigger was activated by an intentional arm muscle twitch. It found the left cheek of Flamboyo's pretend would-be assassin. Another twitch activated the detonator, to blow his head off. But to the bartender's horror, the decapitated person, with only a smoking spinal column stump remaining above the neckline, got off one more shot before he slumped lifeless to the floor. This gunshot shattered the forehead of a government agent, as he peeked out from under the table where he dove for cover. Said agent had been following Flamboyo.

"So what, you scratched at your cheek, tugged at an ear lobe?"

"Too obvious." Flamboyo exercised every last ounce of self-control to affect listless apathy. This, as he untied a rowboat where it was moored on the North Hancock Street Canal, one of a network dug years previous to help control rising-sea-level flooding. The gentle lapping of tidal water against crumbling cement street curbs helped to sooth his nerves. "The code was in how I placed my fingers on my beer can."

"Okay, so now you're sure you've taken the bull's-eye off your back."

"That's right, man. I could be feeding fish and bread to every no-zone kid. The powers that be will still sit by idly while someone turns me into a six-piece dinner, because thank God I'm a target of terrorists! Which means I can't possibly be a part of any terrorist plot myself!"

"And you've got others willing to do what, um, he did?" Engeling had to settle with nodding back behind himself in the direction of the bar. His hands were too occupied with oar rowing, for him to point.

"*I'm* ready to do what he did, man!"

"So long as you don't go soft on me with that delusional liberator of the no-zone."

"Okay, man, why you don't tell me what it is exactly I'm not going soft on you about, huh? Why am I not looking to have *your* head blown off so you can join my most trusted associate?"

To answer that question, Dr. Morel Engeling was not about to tell his whole life's story. Flamboyo was already well aware of everything about Engeling reported in the press. Dr. Engeling had been an applied astrophysicist with highest security clearance. But then he had committed suicide, apparently, diving into water off

Cape Cod after dumping buckets of chum. His bitten-off foot was found washed ashore. Bull shark teeth were embedded in it, including one with a telltale sliver of herring impaled on it. The rest was detail of no particular interest to Flamboyo. There was plenty enough depravity which had led to his own sorry circumstances, without getting haunted by the depravity of others. Flamboyo didn't need to know how Engeling had performed surgery on his own self, attaching a prosthetic foot, to assure nobody else would learn he was still alive. Nor how Engeling had left the boat he took into the Atlantic to drift aimlessly, abandoned, while he rode out a storm on a special raft camouflaged to appear part of the sea, unless and until someone were to approach to within a few feet of it. Most importantly, years prior, there was how Engeling's father handled Morel Engeling's grief over his beloved older brother's sudden death. The rage that had fermented inside Engeling, in response to his father's mistreatment, had served him well when he had succeeded in goading the shark to attack him, once the chum had attracted it over to his boat. His mother considered herself helpless to stop her husband when he bound Morel, only five, to a bedpost with the understanding he would get untied after he stopped grieving. Morel's father took care to tie together his feet closer to the bedpost than his hands, so that once Morel lost his balance, he was falling back away from the bed, inflicting searing pain on his wrists. Grief over his brother blurred together with grief and terror over what his father was doing to him, and of course the relentless pain. Morel Engeling's seething rage against a world he wanted to damn if no God would, he found this rage to finally quiet down, the middle of the night, so his father would untie him. This was the rage that had gotten him through having a shark tear off his foot in aid of having the world believe he committed suicide. This was the rage that had sustained Morel long enough to hunt down Flamboyo Sanchez, after he hypothesized someone like Flamboyo and an organization like Flamboyo's organization must exist in at least one of the no-zones. And most importantly, this was the rage that had fueled the piecing together of a plan for which the likes of Flamboyo and his crew would be necessary to complete its execution. "There is an island in the Atlantic-" The wildness in Dr. Engeling's eyes as he spoke these words was unsettling enough to Flamboyo, he had to steel himself to keep from flinching out of a staredown with the man. "-that is unstable with geothermal activity. You understand what geothermal-"

"I know all about geothermal activity! Don't mess with me, man, don't mess with me!" Flamboyo's cautionary head-shake was as much more as he could add without coming totally unglued. He struggled to contain his furious torment over Luis getting his head blown off to serve the cause.

"It's possible that of its own accord, whether any day now, or in the next hundred years..." Morel wanted to do to Flamboyo what he'd brought himself to wanting to do to this father when he found the rage. But he stifled himself like he'd stifled himself finally when tied to the bedpost; if everything worked out well, Flamboyo and the rest of the unfit species - himself deservedly included for the damnable thoughts in his head - would soon enough be eradicated, a worthless pestilence banished from the universe. He kept reminding himself this was the common purpose that brought him and Flamboyo together. "...an entire mountainside of that island will slide into the sea. This will precipitate a one-hundred-foot tsunami along a forty-mile stretch of coastline somewhere between New York City and Miami. Strategically placed explosives can make the Kennedy Space Center Ground Zero for the wave surge. During the ensuing chaos, we hijack a shuttle pod from the space center. We chart an erratic moon trajectory to allow ample time to retrofit the pod with my hyper-magnet application. Meanwhile, you with your acquired communication skills keep begging off our fellow maggots in pursuit. You know. Maybe something about establishing a new outpost for the next garden of Eden. Somewhere to ferry your hopelessly damned children. You threaten we will blow ourselves up if the authorities try a boarding maneuver or some such. And you keep teasing them with hope they're making progress reasoning with you, appealing to your common sense. For example, suppose they prattle on about how impossible it would be to terraform a stable atmosphere on the moon, especially since we couldn't get away with that on Mars. You make noises like, 'Really? Then why can't we build a temporary settlement underneath some craters? The poor, orphaned children can romp around there while we work to dome over the surface.' You keep feeding them such rhetorical diuretics so they're too busy with their own verbal runs to suspect we're buying time. Once we're around to the dark side of the moon, we're going to send it on a path headed straight for the bull's eye."

"The Earth." Flamboyo let go his oars as it sank in what Morel was talking about.

"The home colony of the supreme pestilence trying to spread outside the solar system."

"You have the ability to push the moon with this hyper-magnet you mentioned?"

"Actually, we will employ two hyper-magnets. One of the hyper-magnets will be carried by the hijacked shuttle pod, the other landed on the lunar surface. Their like magnetic poles will be positioned to face one another, before the shuttle pod is accelerated on a crash course for the moon. Magnified magnetic repulsion will result, literally knocking the moon out of its orbit."

"So, you're- You're talking about- What exactly will happen-"

"The planet gets shattered apart!"

"So all life-"

"I'd reboot the whole universe if I had a plan! Damn!" Morel Engeling was cursing his own self, for having gotten so carried away with his revelry. The thing with the starship captain's daughter alone, Morel *knew*. In so many words he'd even told Flamboyo he knew. Flamboyo's level of nihilism didn't begin to approach his own. Maybe no one else's level of nihilism approached his own. Speaking of reboots... "Hey," he shook his head like he was coming out of a daze. He hoped Flamboyo wouldn't suspect this was calculated backpedaling. "Truth is, the moon will get shattered, not the Earth. It will add to the Earth's mass once all the dust settles out from the infestation-terminating global climate cataclysm. Give a rodent or some such a chance to evolve to do better, maybe."

"Okay, man, before we make even one more row of the oars," Flamboyo pulled in his set and slammed down the handles in the rowboat, "you need to understand something: I am at the point where, you tell me you got a plan to blow up the sun, I am in. If you're worried I might think there is anyone, anyone on this planet better off alive than dead, why not also worry the quarantine barriers are coming down any time soon? What we should be concerned about, I will give you this, is the full extent of your plan getting out to my crew. There probably are a few who still are naïve enough to believe anyone is salvageable, including their own sorry selves."

"That is expected," Morel nodded. He had to work hard to suppress an urge to add, *A man can tell you to your face he has given up all hope, and still be lying.* Because what Morel did trust was that were he to have added this comment, Flamboyo wouldn't have thought twice. He would have reduced his head to a smoldering vertebra stump as had happened to one of Flamboyo's "crew" in the drinking hole. And how ironic, for it would have been from Flamboyo's rage over having been forced to face the painful truth, that he could only dream of climbing to the level of nihilism where Dr. Morel Engeling himself had long since already made his ascent. This was why Dr. Engeling believed that in the last stage of the operation, he would need to commandeer the shuttle pod alone.

# Chapter 1

*Captain's Log: 12, 27, 2062 Earth Calendar*

"The Smoke and Mirrors has safely descended onto the outermost edge of the orbital plane of the Callaway X Centra system. Happily, we haven't lost a single advance guard firefly donut on our return flight here. We replicated the exact course we took out of the system on our limping way home a mere ten months ago. First Engineer Buddy Leung bet that lightning was not likely to strike twice, especially steering so high above the Oort Cloud boundaries. He was right.

"Our mobile tree friends on Oomb, I guess it's no metaphor for them when they pull up their roots to travel to a new location. Okay, I'm also guessing my comedic timing is no better printed than spoken. Best I leave the one-liners for my-"

Captain Taylor looked up from speaking into her paper-thin yet steely-stiff electronic journal sheet. She wanted to make certain her husband Chris was not present on the navigation bridge of the first full-sized spacecraft built by humans that could travel light-speed multiples. She didn't want him to see her delete "my" as in "my husband," and instead pick more neutral words from the choices the journal sheet offered. Her journal sheet arrived at those choices non-telepathically, in contrast to what said "tree friends on Oomb" had evolved to be capable of doing.

"Best I leave the funny stuff for Officer Olsen-Taylor's journal. But time is running short before government observer Louisa Entroper's-" Captain Taylor wanted to say: *Louisa Entroper's pathetic and condescending effort to make herself more useful, and by implication criticize my leadership into the bargain.* However, she opted to go with: "Time is running short before Dr. Entroper's insistently urged team-builder exercise. Still, I wish to dwell on a point of wonder. Suppose the Oombians had developed space travel, instead of deliberately opting not to bother. Suppose they had constructed a base for early warning detection of incoming asteroids and other potentially hazardous objects. Then suppose they had constructed that base on one of their solar system's outer planets, comparable to our dwarfs Pluto and Eris. In other words, it would have been along the lines of what we were expected to set up on our original mission before we got called off, answering the distress message from Fafama. Imagine the Oombians had done this early warning system, well prior to our arrival. For the keepers of such an outer planet outpost, just how would the Smoke and Mirrors have appeared as it swung by, at or near light speed?, assuming it swung by close enough for clear observation?"

Taylor set down her journal pad on her knees, to sit back and reflect. So easily did she shut out what was transpiring around about her on the navigation bridge of Earthling humanity's first starship, she may as well have been seated in an empty room. In her mind's eye, Captain Helena Taylor pictured the entirety of the Smoke and Mirrors in flight mode. From stem to stern, as it were. The captain visualized how an arrangement of petal-thin mirrors lent the likeness of a bloomed tulip, behemothly proportioned, to the starship's front end, and how a different arrangement of petal-thin mirrors made the starship's rear end amazingly comparable to a bloomed rose, also behemothly proportioned. She pictured the twelve-hundred-foot-long, so-called asparagus-stalk hull to which those mirror arrays were attached. Said cylindrical hull was two hundred twenty feet in diameter. A seventy-five-foot-diameter photon exhaust shaft ran its full length, from the "rose" to the "tulip," straight through its center. "To herald the Smoke and Mirrors's arrival," Helena resumed softly speaking into her journal pad, "does a monstrously sized flashlight beam, all dusty with outer space debris, seem to suddenly get turned on? And then, does the spaceship itself appear blurred, little more substantial than that beam it is riding?

"Meanwhile, what about those electromagnetically-charged mirror arrays, otherwise nicknamed the tulip and rose petals? Are they refusing to accept light's behavior as both a particle AND a wave? Is that the secret to what they are doing? No more Hamlet-style "to be AND not to be"? No more to particle photon AND non-particle wave? Rather, are the mirror arrays forcing light to choose its ultimate character? And is sparkling fairy dust the byproduct of that light-speed-cheating choice? Maybe that is not THE question. But it certainly is A question!

"With special interest will I follow the work of our guest theoretical physicist, Professor Timothy Aquinas on leave from Harvard. If I understand correctly, his current thinking is that Buddy's mirror array setups create a small black hole singularity in the photon exhaust shaft. The singularity sucks the spacecraft forward, and it also "sheds" gravity. At the top speed we've managed to accelerate the Smoke and Mirrors, we achieve a gravitational pull close to fifty-one per cent of what we experience on the Earth's surface. In Aquinas's estimation, our mirror array propulsion is far more complex than light merely pushing us along in some hyper version of a solar sail.

"Buddy and the professor do agree on one piece of

the puzzle. They agree that virtually all friction from any source in front of the Smoke and Mirrors, including and most notably all light friction, is effectively neutralized. This is accomplished by the tulip petal array in conjunction with the photon exhaust shaft. A strange enough notion, that light can provide friction resistance to an object moving forward, as assuredly as wind blowing in one's face.

"But the theoretical melee beyond this accepted reality gets even stranger.

"Buddy has his own peculiar notion. The way he tried to explain to training engineer Pedro Perez - and what a story that is in itself, how Mr. Perez has so fully embraced the future into which he was awoken! Anyhow, Buddy Leung's explanation, he has asked us to imagine someone going off the edge of a cliff. We know gravity is pulling that someone to her doom. Buddy suggests that the removal of all friction from ahead of the Smoke and Mirrors sends it falling forward off a figurative cliff. Plus, it's getting a big push from behind by a barrage of light, a barrage of light accelerated beyond its "normal" speed by the electromagnetically charged mirror arrays. Thanks to said profound influence, that barrage of light is pushing the starship against the curvature of space-time. It's like centripetal force combining with centrifugal inertia. A rolling ball meets the edge of a hole in the ground. For example, a golf ball meets the lip of the cup. When the ball rolls there at just the right angle and speed, it does not drop completely in. Rather, the golf ball drops only part of the way in, before it gets accelerated out of and away from the cup. It's what the solar clippers do when they round Mars for the slingshot effect back towards Earth. Officer Leung would have us believe the force of the electromagnetically enhanced light barrage slingshots the Smoke and Mirrors along the space-time curvature. Instead of dropping into the hole of an upper speed limit slower than "normal" light travels, our spacecraft gets accelerated rimming out away from that hole. Our spacecraft effectively gets 'rimmed out' towards a fifth-dimensional experience of its existence, where matter can easily travel well in excess of one hundred and eighty-six thousand miles per second."

Captain Helena Taylor lowered her journal pad to rest on her knees, so as to sit back, muse anew over Timothy Aquinas's behavior. The professor had strained to keep his reaction reserved, when Buddy first broached these curious thoughts on how the mirror array was able to propel the Smoke and Mirrors to speeds faster than light, and do that safely, without ripping apart the spaceship and its occupants. Aquinas had managed to sublimate everything save for an uncontrollable flinch. Then he had feigned nonchalance for uttering, "Well, you're the one who came up with the entire mirror array system in the first place. Until we can design the proper tests, who's to say you haven't also arrived at ultimately the best explanation we're to ever conceive for *why* the mirror array works?"

"Excuse me, Captain Taylor." A small yet spry woman stood before the captain's chair, holding forward a plate full of food.

"Let me guess. You're, um, Ludi's grandmother?"

"Norma Rivera, Captain Taylor. Please excuse my English. Is not so good for that I learning on your spaceship."

"Well, Señora Rivera, your English is much better than my Spanish. But what's this? You have a snack for me? It looks and smells delicious!"

"Is the first arroz- um, rice with- we say 'gandules,' is a

type of, um, yes, a bean we have in Puerto Rico. We say 'arroz con gandules.'"

"Arroz con gandules, mm." Helena had already taken in a sample on the offered fork.

"We grow the gandules fresh in the garden of the spaceship. Are the first gandules we pick, yes. You like?"

"Mm," Captain Taylor nodded, and awkwardly hurried her swallow. This, not because she was just trying to be polite; she really did find the rice with pigeon peas tasty. Rather, she wanted to get in an especially positive remark before what she well knew was the ongoing rush of events soon to be upon them. "Señora Sanchez, not only do I like this very much, it's the perfect complement to the music my- we have playing on the bridge! Um, I was told it's by a Puerto Rican group..."

"Sí," Norma nodded. "Is Haciendo Punto En Otro Son. Is difficult the translation in English. Is something like: Making a different music. Entonces, their music pleases you?"

"It's so full of energy! Maybe our engineers can find how to use that music to power our spaceships so we don't have to rely on mirrors."

"I am sorry, Captain Taylor, I no understand everything you say."

Helena made a dismissive gesture. She was about to assure Norma it was no big deal when-

"Ahh, aquí estás, mi cielito linda!" *Here you are, my pretty little heaven!* It was Norma's husband, Típico, poking his head around the corner of one of the entrances onto the ship's navigation bridge.

"Aye, Dios, no!" Norma blushed and laughed as she dove to one side of the captain's chair in a futile effort to keep hiding from her husband.

On their three-month voyage out to the Callaway X

Centra system, one of the Smoke and Mirrors crew's first priorities was to bring up to mid-twenty-first-century standards the health of the some two hundred people they had spirited out of a poor neighborhood in northern Philadelphia from the turn of the century. Among other situations, Chief Medical Officer Deborah Davis-Murphy and her team had had to deal with drug addiction, five pregnancies which included four mothers dangerously overweight, and Pedro Perez's broken back problem from a car accident suffered the previous year. That was, the previous year back six decades earlier. But one of the more interesting situations had involved the senior citizens. Between a strict exercise and diet regimen, and repair work on their telomeres (the ends of chromosomes that become frayed with aging), they were enjoying the sort of rejuvenation getting experienced by the more affluent members of society back on Earth. As a result, some of the men were turning obnoxiously amorous, with little regard for the decorum expected aboard a starship resettlement voyage to another solar system. Away from the Smoke and Mirrors, knowledge of people having gotten pulled out of the past was restricted to a small handful of government officials. But hardly anyone aboard the Smoke and Mirrors was *not* aware that Grandpa Típico spent most of his free time chasing his wife.

"Bailamos a la música, sí?" *We dance to the music, yes?* Don Típico, grinning from ear to ear, put one hand over his belly with his other hand extended to his side, as he swayed his hips for his entrance onto the bridge. He was dancing with himself until he could grab hold of his partner. Captain Taylor also got the impression he might as well have been wading his way into a party, how some people waded their way into a swimming pool. He was certainly dressed the part in his light-blue guayabera shirt.

"Careful that you don't bump into- Norma, can you please tell him in Spanish-"

"AIIEE!" Norma squealed as she broke into a run for an exit as Don Típico boogied round Helena's chair on his pursuit. He accelerated into a sprinted side-step that still coordinated perfectly with the shifting beats of the Puerto Rican music.

"Great." Captain Taylor threw up her hand not occupied with holding steady her plate of rice and pigeon peas, in resignation to the situation. She wanted to warn off Norma's husband from accidentally bumping against a navigation crew member, thus perhaps causing him or her to mess up some critical starship function. But thank goodness, Helena sighed with relief, Típico didn't turn his attention to trying to pull second-in-command Yoon-hee Park-Smith away from her master navigation console for some salsa or whatever type of wonderful music that Puerto Rican group was playing.

"Captain?"

Helena jumped, nearly let go of her plate, with Yoon-hee's sudden urgent-sounding utterance. Had Officer Park-Smith read her mind?

"Captain?" Yoon-hee repeated. "You're okay?" Yoon-hee's vision was glued to the panoramic view-screen. That screen displayed what was happening to matter and energy in the Smoke and Mirrors' path, anything that could offer the slightest resistance, friction to its forward momentum. It was all getting funneled, concentrated into that persistently mysteriously sparkling fairy-dust stream that did heaven-knew-what inside the photon exhaust chamber. Navigation Officer Yoon-hee Park-Smith often imagined how that stream got channeled by the mirror array "tulip bloom" at the front end of the starship into the cylindrical photon exhaust chamber. And then, how that stream flared out dramatically from the spaceship's rear, to get joined by ambient starlight as well as by laser beams from a laser lantern hung out the starship's rear. All that together, processed by the electromagnetically charged mirror array "rose bloom," in ways far from fully understood. In addition to the fairy-dust trail, Yoon-hee was also contemplating the very bright star that was Callaway X Centra. Still off in the distance, a sinewy thread of its light was nevertheless getting woven into said fairy dust. Despite these many focuses for her attention, however, Yoon-hee couldn't help also noticing the ruckus behind her.

"I'm fine, Yoon-hee, thank you. You were saying?"

"We're decelerating to three-quarters light-speed, Captain." Yoon-hee turned back over her shoulder. "You might want to either finish off your snack, or blanket it before it starts to scatter in the decreasing gravity."

Helena Taylor missed that last part, as – what awful timing! – Officer Louisa Entroper was entering onto the bridge the same instant Norma's husband was making his boogie exit. Típico didn't even have the courtesy to allow Entroper to go first. Rather, he squeezed past her. And to make matters even worse, on his way into that squeeze, he paused, appearing to size up the government observer as a possible dance partner. But then he shook his head dismissively and continued on his way. His side-steps gave the appearance of a one-man tango. Helena wondered what put him off about Louisa. Was it her snow-white mop-top?, in contrast to Norma's curls that still maintained their auburn shades? Was it the severe befuddled look Louisa gave him?, too shocked at his incivility to proceed herself until he had finished squeezing past her?

Whatever it was, Dr. Entroper made a show of closing her eyes and shaking her head, with as much untempered disgust as she could emanate without yielding to the temptation to simply blurt out, *This is no good!* Then she stationed herself directly before Helena to address her. "Captain Taylor,- Oh, can someone turn off that music?" An especially loud passage had kicked in. Several members of the Puerto Rican group, Haciendo Punto En Otro Son, were blending together their voices for a choral refrain Helena wished could be turned up even louder, to totally drown out Dr. Entroper. "Whose idea was it to pump that onto the bridge? I don't know how any of you can concentrate- Ah, thank you. Now I'm not saying I don't like that music." Louisa Entroper held forward a cautioning hand with the palm facing Captain Taylor. "It sounds wonderful! Who is it? Something from some people in your colonization project?"

"It's a Puerto Rican group Officer Olsen-Taylor has in his collection. He thought it might help bring everyone closer together."

"Well there's a time and a place for it, and this is neither the time nor the place. And be sure to inform your husband that some people might not appreciate being forced to listen to his music. It could have the exact opposite effect from what he was going for, and drive everyone further apart."

Yoon-hee was about to throw in that, for what it was worth, the complex percussion passages were helping her to stay focused and invigorated. But her memory of other crew members' experiences caused her to think better of engaging a tussle with Dr. Entroper.

"I will make a note of your concern, Louisa," Captain Taylor forced herself to nod deferentially, likewise steering clear of a tussle.

"Oh, it's more than just my concern, Captain." Dr. Entroper shook her head vigorously. "It's what years of behavioral research tell us. Now," she slapped her hands together and rubbed, "for this session, I'm taking you and Officer Kevin Smith-Park off the bridge. The activity works best in groups of no greater than twelve at a time, and I went to great lengths to get the mix on each team as varied as possible."

"Myself, I find that things get too tangled and the mattress doesn't give enough support when there are more than three." Over having precious moments about to get wasted, Kevin channeled his frustration into saying something crass. Better that than dealing with Entroper's wrath, were he to admit he'd rather hear more from Chris's bizarre music collection than attend her friggin' "team builder."

"Captain, can you twist my husband's ear for me?, especially painfully hard?"

"I'll leave that to you, Officer Park-Smith," Helena paused to say at the bridge exit, while wishing she could tell Louisa where she could stick her team-builder. "Captain's orders."

"Why Officer Smith-Park, I don't know what kind of team-builder <u>you</u> had in mind, but I don't think we'll be utilizing any mattresses," said Louisa. She sensed Kevin's irreverence was meant as a stand-in for the derogatory comment he didn't have the guts to make. But she still tried to react as though it was nothing more than good-natured repartee. Perhaps she could soften his attitude towards her, just a touch.

"Well I'm guessing you're not going to be playing any music for all of us." Helena instantly regretted the venom she couldn't help dripping from her voice. She found the hypocrisy galling, Louisa Entroper lecturing the captain on not leaving the crew any choice but to hear certain music her husband had selected. And yet at the same time, Entroper had made an insistent nuisance of herself until the captain had finally capitulated and allowed her to arrange for everyone to forcibly attend her "team builder."

"No, Captain, I'm not." When Louisa said this, Helena wondered whether her ultra-severe tone was mere reaction to the severity of her own tone. Or did Louisa Entroper know she was getting called out on hypocrisy? No, Helena Taylor decided Louisa was most likely oblivious to how she came off, when she lectured Helena to not impose the music, yet then expressed a strong desire to impose her latest effort to make herself relevant to the mission.

Kevin, Helena, and Louisa wended their way down the hall from the bridge to the circumvator, as opposed to an elevator. The circumvator would bring them around to the far side of the photon exhaust chamber, to where the assembly room was located. Captain Taylor thought on how, early in their first mission, she had gotten haunted in this same hall by specters of some of the perished from the Mars disaster of 2054. As First Engineer Buddy Leung had explained it, cosmic particle conditions must have been just right for catching glimmers of the victims' fourth-dimensional existence. This, through a wound cut into the space-time fabric by so many bodies having their spirits torn from them nearly simultaneously. Such an enormous tragedy happened, thanks to a tornado of unanticipated magnitude. It drew nearly half the fledgling terraformed atmosphere on Mars out into space. Several colonists got drawn out into space as well, including all the volunteers from a poor neighborhood in the Philadelphia quarantine zone. It was one of those volunteers whose phantasm Helena had recognized specifically, for he was her husband's great uncle, Pedro Perez.

In exchange for her crew being allowed to execute a plan that had literally come to her through a voice in her head, Helena had accepted certain conditions for the Smoke and Mirrors' second mission. The starship would get retrofitted with retractable nuclear cannons and laser knives. Plus, it would deliver the necessary personnel and equipment to install a protective laser mesh network around the planet Oomb in the Callaway X Centra system, as well as around the planet Fafama in the Alpha Centauri C system. This militarization was deemed necessary because a vehicle had crashed on Fafama carrying deer-like creatures who communicated the intention of their kind to invade from a more distant star. According to those creatures, their fellow beings' goal was to round up animals on Fafama, Oomb, and Earth to replenish their food supply. Those creatures reported that the cannibalistic targets were animals who, like their fellow beings, had evolved to an advanced level. Anyhow, a Fafaman distress call regarding this threat had led to the secret abortion of the Smoke and Mirrors' original mission. Instead, its maiden voyage got redirected well outside humanity's birthplace solar system, to make first contact with an intelligent extraterrestrial species. Or first completely verifiable contact, if any of certain stories on Earth were true, going back a century or more.

But as for the voice in Helena's head, it had insinuated a plan to use the time-travel ability Buddy Leung had discovered and tested on the redirected first mission of the Smoke and Mirrors. Ultimately, Pedro Perez, his family, and several of their neighbors got spirited out of north Philadelphia. They were gathered up from back when Señor Perez was still a young man. Thereby, Pedro was not going to be around, years later, to go to Mars and meet a terrible fate by way of a monstrous, atmosphere-depleting tornado. Which is what he had suffered, on the original reality trajectory, before the Smoke and Mirrors made a time-travel intervention. Ditto for the descendants of some of his likewise-spirited-out neighbors. Those descendants had originally joined Pedro in volunteering to resettle on Mars. This had not been the case for other spirited-out neighbors. Many of them had originally gotten done-in variously by drug abuse, random shootings, and other health crises. Those particular neighbors had perished well before they could have reached Pedro's old age to even live contemporaneously with Martian colonization, let alone participate. But again, that had been on the original reality trajectory. On this new trajectory, Pedro Perez, together with family and neighbors from when he was a young father, were all given a fresh start on the Garden-of-Eden-like planet of Oomb.

Captain Taylor had argued that this top-secret project might help the tree people of Oomb to look more favorably upon Earthlings. Those curious plant beings had made clear they were even less keen than the captain, where being provided with any measure of militarization to protect themselves from a potential interstellar cattle-rustling operation was concerned.

Prior to what President Carey had termed Captain Taylor's own little do-it-yourself rapture, she had received a special criticism from the president's top military advisors, as well as from Dr. Louisa Entroper. Entroper and advisers, alike, had argued there would be a bad consequence to Taylor's scheme. Sure, six descendants would be saved from perishing in the Mars disaster, when their ancestors were "raptured" away from Earth. But that would only mean other people taking their place on Mars, other people getting consigned to the same fate. Net improvement, zero.

Curiously, however, the history had changed to record fewer fatalities, including no one from either the Philadelphia quarantine zone or any other quarantine zone. Apparently, there was a special uniqueness to the story of eighty-year-old Pedro Perez raising his great grandson, while persisting with his life-long great enthusiasm for astronomy and space exploration. There simply wasn't another narrative out there compelling enough to inspire giving a different group of wretched poor on the wrong side of the quarantine walls a chance to reboot their futures on Mars.

Another issue had concerned how the time conundrum would resolve itself. History had been changed, so Pedro Perez and other denizens from the quarantine zone were not in the Mars colony when the weather disaster struck. On the new time line, there was no need for time travel to "rapture" their ancestors plus a much younger Pedro Perez. Would the voice in Captain Taylor's head tell her to spirit away victims of the Mars disaster who came from more affluent backgrounds?, or send her on some other quest altogether? Would Taylor and her crew lose all memory of the history prior to their "rapture" experiment? Would they wake up one day, wondering how a group of mostly Spanish-speaking, impoverished people suddenly appeared aboard the Smoke and Mirrors? Or would some other unimaginable thing happen?

Well, as it had turned out, nobody involved in performing the "rapture" had any trouble remembering what they'd done, why a Puerto Rican community from north Philadelphia was aboard the Smoke and Mirrors. In fact, this applied to everyone else aboard the starship as well, down to the last Marine.

There was one memory-related difference, however. Captain Taylor's own experience was comparable to that of other people aboard the Smoke and Mirrors. Following the "rapture" of the Puerto Rican community, her memories had persisted long enough to realize fewer lives were lost in the Mars disaster on the new time line. Details were committed to print, and it was a good thing they were; as days elapsed, Taylor found herself steadily losing recollection of Pedro and others in his surrounding community having ever gotten caught up in the Mars disaster. The documentation didn't help jog her memory in the least. After Helena Taylor's recollection faded away completely, she did read what got written down. However, she might as well have been reading what her mother wrote about something she did when she was two years old, that she also couldn't remember. But again, her remembrance of the "rapture" itself persisted, including a vague sense it had saved the "raptured" from *something*. Buddy Leung was taking up lots of his free time fleshing out the hyper-physics equations for a comprehensive explanation, as would have been expected by anyone close to him. He was making noises about intertwined quantum waves that had gotten Professor Aquinas's attention.

*For certain,* Captain Taylor thought to herself as she, Entroper, and Kevin exited the circumvator, *there's only one impact I can foresee coming from Entroper's "team builder." That is, a precious waste of time I would have liked to have spent making one last check that everyone, especially all the children, are ready for a greeting they will be hearing directly inside their heads, bypassing their ears. Of course, in the wake of this activity, Louisa is going to attribute every smooth interpersonal interaction between the various groups aboard ship to her divine intervention. Although,* Helena sighed with a measure of resignation, *if that helps the woman to validate her worth, maybe she'll finally be able to let other matters- No, what am I thinking? She'll just become even more of a pest about, for example, why I don't set a written agenda for meetings.*

Helena found herself gritting her teeth as she reflected anew on how the government mission observer had at last succeeded in arguing for the team builder. Dr. Louisa Entroper had first broached the matter a few days after the time travel to "rapture" Pedro Perez and company. The Smoke and Mirrors was at the forty light-speed multiple and travelling high "above" the outer fringes of the Oort Cloud that enveloped Earth's solar system. The Oort Cloud, of course, was a sort of cosmic scrapheap full of comets and other debris, also found around the Callaway X Centra System and the Alpha Centauri C system. Anyway, Dr. Ali Magabu, the ship's chief counselor, had taken to joking that "truly," he was "the evolutionary missing link between Stress Relief Cookie Provider Chris Olsen-Taylor, and Chief Medical Officer Deborah Davis-Murphy." He had also volunteered that he was arranging a series of dessert get-togethers. He was sending out sets of invitations in a strategic fashion, to bring together people on board from various backgrounds, over fruit, cookies and ice cream. Cheese, crackers, and veggies would be provided for those with less of a sweet tooth. One such invitation set had gone out to a couple of the soldiers, a starship engineer, and a few of the "raptured" parents with their children.

"That's a start," Louisa had jumped in before anyone else could react. She had done this in a firm, commanding voice that Captain Taylor had read as her bid to take charge of the meeting. "Dr. Magabu, what are the structured activities you have planned for these socials once you have lured in people with your delicious bait?"

"Nothing structured, Dr. Entroper. And truly nothing obligatory. People can choose to attend, or not to attend."

"But you will do follow-up on anyone who doesn't RSVP?"

"No RSVP either, Dr. Entroper. I want everything regarding this little project of mine to be as free from stress as possible. I'm also encouraging other venues. For example, I've suggested people might want to join Officer Olsen-Taylor for a round of holographic golf or golf lessons, to prepare for engaging Oomb's tree people in their game of oof. Frankly, Dr. Entroper, since in so many respects we are venturing into the interpersonal unknown, I am most truly reticent about insisting on any one particular course of action."

When Entroper had looked Helena's way to see how she was taking Magabu's remarks, the captain had made a point of nodding emphatically agreeingly.

"Well, here's the thing." Dr. Louisa Entroper had slapped her hands on the table before her; Helena had mused this was in lieu of how Louisa had really wanted to slap her face instead. "Especially, especially since we are heading into that interpersonal unknown of regular, daily contact with an extraterrestrial species, I think it behooves us to establish a common, baseline experience we have all shared."

*Such as being born?*, Second Engineer Kevin Smith-

Park had wanted to ask. But the threat of how this woman might have taken such flippancy made an ear twist by his wife, First Navigation Officer Yoon-hee Park-Smith, seem a gentle prospect by comparison. So he had stifled himself.

"What I have been meaning to bring up with you, Captain, I think now is as good a time as any. Everyone aboard this ship, children included, ought to share the common experience of a team-building exercise I am qualified to provide."

Helena Taylor had intertwined her hands prayerfully before her, and had turned Louisa's direction to ask in as pleasant a voice as she could suppress her true feelings to muster, "What team-building exercise might that be?"

"Captain, the exercise may lose some of its efficacy were I to share it before you experience it. It's best activated with no prior chance to mentally brace one's self."

"Oh. Well, what do you think, Ali? I don't see why Louisa's generous offer can't be thrown out there as one of the choices."

"Captain..." Dr. Entroper had raised forward a hand as in STOP. But then, she had bowed her head, closed her eyes, tried to contain herself. "Excuse me, Captain," she had gone on finally, "but this will not work as a choice. To establish this as that common baseline experience we discussed,-"

*As that common baseline experience YOU discussed,* Helena had fought off an urge to correct her.

"-you have to order, as captain of the Smoke and Mirrors you're in your bounds to order everyone to participate."

"I hear what you're saying, Dr. Entroper, and I will take it under advisement."

"Okay." Louisa had tossed her hands in the air.

And the crusade had begun. At subsequent meetings, Dr. Entroper had reported out any smallest misunderstandings she managed to cull, prying about the Smoke and Mirrors. At each successive such gathering, there were always more such occurrences to report than at the previous one. She had always begun her news saying, "Officer Magabu, I trust you're aware of the situation that developed-" in some certain location. This remark was always vague enough, with an insinuation of something potentially serious, that Ali Magabu had had to fight down squirmy discomfort to respond with some degree of matter-of-factness, "I'm truly not sure to which situation you are referring, Dr. Entroper."

Most of the time, Ali had recognized the situation once Entroper had provided more detail. Usually, it had been something so minor, he had wanted to tell the captain he thought it too trivial to even mention. But trying to steer clear of saying anything the woman could take as an insult, he had limited himself to simply stating how he'd resolved matters. This had not stopped Louisa, when Helena asked her if she was satisfied with Ali's response, from her refrain, "I just hope we're cohesive enough, enough of a team, to handle the far more complex issues that are going to face us after we arrive to Oomb, and later Fafama." When the situation had concerned Placido Perez accidentally on purpose making off with a soldier's lunch so he could skip the cruciferous vegetable salad part of his special diet, and instead indulge an extra-cheesy omelet, Kevin had wanted to comment, *Yeah, it's a slippery slope from trying to avoid eating your veggies to civil war aboard the Smoke and Mirrors; shoving your team-builder up everyone's hairy butt is our only hope!*

The few times Ali was not aware of the situation Dr. Entroper dredged up from her snooping around, the captain had felt no choice but to ask him to check into it. Officer Magabu invariably found that Louisa had blown matters all out of proportion. There was the six-year-old, Silvio Gutierrez, from Philadelphia. Louisa said he came running to his mom, scared silly, because he thought a soldier was marching down the hall after him. Reportedly the mother got so upset, she demanded, demanded!, Louisa arrange for a meeting with the military liaison. "I'm just relaying what the mother told me." Dr. Entroper had spread her hands apart, palms open ceiling-ward, to convey, suggest she was not driving any agenda. "If we hadn't been about to have this meeting anyway, Ali, I would have had to come get you." What Dr. Magabu had found was that the mother successfully assured her son that the soldier in question was most likely in a rush to duty somewhere. Silvio just happened to get in his path. Silvio himself was too busy playing soccer in the exercise room with the other boys and girls on board to be bothered talking with Ali about the incident. "I tink Dr. Entroper, my poor eengleesh confused for her when she ask me eef everyting ees okay. I tink she trying to make a conversation," had explained Señora Gutierrez.

When Ali and Helena had confronted Louisa with what Ali found, she had said, "Well, they must have convinced themselves it wasn't that important. All I'm telling you is what the mother said, how she said it, when she came to me."

You mean, when *you* came to *her*, Captain Taylor and Dr. Magabu had both been desperate to say, if only…

Inevitably, an incident of some genuine seriousness had occurred, mere days out from Oomb. Again, so far as Captain Taylor was concerned, this was the first grave interpersonal matter of the mission. A tribute, she thought, to Dr. Magabu's low-key approach. Among his other strategies, that dessert social was very well attended by a broad cross-section of the people aboard the Smoke and Mirrors, and had resulted in three others over the intervening months. Yes, the first grave interpersonal crisis of the mission, yet the way Entroper had framed it, this was the straw that broke the camel's back, the final outrage, the result of Dr. Magabu's nonchalance and the captain's weak leadership. And ah, yes, wouldn't you know that Chief Medical Officer Deborah Davis-Murphy had a big hand in the initial dealing with it?, to help Louisa grind her ax?

"Captain, I need you in the infirmary, now!" had been Dr. Davis-Murphy's bolt out of the intercom blue to Helena, while Helena was in her office reviewing proposed infra-structure plans for the human settlement on Oomb. What had awaited her in the ship's hospital were Deborah and Louisa standing around the bed of a heavily-sedated young woman, Angie Acevedo. "I'm sorry for calling on you like this, Captain. I trust if you had something pressingly urgent, you would have said I had to wait."

"That goes without saying, Officer Davis-Murphy."

"Captain, Dr. Entroper brought this woman to me in a trembling, sobbing state. I was here to see she really was upset."

*Ah, yes, and wasn't it such a shame earlier on, when you weren't around to confirm that little boy Silvio's actual state?, so we didn't have to rely on the undependable observations of myself and Dr. Magabu?* Captain Taylor had wanted to say this. Instead, she had clenched her teeth, kept her lips pressed together, and merely nodded acknowledgement of what the chief medical officer was conveying.

"Captain," went on Dr. Davis-Murphy, "her name is Angie Acevedo, and she says a soldier tried to rape her."

"Which soldier?"

"She didn't have a name. We're running her description through a profile program, but no matches yet."

"What does Dr. Magabu- What's his input on this matter?"

Louisa and Deborah gave each other a look that Helena read as: *Oh-oh, we got so carried away, we forgot...*

"Captain," Deborah said at last, attempting to cover for them both, "I have a call in to Magabu. Louisa, can you-"

"I'll check on what's taking him so long, Dr." And Dr. Entroper was gone.

"Captain," Dr. Davis-Murphy repeated. Helena recognized instantly that certain pleading tone; it meant that once again, just like during the first mission, her medical officer was going to beg her to see reason. "We know the military personnel on board were so thoroughly vetted, it's highly unlikely whoever this woman encountered was actually trying to rape her. Most likely it's some terrible misunderstanding. But just maybe, matters would not have reached this distress level had we taken Dr. Entroper's advice and gone along with her team-builder exercise."

"I told her she could have offered the activity on a voluntary basis, and she refused."

"Captain, I know that making the activity mandatory was a deal breaker for you,-"

*Oh, so I was the one being unreasonable when I insisted people should have a choice whether to participate.*

"-but I think there is something to be said for getting us all on the same page, at least for one little shared experience. I do plan to argue the case at our next chief officer meeting."

The upshot of the incident from Magabu's inquiry had only served to bolster Louisa and Deborah's persistence. It turned out the woman from Philadelphia had been raped by a police officer back on Earth. That officer had raised his eyebrows at her suggestively, several times, before attacking. Well, as luck would have it, a soldier aboard the Smoke and Mirrors likewise gave her raised eyebrows; that's what set her off. She tried to keep her composure until she was well down the hallway, past said soldier. But then she couldn't hold it together any further, and came totally unglued just when Dr. Louisa Entroper happened to be prowling by. Clearly, the reason the profile program was having trouble making a match with anyone aboard the ship was that the woman's description had a lot of the rapist police officer's characteristics blended in.

Anyhow, after consulting with Magabu, Captain Taylor had decided to pre-empt any further pressing on the team-building matter. She had announced at the outset of the next chief officer meeting that she was squeezing in the activity as a mandatory event during all the last-minute preparations for the return to Oomb.

And so there they were in the ship's congregation center, the last group on Louisa's schedule. Chairs, tables and other odds and ends had been uncoupled from their normal floor anchors and latched to the walls, to leave a wide-open space in the middle.

Dr. Entroper directed everyone to stand in a circle, eleven people she chose for this group, plus herself as the twelfth. Each person was to introduce his or her self, with short give-and-take conversation pursuant to each introduction. "You might think it is ridiculous to be asked to open up more about yourself, in front of people with whom you are already mostly familiar. But consider," she added sternly, "there is going to be at least one person who doesn't really know you, and at least one person who you really don't know, or who you might benefit from getting to know just a little bit better."

Second Engineer Kevin Smith-Park led off, saying, "I gather many of you are still pretty excited to be here. Um, compared to our first mission, so far, for me, this has been a real snooze-fest. I hope those of us working the navigation bridge can keep it that way, so you continue to enjoy yourselves."

Dr. Timothy Aquinas built on Kevin's remarks. He said he was having fun, studying the Smoke and Mirrors's trail-breaking propulsion system, to try figuring out why it worked. Kevin resisted the temptation to tease him that his real goal appeared to be to try to find the ideal location on his nose to rest the bridge of his oversized glasses. Aquinas was constantly readjusting them, even while eating.

Professor Dauntilus Skepticus in turn built on Aquinas's remarks. He said he was "trying to figure out how the so-called ephemeral dragon 'worked.'" Dr. Skepticus repeated what he seized every opportunity he was given to say, plus some he was not given when he would barge in on the conversation of others, no matter their subject. Which was, he was determined to prove, to demonstrate, Effy was a nonbiological phenomenon. Effy, of course, whatever it was, had somehow gotten aboard the Smoke and Mirrors on the first visit to Fafama. It had earned hero status by helping to loosen away a dirty comet that got stuck in the spacecraft's photon exhaust chamber at the outset of the return voyage to Earth. Under certain lighting conditions, it did look like a cross between the Chinese dragon of myth and the near-mythic flying reptile, the Pterodactyl. Captain Taylor's husband Chris was convinced it had to be what translated from the Fafaman tongue as an ephemeral dragon. Ephemeral dragons purportedly dwelled in the Grand Basin, some nine hundred miles east of the multi-mile-tall pyramid that was the center of Fafaman civilization. "It is wonderful for small children to entertain all manner of fantasy creatures in their imaginations," Dr. Skepticus went on at the team builder. Captain Taylor was hearing this line from him for the fourth time, as well as its follow-up. "But what is wonderful for adults is to unravel the mysteries of nature without getting superstitiously spooked by them."

"Forgive me for my saying so, Professor Skepticus..."

Skepticus's wide smile seemed to Helena suddenly somehow to have become an empty shell. The spirit of a smile had drained away, leaving tightly controlled rage to light his beady little eyes.

"...having had the pleasure of seeing the so-called 'Effy' under ideal viewing circumstances, I must confess it does look very much like a biological entity, where it might be too tall a mountain to climb to prove otherwise. I trust you're assembling hypothetical constructs for the biological entity scenario, in case your present hypothesis fails rigorous testing?" Aquinas paused from his spectacle-adjustment nervous tic; he wanted to make sure he didn't miss Skepticus's answer.

"I am trusting that your own worthy efforts, Dr. Aquinas, to apprehend the why, how and wherefore of the mirror array, will not get misdirected by mere sensory input."

"Ah, Dr. Skepticus, so you have discovered a way to take in data without using one's senses?" Aquinas's glasses adjustment got more animated than ever with his excitement over composing the perfect retort to his colleague's insult. "When were you planning on sharing a finding of such historic import as to trivialize the mirror array?"

"Um, I'm Tanya Petrovsky, shuttle pod flight specialist and third engineer." Tanya figured she'd better move the process along, before war broke out between Aquinas and Skepticus during the team-building preliminaries. Louisa thanked her for it.

Also in this hand-picked group, Pedro Perez effused over how excited he was to be heading up the electrical infrastructure team for the human settlement on Oomb. Norma echoed his thanks in Spanish, which he translated, although she spoke in her quietest voice for fear her husband Típico might be lurking close by. "Captain Taylor, before the others introduce themselves," Pedro put an arm around Norma, the grandmother of his wife Ludi, and she gladly leaned into him for comfort and support, "I have to thank you again-"

"You've thanked me enough already, Señor Perez."

"A thousand thank-you's are not enough, Captain. And they are not only for me. They are for all my family, and other people who lived on our block in Philadelphia. For example, Ciela." Pedro pointed across the circle at the young woman, who as a result self-consciously crossed her arms so her hands were cupping opposite shoulders. Kevin thought she was behaving as though she were suddenly bare-chested.

"Can you introduce yourself now, Ciela?" proposed Dr. Entroper. "I'm sure Pedro can translate."

"No, is okay," she shook her head, though she was still most modestly hiding her upper torso, already modestly-enough clothed in the standard issue sky-blue turtleneck. That turtleneck sported the yellow rose breast-patch logo for the second Smoke and Mirrors mission. "My name, like he say, is Ciela, and I thank you also, Captain Taylor. Before you, um, rescued us," she was searching her mind for the correct words, "I was almost graduated from high school. But my grades were so low, for sure no college will take me. Only if I can pay money my family doesn't have, because I am not *bastante* good for any kind of scholarship. *Bueno*, at home there is always the TV on loud, and my family screaming and fighting. Outside the home, my friends get in trouble with boys, and people offer me the drugs. One man says I can make a lot of money if I will be a prostitute. What I want to tell you, my head was not thinking right because there was no place I can go that is a quiet place where I can hear *me*." She left off from modestly covering up her chest to patting it proudly. "Maybe it was the reason I can't do so well in school, because I can't find the quiet place for study. But like I said, my head was not thinking right. Before I woke up like a miracle on your spaceship, I was thinking more and more about that man who wanted to make me a prostitute. He was speaking to me so nice and he always had a flower or a candy for me. And when I told him I wanted to go to college, he bought me a book, *The Seven Habits of Successful People*, was some title like that. I knew he was a pimp – is the name for men who manage prostitutes. But he didn't act like how I thought a pimp is supposed to act. So I was thinking, I will ask him if he can give me that quiet place to study when I am not, um, working for him. I am sure he says yes, yes, yes, of course, anything he has to say so I step into his trap. I see that now, because I am safe on your spaceship. Now, I have all the quiet I need for studying medicine, when I am not helping Pedro's wife with teaching the children."

"This is what I am talking about, Captain," said Pedro. He jumped in before Louisa Entroper, frustrated with how the whole process had gotten bogged down in testimonials, could take a stab at getting it back on track.

"Mr. Perez-"

"Only one more thing, Dr. Entroper!" Pedro held up a forefinger for emphasis. "Captain Taylor, I think you are the busiest person on the spaceship, so I don't know when is the next time I can talk with you. I only wanted to say, if you are too busy for us to ever talk again, that I hope other people will receive the opportunity you have given us."

Captain Helena Taylor beamed. "Señor Perez,-"

Louisa had her mouth half open, about to shush the captain. But she short-circuited her effort with an eyes-closed exhalation of resignation.

"-I thank you for your input, and I can assure you I've discussed what you suggest. Please understand, we must proceed most carefully. First, of course, we need to see how things work out in the long term with our first experiment, if you don't mind getting termed part of an experiment." *You have no idea*; Helena could have gone on at length about a mind-bending conversation over dinner she had had just a month earlier. In attendance had been her husband Chris, Buddy Leung, and Buddy's wife Cathy. Cathy had overcome her anxiety about being around her husband for so much time aboard the Smoke and Mirrors, thanks to the chance to take a crack at solving the mystery of Fafama's sunset storm line. As it had happened, Cathy was also in the captain's team-building group, standing beside Ciela. She gave Helena a knowing nod; she remembered all too well their running amuck with that dinner conversation. Chris had gotten the ball rolling innocently enough by mentioning an old movie trilogy entitled *Back to the Future*, wherein time travel brought some improvement to a few people's lives.

Before the dining companions knew it, they were speculating about eradicating world poverty and overpopulation, well prior to it getting so out of hand, by spiriting millions and millions of people from the past into the present. They would be brought to populate other paradise planets like Oomb that the Smoke and Mirrors might discover, which weren't already overrun with beings of higher order intelligence. The dining companions had wondered whether the experiment with the people from Philadelphia initiated a manner by which eventually all life lived forever, because it would be getting continually re-awoken, reborn to new possibilities. And they knew it was time definitely to end their little party when they stumbled into wondering how to handle if it ever became possible to go back and stop the giant asteroid from hitting the Earth sixty-five million years earlier that caused the massive dinosaur extinction. At the point at which this was accomplished, would they instantly turn into super-intelligent reptiles? Or would every last vestige of humanity vanish along with most mammals, like they'd never existed in the first place?

"So tell me, Ciela, does your name mean something in Spanish?"

"Why don't you tell her your name, and whether it means something in English?" Dr. Entroper seized this opportunity to at long last move along the introductions so she could get to the meat of the team builder. Thank goodness the other groups hadn't taken this long! Especially since any minute from then, she knew that they would be within contact range of the mind-reading telepathic trees of Oomb.

"Well," the man who Entroper addressed chuckled heartily, "Señora, or Señorita, the name is Sergeant Fred Frankly, in charge of military deployment, if and when needed. Some people say my name means trouble." He jabbed his elbow into the ribs of the man standing to his left.

"Marine Corps Sergeant Guy Hanson; Sergeant Frankly is Marine Corps too."

"Outer Space division," added Frankly. "The cosmos is our new sea."

"I head up technical systems deployment," went on Hanson. "But here's hoping the two of us and the rest of our contingent are an unnecessary precaution, and there continue to be no bad aliens with whom we need to contend." Guy went a little more overboard with his remarks than he had intended to go. He had long since sensed, though, that some of the interplanetary settlers, maybe even including that decent Pedro Perez fellow, were wondering why the significant military presence. The reality was that Sergeant Hanson was in charge of the laser mesh deployment around both Oomb and Fafama. Every last crew member and military officer had been cleared for a full briefing early on in Mission Two, about the potential threat from a planet named TicTocTic, as described by the two deer-like entities who crashed on Fafama. Before even boarding or re-boarding the Smoke and Mirrors, they had all signed away their right to privacy, regarding any communication they initiated or accepted with anyone from off the spaceship. This, to assure not a one of them would let anyone else know about said threat. Only the people "raptured" there from two Philadelphia tenement blocks some sixty years earlier were kept in the dark about Tictoctic, where hopefully they could remain. On that much, at least, everyone else was agreed.

"Captain Taylor,-" Sergeant Hanson got these words out just when Dr. Entroper thought she could finally complete the introductory phase of the team builder by prompting a brief remark from Buddy Leung's wife, Cathy. "-like Mr. Perez here, I'm not sure either when is the next time I'd get to talk with you. And so, I'd like to take this opportunity to note my special fascination with how, according to your report, the sentient tree creatures of Oomb were especially admiring of Mahatma Gandhi. I'm not sure that what Gandhi accomplished with the British could necessarily have worked, applying his philosophy to other situations. But I do believe, even as a trained soldier, that his commitment to nonviolent conflict resolution poses one of the great philosophical challenges of recent history."

"And here I thought one of the great challenges of recent history was to carry a fifty pound backpack across one of Sergeant Hanson's sentences! Har har!" Sergeant Frankly slapped Guy on the back. "Personally, I'll settle with getting Ciela to tell us if her name means anything special. You know. Special name for a special lady." The sergeant gave Ciela raised eyebrows that raised Helena and Louisa's eyebrows. They might as well have been the mind-reading tree people of Oomb, because they were both thinking the same thing: This must be the soldier who terrified Angie Acevedo. His must have been the flirtatious glance that caused her to relive her earlier rape trauma. First chance they got, they'd have to have Magabu speak to him.

"Cielo is Spanish for sky." Ciela blushed. "But my name has an 'a' at the end, instead of an 'o.'"

"Sure looks like a piece of heaven to me," Fred whispered to Guy, for his disgust only.

"Dr. James-Leung, I hate to rush you,-" Louisa Entroper hoped no one else, especially Ciela, overheard Sergeant Frankly. "-but could you...?"

Cathy held up a hand for Entroper to say no more. "I'm Dr. Cathy James-Leung. Officer Buddy Leung is my husband, but the real reason I'm along for the ride is as climate geologist. I will be studying the weather phenomenon on Fafama known as the sunset storm line."

"That's real nice, Dr. James-Leung. Real nice," nodded Sergeant Hanson. "Um, by the way, had I known about all the children and newborns that would be on board from the time-travel component of the mission, I would have tried to convince my fiancé, Jen, to apply to accompany me."

As Hanson spoke, Captain Taylor was struck by how much effort he appeared to be making to relate to other people. Was he especially sensitive to civilian discomfort with the military presence? Or was he just naturally this personable? Either way, she concluded, he was great to have along in case Mission Two did not turn out as quite the yawnfest Kevin spoke of.

"Jen works with a preschool program on our base in Myrtle Beach," Hanson went on.

"Well, that's wonderful, but Buddy and I are into more of an absence-makes-the-heart-grow-fonder sort of thing. Hopefully our relationship will survive our seeing so much of each other."

"From what I hear,-" started Kevin as several foreheads furrowed with puzzlement over Cathy's remarks. The exceptions included the captain, who had long since given up trying to figure Cathy out, and Sergeant Frankly, who wondered whether this small-chested, broad-shouldered blond was signaling availability. "-you don't have to worry about seeing so much of Buddy, because he keeps his socks on in bed."

"Well it's funny you should mention not seeing too much of someone, Officer Smith-Park," Dr. Entroper raised her voice, part-admonishingly, and part in case she needed to drown out Sergeant Frankly, "because our little team builder involves not seeing the people you are trusting to literally support you. Under normal gravitational circumstances, we couldn't have more than six people in a circle, because you'd want everyone in close enough to support one another. But now that we are only a little over half our weight back on Earth, and believe me, I'm not complaining! I'm not much less than what I should be under normal conditions! Well, maybe I should show instead of tell. Sergeant Hanson – you notice how I picked one of the strongest? – I am going to fall towards you, and you catch me. Please."

"Roger that, ma'am."

"Isn't he a sweetie? Okay, here I come!"

"Don't say it," Guy Hanson snarled as whispery as he could out the corner of his mouth at Sergeant Frankly, while Dr. Entroper, with her arms folded across her chest, fell face-forward towards him. As expected in the lower gravity, catching Louisa's shoulders wasn't much different for Guy than had he needed to catch a toppling-over piece of cardboard.

As Guy pushed Louisa back to standing straight up, she said, "Nothing to it, right, Sergeant?"

"You're right, ma'am."

"Well it's going to be even easier than that, because three of you can consolidate your strength to catch the next person. Only, that person will be falling backwards, not forwards, with her eyes closed. And after you push her back up to standing, you're going to tip her over towards another waiting group of hands. Who wants to go first?" To nervous laughter, Dr. Entroper added, "Let me rephrase that: Who is willing to go first? Ah, Captain Taylor, the mission leader to show the way."

All Helena could think was, *The faster we get through this, the faster we can get back to assuring we're prepared for the imminent contact with Oomb.* As she turned her back on the group, closed her eyes, and folded her arms across her chest, she thought on how there was no question any of them would allow her to fall. It could even have been Deborah Davis-Murphy standing across from her in the circle. Helena would not have had the faintest doubt her fall backwards would get stopped well before she could have gotten hurt. And as it so happened, Tanya was to be her primary protector, Tanya who had performed miraculously heroic maneuvers with the Smoke and Mirrors' shuttle pod to save her, Chris and Buddy from certain doom on Fafama. What was there not to trust? Nevertheless, Helena did have to admit something to herself. However brief the interval, from her starting to allow herself to fall backwards to when gentle hands protectively firmly checked her movement, it was still plenty long enough to experience doubt. The fall began slowly because for the first few seconds, her feet were still planted to the floor. In fact, had Dr. Entroper not required them to remove special-issue shoes that helped make walking still doable when gravity was negligible or virtually non-existent, this team builder exercise would have sprained their ankles. Anyhow, as Captain Taylor allowed her toes to lift off the floor, that's when her fall backwards both left from her control and began to accelerate. And that's when, if only for a fleeting moment, she experienced doubt. But it was all okay after that first set of unseen hands, like the unseen presence of God in religious faith, warmly yet firmly caught her. This, even though at Dr. Entroper's direction they pushed her past a return to standing, to fall forward into another group of waiting hands, and from there sideways into a third group. "Nothing to it," she said as she left the center of the circle to rejoin its perimeter and welcome the next person into the center.

"I should think, if Dr. Entroper might excuse me, that my most esteemed colleague Dr. Aquinas should be next up, and we should all stand back to allow the so-called ephemeral dragon to catch him, since he seems so confident it is a biological entity!"

"Dr. Skepticus,-" Dr. Aquinas was readjusting his glasses so rapidly with nervous agitation, Kevin wondered how he didn't make himself disoriented enough to fall over, without even trying. "-I thought it was quite clear from what we know already. Whatever the dragon-appearing entity is, it is not comprised of matter in the same sense we are comprised of matter! So it would not likely be able to catch me even if it wanted to! And besides, how many animals do you know of, that could be trained on a moment's notice to successfully perform this activity?"

"Excuse me, my most eminent partner in scientific investigation, presumably, but where is your data to show there are biological forms extant anywhere in the universe that are *not* comprised of matter in the same sense that we know?"

"Under special lighting conditions, Dr. Skepticus, I thought that data was right here, on board this spacecraft!"

"Gentlemen..." Louisa held her hands forward in a desperate plea for Professors Aquinas and Skepticus to drop the argument.

"Ahh," Dr. Skepticus nodded as he went on, heedless of Dr. Entroper's entreaty, "so, were you to have been around thousands of years ago when people were seeing shapes of things outlined by stars in the sky, am I to assume you would have gone right along with that? And then argued with me that a scorpion, a bear, and who knows what else were floating across the- AAAAAAA!!!" There was a sound like a blowtorch getting ignited. Dr. Skepticus grabbed the seat of his pants and went running in circles, yelling, "Ouch! Ouch! Ouch! Ouch!" Grayish-brown smoke trailed behind him.

"I've got the fire extinguisher!" Kevin was already headed for it.

"What's going on, Captain?" said Louisa Entroper,

But before Helena could even speculate on the cause, they heard little boys' giggles coming from beyond the door to the meeting room they didn't realize had been opened a sliver.

Ciela's eyes lit up wide as she shouted, "Tomás and Jorge! Aye bendito!"

"What about them, Ciela?" asked Captain Taylor.

"When I was putting problems on the board for them during their mathematics class, they tried to sneak a chocolate chip cookie into my back pants pocket. Officer Park-Smith, she told me of the dragon the scientists argue about, that it likes to burn your husband's cookies, Captain! I have to go punish those boys! Tomás and Jorge, come here! Now!" she shouted as she ran for the door.

"Oh-oh!" was the perfectly synchronized exclamation of two voices from out in the hallway, before there was the sound of fleeing children's little footsteps accompanied by panicky squeals.

"I want to know how the people you spirited out of the past are able to just roam freely down the halls, Captain Taylor. Especially youngsters!"

"This is a spaceship, Dr. Entroper. Not a prison." No sooner did Helena vent, than a familiar voice filled her head. She was struck by how, even though it was not a voice she was actually hearing, even though there was no sound associated with it, somehow she knew it could be none other than their primary contact entity on Oomb, Oodle-Noodle.

*Welcome back to Oomb, Captain Helena Taylor. We are happy to host the people you have brought to settle here, to share our music and play our game. We have already constructed log cabin habitations for them, if that is okay. And we were careful to leave open the spaces in each habitation where your plumbers and electricians will need to install power and running water.*

"Thank you, Oodle-Noodle!" Helena was so surprised by what the tree person telepathed about the log cabin construction, she was heedless of how observers might react to her. That is, when she responded out loud to the messages surfacing inside her head almost as gently as though they were her own thoughts. "But about the company we were bringing, how did you know soon enough to make the preparations you, uh, mentioned?"

"Are you talking to yourself now, Captain?! What next?!" Dr. Entroper was becoming ever more agitated, looking on helplessly as her circle of people for the team building dissipated after only getting Helena in the center. The worst of it was the sight of Kevin spraying a fire extinguisher at Dr. Skepticus's smoldering rear end.

"It's Oomb. We're within telepathic range already." Once Captain Taylor addressed this remark to Louisa, she looked away from her and said, seemingly to no one in particular, "We can discuss my question later, Oodle-Noodle. Give us a minute so I can alert everyone else aboard that you're about to make your formal welcome."

*Of course, Captain.*

# Chapter 2

Dr. Louisa Entroper's severe regard made Captain Helena Taylor self-conscious, over having appeared to be talking to empty space when she responded to Oodle-Noodle's telepathed welcome back to the planet Oomb. And so, Helena strove to sustain eye contact with Louisa as she slapped at a small button on her uniform. A soft yet distinct boop-boop! issued from Helena's lapel, and she said, "Yoon-hee?"

"Captain?" came over the intercom.

"I need to conduct an immediate system-wide announcement. We're apparently already in contact range with our friends on Oomb."

"Already, Captain? We're just entering the outer fringe of Callaway X Centra at point four light-speed!"

"Already, Yoon-hee. I'm sure an explanation will be forthcoming how Oo- uhh, how they've managed to extend their telepathic range so dramatically." Even though Helena had uttered aloud Oodle-Noodle's name not two minutes earlier, she couldn't bring herself to do that again with Louisa Entroper hanging on her every word. Clearly, Entroper was on the alert, for any other whatever at which she could vent her disgust and outrage, since her reign in charge of a team builder had gotten eclipsed by the onward rush of events. For sure, Oodle-Noodle, not to mention the other silly-sounding names of Oomb's highly intelligent creatures, should have come as no surprise to the white-haired, mop-topped government observer.

Captain Taylor had made no secret of those names in her debriefing from the Smoke and Mirrors first mission. But no matter. Oodle-Noodle could have confirmed for Helena that Louisa was fuming over what might have been. That the government observer was torturing herself thinking, *If only this erratic person had yielded to reason earlier on in the mission, the team builder could have been done and over with, well before approaching Callaway X Centra. And then, who knew what could have been the positive results?* Instead of revealing these if-onlys raging through Entroper's head, Oodle-Noodle telepathed to Helena, *Captain Taylor, I hereby venture a violation of our communication protocol, by responding to your remark to Yoon-hee, despite it's not having subsequently been directed at me. And so: You are quite correct. There will be an explanation forthcoming, for how some of us have managed to extend our telepathic range so dramatically. But this will take place as time allows and the situation calls for.*

"Ready, Captain. It's all yours." Yoon-hee's announcement jolted Helena, as she had gotten herself so preoccupied with anticipation of any more words that might pop into her head from Oodle-Noodle.

"Attention, everyone, including all of our boys and girls on board who can understand me. Uh, before I continue, Yoon-hee, can you locate Ludi Perez and ask her to translate for our Spanish-speaking passengers? Mrs. Perez, I would be honored if you would translate for us."

"Ludi is happy to be helping, Captain. I've rerouted her intercom for system-wide."

"Thank you, Officer Park-Smith, and thank you, I should call you Officer Perez!"

"Sí, Captain Taylor. Is my honor also."

Helena Taylor proceeded, with pauses every few sentences for Mrs. Perez's translation. "Once again, attention everyone! This is Captain Helena Taylor. We are entering the Callaway X Centra solar system. That is where our destination planet, Oomb, is located. As our spacecraft decel- uh, slows down, as our spacecraft slows down to less than light speed, you are probably noticing that anything you may pick up – chairs, books, etc. – they are all becoming lighter weight. You are also probably feeling lighter, and you are realizing your shoes getting magnetized to the floor when you take steps. This is the time when you should be storing in secure locations anything that could float in zero gravity. If you took off the straw caps on your drinks, screw them back on. Boys and girls, your teachers will help you put away any toys you are not playing with. And anything you *are* playing with, hold on to it! Don't let it hit someone in the head! And if you are eating a snack, careful that you keep the bag closed after you take out each piece. We can't have kelpydoodles and wacamacabroccibules floating all over. They could make a big mess." Helena was straining to keep her vocabulary controlled so that even most of the children would understand. But she knew it was going to be even harder as she got to the crux of her announcement. "Uhh," she went on after her latest pause for Ludi Perez to translate, "what I have said should have been a review of procedure with which you were already oriented. That is, boys and girls, you should have heard these same things from your teachers and your family. Maybe some of you remember three months ago, before we went faster than light? Do you remember that loose objects were floating all about?

"Well, my real reason for speaking to you now, like this, should also be a repeat of what you were already told. Boys and girls, do you remember your teachers said you are going to have a voice in your head? That it will be the voice of a very nice person from the planet where we are going?" On the spur of the moment, Helena decided it was important to specifically address the youngest people aboard the Smoke and Mirrors. Surely, the adults would understand why. If someone was going to get spooked out, really upset by telepathic communication, it was most likely going to be a child. Chief counselor Ali Magabu was nodding his head most approvingly at his station on the navigation bridge of the spacecraft, while Captain Taylor continued from the assembly room. "Well, that nice person has just said hello to me with a voice in my head. She wants to say hello to all of you now. Her name is Oodle-Noodle. Again, I think you already know this from your teachers."

"Oodle-Noodle," Tomás and Jorge giggled together in the closet where they were hiding from Ciela. "When we land on Oomb, we can put a chocolate chip cookie in her pants too! Hee-hee!"

"Hey, don't you remember? Ms. Sanchez said Oodle-Noodle is a tree woman! She don't wear no pants, chico!"

"Oodle-f-n'-Noodle," Sergeant Frankly shook his head in a briefing room where he'd been reviewing coordination plans with Sergeant Hanson, coordination between his troops and the laser mesh installation "tech heads." "I don't f-n' trust anyone who goes by the name of Oodle-Noodle. I don't care if she's a friggin' tree, a friggin' bush, or an asparagus that does the f-n' limbo."

"You haven't read Captain Taylor's debriefing report from Mission One?" asked Sergeant Hanson. "They've all got names like that. I remember Woogle-Poogle and Moodle-Mafoodle."

"You're shittin' me!"

"Before Oodle-Noodle says hello to you, boys and girls, plus you big people listening in," was going on Captain Taylor, "she wants to make sure you know about her special rules for conversation. When she says hello, it will be a voice in your head just like there was a voice in my head. To say hello back to her, you simply have to say, 'Hello.' Oodle-Noodle will read in your mind what you spoke aloud. Isn't that amazing? She is millions of miles away on her planet Oomb, and she can still read what is in your mind. But this is where her special rules for conversation come in. Boys and girls, all of us have thoughts all the time, but we only talk about some of our thoughts. We only talk about the thoughts we want to share with others, yes? For example, maybe some of you think some of you girls are very pretty."

"Ewwww!!"

"Shh, Jorge!" Tomás cupped a hand over Jorge's mouth, but it was too late.

"Ah-HA! There you are!" said Ciela. "You boys come out here and let's listen to the rest of what Captain Taylor has to say!" She pulled Tomás and Jorge from the closet by their ears.

"You wanted Ms. Sanchez to catch us because she is the girl you think is very pretty." Tomás pointed an accusatory finger at Jorge.

"Oh, no, chico!" Jorge shook his head animately. "You're saying that because YOU are the one who loves Ms. Sanchez!"

"Hey, chico, you're the one who is using the 'l' word!"

That was it for words, where Jorge was concerned. His face turned beet red, and with a snarl he jumped Tomás to pound his head.

"No!" Ciela re-grabbed an ear of each and twisted hard. "I do not value going to war! And also, you are both too young for me!"

"Ewww!!" Both boys were trying their best to express disgust.

"-or maybe some of you think some of the boys are very handsome," was going on Captain Taylor, oblivious to the reactions her discourse was prompting throughout the Smoke and Mirrors. "However, these thoughts are too embarrassing to share out loud, aren't they?-"

*Like what you were feeling for the supreme ruler of Fafama, the Fafamafalafama,* Officer Chris Olsen-Taylor thought to himself as he listened to his wife on the navigation bridge of the Smoke and Mirrors, right beside Officer Magabu.

"-So here are the rules for conversation with Oodle-Noodle after she telepaths 'Hello' into your head. She will only try to read your mind about the things you say aloud to her. After her 'Hello,' she will only send messages into your head when you talk to her.

"One more thing before Oodle-Noodle introduces herself. She can carry on close to a thousand mind-reading conversations at the same time. That's more than enough for the four hundred eleven people aboard the Smoke and Mirrors. Boys and girls, if she were Santa Claus, it would be like you were able to sit on her lap in a thousand different places at the same time, to tell her what you want. Oh, and since she mind-reads, she will telepath 'Hello' to you by your name, before you can even tell her your name. And this will be in the language she senses you are the most comfortable." Captain Taylor paused for a big inhale and exhale. "I guess that's it. Oodle-Noodle?"

*I was going to comment, Captain, that in my present condition especially, it probably wouldn't work for me to participate in Louisa Entroper's team builder. When it was my turn to topple backwards, my weight would prove too much, even with the lower gravity.*

"Yes, yes, Oodle-Noodle, but please, go ahead with your welcome to the others. We can talk later."

*Captain, remember what you just said, about how I can carry on so many conversations at the same time? My welcomes are already well underway!*

Had Helena been able to watch children and adults throughout the spacecraft, she would have seen a variety of reactions. It made no difference whether or not they had been attentively focused on the intercoms, where those devices were installed at the junctures of wall and ceiling. Their faces lit up simultaneously, whether with delight, shock, or, in the case of Pedro's stepfather Don Placido, total disgust. "Aydiomio!" *Oh my God!*

"Of course," Captain Helena Taylor shook her bowed head with closed eyes. Even though she could clearly communicate about Oodle-Noodle's capabilities, their full import had yet to sink in fully. When the captain looked up, she noted the behavior of Louisa, Pedro, Tanya, Fred and Guy, the ones still left there from the aborted team builder. They were taking the curious step of moving off to different nooks and crannies, for their parallel telepathic conversations with Oodle-Noodle. Resisting the strong pull to follow suit, Helena stood her ground in the center of the room, and she raised her head to vocalize unabashedly, however seemingly to no visible body, "So let me ask you, Oodle-Noodle: Can you explain to me how you knew we would need housing on your planet for our own, um, special passengers?, who I assume you've read our minds and theirs to already know all about? And wait, thank you, we thank you and your fellow Oombians for what is obviously your unflinching welcome of interplanetary immigrants."

*We enthuse with no restraint over any and all peaceful associations with other life forms, Captain, even when they arrive planning to live among us prior to requesting such an arrangement.*

"In our defense,-"

*No need to defend, Captain. We know for certain – I am telling you the truth about this – we know that had we objected to this settlement plan, you would have sought another planet to locate your time travelers, or maybe even have given them some place special, some secret locale, back on Earth. Now, what we DO have a problem with is the laser mesh, to create on the planetary scale what on your Earth used to be termed a gated community. It is clear to us that there are those aboard your spacecraft determined to deploy the mesh no matter our opposition.*

"But they will nevertheless need to give you an audience for you to formally lodge your complaint. And you must know that I and others aboard the Smoke and Mirrors will object to the planned deployment if you are not persuaded of its value."

*As you could have guessed, Captain, by now we have already mind-read every possible argument your special assignment officers might offer, and we find them of no merit. We look forward to that audience to, as you put it, lodge our complaint. In tandem, we will share our game and our music. Also, I think the timing will be such as to allow you witness of our daily celebration.*

"Your daily celebration? Ohhh, I seem to remember your making reference to that on our first visit."

*Yes, Captain. Now as for how we already knew to construct housing, well that is something I can explain presently, in its entirety. Which explanation will also address, incidentally, the dramatic expansion of our mind-reading range. A telepathic range dwarfing even my own, Captain Taylor, is that of a woman from the Earth city of Philadelphia. Not only did she bridge a multi-trillion-mile space gap, she also crossed sixty years into the future, to experience the universe through your eyes and other eyes. As you grew to suspect, she alternated between experiencing through you, and experiencing through your colleagues and loved one, whenever her presence caused too much discomfort. Then, her vicarious partaking of my planet gave her an idea for the deliverance of her neighbors from their variously wretched situations.*

*In essence, she kept whispering this idea in your ear until you came to be convinced of its compelling worth. During which period of her persuasion, her example inspired my self-discovery of how much more widely I could cast my own mind-reading ability. Well, Captain, since much of the Philadelphian's telepathic intrusion on you occurred over the short interval that your husband was on Oomb, I was able to eavesdrop. As I've explained previously, such eavesdropping would not normally be our inclination. Nor would it be something us Oombians felt comfortable doing. But the appearance of such dramatic plans for our planet on your mental landscape stood out in sharp relief not only for me, but for most other Oombians as well. Our consensus was immediate to embrace those plans. Habitat construction was begun probably before you even got back to Earth. Volunteers from all over Oomb helicoptered to our largest single land mass, about the size and shape of the Earth island you call Borneo. Coincidentally, our ancestors named it Boombeeno. Anyway, some of the volunteers offered their carpentry expertise. Others donated lower-hanging branches they were planning to trim off of themselves, no matter what.*

"Such selfless generosity, Oodle-Noodle," remarked Captain Taylor. If the Oombian could see as well as mind-read, she would have witnessed Taylor shaking her head in astonishment. "Surely, this will have to weigh significantly on our special assignment officers when you express to them why you object to the laser mesh deployment."

*We will hope that is the case up until the final indication it is not the case, Captain Taylor.*

"And if it is not the case, Oodle-Noodle? If they go ahead with it regardless of your kind's will?"

Are you *wanting to ask, Captain, whether their insistence on the deployment of the laser mesh would result in our withdrawing our acceptance of your space-time immigrants?*

"Yes." Taylor bowed her head anew, in a shame she couldn't help suddenly coming over her.

*Captain Taylor, we would never imagine holding hostage something we find good until we convince others to desist from doing something we fear imperils us.*

Helena Taylor lifted her head with her startlement. "You believe the laser mesh imperils you?"

*We are concerned it will call attention to our presence, which could be hazardous to your settlers as well.*

"Captain, I need you on the bridge immediately."

"Coming, Yoon-hee, but I want to pursue this, the next chance we get, Oodle-Noodle."

*We are thankful, Captain.*

"I could almost have read your mind that that would be the case." Helena was already down the hall to the circumvator.

"Captain," Navigation Officer Yoon-hee's voice crackled from the intercom in the lift that travelled sideways around the photon exhaust chamber rather than up and down like an elevator, "the only zero-clearance personnel we had to chase off the bridge was Don Típico circling back in search of his wife. I think he thinks we're sheltering her from him here. He shouted, 'Caramba!' but we got him out."

"I know if worse came to worst, Officer Park-Smith, I could have counted on you to slow-dance him to his quarters."

"I would have thought that was more your area of expertise, Captain, after your boogie fest with the Fafamafalafama."

Just that moment, Captain Taylor burst onto the bridge, and noted her husband Chris focusing her way. However poorly developed were the powers of extrasensory perception in most humans, Taylor's own telepathy was still plenty adequate for her to easily discern that Chris was to hang on her every word in response to Yoon-hee's sarcastic remark. This, in search of some sign, some least hint what was actually going through her head. But she knew the circumstances would not oblige him, nor tax her, as it was clear there was a serious matter at hand. "Okay, Yoon-hee, let's hear it."

"Captain, a UFO was detected by one of our rear guard firefly donuts. It was flying directly through the Callaway X Centra Oort Cloud, on a trajectory that took it past the Callaway X Centra solar system, where we are entering presently, of course."

"Coming from Tictoctic, Yoon-hee?"

"If Tictoctic was its origin, Captain, it sure plotted a most roundabout detour."

"Hmm. Based on what we know from their small craft wreckage on Fafama, the ETs from Tictoctic are likely not so advanced as to want to venture directly through Oort Cloud Space, if they can avoid it."

"That's assuming the crashed vessel represented their state-of-the-art capability. Including piloting capability, given that the creatures on board appeared to be acting in open rebellion, Captain. They might not have received the best available formal training, if any."

"True, Yoon-hee," said Helena as she peered intently at the panoramic view-screen. She was trying to figure out which star was Oomb, now that Callaway X Centra was looming ever larger. "But at least if it is a Tictoctic craft, from what you've gathered it is not taking this particular exit ramp, at least for now. Anything else you have apprised about it?"

"The reason I called you here, Captain. The UFO slowed on its way past this system. Then it sped up again."

"Like they were rubbernecking to look for blood at an accident scene, Yoon-hee? Anyway, just how fast were they going, to have passed by in what I take was a very abbreviated interval?"

"Captain, it had to be a couple hundred times light speed. Another reason I am also of your opinion they are not from Tictoctic. I think they are more likely to be associated with whomever, whatever we detected during Mission One."

"A couple hundred times light speed. If they are from Tictoctic, that means they're probably so advanced, we don't stand a chance of stopping them anyway. Maybe that's why they haven't launched their invasion yet, far as we know from Fafaman communications. They're pushing their technology to the max, to scope out other solar systems. They're wondering whether there might be more delectable meat to be found elsewhere."

"That's a very interesting speculation, Helena, uh, Captain Taylor, but, I'm sorry to interrupt. Remember? It's almost time for the video feed to Earth." Husband Chris Olsen-Taylor was standing before Helena with his body cam.

"Yes. The show for the billions we left behind." Captain Taylor was grateful Louisa Entroper wasn't present to witness her slapping hand to forehead in a clear gesture of embarrassment over her forgetfulness. That would have earned Taylor yet another lecture about the perils of not constantly checking, or even having, a daily agenda, to keep track of what she was doing. Maybe, Helena mused to herself, Dr. Entroper was still conversing with Oodle-Noodle on this very matter. Maybe Entroper was asking the tree creature to telepath her how they manage to stay organized on Oomb, and she was hoping she would learn the Oombians adhere to a formal agenda routine. "Just give me a moment, Chris, to collect my thoughts. No, I'm ready." Helena waved a hand to cancel her directive, soon as she gave it.

"Connecting with the oscillating firefly," said Chris Olsen-Taylor as he blinked the relevant code for the eyeglass lens of his body cam. "And we are ready. Take it away, now!" He aimed his right forefinger at Helena.

"Ladies and gentlemen, boys and girls, thank you for tuning in to our latest installment from the second voyage of the Smoke and Mirrors. If it's the middle of the night where you are, I hope what we're about to share with you will prove worth having set your alarm for two, three in the morning, or whenever you set it for.

"Officer Olsen-Taylor, if you would direct your body cam towards the panoramic view-screen, I'll point out some things. Yes, perfect." Helena was checking a feedback monitor set into the ceiling. "In the foreground of the screen, you will note the continuing spray of twinkles from ambient starlight getting funneled into the photon exhaust chamber. You might recall from previous updates that those twinkles are most likely the result of light 'choosing'-" Captain Taylor made quotation mark gestures with her fingers "-its photon properties over its wavelength properties. This is while the electromagnetically-engulfed mirror array 'blooms' like a tulip around the forward end of the photon exhaust chamber. Such 'blooming' virtually eliminates inertial friction ahead of our spacecraft, especially the inertial friction caused by light. Dr. Timothy Aquinas is our special guest theoretical physicist who will try to expand our knowledge of how and why our propulsion system is handily able to cheat the speed of light, and cheat it without tearing apart the Smoke and Mirrors along with us inside it, in fact even contributing to our health by generating artificial gravity. And I'm imagining we could also use a special guest educator. Yes, I think we need someone who can communicate more clearly what we already suppose we do comprehend about mirror array propulsion.

"In any event, you'll notice the twinkle spray is far less pronounced than during our previous update, as we are decelerating below light-speed. Officer Park-Smith?"

"We're down to about three-tenths, Captain, which is around sixty thousand miles per second."

"Friends joining us from Earth, if you've guessed we're approaching our first destination, you're correct. Something else you might recall is that at the conclusion of our first trip to the planet Fafama in the Alpha Centauri C solar system, we were seeking a return route less hazardous than our initial path. We got reduced to only one advance guard firefly donut. We could not afford-Well, I probably don't need to remind any of you about how we limped home from Mission One after a dirty comet shattered most of our mirror array."

Captain Taylor was repeating for the umpteenth time a story that was pure baloney, meant for public distraction. About how the safer return route just happened to bring them through another solar system, where they happened to notice another planet like Earth and Fafama, suitable for life to have proliferated. So why not investigate? What was not baloney, of course, was their amazement when an intelligent creature from said planet established telepathic communication with them as soon as the Smoke and Mirrors descended into an orbit.

On the panoramic view-screen, Captain Taylor pointed out the star that was Oomb, plus the larger star to Oomb's right that was its sun, named Callaway X Centra where Earthlings were concerned. The captain also gave a brief dissertation on how viewing said sun when travelling close to light speed gave it a lovely pastel lavender hue.

Chris Olsen-Taylor's mother, Samantha, was watching from her apartment in the quarantine-free portion of San Francisco, California. What mattered far more for her than what her daughter-in-law spoke of concerned her son, Chris. Samantha knew he was the one filming Captain Taylor's updates.

It was nearly sixty years earlier that a mysterious, mousey-haired old woman – perhaps the same age as Samantha was presently – had given her a golden cylindrical pendant engraved with markings that looked like Egyptian hieroglyphics, but which Samantha's research had established were from no known language on Earth. The mysterious woman had told her to guard and protect the pendant for sixty years. Soon thereafter, it would prove most important for Samantha to share the object with a loved one who had undergone "an awful adventure." Samantha well knew that the time was upon her, when she needed to fulfill the obligation which had haunted her for most of her adult life, and much of her adolescence. Unless the sixty years was an approximation. Maybe it was supposed to have been sixty-three or sixty-four years. Or maybe it was no years at all. Maybe the mysterious woman had set into motion an especially sick joke. Samantha had been fooled by the persisting luminescence of the pendant in the dark, not to mention the gibberish engraved on it. And yet, how exactly had said mysterious woman vanished from the room where Samantha had met her, so soon as she turned her back on her?

Yes, for all those years the pendant had haunted Samantha Perez-Olsen. And indeed, part of that haunting had been over the possibility she had spent endless hours captivated by a bizarre hoax. But no longer. Absent-mindedly fingering the pendant as she watched Captain Taylor's report recorded seven light years away, Samantha suddenly found herself overwhelmed by one particular intuition. The loved one for whom the pendant was meant was her son. So what "awful adventure" – those had been the woman's exact words, staying with Samantha for all this time – what awful adventure was her son about to have?

No, no, no, Samantha shook her head furiously. *I know what this must REALLY be about!*

# Chapter 3

Seventy-year-old Samantha Santiago-Olsen managed to lift herself out of her armchair, losing her grip on neither the mystery pendant nor the brim of her San Francisco Giants baseball cap. However, once she was standing fully upright, she hurled the pendant at the far wall, heedless of the risk she might have sent it crashing into a built-in television screen. This time, there was no going for an imagined strike zone, as she still sometimes did with her Softy Ball. This time, it was aimless fury. And then she buried her face in her baseball cap as tears came gushing and her shoulders heaved with grief.

But grief over what?

At first, she was certain she'd experienced an epiphany, a better-late-than-never realization that this nonsense with the pendant was, in fact, nonsense. And that it would be proven, confirmed nonsense were she, in a final act of desperation, to follow the directions given her so many decades ago, and hand over the mysterious object to another family member. However, each successive day she had taken the thing seriously was one more day she'd invested in the pendant as a personal project. By very early on, before she'd even graduated from high school, she'd already gone too far. She'd already reached the point where, to have given up on the little old lady's directive, she would have had to have admitted to having wasted a ridiculous amount of thought and effort. How could she keep from coming unglued, making such an admission to herself so many years, decades even, later?

Where abandoning that enigmatic assignment was concerned, what certainly didn't help, right from the outset, were events during her family's first weeks back from their unsettling experience in Philadelphia. Samantha's relatives, on her father's side, had mysteriously vanished, leaving beans in tomato sauce still simmering on the stove. Within days of Samantha and her immediate family making that bizarre discovery, there was a visit to Samantha's home by two Philly police officers. Samantha couldn't bring herself to voluntarily tell them about her surprise encounter with the little old woman hiding out in the cousins' bedroom, and the pendant with which that woman had entrusted her. But there was something endearingly special to how those officers removed their hats to enter her parents' townhouse, how they sat side-by-side on the sofa with their heads bowed humbly, and how they each said, "No thanks, Ma'am," when her Mom offered them something to drink. Had they made the teensiest peep about a little old woman and a golden pendant that glowed greenish in the dark, Samantha wasn't sure she wouldn't have spilled every last detail. As it was, though, they focused on the experience of her mother and father. "You two have anything to add?" was their only bid to bring Samantha and her brother Eduardo into the conversation. When both siblings shrugged their shoulders, the one officer unaffectedly scratched at the nape of his neck and said, "We really appreciate you folks taking this time to talk to us. If you remember anything, no matter how insignificant it might seem to you, just any small detail you forgot to mention, or just plain forgot, period, please give us a call. In the meantime, as soon as we have new information about the whereabouts of Mr. Placido or Ms. Rotonda, we will let you know immediately. And what I said about remembering anything, or any small detail, that goes for you kids too." The officer looked straight into Sammy's eyes and her brother Eduardo's eyes as well. "You tell your parents if you noticed something you forgot to tell us, okay?" Samantha was tempted to offer something vague, about thinking she'd heard an old lady's voice, but that she wasn't sure it was real. However, when a different pair of men came knocking a few days later, was Samantha ever glad she hadn't breathed a word of her odd private experience! Even before they came knocking, she'd overheard her parents wondering to one another why there'd been nothing on the television or in the newspapers about the reported disappearance. They'd been waiting for officials to make it general knowledge before they mentioned anything to their friends. Of course, they'd had no way of knowing that living on and near the same block as her father's relatives, close to two hundred other people had also mysteriously vanished.

In any event, the second questioning took place on a Saturday morning when her brother looked not to be waking up until close to lunch time. Samantha's father, José Santiago, answered the door. At first, he thought the two men were Jehovah's Witnesses, what with their black suits and white shirts. Yet, they weren't wielding any Bibles or religious pamphlets, and from the outset they made the Witnesses seem polite by comparison. After confirming he was speaking to Mr. Santiago, one of them said, "I'm sorry, sir, but we are going to have to speak to you and the rest of your family, now." He and his partner shoved past her father into their townhome, and he shouted, "Anyone up there needs to come down here to the living room, this minute! You don't want us to have to carry you down!" For the entirety of his terse command, the man eyed Samantha standing by the top of the stairs. She was clutching at the brim of her Baltimore Orioles' baseball cap, as was usual when a situation made her feel insecure.

"Brian," the other man said in a tone obviously meant to communicate: *You need to take it down a notch.* And then, to Samantha as she descended the stairs in a gallop, "You think the O's will have any better luck next season?"

"Not if they keep trading players before they have a chance to develop some real teamwork." All these many years later, Samantha still remembered having responded emphatically.

"Well you must be a very smart young lady to have thought it through that far. So, what do you make of your relatives just disappearing into thin air?"

Samantha tried to shrug her shoulders with as much nonchalance as she could feign. "Isn't it possible they went on a long trip somewhere and forgot to tell anyone?"

"What do you know about a long trip, young lady?"

"Brian." The friendlier man was using that admonishing tone with his partner again. "Remember, we're not here for an interrogation."

"Oh, cool!" Younger brother Eduardo set aside his *Star Wars* spinoff comic book where he was reading it nestled comfortably into a living room armchair. He'd woken and come downstairs only scant minutes before the unexpected intrusion. "Maybe you guys are like those secret agents in the *Men In Black* movies! You're going to flash a light in our faces to make us forget we ever knew Papa's side of the family, because they got abducted by extraterrestrials!!"

"You have my permission to torture my son until he tells you everything he knows."

Samantha was able to tell her father was as nervous as anyone, unlike her brother Eduardo. Eduardo's head was always too far up in the sci-fi clouds, she was convinced, to ever sense real danger, even if this wasn't it. Obviously, "Papa" was struggling heroically to layer over his dread with flippancy, so she pushed herself to join in, "Everything my brother knows? You guys should be done in two seconds."

"I think what my sis' is referring to is how long she could stand getting tortured before she spilled all the beans!"

"Oh, that reminds me: If you're going to torture my brother, first you're going to want to fit him with diapers, 'cause he'll probably 'spill the beans' both ends!"

"Stop it! Both of you!" It took Samantha's mom that long to finally protest; she had been wrestling open a Life Savers roll. She gave the fellow named Brian a pleading look, as she took a seat beside her husband on their sofa. An orange Life Saver got knocked against her molars when she said, "Please pardon my family's behavior."

"Nothing we haven't seen in our own," Brian's nicer partner waved a hand dismissively. "But look," his suddenly harsher tone was met with Brian's approving nod, "something all of you need to understand. There is no sense in sharing your experience in Philadelphia with anyone else you know."

"We're afraid people would think we're nuts," said Papa José.

"I get it!" If Eduardo was at all concerned about possible danger from the men in black suits, his enthusiasm did not appear the least bit dampened. "You want us to keep our lips sealed about the disappearance, 'cause other people learning that could create a panic! Cool! Wouldn't it be easier to just make us disappear too?"

Even Brian had to grin. However, as he and his partner headed for the door, he turned back and said,

"That's not a part of our plans, at the present, and we'd like to keep it that way."

This last remark was finally enough to give Eduardo visible, if momentary, shivers as the nicer man gently shut the door behind both of them. And it also confirmed for Samantha the wisdom of her not having breathed a word to anyone about the pendant.

For the following two years, Samantha was able to treat it as a sort of game, keeping the pendant secret from everyone. The biggest scare was when she left her backpack under the seat of her school bus, one afternoon in mid-October. Her art teacher, Ms. D'Angelo, had come into an enormous cache of surplus fine-line pens, color inks, and oversized, specially-treated paper from a friend whose comic book company was going over entirely to computer-generated graphics. Sammy's younger brother was the one in the family who originally went crazy over comic books. And yet ironically, she was the one who grew to want to create her own comic characters, inspired by *Archie* comics. So when Ms. D'Angelo had told her class they could help themselves to any of the old-fashioned comic book production products they wanted, until supplies ran out, Samantha had been the first in line with a grocery bag stealthily brought from home. On the bus ride that afternoon, she'd gotten caught up telling her friend Aninha from Brazil about the first complete comic story she was going to draw and write about her imaginary characters, the Gangly Gang. She'd gotten so caught up in this conversation, she was a full block down the road from the bus stop before she realized that while her treasure trove bag of art supplies was safely in hand, she'd totally forgotten her backpack. Which included the mystery pendant securely tucked away inside one of its many zippered pouches. Samantha had worked herself into a tearful panic by the time she reached home, so that she was pounding on the front door desperate for someone to be there. She usually opened it up with her copy of the house key, but that was also tucked away inside one of the zippered pouches. Fortunately, her mom took the whole day off from teaching for a morning dental appointment, so she had been there for her. After her mom called the school, then a harrowing hour wait, the bus driver had been cheerfully lugging Samantha's backpack to the front door. Said driver would have made it there, too, if Samantha hadn't run out to greet her when she saw the bus round the corner. Samantha's mom followed Samantha outside, to join in thanking the driver for such selfless action. However, before she could speak to her daughter, Samantha was back in her bedroom. The door was slammed shut and locked behind her. Not two seconds later, Sammy was probing the backpack's special compartment for that familiar yet ever-eerie green phosphorescent glow of the pendant.

Inevitably, Sammy had to face her mother's stern lecture about "a time and a place for everything." She could tell this lecture had been weeks if not months in the making. Her mama was just waiting for an excuse to deliver it. Well, Sammy had almost lost her backpack full of textbooks and notebooks because she got so excited over receiving a bag full of art supplies. What better excuse for her mom to warn her about "throwing away an education, doodling comics"?

Sammy bit her tongue when her mama proceeded to confiscate her cherished loot, and told her it would be made available for limited intervals only, on weekends. This, provided she kept up her grades. Of course Sammy couldn't let her mama know just how wrong she was, just what an enormous misconnection of dots her mama was making, if she thought her daughter's moment of absent-mindedness signified a lack of appreciation for the contents of her backpack, not to mention the backpack itself. Except for her family, what could Samantha possibly have held more dear than the mystery pendant with the mystery engravings that a mystery woman told her was vital to pass along to a loved one after that loved one underwent an "awful adventure" several decades hence?

Anyhow, what her mama's rationing-out of art supply use made clear to Samantha was that she would need to guard her comic-drawing work nearly as carefully as she guarded the mystery pendant. How could she know that a poor grade on a big test or her report card wouldn't send her mama into an unthinking rage where she sought to shred and trash the Gangly Gang? Samantha couldn't very well tuck her comics into a small pouch like she'd done with the pendant, at least not without ruining them getting them folded up small enough to fit. And anyway wouldn't her backpack be the first place her mama might look in that aforementioned rage? Samantha finally decided the inside lining of her winter coat was as ideal a place to keep her best comic efforts as she was to find, short of constructing a false bottom into one of the drawers of her clothes dresser. Decoy first drafts were left lying in piles on her desk while her proudest work got carefully concealed by manila folders, complete with cardboard backing before she slipped them inside her coat.

Of course, none of this she would have considered necessary were it just a matter of her mama becoming the gatekeeper for the free art supplies. What drove Sammy's paranoia were rumors at school of other parents trashing kids' comic book collections for various reasons. This, plus the comment her own mama had directed at Eduardo a few months earlier when he tried flicking peas into an empty glass with his thumb and forefinger, like they were tiddly winks. "One more pea into that glass," she'd said, "and imagine that was your comics into the recycle bin!" Eduardo would have let loose with a wisecrack that popped into his head, "Okay, so you want me to make sure my peas miss the glass? Cool!" But he'd heard the rumors at school too. Sammy's father had said, "Julia," to her mama in that tone that said, *Don't make such a big deal,* but Sammy wasn't so sure he'd find the wherewithal to flat-out stop her mama from a search-and-destroy mission, if it ever came to that.

Curiously, though, as Samantha progressed through high school, well she wasn't sure if it was on account of her mother's attitude or if she was simply growing out of it. She found herself setting aside the comics of her own volition, and telling herself it was time to get "serious" about her future. What helped in that regard was, at her parents' suggestion, landing a summer job as a waitress at the *Something's Fishy* seafood restaurant in Baltimore Harbor. Her best friend Aninha also got a waitress position there. During their off hours, when she might otherwise have been sketching characters on a notepad at an outdoor café table while waiting for her parents to pick her up, instead she and her school buddy wiled away their time. When the Baltimore Orioles were in town, they joined the crowds outside the fence by the renovated warehouses, where she hoped in vain to bare-hand a homerun ball after it shattered a warehouse window. And incidentally, have it proven to her brother, once and for all, that such a hit was indeed possible. But more often, they just bummed around the harbor, sharing a waffle cone packed with chocolate chip mint ice cream when the temps got especially high. The diversion that had the most impact on her was their visit to the Baltimore Aquarium. There, Sammy pondered the odd combination of complexity with ephemeral appearance of large jellyfish, which she commented to Aninha made them look like lace doilies brought to life. She started to think on marine biology as a possible career of interest, a goal for her education.

Subsequently getting assigned a biology class going into eleventh grade certainly seemed like a most serendipitous development, but then two things happened. One, while Samantha excelled at drawing detailed, accurate drawings of creatures' inners after their dissection, she also found herself unable to resist doodling those inners during especially boring lectures in other classes. Ditto for during leftover time in those same classes, whenever she quickly dispatched an in-class assignment. Moreover, it came to her to have those inners talk to one another in comic strip fashion, with the goal of amusing her fellow students. Her favorite, and coincidentally the one that received the most laughs, was the starfish stomach saying to the frog intestine, "I never know what to say to the visitors the Mouth sends me; they're always having a total breakdown," and then the intestine responding, "Well I have no problem knowing what to say to them when they reach me. Every time it's, 'What is this shit?'" Sammy told herself, *Okay, so I might still be drawing comics, but at least now it's relegated to an innocent diversion, rather than ruling my existence.*

The second happening was a kind of evolution, after going so many years feeling no pressing need to share the secret of the pendant with anyone. Suddenly, Sammy was become obsessed to find to whom she could confide. Early on, she'd known how thoroughly her younger brother would have flipped over the pendant, and the story behind how she ended up with it, what with his passion for all things science fiction. But she'd also known it would have been way too much for him to keep her confidence no matter his best intentions. Eduardo simply wouldn't have been able to resist blabbing to his friends. And even if he'd sworn them all to mum's the word, inevitably one of them would have let the story leak, and it would have gotten back to her parents. Only his persisting fear of the men in black suits had kept Eduardo from telling his friends about the relatives' disappearance. Although, he did develop a reputation for sternly lecturing anyone who ever said something dismissive to him about extraordinary possibilities. Sammy was there the one time his best friend, Greg, had scoffed at a news report of several people seeing an enormous UFO over Phoenix, Arizona. Actually, her brother had raised the subject with Greg; for all she knew, Eduardo was making a first tentative effort, to find out whether he might be able to trust his buddy to be open-minded enough to not think he was nuts if he told him of his relatives' enigmatic disappearance. "Hey, you heard about that monster flying saucer over Phoenix, Arizona? They said maybe thousands of people saw it at night. I think someone even got a picture of it!"

"Yeah, I think I know what happened. You got these people whose Mommies and Daddies never let them stay up late before, past seven. They didn't know nothing about street lamps, so they all pointed and said, 'Wow, look, Mom, we're getting invaded by some Klingon warships!'"

"I think it's too easy for someone to make fun of

somebody else's experience," Eduardo had bristled, "when they haven't had it happen to themselves!"

*My poor brother,* Sammy had thought to herself as she heard him say this. *Part of his defensiveness must be from this jolting realization Greg isn't someone who's exactly going to take him seriously if he tells him about our Philadelphia mystery.*

Greg had reacted to Eduardo with, "Oh, yeahhh! You're right! That is exactly what they would have said, if someone had called them out on their lame-o reports! Too funny, Eddie my man! I can hear them now. 'You can't imagine how it is,'" Greg had gone on in girlish falsetto, "'to see the night sky fill with cosmic invaders for the first time!'"

"Isn't that the real deal?" Eduardo had chuckled. He had affected total amusement as he'd high-fived his oblivious friend.

So Sammy had sensed an added reason not to share the pendant with her younger bro, for how much more alienated he might have ended up feeling from his peers. She was left to latch the possibility, of letting another know her bizarre secret, onto *her* best friend, Aninha. She hadn't tested how Aninha might respond, like it appeared her brother had done with his close associate. But gee, with so much they *had* shared together... Hadn't Aninha been supportively approving when she mentioned she looked into marine biology careers on the internet after their afternoon at the Baltimore Aquarium? "Wow, that sounds so cool!" Sammy could still hear Aninha's voice echoing decades later. Though unfortunately, she could also hear, and see as well, her reaction, late one night at a sleepover that was just the two of them at Aninha's townhome. They'd finished watching one of those horror flicks pretending to be a collection of amateur documentary videos, complete with nausea-inducing, erratically shifting camera angles. Sammy had tried to ease her friend from an abstracted discussion, about the possibilities of real paranormal phenomena, into an explication of what she'd experienced. But she didn't get very far.

"I had an uncle in Rio who said he was talking to his dead wife, but I don't know," Aninha had giggled, "because he was crazy. My papa said he was a Nutty Buddy, not the kind you can eat!"

"Okay, but what if I told you that back when I was nine, some relatives on my Papa's side of the family were vanished when we went to see them? And the police came to ask us if we knew where they could be, because nobody could find them?"

"C'mon, Sammy-Sam! They had to be somewhere! Maybe your papa is loco in the coco?"

"I was *there*, Aninha! Their food was left cooking on their stove! It was like they'd up and left in the middle of doing stuff!"

"Are you *serious*?!?!" As much as Aninha giggled out that question, Samantha could sense a veil of mistrust coming down between them as never before. Sammy backpedalled, not unlike how Eduardo had behaved with his friend. She got nowhere near mentioning the pendant. From there on, she and Aninha drifted further and further apart so that by college, they were virtually little more than nostalgia-inducing photos in a high school yearbook.

The thought came over Samantha that maybe she was dealing with something the world, her world, wasn't ready for yet. That maybe it was like how it wasn't healthy to introduce young children to sex, apart from what they could be taught in the abstract about "the birds and the bees." Any efforts beyond that could prove most traumatizing. In a similar way, maybe humanity in general wasn't ready yet, had not grown enough yet, to be fully inducted into deeper layers of mystery which surrounded them. Maybe when that diminutive older lady told her she'd need to do something with the pendant six decades hence, maybe that was with the idea she wouldn't be ready to deal with what the pendant was about until then. It might as well have been a grandmother's wedding dress getting placed in the grand-daughter's hope chest.

So Sammy went through her first years at Miami State University, studying biology, with her desire dramatically diminished to let anyone else know about the pendant and its attendant experience. That was, until Arturo wanted to give her a first kiss. They got to know one another at a study session for her advanced calculus class, where she helped him manipulate various infinities in quadratic equations. She learned that his biggest hobby, when he wasn't studying to become an architectural engineer, was reading about UFOs. He was convinced the government was hiding what they really knew. By the time he worked up the courage to ask her to see a movie at the student union, she was as excited as anything at the prospect of having someone with whom she might be able to share her secret without damaging the relationship...and as unsettled as possible, at having become grimly aware that she wouldn't be able to bring herself to intimacy with anyone until and unless she could be honest with them about what she was hiding.

Arturo moved in for the kiss on a late November evening under a grove of palms in front of her dorm. This was after paying fifty cents for them both to see the third part of *The Lord of the Rings* in 3D at the student union. Samantha intervened her forefinger on his expectantly pursed lips. Then she said, "Arturo, I was thinking it especially appropriate-"

"Really?! You have to be *that* formal with me?"

"Okay, let me rephrase: It's way cool, I think, that I have something like Frodo's ring. I'm supposed to do something with it, like Frodo was supposed to dump the ring in a volcano."

"What are you talking about?" Already Arturo was darting his eyes nervously from side to side. Sammy got the awful impression, either he was making sure no one else was eavesdropping, or he was looking for the escape hatch. He hadn't appeared comparably worried that someone might see them kissing.

To steel herself to continue with her explanation, Sammy recalled that hey, this was the guy who earlier the same day was repeating his suspicion the U.S. government was keeping detailed information about UFOs away from the public.

But to no avail.

By the time she was done telling him the story, even showing him the pendant and how it glowed that eerie green in the dark, Arturo was backed completely out of the palm grove. He left her so alone in there that, as he started to respond, one passerby misapprehended he was some nut trying to talk to a tree. "This is unbelievable!" he shook his head. "I didn't think I was *that* important to them! They even found someone willing to put her health in jeopardy carrying around a bar of radium like that! They must have decided it's not enough, to neutralize me as a threat to the general public's lack of awareness by having me associate with someone acting like a total kook! They must have decided my untimely expiration is necessary, by radiation poisoning!!"

The most upsetting part of all was how, throughout Arturo's entire response, he never once thought to give Sammy a chance to address his fears. She might as well have vanished right after she spoke, because he was talking only to himself.

It took Samantha five more years to once more let down her guard, become that vulnerable anew. Doing research at the Scripps Oceanographic Institute north of San Diego, on how to revive abalone populations, and thereby pull west coast sea otters back from the brink of extinction, she met Albert Olsen. Albert was investigating starfish disease resistance. At first, she thought the physical attraction was so strong, she could allow herself to get carried away by sheer lust. She could save expecting him to understand about the pendant until they had grandkids or something. But on a coastal hiking trail near La Jolla, when he drew her close to him in his big, papa bear arms for their first kiss, she found herself pushing against his broad chest to keep his lips at bay, to first reveal the secret burden she'd been carrying by then for close to two of the six decades she was told would be required.

On completion of her full explication, Samantha felt certain this no-nonsense scientist would find whatever feelings he'd developed for her turned to dread-pitying aversion, at best. She took off her ever-present Baltimore Orioles cap, and she said into it, "If you want us to head back to the car right now, you don't have to say another word. Please." Then she buried her face in her cap, and her shoulders heaved with her silently kept grief.

"You know, Sam," Albert started to respond, wanting to enfold her in comforting arms, but fearful how she would react before he expressed himself more fully, "what's so ironic is, I was terrified what you'd think when you realized I intentionally mismatch my socks."

Sammy looked up from her cap at him, all teary-eyed. She half-laughed, half-sobbed, "I noticed your socks, the first time we met. You mismatch them on purpose?"

Albert shrugged his shoulders and held out his hands to his sides, palms skyward. It was a silent gesture to the effect he could offer no defense. He just liked his socks mismatched.

Sammy looked into his winsome eyes for seconds, before shaking her head and closing her own two peepers, like she was snapping herself out of a trance. "My putting up with your mismatched socks... As much hell as you can be sure I will give you for that, it can't begin to rise to the level of me with the pendant and, um, the instruction I'm waiting to carry out."

"Where are you keeping it? I assume you've got it tucked away some place safe?"

"You want me to bring it with me when I see the psychologist you try to convince me to see?"

"Let me put it this way, Samantha: I want to be around you- What is it, forty years from now? When you give the pendant to whoever you need to give it to, I want to be there to see what happens."

...Sammy set aside her Giants' hat, to pick up the framed photo of her and Albert from five years earlier. They were all smiles, arm-in-arm with the Golden Gate Bridge in the background. The photo was from just three months before his massive coronary the middle of the night. It took him away without even allowing him a chance to say goodbye, let alone live long enough "to see what happens." She shook her head and tearfully bit her lower lip. *Maybe*, she thought to herself, *my sudden rage doesn't have anything to do with the pendant. I've done a lot of living these past thirty-some-odd years. I haven't been exactly holding my breath all that time waiting on how things turn out with the reigning mystery of my life. Maybe I'm just so awfully pissed over how fleeting short life is, making it seem especially cruel there would be the false promise of some magical, family-related "Ta-da!" at this late stage. True, Chris has set up that telomere repair nanobot surgery for me. It's scheduled for after he and Helena return from their new mission. But what do I want with an extra fifteen, twenty years when Albert is not around? Am I supposed to just forget about him and have a late-life fling with someone else?*

Sammy struggled successfully to lift herself out of her armchair. She shuffled over to her window looking out the direction of San Francisco Bay. Between two tall buildings, she was able as usual to espy a sliver of dull olive, to reassure herself that beyond all the human-made structures, water still ebbed and flowed from the ocean. The difference this time was the degree of despair and resignation she brought to the task.

That's when she heard the voice. "Is only a little while more, and yes, is your son, Chris. His terrible adventure, from which he will require the comfort offered by the engraving on the pendant, his adventure has begun." It was the same voice Samantha had heard in her cousins' bedroom so many decades ago, where presently she could not get to, even were it still there, thanks to the quarantine zoning. And with John Hancock Street transformed into a canal to minimize flooding from the rising sea level.

Sammy spun her head around. She half-expected to see the diminutive older woman with the mousey-gray hair having materialized in her condo, as enigmatically as she had vanished from sight after handing her the pendant way back in 2002.

No one there. Was it an especially loud voice, somehow carrying that clearly through the walls from next door? And it was from someone discussing totally unrelated matters that Sammy was taking the wrong way? *So let's* see, she started arguing with the imagined reaction of her orchid-raising neighbor, Agnes. *The people next door are talking about a different son named Chris, and a different pendant with special engraving, not my pendant with special engraving.*

*No, they weren't talking about Chris nor a pendant with engraving,* Agnes was sure to offer in rebuttal. *For example, maybe "son Chris" was actually "sun-kissed." Whoever-it-was, she was talking about tomatoes or some such.*

*But it was loud and clear; I did not mishear. However, since I know this is how you would react to my account, that is why I will never be sharing this experience with you, Agnes. Would that it had continued,* Samantha went on to lament to herself. *Would that there had been more to it. Would that I'd even witnessed a phantasm of the woman who once handed me the pendant, to accompany the voice. Would that there were just anything else to reinforce, buttress this sand-castle occurrence against the wind and surf of skeptical remarks from those not here to listen. Heaven knows my own doubts will provide erosion enough…*

On the other side of the continent, in the bar in the Philadelphia "no-zone" not yet repaired from a shootout as deadly as it had been contrived, Samantha's granddaughter, Shelly, was seated beside Flamboyo Sanchez, the author of said shootout. They were watching the same report from trillions of miles away aboard the Smoke and Mirrors that Samantha was watching in San Francisco. Flamboyo had received critical information just prior to Shelly's arrival. Unlike for Samantha about the mystery voice, the main reason Flamboyo would be keeping said information from Shelly had nothing to do with fear she'd stoke personal uncertainty whether it was real. No, Flamboyo's concern was more about the threat of what Shelly might do with such knowledge. That threat would have required deceasing her far sooner than the carrying-out of the plot imagined by Dr. Engeling, which was the plot to ultimately decease every one, every human one, on the planet.

"So I want to make sure I understand. Your mother, the famous Captain Taylor, has flown a spaceship alllll the way back to some planet she visited the first time on a whim."

"No, it was more than a whim," Shelly Taylor shook her head how Flamboyo wished she would stop doing. Her golden locks looked so beautiful when they got tossed around like that. He could tell it was an innocent gesture, not intended for more than to express exasperation with him. But were she trying to seduce him, she couldn't have done a better job short of peeling off her blouse. "You might have heard that the Smoke and Mirrors spacecraft was down to only one advance guard probe to warn them of comets and such, when they left Fafama. They were searching for a safer route home, and they noticed another planet suitable for life..."

"Okay, I understand. So yes, it was more than a whim. The first time. But the government has no better way to spend their money, than to finance your father getting to golf on another planet? Then back to Fafama so maybe your Mom can orbit the sun with their supreme

Fafamafafu-" What Flamboyo was about to say, he paused to readjust. "-Fafamaflushalot or whatever they call him?"

"My mom hinted to me there were other things going on...not that!" Shelly blushed and slapped Flamboyo's arm when he presented her with mischievously raised eyebrows. Then she heaved a sigh and went on, "Surely you do appreciate the scientific opportunity of getting to study cultures and ecologies on other planets. We might learn things to help us do a better job down here."

"Sí, those opportunities include joining the first extraterrestrial country club. It's the ultimate in exclusive, the-wretched-of-the-universe-need-not-apply. Also, there's the 'grand opening' of a disco boogie parlor on Fafama. Okay, so I understand. You risked your skin, re-entering the Philly no-zone, so you could share the news with me, about your father becoming the first person from Earth to set a tee time on another planet."

"Flamboyo, why are you acting like this? You haven't been the same since our interview. Maybe I'm at fault; I was thinking I shouldn't have done that segment at all. My televised coverage might have set unrealistic expectations for people here, that things could move faster than they can actually move."

From their barstools where they were nursing two dark beers, Flamboyo looked up and around to grimly remind himself that, as much pleasure as he couldn't help feeling in this woman's company, it only gave him cruel false hope. Her shower-fresh scent set in sharp relief odors he'd otherwise mercifully adapted to not specifically noticing, lest they keep him in a state of perpetual nausea. Stale fryer grease and stale cigarette smoke (nonsmoking rules in public establishments had become rapidly unenforceable once the first electrified walls had gone up) were laced with wafts of stale urine, rotting trash and a pine-scented spray applied in a woefully ineffectual manner, however noticeable its presence. Framed posters urging people to better sanitation, more education, and healthy recreational activities in lieu of gang involvement and drug use were every one of them vandalized to varying degrees, where they were mounted on the walls by government decree. Vandalism included the bashing-apart of the frames, the smashing-in of the protective glass covers, and graffiti. On not a one of them did the official slogan, what Flamboyo termed "verbal morphine," survive undefaced. In many cases, "The quarantine zones are temporary. Let's make them history." had been marked up to read, "The quarantine zones are permanent unless we make those ruling f-ers history."

Flamboyo could have produced a list that went on for pages, of all the ruin and decay just inside that drinking establishment, compounded by glimpses to be had through hairline-cracked windows of other crumbling structures nearby. Those structures would have been better left concealed by curtains, if where curtains still hung they weren't so faded and discolored. One time, Flamboyo had suggested to an associate that they might as well have been used toilet paper put on display. But as wretched as they were, what Flamboyo found to be even worse was the not-so-obvious stuff. It was the stuff that at first glance looked decent, not unpleasant to live amidst. On closer inspection, shorn of the cosmetic benefit of distant inattentive viewing, it revealed itself to be in as much a state of decay as everything else. For example, there was the parkay wood flooring. Its dark staining cloaked for the casual observer how severely splintered it had gotten from years of neglect, until said observer nearly fell flat on his face from assuming he was traipsing across a smooth surface. Even crueler was the reality of the hanging Tiffany lamps. As Flamboyo saw it, those lamps were to the temples of care-numbing drinking and eating what stained glass windows were to the temples of mind-numbing scripted professions of faith. They suggested welcome intrusions from some faraway land of enchantment, until one realized that the specks of unpleasantly bright light issuing from every one of them were the result of bullet holes.

Pondering one of those holes in the heart of a butterfly design so he didn't have to face Shelly directly, he said, "I don't think you should come here anymore. I'm not sure how much longer my people will want to help delude your people that they are the ones who keep you safe when you enter our hell. No, let me amend that: I'm not sure how much longer my people will be able to keep you safe, even if they want to. A growing number of us are getting more and more pissed because each time you enter, it's with additional gifts for the children. You keep giving them this false sense of hope that they will ever be able to live in a better place, have a better future. Maybe one day you can have the shot-out glasses in these lamps replaced. But so what, man? There will be another gunfight soon enough that gets them shot-out again!"

"If all I was going to do was what you said, Flamboyo, I'd have to agree. But today I'm here with something more." She put a hand over one of his hands on the counter.

*Don't do this to me! Get the f-k away from me!* This is what he wanted to shout at her. But he settled with continuing to look off stoically, anywhere but towards her. He kept his eyes anchored on the hopelessness represented by the bullet hole in the center of the Tiffany lamp butterfly design, though he did not move to shake off where Shelly had placed her right hand.

"Today, on the floor of the United Americas House of Representatives, a group of twenty representatives is introducing a bill to experiment with dismantling the quarantine zones."

Flamboyo's lower lip trembled.

"It would start with Savannah, Cleveland, and here, Philadelphia."

"How will they experiment? They will let you take a few children out to the zoo and see if they can control their desire to throw stones at the lions?"

"No," Shelly said to accompany her head shake, because Flamboyo still wasn't taking his eyes off the hanging lamp. "For an excursion out of the no-zone, all a person would have to do is put on a tracking bracelet and verbalize a purpose, for example seeking employment. There would be teams of social workers and volunteers to assist. And as a special good will gesture, all fence electrification would get turned off."

Flamboyo nodded with a cynical chuckle. "Sí, and when someone stays out too long, the police will use the tracking bracelet to hunt him down and return him to his cage."

"On good behavior, there would be no time limit on leaving the no-zone. And, if someone submits proof of acquisition of a workable permanent living situation outside the zone, the bracelet will be removed."

"So by three weeks after selected no-zones are opened up, what happens with the abandoned areas? Are they going to be razed to start all over?"

"Parts of them might be razed, Flamboyo. Actually, we are hoping and expecting that other well-meaning people will feel emboldened to cross over into these areas to make something better happen."

This particular response finally got Flamboyo to look Shelly's way. "Why is anyone in Congress doing this? What are the real chances for success? What, is finding intelligent life on other planets shaming them into this? Are they afraid what the tree people and the Fafama-whatever are going to think if they find out that humans have shut away half the Earth's population? Or maybe they got spooked by that fireworks display worldwide?"

Flamboyo was referring to a mysterious yet brief flash, which had happened a month previous. It was witnessed worldwide, including in day-lit sky. Where the sun was up, it consisted only of numerous star-like pinpoints at regular distances from one another. In the clear-night heavens, a latticework of reddish lines were observed connecting those pinpoints, giving an appearance to many observers of the skeleton of a geodesic dome.

"I thought they said that had something to do with some sort of gamma radiation striking a special influx of particles in just the right manner. It gave the illusion of design, like a rainbow or a diamond crystal."

What Shelly couldn't have known, even though her own parents were so closely involved, was that several people had witnessed the activation of a laser mesh around the Earth to protect it from a possible Tictoctic invasion. Even trickier than disseminating the false story about a natural phenomenon had been secretly getting all spacecraft outfitted with the security-encoded laser circuit completion kit, so none of them would risk getting blown out of the sky on entering and leaving the atmosphere.

"Anyway," Shelly went on, "you might be right. Maybe, um, it shouldn't have taken extraterrestrial contact to trigger this. But maybe it is sheer embarrassment, what the little green men might think of us. Maybe that's compelling more of those who could actually do something to finally listen to those of us who have been clamoring for years to end this retreat from what a loving, caring society should be about." Shelly ventured to give Flamboyo's sweat-greasy hand a gentle squeeze, where he had left it to still rest beneath hers on the bar counter.

Flamboyo suppressed conflicting instincts to either wrest away his hand, or to squeeze back. He left it lying there limply unresponsive, as he thought to himself, *She-They might as well distract themselves with their delusions during these final days. At this point, it's really no more harmful than some of my fellow quarantine dwellers who sing and pray in churches while they await divine providence. Why should I bother her with my news, that I've gotten the first couple of my men infiltrated into jobs aboard the target freighter?, the first of the several we'll need for the hijacking?, any more than a doctor should make a patient's last days any worse than they already were by sharing his news that she's only got so many months left to live?*

# Chapter 4 – The Counsel

"So this is where we're going to meet." Dr. Louisa Entroper craned back her head to an uncomfortably muscle-straining extent, to take in the enormity of the double doors set before her. They were, by far, the tallest doors, wooden doors at that, she had ever seen. She guesstimated they rivaled the most looming closed drawbridges still remaining on Earth.

Helena was struck by how much those doors reminded her of the royal gates to the Emerald City in *The Wizard of Oz,* minus the emerald sheen...or some bioluminescent shade of green, Fafama-style.

*Normally, we meet standing around outside.* Oodle-Noodle's voice filled the heads of Entroper, Captain Taylor, First Engineer Buddy Leung, Sergeant Fred Frankly and Sergeant Guy Hanson. *The few enclosures we do require are for protecting our oof equipment, literature, various research projects, and some of our musical instruments.*

"*Some* of your musical instruments?" The severity of how Dr. Entroper intoned her question gave Helena a most distinct impression. Namely, that this tagalong government observer thought Oodle-Noodle just lent ample grounds for discrediting the tree creature's entire outlook on life. So, the Oombians are convinced peace and love conquers all? How can anyone take that approach seriously when it stems, no pun intended, from beings who intentionally *don't* shelter some of their musical instruments from the elements?

*Some of our musical instruments do not require shelter. This has to do with the nature of their existence, and the resultant singular manner by which they can be accessed. A subject we are sure to expound upon in more depth at a later, less worrisome time.*

*For the more urgent matters set before us, and*

*eventually, hopefully, for the less urgent, more celebratory matters, we have built this great meeting hall. It has been accomplished in tandem with the dwellings you see we have constructed to promote your settlement on our planet.* Oodle-Noodle swung open both doors. They did surprisingly little creaking where the Earthlings were concerned, thanks to maple-syrupy tree-sap lubrication of their hinges. *Inside, you see we have provided chairs and tables for your pleasure and comfort. Especially on days when it is raining, we have ascertained you will find this arrangement more to your liking than standing around in the elements, like we are wont to do. We only request one pre-condition for when we congregate with you and the settlers, for example for our discussion which is about to take place. We request you mentally accommodate our persisting with standing around while you sit; keeping our trunks entirely upright is what gives us most pleasure and comfort.*

"Oodle-Noodle, I would say you, your kind have gone what we call 'over and beyond' to accommodate us. The *least* we can do is welcome your standing presence when we meet! Ha!" There went Buddy Leung with his laughter again, like he'd just said the funniest thing. "And these monstrously proportioned doors…Yes! Of course! Any of you Oombians can enter without first having to get your tops lopped off or sides trimmed back."

Buddy continued to gawk happily at virtually everything all around. He found himself endlessly fascinated, enthralled by his first visit to the surface of Oomb. This, as a member of the team sent down to discuss the military mission with Oomb's treelike intelligent beings, before settlement activities were begun in earnest.

For Dr. Entroper and Sergeant Frankly, on the other hand, to say they were finding the experience harrowing was putting the matter mildly. Only a small part of it was how seemingly, half a forest had stepped aside to reveal the mammoth meeting hall. Entroper and Frankly had received a full briefing, on details of Officer Petrovsky's and Officer Olsen-Taylor's visit down to the surface of Oomb during the Smoke and Mirrors's maiden voyage. But that had made no difference. Entroper and Frankly were still shocked nearly insensible by what had happened, shortly after their smooth descent into the Oombian atmosphere aboard the shuttle pod. As the pod got closer to the beach where they were to land on the Borneo-sized island named Boombeeno, several Oombian tree creatures had lifted off into the sky in huge flocks, to escort the visiting spacecraft. Their palm fronds had spun furiously fast, like helicopter blades.

"They might as well be freakin' monster dandelion seeds!" Sergeant Frankly had exclaimed.

"You're sure they are to be trusted, Captain?" Louisa Entroper had spoken dubiously. "It's at a time like this I'd feel far more secure were we accompanied by a fleet of our fighter aircraft."

"Based on Officer Olsen-Taylor and Officer Petrovsky's experience, these creatures appear to be as gentle as hundred-foot-long blue whales."

"Appear to be, Captain," by which comment Louisa had made Helena regret instantly her choice of words.

*This is what our experience has been, Dr. Entroper,* Helena Taylor had wanted to retort, but she forced herself to let Louisa have the last word. After the government observer's reaction to the Oombians' beach reception, however, Helena hadn't been able to help herself. When the small forest's worth of tree creatures had rustled their leaves in welcome, Louisa Entroper had vented, "You had to insist, Captain, that even the sergeants remain unarmed for our visit?" Captain Taylor had responded, "Excuse me, Louisa, but have you been getting attacked in some manner not apparent to the rest of us?"

"There! There!" Entroper had abruptly pointed towards the surf. "Go ahead and mock me!"

"Wo!" had exclaimed Buddy Leung. Even Sergeants Hanson and Frankly had leapt backwards into a defensive crouch. They had beheld several creatures, reaching heights of fifteen feet and more. Those creatures had emerged steadily up onto the shore, leaving the gently lapping waves behind. The creatures' necks had stretched disproportionately long for their low-hung, squat bodies. Their mouths were a cross between the huge duckbills of a dinosaur such as a Trachodon, and a person with lips pouted to an exaggerated extent. Their short tails were curled up tight against their hippo-like rears. And their smooth skin, comparable to porpoise skin, was mottled sandy brown and aquamarine. Their short, bouncy steps had made their bellies jiggle, and most alarming for the Earthlings, they had appeared headed straight towards them. But suddenly, they had stopped. In pairs, they had twisted their heads towards their respective partners. With a loud SLURP!, they had delivered big, sloppy kisses to one another. Still facing up the pinkish, coral sand beach, they had subsequently jiggle-bellied backwards with more bouncy steps. They had retreated so far backwards, down into the calm surf, even their ridiculous-looking heads had gotten fully re-submerged.

The negotiating team from the Smoke and Mirrors had not been able to overcome the marveling silence into which they were stunned before the creatures' heads were resurfacing. On this new trip onto dry land, they were every one of them carrying what looked to be a tuna-like fish. When they'd reached the level above the shoreline where they sloppy-kissed before, this time in pairs they had given each other a loud SLAP! in the rear with the sea creatures they were holding. Then they had been off on another, bouncy, total re-submergence.

"You didn't have to wait for any of us to verbalize a question about this, Oodle-Noodle," Captain Taylor had managed to spit out despite having her attention still riveted on the pairs of creatures as their heads again sank out of sight below the wavelets. "Whenever you're ready..."

On her numerous rippling roots, Oodle-Noodle had separated from the rest of the reception forest to come closer to the humans as she telepathed, *They are the Oonzy Ootzies. You're arrived at the perfect time to witness their feeding behavior.*

"So they enter and leave the water during their eating routine?" As he had spoken, Buddy had noticed that only the tails of the fishlike creatures were sticking out of the Oonzy Ootzies' mouths as they had emerged from the surf for the third time.

*They enter and leave the water during most everything they do, Officer Leung. The middle of the night, you can hear their collective snore, each time their sleepwalking brings them to attain their highest tide.* Where Helena was concerned, the Oonzy Ootzies had added an exclamation mark to this telepathed claim, on their next ascendance to dry land. At the height of that jiggle-waddle up the beach, they simultaneously had let loose with a most cavernous belch. The fish tails were no longer hanging from their mouths.

*You probably don't want to be around here mid-*

*afternoon, as their synchronized flatus emission leaves what we're sure you'll agree is a most disagreeable stench in the air.*

"Okay, okay, I believe you, Ms. Fu-err, Ms. Noodle." Sergeant Frankly was holding his hands high, palms facing out, as he backed further away from the Oonzy Ootzy spectacle. "Can we get to wherever we're going, like right now? And, if I can speak honestly, Dr. Entroper is right. We shouldn't have come down here unarmed. Yeah, we didn't exactly pack any fighter jets, but I'm talkin' about my ol' buddy, Mr. AK-51. No offense, tree people." Oodle-Noodle and her kind had gotten the sergeant's forehead sweaty with his nervousness. They continued to just blithely stand around, appear totally nonreactive to his remarks. Not even the least rustle.

Sensing his military colleague's jitters, Sergeant Hanson had made a mental note to explain to Fred Frankly later. There was nothing Fred was verbalizing to these creatures they weren't already reading going through his head. His words were unlikely to at all startle or get a rise out of them.

"I'm not saying I'd of had any intention of actually pulling the trigger or anything like that," Fred had gone on. "But it would have been nice to be prepared, in case- How did you know that seeing us, seeing critters that are aliens for them, wouldn't suddenly send your oochie coochies, or whatever-the-hell you call them, on a murderous rampage our way?"

"That's a good question, I have to admit," had nodded Dr. Louisa Entroper.

*Yes,* Captain Taylor had thought to herself, *I'm sure that really pains you, whenever you "have to admit" fault with how our operation is being run!*

*May I point out to you, Sergeant Frankly, Oodle-*

Noodle had telepathed, *your species' own experience with large, potentially dangerous creatures on your planet?*

"Gladly, Ms. Noodle. Are we talking charging rhinoceros, starving Great White Shark, or stampeding wild boar?"

*Yes, we also have creatures on Oomb where great precaution must be taken for personal safety. There are the fifty-foot-long Hoohas. They burrow about the semi-barren summits of Boombeeno and of our other, more-mountainous islands. But the Oonzy Ootzies are along the line of your few remaining whales. Unless the minds we exhaustively probed on your kind's first visit to Oomb were totally delusional, apparently your largest sea creatures are among the gentlest beings on your planet. It is only in the past, when they were hunted close to extinction, that some of them became deadly boat destroyers, especially near the peninsula of Baja, Mexico.*

"Oh, great, so you guys are eavesdropping on all of our most private thoughts!" Sergeant Friendly had actually appreciated his anger about this getting him past his unnerving discomfort.

*No, no. We have learned to be most circumspect, most discreet, where thoughts of an intimate nature are concerned. That is, unless there is a specific request for such thoughts to be tapped. Your mental activities are like panoramic landscapes for us. However, the information-rich aspects are what stand out in sharpest relief, to interest us the most. All the same, though, we do agree with you that we should, as you put it, "get where we're going." That is, unless you'd like to stay here a while longer, to see whether the Oonzy Ootzies feel like mating…*

"Captain," said Buddy Leung, "I'd actually not mind

if we could afford, um... How long would we have to wait, Oodle-Noodle? Might that happen before the flatus emissions?"

"We are on a fairly strict timeline and agenda, however loosely defined," had cautioned Dr. Entroper.

"I don't know about 'loosely defined,' but I'm afraid Louisa is correct, Buddy. I'm sure you'll get a chance..."

"Of course, Captain."

*There is the question, Captain... Our probing did get a bit personal to arrive at this, it must be admitted. The question is how your away team would want to travel to the grand meeting hall we have constructed to accommodate you. We could take what would amount to approximately a two-mile hike, or we could fly.*

"By fly, of course you mean we could take our pod to land closer to the meeting hall."

Captain Taylor had been able to tell, even without Oombian mind-reading ability, that what Louisa really meant to say was, *Please don't tell me you're going to airlift us in your branches!*

*Unfortunately for you, Dr. Entroper, the beach areas of our islands are the only safe places to land your flying craft. Officers Olsen-Taylor and Petrovsky can tell you the wonderful time they had when we transported them to and from an oof course. But if you prefer, the hike would be most fascinating and not too overly strenuous for you, I'm sure.*

"Umm, on this walk, are there going to be more of your, umm, biological phenomena like the Oonzy Ootzies?"

While Entroper's question had oozed with her squeamish dread, Buddy Leung had nodded with wide-eyed, hopeful enthusiasm for Oodle-Noodle to telepath an affirmative response.

*I must admit, the walk will bring us across several of our planet's flora and fauna engaged in a variety of activities likely to be found as striking to you as the behavior of the Oonzy Ootzies.*

"Hey, I was just thinking, Oodle-Noodle…"

Buddy's enthusiasm had had Sergeant Frankly saying to himself, *Yeah, I was just thinking too, how I'd like to stick you up a tootsie wootsie's, whatever-they-call-them ass, where I'm sure you'll have an even more fascinating time than you're already having!*

Buddy had continued, "Do you have any theories, um, is there some suggestion the Oonzy Ootzies' unique behavior evolved to contend with hostile beasts both ashore and in the water a long time ago?"

*Precisely that suggestion, Officer Leung.*

"Yes, believe me, I'm also going to want to hear, um, get telepathed about that," had said Helena. She had wanted to scream at Buddy to give it a rest; for dealing with Dr. Entroper, his sidebar was coming at the worst possible time. Instead, she had asked, "Um, what are we deciding for going to the meeting hall? Walk or get flown as you're each more comfortable doing?"

"I'll go either way, Captain."

*You mean it makes no difference whether they screw you from the rear, or missionary style?*, Sergeant Frankly had wanted to ask Sergeant Hanson. But the only thing worse for him, than how this extraterrestrial encounter was already getting handled, would have been enduring a dressing-down for impolite utterance. Although, he would have asked what the fu— that mattered since the tree people could read all the garbage in his head, whether or not he kept it to himself.

"Okay, look," Louisa Entroper had raised one hand while she put the other to her head like she was having a migraine headache, "whatever we do, however we travel, I think it's better we all stay together. Please. And if it's the same to you, I vote for flying. I'll just keep my eyes shut until we land. At least I know how to hold on to a tree."

*Which you shouldn't have to worry over doing, Officer Entroper. There is no way any of us, with our multiple branch arms, would accidentally allow you to slip from our grasp.*

The Oodle-Noodle delegation held off on their traditional welcome ritual, of offering their guests a choice from among the bizarre variety of fruit hanging from their branches. They saved it until the Earthlings took their seats around a long rectangular table inside the cathedral-height-ceilinged congregation hall.

Dr. Entroper found the wooden chair onto which she practically collapsed surprisingly spongy-comfortable. Nevertheless, the overall experience continued to prove exhaustively harrowing for her. The worst of it was getting pressed by a deciduous palm tree hybrid to pluck off one of its hanging fruit. What should be her choice? The carrot-shaped fruit with an orange's pulp texture? The grape the size of an apple? The fruit with the likeness to a banana, but hairy like a kiwi?

"This is customary for all encounters on Oomb, Officer Entroper," said Captain Taylor, fully cognizant of Louisa's distress. "You did read the full report? Not only are their fruit safely edible and nutritious for us. The two that Officer Petrovsky and my husband, um, brought back from their experience tasted deliciously comparable to the Earth fruit they most closely superficially resembled."

The way Moofle-Moodle spread apart his branches reminded Dr. Entroper most uncomfortably of what she had once read of some pervert spreading open his trench coat to expose himself. It also didn't help, how he crinkled the already crinkled-enough bark around his eyes to open them further as he nodded encouragingly. Ditto for how he then proceeded to turn his back on Entroper, to display even more choices from his surreal bounty. Where she was concerned, that bounty could have slid straight off the canvas of some hitherto-unknown fantasy-fruit-tree painting.

Buddy Leung mused to himself how Moofle-Moodle could have been a fashion model showing off an especially low-cut neckline that exposed the back all the way down to the uppermost swells of the buttocks.

*I'd offer to pluck low-hanging fruit from my fellow soldier for you, but you'd probably prefer something a little larger than a pair of peas,* Fred Frankly censored himself from vocalizing, while Louisa finally, if hesitantly, made her choice, based on its being the smallest one, and assuming the appearance of a conventional tangerine.

*You don't have to be timid about plucking off my fruit, Dr. Entroper. Honest, there is no pain or discomfort for any of us, whatsoever.*

"Mind you, I'm going to save this for when we return aboard the Smoke and Mirrors, so I can wash it off." Louisa waggled a lecturing forefinger at Moofle-Moodle after snapping off her selection.

*Ahhh, the time has so gotten away from us; we really were hoping to tell you all about our mid-day celebration before you experienced it. But perhaps your attention to its significance will be that-much-more riveted by how surpassingly odd we're guessing you're going to find it.*

Louisa shook her head despairingly into her hand not holding on to the fruit plucked from Moofle-Moodle. *Yes, I really need another "surpassingly odd" experience.*

*Now, if you'll all get up to go outside the hall for a moment. I'm afraid-* Oodle-Noodle was bending back and pushing apart many of her branches, all the better to check the sunlight angle through one of the congregation hall skylights. *–there's not enough time for us to join you; I'm sure it has not escaped your attention how slowly we move when we're not flying. We'll just have to improvise from our present location. Hurry!*

Once the Earthlings were well-exited from the meeting hall, which struck Buddy more and more as a cathedral-proportioned log cabin, it was also Buddy who spoke. This, in an attempt to take the edge off the discomfort his fellow humans were clearly experiencing. They were turning anxiously one way then the other. They were wondering, what next?, like Buddy had seen people do when he was standing seaside in La Jolla, California after an earthquake. "One thing you can say for these tree creatures of Oomb," he said. "They are so fascinated by us, they forget where the time goes when they are with us."

"You don't suppose it would help if these palm-deciduous cross-bastardization flyin' freaks took some time off from- What the f-in' shit are they doin' playin' golf?"

"That's 'oof,'" corrected Buddy.

"Potato, potahto, they can call it skippin' to some ass-lickin' loo for all I care! If they'd taken the time to invent themselves a clock, so Oodle-f-in'-Noodle there didn't have to rely on the position of the sun...! How does that work anyway, since the planet's rotational axis is constantly shifting? Wo! What was- No they didn't!" From his military training and experiences quarantining Somalia, Sergeant Fred Frankly automatically spread-eagled himself on the ground. When he looked up, for Buddy he could have been a turtle extending his head, given how flat he was sprawled out there. Frankly looked up to confirm he saw what he thought he saw the first time.

From almost every window of the towering meeting hall hung what looked like an enormous bare wooden butt. This phenomenon seemed to have been precipitated, not two seconds before it occurred, by what sounded to Sergeant Hanson like an echo-y, deeply vibrant harmonization of a harp, an acoustic guitar, and a harpsichord. That music, rather than issuing from any specific location, seemed to just permeate the air, in a rippling, ascending sequence.

Louisa Entroper reacted by modestly averting her eyes. But this effort proved useless. Some trees remained still. They behaved exactly like trees on Earth. Other trees, however, the peculiar ones that had palm fronds for flying sticking out the top of their otherwise deciduous-looking trunks, bent away from her. As they did so, their branch arms pulled apart areas of bark to reveal their own buttocks. Realizing this, Dr. Entroper buried her face in her hands. She shook it there while mumbling, "This can't be happening."

"Careful, Buddy, um, Sergeant Hanson too," cautioned a dazed Captain Taylor. Hanson and Leung actually crept closer for an inspection, to either side of one of the butts hanging out a window. "Yoon-hee?" Taylor continued into her lapel mike. "Are you seeing this on the body-cam?"

"Do you hear Kevin behind me, Captain?"

"Oh, I get it!" went Yoon-hee's husband, Kevin, to laughter from others before he'd even gotten to the punchline. "On Oomb, their full moon shows at mid-day!"

"Yeah, what are you f-in' morons doing getting so close to one of those things?" Sergeant Frankly was shouting at Guy and Buddy. "I'm sorry, Captain Taylor, but if anything starts shooting from just one of those assholes, I'll be breakin' off their f-in' branch-arms, and shovin' 'em up where the sun's not supposed to shine!"

Coincidental to Sergeant Frankly completing his threat, the harp-guitar-harpsichord harmonizing suddenly permeated the air again. This time, the haunting rippling chords were in a descending sequence. Not ten seconds later, nothing but the usual bark was to be seen on any tree person's trunk.

"Okay, Oodle-Noodle, so what was that about?" Captain Taylor was not to seat herself inside the meeting hall before she let loose with this most obvious of questions.

*Captain Taylor and other people from Earth, the full, detailed explanation for this behavior is still lost in the foggy mists of our prehistoric past. But between tales handed down by our ancestors, and our study of the fossil record, we are slowly piecing together what happened. I know you are here on other matters, so for now I will try to keep this short. Allow me to take you back, figuratively, to millions of orbits of our sun ago. This was long, long after our planet, in far drier condition than presently, had necessitated the evolution of our mobile ability to seek water oases. And most apparently, it was also shortly after our evolution of flight capability, to survive our planet's relatively abrupt transformation into an archipelago-dotted waterworld with a temperate climate at all latitudes. The water aspect developed thanks to an assault of huge, ice-saturated comets. And Oomb's dramatic, still-poorly-understood transition from a stable to a constantly shifting rotational axis produced our global, year-round mild weather. Anyhow, about one half of us were bearers of sweet seed-bearing fruit, and the other half were bearers of succulent, not-so-sweet tubers,* comparable to your carrots, potatoes, turnips and yams. The tuber producers had to remain immobile for more of the time, obviously, for their self-sustenance to grow from their feet. Most unfortunately, and something we're still trying to understand how it happened, the tuber-bearing beings ended up congregating mostly on one hemisphere of Oomb, while the fruit-bearers congregated on the other hemisphere.

Secretive trips were conducted by the tuber-bearers to fruit-bearer islands. Those trips were mostly staged at night. The tuber-bearers came away with the impression that the soil of the fruit-bearer islands was richer, healthier than where they inhabited. There were, we're starting to discover, differences in geology that might have accounted for this, such as greater volcanic activity in the fruit-bearer zones. Based on the fossil record, there are reasons to believe that the tuber-bearers were suffering from vitamin-deficiency-related illnesses which prompted their spying on fruit-bearer lands in the first place. Anyhow, from stories handed down, we gather that rumors began to spread on the tuber-bearing isles. They were rumors that at some time in the forgotten past, the fruit-bearers had driven the tuber-bearers off their lands. Those rumors suggest that the fruit-bearers had tried to burn down the tuber-bearers by redirecting lava streams to where they lived, thereby forcing them to fly off to archipelagos of poorer soil. As these allegations got more elaborate, and the tuber-bearers' health situation became yet more desperate, legend has it that said tuber-bearers developed a vast army. Their army was intent on firing torch arrows from the sky, to burn down the fruit-bearers and reclaim the tuber-bearers' rightful land.

While the tuber-bearers prepared for war, however,

*a most curious thing was happening in the fruit-bearer lands. Realizing they were getting spied on by the tuber-bearers, on some nights the fruit-bearers were taking advantage of fog banks to sneak peeks at them. What the fruit-bearers saw impressed them as being the most beautiful creatures ever, made that much more irresistible by their clear craving for more loving care than they could give themselves where they lived.*

"Excuse me, Oodle-Noodle, if this is the short version of your story, remind me to bring my sleeper lounge and a sixpack when you decide to take the full dump on us."

"Let me remind you, Sergeant Frankly, we are guests, some might even call us intruders on this planet. I won't tell you what to think where Oombian mind-reading is concerned, but you will show our hosts the fullest respect whenever you open your mouth. Is that understood?"

"Understood, Captain. Sorry, Oodle-Noodle. Go on."

*No need to apologize. I should hurry this up as, again, I know we have other more pressing matters. So, to put the rest as briefly as possible, our legend has it that the tuber-bearers were about to launch their attack. However, before one of them ever fired a flaming arrow, they looked down from flying over-head, and they saw the fruit-bearers had all bared their private parts. That's when the miracle happened.*

"Wait." Sergeant Frankly held a cautioning hand towards Oodle-Noodle.

Oodle-Noodle was standing behind Captain Taylor, telepathing over her shoulder, as it were.

"You're going to telepath us that the tuber troopers suddenly all got the hots for the fruit loopers? You gotta be shittin' me!"

*Such an event, apparently, is exactly what happened, or at least something somewhat along those lines perhaps in not so dramatic a fashion. Perhaps it occurred over a far longer period of time. However long it took, part of the result is that presently, some of our branches actually grow roots which take in nutrients from traces of volcanic dust in the air. Also, of course, it has been passed down from generation to generation to bare ourselves in as public a manner as possible, every mid-day, to commemorate when love broke out instead of war.*

"So you must be the planet where our freakin' hippies came from, last century, saying to make love, not war!" Sergeant Frankly stuck a forefinger in his ear and shook it vigorously, like what he'd just heard was some especially large glob of ear wax he was trying desperately to dislodge.

"Wouldn't it be nice, Oodle-Noodle, Moofle-Moodle, the rest of you, if other worlds could resolve their problems the way you say you so simply resolved yours?"

*We don't know for certain, Dr. Entroper. Much of what I told you is reasoned conjecture.*

"Oh, I don't doubt that." Louisa emphatically nodded her head enough to shake her white mop-top. "All the more reason to consider most carefully this special video we've prepared for you. Sergeant Hanson, if you will..."

Guy Hanson had already unstrapped his backpack. From it he removed an object about the size of an early twenty-first-century laptop computer. He unfolded it to set up a forty-inch-screen television, mounted on the wooden table where they were seated.

The tree persons, having read the Earthling minds, gathered on the side of the table where they'd have to be to view the screen. They did this before Guy could open his mouth to direct them.

"Citizens of Oomb, my name is Michael Spinner. I'm the Secretary of Defense for the United Americas on the planet Earth, about seven light-years from your solar system. My colleagues assure me I don't need to explain stuff, like what a year means, because you can read the minds of our representatives to your planet for that information. Sorry I can't be there, personally, so you can pick my brain directly. But as you're about to find out, I've got my hands plenty full, making sure we're protected here from what a part of the universe out closer to you might be tossing our way. We have a saying on our planet that charity starts at home. Well the same might be said about watching out for threats."

Captain Taylor crossed her arms and shook her head. She was uncaring whether Entroper took offense, as she thought to herself, *Is Spinner really thinking to charm extraterrestrials with his folksy, Santa Claus appearance and off-hand way of talking?*

"Oh, and before we tippytoe into this thing any further, a word of caution," Secretary Spinner continued, on the pre-recorded video. "We'd really, really appreciate it, if none of you telepath anything I'm about to tell you, to any person from Earth who is not there with you as you're watching this. Indeed, what I'm trying to say is, please self-screen your telepathed messages to ensure you don't even *hint* at any of what you're about to learn, to any Earth people not congregated with you presently for this briefing. I'm referring specifically to those folks along for the ride, the folks you've been kind enough to welcome to settle on your planet. See, they have their hands full starting their lives anew, after some most unfortunate circumstances. They've got plenty to worry about without fretting over what I'm here on this video to share with you."

Secretary Spinner proceeded to describe the threat. Antlered, deer-like creatures from a planet named

Tictoctic were most likely on the verge of making other highly intelligent, sentient beings the target of an interstellar cattle-rustling operation. Spinner explained how the laser mesh around Oomb would protect the planet from possible invasion, but that the Earthlings also wished the tree creatures to consider allowing a terrestrial military presence from Earth. That presence would provide an additional safeguard layer not only for the Oombians, but for the Earthling settlers as well.

"Now I understand. Trust me, I *do* understand," went on the defense secretary. "I've actually read quite a bit of the debriefing from my fellow Earthlings' first visit to your beautiful planet, which we want to help you to keep beautiful. So I know a lot of what you telepathed to our pioneering goodwill ambassadors."

Louisa Entroper was nodding her head encouragingly, with side glances to Oodle-Noodle and the other tree creatures. They were side glances she didn't need to make. The Oombians read her thoughts, that it behooved them to consider most carefully what the secretary was saying, especially since he'd gone to the trouble to read a debriefing of what they had telepathed.

"I think that by far," continued Secretary Spinner, "the most intriguing and laudable aspect to your, let's call it a perspective on life, is your apparently planet-wide commitment to peaceful, nonviolent negotiations on any issue which might happen to arise."

"Make love, not war," a nodding Buddy Leung couldn't help blurting. "Just what you guys were telling us about the origins of your daily celebration." *You guys*, of course, was referring to the tree creature Oombians.

"Shh!" Dr. Entroper shushed as harshly as she could muster, Helena thought.

"It seems to work for you," Defense Secretary Spinner

conceded in the continuation of his video. "More power to you. Sorry to say, though, our experience has been that the rest of the universe doesn't usually work that way. I'll give you an historical example from our planet, where maybe you can draw an instructive parallel. See, on one of the Earth islands, and I understand your world is nothing but islands of varying sizes. Anyway, there were these people called the Tainos. The Tainos weren't interested in war or beating up their neighbors to get what they needed. And they had this ball game they loved, just like you love your oof.

"But here's the deal: The Tainos got attacked by people from neighboring islands, the Caribs. Now you don't appear to have anyone on another planet in your solar system capable of attacking you. In fact, your planet seems to be the only one orbiting your star, fit for life as we know it. However, here's where the parallel really comes into focus: From way across an ocean, like the Tictoctic folks have to travel way across the distance between your two solar systems, there arrived these people named the Conquistadors. In English, we'd call them the Conquerors. They were looking for gold, same as the Tictoctic critters might be looking for food. Long story short, them Conquistador types thought there might be plenty of that valuable mineral somewhere in the mountains of the island where the Tainos lived. So they turned the Tainos into slaves to mine for it. Took only a matter of years, before most of them peace lovers were almost extinct, wiped out, gone. And they'd tried real hard to get along peacefully. Their women even threw themselves at the Conquistadors, but it didn't work. I guess what we're trying to say is, we don't want you to end up like the Tainos." Through this part of Spinner's presentation, photos of wood-carved depictions of

Conquistadors brutalizing Tainos were shown on the screen. "Your women couldn't even throw themselves at the Tictoctic folk since you're two entirely different species. In fact, if one of your women ever threw herself at me, all I'd be doing is yelling, 'Timmmberrrr!'

"I know this is no laughing matter. That's still no reason not to have a little fun with one another, since we're all on the same side. Well I'm nearly done here my end, making my sales pitch. Simply put, unless you have something special up your sleeve, up your bark, whatever, we hope you will accept our offer. Well, as one of our cultural icons Mr. Spock used to say, back when we could only dream about travelling to other planets and having our minds read by extraterrestrials, 'Live long and prosper.'"

"Wow! Now that was impressive!" Louisa Entroper gave Oodle-Noodle and the rest of the tree people a sweeping look that added, *I dare you to disagree with me!*

*Officer Entroper, I will grant you that Secretary Spinner's presentation was interesting on so many levels,* telepathed Oodle-Noodle. *I for one would want to learn more about the Tainos. The memory reserves for all of you present, as well as for those back aboard the Smoke and Mirrors, appear most deficient on this subject. This is true, even for several of your passengers who we are welcoming as settlers, who originated from the island of the Tainos and might carry some Taino blood.*

"What would you like to learn about the Tainos, Oodle-Noodle? I have to confess I'd never even heard of them until now."

Had Sergeant Hanson expressed wonder whether the Tainos' women were especially hot, that would have been cause for Sergeant Frankly to give him a bonding back-slap.

Instead, Hanson's question and admission left Frankly rolling his eyes.

*I'd like to know to what extent it is romanticized, Secretary Spinner's characterization of the Tainos as peace-loving. To be certain, any description of us Oombians as simply peace-loving glosses over our wrestling with what that actually means, in real life application. I would venture to opine, based on our extensive probes of your thoughts, that we have as a whole devoted far more effort and deliberation this direction than you. However, we do have what you'd term 'dissension within the ranks.' There are those of us, even a few here present, who believe Secretary Spinner's argument is not entirely devoid of substance worthy of our reflection.*

"Well how about, Ms. Oodle-Noodle, if we explore what some of your kind consider – how was that? – 'not entirely devoid of substance'? Perhaps we can start to establish some common ground?"

Captain Taylor found Entroper's tone to be whiny, perhaps borne of trying to delay the inevitable, yet rightful presentation by the tree people of their own perspective on the situation.

*We would be happy to do that, Dr. Entroper, after we demonstrate what we assembled here all agree is our most profound concern with Secretary Spinner's plan.*

Louisa scanned every tree being in the room for some least sign, indication, of anything less than unbridled enthusiasm over what Oodle-Noodle telepathed. But everywhere she turned, she got met by rustles of leaves as trunks got nodded in solidarity. "All right." She tossed her hands in the air in resignation, to accompany the you're-making-a-big-mistake tone of her voice. "Tell us or- You said something about 'demonstrate.' Go ahead."

*Yes. We're going to ask you to accompany us to the*

*nearest oof course. It's only a short walk from here, and it's the same one where Captain Taylor's husband is playing.*

"Before we go," Louisa turned to Helena as they were rising from their chairs, "I'm just wondering whether our captain has any input she'd like to offer. Captain Taylor, is it satisfactory for you that we are headed out to an oof course?"

Helena strained as much as she could to keep her voice free of any faintest trace of bristle. "I must admit I am puzzled about what playing oof has to do with how we should handle the potential threat from Tictoctic. On the other hand, I feel I know way too little about what our gracious hosts are thinking, to pass judgment before I learn a whole lot more."

"I think the captain is right, Dr. Entroper," chimed in Buddy Leung. "Everything is so new here, we might as well have been delivered to the planet's surface by a stork instead of by our shuttle pod. Ha!"

The Earthlings experienced the most peculiar sensation of the forest seeming to move alongside them as they passed through it. And Sergeant Frankly said, "Oh, I think I get it. It's like when people conduct business on a golf course. You tree guys, and tree gals as well, excuse me, you believe Churchill should have invited Hitler for a round at Old St. Andrews, then let him win so he'd feel better about himself and stop gassing all the Jews. Something like that?"

*What we wish to demonstrate is actually very far removed from that. But how familiar are any of you with golf on your planet?*

"Why do you ask, Ms. Oodles of Noodles? Haven't you already read our minds about that? Sorry! You're right!" Sergeant Frankly ducked his head behind his hands to fend off the expected admonishment. "These tree people haven't made fun of our names, so I shouldn't be making fun of theirs. Guess I'm lucky you *are* so peace-loving, Ms. Oodle-Noodle, or I could have expected an f-in' twig down my throat for my impertinence, huh?" Then, to Sergeant Hanson traipsing through underbrush alongside him, "How do you like that for a word?"

"Where your behavior is concerned, Sergeant Frankly, it's quite, um, pertinent."

*Captain Taylor, Officer Entroper, if you're concerned about what Sergeant Frankly said, don't be. Remember, whether you voice such things aloud, or self-censor them before they can get past your lips, it's all the same to us because of our so-highly-developed mind-reading ability. And having mind-read, previously, the meanings for the words "oodle" and "noodle" in English, I was actually flittingly amused. But back to why we even bother asking you what we've already mind-read. It is a courtesy we try to extend to you, just as we know you try to extend to us the courtesy of making your verbalizations as patiently respectful towards us as you can manage regardless of how you feel. Not that we are not sensing a great deal of awe from you about us. Ah, here we are.*

The assortment of humans and tree beings entered onto a somewhat elevated clearing. The humans got the odd impression a significant part of the forest they were exiting was exiting with them.

What was laid out before the Earthlings struck Captain Taylor, with her casual interest in art history, as a subject for some fan of both a traditional painter such as Norman Rockwell, and of someone more surrealistic like Salvador Dali. The log cabin clubhouse did not appear to her too different from the Scottish-inspired lodge to where her husband had dragged her, at the Torrey Pines golf course on the west coast of California. Although, rather than containing multiple floors of rooms, one could tell from its tall doors that it contained one high-ceilinged room, to accommodate the entrance of the tree creatures. To one side of the clubhouse, there was what looked to be a practice putting green, also like at Torrey Pines. Beyond both the clubhouse and the practice green, the closest tee boxes and fairways of the oof course stretched out on picturesque, gently rolling hills. Although, this layout did not stretch out so much that it obviated Captain Taylor's general sense the oof course overall amounted to something more humbly proportioned than a typical golf course back on Earth. This was consistent with what both her husband and Officer Leung had advised her was the shortening effect on oof ball flight distances of Oomb's slightly stronger gravitational pull, thanks to its bit larger size compared with Earth. Nevertheless, Helena would not have been surprised to discover, back home, some especially rustic, rural golf course bearing a striking resemblance to what she was contemplating presently...except for one glaringly surrealistic component.

The players.

*Would they be oofers since we call ours golfers?*, Buddy Leung wondered.

Whether oofers or golfers, on a distant fairway two small figures could be espied who looked to be human. Helena was certain they were her husband Chris and Chief Counselor Ali Magabu. Scattered amidst them, however, and scattered elsewhere on the course including on the flag-pin-bearing greens, were various trees moving about. Their rippling roots gave the impression they were floating on a commotion of octopus tentacles. They were either approaching their balls, or they were taking swings at their balls, whether with a branch, with a wooden oof club held in their branch hands, or with their rear ends (modestly covered by bark, of course). In the case of rear-end swings, the ball was elevated atop a multi-foot-tall tee. Some trees at first appeared to just be trees, planted obstacles as on more challenging golf courses. But then, after another tree person hit, their commotion of rippling roots started up and they were on their way. This made clear they had merely been waiting respectfully on a fellow player's shot. Not too far from the clubhouse, the Earthlings saw one ball go into the woods alongside the fairway, then half those woods move apart so the player could get at where their branches pointed that it landed.

Suddenly, the air was filled with music like it had been for two brief intervals by the conference hall, though this time involving a full melody. It sounded like a blend of acoustic guitar with bagpipes, a hybrid fusion of those sonorities unimagined by any of the Earthlings before then.

"Captain, I think it's coming from there." Officer Leung pointed at an especially tall tree standing the middle of the fairway, one over from the closest fairway to the clubhouse. Many of the mobile tree beings the Earthlings had seen, and met, were surmounted by helicopter-blade palm fronds. Those fronds depended from a rotor stem plugged into a hole in the trunk, and said hole was thickly lubricated by sap possessing many of the chemical qualities of antique motor oil back on Earth. However, the especially tall tree to which Officer Leung was pointing was of a totally deciduous nature, no palm fronds atop. Its arm branches were posed as they'd be lifted to hold and play a guitar. And those branches' fingers were in a flurry of motion, as one would expect of human fingers busily engaged in strumming a stringed instrument. Only, there was no such instrument visible in the tree being's branches. *Like the air guitar of yore,* Leung fancied, *only this one seems not imaginary.*

"Oodle-Noodle, can you explain how, uhhh, am I correct that the music is somehow issuing from that creature?"

*From one of our oofadors, yes, Officer Leung. You will find the explanation of unfathomable interest, I am sure. However, there would seem to be some urgency to first demonstrate what most concerns us regarding the military aspect of your mission to our planet.*

"If you're telepathing about what is most urgent, Oodle-Noodle, there is an argument to be made that what is most urgent is to achieve our common ground as fast as possible. I would start with your colleagues explaining what portion of Secretary Spinner's presentation they found to have some merit." Louisa Entroper shook her head for emphasis. Perhaps that had the unintended effect, Captain Taylor mischievously wanted to tell her, of suggesting she should not be listened to.

*Officer Entroper, you might be disappointed to discover that what constitutes a big difference of opinion for us may seem trivially negligible to you. Unless there is an especially strong objection, I suggest we proceed with our demonstration, as who knows? Maybe you or others in your party will likewise find our concern to not be totally devoid of merit. And then, sharing out from both sides, we will* ***really*** *achieve some common ground on which to build.*

"Hmm," hmmed Entroper.

Captain Taylor detected a hint of resignation, but what seized more of her attention was an odd, vaguely unsettling impression she was experiencing. That impression came from trying to focus again on those small figures in the distance who were certainly her husband and Officer Magabu. At how far away they were, they could have been two ants, crawling here and there at the pace of two ants.

"So, your husband Chris and who else is that?"

"Ali Magabu," Helena answered Entroper.

"So, after we established orbit around Oomb, Officers Olsen-Taylor and Magabu were the first off the ship?, in order to go play a game while we prepared to negotiate?"

Before Helena could answer, what looked like a huge sunflower made a surprising racket as it extended outwards from a nearby bush. No sooner doing this, than its yellow-orange-ish face inflated how Captain Taylor remembered once seeing a blowfish puff up in an aquarium. A rapid deflation ensued, which produced a shrill whistle.

The next thing the Earthlings knew, a flying creature entered the picture. It could have been a hitherto-unknown breed of cardinal, with plumage a deep shade of violet instead of bright red. As it continued in view, several more differences from the typical cardinal became apparent. Its wings flapped ultra-fast like a hummingbird's, as it moved from hovering in one location to hovering in another.

The violet-colored flying creature finally chose to station itself before the semblance to a large sunflower. A long, feathery tail uncoiled from the creature's rear, and snaked forward to wrap around the tall flower's stem just below its face-sized bloom. Captain Taylor got another unsettling impression, this time that the flying creature was trying to strangle the plant. The bloom might as well have been someone's face sitting atop a green, disproportionately thin neck. Feeding that impression further, the flower proceeded to writhe about like it was, indeed, getting strangled, until a most peculiar crest unfurled atop the violet-colored flying creature's head. That crest looked like a miniature version of the face-sized flower.

When the flower found itself face-to-face with the crest, it froze. Where Captain Taylor was concerned, the flower could have been seeing itself in a mirror.

The flower's yellow-orange-ish face proceeded to puff up anew. Only this time, it did not emit a harsh whistle as it rapidly deflated. This time, it sprayed a yellowish dust all over the birdlike creature. Helena, Buddy and Sergeant Hanson took that dust to be some form of pollen.

As the immense flower shrank back down into amidst the bush from where it had emerged, the purple birdlike creature opened its beak. A bright pink, forked tongue was extruded. Curling all about, that tongue was able to touch nearly every part of the creature's head and body. It worked incredibly fast to lap up as much of the yellowish dust as possible, save for the dust which had settled on the creature's flower-shaped crest.

Meantime, a second such semblance to a large sunflower poked out from amidst the same bush where the first one grew. In the blink of an eye, the purple flying creature had its feathery tail wound tightly round the second flower stem, before that second flower could unleash its own pollination-summoning whistle. With an audible poof!, the purple flying creature's flower-shaped crest blew much of the dust that had landed on it from the first flower onto the second flower.

*Ahh, forgive my commenting once again before you have asked for a reaction to something I've read in your minds. I see you're especially fascinated by the pollination behavior of the hinky-tinky.*

"No forgiveness is even necessary, Oodle-Noodle." Captain Taylor's head shake looked to Officer Leung to also be bringing her out of the entrancing hold the symbiotic Oombian biological activity was having on her. "Officer Entroper," Taylor went on to Louisa, "to address your concern over Chris and Ali being the first officers to leave the ship, to go play oof, both of them are wearing body cams. Who knows how many other wonders of Oomb they will record, to add immeasurably to our knowledge of the planet, including things about which it might be helpful to warn our New World settlers?"

"Yes, maybe you'll even get clues for how to deal with an invasion from Tictoctic. Maybe a hinky-tinky can grab the Tictoctickians by the neck and not let go until they promise to be nice. I know…" Louisa Entroper threw her hands in the air anew. "I'll never win any awards for diplomacy."

"Don't worry 'bout it, Officer Entroper." Sergeant Frankly put considerable growl into his voice to stave off anyone else speaking before he finished having his say. "Probably just as well I had to come unarmed. I'm not sure I could have controlled myself, to keep from blowing winky-stinky and his flower friends to Kingdom Come, like I plan to do to those antlered interstellar cattle rustlers from Tictoctic when they attack. Sorry, Oodle-Noodle, I don't know what the fudge you'll be demonstratin', but I for one am not going to moon the enemy, to see whether they'd want to get it on with me instead of getting me served on a dinner platter, although I'm glad it worked out for you folks. Like Entroper said, I don't think your planet is the rule, the way things work for you around here."

"Someone from another planet taking a nature walk on Earth might find it comparably overwhelming. For example, watching a squirrel collect nuts," Sergeant Hanson offered. Helena gathered he was somehow trying to take the edge off his fellow sergeant's remarks.

"Yeah, I think there are plenty of nuts for the squirrels to collect on Oomb."

*Shall we enter the clubhouse to select your oof equipment?* As Oodle-Noodle graciously held open the door with one branch hand and gestured with her other hand, Helena thought she read a profound sadness in her eyes. The bark framing Oodle-Noodle's eyes seemed to crinkle even more than usual.

The Earthlings entered the oof clubhouse with mouths agape and eyes looking all around in obvious wonder, save for Louisa Entroper. She kept her head bowed with her mouth tight-lipped from grim determination.

A tree creature was emerging from the back room. He carried a straw basket full of shiny oof balls in his leafy branch arms. *These are freshly cured, guests from Earth. Please help yourselves. You'll also want to select clubs from each basket. Your fellow travelers, already out on the course, knew just what to pick. However, if you're not familiar with your comparable game of golf, please allow me to make your choices for you.*

Louisa intended to protest that she would rather just observe, instead of having to swing any oof clubs herself. She would learn whatever they were supposed to learn by watching what the others did. Before she could open her mouth, though, a low-pitched "Ooooff!" howled from the back room. This noise got followed by the plop, plop, plop of newly excreted oof balls dropping into another curing basket.

"Eww!" This was Entroper's own peculiar sound, as she tried to shake off her revulsion. "What in the world was *that*?" As she said this, she made the mistake, where avoiding additional revulsion was concerned, of taking a peek inside the back room.

What met Louisa's eyes, as well as those of Officer Leung and the sergeants who joined her, was a tree creature that reminded Leung of cypress trees he had seen on the California west coast. Branches, including arm branches, were not in evidence until a little over halfway up the gnarly trunk. Far different from an actual cypress tree, though, was how this particular tree person squatted down on its five root-legs over a basket. An oof ball was slowly dropping out of an orifice clearly located at the intersection of those five root-legs. The face on the creature's trunk, just below the leafy branches, was clearly showing signs of straining. Its bark wrinkled several times over, where the two eyes were squeezed shut.

"I've seen rabbit and deer pellets in open fields, but this is f-in' ridiculous!" The perceived absurdity of what the cypress-like tree person was doing had Sergeant Frankly uncaring how vulgarly he spoke. "Maybe after we finish trying to hit tree poop into the cup, maybe we can teach you critters how to throw a cow patty like a Frisbee! Hell, shouldn't our putts be at latrines dug into the ground?"

"Please correct me if I get any of this incorrect, Oodle-Noodle," said Buddy Leung. "Sergeant Frankly, I think the Oombians found that certain irritants, intentionally inserted into specially trained beings, will cause their sap to accrete around those irritants to grow the oof balls, the same way an oyster grows a pearl. And of course the specially trained beings are on a special diet to promote the production of ideal sap for the oof ball's bounce, roll, spin and uniform sphericity. What I've learned that's new, I think, is why the game was named 'oof.'"

*Correct on all counts, Officer Leung. So Officer Entroper, if I might ask you a question: While it is clear from mind-reading that you have never played the game of golf on Earth, aside from a few rounds of the putting element only, with younger relatives, are you familiar with its basic rules?*

"Well Oodle-Noodle, now I'm really puzzled." Louisa Entroper couldn't have given the tree being a grimmer regard, Helena thought, had Oodle-Noodle threatened to poke out the Dr.'s eyes with her branch fingers. "If you could mind-read my lack of experience playing golf, why can't you also mind-read the extent of my familiarity with the rules for that idiotic game?"

*Officer Entroper, please pardon the clumsiness of my effort to hurry along our dialog to the demonstration of our concern. Yes, you're right; I've gotten too arbitrary in setting the boundary between telepathing to you what I already know is going through your head, and pretending to first need to ask you what you're thinking.*

"No, but this is good. You are reminding us that for your kind, much of this conversation is a waste of time. And what a coincidence indeed that that is exactly how I regard golf and, most likely from what I've seen thus far, your game of oof. Although let me make sure you've also mind-read my profound appreciation for the tremendous effort I understand you have already gone to, to make our settlers feel welcome."

*A tree-mendous effort, yes? No need to worry about that, Officer Entroper. We "get" your appreciation. However, allow me to correct you. By no means do we regard conversation with you as a waste of time. For remember, while we can read your minds, you cannot read ours, beyond most rudimentary, fleeting intuitions. Also, until we share experiences and ideas with you, we cannot be sure just how you will react. To that end, I am now about to comment on something. And then I am going to raise a question regarding that something. It is a question it does not appear has ever occurred to you before, in the way I am going to frame it.*

*Officer Entroper,* Oodle-Noodle continued to telepath, *you say that golf, and presumably oof as well since it is so similar to golf, is a waste of time. However, golf does not involve dropping bombs on people, other living creatures, and intelligent constructions. And, it can be good mental exercise, especially since it also does not involve the psychological trauma from being in a firefight with a so-called enemy. Since in those and so many other respects, golf and oof are beneficial rather than destructive, how is war not a far bigger waste of time?*

"Allow me, Officer Entroper." Sergeant Frankly held up a hand for Louisa to hold off while he responded. "Ms. Oodle-Noodle, I am sincerely happy for you and your kind. For all of you folks." Fred Frankly suddenly was feeling the rapt attention of a forest's worth of towering tree beings gathered round. "From what you – what's that fancy word? – telepathed, from what you telepathed us, if I understood correctly, somewhere in your prehistory, when the bad guys threatened you, your ancestors got away with mooning – what we call mooning but I'm guessing you've already read our minds for what I'm talkin' 'bout."

There was a rustle of leaves as the tree beings nodded.

"So your ancestors mooned the enemy to make them not just friends, but lovers. Then everyone orgied their way to an everlastin' peace where you got both sweet and sour hangin' from your boughs. That's great. Bizarre, but great.

"However, as we were alludin' to earlier- Hey Professor Hanson, how's 'alludin'' for one of your scholarly-type words?"

"Alludin' and his magic lamp, Professor Frankly."

"Yeah? I might as well go ahead and say f- you since our tree friends already know that's knocking around in my head. But anyway, Oodle-Noodle, as we were alludin' to before, it's a big wide universe out there, where there aren't too many wars getting flipped over to love feasts. We've got plenty of nasty characters on our planet who, if you show them where the sun don't shine, well... You might have had one butthole before. However, if you go and do what your ancestors did, you won't be able to count the number of buttholes, for how many bullets our nasty characters will fire your way. That is, if they don't set off an explosive device, blow apart your business end into a thousand itty-bitty bloody pieces."

Louisa Entroper could not have nodded more emphatically in agreement.

"And please, spare me the psychological bull-dookey about how-" Sergeant Frankly broke into an overly-affected, girlish voice, "-somebody looked at them the wrong way when they were kids, and they've been messed up ever since."

*Sergeant Frankly, you must know the situations are often far more complicated than that. And we'd be the first to admit that individuals are born, most tragically, wherein brews a toxic mix of factors. Those factors could include hormonal imbalance, genetic mutation, or an especially poor diet. Their toxic mix leaves such individuals beyond the reach of reason and love, at least until which time as those deeper causes have been addressed. Which is why even on Oomb, we do our own policing of sorts. But again, that is for those fellow tree beings wherein the reception from their divine spirits is as disrupted as the reception from electrical transmissions into one of your antique televisions, when some of its parts are broken or malfunctioning. The notion of an entire society going crazed beyond the reach of reason so that only war, only war, is the remedy, we believe that notion is rooted far less in reality, and far more in a loss of faith in the ultimate benevolence of the universe.*

Fred Frankly glanced around at his fellow Earthlings to see how they were taking Oodle-Noodle's remarks. When he did, he found it upsetting enough that a Marine Sergeant, of all people, Sergeant Hanson, was thoughtfully stroking his chin with thumb and forefinger, suggestive he might actually be giving serious consideration. But what really set off Fred Frankly was genius hyper-physics engineer Officer Leung, how he greeted with an assenting nod the tree person's dangerously irresponsible naïve dribble, where Frankly was concerned. "You know," Sergeant Frankly said at last, "what I've often thought back home is what's knockin' around in my head right now. I'm thinking me and my fellow soldiers ought to just step aside. We ought to just lay down our arms and let the shit hit the fan. Then we can see how well all the ingrates do when nobody is holding back the barbarians. I mean, let's see if it works out when you try stickin' flowers in the enemy's gun barrels! Except of course here on Oomb, where I'm sure the result will be a human marryin' a tree; they'll give birth to these plant-human hybrids wavin' their f-in' cute little leaf-hands in everyone's face! While we're at it, back on Earth let's open up all the quarantine zone gates, de-electrify all the fences. Let's see what kind of a love feast we'll have then! And when the deer people land from Tictoctic, we can serve them some pizza, see if we can get them cravin' that instead of our flesh! Sure!"

*If we could go on with our demonstration…*

"Excuse me, Oodle-Noodle," Louisa Entroper held up a hand for her interruption. "I'm sorry, but I am feeling precisely what Sergeant Frankly is feeling. It is not the least bit clear to me what your demonstration can possibly accomplish, regarding the potential threat with which we are concerned, especially since golf, oof, whatever its manifestation, is of no interest to me. I dare say that's the case for you as well, isn't it, Captain Taylor?"

"Yes, Officer Entroper. Given a choice, I'd far rather be biking down Highway 101 alongside my daughter, than chasing little balls across the ground alongside my husband."

Louisa motioned a hand Helena's way as though to say, *Case in point*.

"However,-"

Louisa proceeded to slap said hand against her forehead.

"-I don't think Oodle-Noodle has telepathed anything about our having to take up golf or oof for their demonstration to be salient."

*Correct, Captain.*

"And I'd be the first to admit I have not the faintest intuition how they are going to tie in that game with our substantial, legitimate concern over a possible threat of military aggression from an extraterrestrial intelligence. But again, it *is* a big, wide universe out here, where I've already experienced things way beyond my imagination. Had you asked me two years ago whether mobile, mind-reading tree creatures existed anywhere, I would have confidently dismissed that notion. Officer Entroper, I gather you are suggesting our most generous, accommodating hosts should not even bother with their demonstration, or that we should not bother giving it any of our attention, because it is beyond your imagination what possible pertinence it could have to our concern. If that is true, I must disagree in the strongest possible terms. But I'm not going to force you to stick around for what the Oombians have to show us, since I'm not running a dictatorship."

"Might I add, Captain," Sergeant Hanson raised a forefinger hoping to be allowed to speak.

"Of course, Sergeant."

"Thank you, Captain. I believe there is considerable truth to what my fellow soldier has said. Those of us prepared to wage war, if necessary, are striving to protect civilization from getting overrun by the barbarism it has taken our species thousands of years to ever-so-slowly leave behind. An important part of what we're protecting is the ability for the sort of disagreement to take place we've been hearing between Captain Taylor and Officer Entroper, without one of them taking up a weapon against the other, and without Captain Taylor saying that since she's the captain, she's going to order around Officer Entroper."

"I think that's more 'n enough with the yappin'. Sooner we get this over with, sooner we can cut to the nitty gritty. So Oodle-Noodle, what? I stuff this bag full of what clubs I think I might need, then grab a couple of those poop pearls?" Fred Frankly had already helped himself to a surprisingly light-weight oof club bag made from sewn-together, palm-like fronds that were bright green with streaks of yellow.

*Those of you who wish to experience the demonstration in addition to witnessing it, yes.*

Buddy Leung and the two sergeants stepped onto the first tee box carrying bags full of clubs and balls.

Captain Taylor stood just off the tee box with her hands knitted together behind her back. She took in a pastoral view which proved most exhilarating. Fluffy cumulus clouds ran shadows along the near ground and the mountainous backdrop. Hints of gentlest breeze carried a sweet, perfume-y fragrance, like honeysuckle. And, what Oodle-Noodle later told her was the Twiddle-

Twaddle, another birdlike creature, soared through the sky in a series of gracefully smooth arcs...and performed a most unusual hunting maneuver. The Twiddle-Twaddle looked not unlike a bald eagle or some other large hawk. However, when it spotted prey along the ground, it flipped upside-down and rolled body and wings together into a feathery ball. This left the bright orange webbing of its oversized talons to balloon out like parachutes in the shape of two mushroom caps, for a slow, pendulum-swinging descent. Oodle-Noodle telepathed that equipped with binoculars, the Earthlings might have been able to spot the Twiddle-Twaddle's target, mouse-like creatures with unusually long necks. The Earthlings might have gotten to see their heads swaying from side to side on said long necks, as they got hypnotized by their hunter's pendulum-swinging, upside-down descent.

Officer Entroper stood further off the tee box than the captain. Her low bow, trying to lose herself in self-sedating meditation, got Buddy Leung's attention from up on the elevated portion of ground. He mused to himself that Louisa's forehead should have been sporting a pair of horns or Tictoctickian antlers, for her to threaten to charge like an angry rhinoceros.

*I'm sure you notice the flagstick for the first hole, about two hundred fifty yards away on a slight dogleg left.*

"Roger that," said Frankly as he took a couple of practice swings with his selected driver, to loosen up. "And it looks like trouble with that creek along the right side of the fairway, and those woods along the left. Can we count on your fellow tree folk to toss or kick our balls back out into the open, in case Captain Hook shows up?"

When the sergeant mentioned the creek, what

looked there to be a flowering lily pad abruptly dropped from sight with a most noticeable splash!

*Many of those are our deeply-rooted, immobile brothers and sisters. Obviously, they are unable to improve your lie, where your ball sits after you have struck it. Not that they necessarily would if they could, any more than we would ever consider freeing you from the consequences of your actions, however much we might try to help you to arrive at the best actions to take. On the other branch, our achieved level of communication with the immobile ones is comparable to how far you have gotten with dolphins and pigs. We really don't know what they might do if they could.*

Buddy Leung turned away from the tee box where he was standing, to exchange a significant look with Captain Taylor. What Oodle-Noodle telepathed about "the consequences of your actions," she wasn't just talking about oof, was she?

"Okay, Oodle-Noodle, so help me out here," requested Sergeant Frankly. But more than anything else, he was wondering why he didn't catch at least a faint whiff of poop when he teed up his oof ball.

*Aim for the fairway, Sergeant Frankly. Think about your ball landing in the fairway.*

"Yeah, I don't want it to go too far right bouncing into the creek, or hook it left in amidst your stuck-in-the-mud relatives."

*Focus on where you DO want your ball to go.*

"Which is not into the crap. Got it." Sergeant Frankly took one final practice swing. This consisted of taking the club only halfway back, then bringing it through with a powerful Whoosh! After that, Frankly stepped up to the ball, waggled his clubhead behind it three times, and took a whack at it. A sharp crack! was produced as the oof ball got compressed, followed instantly by its decompression on its skyward ascent. After starting out on a promising trajectory, Frankly's shot suddenly took an arcing turn right, landing it headed for the creek. His ball took two little hops in the tall grass that had the sergeant hopeful it would stop short, stay dry. The third bounce, though, was so big and projected the ball so far forward, it came down with a loud splash! in the middle of the creek.

"Damn! So what are the local rules? Is that out of bounds, and I have to tee up again? Or do I take a drop just back of where it went in?"

*You take the drop, Officer Frankly. One thing we agree on is that all the world is an oof course, so there are no out-of-bounds, as you term them. There is only a one-stroke penalty for hitting your ball into a location where it can't be played.*

"Of course!" Kevin Smith chuckled in Helena and Buddy's ears via their implanted mikes, from his eavesdropping location aboard the Smoke and Mirrors. "To quote from his play, *Much Ado About Golf,* 'All the world's an oof course, and we are its players.' From that truly great dramatist, Shankspar. You know: To tee or not to tee, that is the question."

"I'll go next and see if I can avoid the right side," Buddy said in a laughing voice as he went to plant his tee. Helena and the tree beings were well aware that his amusement derived from Kevin's remarks, rather than from Oodle-Noodle's explanation of the local rules.

*Remember, Officer Leung, to focus on where you DO wish the ball to go.*

Buddy took a slow and easy, most relaxed-looking practice swing. Then he stepped up to the ball. But he knew he was in trouble, soon as he completed his follow-through after contact. He found himself facing the line of "deeply rooted brothers and sisters" along the left side of the fairway. He watched helplessly, groaning pleadingly, "Nooo! Nooo!" as his ball hooked sharply into a part of the woods where the ground cover grew especially tall and thick.

"Oh, I think I got it now," Louisa Entroper cackled shrilly. "Your demonstration is of how we can scare off the bad guys by playing your game in the worst way possible! Of course! They'll just turn around and fly off, never to be seen again, so they don't have to watch one of you hit another crummy shot!"

Oodle-Noodle made the universal negation sign, twisting her trunk from side to side as she telepathed, *Sergeant Frankly and Officer Leung shared something in common, most significant, before they struck their respective oof balls. Their collective attitude, so pronounced that their verbalizations of it were but what you would call 'the tip of the iceberg,' was that the best way to make a good shot was to dedicate their attention to avoiding a bad shot. Despite my counsel for them to focus on where they wanted their balls to go rather than on where they didn't want their balls to go, they concentrated on the bad. You witnessed the result. When you deny yourself the faith to make goodness happen, and instead you work so hard to defeat the bad, all you do is assure that the bad will happen.*

"There is a certain degree of counter-intuition to golf," Buddy nodded reflectively. "Sergeant Frankly, this is the physics of what happened to your shot. Trying to hit your ball away from the hazard to the right, you swung your club from outside in. As a result, you cut the club face across the ball in a manner that spun it to the side rather than launching it straight forward."

"Okay, now I freakin' understand," Fred nodded to

feign dawning enlightenment. "When I want to smash in the skull of one of those bloodthirsty critters from Tictoctic, I need to stop worrying I'll only give him a glancing blow, and focus on imagining his brain spilling out, lest I accidentally slit his throat instead! Got it!

"Umm, look," Frankly shook his head. For once in his life, he thought better of leaving his snide remark to stand on its own. Most unexpectedly, he launched into an uncharacteristically more diplomatic tack that even surprised his own self. "Like my fellow officer has indicated, there's a lot of barbarism out there you've been lucky enough to get evolved out of your system, save for having to police a few miscreants you mentioned, plus watching out for some of your local wildlife not quite so fun-loving as those ootzy pootzies or whatever you call them. But what we're telling you is this: There's a big, bad universe out there, and we've got the guts and the hardware to keep you safe from it, if you'll let us."

*It takes more courage and resourcefulness to make love work than to stave off violence with more violence.*

"But what if you get yourself killed courageously, resourcefully trying to make love work?" Dr. Entroper emphatically pointed at Oodle-Noodle. Then she swung her forefinger around to open her question, issue her challenge, to the other tree creatures in attendance.

*If we do violence to defend ourselves, our dream is killed.*

"But at least then you live to dream another day. And who knows? When conditions become more favorable…"

*Were implementation of the dream of the creation of the universe, in other words "trying," as you put it, to make love work, were that grand project postponed until conditions became "more favorable," nothing would ever have existed. As I telepathed you about our own history, had the fruit-bearers waited for the tuber-bearers to disarm before they mooned them, war would have broken out instead of love.*

"And as Sergeant Frankly indicated, your evolution apparently took a lucky turn with which none of the rest of us have been blessed," Entroper was quick to respond.

"Hey, could I have some quiet, or doesn't it matter that I haven't gotten to hit yet?" Sergeant Guy Hanson's tone of voice suggested to Buddy that he was trying to lose himself in concentration on his shot, as he waggled his driver over his teed-up oof ball. The stunned silence meeting the sergeant's request lasted long enough for him to take a full swing. With another sharp crack!, the pearly-colored extrusion from the local ball-layer took a high arc right down the center of the fairway leading to the first hole.

"Well, I have to admit," said Guy as he gave the wooden oof club a twirl on its way back into the bag woven out of huge, yellow-striped fronds, "I pretended I was aiming at the bulls-eye on a firing range. I managed not to give the hazards another thought,-"

"And Halle-freakin'-lujah," interrupted Frankly, "you're ready for the WPGA 'cause heaven knows nobody's ever blown a shot when their attention has been exclusively on where they want the ball to go. Just like nobody's ever gotten a window view through their chest after trying to stick a flower in some savage's gun barrel."

*Success can never be guaranteed. However, good shots are more likely the more you focus on where you want the ball to go rather than on where you don't want the ball to go, where you fear the ball will go. This, as assuredly as focusing on the possibilities for peaceful resolutions makes peaceful resolutions more likely. You have virtually no chance of making a dream come true if most of your attention is given over to avoiding a nightmare.*

"I'm sorry, Captain, but enough's enough!" Dr. Entroper burst out in what struck Captain Taylor as virtually a growl. Entroper shook her white mop-top like she was trying to dry off from immersion in the prevailing dialog, how a dog tried to dry off from a bath, the captain fancied. "No insult meant to you or your kind, Oodle-Noodle, but what *our* kind have to remember is that just because you possess this amazing mind-reading telepathic ability doesn't automatically mean your every thought is just oozing with wisdom like sap from your trunk! No! Let's get serious, people! The idea that how you play a silly, meaningless game has any real relevance to staving off bloodthirsty conquest by a civilization apparently more technologically advanced than ours is totally ridiculous!"

Buddy Leung wanted to say Entroper's complaint was short on specifics, and that her belligerence did not confer any more weight to her opinion than Oodle-Noodle's telepathic ability conferred to hers. But he contented himself with knowing the tree creatures could read his thoughts on this matter.

Indeed, Oodle-Noodle blessed him with an appreciative nod before she telepathed, *We're about to get interrupted by a communication from Officer Yoon-hee Park-Smith that will compel you to cut short this visit. So please allow me to express our collective sentiment on the primary issue which has brought you here. And allow me to do that with the full understanding, yes I agree, Dr. Entroper, our telepathing it to you does not in and of itself lend it any more weight than a voiced sentiment. What you do will be what you do. We will not force you to do otherwise, or behave any less hospitably towards your fellow creatures who are taking up residence to form a new life here. But we plead with you, if you are to respect our wishes as natives of this planet, that you do not deploy the laser mesh. It is only more likely to draw the attention to our planet, and your settlers here, that you seek to avoid. I do not understand any difference between this deployment to avoid a hazard, Dr. Entroper, and the aiming away from a hazard on an oof course that sends the ball flying into it. Perhaps you can explain to me...*

"Captain," Yoon-hee's voice suddenly crackled over her earpiece, and the other visiting Earthlings' earpieces as well, "we've got a UFO situation. Its ultimate course is not clear, but it appears to be headed out from Tictoctic."

"Our firefly donut picked up on this, Yoon-hee?"

"The same, Captain."

Shortly before descending into the Callaway X-Centra system's orbital plane on their approach to Oomb, Officer Buddy Leung had engineered the launch of an eavesdropping firefly donut. That donut was programmed to assume an elliptical orbit in and out of the star system where Tictoctic was located. Were the antlered creatures of Tictoctic to detect its presence, presumably its flight path would lead them to assume it was naturally occurring space debris. Hopefully even a close fly-by would not raise suspicions thanks to its photon exhaust trail mimicking a typical comet trail, albeit on a more minute scale. And its data stream back to the Smoke and Mirrors was scrambled to suggest radioactive decay rather than intelligent design.

"Ali?" said Helena Taylor after clicking something on her uniform collar. "You and Chris are going to have to finish your game later. Something's come up."

"Understood, Captain."

"Um," Helena held out a cautioning hand even though Dr. Ali Magabu and her husband Chris were not present to see it, "tell Chris, you can do this as well. Um, ask your guide, caddie, whatever they call them, whether you can mark where your ball landed, to return to it later."

"We just finished putting out, so no problem, Captain. No need to ask. In fact, your recalling us at this particular time probably proves most fortuitous for saving your husband from going completely bald before the next time you see him."

"What, has he been betting a thousand follicles a hole?" asked Engineer Kevin Park-Smith back aboard the Smoke and Mirrors. "And you figured this was as good an opportunity as any to fill in those pesky gaps in your own scalp, Officer Magabu?"

"Truly, Officer Park-Smith. No, what happened actually is that while searching for his ball in some rough, Officer Olsen-Taylor got his curly locks mistaken for the furry hide of a so-called oogoojoobu. The life form committing this error was an aggressively pollen-spraying vine, hanging from a branch of one of the permanently rooted tree creatures. Truly, that vine might as well have been a cobra for how it hissed as it released its fertile dust. Anyhow, the fripe look like a cross between a hummingbird and a turtle, and they are the size of ladybugs. They have been nibbling at Chris's hair ever since he got sprayed with pollen. Apparently, the fripe find his hair every bit as delectable as pollinated oogoojoobu fur. There's also something about the defecated result getting mixed for fertilization with-"

"Please, Ali, we need to save that for another time."

Captain Taylor held out a cautioning hand again that Officer Magabu couldn't hope to see. "We'll meet you back aboard the shuttle pod in ten, fifteen minutes?"

"Of course, Captain."

On their airlifted transport back to the shuttle pod parked on the nearby beach, Oodle-Noodle explained the rest of what Ali was going to relate about Chris's hair predicament. She included assurances Chris's scalp should not suffer any lasting consequences.

When the Earthlings were boarding for the return trip to their orbiting mother ship, the Smoke and Mirrors, Oodle-Noodle made a special rustling commotion to stall Captain Taylor's ascent as last one onto the shuttle pod. *Captain,* she telepathed, *I can't over-emphasize our dread your kind will insist on continuing to plan based on your fears, to the neglect of schemes based on hope.*

"So, are you acting upon this dread?" Captain Taylor couldn't help a wry grin breaking out as she spoke.

*We are planning for such time as you finally realize the futility of violence, assuming any of us are still left alive.*

Captain Taylor was going to let Oodle-Noodle have the last word, telepathed or otherwise. But on a surge of frustration, she did an abrupt about-face, back down the shuttle pod steps. "Look," she already had Oodle-Noodle's attention as that tree creature had mind-read what Helena was about, "you probably already know, but I want to renew your attention to this portion of our mental landscape. Our most revered sociological philosophers had reached a consensus, that no civilization continuing to embrace warfare could advance beyond a certain point technologically without self-destructing, that in fact our own civilization was teetering close to the edge. We had planned accordingly, making our first interstellar flight virtually defenseless, unarmed. And then we received the warning about Tictoctic, coming from their own people."

*Yes, two of their own found something to do other than the violence in which many of their peers plan to participate.*

"What exactly would you have *us* do?" Captain Taylor exhaled with exasperation.

*First, don't deploy the laser mesh. Second, have two of us come aboard your ship – I could be included – to elaborate our ideas and brainstorm with you.* Oodle-Noodle mind-read Helena wondering how so much tree could even fit aboard the shuttle pod for transport up to the Smoke and Mirrors. And so, as the starship captain eyed her most dubiously, the Oombian added, *An extraordinary portion of my flying assembly could be trimmed off with no more harm than from cutting your fingernails.*

"That's an offer I assure you we'll take seriously, Oodle-Noodle."

Pppppptttt!!!

*You'd better go before the stench overwhelms you.*

"Captain, was that-"

"Get back inside, Buddy! You heard what Oodle-Noodle telepathed!"

The Oonzy Ootzies had just erupted with a collective flatus emission on their latest emergence from the shoreline.

## Chapter 5

"Okay, so this much we agree on," said Captain Helena Taylor. She had sat herself down on steps where she could stretch her legs, nearby the captain's chair on the navigation bridge of the Smoke and Mirrors. That was Helena's go-to for making herself comfortable, whenever she conducted a brainstorming session there. Chris sat beside her, his arms wrapped round his bended legs.

Helena's other closest advisers either remained in their regular seats, or they joined her and her husband on the floor.

And Dr. Louisa Entroper, mission observer for the president of the American Union, restlessly prowled back and forth between the panoramic view-screen and the navigation panel.

Post-Velcro innovations were working so well to prevent any of the Earthlings from floating, gravity was hardly missed.

"Whether we decide to deploy the laser mesh here or not," Helena continued, "within the next two days we are bound for Fafama." For emphasis, she tapped together the tips of her forefingers. "The Fafaman government is in full agreement on laser mesh deployment. In the worst case scenario that the UFO heading above the Tictoctic orbital plane is charting directly for Fafama, we have limited time, if any, to outrun them for its installation."

"I'm just thinking, Captain." From his seat at a systems monitoring console, Kevin pointedly stared at Chris's head. Scalp had been revealed there by nibbling fripe while Chris was playing oof. The scattered tufts of hair that remained reminded Kevin of something. They reminded him of patches of grass with bare ground in between, on the field where he enjoyed playing softball back home in southern Maryland. "Maybe we could launch Officer Olsen-Taylor into orbit," Officer Smith-Park went on. "We would mount him inside a transparent sphere strung to a giant mirror. Which aliens, however bloodthirsty or hideous-looking themselves, won't experience sheer terror when they see a magnified image of Chris's scalp? They'll flee at a thousand times light-speed, whether they have that capacity or not!"

Yoon-hee wanted to dig her sharp nails into her husband's armpits for this gratuitous mockery of the captain's husband, whose self-esteem she sensed was not very high to begin with. But she knew the complaint such behavior would rouse from the restlessly pacing Dr. Louisa Entroper. Entroper was having difficulty enough, accepting the captain's occasional habit of favoring the floor to her throne-like chair when there were weighty matters to discuss. So instead, Kevin's wife settled on saying, "My husband is jealous, Chris, because he doesn't have the panache to carry off that look the way you do!"

Chris smiled appreciatively as he nevertheless self-consciously scratched at his scalp. He said, "Captain, if my appearance is too much of a distraction, I wouldn't mind a quick exit to clean up and make myself more presentable. Umm..."

Kevin stifled an urge to react, *Oh, no, don't change a thing. In fact, go bring us some more of your fifty-year-old albums with the twenty-minute-long pieces, to seduce us ever-deeper into your own special brand of crazy.*

Captain Taylor shook her head, "No, Chris, if you can stand the discomfort a little while longer..." She comfortingly patted his hand. "We could ALL use the reminder that as we decide what to do, we are dealing with an extraterrestrial culture and ecology about which we know next to nothing. And when you come right down to it, we are basing our actions almost entirely on mindsets we bring from our own planet." On uttering "ALL," Captain Taylor gave Dr. Entroper a look that would have frozen her still, if only, rather than allowing her restless prowl to continue.

"I'm not sure I understand, Captain." Entroper was not going to take an indirect lecture, even, without a stiff rebuke. "Are you suggesting that perhaps our powers of reasoning are mere cultural artifacts? Let me just say, I think we make a serious mistake if we allow superficial strangeness to mislead us about the applicability of universal truths." She shook her head emphatically.

"Actually, Captain," Dr. Ali Magabu stroked his chin thoughtfully, "I have been personally moved, truly, to reflect upon what my parents told me their ancestors related to them. It was about the incursion into Nigeria of Christian and Islamic missionaries and colonists. On the positive side, they introduced literacy. Literacy proved a most wonderful opportunity to record innumerable oral traditions so they could be preserved for all time. Moreover, my ancestors thereby found themselves challenged to consider how much belief is superstition, and how much actually could have some basis in reality. This was as true, of course, for judging the newly introduced religions as it was for judging the indigenous forms, such as the Kalabari of my great-great-grandparents. Who incidentally would have nodded knowingly if they'd been privileged to meet with Oodle-Noodle and her associates. You see, my ancestors believed most firmly in the Teme, the spirits at the core of all material things.

"But anyhow, on the negative side was the

exploitation of oil and copper resources that poisoned both the politics and quite literally the environment. My parents felt compelled to flee to Cairo. Cairo proved distinctively safer for the pursuit of their academic interests, even after the quarantine fences went up."

"And this has to do with our situation in what way?" Kevin made a circular gesture with his right hand, to put an exclamation point on his impatience.

"In precisely this way, Officer Park-Smith: Here on Oomb, truly we are the missionaries, we are the colonists. Back in Nigeria, the case might be made that the spread of written language was at least as valuable to my ancestors as anything they could offer to the tribes from Europe and Arabia. And yet here, most curiously, it might well be argued the Oombians have far more to offer us than we could ever possibly bestow upon them. I truly hope this situation will not come to parallel the Europeans' first encounters with Native Americans. We all know that the English, the Portuguese and other colonizing explorers depended quite heavily on the misnomered 'Indians' for learning how to survive in the so-called new world. In return for which, many of those colonizing explorers delivered the harshest possible end to much of a way of life, whether by massive, out-and-out slaughter, enslavement, or the unwitting spread of foreign viruses far more lethal than the prancing boogersnot we experienced on Fafama."

"So, if we protect the Oombians from Tictoctickian aggression, that's not doing them all that much of a favor I take it?" spat out Kevin. He surprised himself at how especially irritating he was finding Ali on this particular occasion. He used to always enjoy the counselor's thoughtful input.

"Good point, Officer Park-Smith," grumbled Louisa

Entroper. "And may I add a question, Dr. Magabu, as relates to the missionaries? I wasn't aware we had any on board." As Louisa made her observation, she had to stifle an urge to scale the short stairway and co-opt the captain's chair for herself, since Helena Taylor was so intent on leaving it unoccupied. "I've heard that a few of the women from Philadelphia have converted one of the cabins into a small chapel. But I'm not aware of their doing any proselytizing as such, even to their fellow Earthlings."

Dr. Ali Magabu responded, "Excuse my saying so, Dr. Entroper, but, we have suggested strongly to these beings, have we not?, that they will not be safe unless we militarize their planet. I fail to detect the difference between that, and someone saying you are doomed to hellfire and damnation unless you repeat certain phrases as your own, about Jesus being your lord and savior. Oombian history apparently includes staving off a world conflict, and turning the tide to peace, by nonviolent means not even requiring manufactured artifacts of any kind. Especially since this is their given, the mobile tree creatures here could not be blamed for regarding as superstitious the protective powers of a laser mesh."

"Hey, Ali, for the record I've never insinuated nor believed anyone was going to hell for not becoming a Christian," Yoon-hee bristled. In an aside to her husband Kevin, while Officer Magabu silently mouthed for her a reassuring *I know*, she added, "Eternal tickles without mercy are another matter."

"Where superstition is concerned, Officer Magabu," proceeded Louisa Entroper, her bitter disappointment in Ali not to be distracted by tickle talk, "I'm not sure there is anything more superstitious than treating love as some universal magic potion. I think maybe Sergeant Frankly has the right idea. All the soldiers should just stay home, see how it works out for the rest of us without them on the job."

"But Ali makes an important point, Louisa," said Helena. "We are intruders here. Oomb is not our planet. Their leadership has been crystal clear about their wish that we not deploy the laser mesh. And this comes only after accommodating us in every other way. I think the fact we are discussing whether to deploy the net after getting plainly told they don't want it reveals a certain arrogance on our part."

"Tell me, Captain, is 'our' arrogance at all a match for yours, when you and Officer Leung here held this mission virtually hostage to your insistence no additional protective measures be presented as options for Oomb and Fafama?"

"It is plainly obvious that what you term 'protective measures' are of no interest to the Oombians. And as for-"

"You mean the Oombians of whom we are aware."

"Ah, yes," Captain Taylor nodded knowingly as she got to her feet. Buddy Leung consequently fled from where he was leaning against the navigation console. He wanted to remove himself from the line of fire between Louisa and Helena. "That is how some people operate, isn't it? Search for support for militarization, no matter how meager, and marginalize the opposition to militarization, no matter how enormous? What I was going to say," Captain Taylor went on, though regretting she didn't let Entroper squirm by waiting for her response, "was that I don't doubt the Fafaman leadership would have jumped at the offer of a land- and air-based missile defense system. But after dealing with them, I'm afraid they would have been motivated more by what they thought they could do to their rebel faction, than by fear of creatures who couldn't fly to their planet without accidentally crashing their spacecraft. The bottom line is this, Dr. Entroper: You can characterize my behavior however you wish, but I was NOT going to sell my soul to head up the second Smoke and Mirrors mission. As it is, my conscience isn't sure I didn't agree to too much when I allowed for the weapons retrofit of this spacecraft."

"Well, I'm with Secretary Spinner when he said the terrorist attack on the Fafaman government's traditional ceremony was all he needed to know about the rebels, Captain Taylor," Entroper said most forcefully. "And here's MY bottom line: We have a right, a duty, speaking of conscience, to protect our fellow Earthlings who are peacefully trying to make a new life for themselves on Oomb, whether Oodle-Noodle and her gang approve or not!"

Chris wanted to say, *Shouldn't that be Oodle-Noodle and her forest?,* but he thought better of it. And Helena Taylor thought better of escalating the argument further with Dr. Entroper. To the captain's way of thinking, there were so many holes in the official observer's reasoning, it was hard to know where to begin. Helena could have said to Louisa that the terrorist attack is all she and the secretary of defense *want* to know about the rebels. That she, Louisa, has alarmingly little interest in any pesky complications. For example, there was the possibility most rebels didn't consider themselves represented by the violent actions of those who infiltrated that so-called "traditional ceremony," which was in fact a very untraditional parade of military might. Also, there was the possibility the rebels' grievances with the Fafaman government, especially regarding pollution of the water table, might have some merit. Moreover, Captain Taylor could have gone after Entroper's high-sounding rhetoric about the right to defend fellow peace-loving Earthlings settling on Oomb. Yes, the Oombians did agree to welcome settlers from Earth with open branches bearing fruit and tubers ripe for the plucking. But when did they ever waive their insistence on no change to their non-defense policies?

No, Helena decided. She figured that if she continued to dissect Dr. Entroper's increasingly flustered-sounding remarks, the growing mutual aggravation would be to no good effect. So she settled with, "Look, here is my proposal: We *do* proceed with deployment of the laser mesh shield around Oomb, despite their objections."

Dr. Entroper exhaled like she'd been holding her breath throughout the argument, holding herself in suspended animation until such time as the captain came to her senses.

"However,-"

On this signal of a qualification to Taylor's announcement, Louisa Entroper did a doubletake.

"-as soon as we can return from deploying the mesh around Fafama, and otherwise checking out their situation, I insist on exploring an option Oodle-Noodle telepathed. I don't know whether any of the rest of you may have overheard this, or whatever the tree creatures would call it when someone's mind picks up a telepathed message not directed at her..."

Everyone shook their head to indicate they didn't know what the captain was talking about.

"Okay, what Oodle-Noodle suggested was that she and an associate could trim down, short and narrow enough to board the Smoke and Mirrors. Accompanying us, they could help scheme nonviolent ways to deal with the anticipated threat from Tictoctic."

"And of course, exploring whatever the tree

creatures believe might be realistic options does not necessarily commit us to follow their advice if, for instance, we find those options to be particularly naïve. Isn't that right, Captain?"

"Again, exploring options I think is an excellent way of putting it, Buddy."

"What I find most notably intriguing about your proposal, Captain," added Ali Magabu, so captivated by the idea that he had to stand up to walk off loose energy, "is that clearly, unless they are deceiving us to a truly unfathomable extent, these Oombians have worked for generations at nonviolent conflict resolution. Who knows? Maybe such deliberate focus is at the center of their being able to amplify their telepathic abilities so far beyond ours, we may seem to them like lower life forms by comparison. Whether or not that is their perception of us, it must be admitted that for our own part, we have not come too far along, we are not really very adept, at imagining peaceful outcomes when confronted with threats of violence. Perhaps such imagining is not possible unless you bring extraordinary naïveté to the table; our Oombian friends have only been able to get away with believing there's a peaceful way out because until now, they've been sheltered from the worst the big, bad universe has to dish out. The point as I see it is that their perspective certainly warrants the audience for which you are asking, Captain."

Captain Helena Taylor wanted to thank Ali and Buddy both for piling on their support before Louisa Entroper could even open her mouth. But Helena satisfied herself with remarking, "Something Oodle-Noodle telepathed me I found especially haunting. She indicated that she and her fellow Oombians expect we're going to have to find out the hard way the futility of violence, as she put it. So they are already making plans for what to do in the event any of them survive the consequences of our actions. People, if there is any truth to what she telepathed, if we're the ones who are really naïve, I'd like to give us a chance not to have to learn the hard way."

"Captain, as skeptical as I have to admit to being about that nonviolent stuff – you might as well try to argue World War 2 wasn't necessary – but since you're going along with the laser mesh shield for Oomb," Kevin said in even tones, "I'm in. Can't really see how it would hurt to have Oodle-Noodle prune herself for boarding. Once she's had a chance to sink her roots into the navigation bridge, she can telepath us what she's got."

"So it's agreed?"

After surveying all the heads nodding in the affirmative to Taylor's question, Dr. Entroper tossed up her hands and let them drop virtually lifeless. This was her way of showing how helpless she felt to raise the least objection.

***

"Listen to me, Papi."

"No, you are right, Pedro." Don Placido waved his forefinger like a windshield wiper, Pedro thought to himself. "The faster we stop talking, the faster you can complete your work and turn on the power!"

"Wait! Papi! Look all around you! Everything is different! Every thing is different!" For further emphasis, Pedro Perez made broad, sweeping gestures of his arms. "Look closely at each bug, Don Placido! Each bug is unlike any bug you saw on Earth!"

"I wasn't happy about seeing bugs on Earth! Makes no difference here, unless they taste like gandules when you mix them with rice!"

"Okay, forget about the bugs! Take a deep breath of this sea air nearly always at a comfortable temperature!"

"I'm not complaining about the air, but that's something I can still enjoy while I'm watching TV."

"There you go with the TV again! Okay, you don't like bugs. What about this magnificent scenery? Aren't those green mountains an improvement over gray city buildings? Oh, look at that rainbow! This place is like Hawai'i! A rainbow every day!"

"Ay bendito, Pedro hijito! I have to catch up on fifty missed seasons of baseball games! I downloaded them from the spaceship library! Bueno," Placido huffed in resignation, "I stay outside to admire the scenery for an hour. Then what?"

Ludi set down her gardening trowel to get back on her feet and loop her right arm around Placido's left. "Listen, 'suegro' (*father-in-law*), Doña Rotonda would like if maybe you chased her around how my grandfather dances after my grandmother."

"Sí, and when I capture her, she will give me more work to improve our house!"

Don Placido had just found his stepson Pedro checking electrical current output, and double-checking the wire encasement for a solar panel tower grid. Pedro had overseen its construction at the higher altitude end of the log cabin community the tree people had built for the hundred-ninety-some people relocated sixty years and trillions of miles away from their former tenement district in north Philadelphia. Pedro was also taking measurements to assure the solar panels were following precisely the course of the sun Callaway X-Centra across the sky, a most convoluted course due to Oomb's constantly shifting rotational axis. He'd already noted with pleasure this would be a twenty-hour day followed by only five hours of night before the next dawn. Once the power was turned on in another hour or so, there would be more than enough juice in the system to keep everything lit throughout the darkness. This, even while he was taking down parts of the grid to assure all parts were functioning properly.

Nevertheless, Señor Perez was feeling a certain amount of stress, even before Placido found him to add to it. Pedro wanted to get everything working sooner rather than later. Already he could see the news crew making their way up the hill from the center of Oombinquen. The Earthling settlement had been given that name as a fusion of the planet's name, Oomb, with the Taino Indian name, Borinquen, in honor of the Puerto Rican heritage of the Earthling settlers. Borinquen was the name originally given to Puerto Rico before the Spanish arrived.

*Bueno*, Pedro thought to himself, *I brought this on myself, during our voyage here*. Officer Kevin Smith-Park had found Pedro an especially quick study when he explained the plans to anyone interested, for adapting mid-twenty-first-century technology to the situation on Oomb. And he hadn't needed to ask Pedro twice, where heading up development of the settlement's power grid infrastructure was concerned.

"Bueno," sighed Placido with an exhale of resignation, "I suppose I will go sit in front of my blank hundred-inch screen, and dream of seeing the Phillies Stadium on there."

"Hey, Papi, I wondered what you were dreaming of when you snoozed off with your big screen mistress!"

"'Ay Dios mío'! *(Oh my God!)*" Placido grumbled as he turned around to leave. "After you finish making me wait for the power, how about some cars and some streets? This is a long climb even if you welcomed me with a 'pilón' full of pork!"

"Aye, Papi, are you not feeling like a new man with all

that exercise they made you do aboard the Smoke and Mirrors after your rejuvenation surgery?"

"I feel like a new man because I have a hundred-inch screen to watch fifty years of baseball! If I get tired and want to do something else, I will let you know!"

"Don't you want to play with your grand-daughter before you leave?" Ludi linked arms with Placido anew.

"Hola baylo a-ee-o," was how Alexita's brave effort to say *Hola Abuelo Placido* – Hello Grandpa Placido – came out, as she tentatively opened and closed the fingers of both her raised hands by way of trying to imitate the wave hello.

Before Ludi could finish dragging Placido over to her daughter's side, to have her give her grandpa a hug and a kiss, an Oombian vine snuck out of the grass. It crawled up Alexita's leg to tickle her tummy with its tendrils. As she lost balance and fell over backwards giggling, Placido pointed, horrified. He exclaimed, "Ay Dios! Someone has to stop it from biting her! She is much safer indoors in front of a TV!"

"Ay, Papi, a plant is not going to bite her or give her a pinch, like this!" Ludi demonstrated on Placido's arm held captive by her own, while already the vine was relenting and retracting itself into the nearby woods. "It was trying to make Alexita leave some fertilizer because it mistook her for another animal. Anyway, I like how you waited on someone else to rescue her! Ha! Thanks to God she was not needing your help!"

"Careful down there! We are landing!" It was the husky, laughter-filled voice of Pedro's sister Jerri suddenly raining from overhead, along with the distinctive whup-whup-whup of one of the Oombian tree people in flight.

"Hola Don Placido!" chimed in other sister Gloria as the intensifying whup-whup-whup sent a strong breeze right into Placido's face.

"Aye Dios mío, you brought the babies up in the sky like that?!" Placido pointed at the dozed-off creatures in Gloria and Jerri's arms as the tree person landed. "You could have dropped them!"

"Woofle-Woofle wasn't going to let them drop, were you, Woofle-Woofle?" Gloria stroked Woofle-Woofle's bark with mock tenderness to accompany the mock tenderness in her voice.

*I had safety net branches ready to catch the babies at all times. There was never the least danger to them.*

"Ay! Ay!" Placido frantically batted the air with his arms. It was as though gnats were in his face, Pedro mused. "No more voice in my head! No more!"

"Is okay, Papi!" said Jerri. "Woofle-Woofle apologizes! He telepathed me that he will not speak in your head no more."

"So what brings you girls here?" asked Pedro. "I mean, besides Woofle-Woofle? Oh, gracias."

*De nada.* Woofle-Woofle had just spread his branches wide for Pedro Perez to make a fruit selection.

Señor Perez plucked something off the Oombian that looked and tasted like an extra-sweet strawberry, but in the shape of a carrot, and with the consistency of a well-cooked yam. "Are you here to celebrate the activation of the solar power grid?" he proceeded with his sisters. "I think that's the news crew ascending the hill to make their first TV report, that they can make a TV report finally."

"Ay!" Jerri and Gloria wailed their desperation in unison. "What will Juan and Carlos want with us when there are Ciela and other chicas," whined Jerri, "who are not connected to babies?"

"That is why we were thinking, Ludi preciosa," started in Gloria. Pedro had long since tired of Gloria's manipulative transitions, from her forlorn cry of helplessness one moment to her enthused articulation of hope the next. Such hope always proved false, that if her target audience would just do the favor she asked, they might never have to hear her forlorn stuff, ever again. And so, Pedro looked away and shook his head as his younger sister went on, "maybe Alexita would like to play mama with Espacio and Galaxio for a while. We promise we will pick them up, right after dinner."

"By Alexita playing mama," Ludi nodded knowingly as Placido turned his back on a fruit-pluck offered him by Woofle-Woofle, "you mean *I* will be playing mama. Sorry, girls, but as you can see, I am busy planting mums and petunias in an experiment to discover how well Earth plants do in the soil of Oomb."

"Ay, Ludi, how can you plant when you have to take care of Alexita?" Jerri sounded irritatingly to Pedro like she thought she'd caught his wife in some indefensible contradiction. Since she wasn't likely to get what she wanted from Ludi, she might as well go nasty.

"Alexita helps me a little, and when she can't help, she's fascinated by what I'm doing, and the strange insects we see."

"Bendito…" Gloria sprang up and down on her legs with extra urgency as the news crew of Juan and Carlos was fast approaching; Pedro mused to himself she was acting like she needed to use the bathroom soon, or she would have an accident. "Why can't Espacio and Galaxio help, also?"

"You know the answer to that question, Gloria! Alexita is two, and Espacio and Galaxio are still babies!"

"We thought you wanted to become a teacher with a room full of children, Ludi!"

Again, Pedro could tell that Jerri, his older sister, was determined to shame his wife into a guilt trip if she couldn't get her to take the babies off their hands.

"But you won't even- What is two plus one, Gloria?"

"Two plus one? Let me see." Gloria made as much of a show as she could, of sticking out two fingers on one hand and one finger on the other, without losing hold of her still-snoozing Galaxio. Then she counted off, "One, two, three. Three, Jerri," she nodded.

"So you can't take care for three children for a short time, yet you want to spend entire days with twenty of them?"

"When they finish installing running water and the power, there is a building Ciela and I will be using as a school house for children four and up. We'll be happy to take Galaxio and Espacio on their fourth birthday. Myrta told me she'll watch Alexita for me while I am teaching her six-year-old daughter, Suerta. Maybe she will watch your children also if you can offer her something in exchange. But the building is not ready yet, so I am taking this time for my interest in gardening."

"Aye, how nice for you, Ludi," whined Jerri. "We don't have time for nothing!"

Pedro was about to lay into his sisters, starting with, *You had plenty of time for partying and getting pregnant with those two roosters before you could be sure they cared very much for you.* But all of the sudden, Tomás and Jorge sauntered side by side out of the woods. They were the two eminently school-age boys famous for sneaking a chocolate chip cookie into Dr. Skepticus's clothes, so the seat of his pants would get incinerated by Effy, the ephemeral dragon. They paused from their saunter to belch in unison, then they beat a hasty retreat back into the undergrowth from where they had emerged, enough with their Oonzy Ootzy imitation.

"Ay, look at them!" Melba whined wistfully. "They go where they want, and no mother has to care for them all hours of the day!"

"Hey, what about Don Placido?!" Jerri's light went on, soon as her eyes settled absent-mindedly on her step-father lingering nearby. His descent back down the shallow slope to his new home on Oomb had stalled out, on the chance another unexpected thing might occur to give him even more to variously marvel at or shake his head in disgust. However, Placido knew that attention came from his step-daughters only when they wanted something. The instant Jerri mentioned his name, he realized she and her sister would ask him to watch his grandchildren. So with a quick, "Oh-oh," before Gloria could cry out, "You are not doing anything this afternoon are you, Papi?," Placido spun around on one foot and was hurrying off again. He hunched his shoulders ear level in his effort to use his arms to maintain balance. He would have thrown himself to the ground and rolled if he thought that would get him away any faster.

Whatever. Pedro had had enough of Gloria and Jerri's attitude. Probably nothing he said would matter, but he was determined to take another stab at it. He leapt off the platform for the solar grid, and practically used his shoes as skis to hasten his slide downslope to the news crew.

"What is Pedro Perfecto doing?" Gloria wondered aloud.

"I don't know, but like you said, sister, what we do know is that everything he does IS perfect."

Pedro was finished asking Juan and Carlos to postpone their ascent to the grassy plateau until he took care of a personal matter. And so, with giant strides he quickly returned back uphill.

Placido stopped his own retreat, to try listening in on what would happen next.

"Sisters, I have something important to say to you."

"We don't need your advice," said Jerri as both sisters turned away from Pedro to seek a flight off the plateau by Woofle-Woofle.

"You're not going anywhere until you've listened to me."

"Ay! Save us, Woofle-Woofle!" Jerri regretted Pedro didn't grab her shoulders or something similar when he ran in between her and the tree creature. She wanted to be able to complain he was hurting her, thus making a strong case for Woofle-Woofle's expedient deliverance of her from what she did not want to hear.

*We do not intercede on family or other Earthling matters, unless we comprehend a nonviolent way to rescue someone from threatened violence.*

"Listen, both of you!" shouted Pedro. "The great-grandchildren of your generation have given you, they have given all of us, an incredible opportunity to live lives we could never have dreamed of living before!"

"This is YOUR dream to live on another world very distant in space, dear brother. Not our dream!" Gloria gestured towards Pedro, then back at Jerri and herself, with her hand not cradling the still-napping Galaxio. Both sisters shook their heads 'no.'

"So you want to return to an unhealthy, drug-infested slum, when here you have all this clean air to breathe and such beautiful scenery and weather?"

"But we don't know anyone here. They are all strangers."

Pedro wanted to argue this point, the absurdity of what Jerri said. Close to two hundred neighbors were spirited out of Philadelphia alongside them. Plus, there were all the new acquaintances his sisters had made aboard the Smoke and Mirrors. They'd added at least another couple of good friends. But Pedro knew from excruciating past experience that when Jerri and Gloria wanted to be miserable, wanted to complain, they rejected all contrary indications with profoundly disturbing ease. The second mission's chief expert on both human and extraterrestrial psychological issues, Dr. Ali Magabu, had taken a special interest in their situation. They had both gotten pregnant out of wedlock, and they both had turned down all offered counseling services aboard the Smoke and Mirrors. However, Ali had concluded there was too much on the sisters' plates already. Luring them into a healthier regimen and guiding them through child-birth had needed to take place at the same time they struggled to adapt to literally out-of-this-world circumstances. It was unrealistic to expect to make any major headway in the immediate future on their other issues. With this in mind, and again remembering how futile it had proven previously, to pick apart their life-sucks-for-them-because-they-can't-get-their-way venting, Pedro tried a new tack. "Okay," he said with a wave of both hands, to symbolize sweeping aside everything else. "Let us imagine something. Let us imagine that with the tap of a magic wand, you have no cares, no responsibilities. You have all the time in the world for whatever you want to do. What would you want to do?"

"I would start with him," Gloria giggled as she pointed down the hill at Juan. "I would want to do him!"

Jerri gave Gloria a hi-five.

Pedro closed his eyes and shook his head. He was already despairing over any chance his new tack would achieve even the least bit of progress with his sisters. "In this magic scenario there are no boys. There are only unlimited possibilities for what you can do," he continued nevertheless. "Perhaps you would want to become a professional dancer?"

"No," Gloria shook her own head as she responded in a matter-of-fact voice. "I would want to always be bad. What about you, sister?"

"Me too. Sí, we are evil." Jerri burst into a giggle.

"Pedro..." Ludi's tone of voice was so freighted with the message to her husband, *Don't bother, it's not worth the effort and you will only raise your blood pressure,* his name was all she had to say.

Nevertheless, Señor Perez gave in to his frustration. He reacted, "Someday, I hope you both will appreciate the opportunities you have been handed! At the least, you should figure out how you would answer the question of how you would want to occupy your life if you could occupy it with anything you chose!"

"Pedro..."

"Is unfortunate how people are not thankful for their blessings, how people are not realizing how thankful they should be for their blessings, until they lose them!"

"Pedro!" This time Ludi was shouting because this time, she was not admonishing her husband for getting all weepy, again, over his reflection for the umpteenth occasion on how they'd lost their house in New Jersey. Rather, this time she was calling his attention to a spectacular phenomenon spread out across the firmament, from one moment to the next. It looked like a grid or a luminous fishing net, Ludi thought. Its crisscrossing lines glowed bright red in dramatic contrast to the indigo-blue sky. Moreover, as dramatically quickly as they appeared, those red lines somehow intensified, deepened...and disappeared.

Observers on the ground found when they blinked their eyes, they still saw a purplish residue. It was as though they'd lingered a glance at the sun a bit too long.

Further unsettling was the distinct bang! heard a few minutes later, which seemed to have descended from the sky.

Pedro unaccountably found himself feeling chilled to the bone. If he could only have known, that was his latent telepathic power picking up on Woofle-Woofle's fear.

***

"Sergeant Frankly?" Captain Taylor turned her back on the panoramic view-screen where she had just seen, from orbit, the red-lined net encircle Oomb for a brief yet memorable moment. It was what had been experienced by Pedro and others from the ground. "Maybe I should have known better, Sergeant. Maybe I even missed the briefing. But, I wasn't aware that deployment of the laser mesh was going to produce such a spectacle."

"It's the system signature, Captain, confirming it's up and running." Frankly bluffed his way through trying to seem more nonchalant than he actually felt. "You know, like the beep when you reset a security alarm."

Helena Taylor folded her arms. "It's a signature some eavesdropping sensor of which we're not aware could detect, to announce to, oh, say, Tictoctic, that here we are."

"Captain, if you're so concerned, we could try something different when we activate the mesh around Fafama," said Sergeant Frankly. "We could fan out the light-bending mirror cloak from the interceptor satellites, to conceal the activation signature like they did for the Earth mesh."

To safely approach a laser-mesh-enrobed planet, spacecraft had to be encoded so when they bisected any part of the mesh, they would allow the mesh circuit to remain uninterrupted. The interceptor satellites were to fire disintegrating laser bursts at any incoming, un-encoded spacecraft and space debris.

Taylor sighed. She didn't want to get into how despite the mirror cloak, there were mysterious, red, crisscrossing lines that lit up the skies in scattered locations around the Earth, during most secretive activation of its laser mesh.

A "conventional" explanation had been required for wide circulation. "I guess the point is," Captain Taylor said finally, with her sigh persisting, "even if bad guys find out about the mesh, lots of luck passing anything through it without the encoding program."

"Captain, you can look at the situation as not unlike in the days before the quarantine zones. Posted signs let thieves know which houses were protected by security systems."

"Hmm..." Captain Taylor hmmed absent-mindedly. As she pondered the principle archipelago of Oomb, she wondered, *Did Oodle-Noodle formally telepath me of her concern the deer creatures of Tictoctic could misinterpret the laser mesh? Or, did this occur to me by myself?, perhaps abetted by whatever dormant psychic ability I possess?*

"Captain," said Yoon-hee busily monitoring the navigation panel, "we have confirmation the guinea pig pod with the programmed encoding sequence has made a safe ascent up through the laser mesh. Should I tell Buddy to break out of low orbit now, for rendezvous with us?"

"Yes, and have Officer Leung advise Oodle-Noodle I am looking forward – Scrap that, I'm sure she already knows. Just tell Buddy I'll greet him and our new honorary crew members at the shuttle pod dock in fifteen minutes."

"You heard that, Buddy?"

"Captain," Buddy's voice crackled over the control room intercom, "Oodle-Noodle telepathed me to convey to you again her gratitude."

*And your concern about our laser mesh deployment over your objections is taken most seriously,* Captain Taylor thought to herself. She trusted Oodle-Noodle and the other tree creatures would pick up on that deliberate cogitation as effortlessly as had she told them to their faces.

"Captain, I'll meet you down there after I get the rest of my stuff and check in with Sergeant Hanson." Frankly was following Captain Taylor off the bridge as he said this.

***

"On behalf of the crew of the Smoke and Mirrors, Oodle-Noodle and Wafoodle-Boodle, I welcome you both aboard." Captain Taylor gave the tree people an awkward bow. She was still uncertain, even after several encounters with Oombians, how best to greet sentient beings who knew what you were going to do before you did it.

*Thank you, Captain Taylor.* Oodle-Noodle's telepathed gratitude merged with Wafoodle-Boodle's in Helena's mind. Then, as they spread their branch arms apart for Helena to select what she would pluck from them, Oodle-Noodle went on, *I must apologize for two things. First, as we are sure you've already noticed, we're still shedding sand and soil from our mobile root tendrils, despite our best cleaning prior to boarding the shuttle pod.*

"I'll have Chris sprinkle chocolate shards on them so Effy, our ephemeral dragon, will have your dirt trail incinerated to dust in no time."

*We look forward to assisting Professor Skepticus to ascertain whether Effy is a pronouncedly living entity. Presumably if its mind is readable for substantial thoughts, that will settle the matter.*

"'Pronouncedly living'? 'Substantial thoughts'?"

*You would discover that everything is alive, if you could but perceive everything from far more than three dimensions, Captain. It's only a matter of how removed particular things seem on your level of perception, from the intelligence that animates them,* telepathed Wafoodle-Boodle.

*Wafoodle-Boodle is one of our spiritual explainers,* telepathed Oodle-Noodle as she gave said explainer a most tender, bark-crinkling regard.

"Sounds to me like some wriggle room for Skepticus's predisposition on the matter, so I'll look forward to how that turns out. But, um, what else are you going to waste your telepathing to apologize for that doesn't need apologizing?" Helena Taylor hurried in this question to forestall formally greeting Buddy Leung. However, she could tell from the look Buddy gave her that he already strongly suspected what he needed to do. That he needed to stay behind on Oomb while the Smoke and Mirrors headed for Fafama. And talk about telepathy, Helena sensed the look she gave him blatantly advertised his suspicion was correct.

*Maybe not a big thing for you, Captain Taylor,* telepathed Oodle-Noodle. *However, we can't help feeling impolite, not carrying our usual abundance of fruit and tubers to share. I can tell you are disappointed at the absence of what you would describe as an apple-sized grape. We strove to partially make up for this. After completing the trimming necessary for us to conveniently mobilize about your spacecraft, we plucked off and gathered together all the fruit and tubers from our discarded branches, to carry them aboard in our luggage. Included are several of the monster grapes. Oh, excuse us.* On this last telepath, Oodle-Noodle and Wafoodle-Boodle scurried to one corner on their root tendrils. There, they activated the misting from the water tanks mounted on their backs so they wouldn't dehydrate in the ship's low humidity. Of course, Earthling climate engineers had long since adapted the tree creatures' rest quarters. Not only would the Oombians enjoy a moisture-laden retreat. They would also have at their disposal, any time they required, rich soil down into which they'd be able to sink their root tendrils deep. This, despite said soil being treated with special bio-adhesive material so it wouldn't float off in zero- or low-gravity situations, as was presently occurring with the bits of dirt and sand they were still shedding from underneath their trunks.

Anyhow, the tree creatures' movement over to the side left Helena and Buddy face-to-face finally. Postponing the inevitable was no longer an option. Before the captain could attempt what she'd resigned herself to being a near-worthless expression of regret, Buddy gestured for her to save her breath, and himself offered, "Captain, if you're not going to ask me to stay behind with a shuttle pod, to help monitor the situation here, I wish permission to speak honestly."

Helena was struck speechless, reflecting on how deadly earnest serious Buddy was acting. Under less-ominous circumstances, she could have well imagined her first officer doing more of his endearingly lame comic material that he was always the one laughing at the most. *When Oodle-Noodle was using the pruning shears on herself, she explained to me she was hedging her bets. Ha!* But such flippancy was not to be. "You know you're not going to have to ask permission for that, Officer Leung. Ever," she at last responded.

"Uh, have you told Cathy?"

Helena Taylor could tell his question was as in: *I hope*

*you took care of that to spare me the squirm.* But as bizarre as Buddy's situation with Cathy still seemed to her, under the circumstances Helena was glad to have at least done him that favor. "She was fine with your staying behind," the captain nodded. "Said to tell you she looks forward to missing you so she can look forward to seeing you again. I assured her I was certain the feeling was mutual. Buddy..."

The intensely somber way Helena uttered his name had Officer Leung's heart skipping a beat. It was all he could do to acknowledge she had his full and undivided attention by saying, "Captain?"

"I hope I didn't make a mistake. How that grid lit up and stayed lit like that, even if it was for only a few seconds, we might as well have set off fireworks with a megaphone announcing, 'Here we are!'"

"I know, Captain. But I'm already working on a way to protect the mesh from a sabotage plan I thought of. With set encoding, the code can be broken. However, variable encoding would make it impossible for marauding craft-"

"Because as soon as they did break the code, it would have already changed," Captain Taylor nodded as she finished Buddy's sentence. "They'd have to be solving it simultaneous with testing the mesh boundary. Brilliant, Buddy. What about if they launch a decoy so they can locate the armed satellites, when those satellites unload on said decoy with disintegration beams?"

"Already taken care of in the original deployment, Captain. After every activation, the satellites automatically shift position like musical chairs." When this information got greeted by Helena with a long silence, Buddy Leung added, "I know, Captain. I'm still worried too. Just because I get the mesh to the operational point where I can't figure out how to beat it doesn't mean someone else won't."

"Hey, Cap'n, Officer Leung, hope my yappin' with Sergeant Hanson wasn't holding things up. Anyhow I'm packed and ready."

Sergeant Frankly's arrival at the shuttle pod bay spared Helena and Buddy any further commiseration. "Your unit is all aboard, Sergeant," said Buddy. "I'll be staying with you on Oomb, and we'll have the shuttle pod at our disposal while the Smoke and Mirrors is gone. You'll still be in charge, but I'll be around for added logistical support."

"Don't take this the wrong way, Leung, but I hope we won't need you because if we do, you won't be enough. If those bad asses with antlers break through the laser mesh defense, one extra grunt won't matter a whole heckuva lot. That is, unless you figure on sneakin' us into a wormhole or somethin' on the shuttle, leave the settlers behind to hope the tree people will mess with the antlered aliens' minds. Maybe they can declare deer huntin' season on them! Yeah!"

As much as he was willing to spout off, Fred Frankly wasn't about to share with Taylor and Leung his conversation with Officer Hanson. He'd found Guy Hanson on the edge of his bed, hunched over. Hanson was dripping a tear on his cardboard-thin yet unbreakably-strong, super-flexible textboard.

"What the interstellar f--k is THIS about, Buddy?" Frankly had asked as he'd plopped down beside his long-time associate, and put an arm around him.

"It's Jen."

"Oh, hell no! You got a Dear John from her?! F---in' a! What's her problem?! Huh?!"

"No, it's okay. I need to understand. At these

distances, for this amount of time..."

"You need to understand nothin' from her, Guy! Nothin'! You offered her a chance to tag along! Shit! Ciela could've used the help with those f---in' weasels who think they're so clever stickin' chocolate chip cookies up people's business end so they get toasty marshmallow ass from that f---in' ghost dragon!"

"Look, she found this guy who wants to stay earthbound like her. Sucks for me, but maybe she's happier..."

"I'll bet she 'found' this guy! Was probably all dreamy-eyed about him before you even left! Ya see, this is why I'm a player, man! Why even try to commit to someone when the odds are they don't even know themselves what they want?"

Guy Hanson just gave his fellow sergeant a wan smile through his tears. He'd learned the hard way not to ask again: Who was she? It might not even have been a 'she,' Guy had reflected. Maybe one of his parents deserted the family when he was at an age of maximum vulnerability.

"Look," Fred had slapped him encouragingly on the back, "I know what's for me might not be what's for you. Hey, I've seen pictures of those Fafaman women. How about those eyes? Hey?! You've noticed them too, haven't you?" Fred had punched Guy playfully on the shoulder as Guy blushed with a sheepish grin, albeit still red around the eyes from his tears. "With peepers like that, boobs are almost an optional feature. Almost." While Guy shook his head at how casually his military partner could be so crass, again and again and again, Fred had gone on, "Who knows? Maybe one of the Fafamaf--in'falafel's harem girls is getting tired of being treated as a piece in his f-in' assortment pack, and she'll prefer to roam the cosmos with you."

"Well," Guy had pulled himself back together enough to clutch at Fred's shoulder with brotherly love, "as long as you're wishing that on me, here's wishing you fall hard for one, just one, of the eligible young women in the settlement, and that the feeling's totally mutual!"

"So you think there may be someone who can saw down Sergeant Fred Frankly like a lumberjack would take care of Oodles of F---in' Noodles if she only stopped movin' for long enough? Hell!" Then with a big mutual embrace, Guy and Fred had said, "Semper Fi!" to one another. Fred had no idea, especially lacking Oombian mind-reading development, that midway through this farewell, Guy hadn't been able to stop thinking, *God help us all if the tree people are right about our laser mesh deployment!*

# Chapter 6

"Acceleration to quintuple light-speed is approaching thirty-six percent. Ascendance to course plateau altitude above the orbital plane is approaching seventy-one percent. Distance from next solar flare surf turbulence is closing in from five point two million lek-leks. Your suggestion, most revered Captain Mat-kek-tek, is proving the most brilliant advice possible. Boosting rotation an additional thousand revolutions per pektel has shortened course altitude ascent time by ten percent. Acceleration to quintuple light speed is approaching forty-one percent. Ascendance to course plateau altitude-" So goes this rough approximation of Officer Tak-venk-tit's tongue-flicking running commentary, with a lek-lek measuring about half a mile, and a pektel measuring about three seconds. However, altitude ascent time was *not* shortened ten percent. It was more like half of one percent. Officer Tak-venk-tit rounded way up, from one half to ten, for the greater glory of the captain. Officer Tak-venk-tit hoped such greater glory would buy his latest scar a little extra time to heal, before he had to experience the next assertion of authority superior to his own. All of this, aboard a saucer spacecraft named, again as the translation would go, Dek-Fook-Tek's Third Celestial Breath. Dek-Fook-Tek was the single most powerful creature on the planet Tictoctic, and the saucer was bound from Tictoctic for the planet Fafama.

Captain Mat-kek-tek paused from sharpening his antlers with his custom-made bahvek, to nod his tolerance of Officer Tak-venk-tit's compliment. But he added, "The glory is for Dek-Fook-Tek; my brilliance compared to his is as the light reflected off Tictoctic compared to the sun's direct rays."

With this ritual pronouncement, all officers present on the navigation deck of the saucer craft, save one, rose from their bucket seats. They turned to face Captain Mat-kek-tek, and vulnerably swelled out their chests. In unison, they chanted, "His will be done." It was for the captain to decide to what extent to slash at one or more fellow creatures, if at all. But Tak-venk-tit calculated correctly. His flattery sounded genuine enough, especially since he gave the ten percent estimate as a supporting detail, as an extra-compelling reason for praise. Captain Mat-kek-tek would never know of the exaggeration, from an insignificant half a per cent to an impressive ten percent. Instead, he would feel less need, at least temporarily, to remind the officers of their station in life. Except for the one who did not stand. But he would be dealt with soon enough. There would be plenty of time for that. Presently, the captain was intent on offering up a further suggestion calculated to garner even more praise, however much he might demur and give most of the credit to Supreme Authority Dek-Fook-Tek. To heighten the impression he made, Captain Mat-kek-tek resumed antler sharpening with his bahvek before he clicked his tongue anew. An Earthling might have been reminded of a billiards player refreshing the chalk on the end of her cue stick. The idea was to demonstrate that okay, maybe some of the officers understood far more of the nuts-and-bolts operation of the saucer craft than Captain Mat-kek-tek did. However, what they knew might be blinding them to his brilliance; didn't Officer Tak-venk-tit use "brilliant" to describe the captain's advice? Yes, for certain the other officers were blinded by what little they did know, in Captain Mat-kek-tek's estimation. They were blinded to the brilliant way Captain Mat-kek-tek could simultaneously prepare to defend, to uphold his station in life, and propose something too obvious to occur to them without his essentially divine intervention as one of the hooves of Dek-Fook-Tek. "Here is another suggestion," is how the first in his new series of tongue-clicks might have gotten translated by expert linguist Ali Magabu, after enough language semantics analysis. "Spinning into the next solar flare surf at varying angles, perhaps we discover that particular angle which most minimizes the turbulence."

Initially, Officer Tak-venk-tit nodded hesitantly slowly to this new advice from his superior. As little as Tak-venk-tit understood of their space vehicle's operation, he did know one thing. Officer Kwit-Nik, who neglected to stand with the rest of them to vulnerably tongue-click, "His will be done," had already devoted entire test flights to exactly what the captain was suggesting. In fact, Tak-venk-tit wouldn't have been surprised if Kwit-Nik's preoccupation with minimizing the imminent impact of the oncoming solar flare was what kept him from joining the other officers in their humble obeisance. Tak-venk-tit's mind raced as he wondered whether to let Captain Mat-kek-tek know his suggestion had long since gotten beaten out, by the thoughts of someone well below his station. He could have most humbly brayed something to the effect of, *Honored Captain, that suggestion is so brilliant, Officer Kwit-Nik is hard at work on it, even as we speak*. But would not such a reality check prove especially dangerous? Officer Tak-venk-tit realized, the pektel he considered it, that this approach was only more likely to garner him fresh chest wounds, however superficial, from the Captain's hyper-sharpened antlers. So he opted to accelerate the speed of his nodding acknowledgement of the Captain's new suggestion, as if its brilliance was slow to dawn on him, at first. And he tongue-clicked, "We must consider your advice immediately! Officer Kwit-Nik!?"

To gain Kwit-Nik's attention, Tak-venk-tit lowered his head, and he gently nudged his stubby antlers, kept stubby for his station in Tictoctic society, against the back of Kwit-Nik's head.

Kwit-Nik jerked with startlement, so absorbed had he become by his analysis of data piling in on the navigation panel. Had he received sharp, painful pokes that gave him the sensation of bleeding from a fresh wound, he would have flicked his tongue to click, *Thank you profoundly, Captain, for drawing my attention to you. You so honor me*. But instantly realizing this benign attention-getter had to be coming from an equal, he clicked, "I'm sure the Captain humbles me with how much sooner he was alert to this situation than I was."

The captain rose from his chair to look over Kwit-Nik's shoulder at the multiple data screens. He nodded most knowingly, despite having no idea how to read or interpret anything he saw there.

Kwit-Nik went on, "I give Captain Mat-kek-tek well-deserved and not nearly enough rest, from telling you himself the meaning of what we see here. Our scout saucer specks have picked up a most distressing indicator of hitherto unsuspected sentient creatures. They were unsuspected except, of course, by our Supreme Authority, Dek-Fook-Tek." Kwit-Nik rose to join everyone else on the navigation deck, to turn facing the proximate direction of Tictoctic.

Captain Mat-kek-tek made a show of being the last to this ritual action, by giving every officer an inspection followed with nodding approval. This, as though he needed to assure they every one of them were doing what they were supposed to be doing. But actually, he was saving face for himself; he really did not know which way faced Tictoctic before the other Tictoctickians demonstrated.

"His will be done," said everyone in unison finally, thus paving the way for Kwit-Nik to continue, "The indicator has been detected from the fourth planet around the star between our system and the target system."

*Oh-oh, this is not good*, Kwit-Nik thought to himself. He noticed that in reaction to his news, Captain Mat-kek-tek couldn't control an instinctive twitching of his standing-alert ears. This was the unmistakable sign a deer creature of Tictoctic has been taken by surprise. Implicitly, Kwit-Nik tried to assure the captain that said unmistakable sign had gone unnoticed, by proceeding without delay to ask, "Should I share with the others what we already know about the details of the most distressing indicator?"

Mat-kek-tek silently closed his eyes as he nodded his assent; another terrible hint, Kwit-Nik well knew, the captain would soon be re-asserting his dominance.

Officer Kwit-Nik nevertheless feigned calm to say, "Two specks have transmitted photos of the fourth planet from two different perspectives. Here and here." The officer brought up both photos on navigation panel screens for the rest of the crew to ponder.

Captain Mat-kek-tek nodded knowingly at those photos. What they showed was as much a surprise for him as for anyone else aboard the saucer vessel from Tictoctic. However, he wanted to convey the impression that what was displayed was exactly as he'd suspected...as he brought every last bit of self-control to bear to keep his ears from twitching again.

"The crisscrossing narrow beams of red light lasted less than two pektels on the time-elapse photographic sequence. I believe Captain Mat-kek-tek's analysis was brilliant, as always, when he concluded the intelligence responsible for this unique phenomenon was activating some type of electronic security layer to envelope the planet." Kwit-Nik yet again was seeking to flatter the captain credibly enough to lessen the blow he feared he was inevitably soon going to receive from him.

"Officer Kwit-Nik, please explain to your peers the significance of this discovery. Officer Tak-venk-tit, contact the Supreme Dek-Fook-Tek with the documentation of my pivotal role, and of the new knowledge we gained by it, all thanks to his ultimate inspiration."

"All thanks to his ultimate inspiration," the officers every last one stood back up on their hind hooves to solemnly, ritually reaffirm.

Throughout, Kwit-Nik couldn't help noticing how the lights from the navigation panel illuminated the captain's face. They made it appear Mat-kek-tek was stunned nearly to paralysis by his perplexed state. Obviously, Captain Mat-kek-tek's latest orders for Kwit-Nik to explain the significance was intended to help the captain understand more clearly what had been discovered, without having to admit such help was needed.

This in mind, Kwit-Nik turned to his peers to say, while Tak-Venk-tit accessed the communication hyperspace network, "Here is the significance: There is no good reason for an entire planet to get enrobed in a security layer-"

"-unless its inhabitants are planning an attack, and they want to assure that retaliation will prove impossible!" Captain Mat-kek-tek got so excited that a possible ramification of the discovery had occurred to him, he couldn't help interrupting Officer Kwit-Nik's execution of the order he'd given him.

Kwit-Nik was actually going to complete his sentence

with something about the planet's inhabitants evidently fearing some extraterrestrial threat, not even necessarily intelligent. And certainly not necessarily as a result of those inhabitants planning some form of aggression. For example, there might have been worry over a destructive asteroid shower, as opposed to a counter-attack to which the aliens were plotting to immunize themselves. Well the officer knew, though, especially given Tictoctic's history, not to greet the captain's enthused sentence completion with any less than unbridled praise. "Captain Mat-kek-tek," Kwit-Nik said with a low, sweeping gesture of his right hoof, "I can only nibble on leaves of thanks, for your eloquence has spared us from my comparatively awkward and ineffectual elocution."

Captain Mat-kek-tek responded, "And I must regret our Supreme Authority Dek-Fook-Tek is not here to spare us from my own merely functional speech."

"His will be done," the officers stood to declare anew.

But Flight Engineer Kwit-Nik could tell Captain Mat-kek-tek was still boastfully proud of his deduction, however possibly incorrect. So boastfully proud, in fact, that for the first time, Kwit-Nik entertained real hope he might yet avoid more than a few scratches, as reminder of his subservient place in the Tictoctickian military hierarchy.

"You have news, Officer Tak-venk-tit?" Captain Mat-kek-tek nodded acknowledgement Tak-venk-tit was standing beside one of the bridge control consoles, patiently awaiting attention to be given. Tak-venk-tit's chest was thrust vulnerably forward for an antler-slashing, if that were to be his lot.

"Captain, the hyperspace saucer link has been effected with a ten-pektel oral and visual delay." Tak-venk-tit couldn't help preceding this announcement with an exhalation of relief, though he was nevertheless apprehensive about what he felt obliged to add. "I report this with bottomless shame, because a link worthy of the Supreme Dek-Fook-Tek would transmit his communication prior to his even having to trouble his ever-cherished tongue to click."

"Honor us, Supreme Authority, to carry your burdens whenever, however we can."

Once this oft-used litany was completed by every officer there present, the grainy image of Dek-Fook-Tek himself appeared on the control console television monitor. Captain Mat-kek-tek knew he had no time to spare, before launching into yet another ritual declaration. "Supreme Authority, there is no thanks I can give you worthy of your effort, for this attention you deign to grant, especially with the ten-pektel delay." Mat-kek-tek added that last part off-script.

During the tens of pektels he knew he would actually need to wait for a reaction from Dek-Fook-Tek, the captain said to Officer Tak-venk-tit, "Your inspiration from the Supreme Authority shows through all your deeds, Officer Tak-venk-tit. Do not judge yourself overly harshly when of course your results do not begin to measure up to what mine would have been, had I the least small additional fraction of my time away from my other considerable responsibilities aboard this craft."

"Your mercy illuminates the glory of our Supreme Dek-Fook-Tek." As custom dictated, Tak-venk-tit persisted with his chest thrust vulnerably forward, while the other officers rose anew to declaratively add, "From whom all mercy flows."

Even though he joined in, Kwit-Nik found himself unavoidably thinking, *One of the captain's "considerable responsibilities" must include keeping his antlers wood-splinter sharp.*

"Be as concisely thorough as you can be, Captain Mat-kek-tek, given your most notable limitations in that regard." The Supreme Authority's tongue-clicking came through static-y, like unto how the image on the console monitor was grainy. "Please explain why I should not be through with this conversation in a blink of the eyes, let alone a so-called ten-pektel delay." Dek-Fook-Tek's antlers loomed so imposingly overgrown above his narrow head, Captain Mat-kek-tek had to wonder anew, as his Supreme Authority spoke, at how he didn't lose balance of them. The captain had to wonder at how those bony protuberances didn't tip over uncontrollably to one side, thereby breaking Dek-Fook-Tek's neck and thus requiring consensus around a new Supreme Authority. But naturally, Mat-kek-tek wasn't going to mention any of this to him. He thrust out his own chest before the camera, as though Dek-Fook-Tek could somehow stab him across trillions of intervening lek-leks. And he said, "Supreme Dek-Fook-Tek, thanks without end to your visionary guidance, microsaucer surveillance has documented offensive preparations by as-yet-unidentified sentient creatures. Those preparations take place in the star system which ornaments the celestial tree between Tictoctic and our initial food-gathering destination.

"Officer Tak-venk-tit, tell our Supreme Authority how much longer he must wait to view the evidence at his end."

"There are still seven pektels, even though the seven pektels are counting so that they are already reduced to five, and will be down to as nothing by the time I conclude this useless apology. I regret each pektel you must wait, Supreme Dek-Fook-Tek. Each pektel is like a daughter too many, who I must abandon in the wilderness for an oskynt to devour."

The only reason Tak-venk-tit had time to conclude this traditional grovel was that, in fact, the image transmission to "Supreme Dek-Fook-Tek" of the laser mesh shield activation around Oomb took tens of pektels. This, succeeded by additional tens of pektels for the Supreme Dek-Fook-Tek to react. And then several pektels more for the response transmission of that reaction to reach the giant saucer craft on its ever-increasing distance from Tictoctic.

Several officers and even the captain himself took a breath as deep as it was tense during the final pektels before the Supreme Authority's countenance indicated he'd received the transmission. It would not have been a complete surprise had Dek-Fook-Tek shamed the captain for his inability to previously recognize this new threat, after all the divine guidance Dek-Fook-Tek had given him. Pursuant to which, he, Captain Mat-kek-tek, might have been ordered to crash the Third Celestial Breath into the star of Tictoctic. And well Officer Kwit-Nik knew the difficulty of convincing any of the crew, let alone enough of them, to defy such an order.

Dek-Fook-Tek's actual initial reaction, at least, to his first look at the grainy, black-and-white images (which meant that the glowing red of the laser mesh network went unknown) served to prolong the suspense. The Supreme Authority hastily rose from his throne, and he announced, "Do not speak or otherwise demonstrate your unfitness to draw your next breath, until I have blessed you with my defining ruling on this matter!" Then he dropped down on all fours to gallop off-screen. Officer Kwit-Nik got the unsettling impression the Supreme Authority was behaving like someone at a dining troft who unexpectedly slips away so no one has to watch him vomit from a sudden fit of nausea.

Indeed, Kwit-Nik would have enjoyed vindication if a camera had followed Dek-Fook-Tek. Instead, one of the Supreme Authority's servants filled the screen with his calf-small head sporting two rounded bumps where antlers should have grown. His whiny bleating strained to mask any other noises that might have betrayed a clue to what the offstage ruler was doing. "I am authorized to remind you-" The servant's bleating got so whiny, Kwit-Nik wished anew all his fellow creatures could employ tongue clicks, rather than that skill getting restricted, limited to only persons in certain stations in Tictoctic society. "-of the endless generosity, as vast as the grazing fields of our distant ancestors, shown by the Supreme Authority when he assumes the burden of making the most important decisions. The only thing he asks in return, compounding his bountiful gifts, is that we live the fulfilling lives he knows are best for us."

As it turned out, nothing masked totally, nothing distracted totally from the irregular, abrupt, harsh noises originating off-camera. Not the unnamed servant's continuing blather, as Kwit-Nik could not help secretly regarding it, about Dek-Fook-Tek's greatness. Not fellow officers plus the captain performing the requisite ritual declarations, declarations with which Kwit-Nik himself felt obliged to harmonize, reaffirming that greatness. And certainly not the static in the transmission from Tictoctic. But not even Kwit-Nik could have imagined how extreme the behavior which produced those sounds, any more than Officer Tak-venk-tit could have. Tak-venk-tit's unquestioning loyalty inspired him to dismiss them as most likely stemming from nearby construction work, perhaps another monument to the Supreme Authority.

Soon as he galloped off camera, the Supreme Dek-Fook-Tek had gone directly over to his personal venting wall. There, he turned his back on it and kicked and kicked at it until his hind hooves shattered it into long splinters. A good thing it had been recently replaced, an on-looking servant was thinking to himself. Otherwise, it would have shattered too soon for the Supreme Authority to purge the holy fury. The holy fury was whispered, by his closest advisers, to periodically build in his legs until it must either find release, or perish him away too soon from a planet's citizenry he was born to lead.

Completion of the wall's shattering may have coincided perfectly with completion of the fury purge from the Supreme Authority's hind legs. However, there was other rage yet to be vented. For that, Dek-Fook-Tek turned clip-clopping around on all fours to face the result of his kicking. He lowered his head to snatch up one of the more sizable wood splinters between his teeth, and he shook that splinter with a long, simmering growl. A final, escalated, "GRRRRR!!!" ended with an exhaled snort. The splinter having been considerably misshaped by his chew marks, he unceremoniously let it drop to the striated cement floor of his throne room, and he stood up on his rear hooves to swagger triumphantly back over before the camera. *No one else,* he told himself, *not even my closest advisors, really understands the threat as I do. No one! Yes, of course, they swear unswerving allegiance to me and what I represent like I am some sort of God. But how many of them really believe that? How many are not just trying to avoid my antler-goring, of which they are nowhere near deserving? They make all the right declarations in all the right situations. And yet, how many are just bleating empty words, while keeping an antler's-length distance from passion for what they are saying? They voice agreement the mysterious mesh signifies preparations for acts of unspeakable aggression, but how many are too naïve to learn from our own turbulent history? How many persist in wondering whether the mesh is part of a merely defensive posture?* It was all Dek-Fook-Tek could do, not to turn his back on the camera and try shattering the lens with one of his rear hooves.

Instead, the Supreme Authority managed to stare steadily into the camera. Only a random twitch of one ear or the other hinted at what he would have been the first to characterize as an heroic effort, not to show his minions more than they could handle, given their limitations. Not to burden them with an unbridled revelation of his full passion on their behalf. And he said, "Captain Mat-kek-tek, you have done an adequate job of further chewing what I have regurgitated, but now you must do so much more."

"Supreme Dek-Fook-Tek provides the picture for which our frame is hardly adequate," the officers joined the captain in yet another ritual declaration.

Several pektels later, the captain and officers exhaled relief to see the Supreme Dek-Fook-Tek make his approving nod to their obeisance. This, despite how grainy the video transmission continued to be. Kwit-Nik would have found himself puzzled at the Supreme Authority managing to tip his head, even the least little bit, without the unwieldy weight of his antlers causing it to tip all the way over into a neck-breaking episode. That was, if he didn't know what Captain Mat-kek-tek had refused to notice, even when given the chance. Anyhow, Dek-Fook-Tek thereafter blessed the captain and company, blessed as they were supposed to regard his every utterance, with an explanation of the "so much more" the captain must perform. "Captain Mat-kek-tek, the mission to the original target is cancelled. Proceed directly to the planet that is getting developed into a fortress. After you destroy its offense-enabling shield, implement the full and complete plan as it was originally envisioned for the original target." Dek-Fook-Tek paused, and it was only after precious pektels elapsed that Captain Mat-kek-tek realized he was awaiting a ritual declaration. Panic-stricken, the captain nevertheless managed to appear calm as he initiated a round of approving nods by his officers over the wisdom of what Dek-Fook-Tek decided was to be their new mission. Upon which, the captain bowed towards the television camera, and he led those officers in solemnly baaing, "By your most divine guidance, Supreme Authority."

Dek-Fook-Tek's reaction to this latest praise offering seemed to the anxious saucer crew to take a hundred pektels. But far sooner than that, they got to see Dek-Fook-Tek close his eyes and subtly nod his approval of the tribute. He went on, "All of you I see in the screen before me, you have demonstrated the good sense to stay true to my counsel, even when I might have perplexed or even gone so far as to trouble you."

The captain and his officers vigorously shook their heads in the negative, to try to convey vehement, sincere denial of what their Supreme Authority was speculating.

"Yet, while your sense of duty is indispensable for our mission, you know of special others aboard the saucer craft. Without their willingness to risk the ultimate sacrifice, we cannot hope to build a safe and secure future for our people. Bring them before this camera, at once!"

Captain Mat-kek-tek nodded as though he understood completely; well did he know that any slightest hint at having no idea to whom the Supreme Authority was referring could earn him total disembowelment. Captain Mat-kek-tek forcefully tongue-clicked, "Officer Tak-venk-tit and Officer Kwit-Nik, bring before us those to whom Supreme Dek-Fook-Tek is referring, in enough time for him to view for comment on his next transmission!"

"The Supreme Authority was talking about me," Tak-venk-tit asserted to Kwit-Nik once they were out in the corridor. "Without my regular updates, the captain is incapable of deciphering control panel output to know our mission status. And yet, because of my subordinate relationship, I am always at risk of so displeasing him that I would face full disembowelment. So where are we headed?"

Since Kwit-Nik led the way, Officer Tak-venk-tit found himself automatically following. It only just occurred to him what was happening in that regard.

"The Supreme Dek-Fook-Tek had others in mind, I believe," Kwit-Nik halted his trot down on all fours to turn around and tongue-click. "That was others the Supreme Authority said, not one. And 'others' strongly implicated other than us, who he was viewing on his video feed from the microsaucer hyperspace link."

"But-But he is preoccupied with the well-being of an entire society, rather than with merely the personnel on one saucer craft. It-It had to be he didn't realize that who he was referring to was already in his view. Moreover, he probably was not aware my duties are enough work for at least two people. To preserve his honor, I was thinking we should return to the bridge in a few more pektels, and announce that you have been sharing in my labor. Certainly Captain Mat-kek-tek will understand. Or, at least he will have the patience to await our explanation, once our audience with the Supreme Authority has been brought to a successful close."

Kwit-Nik closed his eyes and shook his head. Then he

turned his back on his fellow officer and broke into such a gallop that Tak-venk-tit imagined no alternative than to follow.

On his gallop, Kwit-Nik experienced regret. He regretted he could not realistically hope they would get transported through a secret porthole, around the last bend in the corridor before their arrival to where he was directing Tak-venk-tit. And that, out the other end of that porthole, they would find themselves in an open field where they could prance about to their heart's content. An open field where they would be free from all worry, and free especially from the hierarchical obligations of the Tictoctic civilization. An open field where, when they tired of roaming restlessly hither and yon, the resources would be available for truly original research and development. That, rather than having to rely entirely on achievements co-opted from others, with no hope of surpassing those achievements, and in some cases no hope of ever actually understanding the least, stumpiest antler-bit those achievements' inner workings. Ever since the conquest of Chonora, it had been almost as though the deer creatures were chanting magic incantations with little or no idea why they were so effective.

But there was no such porthole. Kwit-Nik clip-clopped to a stop before a door engraved with words that roughly translated: Food Preparation Den. There he resumed standing on his two hind hooves, and Officer Tak-venk-tit did likewise.

"Food preparation, what?" literally snorted Tak-venk-tit. "Anybody can take a piece of meat, a sliver of brain, and cook it until it's safe. The spectacles they make of a meal might enhance their appeal, but are not at all necessary."

Kwit-Nik closed his eyes to shake his head anew. "Are you forgetting it is our herd of chefs who will be the first to sample the new food source? That it is they who risk death, if the extraterrestrial biology proves too much for our bodies to safely process without significant genetic modification before-hoof?"

The look in Tak-venk-tit's face reminded Kwit-Nik of the expression on others' faces, he noticed, whenever an especially bright light got in their eyes. With the advent of motorized vehicles on Tictoctic, there had been a rash of night-time fatalities from fellow beings freezing in the middle of the road whenever they saw the headlights of an oncoming car. It had gotten to the point that everyone who could afford them wore special goggles. They were goggles which reduced the glare enough in the evening to avoid the triggering of such a dangerous reflex reaction. Whatever.

For Kwit-Nik, it was even more disturbing, if not as apparently fatal, all the times he confronted his deer-kin when they seemed either unable or unwilling to grasp the simplest logic. Instead, they gave him this same caught-in-the-headlights perplexed, utterly confounded look. "Do you understand what I'm saying?" Kwit-Nik couldn't help bleating this question, which made his frustration clearly evident to Tak-venk-tit.

Before Tak-venk-tit could respond, so confronted, there were rapidly approaching clip-clops bespeaking much urgency. They announced the arrival of Message Officer Trak-mak. Perfunctory "baaaa's" were exchanged to give Trak-mak a chance to catch his breath. Then, he reared up on his hind hooves and, gesturing in the direction of the navigation bridge, he tongue-clicked, "Captain Mat-kek-tek, in his profound wisdom, realized you might not have understood to whom the Supreme Dek-Fook-Tek was referring. There can be no doubt: the Supreme Authority seeks an audience with the pioneer chefs before they begin their final preparations on course for the defense of a new food source. They must be brought to the navigation bridge with maximum haste!" Trak-Mak brought down his right hoof-hand to paw at the floor for extra emphasis.

"I was going to tell you," Tak-venk-tit wasted no time telling Kwit-Nik, "our best course is always to attend most carefully to our captain. His wisdom is an extension of the greater wisdom of the Supreme Authority, even as the river is an extension from the sea. So no more delay in herding the chefs!"

It was Kwit-Nik's turn for the paralyzed-by-the-headlights expression on his face. His reaction stemmed from incredulity over his fellow officer's inanity. When the two deer creatures left Captain Mat-kek-tek's presence originally, Kwit-Nik had asked Tak-venk-tit to understand that the chefs were the ones about to risk their lives for the greater good. They were the others who Dek-Fook-Tek was commanding to see. Tak-venk-tit had reacted to Kwit-Nik's assertion with a look of complete and utter bewilderment. However, when Tak-venk-tit was told by Trak-mak what Mat-kek-tek said, that the chefs were with whom he was certain Dek-Fook-Tek was demanding a remote audience, well, then, that was another matter. Tak-venk-tit understood that as reason to lecture Kwit-Nik on the need to defer to their leader. This, as though what Mat-kek-tek ordered was different from what Kwit-Nik himself had suggested. The least Tak-venk-tit could have done was to acknowledge the two things were one in the same.

But it was even worse than that. Rivers flow down to the sea, Kwit-Nik was thinking to himself. And so, Tak-venk-tit's invocation of a popular saying should have had wisdom flowing from the lesser Captain Mat-kek-tek, down to the greater Supreme Authority Dek-Fook-Tek, not the other way around. From time immemorial, however, this notion that rivers are fed by the sea had been embraced with ridiculously little rumination. Kwit-Nik sometimes wondered how many of his kin understood that reality travelled the opposite direction from the popularly accepted notion.

There was no time for lingering over this matter, though. Kwit-Nik managed to snap himself out of his extreme frustration, fast enough to beat Tak-venk-tit to depressing a rectangular blue button beside the door to the food preparation den.

The door slid aside with a swish!, revealing a vast chamber of the saucer craft. The attention of someone viewing it for the first time likely would have gotten drawn initially to five enormous rectangular containers. They were mounted side by side, up along the wall opposite the entrance. For what was displayed inside them, they might as well have been five most spacious coffins with see-through lids providing easy viewing of their contents. Two of them housed complete corpses, with arms and legs splayed out and strapped down.

No matter how often Kwit-Nik had entered this den, he couldn't help experiencing considerable discomfort at the sight of those mounted containers. It was all he could do to keep from pawing nervously at the floor with one of his cloven hooves. The worst were the contents clearly visible through the other three transparent panels, the contents that were not complete corpses. In two of them, the brain case had been neatly sawed off. In the remaining one, the torso was what had to be strapped down, because both arms and legs were removed.

Yes, Kwit-Nik well understood that without those bodies, he and his fellow apex predators of Tictoctic would have faced imminent starvation. They couldn't hope to live off the meager plants that were all that could still manage to grow on the home world, discounting rumors of relic lush forests still extant in the far northern and southern hemispheres. Those plants made most cuts of meat deliciously spicy, when expertly applied by the chefs. And speaking of such expert applications, yes, Kwit-Nik did relish roasted cerebrum marinated in slotkik herb oil as much as anyone he knew, though he regarded as pure superstition the belief that eating brain somehow added to your own intelligence. And yes, of course, he was well-versed in the barbaric history of these creatures, the havoc with which they'd threatened Tictoctic until Dek-Fook-Tek's brilliant military strategy successfully treated them as a pestilence to be permanently eliminated. For sure, several small tentacles framed their beak-like mouths. Suction cups were scattered down their arms and legs, which had allowed them to scurry across ceilings like certain venomously unpalatable insects on Tictoctic. These features lent terrorizing aspects to even their innocuous corpses. Fellow deer creatures often felt prompted to bleat, "Thanks be to Dek-Fook-Tek that they ARE all dead," whenever they got to see any of the remaining alien corpses.

Kwit-Nik "got" all of this. And yet, there was still so much to be troubled over, so much that Kwit-Nik couldn't help troubling over. The grisly kitchen displays of the corpses bore uncomfortable resemblance to displays of insects in Tictoctic museums. Kwit-Nik knew all the arguments, about how these creatures really didn't amount to substantially more than bugs on a gargantuan scale. But what bugs had ever developed space travel? And since what these creatures had developed was substantially beyond anything Tictoctic's best minds had ever actually conceived, how weren't Kwit-Nik's fellow beings the inferior species instead? This of course being a question none of Kwit-Nik's associates could ever learn was troubling him. It would have more than sufficed to get his body dismembered, then placed in a freezer alongside these creatures. Such had been the fate already of Tictoctic's few known dissidents, excepting that infamous couple who had managed to make away on a solar scout cruiser. But who knew what fate had eventually caught up with them, if they didn't fully understand the maintenance of a vehicle that cheated light-speed?

Ultimately, what Kwit-Nik couldn't fully overcome, fully get past, was that regardless of his culture's teachings, and regardless of how ugly they looked, these creatures at one time surely had had families, loved ones, friends. Plus there was the claim by those vanquished dissidents, about these extraterrestrials not at all agreeing with their leaders' policy of treating the citizens of Tictoctic as a danger to be contained.

These were antlers already shed, though, as the popular saying went. Beating Tak-venk-tit to the charge, as another saying went on Tictoctic, Kwit-Nik overcame his queasiness to take purposeful, clip-clopped strides over to the head chef, Glork-tek, and say, "I am most sorry to interrupt what anyone can see is another of your most masterful meal preparations, Dominant Chek Glork-tek. But I am honored and humbled to announce to you that our Supreme Dek-Fook-Tek insists on an audience with the entire chef contingent, immediately."

Glork-tek stepped back from mixing together finely chopped arm sinew with lukt ferns in a bowl, to hastily wipe off his articulated cloven fore-hooves on his apron. He stole a glance Tak-venk-tit's way before tongue-clicking to Kwit-Nik, "You should be sorry, Officer Kwit-Nik, to characterize informing me of an insistence by our Supreme Authority as an interruption. Far from an interruption of my meager food preparations, an audience with Dek-Fook-Tek can only prove an enhancement, indeed, an inspiration to reach new culinary heights once I return to this task!"

"Only by his supreme mercy am I spared the goring I so justly deserve for my inadequacy." Kwit-Nik bowed low to bleat this, after likewise stealing a glance Tak-venk-tit's way. For some time, he and Chef Glork-tek had shared an understanding these ritualized self-effacements and adulation for Dek-Fook-Tek had to be scrupulously adhered to, in Tak-venk-tit's presence. Tak-venk-tit was always seeking an excuse to encourage Mak-kek-tek to scar someone's chest with his constantly-sharpened antlers, so long as that chest wasn't his own.

"Only by his supreme mercy are we spared the goring we so justly deserve," the other chefs joined the chef in declaring, to the nodded approval of Tak-venk-tit, Kwit-Nik noted with relief.

"Officer Tak-venk-tit, since you are the chief record keeper for Captain Mat-kek-tek, it seems only fitting you lead the charge back to the navigation bridge." As relieved as Kwit-Nik felt, seeing Tak-venk-tit's nodded approval of his recommendation, he well knew that no amount of implicit flattery was too much, where keeping on this creature's good side was concerned.

"I agree to that, Officer Kwit-Nik, only because our Supreme Dek-Fook-Tek is not here himself to lead what we all know would be a far far superior charge." With this pronouncement, Tak-venk-tit reared up his arms way high into the air. Then he landed his hoof-hands down hard on the floor, to spring into a gallop out the door.

As Kwit-Nik joined the others in following Tak-venk-tit, he guiltily mused to himself, *Where does adulation for Dek-Fook-Tek reach its absurd limit?, as much as I consider myself a most devoted follower? The chef herd might as well have postponed Tak-venk-tit's actual leading off the charge to solemnly swear, 'Our greatest regret is that Dek-Fook-Tek is not all of us, so that we have to be ourselves instead.' And why stop at that even? Why not insist that before every bathroom visit, everyone must say, 'I make this poop only because the Supreme Pooper, Dek-Poop-Tek, cannot poop for me instead'?*

"Bahh, Officer Tak-venk-tit." Dek-Fook-Tek's greeting arrived what seemed like far more pektels after the chef herd's entry onto the bridge than was the actual reality. Again, it sounded as fuzzy as his image on the video screen was grainy.

"Supreme Authority Dek-Fook-Tek..." Tak-venk-tit paused, to return down on all fours. He pawed at the floor just one time with his right hoof-hand, and bowed reverentially. "Above all other schedules, Supreme Authority, your schedule ought to be protected by every warship available, if need be. For any time we may have lost you from that schedule, we can only wish that by shortening our own lives, we could add to yours to make up for it."

Receiving this cue for yet another ritualized declaration, everyone else on the bridge got down on one elbow and bleated, "Take from our lives that yours might be extended, oh Supreme Dek-Fook-Tek." Glork-tek and Kwit-Nik exchanged a furtive look on their way to this latest prostration.

After the usual shorter-than-it-seemed wait, Dek-Fook-Tek subtly nodded approving acknowledgement, and he continued the ritual with, "I never allowed even one pektel of my time to get wasted. But you are forgiven the misapprehension, thanks to my bountiful mercy."

"His mercy is limitless," completed the ritual.

On Dek-Fook-Tek's next turn, he was able to far more casually tongue-click, "So Chef Glork-tek, tempt me with your best proposal for preparation of our imminent new food supply."

Glork-tek could have bleated what he well knew would have been some nonsense, about how his preparations would just as well have been scraped off the anus of a lowly Nibbler, were the Supreme Authority to take up the culinary arts. However, enough was more than enough. He butted his two hoof-hands together and zestily kept rubbing them together until sparks flew. At which moment, he tongue-clicked, "Well, assuming a physiology comparable to the Chonorans, we start with thinly-sliced filets from their buttocks, baked with a pan-seared finish. Setting these aside, we julienne strips of fat from around the torso region, and we fry them until they are crispy on the outside yet liquid-y on the inside. Each crispy fat-stick gets wrapped in its own pan-seared buttock slice, which is then delicately rolled in a bed of finely chopped basnelary leaves until thoroughly coated. The finishing step is to tie together each roll with two raw cerebrum strings, one near each end. And there you have it." Chef Glork-tek backed off from the camera and held open his hoof-hands as though he were presenting the completed dish he just described.

Dek-Fook-Tek's first reaction to Chef Glork-tek's proposed preparation appeared reasonable enough. He seemed to Kwit-Nik a bit quizzical, for he nodded his head first to one side, and then to the other. As more pektels elapsed, though, he stepped closer and closer to the camera, until finally he was lapping the lens with increasing urgency. That's when the picture went black on board the saucer craft. On Tictoctic, four of Dek-Fook-Tek's handlers were pulling him away from the camera lens. His legs and arms alike were flailing wildly, and his snout was foaming with his snorts. The camera crew knew not to reactivate the monitor until their Supreme Authority was returned to sitting on his throne, regally composed. Their only regret was having to wait until he'd heard the entire recipe before they could turn off the camera to save him from making the usual spectacle of himself. Which spectacle they were under pain of death were they ever to reveal in its full extent to anyone outside the Supreme Authority's royal chambers.

This wasn't the first time Kwit-Nik had caught a glimpse of the supreme Dek-Fook-Tek at one of his not-so-supreme moments. What always spooked the officer was how nobody was ever willing, himself included, to comment on those fleeting looks into what looked to be a most unsettling reality about their leader. Rather, typically everyone waited quietly for the next appearance of Dek-Fook-Tek before they even moved a muscle, let alone commented on what they saw. Comments, of course, never happened. Had he the reckless courage, Kwit-Nik would have tried leading everyone in a new ritual declaration: *We are but a gentle breeze to your tornado when you are agitated, Supreme Flailer.*

When Dek-Fook-Tek at last reappeared on the video screen aboard the saucer craft, the lens was focused tight on his long snout-y face, to the exclusion of the upper half of his massively unwieldy-looking antlers. As happened on occasion, his handlers were holding balanced that bony extension growth from his skull, having injected him with the requisite tranquillizer to subdue him at his potential worst. Otherwise he would have had to lie down, completely reclined, rather than seated on his throne.

"Chef Glork-tek," said Dek-Fook-Tek, "I salute you for once again saving me from disappointment. So soon as we can be assured the new food source is safe, I look forward to your personally serving me the dish exactly as you have described it. And this is where I want to address the officer chefs under your direction." Dek-Fook-Tek paused long enough to receive the video feed confirming the subordinate chefs had stepped forward and, reared up on their hind hooves, had swelled out their chests. This, to show that not only were they attending obediently to every last tongue-click he was about to produce. They were also prepared to welcome the sharpest antlers possible charged fatally deep into them, were this action so decided upon by any of their superiors.

"Officer chefs," Dek-Fook-Tek at last continued, "your leading Chef might know more about food preparation than you. And other officers aboard with you might know more than any other citizens of our beloved Tictoctic about spacecraft operation. Yet ultimately, what you are offering far out-duels any of their so-called expertise."

Kwit-Nik strained not to let his ears flutter at this supreme dismissal of applied intellectual activity. In his more heretical moments, which seemed to come upon him increasingly often, Kwit-Nik wondered whether Dek-Fook-Tek spoke in this manner because "so-called expertise" lay far beyond his comprehension. The Supreme Authority's only brilliance boiled down to military strategy.

"What you offer are your bodies in sacrifice," Dek-Fook-Tek went on, "as first tasters of the new food supply.

Should you survive, and the new supply does not require genetic modification for us to safely ingest, it will be my honor to personally inflict most profound scars on your chests. To the other antler, should you perish for your efforts, know that statues will be erected in your permanent, historical honor." A nod from the Supreme Authority indicated he was pausing for a response.

The officer chefs collectively went down on one elbow, or it could have been thought of as a front knee for all the galloping they did. They ritually declared, "Supreme Dek-Fook-Tek, you offer more than we deserve, as we are unworthy to even nibble on your droppings."

"You demonstrate all that is best about the spirit of Tictoctic," said Dek-Fook-Tek when he resumed many pektels later. "Captain Mat-kek-tek, Chef Glork-tek, I want you to review for me the collection process as it will apply to the new first target."

"The goal is total incapacitation of all military infrastructure so that species extinction will not be required. We have planned this as a tribute to your bountiful mercy, Supreme Dek-Fook-Tek, which dawns as regularly as the day."

This was the cue for everyone on the navigation deck to rear up on their hind legs, swell out their chests, and declare, "We flourish in the golden rays of your mercy."

Dek-Fook-Tek's approving nod was most gratefully received aboard the Third Celestial Breath after what seemed like endless more pektels. That nod was made possible without embarrassment, by his off-camera handlers carefully tipping his antlers down and forward.

Mat-kek-tek continued, "For the initial roundup, Chef Glork-tek will accompany me to the surface after the incapacitation process is completed. Chef Glork-tek?"

The captain shifted attention to the chef with a sweeping gesture.

Glork-tek nodded his acknowledgement, all he needed to do since he was considered of equal rank to the captain. "On the planet's surface, my goal will be to select out a few specimens for our officer chefs to sample after proper preparations. Also, I will be in charge of directing a contingent of soldiers to properly cage selected bulls and cows for strategic breeding. That contingent will get left behind after we initiate our return to Tictoctic. They will prevent the target species creatures that remain outside the cages from interfering with the cattle-raising process."

"That contingent of course will also have adequate resources to assure the target species cannot rebuild any military capacity," broke in Captain Mat-kek-tek. "And then there is the matter of how Chef Glork-tek will handle those selected specimens."

Again with a nod, Glork-tek tongue-clicked, "Inspired by your most bountiful mercy, Dek-Fook-Tek, once back aboard the saucer, each selected specimen will receive a one-inch-diameter metal bolt hammered through its skull. Instantaneously thereafter, it will be decapitated. For display purposes while making culinary preparations, the heads will be stitched together with the torsos, the same as with the remaining Chonoran bodies. Again, all thanks to the inspiration of your bountiful mercy."

"His mercy is limitless," echoed the ritual declaration throughout the navigation deck, to close out the review asked of the captain and the lead chef by Dek-Fook-Tek.

When the Supreme Authority nodded his acknowledgement of this latest ritual accolade, Kwit-Nik dared think to himself, *That nod is as if to say, 'Of course my mercy is limitless.' What is really limitless is his ego.*

Anyway, Dek-Fook-Tek proceeded after this notable nod with, "Captain Mat-kek-tek,-"

The captain visibly nervously swelled out his chest, as though the Supreme Authority could somehow transcend the trillions of lek-leks of space in between them to gore him then and there.

"-this concludes our audience. As much as you might desire it, my humility demands that this opportunity for you to associate with me NOT become the subject of a commemorative ceremony in future years. Perhaps we can permit such a ceremony, to celebrate the report on the results of first-feasting upon the new food source."

Even though the screen went blank, everyone on the bridge nevertheless ritually announced, "Your humility knows no bounds. It grows as thick as the most impenetrable forest." There was no telling that the monitor wasn't kept going on Tictoctic for Dek-Fook-Tek to check he was continuing to receive proper accolades.

Kwit-Nik incidentally always wondered, tried to imagine an "impenetrable forest" every time it received mention in the ritual. The last remnant of forest, let alone impenetrable, had long since passed into history, almost a full generation before he was born, though rumors persisted of a few remaining near Tictoctic's north and south poles.

"Officer Kwit-Nik, there is one more matter to be addressed before you return to your monitoring task."

With this abrupt announcement from Captain Mat-kek-tek, Kwit-Nik's ears fluttered uncontrollably and his heart skipped a beat. Yet, he still managed to pull himself together to swell his own chest vulnerably forward and tongue-click, not bleat, "Your attention to detail, Captain, trenches the channel through which my actions must flow to have any merit."

Captain Mat-kek-tek nodded approval, but Kwit-Nik

could see he was not to be the least bit dissuaded from his intent.

"The scars I have received from the Supreme Dek-Fook-Tek," the captain tongue-clicked with what seemed to Kwit-Nik to be done with a special edge to each click, as though he'd somehow been able to use the bahvek to sharpen his utterance like unto his antlers, "are as lofty mountain ridges to the gentle hills with which you will now be honored. Display them proudly upon your recovery."

With that, the captain went down on all fours, and he lowered his head in Kwit-Nik's direction.

Officer Kwit-Nik's inhale and exhale in anticipation of the imminent wounding, he couldn't help that becoming a resentful heave. He thought to himself, again he dared to think: *My hard-earned expertise is what made possible the detection of the unexpectedly closer threat to Tictoctic. This scarring I am about to receive is not the infliction of an honor. It is the captain trying to assert his primacy over me, because his own expertise doesn't extend much beyond how to sharpen his antlers. His dim awareness of this fact makes him feel insecure in a way he does not wish to admit to himself or others!*

As Captain Mat-kek-tek trotted nearer, Kwit-Nik closed his eyes and winced in advance of what he could only hope wouldn't turn into a deadly goring from his superior losing self-control, giving in to blood lust raging enough to kill.

There was a halt to Mat-kek-tek's forward motion which lent Kwit-Nik cruel hope, however fleeting, that for some reason he was to be spared. Maybe the captain would frame it in terms of: On second thought, this honor was not deserved.

But no. The next thing Kwit-Nik knew, he felt two slashes diagonally across his unflinchingly swelled-out chest. At first, the odd sensation didn't actually register as painful. On his next inhale, however, the searing feeling was so intense, he passed out.

As Kwit-Nik recovered consciousness some while later, he grew dimly aware he was still lying prone on the floor of the navigation bridge where he passed out. He was receiving stitches from Doctor Hik-tok-tek-tik while Officer Tak-venk-tit was saying to the captain, "Quintuple light speed is sustained at course plateau altitude. Percent of calculated distance traversed from Tictoctic to the target planet is approaching thirty-three point four percent." And all Officer Kwit-Nik could think was: *I have indeed been truly honored by the captain. I should never, ever have doubted his care for us would preclude his highly-sought-after scarring from getting exaggerated into something fatal. For this and other of my recent self-contaminating weaknesses of thought and speculation, I would formally ask the captain's forgiveness. But I am unworthy of having this request even listened to in the first place. Were there any real honor left in me, I would refuse the medical treatment I am receiving. What I must do is rededicate myself to the mission exactly as laid out by the Supreme Dek-Fook-Tek. I must root out all my mental distractions to loyalty as the worthless disease they really are!*

# Chapter 7

"This is an IABC special report: Briefing from Interstellar Space. Now here are IABC news correspondents Paul Berger and Amal Mahfouz."

"Good evening, good morning, and good afternoon. I think that covers everyone." Berger couldn't help a wry smile accompanying the mischievous glint in his eyes. "Or simply good day, if you are tuning in from aboard Space Station 2. In just a few more moments, we will be receiving a live broadcast from aboard the solar starship, Smoke and Mirrors. Captain Helena Taylor has some news for us, en route back to the planet Fafama in the Alpha Centauri C System. Of course, who needs to be reminded that last year, Captain Taylor and her crew made historic first formal contact on Fafama with an intelligent extraterrestrial species. The word is, Amal, Captain Taylor's news has to do with this intriguing detour the Smoke and Mirrors made to another nearby solar system, where they detected yet another Earth-like planet."

"Yes, that's right, Paul," Amal nodded as cautiously as she spoke. "And as you put it regarding the first contact, who needs to be reminded what we found on that detour, which was an amazing water world dotted with island archipelagos. The largest land is only the size of Borneo. Even more amazing are the mind-reading tree creatures who we found inhabit those islands. They have developed an affinity for the Beatles, merengue, and other music from the twentieth century on Earth."

"So tell us, Amal, would you care to venture a guess as to the nature of Captain Taylor's news?"

"Ohh," Amal shook her head and laughed, "not me. After learning about the mind-reading tree people, I think we have to be braced for anything."

"Good advice, Amal. Okay, they're ready. Live, from on board the Smoke and Mirrors, here is Captain Helena Taylor. Captain?"

"Thank you, Paul." For live broadcasts, Helena always got advance word about the correspondent who would be introducing her, so she could create the illusion the interaction happened instantly. This, rather than her audience having to wait out an awkward seven-minute delay between the correspondent's introduction, and her acknowledgement. What happened was, Helena got started on her transmission seven minutes earlier than the agreed-upon time for the correspondent's transmission. Synchronization was never perfect, but on the correspondent's end, Helena's portion got postponed if it arrived too early. If it arrived too late, it was never by more than a few seconds, to answer the correspondent's, "Captain?"

"Welcome back to the navigation deck of the Smoke and Mirrors," Captain Helena Taylor continued, "and let's also welcome, for the first time, our new audience on Fafama. Our technical crew, directed by First Engineer Buddy Leung, has worked closely with the technical crew of the Fafaman news network to facilitate yet another historic milestone, or in this case maybe we should say trillionmilestone: a television simulcast to civilizations on multiple planets. With our next public transmission, we hope to include, as well, our friends on the planet Oomb. But for now, pama." Captain Taylor made the sweeping greeting gesture she had learned the previous year when first arriving on Fafama. "It's a shame, actually, our friends on Oomb won't be seeing this transmission, for what I'm about to share." Captain Taylor came out from behind a railing and approached her husband Chris's body cam, like she usually did for these events. This, to simulate a closer relationship with her unimaginably vast audience. "Before we left Oomb, on the next leg of our second mission," Helena Taylor continued, "our principle contact there, named Oodle-Noodle, expressed a great interest for herself and for an associate, Wafoodle-Boodle. They wanted to accompany us to Fafama. Wafoodle-Boodle is renown on Oomb for her expertise in resolving the few disputes that still arise. She is one among a special group of planet-wide conflict mediators."

Captain Taylor made certain not to allow her eyes to wander anywhere near where Second Engineer Kevin Smith-Park was seated. Kevin always referred to Wafoodle-Boodle as Wafoodle-shake-your-kaboodle. Helena Taylor often found it difficult enough to use Oombian names without a giggle; she didn't need any reminders of how easily those names could be made fun of, to risk an indiscretion on display for untold billions of people. She sweated this out, despite how much worse it would have been. That was, if somehow she were to have inadvertently let slip the least clue to the possible threat which had the Earthlings spending so much time away from their home solar system in the first place.

"After considering Oodle-Noodle's request, we concluded it made lots of sense," continued Captain Taylor. She exuded a tranquil-yet-firm steadfastness of purpose, her husband who was filming her thought proudly. "What better way to launch an outline for future interplanetary cooperation? And where Fafama was concerned, how could we reasonably say no to an opportunity for Oombians to bring their vast peace-making expertise to bear on difficulties between the established Fafaman leadership and rebel forces, some of whom think nothing of inflicting violence on innocents?

"The Fafamafalafama himself communicated his willingness to still welcome us with our Oombian contingent tagging along. And so, our next task became to figure out how fifteen-foot-tall mobile tree creatures were going to even fit aboard the Smoke and Mirrors, short of just carrying them in on their sides and laying them out in a hallway. Either that, or setting them up underneath the skylights on the navigation bridge, which would allow them only a very limited range of movement. Or making them spend all their time in the shuttle pod hangar."

Captain Taylor left out any mention of the American Union government observer Louisa Entroper's untempered objection to bringing along the Oombians. The captain had explained to Entroper why, before the briefing. The report on Entroper's concerns would have had to have gotten boiled down to something vague, about how the Oombian presence would only complicate diplomacy with the Fafamans. And that could have been interpreted as a hint something was going on far more serious than anything being admitted to publicly.

"Fortunately, Oodle-Noodle and Wafoodle-Boodle knew how to solve the problem for us. They were able to trim down their branches, excepting their critical arm branches. They were also able to whittle down their trunk tops, after removing their copter-blade, palm-frond assembly. Now, each of them takes up little more room than a seven-foot-tall human. This was accomplished, happily, with their suffering only a slight bit more discomfort than one of us clipping our fingernails. True, the excision of their palm-frond assemblies has temporarily cost them their flying ability. But they assure us that once they return to Oomb, they will be able to grow everything back to normal for themselves in a matter of months.

"One more item before I introduce the Oombians in their trimmed-back state: You'll notice a woman coming in behind Oodle-Noodle, and a man entering behind Wafoodle-Boodle. You may recognize the woman as our shuttle pod flight commander, Tanya Petrovsky. She has taken it upon herself to voice whatever Oodle-Noodle telepaths to her, in response to my questions. As you may remember, Oombians lost their speaking ability when they came to rely solely on mental telepathy to talk to one another, though they still retain a conventional hearing function. Anyhow, Tanya's husband, our chief mental health and linguistics officer Dr. Ali Magabu, chose to do the speaking honors for Wafoodle-Boodle.

"With no further delay, let me welcome onto the navigation deck the first-ever Oombian space farers, Oodle-Noodle and Wafoodle-Boodle!"

The two tree people came into camera view with Tanya and Ali trying as much as possible to stay hidden behind them. Both Oombians made a point of waving at Chris's body cam.

"As you may also remember," said Captain Taylor, "the Oombians have hundreds of small yet powerfully strong cilia covering the underside of their roots. These cilia allow them to glide across most any surface like starfish on the move. These cilia also ease plunging their roots deep down into the soil when they are doing their version of sleep, or crave a particular nutrient instinctively sensed to lie present beneath them. For these purposes we have filled sunken basins in their rooms with specially selected dirt from Oomb, and we have warehoused additional dirt for replenishment of lost nutrient value during the long voyage. The same as with the soil for potted plants situated throughout the Smoke and Mirrors, the Oombian soil has been treated with a special, biologically-derived adhesive. This adhesive keeps that soil from floating all over everywhere in a low-gravity environment, especially when gravity is near zero because we've dropped way out of light-speed.

"So Oodle-Noodle, and Wafoodle-Boodle, how has the trip been for you thus far?"

Both Oombians knew from perusing Helena's mind not to make reference to the situation of most interest to them by far, which had to do with Professor Skepticus and the ephemeral dragon, Effy. From their mind-reading ability, they became aware Effy was some sort of sentient creature, well before any crew members had thought to warn them of its wandering presence. They were therefore all-the-more amazed that Skepticus remained determined to prove Effy was nothing more than a nonliving phenomenon unique to Fafama, which phenomenon had somehow leaked into the Smoke and Mirrors. Dr. Aquinas had noted that it would have been virtually impossible for clouds or other known atmospheric phenomena to accidentally slip aboard the starship. Said notion had long since been dismissed by Skepticus as irrelevant to the ongoing mystery. But what really surprised the Oombians was how nonchalantly Skepticus speculated away their mind-reading sensing of Effy's presence as a living, thinking entity.

"We're going to discover this gaseous electrical phenomenon also reflects neuron synapse discharges like a mirror. Surely, esteemed creatures of Oomb, you are not going to argue the beings seen in mirrors have any life of their own, are you?"

Oodle-Noodle thought better of rebutting, *I don't know the last time a mirror image managed to torch someone's pants bottom in search of a hidden chocolate chip cookie.*

Presently, the Oombians knew that any mention of the ephemeral dragon could inspire such questions from the news media as would prove especially awkward for the Earthlings to answer, without revealing the treacherous reality of their first mission to Fafama. Suspicion would quickly reach critical mass that something big was being kept secret from the public.

So, instead of saying "boo" about Effy, Oodle-Noodle telepathed for Tanya to utter, "We miss deeply many of the sights, sounds and smells of our beloved Oomb. But Officer Olsen-Taylor's sharing with us of holographic golf, including holographically simulated vistas on your beautiful planet Earth, is making our trip more than merely tolerable."

Chris wished Helena's smile when she nodded acknowledgement of Oodle-Noodle's response didn't seem quite so strained. But he nevertheless kept his bodycam steady for his wife to ask, "And what of our destination? What intrigues you most about that?"

As with Captain Taylor's first question, the Oombians understood that a totally honest answer ran the risk of hinting at the Tictoctic threat being kept from knowledge of both the Earth and Fafaman general populations.

"It's the central pyramid, definitely," was how Ali Magabu started to pass along Wafoodle-Boodle's telepathed response. He strained not to substitute "truly" for "definitely" as he would have done naturally were the sentence all his own. "The architectural techniques to assure its stability, despite its height and the daily onslaught of the sunset storm line, they are of surpassing interest as we prepare for experimenting with our own habitation construction."

Ali left out the telepathed hems and haws from Wafoodle-Boodle. The tree creature was obviously narrowly avoiding unintentionally letting spill a reference to the settlers snuck aboard the Smoke and Mirrors after they were spirited away from somewhat impoverished circumstances some sixty years earlier. Specifically, the tree person nearly spoke of habitation construction for the Earthling settlers.

"Well," Captain Taylor reacted, "if you two can help ease tensions between the Fafaman government and the rebels, the sharing of those architectural techniques would seem the least of what your visit might profit you."

It was all Flamboyo Sanchez could do, not to hurl his almost-empty beer bottle at the flat-screen television, the one mounted above the counter at the tavern where he'd previously orchestrated a gun fight to make an impression on fellow nihilist Morel Engeling. *Yeah, sure,* he thought to himself, *they can teach everyone how to play their version of golf, as if one version of that f-n' useless distraction in the universe weren't enough. Then they can erect quarantine zones for anyone who doesn't join in the fun! Shit!*

"I was going to call your name, but I assume you're moving about incognito since that awful shootout." Shelly Taylor slid onto the stool beside Flamboyo without his realizing until she spoke, so focused was he on Captain Taylor's two-world telecast briefing. Shelly was doing some extreme incognito herself. Her shoulder-length, sandy-golden locks were bunched into the cap on her head. And she sported totally opaque sunglasses, plus a baggy camouflage shirt. That style of shirt was especially popular among quarantined women going to great fear-driven lengths to hide their sex. It was also popular among quarantined husbands and boyfriends anxious to enhance their significant others' safety, as well as among family and friends of lesbian couples. "Oh, wow, those tree people trimmed themselves down to bush league, as my Dad probably punned to my Mom as they were watching this. Random thought number three: I'm so relieved to find you safe, I could hug you." She pulled the bridge of her shades down her nose far enough to give Flamboyo direct eye contact.

"You make it difficult not to curse in a woman's presence." Flamboyo shook his head, leaving Shelly to have to settle with no more than his profile.

"Oh, and which f-n' damn woman would THAT be?" she said in the deepest, huskiest voice she could conjure.

Flamboyo's disgust ground down his chuckle of amusement to an exhaled "Hmmph!" He shook his head again, and he seemed to Shelly to be spitting out more than speaking, "You have no idea how dangerous this is. I don't want to hear about your security entourage hanging around the front entrance, and simulating drunk-senseless over there in the corner. They can be picked off as easily as these nuts." He grabbed a handful of cashews from the bowl on the counter for emphasis, even though he couldn't bring himself to add, *with the right move of my forefinger across this beer bottle. It would never get traced back to me*. "Look," he went on instead, his voice softening, "you have your news segment, you have that video to confirm you are a caring person whenever you doubt it. But my work with the children is terminated. It is too dangerous for them to be anywhere here other than locked inside their rat palaces."

Shelly grabbed Flamboyo's unshaven, stubbly face by the chin and turned it her way. He put up only token resistance, she could tell. Ditto for when she kept it lifted so his eyes had to meet hers. "You haven't been following developments in D.C. at all, have you, you impossible pessimist?" she whispered, and shook her head with her usual infectious grin.

"They are going to build casinos for us like they used to have on the Native American reservations, before those got rezoned inside the quarantine areas?"

Shelly let go Flamboyo's chin lest she succumb to temptation to pull it close for a comforting kiss. Instead, she gave him her disgusted, tight-lipped regard. In a whisper once more, while still trying to affect husky maleness, she responded, "The proposal to loosen the regs on travel into and out of the zones has gained official sponsors in both the House and the Senate. It would include turning off the juice so there would be no more accidental electrocutions. An amendment has already been offered, to subsidize school reconstruction and small business incentives, including proposals from entrepreneurs already working INSIDE the zones!"

Flamboyo turned away from Shelly. Again, he left her with only his profile. He seemed to her to be trying not to fall under the spell of even the faintest flicker of hope. Finally, he said, "So what is his name? Kucinich? That is the junior representative who is offering that amendment to his own proposal? He got Senator Borosage to support it before the entire bill gets defeated by 536 to 1 in the House, so it doesn't even need to go to the Senate?"

If she could have, Shelly would have burned holes into Flamboyo's cheeks with her piercing stare, to pain him into turning back her direction. "Representative Kucinich has over one hundred thirty co-sponsors in the House, and Borosage has forty-three in the Senate."

"What," Flamboyo couldn't help his voice cracking falsetto, "they're hoping to bring some of the action we have here outside the no-zones?"

"That 'action' has had exactly the reverse effect you

would have expected, Flamboyo," Shelly responded instantly. She was ready. "Enough people saw you in the report. The photos of the aftermath of the shooting awoke people's conscience."

"So they can have the no-zone-dismantling proposals defeated seventy-seven to forty-three in the Senate, and four hundred seven to one hundred thirty in the House. Then, these people with the good conscience can shrug their shoulders and tell themselves, 'Oh, well, at least we tried,' and go back to enjoying reports from other worlds when they aren't golfing, no?"

Shelly maintained her steady piercing stare at Flamboyo's profile, as though the attempt to burn his cheeks was making progress. In an unflinching voice, she whispered, "The bill is getting seventy percent support in opinion polls. In the Senate, Borosage has already rounded up enough votes, beyond the bill's actual sponsors, and they're only a few away in the House. The President promises he'll sign it. Flamboyo," her tone finally broke down from tough to pleading, "a collective spirit of good will has been roused at last. Maybe it has something to do with our establishing contact with extraterrestrial civilizations. I don't know. But what I DO know, and believe, is that when the history of this era is written, these quarantine zones will receive only a shameful asterisk, like slavery two centuries ago!"

"Is your boyfriend in the seventy percent?" As much as he wanted to, Flamboyo just couldn't bring himself to turn Shelly's way when he asked this. Still, Señor Sanchez could see from his peripheral vision that his question had at least caused her to finally break off her discomfortingly piercing stare.

Shelly bristled in a low voice, "He's not my boyfriend any longer, and it's none of your business." Her heart skipped a beat. She thought to herself, in a slight panic, this guy must have feelings for her, for him to be asking such a thing. Yet she also cautioned herself not to read too much into what he said. She knew she was vulnerable to doing exactly that, at this early stage right after her breakup with Mike. She shook her head at how so damned soap opera complicated it had all become. Yes, she knew she did care something for this grubby- Was he letting himself go like this to keep women too grossed out to get anywhere near him emotionally, so he could better focus on- What, was he going to head up some secret revolt or something?

Anyway, Shelly still loved Mike, which made their breakup fight that much more painful...and impossible to resist recollecting. Mike was regaling her with a story over wine and dinner, where he forewent his usual rib-eye steak to make common cause with her insistence on always ordering vegetarian. He had the lead role in the story, about his special deal with senior pro golfer Lucas Feuillet. Mike had sold Feuillet on renting out space in the new commercial development wing of Space Station Two, for his special line of Lucasaurus Golf Wear, featuring his trademark growling T-Rex. Right beside it would be installed the world's first chip-and-putt in orbit, made possible for that weightless environment by recent innovations in electromagnetic applications. As with all his sales adventure recounting, this one ended in his refrain, "Let's all remember that nothing happens – including your parents making it to Fafama – until someone sells it to someone else." And this time he added, "Who knows? Maybe I can even sell the Lucasaur on hosting the first interplanetary tournament on Oomb!, once he sees how well he does on Space Station Two! The World PGA goes Cosmic PGA! Yeah!"

*Oh, Mike, you are my comic relief!*, Shelly had always thought to herself. She had always shaken her head and giggled at her boyfriend's typically wild-eyed brainstorming inspired by whatever his latest sales success.

But this time had proven different. This time, he'd set down his wine glass with a significant thunk! on the tablecloth to initiate his own version of piercing stare. "Shelly, there's something I need to sell you on before we go any further. Any further with this dinner, I mean."

Heart suddenly thumping hard, Shelly had given Mike a searching, what's-this-about? look. She'd already accepted his marriage proposal months ago, and the date was already tentatively set for the following summer, so what the-?

"Shelly, especially with recent developments, I want you to stop risking yourself in the Philly no-zone. You've done plenty there already. Maybe if Kucinich and Borosage get their way, you can do some sort of outreach with children, whoever, when they're let out of there on good behavior visits. Heaven knows that will be dicey enough."

Shelly had shaken her head "no" slowly at first, then had sped up as she put some fury into it. She had said, "How can you ask me to do that? How would you like me saying to you, 'Especially with all the corruption going on, I want you to cash in all your chips and walk away from the casino tables; no more big deals'?"

Mike had looked to one side, then the other. It was as though, Shelly had gotten the impression, he was looking for some source of this question other than her self, or where to escape to, before he had finally said, "At least I have some chips to cash in. But, uh, that's what you think of my work? That I might as well be playing blackjack?"

"I try not to be judgmental. I know you're good at what you do, and that there's some truth to your adage about nothing getting done until someone's sold on it. But yes, I have my concerns. Some things that people need to be sold on don't have chips to cash in, but they're just as important, if not more so."

"Yeah, well, not when you could get yourself killed by a bunch of freakin' savages doing it."

There had been lecturing authority in Mike's voice to Shelly's quavering, tearful nervousness, but this last comment had helped her return to a calmer place to ask, "Okay, putting aside whatever you might think of my work, what about Representative Kucinich's bill, Michael? Are you for it, against it, split down the middle, what?"

Mike motioned at his dinner plate like the bill had just been served him there. With a puff out his mouth, he answered, "I'm dead set against it. I get that people like yourself are honestly concerned over fences having been put up between us and them. But hey, it's a hell of a lot more civilized than what our ancestors did, massacring the Indians and such."

Shelly took her napkin off her lap and tossed it aside on the table. "So you're really that ignorant, you really think the people in the no-zone are somehow subhuman?! And as for Native Americans, you still insist on calling them Indians?! Seriously?!"

"Oh, I know your lover boy – What's his name, Flamboyo? Is that what this is all about?" It had been Mike's turn for tearful shakiness in his voice.

"I care about Flamboyo, and I'm wondering what I ever saw in you!"

"Shelly-"

But it was too late; she had already stood up, taken

off her engagement ring, hurled it at him and stormed off.

"Con permiso-" *Excuse me* "-this is my seat, unless I'm taking you two away from measuring who has the longest, stiffest wood."

*Bueno*, Flamboyo Sanchez thought to himself, presently, *Porfirio has sized up the situation perfectly*. "Too bad for you, the only wood you are going to get measured for is your coffin," Señor Sanchez said as he pulled a gun from his belt. Then he let it appear to Shelly that Porfirio's reflexes were too fast for him, that his associate kicked the gun out of his hand before he could get off a shot.

The next thing Shelly knew, Porfirio yanked Flamboyo off his stool, and they were rolling across the floor locked in a fierce struggle. And the next thing she knew after that, the guy in one corner, supposedly drunk senseless, was herding her out the door, where other members of her security closed rank around her. They hurried her into a motorboat that suddenly came speeding up the North Hancock canal producing a foamy, splashy wake that drenched the sidewalks on both sides.

Meanwhile back inside the bar, Flamboyo feigned he'd gotten knocked unconscious as the pretend mortal combat collided with a round table and chairs, seconds after its occupants had fled to get out of the way. Porfirio had already secreted a note into one of Flamboyo's pockets, so there was nothing more for him to do than stand, dust himself off, and belly up to the counter for a drink. At what Flamboyo determined was a suitable length of time later, he acted like he was coming to, and he affected a staggering, defeated withdrawal out the front door. Once a good distance away down the canal in his rowboat, he at last allowed himself a look at the crumpled-up note. Electronic surveillance was so thorough, for his operation all hi-tech com links had to be ditched in favor of centuries-old note-passing.

In any event, as he expected it would, the note confirmed that five of his people had gotten themselves hired aboard the target freighter. One of the few weaknesses in the quarantine zone establishment was that most significant harbors for freight transport were virtually cut off from free areas by no-zones. Yes, there were tightly-secured umbilical routes, both rail and road, linking the harbors to outside the quarantine areas. And as an extra added measure, especially able-bodied men and women inside the no-zones with no officially documented criminal record were allowed to apply for a token number of job openings aboard freighters and tankers. The hope was that the threat thereby got considerably diminished, of no-zoners wanting to try to cut off one of said umbilical routes, isolate a particular harbor, hold it essentially hostage. This policy had also proven politically expedient for responding to critics of the whole quarantine system. *See? We're giving people inside there a chance to come out. At least it's a start.*

Five people were not going to be quite enough to hijack the freighter in such a way as to keep the rest of the world from realizing what was happening until it was too late. But on the return trip from Lisbon, Portugal, eight to ten sailors would be dying from poisoned tuna salad. Salmonella bacteria would have been injected into said salad. However, the incident would get written off as having resulted from tragically negligent food prep, nothing more.

For a successful hijacking, only half of the subsequent new hires would need to be Flamboyo's people.

As Flamboyo Sanchez tore up the note and scattered the pieces in the canal, he was of two thoughts: *Don't let Shelly get to you. Be strong. Once everything's in place and the plan is set into motion, it must be seen through to its conclusion; nothing should be allowed to stop it...*

*...but we're not there yet.*

# Chapter 8

"Wife sixteen, the Varawafawa!" a voice boomed in the ear pieces of Captain Taylor, her husband Chris, Louisa Entroper, and shuttle pod commander Tanya Petrovsky. That voice also boomed through the Smoke and Mirrors navigation bridge intercom.

Down on the planet's surface, the captain and the rest of her away team were sitting in a special guest box, three stories up the northeast-facing side of Fafama's great pyramid. This two-mile-high architectural wonder was surmounted by an abundantly lit antenna tower which extended additional miles into the upper atmosphere.

"Sergeant Frankly, how would you rate wife number sixteen?" Kevin on the bridge of the starship in orbit around Fafama was asking Fred Frankly seated at the laser mesh monitoring panel back on Oomb. The Fafamans had allowed the Earthlings to set up night-vision scanners for their event, staged late evening as was so typical for these extraterrestrials since they were nocturnal creatures. Thanks to those scanners, Kevin and the other Earthlings were able to scrutinize every person who strode into view for the ceremony, as easily as though they were possessed of nocturnal vision themselves. It made no difference whether the Earthlings were seated in the review stand, or were stationed back aboard the Smoke and Mirrors in high, geosynchronous orbit directly above the great pyramid. Or, in Sergeant Frankly's case, were viewing a transmission of the proceedings from trillions of miles away, in another solar system.

Under normal circumstances, Second Engineer Kevin Smith-Park's crass question would have gotten hair clawed out of his armpits by his wife. However, the ceremonial parade leading up to the formal unveiling of the ruler's latest addition, wife number twenty-three, the Varafafafa, went on at incredibly tedious length. Consequently, navigation officer Yoon-hee Park-Smith found she just couldn't get that annoyed over her husband's inappropriateness. Her irritation centered elsewhere, on a slow burn. She stewed over how so many Fafaman women and their families could continue to endure such degrading treatment, yet act like it was a profound honor.

"Gotta love the waist-length hair, but her face is all about the bow-wow," finally arrived Sergeant Fred Frankly's response to Kevin, on a five-minute delay from Oomb.

"I hear you," said Kevin, but Yoon-hee actually found herself pleasantly surprised. She sensed that Frankly's most offensive comment, yet, well exceeded the limits of her husband's personal comfort zone. He was only feigning nonchalant acceptance.

Back down on Fafama, Chris Olsen-Taylor shared a rare moment of camaraderie with Louisa Entroper. Chris removed his earpiece for the feed from the navigation bridge the same time Louisa did, and for the same reason. Namely, a disgust-beyond-disgust reaction to Frankly's last comment.

They were not alone.

For her own part, Helena Taylor felt moved by Frankly's gratuitous crudity to risk making herself a disrespectful distraction from the ongoing ceremony. She spoke above the din of approving Fafaman purrs to hear herself as she said, "Kevin, please advise Sergeant Frankly we don't know for certain that Fafaman surveillance can't tap into our com link and eavesdrop on everything. I'm going to have to order you two to cease and desist with your meat inspection, immediately."

"But Captain, I hear the choicest cuts are yet to go on display." Despite his squirmy sense that Sergeant Frankly had way overstepped the bounds of tolerable indecency, Kevin felt he had to offer this protest. He was more than ready to back down, though, when Taylor responded, "And I'll have Yoon-hee make you one of them, ground up and served to me on a hot plate getting flame-broiled by Effy, if you don't obey this instant!"

"Aye, Captain."

The tedium of the ceremony continued all the same. The Earthlings endured it on the promise that soon thereafter, the Fafamafalafama would give them the audience they sought. The point would be to discuss ideas inspired by the Oombians for dealing with Fafama's homegrown terrorist threat, once the Tictoctic threat was essentially neutralized by the laser mesh shield deployment. At least, this was the point as far as mission leader Helena Taylor was concerned, even though there was considerable rumbling down the ranks aboard the Smoke and Mirrors. For her part, Entroper was hoping to feed those rumblings. In addition to which, she wanted to help nurture any thoughts Fafaman leadership might be willing to entertain, about the utility of further military assistance from the Earthlings. She wanted the Fafamans to imagine how that assistance could help them deal with Fafaman terrorism as well as with the great unknown potential extraterrestrial threat.

Wife sixteen, the Varawafawa, mounted a raised platform when she emerged in her long, bioluminescently lit gown from the subterranean entrance. The Fafamafalafama, already standing upon that platform, faced away from her. He held his arms high, so that the non-luminescent side of his special ceremonial cloak made him to appear, even to his fellow nocturnal beings, as some forebodingly large and mysterious bat-like creature. There was no mystery about it, however. This was his sixteenth performance that evening, in a ceremony he'd starred in every year for the past twenty-two full orbits of Fafama around Alpha Centauri C.

As per the ceremony, the Varawafawa clasped her hands together at her waist, and she gazed heavenward, as though she were beseeching the stars to provide her with divine deliverance. It was then that the Fafamafalafama turned around to face her. His arms still held high revealed to her and all in attendance the light blue underside of his cloak, especially brightly luminescent by Fafaman standards.

The wedding audience let out a collective gasp as though they were viewing the ruler's cloak for the first time, awestruck, not the sixteenth time, which was the reality. The Varawafawa threw her arms wide open, trying to emanate delighted amazement. The Fafamafalafama took her up into his gentle yet insistent embrace.

A man standing off to one side resumed beating on a bulbous-shaped dark object set before him. It was so enormous, he got lost from sight behind it. It was the hollowed-out, rear-body exoskeleton segment of Fafama's monstrous spider, the ahtpah. Its size had been made possible by the planet's bit lower gravity, compared to that of Earth's. Rings on the percussionist's fingers caused the bulbous segment to melodically thunder and reverberate. To Chris's ears, it was like some never-before-experienced cross between a tympani and a steel drum.

In close embrace, the Varawafawa and the Fafamafalafama timed together their pelvic thrusts. Those thrusts coincided with each climactic wave of thunderous rhythm sounded on the hollowed-out ahtpah abdomen. There was one thrust for every child birthed by the sixteenth wife. After the fourth pelvic thrust, the couple separated to both face the pyramid, which meant also facing their audience. They remained in physical contact by only their outstretched hands. They waited as a wagon was rolled into place behind them. Two curtains had been closed together on the side of the wagon facing out at both the royal couple and said audience. Those curtains glowed burgundy red. With staccato taps on the exoskeleton, evocative to Chris of steel drumming, children one by one slipped out from between the glowing curtains, to join their parents. The youngest, a daughter, jumped up into her mother's arms; the second youngest, a son, did likewise into his father's arms; and the two oldest, more daughters, stood on either side of the couple, leaning in affectionately towards them. A climactic flurry of notes, reverberating from the ahtpah's hollowed-out rear bulbous segment, seemed to evolve into a riot of "ee-ee-ee"s and stamping feet from the Fafaman populace.

Chris marveled at how the Fafamafalafama, together with his sixteenth wife and their four kids, appeared to be the snapshot portrait of the heterosexual version of the idealized Earthling nuclear family, albeit cast in considerable shadows.

The wagon and everyone save the Fafamafalafama were rushed off the stage to make way for wife number seventeen. In all, there were six more wives to go before the formal first introduction of the twenty-third one.

"Welcome back to Fafama, 'Cahptahn Taylah.'" Days earlier, this is what the synthesized voice had said. It had boomed from the captain's new, improved, ear-implanted translator nearly as much as the Fafamafalafama had boomed in his original fa-la-las.

Computer engineers had worked wonders off the linguistic algorithms for the Fafaman tongue they had retrieved from the translator Ali Magabu had jury-rigged during the first mission of the Smoke and Mirrors. Those engineers had figured out how to considerably accelerate the translation process, in addition to preserving much of the source voice characteristics. The ruler's translated words had not appeared too much out of sync with his mouth movements on the panoramic view-screen monitor, as the Smoke and Mirrors had slid gracefully into orbit around the planet Fafama. "You know, you took something of ours when you left here the first time," had gone on the Fafamafalafama.

Had Captain Taylor grown the type of ears that grew from the heads of the deer creatures of Tictoctic, they would have fluttered with concern and amazement. *What*, she thought to herself with fresh apprehension, *do they keep count of their ephemeral dragons, and they discovered that one was missing?* "I'm afraid I don't understand, esteemed Fafamafalafama." Taylor had managed to sound believably perplexed, despite her apprehension she *did* understand.

"Why, you stole our hearts, 'Cahptahn.' All of you." The Fafamafalafama's voice had softened from the mock severity of his initial remarks, to something indulgently warm, however persistently booming. "For a time after your departure, news clips of your visit were the number-one-rated shows on television. What aggrieves us to this day, though, are the terrible circumstances of extreme misunderstanding under which you fled our marvelous planet." Woe-is-me had crept into his tone.

On board the Smoke and Mirrors, Kevin had rolled his eyes.

"We discussed what transpired at great length, right

after our departure." Captain Taylor had been unflinching in her tone and demeanor. With her arms crossed, she had looked straight ahead at the Fafaman leader, as his holographic image had projected from the view-screen. Everything she had been about to say was already long since messaged during extensive diplomatic exchanges via the firefly donut hyperlinks scattered between Earth orbit and Fafama. "We now understand how actions your flight personnel took to try to protect us from your native wildlife and rebel forces could have been misinterpreted."

"Not only that, 'Cahptahn.'" The Fafamafalafama hadn't been able to help a smidge of irritation creeping into his voice. His huge, nocturnally-adapted eyes had glinted like cold steel, Captain Taylor had thought, in the pale-green bioluminescence shed by flounder mice surfacing in soil close to where his video transmission was being made. "There is the very hurtful misapprehension, on your part, that you were not free to leave for your spacecraft at any time you chose. That merely asking was NOT all you had to do."

"A terrible misunderstanding on our part," Helena had nodded while still keeping her arms crossed. "It is our earnest desire we will travel some way towards smoothing over our mutual difficulties, starting with the deployment of the laser mesh shield around Fafama. That should, of course, provide protection from any potential threat from Tictoctic. But it is also good for pulverizing incoming asteroids, if THAT threat ever arises." Captain Taylor had nodded her way through this formal introduction of what was already agreed to via the hyperlink negotiations.

"Permission to add something, Captain Taylor?" Louisa Entroper had raised a forefinger and hunched her shoulders as though, it seemed to Helena, she had been bracing for Helena to meet this meek request with a sharp rebuke.

"We HAVE gotten ahead of ourselves, esteemed Fafamafalafama," Captain Taylor had nodded. She had tried to effect as casual an absent-minded sudden realization as possible, yet still with the on-her-guard crossed arms. "We ought to have finished with introducing some of our new passengers on this flight before we launched into agendas."

Entroper had shot Taylor a severe if momentary glare, for terming her simply a new passenger.

"This is Dr. Louisa Entroper. She is tagging along as an official observer for our government. Permission granted, Dr. Entroper." Helena had spun her direction, and dropped one arm from where it grasped the other, to make a sweeping, here-she-is gesture towards Louisa.

"Thank you, Captain Taylor." Dr. Entroper couldn't help injecting some it's-about-time venom into her voice, Captain Taylor had felt.

"Ahh," the Fafamafalafama had nodded, "an official government representative. One step closer to the center of your power. Very good."

"On behalf of that government, esteemed- Now it's Fafamafalafama, am I correct?"

"Very good, 'Dahctah.' It's 'Dahctah Ahntropah,' yes?"

"Dr. Entroper, thank you," Louisa Entroper had blushed.

Helena had thought to herself, *He's working that charm again. Maybe she'd like to compete to become wife twenty-four next year.*

"I just wanted to assure you," Louisa had gone on, "our efforts to secure your planet from this external threat that has us all so anxious does not necessarily have to stop with the laser mesh shield. Yes, we've made decisions," Dr. Entroper had nodded to Captain Taylor. Thereafter, she had seemed to be addressing the captain, lecturing her even more than the Fafamafalafama. "But one would think, where the best interests of a planet are concerned, the political leadership of that planet ought to have some say in the matter, no?"

"One would think, 'Dahctah Ahntropah.' However," the Fafaman ruler had held up a cautioning hand, "it is not we who answered your distress call across vast distances. It is not we who showed up on your space station, then trusted you to land us safely on your planet's surface. It was you who came to us."

Aboard the Smoke and Mirrors, looks of surprise at this remarkable concession had been exchanged all around. This was by far the closest any Fafaman, the Fafamafalafama himself especially, had come to admitting their visitors enjoyed technological superiority over them.

"What you got for your efforts, no matter our intentions, we were not careful enough. You were left with the impression we were actually holding you against your will, and then firing our missiles at you. For that impression, we insist on certain specific reparations during your second landing on our fair planet."

*Did I also misapprehend you were trying to mate with me?* Captain Taylor had had to bow her head not to be looking into the esteemed ruler's eyes as she thought this to herself.

"Each person in your landing contingent will have their own personal assistant to answer their every need."

*And watch our every move. And won't that make it easier for the Fafamans to take us hostage if that was their original intent?* Helena had found herself unable to avoid these suspicions. *Did Ali sneak me a side glance with the same concerns written all over his face?*

"Moreover, 'Cahptahn,' such is our trust in you, we are also going to make available to you any and all designs of our architecture and our technology. That will include every last concealed labyrinth of our central pyramid, plus the full schemata for our most powerful weaponry. Much of this we don't even trust with our general public, as we never know to where the savages have infiltrated."

"Well, Captain, I don't believe we could ask for a better show of trust than that." Louisa Entroper had given Taylor a significant look; the captain had known she wanted to say, *Don't you feel foolish now, having stood in the way of our bringing military upgrades to these people?*

"Esteemed Fafamafalafama, we will look forward to learning from your own most impressive achievements, the central pyramid certainly chief among them," Captain Taylor had responded, deliberately bypassing Entroper's remark. "But, we are feeling we owe you something more for your welcoming us back, especially since we appear to have misunderstood your intents and purposes on our first visit. Among the offerings we bring you, besides of course the laser mesh shield, is a complete retrofit to your shuttle blade craft. We propose to engineer this retrofit before making our return descent to your planet. Of course, your achievement in regard to your vehicle we find most impressive. Availing ourselves of its design plans will doubtless teach us an additional thing or two for our own ground-to-space flight technology. Still, we believe you will find our retrofit gives you a smoother, more comfortable, safer-feeling re-entry to the Fafaman atmosphere than you enjoy presently." The captain had carefully calibrated her remarks to salvage as much Fafaman dignity as possible. She had even stretched the truth a bit when she spoke of Earthlings "doubtless" learning "an additional thing or two" where ground-to-space flight technology was concerned.

"You'll be interested to learn, 'Cahptahn,' we have our own revised, vastly improved version of the shuttle blade under construction even as we speak. If you want to tinker with one of our presently deployed shuttle blades, well and fine. I only hope you won't be too offended should my people conclude there's too much risk in your finished retrofit, so that they escort you to the surface in a separate craft rather than take their chances on your handiwork."

"Of course not," Helena Taylor had shaken her head firmly. It had been all she could do not to grin empathetically at the Fafamafalafama blustering through his face-saving denial of reality.

"Well, then..." The Fafamafalafama had sounded to Captain Taylor a bit flustered. If she hadn't known better, the Fafaman ruler had been expecting some pushback from her, over his insulting insinuation Earth space-flight technology might not be quite up to Fafaman standards after all. Helena had concluded it was just as well the man was oblivious to how silly he sounded, as he had gone on, "Allow me to return to my principle theme for this communication. You Earthlings have stolen the hearts of my people. And so, we have a very special occasion upon us in which we'd like one of you to play a very special role. 'Cahptahn,' can you present before me, on your monitor, the man who I have been advised will be in charge of deploying the laser mesh shield?"

"Sergeant Guy Hanson? He's here with us on the

bridge. Um, Sergeant Hanson?"

"Yes, Captain." Guy had self-consciously run his fingers across his crew-cut-shaven head. He had felt ridiculous since he knew there was not enough there for him to comb or otherwise put back in any other place than it already was. This, as he had risen awkwardly from behind a console, and the Fafamafalafama had grinned with satisfaction over having clearly taken Captain Taylor by surprise.

"The esteemed Fafamfalafama would like to speak to you." Helena had waved Guy to a prime central location in front of Chris's body cam.

"Esteemed Fafamafalafama, sir!"

"'Sahgahnt Hahnsahn,' is it?"

"Yes, sir."

"On behalf of my people, I thank you in advance for the task you have undertaken, to install a defense shield around a planet other than your own. In three days, at the dawn of stars-out- Which reminds me; I am going to go blind if I behold so much brightness on your end for much longer without- Thank you, Frasta." Someone off-camera had handed the Fafamafalafama a pair of sun goggles. Once he put them on, those goggles had made him appear to Sergeant Hanson that much more foreboding and mysterious, in the pale-green luminescence where the Fafaman ruler sat. "You know, 'Sahgahnt Hahnsahn,' we are nocturnal creatures who honestly have to wonder how you Earthlings ever accomplish anything under such constant glare."

"I think it's a matter of what we grow up with, sir, esteemed Fafamafalafama, sir."

"Yes, 'Sahgahnt Hahnsahn.' So I hope that with your own, special, night-vision goggles, you will do us the honor of giving away my twenty-third bride to me at my annual wedding. The winner of this year's competition for that most extraordinary privilege, her maiden name is Yulala, and her name as the twenty-third wife of the Fafamafalafama will be Varafafafa."

"May she bear many magnificent children," had come the translated ritual wish from a chorus of solemn voices off-camera.

What's this?, the captain had wondered. Was this her imagination, or was the Fafaman ruler actually somewhat bothered, a little irritated, by said wish as he had understatedly nodded his acknowledgement of it? Was that why he had blinked his eyes a lingeringly long time on his nod? Or was a deceptive reflection on his glare-reducing goggle lens tricking her?

"Tragically, some thirty-three suns ago, her father met an untimely fate," continued the Fafamafalafama. "In a wilderness area, he accidentally took refuge from the sunset storm line inside a tralalafa lookalike. It was hosting the residence of one of our planet's more lethal creatures. That creature's nerve toxin paralyzed Yulala's father within moments of the lookalike tralalafa protectively furling around him. His body got completely desiccated, well before stars fade. The irony, so they tell me, is he was trying to collect samples of that very same toxin, to look for possible beneficial medicinal uses. Ha! 'Sahgahnt Hahnsahn,' Captain Taylor will tell you I am a most open-minded person. But I was warning our medical researchers long before this particular, most tragic incident. The search for health benefits from nature's reminders of how evil operates is like looking for something of redeeming value from among those savages who have rejected the life of the central pyramid!"

"Esteemed Fafamafalafama," said Captain Helena

Taylor, "I would be the first to agree with you. When collecting samples from such a dangerous source, all care needs to be taken. However, I have to tell you that our experience on Earth, um… Maybe Fafama will prove far different, but our own medical researchers have made enormous strides fighting health problems, working with the most lethal substances produced by creatures on our own planet. Um, I applaud your stated open-mindedness, your clear wisdom allowing such studies to go forward on Fafama despite your most clearly reasoned objections." Captain Taylor had pushed on with her point, despite Entroper off-camera shaking her head *NO* so furiously, her white mop-top got all unkempt.

There had been another of the Fafaman ruler's eyes-closed nods of acknowledgement of someone trying to appease his ego. After this, he had given Helena Taylor a decidedly long, poker-faced stare before at last saying, "Interesting, 'Cahptahn,'" and proceeding, "'Sahgahnt Hahnsahn,' our people grieve over the untimely loss of the twenty-third bride's father. We cannot envision a better way to temper such sorrow, than to have you take the deceased father's place in both the wedding ceremony, and in the sacred visit to the Grand Basin that must precede it. You, the 'Ahthlahn' who brings us protection from an outer space threat!"

Sergeant Guy Hanson had curled into the bow he read about on the trip from Oomb, studying what was known of Fafaman culture. It was the bow that imitated the curling-up of Fafama's ferny tree. The ferny tree, of course, waited for the bioluminescence from a flounder mouse surfacing out of the soil at night, before it unfurled anew. Hanson resumed his full stature, after he had waited the seconds he estimated the Fafamafalafama's subjects typically waited to unfurl, as it were, from their own obeisant bows. "Most esteemed Fafamafalafama, sir," Guy had subsequently said, easily ignoring Kevin's raised eyebrows, "with Captain Taylor's permission, I will consider it an honor to give away the bride for your twenty-third wedding."

*She'll make you forget all about what's-her-face,* Kevin Smith-Park had wanted to whisper in Guy's ear.

"You have my permission, Sergeant Hanson."

"Thank you, Captain."

"Yes, thank YOU, 'Cahptahn,'" the Fafaman leader had echoed. "Now before I must leave to attend to most crucial matters on my end, I understand you have other of your guests I should know about. Especially, there are these tree creatures from another planet where you got distracted. They are supposed to read minds. Is this correct?"

"Yes, but before that, one other humanoid person I should like you to meet. Her name is Dr. Cathy James-Leung. She's the wife of First Engineer Buddy Leung, who unfortunately could not join us on this mission."

*Yeah, it's better for their marriage that way so they don't drive one another nuts like the rest of us are doing,* Kevin had wanted to blurt out. But it was the same as with what he'd wanted to let rip about the invite for Hanson to give away bride number twenty-three. He found the risk of a resulting diplomatic kerfluffle far more inhibiting than merely the threat of his wife number one, Yoon-hee, digging her nails deep into his armpits.

"Dr. James-Leung is here, um, she'd welcome the opportunity to work with your own meteorologists and physicists to gain a better understanding of the sunset storm line."

Cathy James-Leung had imitated Guy Hanson's curled-up-ferny-tree bow and unfurl, and she had even added the customary Fafaman greeting, "Pama," to her diplomatic effort.

"Ah," the Fafamafalafama had nodded with a smile that gave Helena the creeps, when considered together with what he had proceeded to say. "That must be very serious, essential work indeed, to detain 'Ahfahsah Buddy Lahung' away from your charming presence, 'Dahctah Cahthy Jahms-Lahung.'"

*I'll have to warn her about him,* Helena had reminded herself.

With a nervous smile, Cathy had asked to be excused from the bridge; she said she was readying aboard-ship sensors to collect data on the next sunset storm line. That storm line had been soon to be passing directly underneath where the Smoke and Mirrors was holding steady in geosynchronous orbit.

"So 'Cahptahn,' I am mightily intrigued by 'Dahctah Jahms-Lahung.'"

*Oh, how lucky that twenty-third wife is going to be,* Kevin had thought to himself. *He'll be whispering such sweet nothings in her ear as: You're almost enough to make me forget about number twenty-four.*

"But in a far different way," the Fafamafalafama had continued, "I am most anxious to meet these tree people from that planet I am told orbits a star somewhere between us and 'Tahctohctahk.' But I only have a few nininanas left before I really must conclude this transmission. My expectation is that on our next meeting, we will be in the same room together. And there, we will lift glasses of our finest ferment, to exchange your customary toast, 'Up your anal orifice.'"

Louisa Entroper had leaned her forehead into her hand, beyond disgust that Captain Taylor and her fellow insubordinates never found fit to clear up that particular confusion from the first mission, about the "customary toast."

"With you, esteemed Fafamafalafama, we always look forward to that toast," Helena had grinned mischievously, all the more delighting in Entroper's evident discomfort. "But not to keep you on this task any longer than required," she had invoked the popular Fafaman saying, *No more for the task than the task requires*, "I'm going to call our ambassadors from Oomb onto our navigation bridge. A word of caution, though. They do not speak. When you address them, they will respond in kind with a telepathic transmission directly into your brain. If you wish, whatever they telepath to you they can also multi-path to any other of your loyal subjects in attendance with you. Also, understanding their telepathed communication does not require mediation through any translation device. Nor do they require you to telepath in return. It is sufficient if you simply speak aloud whatever you wish to communicate to them. Your oral noises are merely confirmation for them that you desire to interact with them, that you are welcoming them to read your mind for those particular thoughts behind what you are saying. And as a kind courtesy to all of us non-telepathers, they try only to telepath when spoken to."

Captain Taylor had not been able to help noticing that as she went on about the Oombians, the Fafamafalafama's smile had grown more and more expansive. Together with his opaque sun goggles, it had conveyed the sense he thought she was trying to put some huge farce over on him.

"So 'Cahptahn,' what you're saying is that these walking plants of yours can read our every thought, even when we do not engage them in conversation?"

"Yes, but they have learned to respect a certain amount of mental privacy, even among themselves. At least, this is what they tell us. The way they describe it, thoughts intended to be communicated stand out in sharp relief. The tree creatures compare them to peaks of mountain ranges. For more intrusive prying, they have to plunge down deep into the brain wave valleys. They say it's an ability all life possesses. Their special circumstances favored its development more thoroughly than is often the case."

"If we didn't possess mind-reading ability, their telepathing wouldn't work on- Well, I suppose it remains to be experienced, whether the Fafaman mind can receive a telepathed communication, doesn't it, 'Cahptahn'?" The Fafaman ruler had gone from a nodding frown of that-makes-sense understanding back to his expansive smile. "Okay, let's meet your ambassadors from that other planet. And by all means, have them multi-path their mental telepathy to the entirety of my entourage."

"They already know, esteemed Fafamafalafama, and they are moving onto the bridge without my having to go speak to them."

As Oodle-Noodle and Wafoodle-Boodle came into view on the monitor, the Fafamafalafama's grin had seemed to Captain Taylor to have gotten wider than his face, were that possible. "'Cahptahn,' 'Cahptahn,'" he had shaken his head in a manner complementing his deep-throated tsk-tsk-tsk tone of voice, "couldn't you have done a more believable job with those costumes than that? Did your costume designer run out of leafy branches, so he had to top off both your actors with those disproportionately tiny fronds like on our sababalafas? And did he think he was decorating a tree indoors for a festivity, like we also do here, when he had more than one type of flower blooming from them?, an impossibility in the natural world? 'Cahptahn Taylah,' is this kind of joke customary for you in the middle of important negotiations on 'Ahth'?"

Captain Taylor had smiled, shaken her head, and said, "It's no joke, esteemed Fafamafalafama. Should I have Oodle-Noodle and Wafoodle-Boodle, here, explain for themselves?"

Before answering, the Fafaman ruler had ducked out of monitor range. From off-camera, he could be heard delivering a rapid series of fas, las and sas. They had been suggestive of his giving commands. No English version had followed, meaning the translation enabler had been turned off his end, if only temporarily. Then he'd appeared back on the screen and said, translation resuming, "'Cahptahn Taylah,' I have just given my adviser, Wafalawa, you know him, two orders. One is to ask my next audience for patience while I finish with this unexpectedly long task. The second is to assure our airwaves are getting closely monitored, for any special hi-tech trick where you somehow make radio waves enter our heads to simulate telepathic communication. What I am trying to say, 'Cahptann,' is this: If putting on some kind of magic trick is customary on 'Ahth,' fine. But we cannot endure it, we do not have the time for it, here on Fafama!"

Helena had wondered whether the Fafamafalafama was thinking this was her revenge. That this was how she was getting back at him for her time that got wasted on the first mission, when she felt trapped within the deep recesses of the central pyramid while he alternated between trying to seduce her and "servicing" his wives. "Esteemed Fafamafalafama," she'd responded with a pronounced sigh, "on this subject we feel exactly as you do. There surely cannot be a faster way to undermine trust between two different cultures, especially when they are from two different planets, than for one of them to be attempting what you fear we might be attempting."

"Okay," the ruler had nodded with that expansive grin re-dawning across his face, "let's have your plant friends communicate for themselves."

Helena had gotten the impression the Fafamafalafama was yet to be convinced, but that he had resolved to embrace with bemused zest what he regarded as a most bizarre challenge.

Wafoodle-Boodle had turned Oodle-Noodle's way, to direct Earthlings and Fafamans alike to that tree person as the source of the telepathing about to be experienced.

*Esteemed Fafamafalafama, Wafoodle-Boodle and I wish to thank you in advance, for any hospitality extended to us by you and your fellow Fafamans.*

The Fafamafalafama's eyes had quizzically roamed the ceiling of the throne room where he was standing. The long whiskers of his short advisor, Wafalawa, had repeatedly curled and uncurled in total bafflement.

*First, allow me to explain about our appearance. We can well understand how we might puzzle sentient beings from other worlds, unfamiliar with our own unique evolutionary pathways. I will abbreviate this so you can soon attend to your other duties.*

The Fafamafalafama had nodded acknowledgement with what Captain Taylor found to be his most enigmatic smile yet. If only she could have known how thoroughly the Fafaman ruler was enjoying the notion these beings might well have read his mind, only to find out that his "other duties" involved "servicing" wives twelve and thirteen! That those were the "audience" awaiting him!

*Our multiple flower varieties resulted from a long-ago hybridization which set us down the oof fairways of peace. Oof is our planet's expression of the universal game we hope you will get to play one day. The fronds you spotted atop us, when those fronds are fully grown, they facilitate our flight from island to island, safely above our planet's watery surface. To make possible the practicality of our joining the Earthlings on their second visit to your planet, we had to have our frond growth significantly pruned, along with several of our longer branches. This is a trivial issue for us, since our frond assemblies naturally ripen past their usefulness and fall off every two years, in any event.*

"Well still, that is most splendid of you to go through such a process so you could visit Fafama. But I fear you are wasting your time. 'Cahptahn Taylah' communicated to me some days ago that you believe you might be of use to deal with our barbarism problem. I have to tell you, we are not so lucky that there could be a hybridization between us and our savages that would lead to peace. That would be simply impossible, the kind of mass-mating you put in my head happened with your, uh, people back during your forgotten prehistory."

*There is far more hope than you imagine presently.*

"Yes, if your mind-reading can lead us to the caves where the barbarians hide, there is considerable hope we can eliminate them before they wreak any more havoc!"

*We wish we could do that.*

Initially, this telepathed response from Oodle-Noodle had surprised Captain Taylor. How could that tree creature lie so brazenly like that? Of course their mind-reading allowed the Oombians to know where most Fafamans were situated on the entire planet. Further reflection, however, had helped Helena realize some things. Oodle-Noodle's message had constituted the perfect ambiguity for keeping going the dialog with the Fafamafalafama. Oodle-Noodle could have admitted she was fully capable of locating the rebels through her mind-reading, but that she refused to because she knew she would be opening the door wide for their slaughter. Consequently, though, the Fafaman ruler would certainly have not wanted another thing to do with the Oombians nor their advice. By telepathing, *We wish we could do that*, what Oodle-Noodle had been meaning was: She couldn't tell the Fafaman ruler exactly where the rebels were hiding out, not because she was incapable. She already knew exactly where they were hiding out. But she couldn't share this information with the Fafamafalafama, because then he would have had his military move in for the kill. She hadn't been lying, but she had been easing misinterpretation of her telepath by the Fafamafalafama.

As Oodle-Noodle had hoped, the full meaning of her remark never occurred to the Fafaman ruler. If it *had* occurred to him, that would have resulted in his saying, *You wish you could do that, but you can't? Or you wish you weren't fearful of what we would do if you did?* Instead, the Fafaman leader had suggested, "If you accompany 'Cahptahn Taylah' to our planet's surface, perhaps a flying tour of the central pyramid's surroundings will allow you to home in on the barbarians' location?"

*That would not actually add to what our telepathic powers allow us to do,* Oodle-Noodle had responded. *Besides which, from up here in orbit, we will be better able to monitor actions of concern across the entire planet.* Again, Oodle-Noodle had embraced useful ambiguity. Ship's counselor Ali Magabu had joined Captain Taylor in realizing this, most approvingly.

"So you will warn us whenever you mind-read the barbarians are about to launch another terrorist attack?"

*We are concerned about that, of course.*

The Fafamafalafama had puffed air out his pursed lips with his growing frustration. He had not needed any fully developed mind-reading of his own to sense this bizarre tree creature was staying intentionally vague. And yet, receiving her messages telepathically spooked him too unnervingly for him to think through probing followups. This, especially since he was well aware that she, it, whatever way up there in orbit most likely knew what he was going to say before he said it. "Your companion there," the Fafamafalafama had finally motioned in the video monitor, Wafoodle-Boodle's way, "what is your companion's task here? On Fafama we say, 'No more for the task than the task requires.' Is your companion required since, uhh, she has nothing to telepath?"

*While Oodle-Noodle monitors more worrisome activities down on your planet,* Wafoodle-Boodle had mentally stepped in to say, *I will be probing and telepathing more reasonable elements of those groups who have rejected life inside, or supportive of, the central pyramid. I will be generating and encouraging ideas for peacefully resolving the conflict of greatest concern to you. With your permission, of course.*

The Fafamafalafama's grin had grown its most expansive yet, Helena had reckoned, before he fa-la-laed, "There are no reasonable elements. They are all determined to destroy our way of life."

*What if we can find how to take away any cause for them to think they have to destroy you?*

The Fafaman ruler had nodded. "That would mean something IF, again, there were any reasonable elements among them. Um,..." He had suddenly put his fingertips to his forehead.

"Captain, permission to speak?" Dr. Entroper had raised her forefinger.

Taylor had suspected Entroper wanted to offer the Fafamafalafama the same assurance she was about to offer, so she had said, "Go ahead, Dr. Entroper."

"Esteemed Fafamafalafama, what these creatures

asked us permission to come along for, please understand you are in no way obligated to agree to any of it." Louisa Entroper had shaken her head most emphatically. "Yes, we are offering you the laser mesh shield, plus further discussion on what might prove of mutual future benefit. But we have an expression on Earth: no strings attached. Now these creatures have both been very generous with their time, offering up themselves like this." Louisa had motioned towards the Oombians with a sweep of the hand. "However, what they would like to do is in no way connected to what we have unconditionally pledged to do. I just wanted to make sure you understood that."

*Yeah, sure,* Chris had thought to himself. He fought off an urge to focus the body cam on Entroper's posterior. *And while you're at it, you also wanted to make certain the Fafamafullofenema understood that if you had your way, you'd be the captain. And you'd have made damn certain Helena wasn't testing the limits of your authority the way you constantly test hers!*

"No," the Fafaman ruler had shaken his head, "I understand there are no strings attached. A superb way of putting it, though we would switch out 'strings' in favor of 'ahtpah' web strands. But I am most curious to, um, experience whatever it is your alien passengers think they can offer. Perhaps we can teach them about what is actually possible outside their rarified world. Tell me, whichever one of you tree creatures cares to respond, have the 'Ahthlahns' provided you with the laser mesh shield?"

*They have,* had telepathed Oodle-Noodle, *despite our objections. We fear the consequences.*

"You fear the consequences? Interesting."

That is when the audience with the Fafamafalafama had been rushed to its conclusion. His adviser Wafalawa had taken his place, to work out logistics for Sergeant

Hanson to make the traditional journey to the Grand Basin with the twenty-third bride, for the necessary ritual before the wedding. Traditionally, the pre-wedding ritual entourage only included the bride, the bride's father or other male appointed to give her away, two armed security guards, the glider pilot, the first wife, and the official chronicler for the Fafamafalafama's family. No news media nor other members of the bride's family were allowed. For this special occasion, though, featuring the first-ever extraterrestrial to give away the bride, it was agreed that Chief Medical Officer Dr. Deborah Davis-Murphy, from aboard the Smoke and Mirrors, plus a Fafaman physician of comparable rank, would also be in attendance. They would nurse the bride, the sergeant, and anyone else through the peculiar if ultimately benign symptoms sometimes suffered by Earthling and Fafaman alike from exposure to one another's respective alien bacterial and viral fields. In addition, Captain Taylor had pointed out that while the Fafaman ruler said the Earthlings had stolen Fafaman hearts, it turned out the Earthlings had also inadvertently made off with something else from Fafama: one of its legendary ephemeral dragons. "Your society says, 'No more for the task than the task requires,' Wafalawa," had observed the captain. "Well, we have another expression: killing two birds with one stone." Helena Taylor had gone on to ask if it would be too disrespectful of the ritual, or disrespectful at all, for the same flight out to the Grand Basin to be for both the ritual and turning lose Effy, the ephemeral dragon, back into its natural habitat. Oh, and there was this Professor Skepticus who would like to preside over Effy's release. Among his many various science projects aboard the Smoke and Mirrors, he was determined to prove the ephemeral dragon was not any kind of living creature at all. Rather, in his estimation it was some extraordinary chemical phenomenon he'd been on the verge of explaining for the past three months. And her husband, Officer Chris Olsen-Taylor, needed to come also. He would lure Effy, living or nonliving, out of the shuttle pod with chocolate chip cookie crumbs. And "this is the last one, I assure you," there was Officer Cathy James-Leung. She was busily collecting data for developing a working hypothesis as to what originally triggered, and then made to persist for millennia, Fafama's sunset storm line, the phenomenon that had shaped so profoundly the course of evolution on the planet.

Pending approval by the Fafamafalafama, all requests had been agreed to by Wafalawa, however nervous he had made the captain with his whisker-twirling while she itemized them. And as it turned out, the only input Fafama's supreme ruler had made, his only insistence, had been that the ephemeral dragon, or whatever natural phenomenon it was, be released back into its original setting after Sergeant Hanson and the twenty-third bride performed the ritual. This, to symbolize how the Varafafafa's spirit would soar free, once she became wife number twenty-three of the Fafamafalafama.

Chris had had loads to share with his wife, Captain Taylor, in the wake of this special excursion three days later. Nevertheless, there had also been some matters he didn't feel comfortable getting into.

Out near the western shore of the Grand Basin, a shuttle pod carrying the Earthling contingent had rendezvoused with a large glider craft carrying the Fafaman bridal party. Fortunately, there was a large outcropping of shale which provided a reasonably-sized landing strip, not more than a quarter mile from the beach. This rendezvous was scheduled for late night, because the Fafamans needed to wait for the sunset storm line to blow past the central pyramid before they could safely embark on the four-hour flight due east.

On the short hike down to the shoreline was when the bulk of the uncomfortable-to-report stuff had happened, where Chris was concerned. The Varalawa, the first wife, had peppered him with questions about Helena. Was she doing well? Did she order him around the same way she ordered around other crew members under her command? How did she, and Chris too for that matter, feel about working so far away from their daughter? Most awkwardly uncomfortable of all had been when the Varalawa had grabbed one of Chris's hands to stop him in his tracks. With her nocturnally large eyes, she had proceeded to look deeply into his, to ask, "So you are her only husband, and she is your only wife, yes?"

"Um, yes."

With Chris's response, the first wife, the Varalawa, had released her grip on him, and she had gently patted his hand. Then, she'd resumed her trek down to the shoreline at a picked-up pace. This, with what had struck Chris Olsen-Taylor as a satisfied grin, set off in silhouette by the soft-green, bioluminescent glow of the Grand Basin.

Officer Olsen-Taylor would have been happy to focus his attention on simply enjoying the overall ambience. There was the typically cloudless, star-studded sky, post-storm-line; the Grand Basin's aforementioned bioluminescent glow; the gentle crashing of wavelets; the tangy sea air indistinguishable from sea air on Earth...Chris might have asked whether the Fafamans had their equivalent of the Big Dipper, Ursa Major, and other objects and animals that Earthlings long ago visualized by playing connect-the-dots with the various constellations. Instead, he had not only been getting a disturbing reminder of the strange allure of the Fafamafalafama's first wife, she had been giving him serious worry over just what was going through her head. Was she planning for them to go off together? Was she figuring he couldn't have been too happy with only one wife? And if that were her scheme, and the Fafamafalafama got wind of it, couldn't Chris expect to find himself on the wrong end of that big, long sword he always lugged around? *My God*, Helena's husband had thought to himself with a surge of heart-skipping panic, *those guards had to have noticed the Varalawa grabbing my hand! What if they report back on that to the Fafama-what's-ama? Chris, get a hold of yourself.*

As the combined contingent of Earthlings and Fafamans had continued their seaward trek, Helena's husband had made a firm resolution. Were the first wife to confess her undying love for him, he would have to set her straight. He would explain how studies had shown some people are attracted instinctively to others whose gene pool varies significantly from their own, the better to produce strong, healthy children. So what gene pool could vary more than that of a person from another world? Love really didn't have anything to do with it. Oh, plus there was the small detail that he did love Helena, however much he bothered over her own seeming infatuation with the Fafamafalafama.

Anyhow, as Earthlings and Fafamans alike got ever closer to the beach, Chris had noticed something else potentially worrisome, along the same lines as his bother over the Varalawa. It had happened when Sergeant Hanson was introduced to Yulala, the twenty-third bride soon to become the Varafafafa. Their reactions had been such that Officer Olsen-Taylor would not have been completely surprised had a small electrical current passed visibly between them. The Varalawa had fa-la-laaed, "Future sister sharing my union, this is 'Sahjahnt Hahnsahn.' 'Sahjahnt Hahnsahn,' I present to you Yulala, your honorary daughter who seeks your wise counsel." Before the sergeant was to utter a sound, this was the part where Fafaman custom dictated that first, Yulala would bow to rub her head across Guy Hanson's chest. Then Guy would reciprocate. But she accidentally had bumped into his chin because she didn't bow quite low enough. Following which, Yulala and Guy had bumped both their heads together because Guy didn't expect her to try a second time. He had assumed he should proceed with his part of the bowing ritual. What had ensued from there was each tenderly rubbing where the other received a head-knock. Hanson had looked into Yulala's eyes as he had said, "I am so sorry, most honorable bride of the Fafamafalafama." Yulala had shaken her head *no*, as she had searched the sergeant's eyes and said, "I am the one who should be sorry, 'Sahjahnt Hahnsahn.'" Thereupon both had backed away from one another's tender ministrations. Chris and Shuttle Pod Commander Tanya Petrovsky had shot each other a glance; they hadn't required Oodle-Noodle's mind-reading capacity to know they had both been thinking the same thing. Guy and Yulala were exhibiting the telltale signs of shame.

No matter that the marine sergeant had quickly pulled himself back together enough to officiously say, "Honorary daughter, let us go down to the sea, that I might explain to you the joys that await with Fafama's source of all our courage and inspiration."

The Varalawa had congratulated Guy on not requiring any of her prompting to recite perfectly accurately every word of this portion of the ritual. During which, Chris Olsen-Taylor had reflected further on what he observed. Clearly, as far as Olsen-Taylor was concerned, Yulala bumped into Guy's chin, in the first place, because she tried to keep sneaking a glance up at him as she bowed. And Guy was so startled, so entranced, by Yulala's beauty, he was oblivious to her redoing her bow. Certainly, it couldn't have been helping that Guy's fiancé recently unexpectedly broke up with him. Chris had resolved that if he noticed any more evidence of sparks flying between those two, he would warn the Marine Corps sergeant, the first chance he got, of the potential danger for them both.

The ritual on the beach had only served to give Chris more reason for alarm regarding Sergeant Hanson, not to mention reason for alarm regarding all their safety.

The royal family's security detail had stepped out into the sea first, rifles at the ready, until they were waist-high amidst the low breakers. Chris knew they were protecting the gathered entourage from the Faboompa, plus who knew what else was prowling those alien waters. Thanks to the bioluminescence, Officer Olsen-Taylor had even been able to espy something unusual to bring to the attention of fellow Earthlings Tanya, Dr. Davis-Murphy, Dr. Cathy James-Leung, and Professor Skepticus. As Sergeant Hanson had waded out to roughly knee-high in the surf with Yulala, Chris had been able to point out the hind legs of the three Faboompa anchored closest to shore. Those legs might otherwise have been mistaken for the tips of a coral reef showing a bit above the waterline at low tide. As Chris had explained, the Faboompa usually dwelled upside down. Their antlers were kept anchored in the sandy bottom until such time as two or more of the Faboompa bulls decided they must battle for a mate. This was what he learned about them on the first Smoke and Mirrors mission to Fafama, when the Varalawa flew him over the Grand Basin to experience the ephemeral dragons.

"As this Grand Basin is the source for the nurturing water of the sunset storm line, honorary daughter, so shall the Fafamafalafama be the source for your Grand Womb's inner sea of life."

The Varalawa had nodded approvingly at how well Sergeant Hanson recited the ritual phrases. The sergeant had recalled those phrases so accurately, so thoroughly, he was still not requiring any of the first wife's prompting assistance.

Chris had been disturbingly struck by how much it looked like Guy could have been reciting his wedding vows, had he been holding Yulala's hand. Especially given that despite her demur bow the sergeant's way, she was still trying to sneak looks up at him.

"He shall move upon you like the waves move upon the shore, and you will receive and be glad unto him."

"Sheesh!" Kevin's voice had crackled in Chris's earpiece as Kevin was monitoring this event from high up in orbit aboard the Smoke and Mirrors. "They might as well bag and sell the Fafamawackoffalot's crap as holy sacred fertilizer while they're at it!"

Chris was going to respond with something about how he loved when Kevin dropped hints about what he wanted for his birthday. Before he could get to that, though, there had been sudden loud splashes discernible above the din of the surf. "What was that? Oh-oh!" Chris had exclaimed, as he had realized the rear quarters of the Faboompa just offshore were no longer visible. Where the tips of the Faboompa's hind flipper-hooves had been reared, rock-formation-stiff, above sea level, three sets of enormous, bioluminescently pinkish-white antlers that looked to Chris like lit-up coral reef outcroppings had risen slowly. They were followed by three most frightful heads; Chris would have likened them to a cross between moray eel heads and Tyrannosaurus Rex skulls. Two of those heads had turned towards the third, which had offered its own, challenging glare, right back. Then all three, with mouths opened wide, had let out deep bellows. Those bellows could have been blasted through amplifiers from Alpine horns, Chris had imagined.

Sergeant Hanson had already swept up Yulala in his arms and safely deposited her ashore, when one of the two security guards had shouted, "Everyone stay back!" Pursuant to this urgent warning, both guards had raised their rifles to aim them seawards.

"NOOO!!" Sergeant Hanson had shouted. He had waved his arms intensely desperately as he had dashed back into the surf towards the guards, to everyone's surprise and shock.

But the Marine Corps sergeant had been too late for stopping the guards. Both had opened fire on the three Faboompa, and just as Hanson had feared, that had had the opposite effect desired. Those three monstrous sea creatures were about to duel in anticipation of a new mating cycle, oblivious to the happenings near shore. But some of the bullets had found their mark. They had broken off parts of the beasts' antlers in small bursts of shattered bone-like growth. This had turned the Faboompa's attention in the direction from whence this damage issued. What's worse, several of the cows over which they had been about to duel had surfaced, with their antlers as tall and wide as a male peacock's display. That's when the splashing stampede towards shore had begun, preceded by the most deafening collective bellows possible.

Sergeant Hanson had come to a stop in waist-deep water, while the two security guards had retreated to solid land and were trying to herd everyone else back-back-back up the shoreline.

"Sergeant Hanson!!?? There's still time to get out of there!!" Chris had collected himself together enough to shout above the bellow-y, splashy din, seeing whereas the surf was still up to the faboompa's necks, impeding their forward progress.

But Guy hadn't been listening. To the further bafflement of Earthling and Fafaman alike, he had removed his translator from his belt. This translator had been programmed with the latest linguistic algorithms developed after Mission One, but it was not one of the ear implants. Rather, it was a retrofit of one of Officer Magabu's original jury-rigged devices. Guy was holding it in his right hand, stretched out on his right arm behind him and to his side. It had been like he was about to pitch a baseball or hurl a grenade at the approaching Faboompa, Tanya had thought. When Sergeant Guy Hanson had thrown it, he had sent it on a perfect trajectory, high above the antlers of the Faboompa herd. For Hanson and his fellow humanoids, the translator had gotten lost in the night, immediately upon its release from his hands, even with all the bioluminescence from the sea. What hadn't gotten lost was a recorded portion of the Faboompa bellows, on repeat playback at maximum amplification from Guy's translator. It was set so loud, it had been heard easily above the din being caused by those enormous Fafaman sea creatures. It had been loud enough, as the sergeant had hoped, to distract the Faboompa from their rage at whoever had fired on them. The Faboompa had reversed direction, to answer the recorded call of themselves, even as it got drowned out plunging into the sea further offshore than to where they stampeded themselves.

No sooner this, though, than two Fafaman glider jets had been rocketing overhead.

"It is okay," one of the Fafaman security guards had fa-la-laed the pilots over a Fafaman com-link device, before one of those pilots might have opened missile fire on the Faboompa herd. "The Earthling who is standing in for the twenty-third's deceased father, he risked his life on his peculiar scheme to distract the Faboompa from our presence, and it worked!"

The other Fafaman security guard, the first wife, and Yulala had muted their ee-ee-ees to welcome Guy Hanson back to shore, for fear the Faboompa's attention might yet get turned their direction anew.

"Bet they'll want to toast several bottles alllll the way up his ass for that," Kevin Smith-Park's voice had meantime erupted in the away team's non-translating earpieces, except for Sergeant Hanson's. Officer Smith-Park had cut Hanson off from this particular transmission.

"Okay, I don't think they have abandoned the idea of completing the ceremony," Helena Taylor had cautioned everyone, this time Sergeant Hanson included.

Incidentally, Chris hadn't been able to help noticing that the sergeant made a move Yulala's way, then checked himself...exactly the same time Yulala checked *her*self.

"No, keep going." The Varalawa had given Yulala a gentle push. "Remember: the presentation of the Foofafa shell."

"Oh, yes, of course," the twenty-third bride's fa-la-las had translated, in a timid voice tinged by nervous laughter. Her head had been bowed contritely, it had seemed to Chris. Chris had also been struck with an impression – Was it a fleeting mind-read? – an impression the first wife would have pushed Yulala all the way, into Sergeant Hanson's arms, if only...

Yulala had squatted, to pick at and sort through remnant shells of the Foofafa, the Fafaman version of a cephalopod. There was a plentiful supply to choose from. Chris had been reminded of horseshoe crab shells he used to find during shoreline hikes in Delaware.

At last, after considerable searching, Yulala had happened upon a Foofafa shell that was broken apart perfectly, in half, to reveal its spiral design of chambers, speckled with purplish bioluminescent bacteria. She had carefully dislodged it from the sand, rinsed it in the surf, and presented it to Sergeant Hanson as though she were bringing him an offering.

As per the Varalawa's instructions, Guy had put his hands to the shell while Yulala had maintained her own hold on it. Again, Chris had not been able to shake off sensing they might as well have been about to perform wedding vows for themselves, no Fafamafalafama involved. Certainly, they had kept their heads demurely bowed throughout the remainder of the ceremony. Had they been afraid that if they looked into one another's eyes during their recital of the ritual lines, their fascination with one another would have been revealed to any and all onlookers? Or that they wouldn't have been able to resist rushing into one another's tender embrace?

"This Foofafa shell has many empty rooms." From her waist-strapped version of the linguistic device, Yulala's voice in translation had somehow carried above the collective din of surf, plus the Faboompa splashing about, far offshore. The Faboompa were still in a frenzy to locate the source of the repeated replay of their recorded bellows. Which bellows had gone on even after Hanson's translator sank below the surface. In fact, they had continued until the device had sunk to the sandy bottom, and had gotten crushed by Faboompa antlers replanted for resisting the sea's violent ebb and flow during the next sunset storm line.

"By the children from your glorious union, will the-"

"From your glorious union with the Fafamafalafama," the Varalawa had corrected Sergeant Hanson's deletion. She had been on the alert for just such an error.

"Sorry. By the children from your glorious union with the, uh, Fafamafalafama will the empty rooms be filled with unending joy."

"Because I have been chosen by him,-" Yulala had snuck a peek at Guy Hanson on this portion of the ritual utterance. Said snuck peek had had Chris wondering anew whether he was reading too much into completely inconsequential nonverbal behaviors, or... "-joy sweeps across me like the sunset storm line."

"Oh, yeah, a daily hurricane that requires you guys to either live inside one humongous pyramid, or burrow with the rebels underground, that's a great metaphor for true love!" Kevin had commented for Tanya and Chris's earpieces only.

The ceremony had been completed, once Yulala and Sergeant Hanson had gently set back down the broken Foofafa shell on the beach. It had only remained for Chris to lure Effy the ephemeral dragon out of the shuttle pod. Then the Earthlings could return to the Smoke and Mirrors.

Officer Olsen-Taylor's trail of chocolate chip cookie pieces got successively incinerated one by one, further and further away from the shuttle pod. During which, Professor Dauntilus Skepticus had huffed and puffed to

Shuttle Flight Commander Tanya Petrovsky, on their trek back from the shoreline, "So you see, Commander Petrovsky, what we are still to learn is the magnetic resonance relationship of whatever-it-is. What is that special something in Officer Olsen-Taylor's recipe, that draws the gaseous phenomenon in the same way metal filings are drawn into special shapes, special patterns by a magnet? The crystallization of ice might lead someone to mistakenly apprehend that snowflakes are twee little creatures who melt to their doom when the temperature reaches above freezing, but that makes about as much sense as the notion of ephemeral dragons! I must say it is not unlike seeing a cloud shaped like a rabbit, and declaring it to actually be bunny fog!"

Tanya had been reminded of her childhood evenings, when she tried to anticipate where next a firefly would flash after its latest display. She had kept her eyes following each yellow-orange flare-out of each cookie piece that Chris Olsen-Taylor sprinkled, in order to make a trail of them leading from the shuttle pod's exit hatch down to the shore. This, as she had responded to Skepticus's boastful assertion, "In other words, the likeness of the phenomenon in question to a prehistoric flying reptile, when it is viewed under special atmospheric and viewing conditions, you say this is comparable to crystalline ice?"

"Exactly!" Skepticus had halted his trudging across the sandy soil back to the shuttle pod, to dart a wide-eyed glance Tanya's way. He had had a wild, crazed look where she was concerned; she had suspected she had just strengthened, deepened his conviction with a most revelatory example not previously occurring to him. "It is an illusion of life, a mirage if you will. Life is no more present than in a rock formation which bears a striking resemblance to someone's face! I must say," he'd gone on gruffly, "we have the very FACT that this phenomenon could be 'lured'," he had used his fingers as quotation marks, "away from its 'home' to board your craft, at an altitude where the air is indisputably too thin for any other Earth or extraterrestrial life form to successfully respirate. And then, it could just as easily get 'lured' back out of your craft onto a planet's surface, or anywhere else for that matter, merely by a sprinkling of chocolate chip cookie crumbs. No matter how delicious those crumbs might be, this is not the behavior of a sentient creature! Oh no! This is the behavior of a nonliving assortment of chemicals! They are interacting in ways about which I am humble enough to be the first to admit we still have terribly much to learn! Indeed, what we are witnessing here confirms everything I've been arguing!"

As Tanya had walked past the professor to be the first one to reach the ladder to reboard the shuttle pod, she had said, "So you discount the suggestion the phenomenon could be life constituted by matter in a more ethereal form? That it might be far different from anything we have previously studied?"

"My dear Mrs. Petrovsky-Magabu, I must say, there is no need for such an extreme hypothesis, until and unless we have fully exhausted all the marvelous potencies of the physics and chemistry of which we are already well aware or, in the case of the mirror array propulsion system, suspect! Really!" He had shaken his head, it seemed to Tanya, at how she could have been so densely stupid as to initiate such an absurd line of questioning. He had had no idea what was about to happen.

Tanya had been hurriedly, anxiously sealing the shuttle pod hatch behind the last reboarding passenger,

Chris Olsen-Taylor. Chris had already been joining Cathy James-Leung to congratulate Sergeant Hanson on making himself something of a hero, sure to enhance the Earthlings' stature among the general Fafaman population. And that's when the seat of Professor Skepticus's baggy olive pants had suddenly ignited with a whoosh! He had been hopping up and down reminiscent of an Irish jig Chris once saw performed in a Boston pub, but squealing, "YEOWWW!!!" quite unlike the inebriated pub frolicker.

"Please tell me, Professor," had said Tanya Petrovsky while Dr. Murphy-Davis had attended to Skepticus's rear, and Cathy James-Leung had inspected the shuttle pod interior to assure there was no structural or operational damage from the flare-out. "Does this incident, the apparent evidence the phenomenon has not left the shuttle pod after all, suggest to you that maybe a revision to your thoughts about it might be in order?"

"Not in the slightest!" Skepticus had reacted with his most insistent head-shake yet. "What this tells us is that the phenomenon is like a bottle of spilled oil! You drop it on the floor and it stains everything, everywhere! Or it's like a tub of plutonium, contaminating everything within its reach with deadly radioactivity! Yes! That's it!"

Toot! Toot!

Wank! Wank!

Just as Skepticus had snapped his fingers over his latest, any-explanation-but-an-ephemeral-dragon epiphany, a greenish, mucous-y something had burst like a horn from his one nostril. Then something comparable had done likewise out from between his buttocks, in Murphy-Davis's face. This, thanks to the portion of his pants that covered them having gotten completely torched away by the epehemeral dragon. Dr. Murphy-

Davis had thereupon nodded her head knowingly, if also disgustedly. Clearly, Skepticus had been suffering from the embarrassing interaction of Earth-borne with Fafama-borne bacteria.

Captain Taylor's curiously soothing musing over those toot-toots and wank-wanks that had issued from Professor Skepticus's bodily orifices coincided, blended seamlessly, with real trumpet fanfare from hollowed-out Faboompa antlers. That fanfare announced the unveiling of the new wife of the Fafamafalafama, the Varafafafa, at the same time it lifted Taylor completely back to the present, from out of her reverie over prior events on Fafama. Which reverie was indulged to such considerable extent to ease the especially discomforting tedium of the celebratory parade of each of the Fafamafalafama's wives leading up to Yulala.

Upon the conclusion of the fanfare, a collective hush of the excited crowd ensued. Helena and her fellow Earthlings could hear the steady hiss of one portion of wall, a few stories further up the side of the central pyramid above the highest rafter of bleachers and seats. It slid open to reveal the hangar entrance. Traditionally, this had been when a Fafaman glider would have come zooming out. Its preceding noise, as it accelerated rumbling down the interior launch runway, would have echoed like an approaching thunderous stampede that set off anxious "ahh"s by most of the vast audience. However, on this special occasion there was a special alternative, to honor the return visit of the extraterrestrials bearing the planet-encompassing gift of laser mesh defense, plus who knew how many other hi-tech goodies that might be received from them, such as the upgrade to their surface-to-orbit flying craft. As the end segment of the runway tongued out from the pyramid opening, what revved up instead of a Fafaman jet was a shuttle pod from the Smoke and Mirrors. Its wing ghosts, as that electrostatically deployed assembly of a variety of magnetized metal alloy filings was termed, provided stability for atmospheric flight. And at the same time, they lent the shuttle pod a more conventional, jet-like appearance.

On leaving the pyramid with no more than a gentle whining sound, the shuttle pod made a sharp ascent, the same as the Fafaman glider would have done. It beamed only one landing light, also from the tradition established by the Fafaman glider. When the shuttle pod neared the height of its planned climb, the Fafamafalafama pointed his two forefingers at it, to trace its descent to an airstrip parallel to the pyramid. Said airstrip had been swept clean of debris earlier that evening, soon as the sunset storm line had gone through.
The suggestion, Helena and Chris gathered from their seats in the review stand, was that the supreme Fafaman ruler was causing a star to fall from the sky. Only someone heaven-sent could do for his twenty-third wife. *And since Helena doesn't appear to be available…*Chris shook his head in disgust. This, without his even knowing, his wife not having shared with him, what had happened on their first visit to Fafama. The Fafamafalafama had tried to seduce Helena while she was kept under armed guard somewhere in the depths of the central pyramid.

"Swords and sheathes!" the translation of the fa-la-las from the well-concealed master of ceremonies boomed in the Earthling guests' ears.

The shuttle pod, piloted by Tanya after she slipped away from the review stand during the presentation of wife number eighteen, kicked up clouds of sand and dust as it whirred down to a halt, just past the raised platform where the Fafamafalafama stood alone beside the Varalawa.

"Swords and sheathes, please refrain from any and all commotion during the pronouncement of the Varafafafa!"

"What?! So instead of 'ladies and gentlemen,' it's 'swords and sheathes'?" Kevin's exclamation filled the Earthling earpieces. "They might as well say, 'Pricks and-' Ouch! Ticklers! That was all I was going to say, Yoon-hee! Pricks and ticklers! Honest! Stop it!"

Chris and Helena, the starship captain, exchanged a knowing look, a fleeting intimacy that, as much as Chris cherished it, left him strangely wanting. Though they were standing so close together, he still sensed a certain distance between them. But he knew that, were he to try to bridge it with an arm around her shoulders, he would get met with a swift recoil. *Yeah, yeah, yeah, it isn't the time or the place, and yet that dance with the supreme Fafaman ruler on our first mission…*

Chris, Helena and Louisa Entroper came equipped with their night-vision goggles, since they lacked the Fafamans' extra-large, nocturnally-adapted eyes. They were easily able to make out Sergeant Hanson holding Yulala's hand, on her final steps down the ladder from the shuttle pod. Hanson was insuring there would be no risk of the twenty-third wife taking a last-moment stumble-tumble on her flowing, dark cloak. Helena and Chris both wished they could possess Oodle-Noodle's mind-reading powers for long enough to discover what was going through the sergeant's head. Ever since the ritual on the shore of the Grand Basin, their latent extrasensory perception had been telling them Guy was troubled by something. Chris had wanted to work his way into asking about it, inquiring how Guy was handling the breakup with his fiancé. But no particular time had ever seemed a good time. Guy had been continually busy with laser mesh deployment issues. Especially, he had had to keep double-checking that the turbulence set off by the sunset storm line, forever on its march around the alien globe, wasn't having an impact outside the Fafaman atmosphere on said mesh. And how was Chris supposed to interrupt discussions of other significant matters? There was that time, over lunch with Cathy James-Leung. Cathy was explaining how a lack of tilt in Fafama's axis relative to the tilt of Earth's axis might be a major clue to the origin of the storm line. How was Chris supposed to interrupt that to pry into whether Guy was experiencing puppy love for the twenty-third wife? Ali Magabu had counseled that, unless and until the sergeant volunteered or strongly hinted at something, he probably just wasn't ready to talk about it. Plus, there was always the distinct possibility that far more had been read into what was witnessed during the seaside ritual than was really there.

Presently, the Fafamafalafama was circling Yulala. His cape was wrapped so tightly around about him, none of its artificially enhanced luminescence could escape to general view. He picked his way carefully to not take a humiliating tumble over the lengthy train of his next wife's dark cloak. To Chris, there was a resemblance to a vulture he'd one time seen stalking his way around a dead fox before moving in for the scavenge. After several suspenseful moments of this, the Fafamafalafama finally stopped his pacing, directly in front of Yulala, and he unfurled his cape. Pursuant to which, he lifted his arms high to reveal, for the twenty-third time that evening, an array of luminescence muted only a notch below dazzling, in Dr. Entroper's estimation.

"This must be the part where he says, 'I *vant* to suck

your blood,'" Kevin commented from back aboard the Smoke and Mirrors. "That's suck, Yoon-hee, not tickle."

Sergeant Guy Hanson gingerly undid the bow tie of Yulala's cloak around her neck. He appeared overly careful, it seemed to Chris, to not even once steal a glance at her eyes. When Sergeant Hanson finished, the cloak slid off Yulala's shoulders. Hanson averted his gaze. *Holy Wackafafamole*, Chris exclaimed to himself inside his head, *was Guy expecting her to be naked underneath the cloak? Or was he afraid that even if she remained clothed, his undressing her with his eyes would prove equally prurient?*

What the fallen-away cloak revealed was the wedding gown. Its train nearly rivaled the length of the train which had concealed it. It was studded with sequins as abundant as the stars in the Fafaman sky. They shone with the brightness of stars when viewed from on board the Smoke and Mirrors, untempered by an atmosphere in between. The only difference was their greenish hue, in the same league as much Fafaman bioluminescence. The Earthlings well knew this display was supposed to symbolize how the Fafamafalafama made life proliferate simply by his virile presence.

"My title is Varalawa, first wife of the Fafamafalafama," the first wife said as she purposefully strode in between the Fafaman ruler and the dramatically attired Yulala.

Yoon-hee watching from a monitor aboard the starship couldn't help wondering. Was a bit of her own untapped, Oombian-type mind-reading ability telling her the Varalawa wished she could somehow always stand between the Fafamafalafama and this sharer – or rival? – of his attentions?

"Who are you, and what is your desire here?"

continued the Varalawa.

"My name is Yulala, but- but my desire is to change that to the Varafafafa." Yulala kept her head bowed contritely low. For all in attendance, her face got lost in her long ringlet curls. She could have been ashamed of lying, rather than simply approaching the wedding ceremony with deep humility and a bit of modesty-inspired embarrassment. Nobody except perhaps for a mind-reading tree could know the difference, Chris felt certain.

The Varalawa nodded her acknowledgement of Yulala's ritually proscribed response, and she turned to Sergeant Hanson. "Are you the father?"

"The father's spirit has gotten swept up in the sunset storm line, from where all spirits will be let to fall, like ripened fofas from the matured faloola fern, in the wake of the final storm line ushering the eternal sunset across all Fafama. I stand in his place for his daughter's petition."

"Can you vouch for the unpierced purity of Yulala?"

Sergeant Hanson swallowed hard, it was evident to every Earthling and many Fafamans as well, as he answered, "I can."

Another nod, and the Varalawa pivoted to face her husband. "My beloved Fafamafalafama, Yulala stands meekly before you, a seeker of your steadfast affection for as long as you both shall live," went the translation of her next utterance. "How do you find her?"

The Fafamafalafama resumed his prowling around Yulala which had reminded Chris of a vulture's behavior. For the glint in the ruler's eyes, from the reflection of the several luminescent sequins adorning Yulala's gown, Officer Olsen-Taylor would not have been especially surprised had he let slip his tongue from inside his mouth to lustfully lick his chops. Likewise where Kevin was concerned, back aboard ship. If not for fear of a severe reprimand, not to mention mercilessly administered tickles, Kevin would have said, *Mmmmmmmmm, that's some prime grade A tenderloin there! He better eat that up before the Tictoctickians can sink their antlers into it!*

The Fafamafalafama at last ceased his meat inspection, as Kevin would have put it, to make the tradition-bound response to the Varalawa's tradition-bound question. "I find Yulala an irresistible, most treasured addition to my collection. I assure my faithfulness to her for as long as we both shall live, even as I have been faithful to my twenty-two other wives."

*Excepting the small detail of trying to spoon an extraterrestrial while she was presumably asleep,* Captain Taylor shook her head in unconcealed disgust.

Again, her husband Chris still had no idea what transpired between Helena and the ruler when she was under security "protection" deep within the central pyramid on their first voyage to Fafama. And so, he took some comfort from noticing her reacting this way. *No more dancing with the Fafacreepalotama, this hopefully means.*

"What do you say to the response of the Fafamafalafama?"

"I say it is beyond what I could possibly deserve." Yulala humbly bowed her head as she responded to the Varalawa's ritual question exactly according to script.

"And what do you say to his twenty-two other wives?"

"I say that from this day forward, shall they always be my twenty-two best friends, my sisters sharing in a supreme love."

*Oh, whoops, I meant to say they will be my twenty-two most bitter rivals, especially schnauzer number sixteen, the Varabow-wowa, who can only dream of a roll in the tralalafa with the ultimate prick after he lays his hands on me!* Kevin again stifled himself, though hoping perhaps Oodle-Noodle and "Wafoodle-shake-your-kaboodle" were getting entertained reading his mind.

"'Sahgahnt Hahnsahn,' if you will." The first wife turned Guy Hanson's way.

The marine sergeant took Yulala's right hand, and he placed it in the Fafamafalafama's right hand, already extended awaiting this action. Hand in hand, the two Fafamans turned to face the Varalawa.

Chris couldn't help thinking that when Guy took Yulala's hand, they both wanted it to stay that way. The final destination was already reached. Chris also couldn't help thinking, while Yulala and the Fafamafalafama were facing the first wife, something most troublesome about how the first wife stole a glance the vast audience's way. Was the Varalawa seeking out his, Chris's, own face in the crowd? Was she doing this, to think wistfully on their being together, rather than her being stuck with a man for whom she was but part of his "collection," whatever "faithful" was supposed to mean for the Fafaman ruler?

"As the first wife, the Varalawa, I condone-" she swallowed hard, "-this union, and I welcome my newest best friend as the twenty-third wife, the Varafafafa. I welcome her into the one family that, above all other families, secures our future as assuredly as the central pyramid secures us from the daily ravages of the sunset storm line!"

"Swords and sheathes, I present to you my twenty-third wife, the Varafafafa!"

Wild monkey ee-ee-ees and thunderous foot-stomping of bleachers broke out in the review stands as the twenty-one other wives plus their fifty-six collective children filed back onto the raised platform, all waving on their ascent. One by one they gave the Varafafafa a welcome hug while a syncopated beat was played on the hollowed-out ahtpah shell. Far behind them, fireworks were exploding across the sky of the most peculiar sort for the Earthlings. They appeared like smoke bombs, billowing more than bursting. Their bluish-gray hues dampened the flashes of light within them, so that those flashes had the same, muted, color tones of Fafama's typical night-time bioluminescence. It was comparable to watching lightning flashes illuminate the clouds that enveloped them, Chris thought. And with his night-vision goggles, the dissipating smoke took on the appearance of monstrously long, ghostly, spindly spider legs, as it drifted off on gentle upper-level winds.

"Captain," Yoon-hee's voice suddenly erupted in the away team's earpieces, "was Sergeant Hanson supposed to sprint back inside the shuttle pod, the instant the Fafamafalafama officially presented his twenty-third wife?"

As soon as navigation officer Yoon-hee Park-Smith said this, the distinctive if faint whine of the shuttle pod, revving up its propulsion system for more atmospheric flight, could be easily heard despite the celebratory racket.

"No he wasn't," said Captain Taylor rising from her seat, straining to get a better view of what was unfolding.

Chris Olsen-Taylor was noticing that things leaving contrails were piercing through the dissipating Fafaman-style fireworks. Said things were on a shallow trajectory that Chris intuited would have required their original launch from a location well beyond the launch site for said fireworks.

"Officer Petrovsky!? Report to me what's going on!" Helena couldn't help a mix of panic and exasperation in her voice.

"We'll explain, Captain!" was what Tanya offered back, as the pod's electrostatically deployed wings sparkled like the Varafafafa's gown, although orange rather than pastel greens, blues and purples. The shuttle was turning around at one end of the runway to initiate final departure.

Dr. Entroper rubbed her forehead as she was shaking it in disgust.

*Sure*, Helena thought to herself when she noticed, *she's thinking to herself how it wouldn't be going like this, were she in charge.*

"Captain," this time it was Kevin, "are you seeing what we're seeing? Not the shuttle pod, but floating down from the sky, just beyond where it's taking off!"

Chris noticed first, but was too stunned to talk and any way wasn't sure he could believe his eyes. Those things with the contrails, that seemed to have come from much farther away than from where the fireworks were launched, they were resolving themselves into a multitude of parachutes with shiny round things hanging from them.

"Maybe this is something to do with the ceremony we didn't know about?" the captain speculated in lame desperation as the Fafamafalafama and family continued waving at the audience, blithely oblivious to everything else, even the shuttle pod taking off behind them.

"Don't think so, Captain!" responded Yoon-hee. "We're picking up a sharp spike in Fafaman security operations! What IS that?!"

One of the first parachutes had gotten separated by a rogue breeze from the rest. It came drifting lazily into the bleachers not far from the Earthling location. And on its final few feet of descent, spindly legs reached down from the circular object hanging from it. They latched onto one hapless Fafaman's shoulders, for razor-sharp pincers to neatly shear off his head.

"The ahtpah!" gasped Kevin. "Holy shit!"

The crowd let out a collective roar of panic punctuated by shrieks and wails. The adolescent ahtpah, Fafama's monstrous spider made possible by the planet's slightly lower gravity relative to Earth's, sucked out its victim's fluids through a feeding tube inserted into his neck.

*We're going to get crushed in the stampede if one of those awful things doesn't get us first,* was all Louisa Entroper could think as more young ahtpahs landed gently with the parachutes, mere yards from the raised platform packed to bursting with the Fafamafalafama's family.

The next thing the away team from the Smoke and Mirrors knew, Fafaman troops were surrounding the platform with weapons pointed upward and outward in all directions. Chris noticed the Fafamafalafama himself ducking down between wives whose number identities he'd already lost track of. This was the last thing he noticed before he, his captain wife and Dr. Entroper found themselves hemmed in, shoved against on all sides by the mounting, panic-driven stampede. Immediately thereupon, to Louisa's faint-inducing horror, an ahtpah with its eight legs all in an excited commotion was descending their way. It was trailing streamers of webbing that were tangling together tens of Fafamans as those streamers blanketed them.

Captain Helena Taylor's last thought before she passed out, with the ahtpah's legs within inches of her head, was that there was a hint of acetone in the air…

When the away team Earthlings came to, they found their heads each resting in the lap of a wife of the Fafamafalafama. This was happening near the platform to where they had been carried by those Fafaman troops who had heeded the call inside their heads from Wafoodle-Boodle. That call had been for them to remain within the confines of the pyramid until the knockout gas had dissipated to safe levels.

When Chris opened his eyes, he saw the Varalawa looking down at him attentively while gently stroking his hair. But he immediately set aside any feelings he might have been wrestling with in regards to her, to lift himself up on one elbow and searchingly glance around. Soon as he spotted Helena likewise reviving, his eyes swept a wider perimeter. Fafaman troops were variously engaged in helping fellow troops back onto their feet, herding citizenry back into the pyramid as they regained consciousness, and dragging still-unconscious ahtpahs by their respective parachutes to a bonfire that was already in full rage, sending smoke spiraling high into the otherwise clear night sky.

"'Cahptahn Taylah,' I want you to know that, if all my wives and children had trusted my example and flattened themselves against the dais, they likewise would have avoided the effects of the fumes which unfortunately were necessary to nullify the peril posed by the 'ahtpah.'" The Fafamafalafama towered over Helena as he stated this with both hands clutching firmly onto the hilt of his golf-club-length sword. "They are those wives who received my wisdom into their hearts who are ministering to you now. However, this in no way detracts from the satisfactory deeds of your 'Ahfasah Petrahsky' and 'Sahgahnt Hahnsahn.' Plus, a special glow of the flounder mouse for your telepathic passengers from the planet 'Ahmb.'"

"Translation, Captain." Kevin didn't care who might overhear. "Only a few of my wives were as let's-hide-from-the-threat chicken shit as I was. And oh, what your crew and tree person guests did, saving our lives, while it doesn't rise to the level of shmuckdom of my anti-heroic cowering, I'd still give it a passing grade."

"'Cahptahn Taylah,' one additional thing." The Fafamafalafama paused to draw his sword and pierce deep into the bulbous rear of an unconscious ahtpah for a TV camcorder, before two troops finished dragging it over to throw onto the bonfire. "Clearly, you and your fellow officers will need to recuperate from this unpardonable, barbaric attack, back aboard your space vessel if you wish. But after that, I should desire an audience with you, your fellow 'Ahthlahns' who delivered the knockout gas, and most especially your guests from 'Ahmb.' I am a little unclear on the details of exactly what happened, and have some questions to ask."

"Believe me, esteemed Fafamafalafama," Helena nodded, still too groggy from the effects of the gas to even sit up as Chris was doing, "I am in a fog myself about events. I will have several questions of my own."

# Chapter 9

"About your new extraterrestrial friends: In case there are any others, I speak of the mind-reading plant people who leant you the means to assist our dispatch of the latest attack by the barbaric rebels. They still don't feel they can make a personal appearance before me? 'Cahptahn,' I am SO disappointed." The Fafamafalafama made an exaggerated frown, complete with pouty lower lip. He turned it first Nanofafo's way, then Wafalawa's way. Those two closest advisers flanked his seat on the provisional throne, the throne away from throne, in his heavily-secured, specially-reinforced reception area on the southwest-facing outer perimeter of the central pyramid. Nanofafo and Wafalawa's lengthy whiskers curled and uncurled empathetically, as Nanofafo and Wafalawa themselves shook their heads in we-don't-comprehend-this incredulity.

*Esteemed Fafamafalafama, I should like to explain,* Oodle-Noodle telepathed. *Where those you term the barbaric rebels are concerned, mind-reading from up here in orbit allows us a far wider range of mental probing than would be possible from down on the surface of Fafama, standing beside you. We thought such mind-reading was what you valued most from us.*

"I understand," the Fafamafalafama nodded at the view-screen, where he could see the tree people looking back at him. Their eyes were open sideways, rather than lengthwise, amidst the corrugations of their trunk bark. The Fafaman ruler would have characterized the Oombians as perpetually sleepy-looking. However, despite the exceedingly odd impression they made on him, he still proceeded to return his attention to the audience in his immediate presence. This audience included Sergeant Hanson, Tanya Petrovsky, Helena Taylor, and Louisa Entroper. "I would simply hope, 'Cahptahn,'" the Fafamafalafama went on, his focus even more specifically on Helena. "I would hope that baseless worry over getting held captive did not play any part in the decision for the beings from 'Ahhmb' not to accompany you."

"Esteemed Fafamafalafama, if there is such worry, how do you explain our presence here?" Captain Taylor locked eyes with the Fafaman ruler.

"Not without some difficulty, 'Cahptahn,'" the Fafamafalafama nodded, albeit in a tone of voice mischievously suggestive he had not actually conceded her point.

Helena couldn't help a trace of grin escaping her tightly-pressed lips as she gave a reciprocal nod. Of course they would have worried, the Oombians and her both, were Oodle-Noodle and Wafoodle-Boodle to get within a burning torch's length of the Fafamafalafama.

Hours ago, back aboard the Smoke and Mirrors, there had been a debriefing as to exactly what transpired, leading up to the rebel terrorist attack via parachuted adolescent ahtpahs. Helena Taylor had had crammed into her office the two tree people, Tanya Petrovsky, Tanya's counselor husband Ali Magabu, Sergeant Hanson, Dr. Entroper and Officer Yoon-hee Park-Smith.

Dr. Louisa Entroper had complained about why Yoon-hee's presence was necessary, when Louisa herself could have acted as the fully impartial onlooker. Taylor had explained that Yoon-hee's input would prove invaluable since she was monitoring Fafaman communication during the incident. But the truth had been that Helena *did* want Yoon-hee to play impartial onlooker. She well knew that Louisa Entroper would prove anything but impartial. Most likely, Louisa would grind her ax early and often, on the need for stronger leadership and more involvement by Earth-originated military. Moreover, Yoon-hee had earned extra respect from the captain for her quick thinking at the height of the terrorist attack. Soon as Helena and company had returned on board the Smoke and Mirrors, Yoon-hee had assured her the firefly transmission back to their home solar system was suspended well within the five-minute delay range. None of the video of the terrorist attack went out. Yoon-hee concocted the pretext that the climactic wedding hoopla was considered too sacred for filming by the extraterrestrials.

Everyone but the tree people had settled into chairs. Those chairs were lined with a Velcro-like material. This material kept their occupants from floating about in the weightless environment, with the Smoke and Mirrors in orbit around Fafama at speeds considerably lower than the usual constant for light. Oodle-Noodle and Wafoodle-Boodle found themselves plenty comfortable, clinging to corrugations in the floor by their root cilia. Thusly had Earthlings and Oombians alike been situated for the debriefing, again with Yoon-hee having given an assurance that back home on Earth, nobody yet knew of the violent disruption to the conclusion of the Fafamafalafama's twenty-third wedding.

Captain Helena Taylor had begun, "Officer Petrovsky, Sergeant Hanson, first allow me to make clear I am nothing less than eternally grateful for your intervention. There is no doubt in my mind you saved lives by your actions; woe be it for me to second-guess you."

"Yes, that's right." Louisa Entroper had nodded her usual, emphatic nod, in response to which Helena Taylor had darted her a steely, who's-in-charge glance. Taylor knew full well Louisa would have wanted to go on. Louisa would have wanted to say that Tanya and Guy's actions weren't the actions she'd been ever-intent on second-guessing, from the first time she stepped foot on the bridge of the Smoke and Mirrors. That she was far more concerned about the leadership they were receiving, or the lack of it, from their captain.

"What I want from both of you, before I have our Oombian friends telepath their roles, is to just walk us through your decision-making process."

Nods back and forth had silently settled on who should speak. Guy Hanson had said, "Captain, four days ago, before the ceremony on the shore of the Grand Basin,-"

"Four days ago," Louisa hadn't been able to help repeating, in a tone that said, *Well this ought to prove something.*

"Um, yes, four days ago, before that ceremony with Yu- uh, with the twenty-third wife, I received a telepathed communication from- I believe it was from you, Ms. Wafoodle-Boodle?"

*Yes.* She had rustled her leaves as she confirmed telepathically.

"Ms. Wafoodle-Boodle mind-read that an attack might be imminent during the Fafamafalafama's wedding ceremony. To prepare for it, she suggested I should ascertain the shuttle pod's weapons retrofit was properly functioning to facilitate the use of knockout gas."

"What was your response?"

"Captain, my response was to query whether the extraterrestrial had observed the chain of command, by first going to you with her concern."

"And what was your response, Wafoodle-Boodle?"

Having read the captain's mind, Wafoodle-Boodle knew better than to prevaricate with some preamble about the high regard in which Helena was held by any Oombian who made the effort to read her mind. Instead, she had telepathed, *Captain, once we were clear there was a threat of massive violence that could have the additional harmful effect of sabotaging our peace plan-*

"YOUR peace plan," Louisa had interjected, with the same tone she'd repeated Hanson's words.

*Okay, once we realized this, we also realized there was a way to diffuse the threat, although tragically not to eliminate it altogether without opening a path for the Fafaman leadership to commit massive violence. Our task, our commitment, was to see our peace plan receive its greatest opportunity for implementation. I telepathed Sergeant Hanson what Oodle-Noodle and I extrapolated would have happened had we gone to you first, Captain. From your prior behavior, we guessed that you would have asked for the location from where the ahtpah attack would get launched. You would have argued that a knockout gas attack on that location would have been possible. Thereby, dangerous injury to anyone would have been precluded, well in advance of the ceremony. I would have explained that that was not going to work. Without the distraction of the fireworks display and the laser mesh shield deployment, the Fafaman military would have easily identified your shuttle pod craft's presence within the Fafaman atmosphere. They would have gone to investigate, in plenty of time to locate where you released the knockout gas. Having thereby identified the rebel stronghold, they would have run a devastating bombing raid. Such a raid would have led inevitably to an even worse terrorist attack, taken in retaliation. We would have argued back and forth what could be done, Captain, but inevitably you would have opened up the dialogue to include most significantly you, Dr. Louisa Entroper.*

Louisa could not have spasmed more had she received an electric shock.

*And it would have been Dr. Entroper who shared our information with the Fafaman government if you decided that should not happen, Captain.*

"You don't know that, Wafoodle-Boodle AND Oodle-Noodle! Neither one of you!" Louisa had shaken her head adamantly. "How dare you accuse me of being capable of..." She had paused, flustered, to reformulate, "How dare you presume my insubordination on no basis whatsoever!"

Captain Taylor had hunched her shoulders and tilted her head. Even without this nonverbal, Yoon-hee and Ali knew she would have said, *Wellll...* if she didn't fear Louisa would have devolved from flustered to a paroxysm of rage. Which actually might have given them a welcome excuse to place the government observer under guard in her quarters. Although, Ali Magabu well knew she'd likely have to commit murder before Dr. Davis-Murphy would sign off on such a recommendation, in order to make it enforceable.

Anyhow, while Helena Taylor was partially stifling her reaction, Oodle-Noodle telepathed, *Far from casting any aspersions on you, Dr. Entroper, we are recognizing and respecting you would have felt honestly torn about the best course of action. In such a conflicted state, you might well have concluded that following the captain's orders presented so terrible a risk to the Fafaman pyramid society, you most nobly would be willing to face the consequences of insubordination to warn the Fafaman pyramid leadership. Part of your calculation – as it was ours – would certainly have been that under no circumstances, especially fear of an attack, would the Fafamafalafama have agreed to postpone the ceremony, the only scenario in which we were able to extrapolate no harm.*

Dr. Louisa Entroper had not been able to get past her puzzlement to mount a response.

Captain Taylor was amused by how ingeniously the tree person from Oomb strove to empathize with Louisa. But she was not so amused that she hadn't been able to go right on to say, "Oodle-Noodle and Wafoodle-Boodle, I guess what I don't understand is how you figured Segeant Hanson would be likely to follow your lead without breathing a word to me. But I must admit your concern seems well-grounded, about the whole course of interactions that might have gotten set off had you come to me first. Now obviously," she'd waved a here-he-is hand Guy's way, "the sergeant was willing to play by your rules, but… You can really read into our minds that deeply?"

"Captain, if I may," Sergeant Hanson had uncharacteristically spoken the same time he raised his hand, rather than waiting to be called on.

"Make it brief, Sergeant. We can explore this more deeply later."

"Thank you, Captain. I just wanted to say that when they telepathed me, my biggest concern was your being able to attend the ceremony with plausible deniability, especially were the attack not to happen. For sure, the Fafamans can't mind-read like your Oombian guests. But it still made me anxious, the prospect of your attending the ceremony in full knowledge of an impending attack, and the plan to thwart it. Something in your demeanor, a look of preoccupation uncontrollably casting a pall across your face, who knows? Something, a feeling, an intuition, could have made our Fafaman guards suspicious to such an extent that they decided to interrogate you, place you in confinement. Nevertheless, I fully understand it was not for me to make these judgments. This was an act of insubordination on my part and my part alone; Officer Petrovsky got brought in on the situation by Wafoodle-Boodle well after the ceremony was under way, at the last possible moment. I am prepared to accept the consequences for my behavior immediately, with full cooperation, no resistance."

Captain Taylor had waved a dismissive hand at Hanson as she fixed her sight on the tree people and said, "So, how much of this was your just knowing Sergeant Hanson would be predisposed to accepting your plan unmodified? And more worrisome, how much is there something about telepathing that goes beyond persuasion to some form of mind control?"

Oodle-Noodle had paused from checking her severely-pruned trunk top for signs her rotator frond assembly was continuing to regenerate. She had wanted to give her next telepathic communication her fullest attention. *Captain, were that persuasion element actually possible, believe me, we would have been bombarding the instigators of the attack with our transmissions in order to stop the problem at its source. No, Captain, what decided us on Sergeant Hanson was that ultimately, he was your one crew member with full working knowledge of the gas-dispersion weapon retrofit of your shuttle pod. Were he to accept our reasoning, nobody else would need to be brought in on the plan excepting, as he pointed out, Flight Officer Petrovsky, at the very last possible moment. It seemed a safe bet that, seeing all the ahtpahs getting parachuted in, she would postpone asking questions until later.*

*While we are on the subject of our potential brainwashing ability, there is one bit of fallout from this operation which proved a big disappointment, apart from the unavoided fatalities at the outset of the attack. This was the action taken by the Fafaman security people who didn't pass out from the gas. We telepathed them that they should gather up the unconscious ahtpahs in a huge net, and airlift them to a wilderness area far west of the central pyramid. There, they could be harmlessly let go. Imagine our disappointment as the Fafamans rejected our counsel, and killed the netted ahtpahs in a huge bonfire instead.*

"Just think, Oodle-Noodle, and you should think about this too, Sergeant Hanson, especially since Captain Taylor appears unwilling to deliver you the proper consequences for insubordination,-"

"Hold it there, Dr. Entroper." Helena Taylor had raised a hand for the government observer to stop. "As captain of this starship, I reserve the right to make a distinction between justified insubordination and unjustified insubordination. In my estimation, only an arrogant fool would insist their every decision be free from all second-guessing by their subordinates. As captain of everyone aboard the Smoke and Mirrors, Dr. Entroper, not of everyone minus a certain government observer, why do you think I regularly put up with what I'm sure you regard as your own most well-founded expressions of dissent from both my decisions and my decision-making processes?"

Ali Magabu wanted to say, *Bravo, Captain; I didn't think you had it in you,* but he had decided to stifle himself so Entroper wouldn't come to feel they were ganging up on her.

"Well," Louisa had made a production of sighing, "all I was going to point out, Oodle-Noodle," like she didn't say a thing about anyone's insubordination, "was this: Had you shared the location from where the attack would be launched against the royal family of Fafama, we could have wiped out the enemy's base of operation. We would have thereby prevented not only that particular act of terror, but who knows how many more future attacks."

*Take a close look at your civilization's history, Dr. Entroper, and ask yourself: How many times did destroying "the enemy's base of operation," as you put it, actually succeed in preventing other acts of violence? Especially since the close of your second world war, what has been the case, far more often than not? That is, unless the real reasons for the violence have been addressed? Weeks or months later, however much time it takes for the believers in violence to regroup, haven't there been other spasms of expressed rage?, whether a series of car bombings, or actions even more widespread? How many of your military "surges" have actually worked in the long run?*

"Well, Oodle-Noodle." Dr. Entroper had uttered *Oodle-Noodle* in a forceful tone suggestive she wanted to admonish the tree creature for adopting such a silly-sounding name, not at all appropriate for the gravely serious circumstances. "I trust you understand the ineffectiveness of violence can be a two-way street. I assume this is an expression you have already picked our brains sufficiently to understand."

*You're right. I have.*

"What I am saying is, if you think the, uhh, the Fafaman king might have been amenable to a proposal to deal peacefully with their insurgents, well, I can't imagine his agreeing to anything less than full retaliation after the bloodthirsty disruption of a sacred Fafaman ritual."

*That is precisely the problem, Dr. Louisa Entroper, government observer. Your imagination, the imagination of your civilization's culture, is ample, nearly boundless, for the usefulness of violence to counter violence, while any attempts to imagine anything other than violence to counter violence are automatically considered naïve and ineffectual, despite your society's religious icons having preached love and nonviolent interventions as the true solutions to society's ills. You best said it yourself, Dr. Entroper, when you labeled any possible alternatives "less than full retaliation." Yes, peaceful, loving conflict resolution is less, while war is more.*

"Ms. Oodle-Noodle, I am happy for you, I really am, because the notions you express seem to have worked for you. But forgive me if I wonder over the prospects for your survival without what you seem to characterize as our violent intervention. That is assuming the threat from Tictoctic is real."

***

"Well, then," the translation presently crackled from the Fafamafalafama's translator, in virtually his same voice, as he slapped the arms of his throne-away-from-throne. Those Earthlings who had slipped into a daydream over the hours-ago debriefing in the captain's office aboard the Smoke and Mirrors were snapped out of it, brought back down onto the planet Fafama inside the central pyramid. "I do want to thank you, 'Cahptahn Taylah,' for delivering on the laser mesh grid, and I want to thank you as well, 'Sahgahnt Hahnsahn,' for presiding over the details of its deployment."

Captain and Sergeant both acknowledged the Fafamafalafama's gratitude with restrained nods.

"The lightning flash of that grid across the sky possessed a rare beauty." The Fafamafalafama elevated his gaze ceiling-ward, and he waved his hands like he were showing off the spectacle. "Such a sad misfortune, the grid activation's necessary postponement until well after the twenty-third wife ceremony. Due to all-consuming work commitments, so few got to enjoy the event signifying our added protection. Including myself, of course. I depended on a report from the Varalawa. She was able to indulge this pleasure while she cared for the eleventh son."

*Yeah, he was too busy humping wife twenty-two, telling her she was the only one for him until the newbie finished taking off her wedding gown.* Kevin Smith-Park thus wanted to fill the away team's earpieces. He knew better, given the delicate negotiations just ahead.

"Anyhow, I should be infuriated over the necessity to so distribute the knockout gas that several of my wives, children and my own self suffered from its effects. And yet somehow, I am not." The Fafaman ruler cast around a most satisfied-with-himself grin, Ali Magabu thought.

Nanofafo and Wafalawa said in unison in their deepest, most solemn fa-la-las, "Such is the mercy of the Fafamafalafama."

*I'm surprised he even got a whiff of the stuff,* Kevin again censored himself from muttering back aboard the Smoke and Mirrors, *the way he ducked down amidst his harem, courageously using them as a protective shield.*

"I am wondering, 'Oodahl-Noodahl,'" the Fafaman ruler continued, "how that search for what you termed 'reasonable elements' among the barbaric rebels is going for you. As you tree people collaborated with

Captain Taylor's crew to foil the barbarians' plot to destroy my family, did it ever cross your mind you would enjoy better luck attempting to surgically transform yourselves into humans of either the Earth or Fafama variety?"

If Chris didn't know better, he could have sworn a look of sympathy flashed across the Supreme Ruler's usually stony-appearing visage. Perhaps it was genuine sorrow for the Oombians having had to discover the hard way how naïve they were with their silly pacifist notions.

"Before one of the Oombians answers, Fafamafalafama,-" Captain Taylor held up a hand, palm facing Chris's body cam. This, to visually impress upon the tree creatures watching from aboard the Smoke and Mirrors what they were nevertheless reading in her mind. She wanted them to hold off on their response. "-you might have already deduced this. But, when our extraterrestrial guests grew aware of the terrorist plot under way, we concluded that trying to alert you ran the risk of rebel eavesdropping. Which might have led them to move forward the timetable before anything could be done to thwart-"

"'Cahptahn, Cahptahn,'" the Fafamafalafama shook his head and dismissively waved his hands with his sharp interruption. "When I commented on how I was not infuriated, of course I should have added that I deduced your adequate line of reasoning. I deduced it the moment I regained consciousness from the gas attack. Now let us hear or..." He waved his hands randomly, like he wasn't sure what to do with them "...or sense, whatever it is our minds do when the plant creatures telepath to us, let us discover how your guest passengers from Oomb feel now, about their prospects for happening upon rebel minds at all capable of even the most inconsequential negotiations. Their efforts might better be employed trying to domesticate an ahtpah." The Fafaman ruler cast a wry grin Captain Taylor's way.

*Esteemed Fafamafalafama,* Oodle-Noodle responded, *how the tragically regrettable events played out has served to confirm we have, indeed, already located a reasonable element within the rebel faction.*

The Fafamafalafama was starting to settle back on his away-from-throne throne, to savor the plant people's squirming, timid admission he was right about the hopelessness of dealing peacefully with the rebels. However, Oodle-Noodle's new assertion, which he sensed got telepathed with total confidence, jolted the Fafaman ruler into leaning forward with an especially wide-eyed double-take, even for a nocturnal creature. Nanofafo and Wafalawa's prodigiously long whiskers coiled and uncoiled at a panicky rate, from their own surprise. In fact, Nanofafo's coiled so tight the third time, his left whiskers somehow got entangled with his right whiskers. They strained painfully unsuccessfully to uncoil once more, until the adviser to the Fafaman ruler could calm down enough, stop his fingers from trembling so much, to unsnarl them.

What certainly did not help the Fafamafalafama or his advisers, where calming down was concerned, were the steady looks on the faces of both Captain Taylor and the rest of her away team. Like what Oodle-Noodle telepathed came as no surprise to them. In truth, Oodle-Noodle's news about the "reasonable element" caught the Earthlings off-guard as much as it did the Fafamans. But the Earthlings were able to do a far better job of suppressing their show of surprise than could their extraterrestrial hosts. They were grown used to unexpected telepaths from the tree creatures of Oomb.

Ultimately, however, not only did the Fafamafalafama manage to settle back on his throne. He also managed to settle back into his world view. A wry grin crossed his face anew, as he thought on how ridiculously naïve all of these extraterrestrials must have been if they believed they understood such a deadly important aspect of Fafaman life better than he. And he kept grinning, to say, "So send us your thoughts, Oodle-Noodle, on this 'reasonable element' among the barbarians you believe you have located."

*Of course. It is someone already in your detention, esteemed Fafamafalafama. He tried to warn outer-perimeter pyramid guards about the attack. But when he prefaced that warning by saying he had come from amongst the rebel faction, they refused to listen to him. They simply locked him up.*

"Guards?!" The Fafamafalafama snapped his fingers as he shouted.

Ten armed men burst into the room so suddenly, for Captain Taylor they seemed to have materialized out of the walls. Enhancing this illusion was the scant, green-tinted lighting leaving the entrances cast in dark shadows. Had the Fafaman ruler ordered those men to kill all the Earthlings, they would have mowed them down with their machine guns before any of those other-worlders could have even uttered, "But…," let alone tried to avoid getting shot. As the situation was, though, the Fafamafalafama said in a continued shout, "I've been told you have someone in custody who tried to warn about the attack on the wedding! I want him brought before me, immediately!"

"Immediately, most righteous Fafamafalafama." The guards made a deferential bow as they chanted in unison. "Every extra nininana you have to wait is a crime-"

"GO!!" The Fafamafalafama rose from his seat and pointed outward with a stabbing forefinger.

Every last guard who had just burst into the room instantly ceased from their extended fawning, and silently hustled themselves out side exits.

"Did this come as a surprise to you, 'Cahptahn Taylah?'"

A surprise how he snapped at the guards, impatient with their bootlicking? A surprise what Oodle-Noodle just telepathed? Helena wasn't sure which, but she was thankful no guards remained aside from the ruler's advisers, on the chance her response might anger him enough to order "Open fire!" on her, were that temptation still extant. "I thought this was an important development, esteemed Fafamafalafama." As Helena offered the most subtle deferential nod, she experienced thankful relief for having so quickly arrived upon an answer as perfectly ambiguous as the question. The truth was, neither Taylor nor any other human aboard the Smoke and Mirrors knew before then that the Oombians had located such an individual as Oodle-Noodle had just telepathed about. All they had known – providing the basis for their seeking this audience with the self-declared high ruler of Fafama – was the insistence by Oodle-Noodle and Wafoodle-Boodle that they had mind-read pockets of general unease over the use of terrorism in amidst the rebels.

"Very good, 'Cahptahn.'"

Helena sensed appreciative laughter in the Fafaman ruler's fa-la-las. Appreciation for a worthy competitor.

Meantime Oodle-Noodle was telepathing to the Earthlings only, by way of apologetic explanation, *We had to await the prisoner's reaction to hearing word of the wedding ceremony attack, to confirm his sincerity and that we didn't misread him. Confirmation of his heart-felt regret has only just in recent minutes been definitively mind-read by us.*

"Umm, if the prisoner is being kept, say, on the far side of the pyramid, how long do you suppose it might take for your security personnel to actually bring him here? We can wait." Helena held up a cautioning hand as in, *No problem. Your people can take all the time they need.*

"Yes, 'Cahptahn,' 'immediately' might not be for a while," the Fafamafalafama nodded his concession, clearly bemused. But then his facial features hardened into an animated geologic formation as he shouted, "Security?! Give me a nininana countdown to the production of the prisoner before me, whose warning you ignored!"

Taylor did not need the Oombians' mind-reading ability to sense that the pause in the intercom response to the Supreme Authority's command was about more than the security personnel simply calculating nininanas. It also included those officers processing fear over what consequences might accrue to whom, for ignoring whatever was the warning. This, as well as quickly weighing the risk-reward of offering an apology. Which resulted in a zero-confidence judgment call not to. Wherefore, the discernible nervousness in the fa-la-las that seemed to fill the room from no particular source as Tanya's ambient-mode translator erupted with, "Forty nininanas, Supremely Patient Fafamafalafama. The subject has been located and is on his way to you via express shuttle."

Helena Taylor well knew from her first mission to Fafama what "express shuttle" meant. That is, people not exiting fast enough from the subway car seized for transport services were getting bodily hurled out onto a station platform. Broken bones and other injuries were of no concern for those doing the hurling.

"So, 'Oodahl-Noodahl' I think was one of your names?" The Fafamafalafama looked aimlessly about the room. He tried unsuccessfully to appear nonchalant about communication with a mind-reading entity thousands of miles away, in orbit around his planet.

*Oodle-Noodle, correct. And my fellow traveler is Wafoodle-Boodle.*

"'Wahfoodahl-Boodahl.' Of course," the Fafaman ruler smiled. Anew, the sheer ridiculousness of their names took the edge off the reality of their mind-reading abilities. "Please explain to me where I have any part of this wrong, as we await the presentation of the prisoner. This is not an exceptional event. Someone living with the terrorists realizes he has put in his lot with a group scarcely more than animals, worse than animals for how much better they should know than to live the way they do. He discovers a means to escape from them, and then he throws himself at our mercy, offering something to prove he has renounced sheer barbarity. In this case, it is an attempted warning about one of the terrorists' heinous, entirely unprovoked attacks. Persuaded of the person's sincerity, I grant amnesty conditional on his providing a certain degree of sacrifice to our society, and that's that. The war against the barbarians goes on. What am I missing, Ambassador 'Oodahl-Noodahl?'"

*What we have mind-read from your prisoner's home community is a smooth, rolling mental landscape where the general agreement is with him, and the commitment to violent tactics stands out as a vanishingly sparse scattering of sharp peaks. The only unifying provocation is concern over what your society's industrial complex is doing to their fair share of the groundwater supply and sunset-storm-line runoff, before both make their way into the Grand Basin.*

The Fafamafalafama did not get to see, of course, what was happening on the command bridge of the Smoke and Mirrors, from where Oodle-Noodle was telepathing. Dr. Cathy James-Leung was exchanging bows of satisfaction with Oodle-Noodle, her husband Buddy, and Ali Magabu. Her satisfaction was over this first official broaching of a theme the Earthlings were hopeful would advance the Oombian cause of peaceful conflict resolution. Cathy had originated the plan, wherein husband Buddy provided his outer-edge-of-applied-physics technical assistance.

Engineer Kevin Smith-Park did not join in the celebratory bow exchange. Instead, he was gritting his teeth as he watched the proceedings unfold on the panoramic view-screen, transmitted there by Tanya's body cam. He worried how Fafama's supreme ruler would react if he picked up on Oodle-Noodle directly contradicting his assertion the terrorist attacks were "entirely unprovoked." Of course the tree creature did this when she telepathed about a "unifying provocation."

"Ahh. The water pretext again," the Fafamafalafama nodded knowingly, like he'd heard it all before.

To the Fafamafalafama's reaction, Louisa Entroper took her own turn at nodding knowingly, although no other member of the away team showed any inclination to join her.

"Tell me this, 'Oodahl-Noodahl,' or send me your thoughts. Whatever it is you are doing. If, as you suggest, the majority of the rebels don't believe in terrorism, why have they not overruled what you seem to imply are a small minority? Hmm?" On concluding this query, the

Fafamafalafama could not conceal a smile of delight, for he realized Dr. Entroper was directing her knowing nod at her fellow Earthlings. It was suggestive that if she'd opened her mouth, she would have been saying, *I hope you're getting this, Captain.*

Anyhow, before the tree person could telepath her response, Captain Helena Taylor said, "Esteemed Fafamafalafama, what we want to find out, the goal of our proposed meeting with the rebels, if we can arrange something with your prisoner, is whether there IS any general support among them for negotiation. Or whether, as your experience suggests, this is a fool's errand. If this situation is anything like situations we have had on our planet, the rebel leadership either might have no control over the actions of a few, or might be conflicted over the use of violence. In which case, we might be able to tip the scales a better direction."

"You mean, by bringing your superior military technology to bear on them if they don't, as you say, 'tip the scales a better direction'?"

Captain Taylor hesitantly nodded in the affirmative. She knew that had she not jumped in, Oodle-Noodle would have responded. The tree creature would have telepathed that it's not easy to "overrule" people with weapons if you are yourself unarmed, even if your numbers far outweigh those with the guns. Also, Taylor was convinced that, if Oodle-Noodle telepathed there was "general agreement" among the rebels against violent tactics, then this was an indisputable fact. But she was equally convinced the Fafaman ruler was nowhere near willing to accept the infallible accuracy of a telepathic tree from another planet, especially when what that tree was reporting he clearly found so hard to believe. Helena Taylor needed to indulge him, allow for his possibly being correct. She needed to frame the proposed meeting by the Earthlings with the rebels as a way to prove he was right not to want to negotiate with them. She needed to make it something he could go along with, thereby hopefully taking a first baby step towards negotiation with "the barbarians" after all. Like Kevin back aboard the Smoke and Mirrors, she fretted as well that it was too soon to expect this guy to even begin to understand that military missions undertaken by his kingdom might have led to terrorist acts, however tragically unhelpful such acts obviously were.

Thankfully, where Helena was concerned, before an awkward silence could set in that might have resulted anew in Oodle-Noodle pushing the Fafaman ruler further and faster than she feared he could go yet, the intercom abruptly ejected static. This static was succeeded by fa-la-las which translated into, "Most supremely patient Fafamafalafama, the prisoner you have ordered brought before your presence is under guard just outside-"

"Send him in NOW!!" The Fafaman ruler impatiently pounded the right arm of his throne with his fist.

Double doors seemed to swing open of their own accord. Guards on the other side took care not to show themselves as they fulfilled their duty. An armed prison warden shoved the prisoner across the entrance, even though he had already started moving forward of his own accord. The prisoner almost lost balance, but managed to stay on his feet, albeit stumbling a few steps. His chains from wrist to wrist jangled more noisily than they might have, had he not been shoved. He staggered up before the seated Fafaman ruler. Guy, Tanya, Louisa and Helena all were struck by the contrast between what they could discern of his unkempt face, and his clothing. Tousled hair, a chaos of mouse-y whiskers which had not gotten trained into anything even remotely like the handlebar moustaches of advisers Nanofafo and Wafalawa...and yet, the sleek, unsullied silkiness of the prisoner's tunic managed a velvety shimmer from the throne room's faint bioluminescence. What the Earthlings did not know was that most rebel clothing was woven from webs spun by the ahtpooloo. The ahtpooloo was a hamster-sized spider not a bit the threat posed by the ahtpah. It was so tame, in fact, that rebel children liked to keep them as pets. Ahtpooloo web filaments created a silky smooth material, once the adhesive spat upon it by the ahtpooloo for catching insects was baked off. And it was so strong, it proved nearly impossible to tear, try as much as Fafaman prison guards might have tried, whenever they threw their arrested wearers sprawling out on the floor in their jail cells.

The prison warden committed more such abuse, before the Fafamafalafama finished rising from his temporary throne. He latched onto the prisoner's shoulders, and he pushed him to his knees as he grumbled, "Bow down to the..." The warden hesitated, as he realized that in echo of his fa-la-las, unintelligible gibberish was crackling out of the supreme ruler's translator. "Bow down to the Fafamafalafama!" he completed his command finally. Thereafter, he went down on his own knees. He circled his left hand round the back of the prisoner's neck, to assure that person was bowing while he lowered his own head into a show of obeisance.

Fortunately for the prisoner, his dress-length tunic protected his knees from getting scraped against the gray shale floor, if not still painfully banged up. He winced in agony, trying not to cry out for fear how much worse it could consequently go for him. He hoped neither of his knees was suffering from bone fractures.

The prison warden watched from the corner of his eye for the Fafamafalafama to stretch out both his arms like a Watfatasa drying its wings in blinding light. Once the supreme ruler did this, the warden returned to his feet, and he pulled on the back of the prisoner's tunic. Said prisoner hastened to return to his feet as well.

"Esteemed Fafamafalafama, your enlightenment makes my spirit to bloom, even as the flounder mouse glow makes the ferns reawaken to their glorious full height after the sunset storm line has passed."

"Yes." The Fafaman ruler could not quite keep the impatience out of his voice as he nodded acknowledgement of this required ritual deference to his authority by the prison warden. "Who are you, who is he, and what exactly did he say regarding the attack on my twenty-third wedding?"

"My name is Mulualla, second keeper of prisoner chain gangs assigned to shuttle station refuse pickup. His name is Zarif. As for what he said, what barbarian infiltrating into our midst has not promised valuable information about his kind? I do not make a habit of paying attention to barbaric grunts." With all his might and fury, Mulualla again grabbed Zarif by the shoulders, and he hurled him sprawled out across the floor at the Fafamafalafama's feet. Easy to accomplish, given the prisoner's chained-together hands and wobbly knee condition, and fueled by resentment over the trouble Mulualla feared he might be in, thanks to this wretched creature. "The security detail that first detained Zarif clearly didn't listen to him either, given how they laughed off his noises." Mulualla hoped this remark would divert the blame to others, for being the first not to report up the chain of command what Zarif said.

"None of you could have known." The Fafamafalafama made a dismissive hand wave. "And I'm not sure yet, that you're not correct in your assessment, that it is not just a lucky coincidence this Zarif animal's concocted story aligned with actual events." The Fafaman ruler pointedly stared into Captain Taylor's face, which he delighted in finding plenty enough apprehensive already. "So," the Fafamafalafama looked down at the prisoner still sprawled out on the shale floor, "you have my attention, Zarif. I am listening. You can make your case to me, although you must understand the stakes have risen immeasurably high now, for both of us. Persuade me of your sincerity and realism, and I will allow our guests from other worlds to pursue this strange dream of theirs with you, so that perhaps a full measure of disillusionment will bring you all to a deeper appreciation for my empire's predicament. However, leave me with the smallest doubt as to your motives, and I will order you flown far away, to be tossed into an ahtpah web."

"The mercy of the Fafamafalafama." Wafalawa and Nanofafo extended open hands their supreme ruler's way, followed by most deferential bows.

Zarif managed to prop up his head on his chained-together hands, which he had lifted off the floor on bent elbows. Then with knuckle and tongue, he wiped away blood from the corner of his mouth where it had gotten scraped on the edge of one of the shale floor tiles, and he said, "I am here because I don't want my wife, and baby daughter especially,-"

"Ahhh-CHOO! Sorry, esteemed Fafamafalafama." Louisa Entroper bowed for the ruler's benefit. After which, she turned towards Captain Taylor and gave her a helpless look as she said, "I guess this means..."

"Our chief medical officer, Dr. Murphy-Davis,

developed what she hoped would prove at least a partial protection from the peculiar immune system reactions we experienced on our first mission here," the captain explained to the Fafamafalafama. "It might have only postponed them rather than eliminated them altogether, at least in Dr. Entroper's case." Then to Louisa, "If you would like to wait for us in the antechamber until we're done, or until you know better how you're doing..."

"No, sniff!" Louisa shook her head resolutely. "I need to be here for this."

*Because none of the rest of us can be trusted to get anything straight, especially the captain,* Helena thought to herself as she made a display of shrugging her shoulders. She had to bite her tongue to stifle herself from saying, *Have it your way.*

This interruption was just as well where Zarif was concerned. It allowed him to adjust better to the noises emitting from the translator, noises towards understandable fa-la-las as well as away into extraterrestrial gibberish. "It is bad enough for the men," his own fa-la-las went on, "but my wife and daughter, the women and children of our community have to suffer in so many respects. As more of our underground aquifer pools become contaminated by industrial waste from your technologies, the drinking and cooking situation becomes increasingly dire. Our filtration systems can't be constructed quickly enough to keep up. Yes. Go ahead and decapitate me so you don't have to hear any of this." Zarif was noticing with his nocturnal eyes that the Fafaman ruler's nostrils were flaring, his eyes were bulging, and the fingers of his left hand were moving upon the hilt of his sword like the legs of an ahtpah spinning its web. "Anything is better than seeing my family too dehydrated and hungry to move, towards the end of each ration cycle." He paused to swallow blood from his injured gums rather than spitting it out.

The Fafamafalafama's rage was mounting, at Zarif's insinuation there might be good reason for the terrorist attacks. He was inclined to take up the rebel's decapitation offer, depending... The Fafamafalafama resolved to make an observation that this barbarian, as he regarded him, appeared rather well-fed, and far from dehydrated. If Zarif's response didn't provide pause for thought... However, as the Fafaman ruler's mouth opened to utter the first syllable, a sudden realization swept away his fury and substituted bemused curiosity. "Your plant people, 'Cahptahn Taylah,'" he started instead, "'Oodahl-Noodahl,' you were thought-sending that water supply problems were the excuse for barbarian violence inflicted on my empire, yes? It appears our prisoner here does support your theory."

*Zarif, are we correct in telepathing you DON'T think of the violence as excused by the water issue?*

Zarif would not have convulsed more dramatically had he received an electric shock.

"Ahh," the Fafamafalafama nodded with contentment, "so this is the first time you experience the reception of thoughts from these other-worldly creatures. Correct me if I am wrong, Nanofafo, but doesn't this mean we needn't worry there has been any sort of collusion between this barbarian and our strange, strange guests from the far reaches of space?"

"Your wisdom is boundless, Supreme Fafamafalafama." Again Nanofafo and Wafalawa both opened a hand stretched out towards their ruler, as though they were presenting him to the Earthlings for the first time. When they bowed low, their moustache-groomed whiskers curled and uncurled with their relief over the possibility receding, that they would have to bear witness to someone's head getting lopped off. Not to mention the extreme unpleasantness of having to preside over the subsequent cleanup.

"Where did that voice in my head come from? You heard it too? You know about it?" As he worked his way to sitting up despite the awful pain in his left knee, Zarif directed his anxiety-ridden questions towards the beings with unusually narrow eye-slits he had heard came by spacecraft from another solar system.

"Th-" was as far as Louisa Entroper got, wanting to eclipse the captain's own intention of assuring the prisoner he should be grateful rather than apprehensive. Entroper's immune system's mounting reaction to Fafaman atmospheric microbes choked her off, so Helena got to be the one to say, after all, "That voice, amazingly, came from thousands of miles away (the translator substituted hundreds of pektels), from aboard our space vehicle. It was from a creature named Oodle-Noodle. She and her fellow creature, Wafoodle-Boodle, joined us when we visited their planet, Oomb. We all 'heard' what she asked you, and you need not fear her. In fact, you can be thankful for her intervention. Her general mind-reading of your populace has revealed for the leadership of Fafama that you are not alone in wanting cleaner, more plentiful water for your family. And her question of you is allowing for you to confirm her other finding. Namely, that you also are not alone among your people, when it comes to renouncing violence to deal with your concerns."

"I am *not* alone...Can they, she, hear me?" Zarif craned his head as much heavenward as his aches and pains would allow, turning one way then the other seeking some sort of sign.

*Please, Zarif, do continue to speak aloud for the benefit of the others. Wafoodle-Boodle and I will facilely grasp the full intent behind your utterances.*

"Okay," nodded Zarif. In any event, he found himself wanting to give his full attention to the Fafamans and Earthlings, the non-telepathing creatures in his immediate presence. "I am *not* alone in considering the violence done on our behalf as only putting us in greater peril from attacks by your military, Fafamafalafama. However, I do feel isolated when it comes to believing something can be done to change the course of action of a fanatical few. It's like everyone is crazy. For example, there is when Chief Vituf announced the forthcoming ahtpah attack on your ceremony, the attack I tried to get through to warn you about. He said if such attacks continue, you will have no choice but to finally accede to all of our demands. But I can tell, my associates can tell, he doesn't believe a word of that. He is going along with what a few people holding all the weapons order him to say. Otherwise, he'll lose his position and probably his life, to be replaced by someone who will be far more enthusiastically willing to spout such nonsense.

"The rest of us are put in an impossible position. One way or the other, most work that provides enough compensation to live supports the war effort. Those few laborers who speak out against this arrangement are fired. Effectively, they and their families are left to starve except to the extent others sacrifice part of their own meager rations to assist them. Those who do not speak out have to live with their conscience, the result being more suicides, more people smoking hallucinogenic plants, and more people, by far the greatest number, sitting immobilized in front of televisions when they are not at work."

"So, there is no shortage of televisions in your, um, society?" As Guy Hanson asked this, Captain Taylor found the expression on the prison guard Mulualla's face especially fascinating. The way Mulualla pursed his lips, she suspected were he to have spoken at that point, it would have been to ask about what's the big deal with watching lots of television.

"If televisions were food and water, we'd find ourselves perpetually stuffed," responded Zarif. "But this is what is even stranger: Of course there are the propaganda spectacles, exhorting us to support our military. And the devastation and pollution from the Fafaman Empire's attacks and industry are covered in the most gruesome detail. However, nothing is mentioned of the havoc I know must be wreaked on your people, Fafamafalafama, when our side unleashes missiles and parachutes ahtpahs into your midst. However, by far the most popular program among my people is the chronicle of how your next wife is chosen."

The Earthlings turned their sights on the Fafaman ruler, to watch how he took this. His assistants and the prison warden fought off an impulse to follow suit. They continued to keep their gaze respectfully averted from their leader's face, lest they engender his punishing rage for such impudence, impudence that was understandable in ignorant aliens, but was otherwise unpardonable.

The Fafamafalafama made not the least effort to reciprocate Earthling attention his way. If anything, he appeared to Helena Taylor to have lifted his chin a bit higher, on his steely resolve not to give any indication how he was reacting to Zarif's account. Helena wondered whether that resolve included the Fafaman ruler trying to image a blank slate in his mind, so even the

Oombians wouldn't know what he was about.

"It is not uncommon for, um, it is rumored that some of our warriors place bets on those candidates for the next wife who they think- I have argued with associates that we need to spend our evenings instead discussing our dilemma, to seek a better plan of action..." Noticing the Fafaman ruler's fingers resuming their ahtpah legs imitation on his sword's hilt, Zarif abruptly changed the course of his account. He grew increasingly apprehensive that from one moment to the next, this especially tall man could transition from insistently nonplussed to murderous fury. Nevertheless, Zarif felt past the point of caring, thus having made possible his going on at such brutally honest length. "The response I get is always the same," he continued. "'You're right, of course you're right,' someone will say, yet then that same someone will go on, 'but what can I do about it?' I always answer, 'Maybe continuing to discuss our terrible circumstances, maybe we will indeed not happen across anything we can do about them. However, if we don't continue to discuss them, there is absolute certainty we will have no chance of happening upon a plan.'

"Then one evening, my wife too weak to move asks me to turn on the TV for her and my daughter, who trembles visibly from a fever. And that's when I resolve: If everything that means the most to me is likely to become lost in any event, I might as well die trying for a different outcome, no matter how hopeless the odds."

"Wait." The Fafamafalafama took his itchy fingers off the hilt of his sword to raise his hand high in a universal nonverbal gesture to stop. "You appear sufficiently well-fed yourself." This was what he was going to ask about earlier. "If your wife and daughter are so famished that they are weak and sick, why aren't you simply sharing more of your rations with them? In other words," he brought down his hand for a firm, non-itchy grasp of his sword, "why shouldn't I believe you are making up this entire story?"

"I don't take even a bite of any of my family's rations. What I am fed at work, we are not allowed to smuggle any of it from the work rations hall. I have scars I can show you from when I did try to sneak out a 'fladahl' of 'wahskootoolah.'" Zarif's voice broke with a combination of frustration, anger, and grief as he turned his back on the Fafamafalafama. He tried to lift his tunic to bare his scars, even though his wrists were still manacled together. He was also wincing from the continuing pain in his left knee. It was bad enough what he knew his family suffered, without getting doubted on whether he'd done all he could to help them.

"No!" The Fafaman ruler stamped his right, booted foot as hard as he could against the slate floor. "I do not need my vision further soiled than it already is! I left off needing any additional confirmation of the savagery of your people, several orbits ago! Leave your clothing on, and tell me your work that leads your overseers to treat your family as so expendable!"

"And expendable is exactly how my family is regarded. Before I left home, I was among those assigned to gather our people's refuse, and bury it in a deep grotto. But this was not always my task. Two solar orbits ago, I used to be an instructor for older children. I have to assume it was one of my colleagues who betrayed me. I have to assume he relayed to our mutual superior my doubts we can fight and kill our way to more and cleaner water. To accompany my subsequent demotion, I was lectured on how appreciative I should be of the mercy of Chief Vituf. He could just as easily have had me chained to a boulder above ground so that after glaring light had blinded me, the sunset storm line would have finished me off. I was also advised my daughter's deprivation, now, would lead to her greater appreciation and dedication for her people once she was of female-chores-training age. During such training, I was promised she would return to receiving more adequate rations. However, what will that promise be worth, if my daughter starves to death before then?" Zarif let out a significant exhale and gave the Fafamafalafama a searching look. Captain Taylor could tell the poor man was wondering, more wearily than desperately, how much more he would have to explain before his fate was determined. Part of Zarif almost would have been relieved had the Fafamafalafama suddenly unsheathed his sword and lopped off his head, especially with his left knee in such throbbing pain.

The Fafamafalafama gave Zarif a long, quiet staredown, no further questions. Finally, though, he did make a sudden move. But not to wield his weapon. Instead, he turned his head Captain Taylor's way, leaving the rest of his chest still facing the prisoner, and he said, "'Cahptahn Taylah,' please confirm something for me about this curiously named individual."

*You should be one to be talking about curious names, Supreme Fafamafullofhimselfama,* Kevin fumed, watching from aboard the Smoke and Mirrors.

"Am I correct?" went on the Fafaman ruler. "We have someone here who can lead us into the center of power for his people? And note this well: I feel generous far beyond what they deserve when I term them people." Before the starship captain could respond, the Fafamafalafama's head swiveled Zarif's way again. "You know where this chief you spoke of is stationed?"

"I know the rotation schedule for his location based on my trash pickup schedule, yes." Zarif winced again on this last part, due to stabbing pain in his left knee when he moved to try to get more comfortable.

The Fafamafalafama nodded acknowledgment of the reasonableness of what Zarif said, if not any least awareness of or care for his agony. It made sense that a cunning beast would not stay in any one place for too long, lest the civilized hunters of the Fafaman Empire finally catch up to him. "So what is the plan, 'Cahptahn?'" His attention was turned back to Helena Taylor anew. "If it is true what this creature claims, that a minor number within his society prosecute a terrorist campaign against my people contrary to even their own leader's wishes, why not use him-" He pointed with his left forefinger down at Zarif. "-to find and surgically excise those few? Then we can address these alleged water shortage issues!"

*There are problems with that approach,* telepathed Wafoodle-Boodle. *In the abstract, you can speak of surgical excision of people, in this case people who believe in violence to advance their ends, like it's no different from removing a wart from your toe. Yet in the real world, application of your own violence to accomplish this goal will likely get more innocents killed in the process. But let us imagine this were to be one of those few, rare instances when 'surgical excision' did NOT also result in the deaths of those not at fault. Fueled all-the-more by grieving family members, the believers in violence who you went after will come to be regarded as martyrs. A new, probably bigger crop of soldiers will arise from their figurative ashes, because you will have dealt only with people who responded poorly to a problem, rather than dealing with the problem itself.*

The Fafamafalafama had to grin at the foolish naivete of the mind-messaging Oodle-Woodle-Whatever-he-she-it called itself. He shook his head in wonderment at how this extraterrestrial could be smart enough to telepath, yet dumb enough to believe what it was saying. Although at the last, before he finally spoke again, his head-shaking resolved into a knowing nod. He concluded the telepathy stuff was just another fantastic ability some creatures are born with, like the ahtpahs with their web-making. It had nothing to do with intelligence. "So what do you propose? Should I remove my sword, and then offer bottles of water and big hugs to the terrorists, as though I were a human tralalafa?"

*Actually, that is not too far off the mark of what our ancestors did to defuse a potential planet-wide conflict between those who were fruit-bearers and those who were tuber-bearers. The fruits bared their butts and love broke out.*

The Fafamafalafama's brow furrowed from puzzling out how the reproductive function worked for the tree creatures. What he knew about plant reproduction was entirely flower fertilization and cross-pollination, no butts about it.

Louisa Entroper vigorously shook her head skyward and said, "We're very happy for you, Wafoodle-Boodle, that that worked for you. But unfortunately, you seem to be a special case not anywhere- ah- not anywhere near-ahhh-CHOO!! I'm okay." Louisa waved off pre-emptively anything Captain Taylor might have wanted to repeat, regarding whether she ought to continue there in her present condition. She tried unsuccessfully to blow her nose, managing to break off only a tiny bit of the elastic greenish mucous she could tell was accumulating to headache-promoting effect in her sinuses.

Meanwhile on the navigation bridge of the Smoke and Mirrors, Kevin was turned to Oodle-Noodle, saying, "All that telepathing about tree ass appears to have gotten the Fafamawhat-the-hell-ama's aides all hot and bothered; look at those whiskers go!"

"My thinking is to move cautiously, step-by-step." Back down on Fafama, Captain Taylor strained to sound as resolute as possible. "Oodle-Noodle, you or Wafoodle-Boodle would take the lead. If you would, one of you would telepath specifically to Chief Vituf, but make your message generally available to his associates. You would telepath that with the Fafamafalafama's reluctant consent, beings from other worlds wish to intervene with ideas for solving the water supply issues. That other-world group would be led to the present headquarters of the rebel government by a rebel who had the courage to seek solutions that did not involve showering young ahtpahs on innocent people. The purpose of this initial meeting would be simply to share the ideas with the rebel leadership face-to-face, so that they might take a full measure of the other-worlders' character. Oodle-Noodle, you would telepath Chief Vituf that during this time, you and Wafoodle-Boodle will be doing continual mind-read sweeps, for any violent schemes their terrorist element might want to take advantage of the meeting to attempt. You would observe that that is how the attack on the wedding ritual was foiled. And you would add that our spacecraft is sufficiently armed to transform their occupied area to ashes, were we to so desire."

*I think we would prefer, Captain, to put this in terms of your non-interest in actually using any of the vast array of weaponry with which your government insisted on arming the Smoke and Mirrors.*

"Very well."

"Esteemed Fafamafalafama, I sense a far greater problem to the alien spacecraft captain's plan." Nanofafo bowed his head low with arms extended way out to his sides. This was the traditional unresisting submission to the will of the Fafaman ruler, should he take so much offense to an adviser's remark that he wanted to lop off his head. Evidence for this adviser's apprehension could be observed in the twitching manner in which his whiskers were curling and uncurling; well Nanofafo knew that were the Fafamafalafama to take such offense, a resulting decapitation wouldn't be the first time.

"Resume your official posture, Nanofafo, and let us hear whether you have discerned the same issue as occurred to me several nininanas ago."

"Truly fascinating, Captain," counselor Ali Magabu whispered from back aboard the Smoke and Mirrors. Helena could just barely make out what he was saying through her earpiece. "I am guessing that whatever Nanofafo says, the Fafamafalafama will get away with claiming he thought of it first, whether or not he actually did. Only our Oombian friends will know for sure."

"Your patience with the sluggish intellects of your nevertheless loyal subjects is a miraculous blessing, Fafamafalafama." Nanofafo stood back up to his full, if short, height. His recitation of the ritual self-debasement most appropriate to the occasion got injected with a strong semblance of sincerity by his relief over the Fafaman ruler's tame reaction. "It is not clear to me how we can trust this proposed dialogue with the rebel barbarians will not digress into a bonding of our enemies with our other-world intruders. Perhaps the barbarians will try to demonize the pinnacle of civilization we have achieved, as symbolized by the central pyramid. All I am hearing is how we have poisoned and diminished the barbarian water supply."

Helena noticed Dr. Entroper nodding to Nanofafo's remarks as though to say, *He does have a point*. This fueled Helena's voiced reaction into something far stronger than she moments-ago contemplated. "This man," Helena pointed down at Zarif rubbing his left knee, "came here to denounce the violent ways of some of the rebels! He told us of how he and his family have gotten mistreated for his complaining to a co-worker about the terrorism supposedly done on his behalf! Believe me, I am not hearing anything particularly appealing going on with the rebels! This includes their chief, who Zarif says is too concerned with maintaining his own power to try putting an end to the attack schemes! I am not hearing anything that makes me at all attracted by, feel any romance towards their side!"

The Fafamafalafama's nocturnally adapted eyes opened even wider than normal, on Helena Taylor using the term, romance. At least, that's how it seemed to Tanya and Guy standing there beside the captain.

Back aboard the Smoke and Mirrors, Helena's husband Chris, viewing the scene on the video monitor in the privacy of their bedroom suite, experienced his stomach feeling like it descended into a bottomless pit. *What*, he thought to himself, as much as he knew he really needed to stop being so paranoid, *was Helena trying to assure the Fafamafalafama that the rebel chief wasn't her type?*

"'Cahptahn Taylah' makes her points." The Fafaman ruler appeared to be addressing the ceiling, which meant he was addressing the tree creatures from Oomb up in orbit around Fafama on the Smoke and Mirrors. "But my brilliant counselor's observations, comparable to what I was thinking the moment this creature came into our presence, do contain some merit."

Zarif was still fighting down spasms of knee pain to keep from moaning. But Captain Taylor thought the way the Fafamafalafama motioned towards "this creature," Zarif might as well have been a sack of rocks someone had unceremoniously dumped on the floor.

"'Cahptahn Taylah,' if we are being honest with one another, ultimately our initial encounters on your first trip to Fafama-"

"Answering your distress message, esteemed Fafamafalafama." This time Helena was the one bowing low, her arms spread far out to either side, aping Nanofafo's moments-earlier submissive gesture.

"As I would have expected you to have been assigned to do, by a civilization containing advisers of 'Dahctah Ahntropah's' caliber." The Fafamafalafama made a subtle bow combined with a subtle gesture Louisa's way. "What I was saying, 'Cahptahn Helenah Taylah,' we did not conclude our first encounters on an especially trustful note, did we?"

"Permission to interject, Captain?"

"Sergeant Hanson?! Uh, yes, of course. Permission granted." Helena couldn't conceal her surprise.

"Thank you, Captain." Guy Hanson took a step forward from his position standing between her and Flight Officer Tanya Petrovsky.

Louisa Entroper was stationed the captain's other side, nursing her increasingly distressed nose as well as favoring growing discomfort getting experienced inside her ears and navel.

"Esteemed Fafamafalafama," went on Guy, "to help satisfy your understandable concern that you don't know us well enough to be able to trust our motives and steadfastness of intent, I make an offer not yet vetted by

Captain Taylor."

"I'm sorry, Sergeant Hanson." Dr. Entroper's stern voice conveyed disapproving alarm pitched perfectly to her words. "The last time I checked, a Marine offering anything in the midst of delicate negotiations, without first clearing it with his superior civilian officer, was considered an act of extreme insubordination! Sniff!" Entroper exercised every last bit of willpower she could conjure, to stifle a sneeze finishing off this reprimand.

"Excuse me, Dr. Entroper." It was Helena's turn at the stern voice. "The last time I checked, it was also for the top civilian officer to decide when a subordinate's behavior constituted insubordination, not another subordinate."

Due to her sinus distress, all Louisa could do in response was to try to blow her nose again, with continued lack of success.

"Please proceed, Sergeant Hanson. Under these unusual circumstances, your brainstorming is in exact accordance with my orders."

"Yes, Captain. Thank you, Captain. My proposed offer is this: that I accompany the captain's negotiating team with an explosive device lock-strapped to my body. The Fafamafalafama would have possession of the remote trigger mechanism. Suppose during the meeting with the rebels, he starts to get the impression, in any way, we are here to take sides with them to plot against the Fafaman Empire. With the press of a button, he can take us out, along with a good portion of the rebel central leadership."

For thirty seconds that seemed to observers aboard the Smoke and Mirrors like a whole lot longer, the only sound to be heard when Hanson finished was Entroper sniffling.

"I would need to make one additional stipulation, 'Cahptahn Taylah,'" the Fafamafalafama said at last. "The device would have to be of our own design and installation onto your courageous subject's body. With oversight by one of your own technical advisers for such things, of course."

"That stipulation could be easily accommodated, Fafamafalafama." Helena strained to keep her tone steady, unperturbed. "But certainly you must understand that were Sergeant Hanson's proposal adopted, there is a huge risk for us, which gets back to that trust factor you mentioned."

"Of course, 'Cahptahn,'" the Fafaman ruler nodded with an expansive grin. "What is to stop me from seizing an opportunity, once your negotiating team arrives at a central meeting place of the barbarian leadership, to kill off the destructive plant at its roots? Apart from the possibility your remaining crew aboard your spacecraft would likely respond with a devastating attack on our central pyramid? In which case, maybe it is better to have that explosive device deployed with our guards aboard your spacecraft. But no. Such destruction of your so-called Smoke and Mirrors would likely result in a second craft of its type arriving to avenge the destruction of the first craft. But back to the original, generous proposal by your loyal subject 'Hahnsahn.' 'Cahptahn,' you might not whole-heartedly endorse, free of any reservations, the no-violence-under-any-circumstances stance of your tree person guest passengers. However, I apprehend that even were I to press the button, and turn your 'Sahgahnt Hahnsahn' into so much fleshy shrapnel, your fellow crew members would not find the strength to exact the cost I would have so richly earned."

*On our planet Oomb, we do not consider the use of*

*violence to be any kind of strength. Rather we regard that as a powerful indicator of weakness.*

The Fafamafalafama smiled like Helena imagined he smiled when one of his multitude of children did something childish, such as casting off a diaper to go running around the room giggly naked. Then he went on as he was going to, had Oodle-Noodle telepathed nothing, "It is clear to me, 'Cahptahn Taylah,' that for this meeting plan to proceed, I will have to offer a counterweight to the personal risk 'Hahnsahn' has volunteered. So this is my offer: Accompanied by a pair of her security guards, the Varafafafa, my twenty-third wife, would travel with you and this Zarif creature into the ulcerous belly of barbarian territory."

"Yula-Oh." Sergeant Hanson wished he could have stifled himself before the first syllable left his mouth.

"Yulala, yes, 'Hahnsahn,' that WAS her name before she officially joined my family." The Fafaman ruler turned his attention away from Captain Taylor to nod at Guy with a knowing smile. "You would agree with me, yes?, that I am not going to want to endanger her by setting off your explosive gear?"

"In other words, Fafamafalafama," Helena sought to draw his attention away from Sergeant Hanson, as much as to pursue this balance-of-risks thing further, "you would not be willing to sacrifice your wife for the sake of maybe dealing a devastating blow to the command center of the rebels?" She was careful not to say *one of your wives.*

"To be honest with you, 'Cahptahn,' the insertion of the Varafafafa into this situation would only be to assure you I do not see the worth of pushing the button on a bomb-rigged 'Hahnsahn,' especially for what that could do to our future relations with you people from Earth. Unless of course you DID evidence any desire, any further weakness, to collude with our enemy against us. As I see it, the whole reason for one of your own to so put his life at risk in the first place is to deal concretely with that trust issue of which we have spoken.

"To go even further, 'Cahptahn,' and read my mind well on this matter, 'Oodahl-Noodahl' and your 'Boodahl' associate, I expect this project of yours to come to nothing. Zarif, were you thinking you are setting up some sort of ambush, you now know what consequences would result. They are consequences where yes, the Varafafafa's life WOULD get sacrificed, to her greater glory and the honor of her original family. But assuming you are as you present yourself, you are about to find out how lonesome are people of good intent among the barbarians. The result, I should hope, will be to move to a new level of understanding between us, 'Cahptahn Taylah.' Then 'Dahctah Ahntropah,' I receive the most positive impression you can help us to negotiate not only additional protections from the potential threat of the creatures of 'Tahktohktahk,' but also additional plans we might be able to implement to cope decisively with the barbarians."

Nanofafo and Wafalawa's nodding approval of their ruler's remarks got so prolonged, Tanya wondered whether they were going to be able to stop without someone slapping them in the face.

Louisa Entroper had her own affirmative head shake, saying, "Of course we must first vigorously pursue every last chance-" This was as far as she got, in an increasingly nasal voice, when WANK! WANK! TOOT! TOOT! Bioluminescent pastel-violet mucous secretions took the shapes of little trumpets that shot from her nostrils and ears, and made a bulge in her sky-blue Smoke and Mirrors uniform, where one was projecting from her navel.

The Fafamafalafama unsheathed his long sword so quickly, its swish! proved loud enough for the observers on the navigation bridge aboard the Smoke and Mirrors to hear by way of Tanya's body cam.

WANK! W- TOOT! T- Before the bizarre products of Dr. Entroper's immune-system interaction, synergistically, with the Fafaman biosphere could complete their second fanfare, the Fafamafalafama had yanked them from ears and nose and, tossing them in the air, sliced them up into confetti-sized bits which fluttered gray and lifeless to the floor. His remaining task was to slice open Entroper's uniform at waist level, careful not to even prick her skin, then lightning-fast pull a mucous horn from its navel generation site to meet the same fate as the rest.

When Entroper finished doing double-takes, she turned to Helena and said, "You see? You see, Oodle-Noodle?" She lifted her head ceiling-ward before returning her focus on the captain. "The Fafamafalafama's weapon has proven useful for something."

"Mm-hm," Helena made the curtest nod. She couldn't help thinking about how the first time she experienced this peculiar nasal discharge, the mucous trumpets had leapt from people's bodily orifices on their own. They had seemed to lock themselves in something like a square dance, from which they had collapsed into harmless puddles. The bizarre discomfort had ended with no sword play necessary.

## Chapter 10

"Sergeant Frankly?! Sergeant Frankly?!"

"Wait for us, Sergeant Frankly!"

"Hola? Hello?!"

Marine Corps Sergeant Fred Frankly pivoted around so he was continuing his jog backwards. That way, he confirmed who called out to him without interrupting his daily six-mile run of the beaten path encircling the Earthling settlement on Oomb named Oombinquen. *Yeah, so it IS Pedro's two nothin'-but-trouble sisters. Wonder what they're dribblin' their bosoms after me about? Shit, if I had any sense I'd leave 'em in my f-n' dust. Maybe I can scare them away for good, by giving them a little peek inside my twisted head. Ask them who wants to take a ride on my heat-seeking missile. Naw, better not. Not after the incident back aboard the Smoke and Mirrors, with that woman who got in a panic fearing one wink from me meant big trouble ahead.* "Okay," Sergeant Frankly huffed reluctantly, as he ground to a halt. With Gloria and Jerri catching up to him, he self-consciously patted at the shower cap he'd donned to keep off nibbling fripe. For some reason, the fripe only confused men's hair, not women's, with the fur of critters native to Oomb. Frankly had to remind himself for the umpteenth time it was either the shower cap, or he would have to put up with bald patches amidst his crew cut. "What do you two moooochachas want?" He drew out the "moo" like he were a cow. "Hey, don't you have two little caca-makers? What'd you do with them? C'mon, don't tell me you got all out of breath from just speed-walking!"

"Aye, no!" Gloria and Jerri shook their heads emphatically. They giggled over the simultaneity of their responses. And the thinner one, Gloria, didn't wait for her chest to stop heaving, from her exertion running down the sergeant, before she added, "That uniform you are wearing, how you say? It takes our breath away! Yes!"

"Sí!" Jerri nodded vigorously in agreement.

"Even with this cap on my head so I look like Granny came out of a shower or somethin'? C'mon!"

"Is better we not see your full head or we faint! Yes!"

Gloria slapped Jerri's arm. "Que tu dices con una cabeza llena? Ay, Chica!" *What are you saying about a full head?*

Jerri turned on Gloria with a wide-open, gasping mouth. How could her sister be thinking something so nasty?

Sergeant Fred Frankly rolled his eyes. "Back to my question about your bundles of crying and caca: What did you promise someone, for her to carry those two hot poop-tatoes while you're out here?"

"Ay, you think those were our babies?" Gloria gave Jerri a look that would have telepathed, were she able, *You have to back me up on this.*

Fred turned Jerri's way. He gave her an arched eyebrow that dared her to vouch for what he was near certain was a lie, would have been certain was a lie had he cared to keep better track of the time-travelling settlers from some fifty years in the past.

"You know Dana and Mariela?" Jerri rose to the challenge with an unflinching, unblinking stare-down of the sergeant. "We were watching their preciosos *(precious ones)* for them so they could work in their garden. Sí." Jerri nodded with determination. It helped that the part about Dana and Mariela working in the garden was true.

"Okay, whatever." Frankly still wasn't convinced. "So

back to yours truly. You stopped me on my run so you could pass out from my good looks, granny cap and all? Better be something more than that!"

"After your run, there are two boys we want you to make very jealous for us." Gloria gave Sergeant Frankly her most pleading look.

"Juan and Carlos," Jerri chimed in.

"Oh yeah, Juan and Carlos," Frankly nodded with easy recollection. "They work at the television station. Are they the ones who did some of their own gardening, planting seeds in you, I mean in Dana and Mariela?" He tripped up on purpose to watch Jerri and Gloria squirm. "What is this, anyway, high school? Maybe after I make them jealous, we can all go out for milkshakes?"

"Aye, no," Jerri whined. "You have to believe us. The fathers of our children were not included when they raptured us."

"Sí, they are old men now," Gloria giggled. "So tell us, Mister. If you have to choose, which one of us you choose? Then maybe you have a friend who can go with the other, and we walk arm-in-arm past the TV station like we are two couples. And what is wrong with acting like we are in high school?"

"When they raptured us here, we WERE in high school!" Jerri added.

"Aye, sí!" Gloria nodded as if they were both effectively hammering their point home.

Sergeant Fred Frankly moved his eyes from Gloria to Jerri, then back again to Gloria, then back again to Jerri. With a dawning, mischief-laden grin, he said, "Why do I have to choose?"

That is exactly when Gloria noticed something extraordinary above the sergeant's head. Well up in the sky, a red beam ended in a white flash. Another and another and another ensued, until several red beams ending in white flashes happened at the same time.

"What is that?" Gloria pointed. "Are we getting attacked?!"

Frankly had already spun around to see what was distracting Gloria. From down the hill in the settlement, he could hear people's various exclamations as they were noticing the light display covering an ever-broader area of the pastel-blue firmament.

"Dunno. Maybe something's gone bonkers with the laser mesh shield!" Frankly was already sprinting towards the command and control underground entrance; Gloria and Jerri were nowhere near to hear his response.

***

"Meteor shower." Buddy had his eyes glued to read-outs from an infrared spectroscopic scan as Fred Frankly joined his subordinates, already gathered around the civilian officer from the Smoke and Mirrors.

"Looked like it was petering out by the time I got here." Sergeant Frankly couldn't help relief suffusing his voice. "Adkins, Koher, Robertson: Spread the news. And watch out for the Perez sisters, 'specially if you're a family man; those rocks aren't the only things burning up in the atmosphere!"

"Actually, the laser shield is doing an excellent job of incineration well before the meteors descend to anywhere near those highest-altitude traces of air. That's the good news." Buddy Leung swiveled around in his chair to face Frankly and the other security personnel who remained after the three marines had left, under order to assure the colonists all was well. "We can be confident the mesh won't allow even the tiniest missiles to sneak through. But what's not so good news, maybe, um, well, puzzling for me and hopefully nothing-"

"What's not so good news, Officer Leung, is that you can't simply f-n' spit out what you're goin' to say! Cripes!"

"Sorry, Sergeant," Buddy responded, plainly conceding Frankly's point, however brutally it was delivered. "Back when we were descending into the orbital plane aboard the Smoke and Mirrors, I thought I had correctly identified and tracked the asteroid cluster in question. It looked like it was going to miss Oomb by a million miles. I'm going to have to launch a probe to double-check my trajectory analysis on other potential space junk hazards in this system, see where I might have gone wrong. I suppose it is not that big a deal since Oomb has the laser mesh protection."

***

"Ha! I finally have you!" Don Típico made this celebratory shout in Spanish as he grabbed Norma in his arms next to the experimental garden. "Like a butterfly with the most beautiful wings, I knew that sooner or later you would stop by some flowers long enough for me to seize you!"

"Ay! Bruto! (*Brute!*) You care nothing for the strange lights in the sky?!" Norma only pushed against Típico's white-suited chest with her left hand. Her right hand was pointing upwards.

"Ay, woman, you did not hear the security people? That was only a meteorite shower the lasers were destroying, before it could hit the surface of Oomb!"

"There they are again!" Ludi exclaimed nearby.

Típico got distracted just enough for Norma to wriggle free. "Caramba!" he complained.

That is when so many additional fireworks sparklers, to what Pedro would have likened them, filled the sky.

***

*Oh-oh. Well, I'm going to have to alert Mafoosoola as well as Sergeant Frankly.* Buddy Leung was left alone at the console monitor; all the security personnel were busy reassuring the settlers and the tree people they were likely experiencing a second wave from the same meteor shower. Or at least Buddy was still officially deeming it a meteor shower, despite something else curious besides his having totally mis-extrapolated its path, apparently. All the rocks from the first shower and all but one from the additional onslaught proved composed of pretty typical stuff, before their laser incineration. But that one exception was the first of its kind ever recorded, if it was a meteorite. The typical stuff included iron metal alloys mixed with feldspar and pyroxene. They were classic equilibrated chondrites. And the laser mesh had turned them to ashes before they could develop a fusion crust entering the atmosphere. The exception registered as having contained, prior to its incineration, an aluminum alloy unknown to Earth civilization, plus known as well as other unknown alloys of various metals, plus trace amounts of several substances including diamonds. In other words, it had to have been intelligently manufactured. Debris from some extraterrestrial civilization's accident? A probe of some sort intentionally sent to join the fate of the meteorites? It was impossible to tell.

*I should also alert Helena.*

***

"Officer Kwit-Nik," Captain Mat-kek-tek tongue-clicked aboard the saucer craft from Tictoctic, as he pawed anxiously at the corrugated metal deck of the navigation bridge with an articulated, cloven hand-hoof, "were our mighty Dek-Fook-Tek available, I would have him confirm what I am gathering from the data output screens. Nothing is so obvious to me that by comparison, his grasp of the situation does not prove me blind."

"We are not capable of giving the thanks Dek-Fook-Tek deserves, for the clarity of his vision with which he blesses us," all deer-like creatures assembled on the navigation bridge rose up on their hind legs to ritually chant.

"Oh, no," Kwit-Nik shook his head as he resumed his seat at the data screen console. He well knew if he did not protest his commander's self-deprecation fervently enough, more chest scars could be in his near future, before the pain had fully subsided from the last time such an honor had been bestowed on him. "It is my obligation to share out, as fast as possible, all impressions I dare to suppose I might be gathering from these screens. That way, Captain Mat-kek-tek, my frequent misapprehensions can be cleared up by your Dek-Fook-Tek-inspired interventions, before they can fester into tragically misinformed decisions." Kwit-Nik well anticipated the result, were he to put Mat-kek-tek on the spot. That is, were he to challenge Captain Mat-kek-tek to be the first to say what data he was gleaning from those output screens. And Kwit-Nik knew what to expect, were he to ask the captain what that data meant, especially in conjunction with the videos the scout saucer sent, before it was itself disintegrated by the laser mesh network. The saucer's captain would have been hard-pressed to say a thing. Such was the depth of his ignorance, the extent of both his science and math illiteracy.

"Please proceed," the captain nodded his approving acknowledgement, "and let us hope that this time, Dek-Fook-Tek's inspiration, enough of it, has finally made its way down to your level."

"I can only hope, Captain." At least, Kwit-Nik gathered gratefully, it didn't sound like he was going to have to trick Mat-kek-tek into thinking he'd arrived at the data analysis by himself. Kwit-Nik could give the results, and his superior could say, *Congratulations on only needing double the pektels to reach those conclusions as I did.*

It had been a far different matter with staging the meteorite showers in the first place. Fresh from the doctor patching up his antler wounds, Kwit-Nik had known he needed to lead the captain into voicing the plan first. Or else, he would face additional chest-piercing way too soon, possibly to a fatal extent. "I don't know how we are going to test out their defense capabilities, Captain Mat-kek-tek," had crisply tongue-clicked Officer Kwit-Nik, "without giving away our presence and thus removing the element of surprise. All we have are our scout saucer missiles, and our detection-cloakable translucent globules. We think the former owners of those globules used them to exert subtle, gravitationally-induced shifts in certain object trajectories. Huge trajectory shifts resulted, the farther the objects travelled. And of course there are random asteroid and meteorite clusters scattered about the target solar system." Looks had gotten exchanged between Kwit-Nik and every other intelligent being from Tictoctic aboard the saucer craft, save for the captain. Everyone else had easily figured out from Kwit-Nik's clues the best course of action. They were just waiting for it to dawn on the captain so he could be the first to say it. Ears had been twitching because well they knew, had any of them been the one to make the connection, it wouldn't be only Officer Kwit-Nik requiring his bloodied chest to get patched up.

"Ba-" As fast as it had spontaneously issued from his

mouth, the captain had stifled his bray of delight over having finally solved the puzzle. In the depths of denial as to his own mental sluggishness, he had felt he needed to admonish his crew for THEIR mental sluggishness. "I have waited long enough for one of you, any of you, to deduce what was so very clear to me before Officer Kwit-Nik got through half of what he had to say. And I am surprised at you in particular, Officer Kwit-Nik, that given your areas of expertise, I should now have to advise YOU!"

"Just another reminder of how helpless we are without your leadership, Captain Mat-kek-tek, especially since Dek-Fook-Tek is not available." Kwit-Nik had turned the captain's way to bow way low. He was grateful for thereby being able to roll his eyes, unnoticed.

Nodding satisfaction with Kwit-Nik's self-effacement, the captain had gone on, "It is really so simple. We launch one of the globules, cloaked, to redirect a meteorite cluster otherwise more than likely to miss the target planet, so that the cluster will score a direct hit. And we embed a scout saucer to record the results. Of course, that saucer gets hidden from detection by the meteorites in its midst."

The rest of the crew on the navigation bridge had flopped themselves back into their respective chairs as though someone had forcefully pushed them there. Technical Officer Tak-venk-tit had made like it was all he could do to gather his wits. "Captain Mat-kek-tek," he had bleated faintly, "you are perhaps the only one aside from Dek-Fook-Tek-"

"Dek-Fook-Tek is the only one who can be only," went the tongue-clicked chant from the others, including the captain.

Officer Tak-venk-tit had swallowed hard as, with a

head tilt, he had affected to have graciously accepted this chastening. Pursuant to which he had said, "Officer Kwit-Nik, do you have anything to add?"

"Officer Tak-venk-tit, do I have anything to add to the beauty of the sunrise that does not cast a shadow upon it? What I have instead is a confirmation of just such a meteorite cluster of which doubtless you were already aware, Captain."

Mat-kek-tek had nodded approvingly, as he had told himself this little detail was too trivial for someone in his position to have to bother to keep track of, but for which he deserved credit all the same.

"The meteorite cluster is not two million lek-leks out from the target planet."

"Officer Kwit-Nik, implement my plan immediately!"

That was then.

"As we can see on this screen overlay," Kwit-Nik was proceeding presently with his findings, "the network of satellite-based lasers that vaporized the first swarm of the target meteorite cluster got reconfigured. This complicates our task. We won't be able to pick off the satellites very easily, once our new decoys betray their new coordinates. Clearly, those coordinates shift automatically after each laser discharge. Now there is another rock cluster close enough by, mostly iron alloys, and we do have a magnetic pulse cannon..." This was where Kwit-Nik sensed he should again allow the captain to assemble the puzzle pieces to the captain's greater glory...and his own chest's longer time to heal.

"No," Captain Mat-kek-tek shook his head, still bathing in the fantasy that they'd depended on him for how to go about the initial probe into the fourth planet's defenses. "The implications were like a sharpened set of antlers, impaling my brain hundreds of pektels ago. And so, I waited endlessly for you to ruminate on the data about the first wave of the meteor shower."

Here Kwit-Nik couldn't help realizing that hundreds of pektels ago was *before* the data had started coming in, about the first wave of the meteorite shower.

"I might as well wait on you, Officer Kwit-Nik, to express the plan for others assembled here who might be even slower than you."

"An honor I do not deserve, Captain." Kwit-Nik hoped no trace of sarcasm seeped through his baaing. "The proposal would be to again use a detection-cloaked globule. This time, we lure an iron-alloy-heavy meteor swarm onto a collision course with the target planet. We follow directly behind. As the swarm approaches the boundary horizon for the laser network, we send out a magnetic pulse which will cause the meteors to cluster in a circle. Then we speed through the center of that circle. That circle, rather than our spacecraft, will take all the fire. During our subsequent occupation, we find and destroy the control center for the laser defense network, so reinforcements will not have trouble arriving should they prove necessary. Have I gotten the details essentially correct, Captain Mat-kek-tek?" Kwit-Nik felt he had to add this question, as he noticed the captain make a telltale huff midway through his explanation. It was, Kwit-Nik well knew, Mat-kek-tek's huff of jealousy over being incapable of having formulated anything close to this plan, even had he been given days to mull over the information garnered from the scout saucers.

"Essentially correct, Officer Kwit-Nik. You will need to make a few tweaks, but I am sure if you keep yourself adequately surrendered to the glory of Dek-Fook-Tek, we can be confident those tweaks will occur to you as you proceed." Mat-kek-tek was gone delusional, fretting over his subordinate getting a little too boastfully carried away with himself again. *Officer Kwit-Nik might be in need of an even deeper slashing than I bestowed upon him recently, to be reminded of how appreciative he ought to be for his multitude of blessings.* But this would have to wait until after the occupation was successfully achieved, so Kwit-Nik would not have the excuse of needing recovery time to avoid fulfillment of his duty.

"Captain Mat-kek-tek, the brilliance of your strategy so stuns me into immobility, I could be trampled under foot by you before I could even take my next paw at the floor." Officer Tak-venk-tit had also noticed the captain's huff, and he concluded further fawning over his superior was well advised.

"It is but a dull reflection from the blinding power of Dek-Fook-Tek, Officer," the captain responded, down on all fours with one leg genuflected facing the guesstimated direction towards their home planet, where Dek-Fook-Tek was located. "And now I must go off alone, to make my own special preparations." With that, Captain Mat-kek-tek literally galloped off the navigation bridge. He was bound for his own stall where he could continue sharpening his antlers with his bahvek, and not have to endure the mindless surveillance of his subordinates who did not yet understand that keeping his antlers knife-edge point-y was as crucial as anything else they did.

# Chapter 11

The river vessel carrying Zarif and his entourage from another planet slowly rounded a stalagmite-strewn corner, deep within the rebels' cavern complex. It came into view of construction workers completing the latest staging area for Chief Vituf's subterranean command. Chief Vituf himself seemed to hardly notice. He appeared to have his attention given over to watching his staff re-assemble his regal throne. But certainly, Captain Taylor thought to herself, he must have witnessed that re-assembly enough other times, it couldn't possibly still hold him so enthralled. Zarif had said the chief's base of operation got moved at least once every seven days. *No,* Counselor Magabu thought to HIS self, *this is the behavior of a truly troubled spirit. He seizes every moment he can, to brood most despairingly over his circumstances, even when he has to hide away what he is doing in full view.*

What also struck both Ali and Helena was the enormous, mottled-gray mushroom hollowed out to serve as the crown on Chief Vituf's head. The way it glinted in the surprising amount of ambient light suggested a protective glazing, like ceramic glazing.

That mushroom crown was only the latest in a series of fascinating revelations about life among the rebels.

Even though it was only a few hours ago, it seemed to the negotiating team like it could have been a full day earlier they had landed in rebel territory, for all the novelty with which they had been bombarded. Not the least of it had met their ears, as soon as they de-boarded the shuttle pod. "They" had not included Ali Magabu's wife. Ali's wife, Tanya Petrovsky, had piloted down from the Smoke and Mirrors, and she was to remain strapped in the cockpit for the duration of the diplomatic mission.

Anyhow, Zarif had led the procession off the hybrid flight vehicle, followed by armed Fafaman guards escorting the Varafafafa, Captain Taylor, Counselor Magabu, and Sergeant Hanson.

No surprise, the rebel troops had greeted their guests at gunpoint. And they had greeted the shuttle pod with a surface-to-air missile aimed its way from one of their three armed launchers.

Ali had taken curious comfort from the one rebel trooper's fa-la-las translating so rapidly. "If we detect that any least aspect of this imposition of your presence upon us is a trick, the only uncertainty about your doom will be whether it is to be swift, or lingering." *Truly suspicion-laden bitterness,* Ali would have conceded, but at least the sentence itself confirmed the rebel language's significant similarity to that spoken within the Fafaman Empire. The ease with which the translator previously handled Zarif's speech was not some fluke caused by the rebel prisoner having had to hang around guards within the pyramid for so long.

The real surprise had still awaited, as Zarif and company had stepped down onto a plateau worn so smooth by the daily onslaught of the sunset storm line, aircraft including the shuttle could land there with ease. The real surprise had been hearing the unmistakable roar and hiss of crashing surf. This gently rhythmic noise had seemed to be emanating from a complex of baked-clay adobe apartment dwellings set into the base of a red sandstone cliff, like a scene out of the American southwest, Helena had marveled.

Meantime, the jagged ridgeline above and beyond had gotten set in such sharp relief by the rising sun, the Varafafafa had imagined with a discernible shudder some awful, unknown monster's impossibly large, tooth-laden lower jaw.

Sergeant Hanson had noticed the Varafafafa's distress. He had wondered what he could do to comfort her without provoking her guards to train their rifles on him, the same as the rebel troops were already. The way she had held her elbows to tuck her arms under her chest, she had appeared chilled with fright.

Captain Taylor had been oblivious to the sergeant's focus, her own self wondering whether there was some peculiar air circulation through the deserted-looking adobe apartment complex that simulated the surf. Could that sound be a cinematic version of what one heard, holding up a conch shell to one's ear?

For his part, Ali Magabu had marveled at how the pitch-black openings in the adobe edifices seemed to amplify the haunting quality of those mysterious surf sounds, especially as daylight spilling down the hillside brought out the reddish-oranges of the dried clay.

Before any of the Earthlings had even been able to ask Zarif if he knew wherefore the surf ambience, a rebel trooper had taken a few steps towards the meek-seeming Varafafafa. The twenty-third wife's guards had trained their weapons his way, as Hanson imagined might have been his own reward for showing concern over her comfort. Said rebel trooper had held up before himself what resembled an antique laptop computer. He had proceeded to pick confidently dexterously at its keyboard with one hand, his other hand balancing it with apparent ease. He had emanated nonchalance regarding the weapon-brandishing directed his way by the Varafafafa's security personnel. He had even stepped provocatively closer to the twenty-third wife, and had alternated looking up at her with looking back down at the laptop screen.

Sergeant Hanson had craned his neck as much as he

thought he could without being too obvious about it. He had wanted to see exactly what the rebel with the laptop was about. So he hadn't been surprised when at last the rebel had announced into a microphone embedded in the computer, "I can confirm this is the Varafafafa, Chief Vituf!"

What the sergeant had espied was that the computer-literate rebel trooper was studying selected screen shots from the Varafafafa's wedding ceremony. Those screen shots were from the portion of the ceremony before the young ahtpahs got parachuted in to disrupt the proceedings, and television coverage got blacked out for the civilian population on Fafama as much as for humans trillions of miles away on Earth. No wonder, Hanson had remarked to himself, that the trooper had given him a significant look while reporting back to Vituf he confirmed the woman's identity. Several photos showed the marine sergeant plainly visible beside the twenty-third wife for the ceremony.

"Continue to proceed with extreme caution, defense worker." Chief Vituf's voice had gotten emitted in static–decayed fa-la-las from the computer as it was near-instantaneously translated. "The strength of the ahtpah web, the stealth of the blinding-light prowler."

"The strength of the ahtpah web, the stealth of the blinding-light prowler," the trooper had repeated. He had hooked his hands together by curled fingers, pulling for strength. Then he had flattened their palms together, prayer-like, with a wavy motion signifying stealth. The laptop was set aside so he could execute these customary gestures of rebel unity.

What had happened next, Ali had mused to himself, could hardly have been more unexpected, truly, had one of the rebels extracted a chocolate chip cookie from his nose. Perhaps there would have been some marginal tempering of the mental jolt, were the Earthlings not so variously distracted by the out-of-place seaside ambience, the one trooper's identity-confirming scrutiny of the Varafafafa, and the odd vista spread out before them. Without this competition for their attention, they might have noticed more specifically what adorned every rebel's neck. Then not have been quite so surprised when one of the rebels had emerged from behind a group of them, to force upon every guest save Zarif a necklace round his or her neck. Each necklace had come from a collection of them, draped neatly across the rebel's right arm raised for that purpose. It had been as though he were a napkin-wielding waiter in some snooty restaurant, Sergeant Hanson hadn't been able to help thinking as he received his own. *At least he isn't trying to give me a peck on the cheek like this was Hawai'i or something,* Guy had further reflected to himself.

In the same vein, Helena Taylor would have been reminded of her and Chris's Hawaiian honeymoon on the Big Island, when they were likewise greeted with leis. Only these were not real or simulated wreaths of Hawaiian flowers. These necklaces were composed of strung-together, ceramic-glazed mushrooms. They had glowed in the early morning shadows with the same pale-green bioluminescence of many other Fafaman nocturnally-adapted life forms.

One Varafafafa guard had trained his weapon on the small of the necklace bearer's back, which was covered in the silky smoothness of a simple gray tunic. And rebel troops had trained their guns on both Varafafafa guards. But the necklace bearer had feigned all-around, nonchalant obliviousness as he had adorned, with the strung-together Fafaman mushrooms, the neck of the Varafafafa guard who was not training his weapon on his back. Topping that off with which, he had said, "As you can tell from our necklaces, after not too many sunset storm lines, the glow of the tapastrahs fades to a most dignified mottled gray. This symbolizes how wisdom gained over time is the province of all. It is not the province only of some arbitrarily chosen leader worshipped as though he alone were the supreme creator of life. Our Chief Vituf assumes the heaviest burden. Reluctantly yet determinedly, he sacrifices such pleasures as the rest of us enjoy when we sire children with a mate. He devotes his time to studying the proper applications of that wisdom."

"Ahh, 'some arbitrarily chosen leader.' You know to whom Chief Vituf is referring," the Fafamafalafama had fa-la-laed to his closest advisors plus his first wife, the Varalawa, with no Earthling translators around. The Fafamans had been gathered in the comfort of his main throne room, centrally located at the apex of the third, hundred-solar-orbits-old accretion of the central pyramid. They had been eavesdropping on Captain Taylor's stubbornly naïve diplomatic mission, or at least that is how the Fafamafalafama had viewed it.

Where the Fafaman ruler was concerned, the aliens from Earth were in the thrall of the ridiculously mobile tree creatures possessed of equally ridiculous names. But at least the "Ahthlahns" set up an oral and visual monitoring of their disgusting proceedings with the rebel barbarians, as he thought of them. That way, the Fafamafalafama could decide directly for himself whether anything was transpiring, too terribly inimical to the welfare of his kingdom. With a simple flick of a switch succeeded by a press of a button, he could detonate the recklessly bold

Sergeant Hanson. At any moment, he could put a quick end to it, even if this meant possibly injuring if not outright killing his newly-married twenty-third wife before they had even consummated their union. Not to mention Captain Taylor and – the only clear positive guaranteed by such a decision – lots of rebels, perhaps a significant portion of the rebel leadership.

Of course, the Fafamafalafama regretted those foolish alien beings were going along with such a foolish plan in the first place, where they were trusting what this Zarif animal said about enough rebels prepared to do civilized business. However, the Fafamafalafama regretted almost as much the "Ahthlahns" not arranging to carefully monitor his reactions to what he was monitoring of their foolish mission. What fun he could have had! He could have feigned such boiling rage, about to blow up Hanson, again and again, just to watch Captain Taylor squirm!

However, his audience had consisted of only the people he trusted the most. The Fafaman ruler knew that any such eruption-threatening anger he might express would have been liable to precipitate among them the most irritating competition possible. Which was: Who could have offered him the greatest ritual fawning that also sounded the least calculated to patronizingly salve his vast ego? This in mind, the Fafamafalafama had gone on, "Let us suppose that, by some impossibly good fortune, 'Cahptahn Taylah' and her crew from 'Ahth' could convince the barbarians to accept my plan, to have the 'Ahth' people satisfy their water demands in exchange for no more terrorist acts waged against us. Do we doubt this Chief Vituf would, in his great modesty, have a statue carved to honor his having said, 'Yes'? Ha!" The Fafaman ruler had concluded with a rare booming outburst, well satisfied by his formulation of something so witty.

"Hee! Hee! Hee!" had cackled, like Earth chimpanzees, his advisors and even his first wife. But actually, they were more relieved than amused that the Fafamafalafama found a way to laugh off the rebel leader's insult.

"Chief Vituf, pah!" the Fafamafalafama had spit. It had seemed to the Varalawa as though the barbarian's mere name was the same on her husband's tongue as a flafla accidentally flying into his mouth. "If only 'Cahptahn Taylah' were not living in a fantasy world. If only it were true the barbarians could be so easily pacified, we never need interact with them, ever again!" He had proceeded to reflect to himself, *I should terminate the 'Ahth' people's hopelessly naïve task right now. I should make a simple transmission to their shuttle officer, to inform her I am giving them a sixty nininana countdown for turning around and leaving barbarian territory before I flip the switch and press the button...as though I would be capable of such unprovoked barbarity myself! But most likely, their even-more-naïve 'Oodahl' acquaintances would tell them to ignore my bluster. That they had read my mind to know I could not really bring myself to perform such an act. Am I correct, tree people of 'Ahmb'?*

*You are correct, esteemed Fafamafalafama.*

*Hmm,* the Fafaman ruler had nodded with a smile the first wife, the Varalawa, had found most curiously enigmatic. Her own self not a mind reader, she would never know what was occurring to him. Namely, that whenever he was referred to as "esteemed," especially in the case of the tree creatures, those saying or thought-sending this weren't necessarily doing the esteeming themselves. They could merely be describing how they had witnessed others behaving towards him.

***

"Traitor! We should have had your wife and daughter fed to a noonthrah!"

What had gotten ugly tense was when the necklace bearer came before Zarif. Knowing what question was coming, Zarif had volunteered before he could be asked, "Whether I had left it at home or not, either way I was not going to be able to get this far wearing my necklace. As it turned out, I realized it was still with me when I was clinging onto an ahtpah web filament. That filament was depending from the leg of a fahtahmahpah in flight, a supernaturally strong fahtahmahpah to have made such an escape from an ahtpah web. Anyhow, I shed my treasured tapastrah chain mid-air, as I was crossing into Fafamafalafama territory. Otherwise, the first people I came across there, once I separated myself from the filament, would surely have impeded my progress any closer to the pyramid with my information. And because I took this chance, look who we have here with plans to alleviate our water problems!"

This was when the necklace bearer had called Zarif a traitor, and suggested his family ought to have met an especially horrific fate.

Ali Magabu received Captain Taylor's nodded approval to attempt to defuse the situation, or at least to return the tension to its previous level. And so he had interposed, "Zarif was arrested, and his warning about the impending wedding ceremony attack ignored. Only because our new friends from another planet were able to read the minds of the plotters of that senseless, deadly act, only because of their intervention were we able to stop it before it could get worse than it already had.

What Zarif served to do, once he finally received an audience with the Fafamafalafama, was to challenge him. Zarif challenged the Fafamafalafama to consider the prospect that several people among the rebels wanted to work out practical solutions with the Fafaman Empire, not start a war. Truly, Zarif and his family deserve special commendation, rather than getting fed to the noonthrah, whatever THAT is!"

"The noonthrah one can encounter in a most unpleasant way, should one take a wrong turn on his unassisted exploration of our cavern network." The necklace bearer had stuck his face in Ali's to say this. His teeth had glowed with the bioluminescence from his latest mushroom snack. His breath reminded Ali of the peculiar odor left on his hand after handling a dirt-encrusted earthworm in the bio-lab garden. "Initially, it seems to the victim that he has stepped into some sort of tar pool with an odd row of stalagmites lining each side. But then, he feels a thick, viscous liquid pulling him further and further down. Bubbles pop on its surface, releasing a gas that makes him too groggy to resist. The supposed stalagmites lean in towards him. They crisscross over his head, and he feels already the digestive acids eating through his footwear. There is a growing fiery sensation on his feet which spreads rapidly up his legs. His final thought before a helplessly screaming descent into lost consciousness is that this is one way how it feels to get eaten!"

"Again," Ali had tried to sound sternly, dismissively unaffected by the grisly picture the necklace bearer painted, "not exactly the type of treatment, truly, one would think awaited anyone associated with finally alleviating your water pollution and water shortage problems."

To this, the necklace bearer had turned his back on

everyone, aimed his rear end Zarif's way, squatted and, with a concerted strain, let out a long fart, staccato-style. "Fine! Maybe you are not a traitor," he had said as he had resumed facing the guests. The necklace bearer had taken a tone Helena Taylor would have likened to a child saying *Sorry* when she didn't really mean it, after being so compelled by her parents. "You, and anyone else who actually believes we can make business, make anything constructive, with the Fafaman Empire, you are hopelessly naïve. Who is the leader of the people from the planet who came here last year? No, wait, it's you." He had pointed at Helena. "'Cahhptahhn Taylahh,' I recognize you from the news on our television. But you are not the ones who telepathed Chief Vituf, about volunteering the twenty-third wife of the Fafamafalafama as collateral so he would agree to meet with you. The telepathers are from another planet altogether, yes?"

Captain Taylor had made the universally recognized affirmative nod.

"I should like to warn them personally, as I am warning you." The necklace bearer did not want to take his admonishing eyes off Ali nor the captain, to pull down into place his protective shades, as his co-rebels were doing with the growing glare of stars-fade. So, he had squinted them to the thinnest possible slits instead, as he had continued, "Soon enough, the Fafamafalafama will demonstrate the full extent of your naiveté. That is, if you really believe there is any kind of reasonable agreement to be had with him and his supporters, by which they will abide."

*The Fafamafalafama agrees your guests from another world are hopelessly naïve. He thinks Captain Taylor and the rest are beyond foolish for believing there is any kind of reasonable agreement to be made with*

*Chief Vituf and HIS supporters! For us beings from Oomb, what this goes to show is that in an ideal world, everyone on both sides of your water-supply-based conflict would all join together in being hopelessly naïve!*

The gun-toting rebels had tilted their weapons skywards to go with their lifted eyes. They were fearfully searching out the source of the voice that simultaneously had entered all their heads.

The two of the three mobile missile-launchers not trained on the landed shuttle craft from the Smoke and Mirrors had been likewise tilted, and gotten wobbled about to fix on a target unknown.

The twenty-third wife's security had finally found themselves blinded by the growing, flooding sunlight. So they had been donning their visors, just when Sergeant Hanson noticed Yulala sneaking him a glance before she donned hers. She had curled her mouth in a manner suggestive she was trying to share with him nonverbally how frustrating she was finding the displayed behaviors. Or was she? Guy had shrugged his shoulders in empathetic helplessness. He had hoped his shoulder-shrugging made sense to Yulala as having established common ground with her. That his smitten-ness with her wasn't causing him to become delusional, to read into her behavior something that wasn't really there. Well he knew such smitten-ness wasn't a good thing, since she was a wife of the Fafaman ruler...however much he might personally disparage one man laying claim to multiple women.

"Excuse me. I did not hear your name." Once again with Helena's blessing, Ali had spoken to the necklace bearer.

"I am Mituv, the official coordinator for this contingent of our perimeter guard." The necklace bearer had made a broad, sweeping gesture with his right arm, the one not burdened by necklaces. He did this to indicate the other rebels still occupied with scanning the heavens for trouble.

"I am Ali Magabu, chief counselor aboard the interplanetary spacecraft from the planet Earth." Ali had made a slight bow. "Mituv, are you perhaps suggesting your Chief Vituf is naïve for agreeing to an audience with us, despite our bringing along one of the Fafamafalafama's wives as collateral?"

Of course, Ali had been unable to see past the ultimate poker-face black of Mituv's sun visor lens, to gather the entirety of his nonverbal reaction to his challenging question. But the writhing contortions of Mituv's mouth had made clear it was all he could do to restrain himself.

During which, Sergeant Hanson had wondered whether behind *her* sun visors, Yulala was secretly wistfully regarding the Earthling soldier with thought of what might have been. And he had been uncertain whether her security detail was eyeing him suspiciously. He had been blocked from knowing for sure by their own visors. Otherwise, he would have directed another helpless shoulder shrug the Varafafafa's way.

"Chief Vituf does not want it to ever be said he did not give a proposal for a peaceful resolution a chance, however dubious the source!" Mituv had finally uttered in a most declarative fashion. Ali had gathered Mituv was trying to make it sound like he was merely giving the plainly obvious response to Ali's provocation all along, rather than something he labored mightily to formulate. "Now you will enter the façade through our security checkpoint, except for you." Mituv had marched over to put himself in the way of the twenty-third wife and her security entourage. "You will return aboard the shuttle craft to await further instructions."

"Yoon-hee?" Helena had spoken under her breath.

"I'm patching through to the Fafamafalafama now, Captain," Yoon-hee's response had gone off in Helena's earpiece. Yoon-hee had easily anticipated the concern Mituv's unexpected protocol change would create.

Ali Magabu had offered up himself to be the first to undergo the security inspection before entering what translated as "the façade."

Meanwhile, Captain Taylor had turned her back on the rebels, and Sergeant Hanson had gone over beside her, to make it appear she was engaged in conversation with him. They had hoped to avoid suspicion over what she was really about.

"Patched through, Captain."

"Esteemed Fafamafalafama," Helena had spoken as close to a whisper as she thought could still be heard on the other side of the patch-through, "just want to confirm you're comfortable with this change. Obviously, there are things, or something, we are going to see they don't want your people to know about. They must be assuming we will keep it to ourselves, not share it with you. This, um, seems naïve, unless they think they have something to hold over our heads to assure we do not share it with you. Maybe they plan to keep one of us hostage. In which case, there are worse places for the Varafafafa to be than by Flight Officer Tanya Petrovsky's side aboard the shuttle. She is probably safer there, even with the rebel missile launcher trained on it."

"Ahhh, 'Cahhhptahhhn,'!" The Fafamafalafama had pointedly bellowed "captain" in a most deep-throated English, to not require translation. "I am surprised," he had gone on, back to fa-la-las, with easily discernible amusement in his voice. "You neglect to mention another way this change makes the Varafafafa safer. That is, should I decide to detonate 'Sahjahnt Hahnsahn'! 'Cahhhptahhhn,'" the Fafaman ruler had employed his admonishing you-should-know-better voice, "I need you to stay alive long enough, at least, for me to hear you concede what I have known the whole time about those barbarians."

"I am glad you still care, esteemed Fafamafalafama," had been the captain's last words to him as she had allowed armed rebel troops to direct her over to someone wielding a baton covered in a black, foam-appearing material. Which baton had reminded her of the airport security baton she saw on display in the American History Museum back on Earth in Washington, D.C.

"Captain, I'm not sure the Fafamafalafama does not have a point. You might want to consider-" That had been when Dr. Louisa Entroper's lecturing voice had cut out, mercifully where Helena was concerned. The captain had just stepped through a door-sized aperture in the impressively multi-tiered adobe structure. The baton did beep-beep a couple times, but the security inspector had seemed satisfied Captain Taylor's night-vision goggles and translator were all that set it off; he didn't go searching for other electronic stuff on her, such as the implanted earpiece and mike. Same for Ali Magabu. As for what was worn by Sergeant Hanson, his shirt buttons were full of plastic explosive. They could have been remote-detonated by the Fafamafalafama, if Yoon-hee weren't putting out a steady, automatic transmission on the radio frequency guaranteed to disrupt that remote. The baton wasn't going to sense plastic explosive in any event. There were also the nanobots Hanson periodically needed to scratch out of his scalp like so much dandruff. They were intended to maintain a communication relay system with both the Smoke and Mirrors and the Fafamafalafama. This, in case some geological features were to disrupt the direct body cam feed from Magabu's night-vision goggles. Sergeant Hanson had needed to assure a nanobot always got itched off his scalp, close enough to Magabu to receive his body cam transmission. Said nanobot was then to send along that transmission to the other itched-off nanobots. The nanobots were hi-tech breadcrumbs, leading Ali's body cam transmissions' way out of the rebel stronghold interior. Fortunately, the security baton hadn't sensed the nanobots, and fortunately for Helena, there was a small gap between Ali entering "the façade" and the first dandruff-shed nanobots activating. That gap had spared her the full brunt of Entroper's counsel.

Once the Earthlings had gone a few steps in, past the façade, they had looked back from where they came. This mere action had yielded the next significant revelation. They were expecting to see the only daylight streaming in from the doorway-sized aperture through which they entered, with a ceiling low enough to foster claustrophobia. Instead, there were several shafts of light coming from all different heights, and as much as one hundred feet to either side. It had been enough light for the night-vision goggles to not yet be necessary, and for the rebels to have to keep on their sun visors.

*The façade, of course*, had been what Hanson, Magabu and Taylor had thought simultaneously. This was not an adobe apartment complex set into the mountainside at all. This was an empty shell that might as well have been a movie set, Hanson had marveled. No wonder it looked so spookily abandoned from the outside.

From this most unexpected revelation, the Earthlings had guessed easily why the rebels didn't want anyone with the Fafaman Empire to see what the façade was. Better the Empire's troops, even the Fafamafalafama himself, believe the rebels positioned their missile launchers in amidst a virtual hive of family homes. Clearly, the idea was that fear of harming innocent women and children would inhibit the Fafaman Empire from an all-out attack on rebel military resources. Moreover, maybe many of the rebels' own people did not know about the fakery of this adobe structure. If the Fafamafalafama were to order it destroyed, oh the propaganda advantage to then be gained so painlessly! Were subjects of the Empire to learn of such an attack, it might even garner the rebels some support from behind enemy lines, beyond who-knew-how-many already doubted the Fafamafalafama's leadership. Additional potential recruits for future violence against the Empire…

The rebels had herded the Earthlings and Zarif towards an open-air car with a seesaw lever in the middle, sitting on a railroad track. As they did so, it had quickly become clear no explanation for the façade was to be offered. However, Captain Taylor had resolved that something else they noticed was not going to go unremarked upon. "Umm, I have to make an observation, Mituv," she had said. "The ambient surf noises I thought I heard outside the façade, they are that much more evident inside."

"And a sea-air fragrance is mixing with the cavern dankness in a truly most pungent way I would add, Captain," had chimed in Ali.

Some rebel troops had brought their rifle-like guns to the ready, and anxiously turned from Taylor to Magabu, and back again. An observer might have thought those two starship officers were suddenly brandishing swords rather than mere words. As everyone piled onto the rail car, Mituv had made a once-again, universally-used gesture, this time for the troops to cool it and lower their weapons. With everyone seated aboard, he had tsk-tsk-tsked, "'Cahhptahhhn Taylahh,'" followed by fa-la-las of, "you should also have noticed the ebb and flow of wind-tunnel-effect breezes! We are on an ancient fault line that extends from here to the Grand Basin! Over millions of orbits of our sun, the sunset storm line has filled in this profound crack in our planet with rock and dust debris, while transverse tectonic upheavals have raised a mountain range parallel to the Grand Basin coastline!" Mituv had been shouting because two troops working the seesaw had set the open-air car into loud motion, making a clickity-clack noise. "More recently, burrowing ahtpahs have dug a network of tunnels! Those tunnels have included an especially long one from where we entered, all the way out to the Basin! Maybe instinct compelled them to follow the fault-line path! For whatever reason, the resulting incursion of Grand Basin waters has awarded them with decimating attacks by Basin creatures more terrifying even than trapdoor ahtpahs! We keep the few remaining ahtpahs penned up, safely blocked away from us by noonthrahs! Those noonthrahs are either naturally situated, or we labored to re-establish them on the threshold of those passageways where ahtpahs still dwell! And steel cable nets stretched across the three exits to the sea prevent the fearsome Basin creatures from decimating us! However, thankfully!, those nets do not keep out the winds, including especially the sunset storm line winds! If anything, a tunneling effect enhances them! You shall see how we depend on those winds for our energy requirements!"

"So you're saying the sea air and echoes from Grand

Basin surf make it all the way to here from the coast?!" Captain Taylor had shouted above the clickity-clack din.

And Sergeant Hanson had scratched at his scalp to release more nanobots for the hi-tech breadcrumb trail.

"Yes they do! Would that they were carried on enough wind to blow away the damage we suffer from the Fafaman Empire's industrialization, 'Cahhptahhn Taylahh'!"

As Helena expected, their subsequent grand tour of the rebel subterranean network before their audience with Chief Vituf had built on this theme. The Fafaman Empire was laying waste to the noble endeavors of the rebels. Apparently, if you went back far enough in the history of Fafaman civilization, there used to be a collective of tribes. Only one of those tribes was under sway of the earlier Fafamafalafamas with their central-pyramid-building scheme. Healthy commerce flourished among all the tribes. But, as the central pyramid grew in both size and stature, more and more tribes aligned themselves with the Fafamafalafama. That forced those tribes living closer to the Grand Basin to bond together in their efforts to transform the naturally occurring caverns and burrowing ahtpah tunnel networks into an alternative to pyramids. Which alternative for shelter from the sunset storm line also proved safer than the former daily retreat into the closest available tralalafas. The pyramid and subterranean life styles might have been able to peacefully co-exist if not for the pyramid society's increasing reliance on polluting fuels drilled out of the ground, especially for a space exploration program. "You need to thank your new, other-world acquaintances who read minds and transmit thoughts! If they had not told us of how you developed starlight-powered space vehicles, not requiring fuel burning," Mituv had pointedly noted,

"Chief Vituf would never have agreed to talk with you!"

The sequence of the guided tour of the rebel's subterranean world had played out in a way expected by both Taylor and Magabu. It had supported, it had documented, their version of Fafaman history. Training to implement terrorist plans had been neither shown as an officially sanctioned activity, nor condemned as something beyond Chief Vituf's control. Instead, nothing but positive greatness had been revealed of rebel industriousness. Captain Taylor had guesstimated that one dramatically enormous cavern, right on the fault line, dwarfed the largest grotto in Mammoth Caves back on Earth. It featured a row of windmills. Their propellers turned majestically slowly, animated around the clock by the wind tunnel effect. Those subterranean windmills were said to supply ample electricity to the entire cavern and tunnel network.

"Bomb the façade to rubble, plus other façades they alluded to, and no more wind tunnel effect, no more electricity, Captain," Kevin's voice from aboard the Smoke and Mirrors had crackled faintly in Helena, Ali and Guy's ears, after said voice's sojourn through numerous nanobot "breadcrumbs." "I'd say that's their most important reason for their adobe village mockups."

*Thank you for confirming the nanobots are operating, and yes we agree*, Captain Taylor had focused on thinking. She had expected Oodle-Noodle back aboard the Smoke and Mirrors to read her mind, then pass along what was read to Kevin. Why risk the rebel troops wondering why she appeared to be talking to herself? She would have had to have raised her voice to a shout, for Kevin to have made out what she was saying above the combined din of the railroad car's clickity-clacks, and the underground wind mills' whup-whup-whups, as relayed from Magabu's body cam through the breadcrumb-trail nanobots.

Along with the tour down the main fault line, there had been side trips to branching-off tunnels. Those tunnels were Fafaman-excavated in recent times, as well as ahtpah-burrowed from ancient times. There were tapastrah gardens, where mushrooms grew as tall as coconut trees. Their log-sized stems got sawed up and specially cured to build the cubicle-like walls that defined rooms inside a typical rebel family burrow. Their caps got slivered and cured with a process that gave them a rubbery texture, to stuff pillowcases woven from ahtpooloo webbing.

By far the most curious side trip to show off rebel ingenuity had been to a rebel dairy farm. There, they milked albino-pink-ish aphid-like creatures the size of goats, named foolapahs. The foolapahs clung to the sofa-sized caps of very short-stemmed squat mushrooms, and they nibbled away at them as they got milked. The visitors would have been offered samples to sip, but such luxury could not be afforded. There was not nearly an adequate milk supply for the rebels, the children especially. Which observation had led naturally to a consideration of the awful consequences of activity by the Fafaman Empire.

"The area we have to quarantine is growing more and more expansive," Mituv had said as they waited, rail car temporarily brought to a halt, for a stainless steel wall to slide aside. "And as we will also show you, where our people's general welfare is concerned, no area is safe from the corrosive impact of the Empire's industry and militarization."

The guests had been brought to another grotto chamber stuffed full of tapastrahs of all varied sizes. Only, that wasn't what was supposed to be growing there. Petroleum contaminating the ground water proved lethal to the subterranean crops which used to flourish. The smaller, edible, mushroom-like tapastrahs could have made up for the lost food supply, since they broke down the petroleum into innocent, nutritious substances before drawing them into their growth cycle. But they were also drawing in toxic metals. And the tree-sized tapastrahs provided far more wall and pillow material than the rebels could possibly use, AND it had become impossible to trade them with the empire for any items, additional food especially, that they COULD use.

Then there was the grotto lake which had to be cut off from the rest. A new diversionary channel was excavated around it, to connect two other lakes to either side of it. This way, lethal metals such as copper that leeched into it wouldn't kill off other blind, albino sea life. The grotto itself had reeked of dead fish and petrol fumes. On its shores, greenish water had lapped gently at washed-up carcasses. Still shedding their remaining bioluminescence, those dead bodies had included one seven-foot-long, ghostly white creature bearing a striking resemblance to artists' conceptions of the aquatic reptile Plesiosaurus, that lived during the dinosaur epochs millions of years ago back on Earth. It had been complete with four flippers comparable to a sea turtle's, and a long, snake-like neck.

Other nightmare tour stops had included a pile of rubble claimed to have been the result of an Empire bombing raid. That alleged attack purportedly caused a cave-in of one of the habitation burrow chambers. Dozens of women and children were buried alive. Amidst the rubble, the Earthlings had noticed fragments of cubicle walls cut from tapastrah stems, and broken toy ahtpahs said to have been carved and assembled from bush-sized tapastrahs.

Such amazing vistas of both a distressingly nightmarish and eerily dreamy quality! There had been so many of them, the encounter at long last with the rebel leader seemed anticlimactic to the Earthlings. Truly pathetic, Ali Magabu thought to himself, how helpless Chief Vituf looked, sporting his oversized, mottled-gray tapastrah crown. This, while he seemed to camouflage contemplation of his troubled circumstances as distraction by the umpteenth reassembly of the rebels' lead command post, kept nomadic for security reasons.

"The strength of the ahtpah web, the stealth of the blinding-light prowler," said Mituv.

Captain Taylor intuited that Mituv's impatience, waiting for Chief Vituf to officially recognize his newly-arrived guests, moved him to speak before he was supposed to.

To the open-mouthed gasps of advisors and armed security flanking him, the chief made a dismissive hand wave as he wearily responded in kind, "The strength of the ahtpah web, the stealth of the blinding-light prowler. You tiny-eyed creatures from another planet, there are these nonsense noises I hear, issuing from your direction whenever one of us speaks. You are armed with devices which cleverly convert our language into something you can understand?" He had gone on to this question without skipping a beat from his repetition of the rebel solidarity phrases.

"And they just as cleverly also convert our 'nonsense noises' into something YOU can understand." Captain Taylor patted a translator strapped to her belt as she spoke. "Chief Vituf, you honor us by your acceptance of an audience with us. Especially since, as I suspect you are already well aware, we have spent so much time in the society of people with whom you are in conflict." Captain Taylor offered a subtle bow in line with the bow she'd witnessed the rebels making to one another. She'd easily figured out she would have come off as patronizing, had she messed with the rebel solidarity phrase...not to mention how the Fafamafalafama, eavesdropping from afar, might have taken that particular diplomatic gesture. "My name is Helena Taylor, captain of the light-powered space vehicle, Smoke and Mirrors. This is my counselor, Ali Magabu, and my security assistant, Guy Hanson. We have come here from the planet Earth, in a different solar system. Light takes five years to travel from Fafama to Earth, but we are able to make that trip in a matter of weeks."

Once all the fa-la-las of the translation were done with, Chief Vituf redirected his attention from Helena to Mituv. "Where is this man's tapastrah necklace that even the people from 'Ahth' are wearing?" He motioned towards Zarif.

"Chief Vituf," Mituv said, shooting Zarif a dirty look, "this is Zarif, Zarif the traitor who went over to the enemy to warn them about plans to resist the Empire's authority! Of course he needed to cast aside any symbols of his former allegiance!"

Chief Vituf made a nod Zarif's way for him to respond to this allegation.

"Chief Vituf, what he calls 'plans to resist the Empire's authority' constituted a plot to have adolescent ahtpahs kill as many people as possible at the Fafamafalafama's latest wedding! I was acting on behalf of my people, because you know how destructive the retaliation would have been, had such plans succeeded! But I was put under immediate arrest! My warning was ignored! It was the creatures from other worlds who prevented a full-on ahtpah rampage! What I got to do was argue before the Fafaman emperor that the terrorists do not represent most of us!, and that we ought to give these beings of 'Ahth,' and from another planet where they read minds, an opportunity to help us solve our problems!"

"I have to wonder whether you concern yourself even half as much with the terrorism we feel each day inflicted by the Fafaman Empire!, the terrorism of neglect for our circumstances!" Chief Vituf turned back to Mituv and said, "Bestow upon Zarif a new necklace."

Captain Taylor got the feeling that as Mituv "bestowed" one of the extra mushroom necklaces round Zarif's neck, he would have strangled him with it, had he thought he could get away with that.

There was too much glare from her night-vision goggles for Captain Taylor to tell how Zarif was receiving his new necklace. By the time she removed them to get a better look, it was already too late. But she did finally determine why generally, the labyrinth of rebel caverns seemed better lit than inside the central pyramid. The rebels could not benefit from the bioluminescence of daily-surfacing flounder mice, with their pale-green glow comparable to fireflies on Earth. It was impossible for flounder mice to survive in cavern environments, where Fafama's tree-sized curly ferns could not grow. Those pancake-shaped furry animals depended on such plants for a symbiotic relationship. And so, the rebels had installed pearly-looking objects the size of basketballs all about their various underground lairs. Those objects glowed with enough bluish-green light to provide far better illumination to a far larger area than did the ubiquitous bioluminescent cavern-wall lichen.

Up until then, the luminescence had seemed to be

emanating from stalagmite clusters near cavern and grotto walls. It might well have crossed the Earthlings' minds to ask about it. However, there had just been too many other features, both good and bad, on which to focus, including features to where Mituv's guided tour had been drawing their attention. Ali Magabu had assumed there was some relatively prosaic explanation. Perhaps there was some sort of bioluminescent moss or fungus far more naturally prolific with its light expression than that aforementioned lichen. As a consequence, illumination was the one thing which these nocturnal humans did not have to bother over supplementing, especially given their ever-nocturnal nature.

What Captain Taylor noticed, she right away figured probably went on elsewhere during the tour. However, the rebels involved were so low-key unobtrusive about it, neither she nor her fellow Earthlings had noticed previously. That was, they lifted orbs from where they had been concealed, orbs with a glow that was fading, to replace them with other orbs in full radiance.

"With your permission to initiate an address to you, Chief Vituf..."

The rebel chief nodded his assent to Helena Taylor.

"We have topics of far more import to discuss, but I am curious about the glowing orbs your people trade out when their light becomes too diminished. Umm..." Helena thought her concession, about there being higher priority items, might help break the ice. That is, the ice she sensed when Chief Vituf met her prior utterance with his non-sequitur obsession over Zarif's lack of a tapastrah necklace.

"The glowing orbs? Ahh, yes! The clapastrahs! There must not have been time for you to visit one of the few remaining unpolluted grotto lakes where they can still thrive. The clapastrahmoo layers over a grain of sand irritant with enough special mucous to fill a hollowed-out tapastrah top. This mucous hardens into a smooth, perfectly-round material that glows for several days with the blue-green luminescence. We use that luminescence to enchant our stalagmite clusters. Anyway, once the mucous hardens to become a clapastrah, the clapastrahmoo's top shell opens wide at the bottom of a lake. The clapastrah's glow attracts a fish named the foofoofamoomoola, when it is ready to mate. The luminescent clapastrah highlights the porous irregularities inside the roof of the clapastrahmoo's top shell. As a result, foofoofamoomoola couples cluster there to deposit eggs and sperm inside the pores. They believe it is a coral formation. This reproductive function is their final act before the shell clamps down on them to digest them. Days later, the fertilized eggs hatch foofoofamoomoola youth allowed to leave for the open lake, where they mature for the next fatal mating.

"'Cahhptahhn Taylahh,' an apt inquiry you have made into our principle lighting source. It seems to me another clapastrah of sorts by which you might be attracting us to a trap equally deadly to us. Yes, there is a problem." Chief Vituf paused for an extended sigh. Helena, Ali and Guy all got the same impression, whether or not the chief was going overly melodramatic. He winded himself, was physically exhausted, simply from the exertion to say what he had thus far said. "You know, do you not?" he turned, finally, to ask the man beside him wearing a much smaller mushroom cap. That mushroom cap was so diminutive, in fact, Guy would have likened it to a skull cap that ballooned out at the top.

"I do know." The man sporting the mushroom skull cap made his own subtle nod of acknowledgement.

"'Cahhptahhn,' I will have my leading advisor, Chuzzle, explain to you." With that, Chief Vituf stood on one leg, crossed it with his other leg, and squatted to rest his elbows on the crossed leg with his face set contemplatively between his hands.

Chuzzle made a sweeping gesture towards Chief Vituf as though, Ali thought, he was a magician drawing attention towards his beautiful assistant. The chief's over-sized tapastrah crown completed the ridiculousness of this tableau for the Earthling counselor.

"The problem is this, 'Cahhptahhn,'" Chuzzle went on with a severe tone to his voice. "The Fafaman Emperor may well have put his twenty-third wife at our mercy to emphasize, to suggest the sincerity of his faith in your plan to deal with the empire's one-sided contamination of an already-meager water supply. He may well have done this, even while his Empire continues with acts of aggression against us. And we have no reason to doubt the sincerity of your intent. But the fact remains that you have toured our society, you have closely examined our vulnerabilities. You could return to the Fafaman emperor and share with him all he would need to know for his massive military structure to deal us a crippling blow from which we would never recover. So the problem becomes how we could ever allow any of you to leave here alive." The awful import of what Chuzzle said gave his mirthless grin with which he topped it off a decidedly sadistic edge for Captain Helena Taylor.

"Ah-ha." Helena made a knowing nod. She was straining not to allow the rebels to see any least nonverbal sign of her growing panic over the obviously heightened perilousness of the diplomatic mission's circumstances. "So, perhaps WE are the ones who have been led into a clapastrahmoo type of trap by the glowing promise of Zarif's reasonable noises. I am not finished." To Chuzzle starting to open his mouth, she held up a "halt" hand. "There is some history to our arrival on your planet you ought to find useful, if you know what is good for you. One orbit of your sun ago, we received a distress signal from scientists of the Fafaman Empire. This signal contained a message, explaining their fear of an invasion from another planet intent on collecting and harvesting sentient beings such as yourselves and ourselves for their food supply. Closer examination of the relevant data has convinced us the threat might be real. It is on account of this horrific possibility that we make a presence for the second time on your planet. We do care about the ramifications for the future of your species. But to be perfectly honest with you, if we did not suspect there was the strong potential of considerable danger for *our* species, I doubt we would have returned to Fafama. Especially after the treatment we perceive we received on our first visit. And so, suppose we get ourselves killed by you for our efforts to mediate your dispute with the Fafaman Empire. In that case, I can guarantee you that all of you, both sides, will be left by my fellow Earthlings to fend for yourselves against this threat far greater than any you pose to one another. Moreover, I cannot guarantee you my fellow Earthlings will not retaliate in ways that would make you beg for the tender mercies of the Fafamafalafama. That is, if they don't decide to mount an offensive against you very soon to rescue us, thanks to your clear threat to our well-being. You see, they have been monitoring every last detail of this meeting. They could forward everything we have learned about you to the Fafaman leader, whether you executed us or not." As much as Taylor wanted to repay Chuzzle's mirthless grin with interest, she disciplined herself to maintain her mouth grimly, determinedly flatlined.

Chuzzle strained not to snarl back at Captain Taylor, bare his teeth, as he made another sweeping gesture towards Chief Vituf.

"You have my attention, 'Cahhptahhn,' and you also have my personal commitment to your safety for the duration of this mission you haveso generously undertaken." Chief Vituf maintained his one-legged, oddly contemplative-appearing posture for this announcement. The throne reassembled for the umpteenth time behind him remained decidedly neglected.

"Chief Vituf, I petition your permission to be excused for a return to other pressing business." Chuzzle swung both arms aside, thereby leaving his body vulnerably wide-open between them. This, for an at-the-mercy-of-your-decision bow.

"Permission granted," was how the chief's response translated as he made no effort to achieve eye contact. Rather, he kept his tapastrah-capped head turned downward into the cupped palms of his hands.

"The strength of the ahtpah web, the stealth of the blinding-light prowler," Chuzzle said as he gave Ali and Guy the impression he slithered more than backed off into the shadows.

"Yes, of course." Chief Vituf made a dismissive gesture with his left hand, and quickly returned it to joining his other hand cupping his face. "Please go on, 'Cahhptahhn Taylahh.'"

"One last thing before I do, Chief Vituf." Helena unfolded her steely-rigid, yet paper-thin, thirty-inch, flat-screen video monitor before she proceeded to ask, "What was your involvement, if any, with such terrorist acts as the ahtpah attack on the wedding?"

"We are aware of such activities, and we are concerned about them, 'Cahhptahhn.' Should we find your proposals acceptable, we will do everything in our power to stop them in the future."

"We see such activities as reminders of our capabilities, 'Cahhptahhn'!" Chuzzle's voice echoed through cavern chambers in tandem with the whoosh of distant Grand Basin surf. "Let us say they provide the incentive necessary for the Empire to get serious about what you offer!, if it is indeed for taking seriously!"

"Once you can assure us as to the wisdom of your plan, 'Cahhptahhn,' and definitively confirm the willingness of the Fafaman emperor to abide by its terms, I assure you, we will stop that." Vituf made another dismissive hand gesture, on this ccasion towards from where Chuzzle's voice had echoed.

"Chief Vituf, we will now connect to a live video stream from aboard our spacecraft." For the time being, Captain Taylor decided she couldn't expect anything more from the rebel leader, that it was unwise to press him further about terrorist involvement, until she explained what her fellow Earthlings were bringing to the table. "Allow me to introduce you to our chief geophysicist and meteorologist, Cathy James-Leung." Helena left off Cathy's "Dr." assignation. She figured it would mean nothing to the rebels, that it would fail to translate meaningfully.

Cathy beamed a big smile. Such a big smile, Ali Magabu mused to himself it nearly made useless the consideration that had gone into dimming the lights on the navigation bridge of the Smoke and Mirrors, so the rebels would not need to don their anti-glare visors to view her presentation on the portable video monitor Captain Taylor had just unfolded. "Chief Vituf, it has been so exciting for me to study the fascinating mystery of your planet's sunset storm line! I believe I've made some progress in solving that mystery. The geological record, what I've had the opportunity to examine, places a dramatic shift in the planet's orbital axis at roughly fifty million solar orbits ago. That is the same time as the inception of the storm line!"

"I am sure it is entertaining for you to study our principle weather mystery, 'Cahthy Jahms-Lahung.' But, what of the plans your 'Cahhptahhn' promises will solve many of our pollution problems caused by the Fafaman Empire?"

"Chief Vituf, I am sure Officer James-Leung fully appreciates the urgency of the situation your people face, and would be happy to leave for later how her storm line research relates."

"Oh, absolutely, Captain Taylor." Cathy James-Leung wobbled her head about most wildly, with her eyes closed. Helena seeing her on the video monitor was reminded of a spinning top when it slows enough to tip over. Cathy was reproaching herself for having so selfishly focused initially on what gave her so much personal pleasure to study. "Chief Vituf," she said finally, "to deal with Fafama's water shortage, I propose something dramatic. We have discovered a large ice comet wandering your solar system. I propose we bring that comet into orbit around your planet, from where it can daily shed copious new amounts of moisture into your atmosphere."

"You can do this?" The rebel chief couldn't help emanating a mix of astonishment and excitement.

Cathy nodded confidently. "Flying our spacecraft close enough to the comet, we can use our gravitational influence. A minute gravitational influence it might be, less than a tenth of a percent course correction in the comet's trajectory. That change might be only as wide as you are tall, after the first labada." In her explanation, Cathy was careful to use the Fafaman unit of distance, the labada, which was equivalent to roughly three-fourths of one mile. "However," she continued, "it becomes a million or more labadas-wide course change after the comet has travelled far enough. Plus, we can accelerate that travel to happen in days rather than years, by electrostatically 'caging' the comet. For sure, the added moisture from one giant space rock alone will not be enough. But it will be a big start.

As for dealing with pollution issues, it was interesting to see what you have done with windmill technology, how you make benefit from open-ended cavern network wind tunnel effects. We also plan to introduce windmills to the Fafaman Empire. They will get built, and anchored deeply enough into the ground to easily withstand the brunt of the sunset storm line! Together with solar technology, plus a few other tricks we have developed, we think we can wean the Empire off petroleum and natural gas completely, for all their energy needs. We will also help you to expand and improve upon the breakdown of the pollutants from which your people suffer. We will accomplish this with pollution-gobbling bacteria genetically engineered from Fafaman bacteria sources."

"How does this sound to you, Chief Vituf?" asked Captain Taylor.

Chief Vituf remained mute for seconds that seemed like minutes for the Earthlings. With better lighting, they would have been able to discern a lone tear coursing down his cheek, eventually dripping off his chin. "Do not give us false hope, 'Cahhptahhn,'" he said at last, head still downturned into his cradling palms as he remained balanced on one leg.

"The hope becomes false, Chief Vituf, only if terrorist acts continue...and the Fafaman Empire continues to retaliate. The cycle of violence has to stop. There is also the matter of not wanting to leave Fafama's future in the hands of creatures from another world who would simply see you as so much meat."

As the final fa-la-las of the translation of Captain Taylor's none-too-veiled warning echoed off through the cavern network, Chief Vituf meditated on the likelihood these strange beings' resolve to essentially save Fafamans from themselves would get sore challenged. Then, he stood back up on two feet to look Captain Taylor square in the eyes. He said, "Like I told you before, 'Cahptahn,' we will do everything in our power to cooperate with this bold plan of yours. But everything depends on the Fafaman Empire."

"Everything ALSO depends on the Fafaman Empire," Helena pointedly edited the chief's remark. She was about to explain how Earthlings seal agreements with handshakes, and to seek knowledge of how the rebels seal agreements, when her earpiece erupted with, "Captain Taylor?!"

"Yoon-hee?" Helena felt her stomach falling through the cavern floor. She turned to check the still-unfolded, set-up video monitor, but the picture had already gone blank.

"Captain Taylor, Officer Leung has just reported that Oomb is under attack, and it IS by creatures from Tictoctic."

"The laser mesh shield…?"

"Apparently that didn't stop them."

"Can you patch me through to Buddy?"

"He said he'll check in when he's able to. Something

about the risk of getting monitored, and that he has his hands full besides."

"Yoon-hee, please explain the situation to the Fafamafalafama. We're headed back now." Of course the Fafamafalafama already knew the situation from the bread-crumb-nanobot surveillance patch-through for him to monitor the Earthling meeting with the rebels. Helena well understood, though, she couldn't expect the rebels to be understanding of that part of the arrangement. So she felt she had to maintain a certain pretense.

"See you soon, Captain. Wait, Dr. Entroper wants to say something."

"Captain Taylor, I'm just throwing this out there: If you wanted to continue with your critical business on Fafama, and delegate the power to me to investigate what is happening back on Oomb,-"

"I appreciate the offer, Dr. Entroper,-"

"I'm sure you do, Captain."

"-but please continue in your assigned role as mission observer." Taylor tried to sound as matter-of-fact as possible, despite how irritating she found the pettiness of Entroper's last comment. "Until Buddy checks in again with more details, my initial reaction is uncertainty over the wisdom of rushing into the situation virtually blind. For all we know, Tictoctic could have battleships surrounding the planet."

"Which is why it might have been wiser to take up the defense secretary's proposal to arm Oomb with both land- and sea-based defense shields to supplement the laser mesh."

"Dr. Entroper, I don't have the time just now to relitigate that decision. Again, we need to find out more and I need to get going here. See you soon."

"You're the captain."

As Helena Taylor explained to Chief Vituf what was happening, she thought to herself how Louisa Entroper would like nothing better than to take charge of the Smoke and Mirrors. She could race back to Oomb, riding in like the cavalry of old to the rescue, with all the starship's retrofitted weaponry blazing. What a striking choice between that attitude, and what she still wasn't sure wasn't just wishful thinking on the part of the Oombians!

Midway through Helena's conversation with Louisa Entroper, Chief Vituf resumed his one-legged, crouched-over contemplative stance. After she finished, there was a moment of nothing more than the echoes of distant surf, punctuated irregularly by water making a plop! into a nearby pool after dripping off the end of a stalactite. The rebel leader's eyes were fixed on the Earthlings' sneaker-type shoes that he found very unusual, compared to rebel moccasin-wear stitched together from dried and cured old tralalafa leaves. With that footwear thus consuming his visual attention, he said, "There are two more you will have to take with you. They cannot have a place here."

Helena shrugged her shoulders and nodded. She was long since resigned to this rebel leader's responses often having the least possible to do with what she said. Maybe, she thought, this was his way of re-asserting control over the situation. Still, it would have been nice of him to at minimum express some sort of regret over the news of an attack. This, not to mention appreciation for how other-world creatures were putting themselves out, to try and help Fafamans with their seemingly intractable problems. Chief Vituf could even have made his appreciation conditional. *Assuming this isn't some devious trick, I thank you, blah blah blah…*

"Bring them out!" Chief Vituf raised his voice for the benefit of someone in a hidden recess behind his throne.

Thereupon, a guard dragged forward a young woman in rags, with her very young daughter in rags clinging to her. He pushed them towards Captain Taylor so hard, they nearly lost balance. What helped them keep from spilling, scraped-up, onto the stony cavern floor was their catching sight of Zarif. "Zarif!"

""Mafamoof!" cried Zarif.

"Father!" came the translation through Helena's communicator, of what was said by the very young daughter, named Meelamoof.

The next thing Captain Taylor knew, they were all rushing into one another's arms, heedless of any risk or protocol.

"There is no place for any of them here," Chief Vituf sounded his weariest notes yet. "Captain, we will await your next move."

"We will see what we can do. In the meantime, a lot will come down to how you and the Empire treat one another." Helena couldn't help her curtness.

*I could have finally had my way with Mafamoof,* Chuzzle was meanwhile thinking after monitoring developments from another location. *I could have told her Zarif had gotten himself killed, and left her to me in his Will. Or I could have settled with any of several concubines corralled for the unattached troops. But denying myself these pleasures has kept my thoughts from focusing on where they must not focus, given those mind-readers from some distant planet. Cupping "Cahhptahn Taylah's" breasts, ahhhh... Her entrancing beauty, is that how she has managed to enslave so many men who she should be the one serving? Even pleasuring myself brings its own special risks at this point. In the relief afterwards, my thoughts will tend to wander...It won't be* long now!

# Chapter 12

"You see what I'm seeing, Leung?" Sergeant Fred Frankly's head was poking out from amidst a bushy clump of Oombian ferns. His eyes were glued to the sky as he communicated with Buddy Leung.

Buddy Leung was parked in one of the Smoke and Mirrors' extra shuttle pods on the dark side of Oomb's irregular-shaped moon, a giant asteroid that had fallen under the planet's gravitational sway a mere two million solar orbits earlier. Buddy had sunk the small, hybrid-propulsion vehicle into a thick layer of asteroid dust. Other spacecraft passing by would not be able to tell what was concealed there, even when that region got periodically illuminated by Oomb's sun, Callaway X Centra.

"There is definitely no mistaking it for random, non-intelligent activity, Sergeant Frankly. And I'm picking up something big, should be within range of the laser mesh within two minutes! Oh, I see what they're doing!" Buddy Leung closed his eyes and shook his head in despair. Up until then, Buddy had held out hope that any hostiles' plan for successfully breaching the laser defense grid would prove a spectacular failure. He had clung to such hope, despite the Oombians having mind-read confident anticipation of success from the approaching aliens. But presently, it was dawning on Buddy what the creatures from Tictoctic were doing, and that its success potential was quite high, indeed.

The first wave of asteroids, part of a naturally occurring shower, had fallen towards Oomb. This meant they had also fallen towards the laser mesh enveloping that planet and its atmosphere. A magnetic pulse from the Tictoctic saucer craft had organized those boulder-sized space rocks into a circular pattern. Buddy had fancied it was as though a stone dropped in a pond had sent out ripples in perfect concentric circles. As that first wave had set off the mesh defense, Sergeant Frankly had enjoyed a ring-side seat from ground level, looking way up into the bright blue firmament. He had clearly discerned red beams radiating from varying distances, inward towards a common center. Before those beams had reached that center, each one had ended in a bright flash like a fireworks sparkler, the Marine Corps Sergeant thought. And all those flashes together had produced a circular formation.

Buddy Leung realized this was the practice round. On the next round, the Tictoctic spacecraft would slip through the common center. It would get protected from laser-beam damage by a second wave of asteroids providing the wagons to encircle the camp, as Frankly would have characterized the event. The new laser beams would strike the new asteroids, not the alien spacecraft.

That is how it happened. The saucer craft spun straight down through the center of the new circle of sparkly laser-beam explosions of asteroids. The saucer was but a pinpoint of light to Sergeant Frankly on the ground, and to Buddy Leung on his view-screen monitor. But for the sergeant, as this space vehicle from Tictoctic continued on its rapid descent, it grew in size to a glistening oval. Across the sky behind it, red lines ended in sparkly flashes going off at random locations. The laser mesh was continuing to easily dispatch the rest of the incoming asteroids, which were no longer getting organized like iron filings by magnetic pulses. The flying saucer slowed to a hover Sergeant Frankly guesstimated was about a mile high. He instinctively drew his machine gun to the ready. Ditto for the twenty other marines under his command crouched down behind him, all wearing camouflage. However, they every last one of them suspected their weapons would prove useless.

Suddenly, the saucer zipped to another portion of sky, where it stopped just as abruptly, to continue to hover. Then it was off again, at a right angle to its previous zip, only to stop on a dime again for more hover. Sergeant Frankly would have likened this continuing maneuver to a buzzing bee in search across a meadow for a flower upon which to alight. He said to Buddy, "Okay, Leung, so they f-n' impregnated our first and only line of defense. It's a big planet, and they still have to figure out, errr… What're the chances they'd ever imagine a bunch of ass-baring, golf-club-swinging footloose trees were able to hide virtually every constructed edifice on the entire f-n' planet? Sure, the manicured fairways for - Why the sweet Jesus do those sons of bitchin' seeds call it 'oof'? Sounds like the noise someone would make after getting kicked in the balls! So they keep their f-n' fairways looking unnaturally neat and tidy. Still, isn't there a chance the aliens will conclude the laser mesh was left behind by some f-r wasn't full of enough piss to mark this territory for himself, so he did that instead? Couldn't they conclude 'nothin' to see here, folks, so let's just move it on along'?"

"We can still hope, Sergeant Frankly." Buddy Leung shook his head. He had to smile at the officer's colorful vulgarity, as he reflected on the enormous hiding task that had been accomplished in such a short time by the tree people. That is, once Moofoosoola and a few of the other most-skilled, long-range mind-readers realized an arrival of creatures from Tictoctic was imminent. The entire Earthling colony had been evacuated from their recently completed settlement, to a clearing in nearby immobile woods. Especially tall Oombians had joined them there. Said

Oombians hid the Earthlings' presence by making said clearing appear to actually be the densest, most impenetrable part of the forest. To complete this part of the coverup was a matter of keeping the children's noise level, if not perfectly quiet, at least below that of the chirping, whirring, goomping and other assorted sounds of Oombian wildlife.

Meantime, other tree people had found they were able to drape enough of their boughs across the roofs and minor roadways of the Earthling settlement to totally obscure them from view, even from ground level. Oombians who were especially viney-branched had flown in to help from a nearby island. They had lifted their upper extremities way past their palm-frond helicopter blades, to wrap cloakingly around the settlement's photovoltaic solar energy tower and water tower. The most difficult task for the Oombians had proven to be covering up the clubhouses for their oof courses all across their planet. Said enclosures were the only ones ever built by Oombians, for Oombians, for the sole purpose of protecting their oof equipment and science research. They were adequately spacious, including high ceilings, to accommodate the tree people, even if the larger of those tree people still had to bend down in order to enter them. Hiding the clubhouse rooftops was easy enough, with Oombians of all sizes straddling them. However, to cover over the sides of the clubhouses, the smaller Oombians had to scale the taller, and they often broke the taller ones' helicopter fronds in the process.

"Shit!" Sergeant Frankly spat out a sliver of an Oombian plant he'd been chewing on like sugar cane. "Must be a thousand gin joints to choose from all over the planet, and those f-ers are landing their saucer on the first fairway here! Hope our little runts are keeping their traps shut, 'less they want to experience what it's like getting turned into veal cutlets!"

Earthlings and tree people alike heard a high-pitched whir from the massive saucer as it lowered slowly towards the flattest, widest portion of the first fairway. The associated air turbulence ripped the helicopter fronds clear off the tops of a timber stand's worth of Oombians lining that fairway. It was all they could do to resist the urge to lift lower branches to feel how bad the damage was. Fortunately, the associated pain wasn't any worse than from cutting a fingernail too close to where it was attached to the skin.

Other trees more similar to Earth trees in their immobile rootedness got bent over way backwards.

Sergeant Frankly's nanobot "bee" cam arrived at the landing sight just in time to record the saucer touching down, for both his and Buddy's remote monitors. As the saucer's spinning slowed significantly, Fred and Buddy could make out metallic slats encircling its upper half. Those slats were rippling successively open and closed, alternately clockwise and counterclockwise. During this, the whirring sound grew louder, and the entire craft's shiny appearance faded to a dull gray. Then three slats slid open in a triangular formation on its underbelly. This allowed for the protrusion of tripod legs. The Tictoctic spacecraft was become wobbly, but the rippling of the topside slats ceased. In their stead, five stabilizer fins appeared, spaced equidistantly around the saucer's rim. They clearly helped the extraterrestrial vehicle to make a final, smooth touchdown on its tripod legs.

"F-k us!" Frankly swore. "There must be fifty of them hustling their butts down the ramp!, and most of them look armed! Even with the element of surprise, I don't like our chances! And shit!, what are galloping deer doing wearing clothes in the first f-ing place?!?!"

"Taking them on is probably not a good idea in any

event," said Buddy Leung. He thought he better heavily reinforce the Marine Corps Sergeant's first impression; Buddy could sense the sergeant was still weighing the merits of an ambush, despite what he'd exclaimed about not liking their chances even with the element of surprise. "I'm detecting another UFO skirting the Callaway X Centra system just above the orbital plane. For all we know, that one is carrying reinforcements."

"You checking this out, Leung? One of them with a shoulder strap bag, stopping to smell the f-in' flowers?! Now he's picking them?! What, if all they came here for was for makin' some f-n' flower arrangement, why do they need all those guns?! Afraid someone's goin' to shove a rose up their ass or somethin'?"

"I would guess he or she is a biologist collecting samples, Sergeant Frankly. If they ARE planning to make meals out of creatures they find here, it makes sense they would want to learn more about the ecology. Maybe they'll have their version of lab rats munch on some leaves, see whether there are any adverse reactions, fatal incompatibilities of this biosystem with theirs." Buddy was half-expecting Mafoosoola or another Oombian to any moment telepath an interjection clarifying what the deer-like creature from Tictoctic was about. That this did not happen gave him an additional sinking feeling in the pit of his stomach. The tree beings might be wanting to spare them information of a horrifyingly disturbing nature.

Correct. Chef Glork-tek, amazed at the abundance of flora, was thinking an especially exotic meal preparation might prove possible with never-before-tasted spices from this planet. But first, regarding the expendable Tictoctickian officers...the chef had two in particular in mind, who had been getting on his nerves. Originally, he was going to recommend Captain Mat-kek-tek dispatch them if the current on-board meat supply ran out before a safe extraterrestrial source was located. Under the new plan, the expendables were to enjoy a new, more dignified title, albeit also more full of double-talk. They were going to be referred to as drafted volunteers, grateful and honored for being forced into doing what they would have otherwise been too stupid to have thought to sign up for. There would be a special celebration hailing their heroism in the service of Dek-Fook-Tek. Afterwards, they would get locked inside an isolation chamber. From a front row seat outside that chamber, Glork-tek would watch them eat. He would see whether a meal seasoned with flower petals and other plant parts from this planet proved survivable, or deadly. If deadly, of course genetic modifications would be required. And fortunately, there were other expendable volunteers, perhaps not quite as exasperating as the two who Glork-tek had in mind, but still... The good news was that even if making food sources from this planet safely edible proved a daunting task, at least the process would reduce the number of mouths to feed. The current safe meat preserves would go further, all praise be to Dek-Fook-Tek.

"Shit! Is that one beastie wielding a heat sensor, Leung?"

"I'm afraid he is, Sergeant. If he continues his survey with it like that, inevitably he will hit the jackpot, locate where the colony is hiding!"

*We are going to have to reveal ourselves now for the diversionary measure, Officer Leung and Sergeant Frankly.* Immediately upon telepathing this, Mafoosoola redirected her extrasensory ability towards the reconnaissance team from off the Tictoctic saucer, headed up by Captain Mat-kek-tek with Officer Kwit-Nik along for advice. *Welcome to our planet Oomb, Captain Mat-kek-tek.*

Mat-kek-tek's ears shot up on high alert. He stood as erect on his hind legs as a deer-like creature could stand, and he made a full, three-hundred-sixty-degree perimeter sweep with his air igniter. "That voice in my head!" he brayed his tongue-clicks due to his high anxiety. "Who else is hearing it?"

All the other deer-like creatures followed the captain's lead, making full perimeter sweeps with their weapons. Soon as they every last one confirmed nonverbally by looks and nods that their experience was the same as Mat-kek-tek's, Officer Nekamek tongue-clicked, "Your powers of hearing are only exceeded by your wisdom, Captain Mat-kek-tek. Yes, we are also noticing a voice in our heads, though we can be certain it is not with the depth and clarity of your aural prowess. It can even be said your superlative attention led the way to our far duller sensations of a communication which otherwise we might have missed altogether."

"All thanks to the ultimate inspiration of the supreme Dek-Fook-Tek. Without whom, there can be no uncertainty that I most assuredly would have missed, NOT might have missed, this alien communication." Captain Mat-kek-tek lifted his eyes to the heavens, in the proximate direction of where he guesstimated his planet Tictoctic hung in the vast firmament presently veiled by blazing-blue sky.

"All thanks to his ultimate inspiration," every last deer creature disembarked from the landed saucer solemnly, ritually tongue-clicked.

*Captain Mat-kek-tek,* Mafoosoola went on, after waiting patiently for the time she knew it would take this new assembly of extraterrestrial creatures to process her initial telepathic outreach, *please rest assured. To speak to us, whether we stand present before you or are communicating remotely like we are doing now, you need only speak aloud, directed to our attention. We will respond. And we pledge to only demonstrate awareness of those things in your mind of which you explicitly wish us to be aware. Although we do take for granted you will accept our showing familiarity with your names and titles without your having formally introduced yourselves.*

"Do not insult Captain Mat-kek-tek!" Kwit-Nik raced to tongue-click. He dreaded what personal consequences might accrue – another antler chest-slashing, perhaps – were an awkward silence to develop as Mat-kek-tek puzzled over what to do next. "Do not suggest there was the smallest chance he might not have known he can speak up right now, just as though you were standing before him, to continue this initial dialogue with you!"

Captain Mat-kek-tek held out a cautioning hoof-hand towards Kwit-Nik. "There is no need, Officer Kwit-Nik, to presume that the ignorance of this thought-transmitting being rises to the level of insult."

"Your humbleness is unbounded, Captain Mat-kek-tek," Kwit-Nik bowed. But he thought to himself, *No, not humbleness! What lacks bounds is your prideful unwillingness to acknowledge anyone else's help! Clearly, you were uncertain how to proceed, until I tongue-clicked about continuing to speak as though the mental telepather were standing there before you!*

"All thanks for your unbounded humbleness." This time, the rest of the deer-like creatures made the captain the center of their attention, rather than the guesstimated direction of their distant home planet, Tictoctic.

"Who are you? Where are you hiding?" Captain Mat-kek-tek brayed after a nod of acknowledgement to his troops for their praise. He would have made the usual ritual self-effacing reference to Dek-Fook-Tek. However, he was anxious to get on with this very uncomfortable manner of communicating, especially to force whoever was putting the voice in his head to show his self.

*I am Mafoosoola. My fellow Oombians and I are not actually hiding. We are all around you. But we have apprehended that an explanation of WHAT we are might spare you much unnecessary anxiety before we make our presence more obvious. We look somewhat like the few trees maybe still remaining on your home planet. Only, we have eyes, and we are able to up-end our roots to move about, amongst other things you are not accustomed to trees being able to do.*

The creatures from Tictoctic nervously galloped to encircle their saucer craft. Pursuant to which, they aimed their air igniters outwards at the surrounding foliage.

*Many of the trees you are now eyeing so suspiciously are, in fact, much like trees as you have read about them. Some of us are going to slowly start moving. When we get closer to you, we will open our eyes. We wish to share our food with you, perform our music for you, and have you play our game of oof with us. And of course, answer your questions to the best of our ability. Are you ready? And thank you, Captain Mat-kek-tek, for so impressively remembering my name is Mafoosoola.* Mafoosoola had long since determined that face-saving flattery was the way to go, including crediting Mat-kek-tek with an achievement not yet evident. That this was the route to the greatest potential for precluding violence from these extraterrestrials.

"'Kakookooka.'" The captain tried to repeat this strange-for-him name before it slipped his mind again, but he tongue-clicked it into unrecognizability for

Sergeant Frankly and any other Earthlings who happened to be eavesdropping. "I insist you specifically make your presence known to me by coming to stand before me. I command this! And you must set down your arms, or hand them over to my men!"

*Very well, but we do not carry weapons of any sort.* With this telepathic transmission, Mafoosoola started her leaves rustling as she carefully made her way to climb down from where she was perched high atop the local oof clubhouse, straddling the peak of its towering roof.

Other Oombians straddling that roof joined her. They vined their way down the sides of fellow tree creatures. Those fellow creatures had gathered all around the clubhouse at its base to help hide it entirely. They had wanted to create the impression for their dangerous visitors that there was nothing other than an imposingly dense stand of woods.

The deer-like creatures galloped over beside Captain Mat-kek-tek, from where they nervously, bleatingly trained their rifle-shaped air igniters on the Oombians in motion. Most of said Oombians rippled their roots cautiously slowly across the ground to form two rows. In between those two rows, Mafoosoola approached the saucer captain from Tictoctic. She moved ever more slowly, until she sensed she had gotten as close as she could to Mat-kek-tek, without panicking him into an order to torch at least her if not also several of her fellow beings. Forthwith, she dug her roots into the topsoil to halt her forward motion, and she opened her eyes gradually. Two sideways slits in her bark spread apart. Her upper branches including her helicopter fronds reached several feet further up, yet her eyes were level with Captain Mat-kek-tek's eyes. *Again, Captain, welcome to Oomb. It is customary when we greet one another to offer a choice of the fruit and tubers hanging from our branches. So I am now going to spread apart my lower-level branches for you to see the full variety from which you can pick. Well do we understand you might wish to run tests, to assure our biochemistry is compatible with yours, before you actually consume your choice. Other Oombians will also here-upon spread apart their branches, so your associates from Tictoctic may likewise each select a fruit.*

"I command you other trees to hold your branches still!, not offer your fruit to my troops! Chef Glork-tek, you will step forward and add one fruit from Mafoosoola's branches to your condiments pouch!"

"Captain Mat-kek-tek," Officer Nekamek tongue-clicked as Mafoosoola spread her lower branches wide, "your decisive orders must surely honor the pride of Dek-Fook-Tek, whose only disappointment, we can safely assume, is not being here to bear witness to them!"

"All honor to Dek-Fook-Tek," the other armed creatures brayed in unison.

"My orders must strike Dek-Fook-Tek as irresolute by comparison to the granite-hard firmness he brings to every move he makes! However, since he cannot be here to personally manage this situation, I hope he can forgive my evident weakness!"

"Dek-Fook-Tek's resolve splits the hardest diamond," the pertinent ritual chant went for all the creatures from Tictoctic.

As Chef Glork-tek gingerly snapped off a fruit that looked like a red pepper with a carrot sticking out of its bottom, Captain Mat-kek-tek went on, "Tell me about the food you wish to offer us, Mafoosoola. From which kind of animals in this place do you take the meat, and how do you prepare it?"

*Apart from nutrients we absorb through our roots from the soil, the fruit and tubers we offer you are our only other food source. We do not eat meat. We are very different from you in that respect, we know.*

"What?!" Captain Mat-kek-tek tongue-clicked as sharply as he could, to express his shock and disapproval. He grabbed at a purple-polka-dotted green fruit in the shape of a pear, with his hoof-hand not occupied gripping his own air igniter. He yanked it off with a violent motion, uncaring of any possible pain he might inflict upon Mafoosoola. Although, despite the branch getting broken to which that fruit was attached, the Oombian experienced roughly the same sensation as an Earthling cutting one of her fingernails. "This is not food! At best, this is something with which to dress-spice food! Baaa!!" he brayed as he hurled it past Mafoosoola, down the shaded lane formed by the parallel lineup of Oombian trees.

***

"You're gettin' Ma-f-in-soola's telepathed blow-by-blow on their first contact with those f-in' stags from Tictoctic?" Sergeant Frankly hardly more than breathed, fearful over how acute might prove the hearing of the deer-like extraterrestrials.

"I've finally managed to send off two SOS fireflies, Sergeant!" Buddy Leung responded from his shuttle pod parked on the irregularly shaped moon of Oomb. He had just reburied the vehicle in a thick layer of dust on the moon's dark side, after having to expose part of it for the firefly donut launches.

***

"So, um, you call this a clubhouse," tongue-clicked Captain Mat-kek-tek. He was following Mafoosoola inside, followed in turn by Officer Kwit-Nik, Officer Nekamek, and two other armed troops he ordered to accompany him. "When you were piled like vines all over it, by any chance were you trying to hide it from us?"

*We were resting in the manner we feel most comfortable, clinging to one another.* Mafoosoola was not lying about this, but she had to wince at the discomfort of not having told the whole truth. *So these various clubs you see in each barrel are not familiar to you from any games you play on Tictoctic?* She delighted in changing the topic. She was even wondering whether something she was working on in her own swing would show up on the course. That was, assuming she succeeded in persuading these aliens to try their game, or at least watch while she played.

"One more question first, if your answer is sufficient. We are experiencing a low level of technology from you. Close to zero, actually. Where are you keeping the equipment you used to launch the laser mesh shield around about your planet? We demand you turn over to us the functions for disarming it!, so we can safely come and go of our choosing!" For this last, abruptly belligerent braying, the captain swelled out his chest.

*We did not desire nor feel we needed the laser mesh shield.* Mafoosoola gave the captain the saddest-looking eyes with this mentally telepathed communication. *Beings from another planet insisted on deploying it here before they left.* Again, part of her sadness stemmed from her selective, as opposed to full, recounting of the truth. Those beings hadn't *all* left. Far from it. *You are correct about our own low level of technology. The other beings did not leave us with any means for disarming the mesh. Even if they had, we would not have known what to do with it, despite our mind-reading capability. Now please, every one of you select a bag, and fill it with an oof club from each barrel.*

*Then you will want to take three or four freshly-cured oof balls from this barrel.*

Captain Mat-kek-tek and the officers and troops he had ordered to accompany him all froze in a disquieting-for-Mafoosoola stare-down. They were to the last one resisting an instinctive urge to either flee, or torch the clubhouse with their air igniters.

"Our technical officer, Tak-venk-tit, will soon enough discover for us whether or not there are laser mesh controls on your planet, and if there are, whether or not they are yours!" The captain was bluffing for what little he knew or understood of Tak-venk-tit's capabilities. "And as for games, games are for children! Games we put away as we mature, to dedicate ourselves to inspiration from the wisdom of the Supreme Dek-Fook-Tek!"

"He warms our understanding with every word that dawns like a new day from his tongue," the ritual chant went as the Tictoctic creatures lifted their eyes reverently towards the clubhouse roof.

"I can only hope I am not imagining too imperfectly what his intent would have been, were he here to guide us directly, when I suggest we try this game. That we try this game for the sake of judging its utility for our children, after, of course, the Supreme Dek-Fook-Tek makes modifications which will only make it better!"

***

"Hey, Leung!" Sergeant Frankly exclaimed under his breath, "I'm surprised Captain Stag and his crew even have to search for another food supply! Why don't they just eat their Supreme Dick-F--k-Dick's shit? I'm sure the way they see it, no other meal could possibly compare with what comes out of his supreme ass!"

"What I'm having trouble wrapping my head around,

Sergeant Frankly, is this. How could creatures operating on their mental level have possibly developed such an advanced application of the mirror array light acceleration principle that I accidentally stumbled upon, to construct that saucer craft?"

"It's their Supreme Dick-F--k-It, Leung! And that's why you've got us Marines, to figure out how to deal with such overgrown antler-wielding rat bastards! I know you and Captain Taylor are all against it, but we really are going to have to bring in some big guns to deal with their special brand of civilization-threatening bullshit! You can't like the translation of the name for their guns, which is air igniters! What the f- are air igniters?! Can't be good!"

"It is perplexing." Buddy closed his eyes and shook his head.

"Shit." Sergeant Frankly could tell the well-intentioned nerdy genius was yet unwilling to concede the point, about necessary violence.

***

"You will stand guard while Kwit-Nik and Nekamek play alongside me!" commanded Captain Mat-kek-tek of two unnamed troops as they all followed Mafoosoola up onto the first tee box. The remaining forty-some Tictoctickian soldiers who had disembarked from the saucer tried to sneak as many peeks as possible at what the captain was doing. They did this while they obeyed his orders to keep their air igniters trained on the Oombian reception committee. Which committee was comprised of two rows of tree creatures, who had reached unanimous agreement among themselves that the best move presently was not to move.

Mafoosoola preferred swinging her butt into the oof ball, teed up three feet off the ground for that purpose.

However, she sensed the visitors from Tictoctic might better handle her using oof clubs, the same as she was expecting of them. She did fear that using those clubs would set back progress on her butt swing. And yet she knew that under the circumstances, this was a small branch to snap off, as the Oombian expression would have translated. Grooving her swing of choice wasn't going to be worth perturbing the antlered aliens so much, their captain ordered them to fire their air igniters. So, she grabbed the golf equivalent of a three-wood, and she placed her ball on a short tee.

Mafoosoola hit a few oof balls towards a stand of trees from where they were tossed right back. Her idea was that the creatures from Tictoctic would take a few practice swings, and then they would try to hit balls towards that same stand of trees. She wanted to counsel Captain Mat-kek-tek on making nice and easy swings, a smooth tempo. But first, she had to convince him it would be much easier if he set down his air igniter, rather than tucking it under his arm to keep hold of at the same time he was using a club.

"My most brilliant Captain Mat-kek-tek, if I may..." Nekamek went down on one knee to beg speak.

"Proceed, Officer," sharply tongue-clicked the captain. He was trying to look as casual as possible with an oof club in his right hoof hand, and his air igniter slung by a shoulder strap under his left arm.

"I regret 'Thank you' is all I can offer in return, Captain. But this is the thing. We know these creatures have played this game their whole lives. And that regardless, they would still have much to learn from you, even when you are holding on to an air igniter while you are hitting the ball. However, why humiliate them any more than is necessary?"

"Officer Nekamek, you always are an attentive

listener to the words of the Supreme Dek-Fook-Tek," the captain nodded as he handed over his weapon to one of the nonplaying troops. "I should, after all, play this as one of our children would play it, and hopefully not fall too far short of Dek-Fook-Tek in the accuracy of my judgment."

"His judgment guides us home to truth with such accuracy that by comparison, the best compass leaves us lost." Officer Nekamek led the other deer creatures in this particular braying litany.

Mafoosoola explained to Captain Mat-kek-tek that he should allow the club to fall freely from the top of his backswing before he started guiding it towards the teed-up oof ball.

The captain mused to himself, *Such a silly creature! Here she must know that at any moment, I could torch her to cinders with the air igniter, order them all torched to cinders. And yet here she frets over my technique swinging this silly- Look how that ball flies! It is almost to those woods!*

"Baaaa!!" all the other deer creatures from Tictoctic brayed appreciatively over Captain Mat-kek-tek's first, wildly successful attempt to hit an oof ball. Kwit-Nik knew they'd be braying appreciatively, even had the captain only sent it the length of two air igniters laid end to end. Which is what the captain did on the first tee, and which did get succeeded by lots of baas. If anything, these Tictoctickian officers made even more of a ruckus than they made over Captain Mat-kek-tek's lucky practice shot. Fearful what consequences might accrue for them, the captain's fellow creatures from Tictoctic were desperate to overwhelm any humiliation he might have felt. And Nekamek thought better of praising his superior for wisely choosing, after only one lesson, not to show up the tree creature with a series of better shots, better ball-striking, than Mafoosoola had developed over a lifetime of playing. That would have been received as an admission the captain had done something not so well, whether or not on purpose.

Matters got tenser when Kwit-Nik pured his ball down the middle of the fairway. He sent it even further than Mat-kek-tek had sent his practice shot. "That shot would not have been possible had I not learned from carefully observing your technique on your shot, Captain," Kwit-Nik was quick to disingenuously observe. "My goal was to get my ball to reach half the distance of yours."

"And at that, Officer Kwit-Nik, you have failed miserably!" Nekamek declared admonishingly, whilst thinking to himself that he had better intentionally mishit the oof ball when his own turn came.

"Captain Mat-kek-tek, we have something here you need to see!" This is how they would have translated, the static-y tongue-clicks suddenly erupting from the walkie-talkie strapped to the captain's waist.

"Everyone back aboard!" the captain brayed with all his might. He dropped his oof club to the ground, and he also dropped himself down on all fours, to initiate the hastiest gallop possible back to the disembarkation ramp left open underneath the landed saucer craft.

***

*The Tictoctickians have compared the magnified reconnaissance images, from their earlier experiment directing a meteor shower into the laser mesh, with their new images gathered while bringing in their saucer craft for a landing,* Mafoosoola telepathed to both Sergeant Frankly and Buddy Leung. *The colony we helped you construct, they are realizing the new images reveal heavy foliage in its place. And with what they have learned from watching us climb down off our clubhouse...We have asked them what the violence will achieve, but they are not listening.*

***

The flying saucer ramp lifted back into its underbelly, and a high-pitched whine started emanating from the craft, as the tree people covering over the deserted human village fled to re-populate forests. By the time the saucer had retracted its tripod landing gear and was rising rapidly skyward, the human settlement was back in full view.

At about a one-mile altitude, the saucer zipped from one stationary position to another and then another. Again, Sergeant Frankly was reminded of a bumble bee checking out its choice of flowers before moving in for cross-pollinating honey gathering. Finally, from one of its hovering positions, it sent down a narrow white beam. That beam was like lightning without the zigzags, sustained for seconds rather than gone in a flash, Frankly thought. The same as natural lightning, the sergeant concluded it must have been incredibly hot, for there was a deafening, rolling crack of thunder from instant heating of the atmosphere. This thunder nearly drowned out the plenty loud enough explosive noise from the artificially produced lightning's flaming destruction of Don Típico and Doña Norma's cottage. Pieces of said cottage, including shattered parts of their hundred-inch-screen television, got sent flying all directions. Another electrical bolt from the saucer snapped the windmill tower in two like a pretzel stick, Sergeant Frankly couldn't help imagining. The windmill itself fell crashing through the roof of the community center. A third, final beam exploded to bits the two-bedroom home of Ciela and her parents.

When the flying saucer returned to where it had landed the first time, Mafoosoola was waiting to greet Captain Mat-kek-tek. The captain was joined in galloping back down the disembarkation ramp by a contingent of his armed troops that was even larger than before.

"Damn!" Sergeant Frankly cursed under his breath to Private Adkins crouched beside him. "If we'd only been allowed to weapon up with a ground-to-air missile launcher before we left home, we could have blasted those antlered f-ers to Kingdom Come!"

"We don't know that that wouldn't have brought their full cavalry charging here from Tictoctic to overwhelm us," cautioned Buddy Leung eavesdropping from aboard his moon-dust-concealed shuttle craft.

"Why we also need a couple of battle cruisers into the bitchin' bargain, Leung! Or maybe you're enjoying feeling so f-n' defenseless!"

***

"I don't want to hear about your friends' resting together just happening to conveniently cover over buildings and other constructed things!" Captain Mat-kek-tek's angry braying at Mafoosoola got so deep-throated, several of the Marines crouched hiding in nearby immobile foliage were reminded of a complaining cow or bull. "Come over here so I can show you something!" He motioned threateningly at the tree person with his air igniter.

Once they'd reached the smoldering ruins of the community center, Captain Mat-kek-tek directed his weapon towards an adjacent dwelling. A door which had gotten blasted flying away from the community center was lodged in that dwelling's bay window. The

Tictoctic saucer captain trotted over to the front door, and he reared up on his two hind hooves to aim his air igniter at it. After making a slight adjustment, he pulled the trigger. At first, nothing was audible to Mafoosoola, but then there was a distinct "fwuh"! Sergeant Frankly would have likened that noise to a propane grill igniting. A trail of fire through the air, as from a blow torch, had the effect of instantly turning a two-foot-diameter circular portion of said door to cinders. Those cinders burst away as though they were just so much black confetti, Frankly would have thought had he enjoyed a clear view of what was transpiring.

"Take a look inside at the ceiling!" Captain Mat-kek-tek waved over Mafoosoola with his weapon. "I knew as soon as we reviewed our surveillance photos that the ceiling levels were too low for beings of your height to comfortably fit inside!"

Actually, the captain had Officer Tak-venk-tit to thank for this realization. Captain Mat-kek-tek had had the technical officer study the photos in question while he had offered nothing. Rather, he had quietly taken out his frustration sharpening one of his antlers with his bahvek. "I am certain, Captain Mat-kek-tek," Tak-venk-tit had humbly baaed after he sensed that enough time had elapsed, "your superior powers of observation made it glaringly obvious to you, long before it came into even blurred focus for me. Those alien habitations are too low to the ground for tree creatures to live inside. Especially when compared to their clubhouse. Whoever did live there, they might have something to do with who the tree creatures say were responsible for deploying the laser mesh shield. If that group of other-worlders has really long since departed, why would they feel they had to cloak their abandoned stables from us? Again, a most profound thank you for your patience awaiting at least one of us to join you, finally, in realizing the most significant import of these before-and-after photos."

"You are forgiven as are your fellow soldiers still racing their feeble minds to catch up," the captain had nodded his pompous appreciation before giving the attack orders.

*Yes, the visitors from another planet did live here. But since the deployment of the laser mesh, they have abandoned this place, as I previously telepathed to you.* The tree creature turned to face Captain Mat-kek-tek with an especially heavy sadness in her eyes. *They fear you. They fear you so much, they ignored our entreaties not to fight your potential violence with the risk for violence posed by their laser mesh shield. That is, the violence to you that would have resulted, had that shield successfully destroyed your spacecraft.*

"Permission to speak to the tree creature, Captain," Nekamek baaed after himself taking a peek through the perfectly circular hole in the front door.

"My only regret is that Dek-Fook-Tek is not here to grant this permission. He would have anticipated your request, to spare you having to make it." Captain Mat-kek-tek's ears fluttered proudly over his having recalled the proper ritual response for the situation.

"I would alert the Supreme Dek-Fook-Tek to how admirably you have handled my nuisance presence, Captain Mat-kek-tek, if not for how egregiously I would thereby be taking him away from assuredly far more urgent matters. As for you, tree being of Oomb," continued Nekamek, "you sorely try Captain Mat-kek-tek's patience, waiting on you to admit what you can be certain he espied through the destructed bay window before he fired his air igniter," went on Nekamek. "There are items for everyday use left lying around within that dwelling! How do you telepath us honestly that these places have been abandoned when clearly they have not? Baa!!"

"Baa!!" angrily joined Captain Mat-kek-tek in the admonishing braying at Mafoosoola.

When Mafoosoola said the other extraterrestrials abandoned their colony, she didn't exactly mentally telepath that they abandoned the entire planet. But she thought better of making that too-clever-by-half observation. The rageful, destructive reaction that would have ensued was clear. So instead, *When they knew you were coming, they headed into the protective sanctuary of the woods.*

"Then they must come out to reveal themselves! Or, we torch you and every other plant in sight!" Captain Mat-kek-tek sounded like a roaring bull from over where Sergeant Frankly and his men were concealed. "Officer Kwit-Nik! Have every soldier commence air ignition into every stand of trees they can, until these other-world-ers surrender themselves!! Officer Nekamek, reactivate the heat sensor so we might locate where they are hiding!!"

Telepathic consultation by the tree beings concluded that an airlift of the Earthlings to another island, thus revealing the Oombians' helicopter powers, would only result in several deaths, even more than presently anticipated. And so...

It was too late, by the time the deer creatures from Tictoctic realized the Oombian tree beings were obliging Captain Mat-kek-tek's demand. They already had a stand of dense woods under flaming, air-igniter attack.

Mobile Oombian tree creatures thinned out a different stand of woods, thus revealing groups of humans variously clinging to one another, or children running to hug tight their relatives. Mobile trees and humans alike escaped any serious injury.

Not so for the deeply rooted immobile trees of the aforementioned dense woods. Flames shot up from them, forming thick black wreaths of smoke. Mobile Oombians in their midst rushed as quickly as their root cilia would carry them, to the nearest water hazard on the oof course. There, they doused the roaring fires consuming their helicopter fronds and other branches above eye level. Such dousing produced clouds of hissing steam which billowed off the creek running down one side of the oof course fairway. Some tree creatures bent down even further, to fully immerse themselves in the muddy water. On their leaves that escaped singeing, they collected water to carry back over to their immobile, only dimly conscious distant cousins. They hoped to shake off enough droplets on said cousins to save them from burning to the ground.

That was what some of the Oombians busied themselves about. But Kwit-Nik noticed two unscathed-appearing tree beings there, simply shutting their eyes. The bark around those eyes proceeded to get wrinkled even more than usual. This conveyed the sense they were focusing, concentrating extra intensely on something.

That was Kwit-Nik's last thought before he got overwhelmed by silent screams in his head. They grew amplified to a more painful extent than the worst headache he'd ever experienced. This sudden agony made Kwit-Nik feel like retching up his last meal of deboned finger-and-toe salad. But he still managed to notice, he still managed to realize, that his fellow deer creatures were also obviously suffering like he was suffering. Some even let their air igniters fall from their grasp, in order for them to lift their hoof-hands to hold their heads in helpless agony.

Sergeant Frankly was about to order his men to take advantage of this situation to attack, when Captain Mat-kek-tek roared through his own pain, "BURN THEM!! BURN THEM ALL!!," and Mafoosoola telepathed, *There are many more aboard their saucer, Officer Frankly. Enough still have the presence of mind to yet lift off and incinerate all of you in a flash. Oombians of lost faith have resorted to this form of mental telepathic violence. We are encouraging them to stop.*

"Well f- me, and f- you!" the sergeant swore under his breath. "Did you ever stop to think that if more of you went in on this so-called 'violence,' whatever it is that's obviously giving these SOBs the fits, you might not only save us from who-knows-what-f-ing-shit they have in store for us? You might also spare some of your own from getting turned into walking campfires?!?!?"

*I understand your fear and frustration, Sergeant Frankly. However, you are talking a temporary solution until their reinforcements arrive and avenge their pain. Perhaps they will even determine how to electronically interrupt the silent scream.* Mafoosoola telepathed this as she approached Captain Mat-kek-tek.

The captain was still overcome by the wordless shouting in his head. He could not re-grip his own air igniter from where it was slung over his shoulders, and follow through on his own directive to torch as many Oombians as possible.

"Yeah, well wait until OUR reinforcements arrive – Captain Taylor has GOT to understand this now – and f-ing blow their bushy-tailed asses to Kingdom Come!" Frankly muttered, more to himself than to Mafoosoola or his fellow Marines.

*Captain Mat-kek-tek, I take full responsibility for this terrible assault on the mental processes of you and your* crew. As Mafoosoola directed this telepathic message at Captain Mat-kek-tek, she also made it generally available on the extrasensory horizon of her fellow Oombians.

With this, the silent scream suddenly ceased. Several troops from Tictoctic held their fire, after having already torched the upper halves of several trees both mobile and immobile. Those troops ceased their fire not to show their appreciation, in sudden defiance of their captain's orders. Rather, the abrupt cessation of indescribable mental anguish temporarily overwhelmed with relief their ability to do anything.

Again, they were two Oombians who had wrinkled their bark even more than it was already wrinkled, their eye slits folded closed with their intense concentration. They used their helicopter fronds to rush themselves both over beside Mafoosoola. They flew so low to the ground, their roots skimmed the sandy soil.

*We cannot allow Mafoosoola to assume the blame for something we did,* explained one of them.

*We are prepared to accept the consequences,* nodded the other.

Captain Mat-kek-tek pondered the tree creatures, totally mystified. His silence got amply filled by a mix of crackling flames, hissing steam from where Oombians were dousing their fires in creek water, urgently fervent leaf rustles from other Oombians shaking moisture off their drenched leaves onto burning immobile trees, the whimpers of terrified children, and the soothingly soft voices of their parents attempting to calm them.

"Chef Glork-tek, I command you to gallop over here!" the captain tongue-clicked finally.

The chef dropped down on all fours to do as he was ordered, careful not to spill any of the leaves or flowers he'd collected in his multi-pocketed bag. Back up on his hind legs after his gallop, he didn't give himself a chance to finish panting. Rather, he breathlessly baaed, "Captain Mat-kek-tek, I do not deserve the patience you have so dramatically demonstrated, awaiting my arrival at your side."

"His patience shames us," went the ritual litany as all the disembarked Tictoctic troops went down on one knee.

"I know it does," the captain reacted flippantly, and added, "At least you're not wasting Dek-Fook-Tek's time. Chef Glork-tek, I have something for you to consider."

The chef nodded acknowledgement. With that, Mat-kek-tek used his air igniter to torch the upper halves of the three non-resisting Oombians standing before him. This was at such close range, their upper branches including their helicopter assemblies were turned instantly to ash. This ash fluttered away on the gentle breeze like so much gray confetti, Pedro Perez thought. He was watching, huddled together with the other settlers.

From just above Mafoosoola's right eye, Captain Mat-kek-tek snapped off a twig that was only slightly singed, and he handed it over to the chef. "In your culinary estimation," said the captain, "will flame-broiling with this particular wood add any significant flavoring to your future preparations, Chef Glork-tek?"

The chef sniffed at the twig with his snout twitching rapidly; Pedro was reminded of a rabbit sniffing at a carrot before starting to nibble on it. Then the chef trotted over to lift one of Pedro's arms to his snout. He didn't bother to inquire, even by the merest gesture, whether this would be okay. Chef Glork-tek sniffed at that arm, and he sniffed at a few contents of his collection bag. Whence forth, he took a flower petal he'd gathered, and he rubbed it on Pedro's sniffed-at arm. Then he sniffed at it again, sniffed at the singed twig again, and at the last returned to Captain Mat-kek-tek's side to bray, "Captain Mat-kek-tek, the occasions are countless that your wisdom inspired by the Supreme Dek-Fook-Tek lead me to novel ideas for meals. This is but one more. And should our aids heroically perish in our first effort to replenish our food supply, at least they will perish, having fully relished their poison."

"Excellent, that is, good enough, Chef Glork-tek." The captain corrected himself on the precipice of blasphemy. Only the Supreme Authority was capable of excellence. "Since Dek-Fook-Tek is not here to prepare our meals, clearly your relatively meager efforts will have to do. So, should we load these three onto the ship?"

The chef carefully picked his way around each half-burnt Oombian. "There is enough wood here to last for several preparations. We can load it aboard now, and chop it up later."

With a slight shift in the breeze, Captain Mat-kek-tek's snout got rabbit-wiggly like Chef Glork-tek's had been, and his ears shot most attentively straight up. "We need to know," he directed this at Mafoosoola, "there are other clothed animals like the group you have revealed here? I must warn you that regardless of your answer, we will search the immediate environs with our thermal imaging device. We will also send a surveillance scout from our landed mother ship to do a likewise scan of every land mass on this planet. Any forests concealing such creatures that you do not immediately reveal to us will get summarily burned to the ground! No more halfway measures!"

Putting an exclamation on the captain's announcement, a rectangular aperture slid open along the rim of the saucer craft, and a small saucer-shaped vehicle shot out. It looped silently around above one stand of trees, then shot over to loop around above another forested patch.

Just before the surveillance scout could scan a third area, Sergeant Frankly led his contingent out of hiding. Their hands were held high in the universally understood surrender mode. Several deer creatures hastily galloped close, to relieve them of the various weapons slung over their shoulders.

"Mafoosoola, I am sorry so many of you got burned trying to protect us!" Pedro Perez spoke loudly, careless of the deer creatures hearing what for them would be nonsense noises. He was also uncaring how they might react to those noises, if the tree creatures didn't intervene telepathically. "But, you specifically telepathed us a translation of what their captain said, about the consequences for your tree people if they conceal any more of us. Why did you telepath this, and yet you told us nothing about the conversation between the captain and his fellow alien who came over to check how my arm smelled?"

Pedro could easily discern the shininess of the golden sap pooling in the corners of Mafoosoola's eyes and running down her bark-creased face. Subsequently he stepped forward from his family. However, he was unable to prevent his wife Ludi from re-grabbing him at the waist and burying her face in his shoulder. Nor could he stop his daughter Alexita from continuing to hold on to his left leg while hiding tremblingly fearful behind him. "You don't have the heart to explain to me what they are planning, yes? Well I know!! I can sense why the one alien was sniffing at me and then at the small branch burned off of you! He was trying to decide how I would taste roasted over your burning body!"

"Aye, no, Pedro!" Ludi's voice was full of admonishing tone as she shook her head in his shoulder.

"Aye, sí, Ludi!" Pedro nodded vigorously, though making no attempt to push her away. "We cannot sugarcoat this! Mafoosoola, do you mind asking their captain why they can't eat the fruit you offered them, instead of our bodies?! Or, there might be plenty of small animals they can hunt here! Why can't they do that instead of tearing apart our families?"

"Hey Mafoo-foo-platter," interjected Sergeant Frankly, hands still raised in surrender mode over his head, "why don't you also telepath Captain Suck-my-Dick they can eat the Marines, and we hope they all choke on our tight asses! That is, if you Oombians aren't willing to try disabling them again with whatever you were pumping into their heads previously!"

Captain Mat-kek-tek ignored the hardy, deep-throated cheers that went up from the full group of Marines endorsing their sergeant's remarks. Instead, he eyed Pedro as he brayed, "Chef Glork-tek, once we sort out the status of all these beasts, I demand you serve me his heart and brain with your most brilliant preparation; I will take my chances on the ill side effects. Just make certain he is cooked through completely!"

# Chapter 13

Back on Fafama, the diplomatic mission headed up by Captain Helena Taylor was returning to where they had left from the shuttle pod. Said pod sat parked just outside the faux-adobe-settlement-complex in rebel territory.

The trek went quickly. It went so quickly, in fact, Helena and Ali Magabu both had to wonder whether Chief Vituf's most recent staging area for his command center was really all that far away from the shuttle pod's parking area. Yes, the Earthlings (with a Fafaman family added into the bargain) were not making the detours they had made on their journey to meet with the rebel chieftain. That is, the detours they had had imposed upon them, to learn more about rebel life, and how that life was getting steadily wrecked by pollution, courtesy of the Fafaman Empire. And of course there was the truism that forays into the unknown always seem to take longer than returns to the familiar. But still...

"Careful... What is your name, little girl?" Sergeant Hanson was guiding Zarif's daughter up the shiny aluminum gangway into the shuttle craft, and she was leaping two steps at a time. Taking together her impulsive behavior with her sun visors and wild lengths of curly black hair, Guy couldn't help but be charmed by this frisky four-year-old.

"Her name is Meelamoof," mother Mafamoof answered from further back. Mafamoof had opted to linger arm-in-arm with her husband Zarif, over trying to keep up with her so-easily-excitable daughter. Only an hour earlier, Mafamoof was fearing she would never see her husband again.

"Welcome aboard a flying craft brought here by

those aliens from outer space, Meelamoof," the twenty-third wife, Yulala, fa-la-laed. She reached down to take one of the little girl's hands, to assure her not tripping on the final couple of steps, hopping up into the shuttle. As Sergeant Hanson completed passing off Meelamoof to her, Yulala added, with a bemused look his way, "They are friendly aliens, too!"

"They better be, or poom-poom!" Meelamoof punched at thin air. "My father will give them trouble!"

Everyone laughed, even Yulala's two security guards. Ali Magabu noticed Guy and Yulala's regard oscillating between themselves and Zarif's daughter. *Good heavens,* he thought to himself, *if I didn't know better, most truly I would suppose those two are yearning wistfully on what it would be like to make one of these little bundles of joy together!*

*Captain Taylor, everyone with you, you must remove your mushroom necklaces and leave them behind, the sooner the better!* Oodle-Noodle's voice suddenly telepathed most urgently.

"Captain, you're getting this?!?" Tanya Petrovsky-Magabu's face paled like she'd seen a ghost, Helena thought, as the shuttle pod pilot poked her head down the gangway over Yulala's shoulder.

"You know we are, Tanya." Captain Taylor was already lifting off her necklace. "Tell us more, Oodle-Noodle!" she went on. Taylor was addressing the mind-reading Oombian who telepathed from aboard the Smoke and Mirrors, way up in orbit around Fafama. "Is it okay to just toss the necklaces aside, or do we need to set them down gently?"

*I'm not sure, Captain, so everyone go with that setting-them-down-gently idea. I picked up an anxious thought on a consciousness horizon. It was thankfulness your delegation was leaving sooner rather than later. I probed deeper. It was emanating from someone who recently left your presence.*

Ali and Helena turned each other's way with significant looks. "Chuzzle," said Ali, and the captain nodded.

*He strains not to contemplate what he prepared. Which was by himself so there would only be one person having to keep the secret unavailable to our mind-reading. He is exercising extreme mental discipline, to try avoiding us accessing his memory of what he did. He keeps reflecting on the fact that whatever it was, it was accomplished single-handedly. And when that reflection comes too close to thoughts entering his head about the exact nature of his actions, he shifts to mental indulgence of his lustful cravings. The best I can make of what has nevertheless leaked into his consciousness is that air-pressure-sensitive explosives have been concealed in your mushroom necklaces. They were meant to go off when your shuttle reached a certain altitude.*

Helena Taylor had just rubbed her forefinger across the nape of her neck and taken a sniff. "Oodle-Noodle, I'm noticing an odd scent. It's something I think must have rubbed off the necklace, even though their mushrooms they call tapastrahs have this ceramic-type glaze on them." The captain corralled Zarif and Mafamoof back down the gangplank, to stand aside on the ground with her.

"That is okay, Captain." Zarif beat Oodle-Noodle to a response, having understood the fa-la-las crackling out of the Earthling's waist-band translator. "The glazing actually sweats from the tapastrahs after they are baked. The odor that rubs off on us from them for a full orbit of our sun, we consider that a soothing fragrance which proudly marks us as people of the underground."

Mafamoof, snuggled in at Zarif's side, nodded confirmation.

*My guess is, Captain, there is at least one tapastrah on each necklace that is not shedding any fragrance. It is a tapastrah that is not a real tapastrah. Rather, it is a tapastrah-shaped container, concealing the explosive and who knows? Maybe there is some friction component with the necklace cord threaded through it!*

"But with our emergency back on Oomb, we don't have any time now to investigate," Helena Taylor shook her head regretfully. All the tapastrah necklaces were shed outside the shuttle pod, and the entire away team plus Zarif's family was safely rushed aboard. "Everybody, strap yourself in! Tanya, prepare for liftoff as soon as I've sealed the hatch!"

"Aye, Captain!"

***

*I failed the plan, I failed the plan, I failed the plan.* Chuzzle kept chanting this to himself as he stepped over a row of stalagmite-appearing teeth of a noonthrah. The entire time, he held a pistol to his own head. He quickly sank ankle deep into the noonthrah's tar-like center, exactly as he had expected to do. Once he pulled the trigger, it would all have been over for him...if it hadn't been for this creature's rippling convulsion in response to fresh prey. Said convulsion threw Chuzzle off balance. To steady himself, he grabbed at one of the teeth, already tilting in towards him. But in so doing, he accidentally knocked his gun against a tilting-in tooth on the opposite row. It fell irretrievably into the creature's extremely acidic tar. Chuzzle bent over to try to retrieve the weapon anyway, and he only succeeded in getting one hand stuck there as well. That's when limitless terror possessed him, and he screamed helplessly.

It was supposed to go that he shot himself before he could experience the full horror of death by a noonthrah.

***

*Captain, I urgently recommend all of you abandon the shuttle as fast as possible! The being who sabotaged the necklaces has committed suicide to avoid any thoughts given over to a plan that can still succeed! He must be referring to-*

"Yoon-hee, Kevin," said Tanya urgently, "I'm putting the shuttle on auto-pilot-"

"So we can control it, see whether we can diagnose anything that might have been done to it! Roger that, Tanya! We'll maintain the pod at low altitude while we run diagnostics! Just get out of there!" Kevin completed Tanya's sentence for her, having also telepathically received Oodle-Noodle's urgent recommendation while that tree creature was standing right beside him on the bridge of the Smoke and Mirrors.

"Captain, we're two short on low-alt cushions!" Tanya shouted to be heard above the din of everyone unbuckling their seatbelts, plus the hum from the shuttle pod's jet engine. "Two of you are going to have to double-up with someone else!"

"Meelamoof you can come with me?" Helena reached down her arms.

Meelamoof looked to her mother, not to protect her from this strangely dressed space alien, but rather for nodding approval. Which she received, so she leapt into Captain Taylor's arms with total abandon.

A member of Yulala's security detail gathered her up into his own, protectively broad-shouldered embrace as

Ali Magabu outfitted him with a cushion and explained how it worked. Ali was not so distracted by this task that he did not notice the resigned glances Hanson and the twenty-third wife snuck one another. Obviously, they were both yearningly wistful over the sergeant not being the one to share the cushion with her.

"You roll backwards out of the shuttle, like a skin diver! Uhhh, that's not going to mean anything to you! Just watch me!" Those were Captain Taylor's last words to Zarif and Mafamoof, who would be following after her, before she trustingly let herself drop out the side emergency exit from the shuttle. Within seconds, a vast cushion ballooned open all around and under her with her precious responsibility, Meelamoof, in firm embrace. The so-called "low-alt cushion" was intended for sky jumps too short for a parachute. Helena and Meelamoof's combined weight down through the center of it kept any breezes from tipping it to one side or another. Seconds more, and Helena was bouncing safely on a patch of arid ground, and she was hearing and noticing others bouncing about around her. After the low-alt cushion's gently automatic deflation, she was able to stand up, uncurl from her protective fetal embrace of Meelamoof, and unclip said cushion from around her waist. As she helped Zarif and Mafamoof unclip their low-alt cushions, she noticed the shuttle craft was maintaining a low-altitude circular flight formation. It was getting kept far enough away from the bailed-out passengers and crew not to hurt them in case it suddenly exploded, but close enough to monitor their condition. However...

"Tanya, are you hearing a humming sound in addition to the hum from the shuttle?"

"Captain," Ali Magabu pointed towards a large sand dune bristled with stalky dune grass, "it truly seems to be issuing from over there! I fear it is more of a buzz than a hum!"

The next thing they knew, a virtual sand storm was erupting from behind the dune. The dune grass stalks shot out like sparks, so Tanya thought. As the buzz from over that direction grew deafening, an enormous compact shape rose into view. Long, segmented legs dangled from underneath. Its wings were a blur of wind-whipping motion, and the rest of it proved too hard to make out in fine detail by the Earthlings, for all the sand getting blown stinging about.

"The blinding-light prowler!" Zarif fa-la-laed. But there was so much noise from the enormous beetle's wings, none of the Earthlings' translators were able to discern enough of his warning for them to emit anything intelligible.

Immediately after realizing the translators weren't working, Sergeant Hanson felt two of the blinding-light prowler's prickly-feeling lower leg segments pushing in on him from both sides. They were not pushing hard enough to crush him as well they could have, rather just hard enough to lift him airborne.

"WAHH!" This was Yulala fa-la-laing "NO!" in her language as she ran away from the protection of her security guards. With all her might, she leapt at one of the dangling rear legs of the monstrous beetle, and she grabbed hold. Her effort was abetted by the beetle's prickly hairs. In reflex reaction, the other rear leg bent against her, keeping her well secure as this creature slowly gained altitude.

Yulala's guards fired their rifles at the blinding-light prowler's rear segment, but to no avail. Guy and Yulala both heard the metallic ping! ping! of bullets ineffectively getting deflected off quarter-inch-thick exoskeleton.

Something else happened, even worse. Distracted by their own efforts, reacting too late to the twenty-third wife's unexpected bid to rescue the Earthling, her guards did not realize what was going on several feet behind them. Two, desiccated, giant round cacti, the proportion of two manhole covers, had been flipped open where they had been dragged on purpose. Out from the burrows they concealed, lengths of webbing were shot by two trap-door ahtpahs. Those particular spiders were closer in size to sheep dogs than to cows, unlike their more enormous cousins.

Meanwhile, Zarif and even his wife Mafamoof grew well aware that the sand eruption from beyond the towering dune was yet continuing. Zarif alone further realized how his initial warning got lost in the deafening buzz. He bent to Captain Taylor's translator to shout directly into it what came screaming out as, "There are more blinding-light prowlers on the way! They will take all of us, too, if we can't find overhang shelter behind that rock shelf!"

Tanya, Ali and Helena followed Zarif's lead. None too soon, as three more blinding-light prowlers were looming up from beyond the dune presently wing-whipped down to less than half its original height. Mafamoof, with Meelamoof gathered up into her arms, had already gone from sight behind the geological feature the father indicated.

As the Earthlings led by the Fafaman fled for shelter, the guards for Yulala were firing their rifles desperately towards the two pairs of eyes, one pair from each burrow, as the webbing dragged them closer and closer to an awful fate.

"Captain! There has to be something we can do for them! Truly!" Ali shouted above the din of multiple monster beetle buzzes, as he and the rest of the humans crouched beneath the rock-shelf overhang. Fortunately for them, this formation had gotten eroded out into the open over millions of years of the sunset storm line activity.

"NO!!" Zarif's WAH!! had come booming out from Helena's translator strapped to her belt as again, he labored to speak directly into it. "Each trapdoor 'ahtpah' can send out multiple fishing lines! More of us will be doomed if we try to help!"

*Truly fascinating how Zarif would make that fishing line comparison*, Ali thought to himself.

Zarif's latest words were no sooner translated than something miraculous happened. At the midway point in one of the web lines between the guards and the trapdoor ahtpahs, flames burst. It was like someone lit a giant match, where Tanya was concerned. As those flames flared out and left a wobbly trail of cinders across the barren ground between the ahtpah and one of the guards, the same thing happened to the web dragging the other guard. Only seconds later, both Fafaman security people were joining everyone else underneath the shale rock-shelf.

Both trapdoor ahtpahs were a blur of motion, repositioning their respective desiccated cacti to conceal their respective burrows.

"I was thinking to use these for purely diplomatic purposes!" Ali Magabu shouted as he pulled forth a small plastic container from his excursion bag. He clicked it open to reveal a little pile of Chris's chocolate chip cookies. "But I truly believe our good friend Effy so richly deserves them!"

"Now, now!" Tanya shouted in a sarcastically cautioning voice to still be heard above the racket yet being made by the three monster beetles buzzing overhead. She was feeling relieved enough to indulge a bit of levity, as said beetles obviously had not figured out exactly where the objects of their frantic interest were hidden. "Do not think for even one moment the ephemeral dragon is an actual life form of whatever sort!"

"What was I thinking?!" Ali Magabu played along. He hoped that somehow, poor little Meelamoof would get diverted from what were terrifying enough circumstances for the adults, let alone children. Each cookie Ali lifted out from its container flared to cinders, soon as he gently placed it on the sandy soil. "Professor Skepticus should have been present to save us from our faulty perceptions!" Ali went on. For an instant, in the shade of the overhang, one of Effy's incinerating blasts, directed at a chocolate chip cookie, made its head clearly visible to all, albeit of a ghostly translucent nature.

Tanya got reminded of one of the more elaborate dragon heads she had seen worn on Earth for a Chinese New Year's parade. "Yes! Of course!" she said. "A special, gaseous, chemical phenomenon which accidentally, under special lighting circumstances, assumes the appearance of a winged dragon,-"

"-that accidentally drifted into the shuttle craft before we left-" Tanya's husband Ali continued.

"-then accidentally randomly followed us out of the shuttle craft-"

"-after which its random blasts of energy just happened to save these guards' lives rather than burning a hole in one of us! Truly chance occurrences! Life and intelligence had nothing to do with any of them!"

"But to play devil's advocate," Helena jumped in, "were Skepticus present, I'm sure he would also have pointed out to you that this whatever-it-is we named Effy only seems to go after ahtpah webbing, chocolate chip cookies, and a few other selected items! He would argue it's behaving like a chemical compound that only reacts with certain substances! I'm just sayin'! But anyway-"

THUD!!

Captain Taylor was going to go on to ask how did Effy end up stealing aboard the shuttle craft in the first place. To which inquiry, Tanya would have responded that when she was arriving to the shuttle bay for her pre-launch prep, she had happened to notice Helena's husband Chris coming from that same direction. Had she not been so preoccupied by her concern over the impending mission, she was going to ask him what he was doing there. Instead of this conversation, though, the unexpected THUD! from close over their heads prompted Helena to say, "It sounds like they are pounding into the rock shelf to try to get at us! But what I don't understand!, this is just occurring to me! When Yulala's guards were freed from the ahtpah webs!, when they were running for shelter here!, those flying bug monsters had plenty of time to grab at least one of them! Why did they keep buzzing where we're hiding, instead?!"

THUD!! THUD!!

"And now they seem to be trying to bring down the roof on top of us!!"

Zarif was suddenly sniffle, sniffle; Ali would have likened the Fafaman's nostril motions to a rabbit's. "If I might, excuse me!" he said as he sniffed at Tanya's neck, then Ali's neck, Helena's neck, and finally one of the guards' necks. "Maybe you cannot smell this!" Zarif said as he wiped sweat from Helena's neck with his forefinger and held it to her nose.

THUD!! THUD!!

"You told us it's just from the tapastrahs in the necklace!"

"But with our sweating from the heat," responded Zarif, "I am realizing there is something more! What I am smelling is the scent sprayed by the blinding light prowler female, when she is attracted to a mate!"

THUD!! THUD!! THUD!!

"Someone must have mixed it into the tapastrah necklace glaze!" went on Zarif. "And since the Empire guards did not keep their necklaces on...!"

Loose sediment was falling on the group of Earthlings and Fafamans from the beetles banging into the shale shelf above them. And Meelamoof was burrowing her weepy face into her mother's shoulder as she wrapped her arms tightly around her mother's neck.

"Oh, no!" Taylor's eyes grew nocturnal wide, Ali thought, as she realized what had happened. "The backup plan for having us destroyed!, after Oodle-Noodle read Chuzzle's mind to realize the necklaces were rigged with altitude-sensitive explosives! It was to trick us into fearing the shuttle itself might be rigged!, so we'd evacuate it!, only to become sex attractants for the prowlers! He committed suicide before Oodle-Noodle could probe that far, so we had to assume- I have an idea!

"Yoon-hee??!! Are you hearing this?!?!?"

THUD!! THUD!!

"I'm hearing everything, Captain!!"

"I'm hearing everything too, Captain!" Louisa Entroper. "You know, if you had allowed more than one shuttle to be retrofitted with some defensive devices, Yoon-hee could have used the remote control to have it dispatch those monsters!-"

THUD!! THUD!!

"-But now..."

"Don't think we'll need them! Yoon-hee, can you bring the shuttle down to stationary hover, as near to our location as possible?!!"

"Yes, Captain! But you're going to get your hands roasted trying to rub the pheromones off you onto its underbelly!" Yoon-hee successfully anticipated Helena's thinking.

"We won't use our hands!!" Helena tore off her blouse, and Ali and Tanya followed suit with their own above-the-waist wear. All three furiously rubbed sweat from their necks with their torn-off clothes, while the whiny hum of the shuttle craft got closer and closer until it was extending the shadow of the shale-rock outcropping overhang.

THUD!! PING!! The enormous beetles were ramming into both the outcropping and the shuttle, as Helena succeeded with something to her immense relief. When she held up her uniform blouse, brought it to within yards of the air-and-space vessel's underbelly, electrostatic cling caused it to jump the short distance to adhere flat against the hull. Steam hissed from all the moisture getting vaporized off said blouse. Ali and Tanya followed suit with their own removed garments.

As Yoon-hee continued to maneuver the shuttle pod remotely, from way up in orbit on board the Smoke and Mirrors, the three monster beetles sought to embrace it with their dangling legs. They fought with one another for that pleasure, insensitive to the outer hull's tremendous temperatures.

Meanwhile, Captain Taylor and company got out from under the shale outcropping mere seconds before it collapsed from the monster beetles' earlier assault.

***

"Varafafafa!? What is this creature trying to do?!?! Sting me?!?!?" Sergeant Hanson was shouting with all his desperate might, from where he was being held securely to the flying monster beetle's underside by its two middle legs. He was referring to how the blinding light prowler was trying to curl in its abdomen towards him. He hoped he was raising his voice enough for his translator to operate, and that if it did operate, the result would prove loud enough for the twenty-third wife to hear from where she had glommed on to one of the flying beast's rear-most legs, twitching frantically to try to get her to let go.

"Call me Yulala!!"

Hanson felt the slightest bit relieved to hear fa-la-las issue from his translator, and then for said translator to convert the royal wife's own fa-la-las back to something he could understand.

"I am sorry!" Yulala went on. "I don't know what it is trying to do!"

"Wait! I've just received word from Captain Taylor in my earpiece! Someone smeared female prowler scent on those tapastrah necklaces we were wearing back to the shuttle until we got warned they were implanted with explosives!!"

"Then I DO know what HE is trying to do!!" Yulala's fa-la-las translated as the monster beetle's curls got rhythmically more intense. "He's trying to mate with you!!"

"In mid-air?!?!" But just as Hanson exclaimed this, he recalled seeing certain Japanese beetles mate in mid-air back on Earth. And the next thing he knew, he was soaked in a foul-smelling, honey-colored, sticky gloop that most unfortunately clogged his left ear. "Hello?!?! Captain Taylor?!?! Officer Park-Smith?!?! Please come in!! Damn!! My earpiece is ruined!!"

*Sergeant Hanson?*

Guy knew instantly this soothing voice in his head came from Oodle-Noodle.

*I have informed the captain of what has happened. Unfortunately, my mind-reading capacity does not extend to location discernment when the location is constantly shifting. But, if you can describe where the prowler is flying you, I can relay this information to officers both aboard the Smoke and Mirrors and down on the ground. Maybe the rest of the away team can rescue you, once they reoccupy the shuttle craft.*

"Okay! We appear to be headed roughly northeast!!, approaching a cliff face!! That can't be too far from the Grand Basin!! Wait!! I think I hear the shuttle behind us!! With more buzzing!! And now there's an even louder wing-whirring sound that's drowning out the rest!! Yulala?!?!!?? Can you see what is happening?!?! I'm facing the wrong direction and can't get my head turned around far enough to- Shit!!!" Sergeant Hanson realized nothing was fa-la-laing from his translator. The new sound had grown way too deafening loud, drowning out his shouts.

Yulala was so transfixed by what she saw, she might not have been able to get words out of her mouth in any event. As the three beetles kept vying with one another for sole, loving embrace of the shuttle craft, a creature the appearance of a praying mantis and the size of a small jet quickly overtook them. Flying just above the melee, it spit two buckets worth of brown liquid from its feeler-parenthesized mouth. One bucket splashed on the head of one of the prowlers, and the other splashed on the head of a second prowler. Both of those impacted prowlers appeared to Yulala to suddenly go limp, give up their battle over possession of the shuttle pod with the third powler. The next thing the Fafaman ruler's twenty-third wife knew, the monster mantis had one monster beetle held by one of its "praying" claws, and one held by its other set of claws. It was flying off, presumably to its lair for a feast. The lone remaining monster beetle of those three was left with the shuttle craft all to itself. It sped off a different direction from the giant mantis, to follow behind the beetle carrying Sergeant Hanson, the same beetle to which Yulala was hanging on.

"There is one other prowler left!!" is how Yulala's fa-la-las resumed issuing from the credit-card-sized translator attached to Guy Hanson's belt.

The resumption of understandable communication from the twenty-third wife of the Fafamafalafama lent Hanson a measure of relief, compounding his relief due to the deafening racket diminishing. Said communication gave Hanson hope that the gross spray from his insect captor's business end hadn't ruined his translator, in addition to ruining his earpiece.

"It is following us!!" Yulala went on.

"I see a dark opening in the cliff face! That must be where these things live!!"

"Hopefully he leaves us alone in a nest, to go fight off any other suitors while he waits for you to give birth!"

"That might not be so funny!" The fa-la-laed translation of this line from Hanson echoed off the cavern walls as the prowler left daylight for darkness. The monster insect flew deeper and deeper inside. Hanson could hear, echoing from the cavern entrance, the buzz of the other prowler, accompanied by the steady hum of the shuttle craft left in hover mode. *Good,* the Marine Corps Sergeant thought. *Hopefully, that other prowler sets down gently his true love, aka the shuttle pod. Then, once we get away from this overgrown critter, we can fly out of here and go retrieve Captain Taylor along with the rest.*

No sooner did Hanson think this, though, than the buzzing from that other prowler abruptly stopped. There was an explosion so devastating, it caused a cave-in totally blocking where he had entered carried by a blinding light prowler. What Guy and Yulala could not know was that the second male prowler was unaware of just how big was his burden he had mistakened for a mate. He had run it crashing right into the cliff face below where he was entering the cave. The collision instantly transformed the shuttle craft into a fireball from which the blinding light prowler was left a hollowed-out exoskeleton, its inners completely scorched away.

***

"Captain, I've just lost the shuttle craft's signal! It appears to have been destroyed!"

"Copy that, Yoon-hee!"

"'Cahptahn,' what is happening?" asked the Fafamafalafama. "First, you lose contact with your Hanson officer and my Varafafafa, and now your Officer Yoon-hee is reporting the loss of your shuttle craft!? I am dispatching a jet squadron to secure you immediately! They should be able to find your location well in advance of the sunset storm line!"

"Thank you, esteemed Fafamafalafama." Captain Taylor crossed her left arm diagonally down across her chest, and she bowed for the benefit of the two security guards, even though she strongly suspected that would make Zarif wince with displeasure. "After we are rescued, our other space shuttle vehicle can take us back to the Smoke and Mirrors for us to follow up on the distress call from Oomb. Although, I do intend to leave Ali and Tanya here to help you locate Sergeant Hanson and the Varafafafa."

"No, 'Cahptahn,' I must insist all of you stay. I warned you. Dealing with the rebels would prove a complete mess, and a complete mess is exactly what you have. We will require much time to sort through this, even after the Varafafafa is safely returned."

To put an exclamation on his command, the two

security guards thereupon trained their rifles on Helena, with intentional wavering back and forth between her and Ali and Tanya.

Tanya rolled her eyes and said to the guards, "Seriously? Our pet ephemeral dragon saves you from the trapdoor ahtpahs, and Captain Taylor concocts the great scheme that diverts the blinding light prowlers' attention away from us, and this is your thanks?!"

The guards' reactions were unreadable, shielded by their opaque sun visors. Their visors gave them a poker-faced demeanor, Ali thought, as they continued to waver their rifle aim among the three Earthlings, with an occasional nod Zarif and Mafamoof's way.

Captain Taylor and Ali Magabu flanking Tanya, both gave her calm-down pats on the back while the captain explained, "What Officer Petrovsky is trying to say is, you have no need to worry we will try to make a run for escape or something. It IS our intent to satisfy the concerns of the Fafamafalafama." Taylor lifted her eyes towards the eastern quadrant of the cloudless sky where the sun wasn't blazing, and she said, "Yoon-hee?"

"Yes, Captain," answered Navigation Officer Park-Smith from her control console on the navigation bridge back aboard the Smoke and Mirrors.

"Excuse me, Captain, before you go on with Officer Park-Smith," interceded Dr. Louisa Entroper, "but from what I'm hearing you dealing with down there, would you like me to temporarily assume command of the Smoke and Mirrors for a more immediate response to the situation on Oomb? Via firefly donut, I could initiate a constant flow of status updates so you would be kept apprised while you are working through matters here."

"I appreciate the offer, Dr. Entroper." Captain Taylor tried to sound far more thankful than she actually felt, which was not at all. "I'm asking Officer Park-Smith to do exactly as you describe, since the only other person left on board who has as much experience as her, operating the ship, is her husband Kevin."

"So you would like me to be assistant to your temporary captain, Helena?"

"Actually, I ask that you continue in your role as government observer of the mission. I'm sure Officer Park-Smith will consider carefully any input you might offer. Yoon-hee?"

"That is correct, Captain. Good luck to you and the rest of the away team. I'm going to announce we're preparing for departure."

Louisa was going to ask who WAS going to play second-in-command. With a shrug of her shoulders, though, she shook her head disdainfully. She hoped others on the bridge would notice, besides those tree people from Oomb, who she wished were not endowed with their mind-reading ability. She asked herself: *Why do I even bother? Yoon-hee is probably going to listen to Oodle-Noodle whispering naïve nothings in her head before she ever listens to me, in any event.*

"Captain Yoon-hee-er, Captain Park-Smith, sorry," Chris panted, out of breath from running to the bridge as soon as he heard Yoon-hee's announcement from the ship's kitchen. He realized too late he could have saved himself so much extra effort, had he propelled himself floating down hallways rather than trying to sprint with the special boots that always stuck to the floor like Velcro. They were the boots everyone needed to wear when they were virtually gravity-free at spacecraft speeds such as orbital velocity, well below even one-quarter light speed.

"That's okay, Officer Olsen-Taylor," Yoon-hee smiled.

She was re-checking the flight path for bringing the Smoke and Mirrors above the orbital plane, out of the way of most potential asteroid and comet mischief. "What's up?"

"Captain, I respectfully request permission to stay behind on Fafama, to make sure my wife will be okay."

"Hmm..." Yoon-hee was thinking, *Great. A tricky decision already.*

"Someone can drop me off on their space station and I'll take their shuttle blade down to the surface."

"You'll risk another shuttle blade flight, Officer Olsen-Taylor? THAT is true love."

"And I've left plenty of chocolate chip cookie batter dough in the refrigerator, in case it proves useful."

"Don't you think you should bring some with you?, see whether the Fafamafalafama might not be more reasonable with a cookie in his mouth?"

*I also want you to take this oof club along, or one of your own if you choose.* Oodle-Noodle handed Chris a big-headed driver.

"So I can go?" Chris couldn't help the excitement in his voice.

"Well," Yoon-hee sighed, "I guess Helena may actually need you down there."

"Yes, Captain. Thank you, Captain."

"Kevin, before you bring Chris over to their space station, can you prepare two additional advance guard fireflies besides the four quadrants?"

"One to check what we're getting into back closer to Oomb, the other to bring the home front up-to-date, Captain?"

"Great minds think alike, Officer Smith-Park."

Louisa Entroper hurried off the bridge, making a concerted effort to not appear to be hurrying. She needed to attach a secured, dedicated memo for Defense Secretary Warlor to the homebound firefly, wherein she would detail the full situation. *They need to know,* Louisa determined, *how the captain has been treating everything like a big joke, allowing ethnic food on the bridge that could have spilled into and damaged expensive equipment, having a Marine Corps Sergeant give away the bride at the Fafamafalafama's twenty-somethingth wedding. Maybe those sorts of things were merely careless, including letting those little Puerto Rican children run wild so that one even stuck a cookie down Dr. Skepticus's pants. But there is some super serious stuff, including trying to negotiate with terrorists on Fafama. And also including listening to those Oombians inexperienced in the crueler ways of the larger universe, when she refused to accept the full defense package if she were to head up this mission. And now look at her failures! Oomb is under attack, helpless to defend itself at least until we return. And even when we do return, the retrofits might not be nearly enough to cope. And here on Fafama, a royal wife is missing and one of our shuttle craft is destroyed!! I just have to hope they went ahead at home, and completed crash-course construction of the starship battle cruiser!*

# Chapter 14

"Mami?!" Alexita was shivering as she quizzically addressed Ludi. If she had been old enough to access the necessary words, she would have cried out, *Why are those deer wearing clothes?! And why are they taking Papi into a spaceship?!* Instead, she had to settle with pointing from a Tictoctickian soldier who was leading Pedro away, from him to the landed saucer craft, and back again. "Mami" understood fully, nevertheless.

Alexita and her mother Ludi were gathered together with other women and children in a clearing beside their partially destroyed settlement. They found themselves under guard by deer-like creatures from Tictoctic, creatures armed with air igniters. It had taken a while for Ludi and Pedro's two-and-a-half-year-old daughter to calm down enough to say anything at all, especially since other children around her were continuing to whimper in fear. Not to mention their mothers.

"Alexita, they want your Papi and those other men to meet some more people on the flying saucer." Ludi bit at her lower lip. It took all of her willpower to maintain her composure. She kept telling herself she had to be strong for her daughter. She also kept telling herself that surely, this amazingly wondrous journey, waking up aboard the Smoke and Mirrors and then getting transported to a new planet covered in island paradises, was not all for naught. Surely, this adventure was not going to end on such a horrific note, with her husband herded away for slaughter, and the rest of them imprisoned like cattle by the tall chain link fences getting erected throughout the settlement.

*I don't want Papi to meet some more people on the flying saucer! I want him to meet us!* was what Alexita wanted to complain. Again, she couldn't find the words, so she simply made a tearful whining noise.

"Alexita, you see your Papi waving at us? He is about to enter there; you want him to see a smile from you to take with him, don't you? You don't want him to see you like this, no?"

Alexita coaxed a wan smile from her deepest resources, accompanied by a hand wave. But the moment Pedro disappeared into the underbelly of the saucer, she sobbed, "Paa-pii!!"

"That one with the child, I think I might want a taste of her as well." Captain Mat-kek-tek extruded his thick yet narrow, tapering tongue to lick his chops as he pointed Ludi's way with one hoof-hand.

"I commend your instinct for what has greatest flavor, Captain Mat-kek-tek." Kwit-Nik at his side made a typical Tictoctickian bow, kneeling down on one forelimb.

On this cue, the two other troops in the captain's immediate presence joined Kwit-Nik's obeisance, and all three ritually chanted, "The quality of what you deem worthy to ingest is such that, were we permitted to partake of your defecation, still would our usual meals leave us nauseous by comparison."

"Captain Mat-kek-tek," Kwit-Nik went on as he reared back up onto his two hind legs, "my only hesitation in promptly herding her over to join the first sampling, you might want to consult Chef Glork-tek. With her wide hips, isn't she especially suitable for birthing additional calves, so that the supply of what you sense to be superbly delectable will be that much more ample?"

"A very satisfactory observation, Officer Kwit-Nik!" brayed Chef Glork-tek just trotting over beside the captain. "You are tongue-clicking about that one, correct?" He also indicated Ludi. "Standing so close to

Captain Mat-kek-tek must have profoundly inspired you!"

"I can only hope." Kwit-Nik again bowed the captain's way.

"You have adequately completed my trial, Officer Kwit-Nik," the captain nodded approvingly. With great self-satisfaction he concocted his bluff, and deluded his own self it wasn't a bluff. That he really had NOT drawn attention to the female alien beast simply because he thought she might prove a savory treat. "I need to administer these little tests from time to time, as you well know, to assure the judgement of my closest advisors remains bahvek-sharp.

"But tell me, Chef Glork-tek," the captain continued, quickly changing the subject. He made a sweep of his front right leg to indicate the entire human settlement. "I understand the generously sized pens for the bulls. But why the other large spaces? It appears that all you are doing is adding fencing around each habitat. Isn't it more efficient, easier to keep track of each animal, when they are filed away in cages proportioned to restrict their movement?"

"Aboard ship, Captain Mat-kek-tek, limited space necessitated exactly as you said, for our share of the remaining Chonoran population." Chef Glork-tek wondered how far he should proceed with his explanation before offering yet more ritualized praise. "However, in my humble effort to catch up to what we can be sure you and even moreso Dek-Fook-Tek intuited long ago, my gastronomic studies are revealing that the production of taste-compromising biochemicals due to stress is far less evident in free-range animals than in caged animals."

"His intuition is the rainbow we can never reach," ritually brayed Kwit-Nik, going down on one forelimb again.

"But its beauty across the sky always guides us," the

other deer-like creatures assembled around Captain Mat-kek-tek answered ritually in unison as they also went down on one forelimb.

When Chef Glork-tek reared back up on his two hind legs, he suppressed a baa of relief that the praise was dispensed with, to go on, "I hazard to assure you, Captain, you will find the heart and brain of the one you have so bravely selected, to help us with the cross-biological risk assessment, to be especially flavorful. Before today, he cannot have known any significant stress, being a wild-caught specimen."

"Your bravery is the long shadow that casts across us the dark night of our cowardice." By the time Kwit-Nik was halfway through this less-used chant, the rest of the deer-like creatures assembled had joined in, with a new bow to Captain Mat-kek-tek.

"Of course it does," the captain nodded nonchalantly as they rose. "But tell me, Chef Glork-tek, why don't we also sample one of the calves for their sweeter, more delicate flavor?"

"The calves' behavior is indicative of excessive, unreasoning fear, as you would expect from any young beast facing a new, unfamiliar situation. We all know this. And what we also know is that as a result, their flavor-compromising biochemicals must be surging, Captain Mat-kek-tek. For myself, I would especially like to try that one." Glork-tek pointed an articulated cloven hand-hoof Alexita's direction. "But now is not the time, if I don't want my taste buds to experience a literally bitter disappointment. On our second sampling, upon our return here... Who knows? We should find the younger creatures in a far more relaxed state. One of them might even have been sired by the bull who will be providing your next full meal."

"Chef Glork-tek, it is always a relief when you or someone else can logically deal with these matters so that I might attend more carefully to our most significant challenges, whatever shortcomings we know that anyone besides Dek-Fook-Tek brings to any situation." Captain Mat-kek-tek re-sharpened one of his antlers with his bahvek as he wallowed, it seemed to Kwit-Nik, in his self-satisfaction. "One last question for now, however: What is the plan you know I would be about with those aging cattle?" He casually waved his left foreleg not occupied with antler sharpening towards where Norma and Típico, and Rotonda and Placido, were holding on to one another for dear life. "Their flesh will doubtless prove too tough and unpleasant-tasting, based on our prior experience with aged animals of Chonora. And I have never favored the broth brewed from old bones. Plow them under for fertilizer, perhaps?"

"We can first transport them to another location where their sounds as they are dispatched do not unnecessarily spike the stress chemicals in the younger herd," Chef Glork-tek baaed approvingly.

"Captain Mat-kek-tek, if I may," anxiously tongue-clicked Kwit-Nik with the requisite bow especially low for the circumstance.

"Yes you may."

"My thanks are beyond inadequate."

"Your thanks are far short of inadequate. Inadequate is the hill as a distant horizon you will never reach. Go on." Captain Mat-kek-tek found himself thinking impatiently he must soon find a reason, okay an excuse, to honor this most irritating inferior with another of his antler slashings. *I feel too strongly the insincerity of his ritual adulations!*

"Mighty Captain Mat-kek-tek, I am certain you observed far more of this than I did, how the aging cattle interacted with the calves. For additional free-range benefit, it might make sense to keep them around. The fertilizer made from them when they die of natural causes should prove just as effective. But again, you would know far more about this than I."

"Officer Kwit-Nik, you have always had rather too much empathy for dumb beasts. In this case, however, you are reaffirming what I already have long since suspected." The captain gave Kwit-Nik a lingering stare as he continued to sharpen an already needle-sharp antler with his bahvek. When he abruptly broke off this intentionally unsettling look, he lifted his head high to bray, "Whichever tree person of Oomb, you decide amongst yourselves who will translate for the cattle what I am about to say. And remember this well: I can no longer be bothered with your silly names, so you will not waste my time relating to me who among you is chosen for such an undeserved honor."

*I am ready!*

"Good. Cattle of Tictoctic's first ranch on Oomb!" Captain Mat-kek-tek reared up as imposingly tall as he could on his hind legs, while he brayed with all his might, "You are welcome for the several mercies we show you on behalf of our Supreme Authority, Dek-Fook-Tek!!"

Every soldier from Tictoctic there present went down on one knee to ritually baa, "He spares us his antlers through our chests, that we might share his women."

The translating Oombian decided not to bother to telepath a translation of this particular ritual assertion.

"Your children will stay with your women, instead of their being isolated in their own separate pens!" went on Mat-kek-tek. "Your men and women aged past their prime will be allowed to live out their remaining days grazing peacefully in your midst!, so that they also might aid in the care of your youth! And I assure you, those fellow cattle we have taken aboard our spacecraft will be dispatched (the Oombian telepathed this as "treated") according to our highest standards of kindness! Lastly, we leave behind a contingent of our troops to protect you from misjudgments by the tree creatures!, as well as to facilitate the orderly rotation of your females into your bull dens for mating purposes! What only remains is for you to bow before me as the representative for Dek-Fook-Tek!, to show your thanks for his tender mercies! NOW!!"

The Oombian gently telepathed how every human would be wise to go down on their knees and bow, to avoid any further harm. The only ones not immediately complying were some of the Marines not herded aboard the flying saucer. These included Sergeant Frankly, who two soldiers had just finished dragging up before the captain, accompanied by tree creature Woony Woonle for translations. Woony Woonle's helicopter fronds were still smoldering from an air-igniter assault. Woony had wasted his energy trying to assure the soldiers assigned to him that the assault would not be necessary to gain his cooperation.

Armed troops entered the pens of the uncooperative Marines, to kick the back of their legs with their rear hooves, thereby painfully forcing their knees to buckle.

Meantime, Captain Mat-kek-tek's slobbering tongue-clicking covered Woony Woonle's face with his foul-smelling spit, at least as Woony would have characterized it.

*To avoid our pulling off your fore legs and hind legs like the appendages of an insect,* Woony Woonle telepathed in translation of the captain's uncouthly delivered message for Sergeant Frankly, *you will tell us the location of the control center for the laser mesh, and you will tell us the pass code for safely traversing it.*

"Go to hell!" Woony Woonle telepathed this growled response from Fred Frankly as, *Sergeant Frankly has indicated a predisposition not to cooperate.*

Captain Mat-kek-tek's nostrils flared with rage. He lowered his head to charge at what he saw as this dumb beast's chest, vulnerably thrust forward thanks to Tictoctic troops flanking Fred Frankly and holding his arms firmly behind his back. However, at the last moment Captain Mat-kek-tek thought better of goring him. Mat-kek-tek decided this pathetic animal, pretending to be something more with its clothes and such, was not deserving of the honor of having its chest ripped open, or even simply slashed, especially by his own antlers.

"Captain Mat-kek-tek! Captain Mat-kek-tek!" one of two troops breathlessly brayed as they galloped up beside Sergeant Frankly.

"You know that by your impulsive interruption of these most serious proceedings, you both have earned my goring of you!"

The troops reared up on their hind legs and swelled out their chests for their captain to do as he saw fit.

"But I am feeling in a most merciful mood today!"

"We are not worthy of a meal made of your ruminations upon the foulest parts of these beasts," both troops went down on one knee to ritually baa.

"Go on with your news!, what must be extremely vital news for you to behave this way!"

"We leave you to judge that," crisply tongue-clicked trooper Mook-ket. "We have located, we believe, the control center for the laser grid. Need I continue, with what we were sure you must have already suspected?"

"I was wondering how much time you would have to

waste before you determined what was so long ago obvious to me. For the benefit of Kwit-Nik here, though, my modesty demands you relate the information rather than I." The captain made a graciously flowing gesture towards Kwit-Nik with one cloven hoof.

"Your modesty is such that, were we to proudly serve your excrement for dinner, you would demur from taking credit for having made it," both troops chanted in unison down on one knee again. Then back up on their rear legs, Mook-ket continued, "The laser-grid console appears locked inside an instinctively constructed beast nest. It is a beast nest different from the one where they keep the master controls for their instinctively built power grid."

"As I suspected all along!" the captain nodded boastfully braying, as he proudly swelled out his chest. He was yet curious, though, about exactly where said laser-grid console was located, which location he was going to take credit for having already deduced, despite in reality not having the faintest idea.

"It's in a back room over there." Mook-ket pointed towards the supply warehouse of canned food from Earth, food to be managed presently by Tictoctic troops. "Here, we were keeping it under guard the entire time, keeping our own from sniffing around inside it, the very place we needed to explore!"

"Precisely!" Captain Mat-kek-tek tongue-clicked. "And by solving this without my assistance, you have saved my time for even more urgent matters!" He pointedly worked his bahvek atop one of his most elevated antlers. Then he turned to Kwit-Nik and tongue-clicked at his crispest, "Once we are aloft, we will incinerate the warehouse until there is nothing left but ash, for gentle breezes to remove all evidence any of it was ever there. That should disarm the laser grid. But before we leave for outer space, we will launch a probe to assure it is no longer operational. What is stunning is how the forces of nature operate. With no conscious design, these dumb beasts are able to instinctively, as has been previously remarked upon, construct such elaborate edifices as back on Tictoctic the twikky-twiks spin their sticky webs!"

*Before you leave, we make one last plea.*

Captain Mat-kek-tek and the other deer creatures looked all around. This time, they found themselves befuddled by a chorus of Oombian telepathers. Those telepathers were harmonizing their message on what they had mind-read to be a most popular, alluring melody back on Tictoctic. Although, despite this distraction, the troops easily persisted with their duties, whether they were holding back Sergeant Frankly from any reckless behavior, or guarding the bull pens.

*Your meat diet is not nearly as beneficial for you as would be the fruit and tubers we offer from our branches. We can show you how to combine those fruit and tubers with savory grasses that grow abundantly here on Oomb, to provide you a delicious, healthier diet. This new diet will lessen your incidence of heart disease and cancer, which incidence you must realize shortens and adds unnecessary pain to your lives.*

Captain Mat-kek-tek noticed some tree creatures appeared to be plucking at thin air, like they were plucking at non-existent guitar strings. Nevertheless, they were seeming to produce an ethereal-sounding instrumental accompaniment to their telepathed chorale-singing of their message.

To Sergeant Frankly's thought, *Now what the f- is happening?*, another Oombian was explaining telepathically, for both him and the other adult Earthlings, what the tree creatures were attempting.

*Return our fellow Oombians and the humans to us, then we can all tell stories, play our game, and create music together. Thereby, will you learn to enjoy happiness how you will otherwise never learn it! We can help Tictoctic towards a new society free from violence. This is our counsel to you as much as to the humans.*

"Baa!!" Captain Mat-kek-tek brayed scoffingly. "These are mental webs you instinctively weave to catch us as though we were tiny nik-niks for the twikky-twik webs! You know nothing of our nutritional needs, and what is that music??!! Stop it!!" The captain fired his air igniter at Woony Woodle and inflamed his upper half, again. The Oombian waved about his unburned branches, most frantically. He hoped there was enough moisture left on his leaves and juicier fruit to snuff out where he'd been newly torched. This, as he telepathed, *For those of us whose visions and dexterity have been extended to five dimensions,-*

The ethereal instrumental accompaniment was ceased.

*-we pluck the various flight paths of struck oof balls. Thereby do we discover melodies, chord progressions,-*

"I don't have time for this!" sharply tongue-clicked Captain Mat-kek-tek. "You can bore our cattle, perhaps keep them sedated with your pointless mental bleating, once we've left! Now translate for the dumb herd what I am about to say!

"Edifice-making animals of Oomb!: In a short time we will be lifting off in our spacecraft to leave this planet!, concluding our first roundup here! Our final action on our departure trajectory will be the complete destruction of your storage warehouse!, to deactivate decisively your laser mesh shield you no longer need, since we are here to protect you forthwith! Anything you may want from the warehouse, all your pens will now be temporarily opened so you can gather them! You better hurry! As soon as our craft is in position, there will be no further delay before we strike with our incinerating pulse beam!"

People could be heard stampeding, how the deer creatures of Tictoctic would have put it, to take away as much food and supplies from the warehouse as possible. Troops intervened threateningly with their air igniters, whenever couples not considered too old to matter tried getting back together for a tearful hug. Captain Mat-kek-tek ignored all of this to lower his head, stare directly into Sergeant Frankly's eyes, and bray without asking an Oombian to translate, "I hope one or more of your sons will grow up to be just like you, so I may feast on their rippling muscles and stubborn brains towards the furtherance of my eternal existence!"

"Yeah? Well f- you too, whatever you f-in' said!" the sergeant spat out as his keepers yanked him around to return him to his pen.

Soon as the saucer got airborne, people fled from anywhere near the warehouse. They did not resist as troops guided them at air-igniter gunpoint back to their assigned living spaces. And a good thing they did, Ludi thought to herself with her arms loaded down by bags of rice and beans. With the Third Celestial Breath, no time was wasted, zipping the giant saucer craft over to be stationed hovering above the warehouse. A blinding white ray beamed straight down from its underbelly. That ray sent thunder rolling outwards in all directions on superheated air. The humans felt like they were experiencing an immense earthquake. By the time the beam was shut off, there was nothing left of the warehouse but its partially melted perimeter walls. Those walls proceeded to slowly cave inwards with a shrill, metallic groan. Thereafter lifting their eyes skywards, everyone planet-bound could see parts of the laser mesh randomly flashing on and off their red beams. The entire system was in danger of shorting out, Sergeant Frankly realized.

"Captain," reported Kwit-Nik on the control bridge of the saucer, "the laser mesh is definitely malfunctioning, now that we have destroyed its control center! Destructive beams are getting emitted even though no object is breaking the mesh circuit! And the laser emission spheres are repositioning after each time they fire! They are doing so with such frequency, I have already been able to extrapolate their next several locations! This will allow us to lock on to enough of them to punch a hole in the defense shield for our exit! As you would have predicted!"

"I hope you fully understand it is as I would have predicted, Officer Kwit-Nik!" What did not go unnoticed by the captain was the perfunctory, tacked-on quality of this most irritating officer's adulatory remark. "Proceed with my exit strategy!"

"An honor I do not deserve, Captain!"

*An honor for which you will receive, at the first opportune moment, the most brutal antler slashing I can give you! It is a feces-ruminating shame you must not be crippled too much, since unfortunately your most wretched services are still required!*

***

"No! No! No!" Buddy Leung was talking to himself as he furiously raced his fingers across the console of the shuttle craft buried in dust and dirt on the dark side of

Oomb's irregularly-shaped asteroid moon. He was struggling to take over remote control of the laser mesh shield, to shut it down temporarily. He knew that were Kwit-Nik to succeed in destroying one or more of the geodesic coordinate spheres from where issued the laser beams, several others would focus their fire power on the saucer and cause it to crash, killing off Pedro, Oodle-Noodle, and everyone else aboard. Not that the humans and Oombians might not be doomed regardless, if Buddy wasn't able to concoct some scheme. Officer Leung had incidentally long since decided not to convey any false hope via the captive mind-reading trees to the humans seized for slaughter, especially since one plan was particularly gruesome in the short term. And for the first time, he found himself reluctantly wondering whether it wouldn't have been better, after all, to have gone along with total arming-up for this mission. That maybe the Oombians were dangerously naïve, however well-intentioned...

***

Kwit-Nik got off successful shots at two of the spheres, causing them to blow apart. From ground level, they looked like two reddish fireworks going off. Laser beams issued from five other spheres, all converging on the saucer craft. However, they gave out a fraction of a second after they fired; their malfunctioning activity had drained their power reserves faster than their solar cells could replenish them. What did get emitted proved enough to jolt the saucer into a wobble, nothing more. In seconds, the spacecraft from Tictoctic had been righted by Kwit-Nik working with Tak-venk-tit. A minute after that, the Third Celestial Breath spun out well past the orbit of the asteroid moon. Its crew was oblivious to the firefly donut launched from there to track it, leaving behind roiled up clouds of lunar dust.

# Chapter 15

"It is all too clear what happened, esteemed Fafamafalafama," the squadron leader's fa-la-las crackled translated out of Captain Taylor's translator. "The shuttle vehicle from the 'Ahth' spacecraft got crashed into a cliff face by a blinding-light prowler. Its resultant explosion there caused the entrance to the prowler den to collapse. The debris down at the base of the cliff includes burnt wreckage from the shuttle, and what looks like one of the wings from the prowler."

The squadron leader's jet was swinging past the cliff towards which the prowlers had been seen headed. This, after landing to pick up the stranded Earthlings, the family from rebel territory, and the security detail for the twenty-third wife.

"If another prowler carried the soldier from 'Ahth' and the Varafafafa into this den, their fate is not clear," the leader's report continued. "With the sunset storm line due soon, there will be insufficient time to search for them."

"But there will be ample time to meet up with your partner jet for the retaliatory bombing mission before you return home, yes?"

"Of course, esteemed Fafamafalafama. Partner is parallel to us now!"

"And partner understands he is to exercise diversionary tactics if you receive incoming strafing, since you are carrying the 'Ahth' creatures?"

Ali and Tanya, seated together directly across the aisle from Captain Taylor, traded significant glances with her. They were thinking the same thing, as they discovered when they compared notes later: The Fafamafalafama might feel good about inflicting revenge for the actions of what might have been one lone terrorist, but what was he actually accomplishing?, other than risking their bombs accidentally causing cave-ins that will bury alive innocent people?

***

By the time the Fafaman bomber was flying alongside the cliff face to search for any signs of Yulala and Sergeant Hanson, those two had already long since climbed out of a nest of dried-out, desiccated foliage the male blinding-light prowler had pieced together for his prospective mate. They were headed down a steep tunnel out of the prowler hive. The giant male beetle had dropped Guy into said nest, thinking it had just mated with a female of his species. Simultaneously, Yulala had let go one of its prickly legs where she ran to grab hold when it first assaulted the Marine. Soon as the male prowler had flown off, the twenty-third wife had urgently fa-la-laed, "Fortunately, what the prowler ejected on you marks you as his territory so no other prowlers will approach this nest! And also, fortunately, he is preoccupied with joining the effort to clear away the debris from the cave-in! However, when he returns and finally realizes you are not a female prowler, he is not going to be happy. He is going to think you stole the nest away from his mate. And then you will see what he is capable of doing with those mandibles that bracket his mouth! We need to get out of here now, while he is otherwise engaged!"

"Any guidance you can provide, Oodle-Noodle?" Guy Hanson had voiced aloud, albeit softly, as they had made their way off the nest. When no response had entered his head, he had explained to the twenty-third wife about the telepathic tree creatures from Oomb.

"Our spaceship must have departed for Oomb," he had concluded. "It makes sense that neither tree creature would have wanted to remain here to help, since their home planet is reportedly under attack."

"Do you feel that?" Yulala lifted her button nose high. Its profile was spotted easily, thanks to Sergeant Hanson's night-vision goggles. The sergeant was reminded of a guard dog he used to train back on Earth, how he would lift his own snout when he picked up an important scent in the air rather than along the ground. "We're getting a hint of breeze, which means there must be at least two exits, somewhere around."

The steep hole they had been descending opened onto a narrow yet flat grotto.

"Ah! And here are some tapastrahs, yes! Of the edible kind!" Prior to making this pronouncement, Yulala gave a close inspection to the squat mushroom she pulled from among several which covered a portion of the muddy floor. "One other necessity before we proceed any further: We need to get the prowler's love juice washed off of you. While it kept us protected leaving the prowler colony, it will not help us where other creatures we could encounter are concerned. It could signal mistakenly that you are part of their diet! If we can be rid of any scents other than our own, we should be okay. With the mud underfoot," she lifted one leg for emphasis, "I am guessing we are not too far from a grotto lake, a good place for your cleansing."

Guy Hanson shook his head admiringly. At the same time, he wondered whether he was imagining it, or was there a certain nervousness about Yulala? Now that they were alone, far away from any other people, she seemed to keep avoiding eye contact with him. "Where did you learn so much about survival skills?" he asked.

"Hiking and exploring are as exciting for me as the sunset storm line is for some people."

"I love hiking and exploring."

"A lot of people don't know about the far northwest corner of the central pyramid," the twenty-third wife went on like she hadn't noticed his chiming in, Guy thought. This, while she busied her hands, feeling along the smooth, slimy-wet grotto wall. Guy got the impression that was helping her locate the grotto lake. "The far northwest corner is seriously compromised by a 'kamakala' colony. The 'kamakalas' are like the prowlers, but instead of having one big yellow shell, polka-dotted pink, that opens into wings, their bodies are segmented into three parts, all black, and they do not fly. Nor do they make webs, like the ahtpah."

"Huh."

"They do dig a complex network of tunnels, similar to rebel behavior."

"They sound like a monster-sized version of our ants back on my planet Earth."

"I and a few friends made discoveries three solar orbits ago, before my parents got me to qualify to try out for the Varafafafa. Inspired by rumors, we snuck over to the northwest corner, and we explored the 'kamakala' colony. We learned how to fool them into thinking we were just big stones they needed to clear from their tunnels. We also learned lots of other useful information, such as how to tell when there was an exit to the outside. I guess the scariest part was when we bumped into the side of a hibernating Namanacasa. One of my friends snuck a note to the police, and before the passing of three more sunset storm lines, there were news reports the Fafamafalafama had a dream about a Namanacasa hibernating near the northwest corner of the pyramid.

After its existence got confirmed, nationally televised underground detonations were set off to destroy it. We didn't learn whether the dying Namanacasa shed its poisonous fumes into the 'kamakala'colony, killed them all off as well. Who knows? Maybe those fumes, if they were shed, have lingered there, making those tunnels completely unsafe for future exploration. Or maybe the detonations have caved in the tunnels. Maybe there's nothing left to explore."

"There are lots of amazing caverns I could show you, we could explore on my home planet Earth. My favorites are along an ancient mountain range called the Appalachians, and a network they discovered on a small island named Puerto Rico."

"When the Fafamafalafama is finished with his present preoccupations, which of course includes determining my whereabouts," Yulala continued to feel across the grotto wall, not deigning even the briefest glance Guy's way as she spoke, "I will ask him whether he would consider our taking a trip to 'Ahth' together to have you guide us through these places of which you speak."

"Okay," Guy gulped awkwardly.

"You could regard it as a favor to us since I grabbed the prowler's leg to join you. You must understand, 'Offasah Hahhnsahhn,' I only performed such a feat because of doubts you could survive here very well on your own, despite your training. That is, without the assistance of someone at least somewhat familiar with Fafaman ecology and geology. Wouldn't have wanted you to ingest a poisonous tapastrah, for example."

"Then I thank you; being your guide will be the least I can do for the Varafafafa, twenty-third wife of the Fafamafalafama." As he thus spoke, Sergeant Hanson made sure he was himself also preoccupied feeling across the grotto wall, no longer trying to make eye contact with Yulala.

So he missed her stealing a look his way.

# Chapter 16

"From IABC News, this is a special report: Update on the interstellar mission of the Smoke and Mirrors. Live from the New York anchor desk, here is Paul Berger."

"Hello. Earlier today, at nine thirty a.m. Eastern Time, IABC News was contacted by the provisional captain of the Smoke and Mirrors for an exclusive interview, to be shared for distribution with other televised news feeds. That's right; the provisional captain. There is much more we're just learning, in the first substantive mission update since a news blackout abruptly suspended coverage of a wedding ceremony on the planet Fafama for their king, the Fafamafalafama. We have been receiving a series of short messages since that event. Those messages have been thanking everyone for their patience, while complex negotiations are being conducted between the Fafaman central government and a rebel group accused of conducting terrorist attacks. We have also been informed that midway through the wedding ceremony, the Fafaman government suddenly decided it should not be aired five light-years away.

"This morning on the east coast of the United Americas, we received word that the provisional captain finally agreed to our request to answer a series of questions. We made this request based on the concerns expressed by many here on Earth, over the lack of information during the past three weeks. The problem with arranging for such an interview, of course, is the seven-minute delay for a transmission to be broadcast and received between Earth and the current location of the starship Smoke and Mirrors. Not that anyone is complaining. Without the hyperspace relays provided by the so-called firefly donuts, the delay would stretch far longer. Years, even. Anyhow, we had thought about filling the delay time for each response with analysis and commentary. But we concluded that more people would want to hear the entire interview without such interruptions, especially since we were asked to share it with several other televised news feeds. Just minutes before I came on the air, we finished splicing together our conversation, editing out those seven-minute delays. Should you wish to see and hear what we were doing here while awaiting each response, the full video is available at IABC News online. You can learn, among other things, why I don't take cream in my tea. But don't let that scare you away.

"Um, with no further ado, here is my interview with the provisional captain of the Smoke and Mirrors: Chief Navigation Officer Yoon-hee Park-Smith. Oh, and one last thing: We hope you will stick around afterwards for analysis and commentary, when my co-anchor Amal Mahfouz will be joining us from our bureau office in Washington, D.C."

"Thank you for agreeing to this interview, Captain Park-Smith," news anchorman Paul Berger went on in the previously-taped interview. "We understand from the initial information we've received that Captain Taylor has temporarily turned over command to you, so she can stay behind on Fafama while you return to Oomb. Does this indicate that Helena Taylor is making good progress on Fafama, helping with government and rebel negotiations? And I'll ask a second question now, to help minimize how often we have to go back and forth on these seven-minute delays: The crew manifest clearly puts First Engineer Buddy Leung in charge, should Captain Taylor be unable to fulfill her duties. Where is Officer Leung that he is not the one temporarily assigned to be the captain?"

"Thank you, Paul, for this opportunity to bring up-to-date everyone home on Earth." Yoon-hee spoke from the captain's chair. The captain's chair was pivoted around so its back was to the control console it usually faced. That was the console Yoon-hee sat at, before she got assigned her new duty. Oodle-Noodle's body cam took in not only Yoon-hee, but also what showed on the panoramic view-screen behind her. What showed there was the video transmission from a camera mounted on one of the Smoke and Mirror's stabilizer "thorns." This way, the audience for Paul Berger's interview got to ponder the vastness of outer space into the bargain, the brightness of innumerable stars undiminished since there was no intervening atmosphere. "Everything has been so hectic since we cut our last full transmission; we regret having had to forgo our usual updates," Yoon-hee went on. "Captain Taylor, with the assistance of our chief counselor Dr. Ali Magabu, is very very busy, yes." Yoon-hee wanted to bang her head against the nearest wall for laughing nervously at this juncture. "They are trying to help the Fafaman government and the rebels get to the root of the difficulties they are having. The negotiations are so complicated, it is a little too soon to characterize how well they are going. However, Dr. Magabu does bring enormous cross-cultural expertise to the situation, and the- and there is the rapport Captain Taylor has already developed with the Fafaman government, stemming from the first mission. Clearly, this is not the time, not yet, for us to just fly away, and keep our fingers crossed the Fafamans can work out the rest on their own, especially with what we're offering to bring to the table, which I'm sure we'll get to.

"Now as for Officer Leung and why I am stuck with this instead of him..." Again with the nervous laughter.

Yoon-hee wanted to strangle herself, especially after the eyes-closed, can't-believe-she-said-that head shake Dr. Entroper made over her "stuck with" word choice. "It is of course an honor, a duty I take most seriously and proudly that Captain Taylor has assigned to me," Yoon-hee said in an attempt to walk back her "stuck with" characterization. "You are correct, Mr. Berger. Under other circumstances, this would have been Officer Leung's assignment. Well what was happening, Officer Leung stayed behind on Oomb while we headed back to Fafama. He was monitoring, uhh, this is part of what has made things so hectic. We didn't feel we had time to do justice to a full update. Not that I'm exactly calving the glaciers, as I think the current saying goes."

"Do you want to start over, Yoon-hee?" Louisa Entroper broke in. "Since this is on a delayed basis,-"

"The CAPTAIN is doing fine, Officer Entroper." Yoon-hee's husband, Second Engineer Kevin Smith-Park, held up a hand out of camera range for Louisa to stop. "Our friends on Earth aren't looking for a polished acting performance. Captain Park?"

"Thank you, Officer Smith. Anyway, Officer Entroper, I doubt my second take would go any smoother than this."

Officer Entroper out of camera range made a face at Yoon-hee that said, *OOOkaaay, but don't say you weren't warned*.

The provisional captain continued, back directly into the body cam, hung like just another fruit from one of Oodle-Noodle's branches, "Officer Leung picked up on what looked to be an asteroid cluster that could be headed towards Oomb. Well, - and this maybe anticipates your next question, Paul – turns out it WAS headed directly for Oomb. It breached the security, uh, the stability of the rich, life-enhancing Oombian atmosphere." Yoon-hee was having trouble with outright lying about what had happened, so she was fudging with "It," and she nearly slipped up when she started to speak of breaching security. "Unfortunately, significant damage was inflicted upon our research settlement and the Oombians, with possible casualties. If you were going to ask next why the rush to return to Oomb rather than waiting out the captain's negotiations, this is the answer."

"Yes, you're right, Captain, one of my next questions WAS going to be about why the rush. But let me make sure we understand correctly from five light-years away, as you referenced earlier: A meteorite shower apparently did not burn up completely in the atmosphere. Enough meteorites were so large, they made it all the way down to the surface of the planet Oomb, where they caused considerable damage plus 'possible' casualties. I'm not clear whether the possible casualties were only Oombians. Did they also include any of our people at the research settlement? Um, is Officer Leung okay? You see, I'm stumbling around too, especially with this delayed-response format, and here I'm the news anchor! I have another question, but, um, let's save it for the next batch."

Yoon-hee had Oodle-Noodle pause the body cam for a minute after transmission reception. She wanted time to think on how she could respond without lying. Finally, she said, "The supply warehouse and two living quarters were utterly demolished. As for casualties, Officer Leung is fine, but we are concerned about some members of the expeditionary team as well as some of our kind and gentle Oombian hosts. And if I can anticipate one of your next questions, the spacecraft that recently left Space Station 2 under such a cloak of secrecy is a second large craft propelled by mirror array technology. It will be rendezvousing with us just outside the Callaway X Centra system, the same system where Oomb is located. Basically, it is a supply ship carrying, among other things, a new- something new, a laser mesh shield for Oomb, to protect it from any additional extraterrestrial objects capable of causing damage. And the other exciting project, we hope that one is going to help negotiations with the rebels on Fafama. It will involve herding an enormous ice comet into orbit around Fafama. That comet is to be set close enough to Fafama, significant water will get shed into the Fafaman atmosphere. We hope this will defuse water shortage as a point of tension and political unrest. Conventional hydrogen fuel rockets will get burrowed into the comet we have identified. Intermittent rocket blasts will make orbital corrections, to assure the comet will not fall all at once, down into the Oombian atmosphere. Those blasts will also accelerate the comet's water-shedding diminution. A fascinating topic for one of our future updates, I should think."

"Wow. Just wow, Captain Park." Paul Berger shook his head, stunned. "You have raised enough topics to fill several updates. But for the time being, we can more fully appreciate, I think, how busy you must all be with so much happening and so many plans. Let me first say that our thoughts and prayers are certainly with any of the expeditionary team members as well as their Oombian hosts who might have been injured. We can only hope nothing has proven life-threatening. But, I don't want to make more of this than is actually there, but you said Officer Leung remained on Oomb to track meteorites before they hit. Has he indicated whether any of them cratered the surface on impact? My only other question on this round will be about that second light-powered spacecraft. Everyone suspected that was what was going on, underneath the same cloaking tarp used to conceal the Smoke and Mirrors as it was being assembled in dock on Space Station 2. Why so much secrecy? Is it just that secrecy is something the government does well, so they do it as often as they can whether it's called for or not? Or is there something- I'm sure you can appreciate how imaginations can get out of hand, with all the wild stories, rumors, that were spread about the Smoke and Mirrors during its first mission."

"I think you're right about people letting ideas go crazy, especially when they are dealing with the unknown." Yoon-hee appreciated the news anchor virtually feeding her lines she could repeat on her slow ease into another evasive response. "And it does seem," yet again with the nervous laugh she wished she could totally stifle, "sometimes the government is secretive for the heck of it. But we were under the impression it was not so much secrecy with the construction of the new starship. Anyone who could have provided useful information about it, they were also deeply involved in the process. Given the urgency of deploying sooner rather than later, especially to bring us the comet-herding equipment and another- another thing, the laser mesh, they just didn't feel they could spare the time for a press briefing. I know with the construction of the Smoke and Mirrors, it was more a matter of Engineer Leung not wanting to reveal anything about the mirror array assembly, until he was certain it would actually piece together." Yoon-hee expounded easily on this particular subject because, at least to the extent of what she was aware, no evasiveness was required...But then it was back to addressing the damage done to Oomb by what she was allowing Berger to believe was a meteorite barrage. "About the incident on Oomb, we'll be sure to extend your kind remarks to everyone there including the Oombians themselves. Oodle-Noodle on the bridge here filming me, if you were within her telepathic range, you can be certain she would be sending you her expression of appreciation directly. As for the impacts, we do know that fortunately nothing impacted so powerfully as to cause any deep cratering."

"Very well." Berger couldn't help a vague sense the provisional captain was eluding him pinning her down. On what, he couldn't figure out exactly. Yet he was resigned to letting it go, at least for the time being, to move on to a last big question. And also leave for later the matter of whether there was more than simply cultural discomfort, modesty on the part of the aliens on Fafama, over their allowing a telecast of the rest of the Fafaman ruler's wedding ceremony. "So Captain," he went on, "this is all very noble of you and your crew, and apparently of the crew on the second starship that is going to rendezvous with you. Protecting Oomb from meteorite hazards, adding water to Fafama to quell disputes between the government and rebel forces...some people would argue, with the multitude of problems we have back here on Earth, that the old saying, 'Charity begins at home,' pertains. Maybe our resources ought to be re-directed towards projects to help with problems more local. Leave the Fafamans and the Oombians to fend for themselves. Water shortages on Earth, aggravated by a population of eight billion plus, those shortages are definitely not helping with our own, terrestrial peace efforts. What do you say to people who put it in these terms? Why not drag that ice comet into orbit around Earth instead?"

Yoon-hee nodded to convey nonverbally her

appreciation for the argument the news anchor was making. "Sure," she said finally, "there doesn't appear to be any national, or in this case planetary, interest we are serving, based on what, um, we usually think of, based on how we think of our national or planetary interest." Yoon-hee caught herself about to say, "based on what people know," which would have been a dead giveaway that something huge was getting kept from the general public. "And there was the rule on that old science fiction series, *Star Trek*; anybody here remember what it was called?"

"The Prime Directive."

"Thank you, Officer Smith." Yet another nervous laugh. "Yes, the Prime Directive was this rule the Starfleet Federation had. They were to avoid involving themselves in any significant way with the history on other life-bearing planets.

"Okay, well, I think this is the thinking. The same as during the first century of the space program, we are constantly coming up with things out here that will have practical use, to help make life better back home. The laser mesh shield is a perfect example. If it works for Oomb, we can be sure it will also work for protecting Earth from large space debris." People back home were wondering what that odd red flash was they saw in the sky, as reported in one of the news capsules the Smoke and Mirrors received early on in the second mission. Yoon-hee figured what she just said might well confirm their suspicions such a protective system had already been deployed. But so be it. She told herself she could not be expected to perfectly bluff her way through this necessary interview, without letting at least a little kitty out of the bag. "Now as for what we are going to attempt with an ice comet: Fafama is as arid a planet as a planet can be, and still have gaianized a prolific evolution of life. Earth, on the other hand, does not lack for water. What we lack are desalinization strategies on the scale they are needed. The global warming of the ice caps immediately rushes most of its resulting runoff into salty seas, before we can corral much of it. The occasional city-sized iceberg we have managed to tow to a coastal city only begins to address the real issue. Adding an ice comet's water to our atmosphere would even more dramatically raise the sea level, flood even more coastal areas than global warming has already done. That would decrease even further the already significantly shrunk area of livable land."

***

"Bullshit! I don't know what she is hiding, and I don't care, but it's some f-ing big shit!" complained Flamboyo Sanchez. He was seated at the counter of the shootout-dilapidated tavern, to watch the provisional starship captain, Yoon-hee Park-Smith, getting interviewed. Sanchez swore for the benefit of the person disguised as a man who had slid onto the stool beside him only moments earlier.

"So, instead of watching more of it, could you follow me outside to a canoe, where we can talk in private?" Shelly Taylor spoke softly, in the deepest, manliest-sounding voice she could coax from her vocal chords. She stared down into her tall glass of dark beer, trying to shake off a vague yet chilling presentiment of something awful from how Flamboyo spit out, *I don't care*...

"You can say whatever you have to say here, Ms. Taylor! Yes! What? You think that when your secret service people precede you and fill this place, nobody, nadie, here is going to know is you? With a snap of my fingers, or the tracing of a pattern into the condensation on this beer mug, I can have you all shot before your quickest-on-the-trigger gunman even touches his weapon!" Flamboyo shook his head with eyes closed, then he proceeded on a softer note, "I imagined you were going to return here soon. Congress was voting on whether to open the quarantine areas, yes? You are here to tell me this miracle occurred?"

Flamboyo disciplined himself to keep his reopened eyes glued to the television above and behind the bartender, who himself was carefully scanning the room for any signs of potential trouble. Said bartender held a soda water trigger by one hand, and an automatic weapon trigger by the other.

Shelly's hair was already slipping out from where she'd crowded it into her wool ski cap. Señor Flamboyo Sanchez did not see this, nor how Shelly was straining to stop her lower lip from quivering as she said, "Could I persuade you to appear before Congress?, to tell your own story? I've managed to get you a three-day pass out of here for that purpose."

That was when Flamboyo couldn't help turning Shelly's way, reacting almost involuntarily. He gave her what he would have insisted was not an affectionate regard, rather that he was overcome by curiosity over her disguise. Was that a sideways glance she stole his direction? He wondered this as he noted her pathetic makeup effort to appear to have a sweaty five-o'clock shadow. He also noted strands of her hair, matted together like golden wayward vines, he fancied. Those strands had snaked out of her gray cap to meander across her ear lobe and down her cheek. That's as far as he got with his cherishing look when the television erupted with, "This is a special report from IABC News."

*Oh-oh,* Shelly thought as she made to latch her hand onto Flamboyo's wrist, and he flinched to wrest it out of reach.

"Here at our Washington, D.C. bureau desk is Amal Mahfouz."

"Good afternoon. Three minutes ago, the House of Representatives in a close, 250 to 242 vote, with the rest abstaining, decided not to approve a bill which would have provided for experimenting with loosening the quarantine no-zone rules. With more-"

"The sponsors haven't given up, Flamboyo. They have a new version of the bill. They think they can get the extra votes they need. Your testimony could make the difference..."

"Puta madre!" Flamboyo tried to speak in as soft, as calm a voice as possible, belying his cursing in Spanish. He seemingly convulsively shook off Shelly's attempt to latch on to his shoulder, and he kept his eyes focused straight ahead. He saw nothing but the tears welling up in them. "Get out, get out now, and take your doomed dreams and the hopeless rest with you."

"I care about you, Flamboyo." Shelly made one last grab at his shoulder.

"Before I give the orders to shoot..."

The steely cold way Flamboyo was able to issue this threat, without raising his voice, spooked Shelly off his shoulder before he could shake her off. The next thing Flamboyo heard was the entrance to the tavern creaking open, then shutting gently of its own accord. Not in the least was it helped along the way, let alone slammed. Subsequently three other people left, one by one at random intervals. *F-ing idiots,* Flamboyo grumbled to himself. *What, they thought I had no idea they were there wasting their f-ing breath trying to protect her?*

Flamboyo exhaled relief, even smiled grimly, thinking to himself, *That f-er Engeling ought to have been here to see this! In case he had any lingering worries I would f-ing permit my sperm machine to f-up my determination! I suppose I should tell him how his shark adventure has inspired me.* Flamboyo felt around in his jacket for the umpteenth time, for the Ziploc baggie full of his original set of teeth he'd had removed, as he also worked his tongue around behind his new set of upper dentures. *The poor bastard we are going to have to torch to stage my death before I head down the coast, he is actually the lucky one. If there is some f-ing reboot of creation, to f-ing try and do a better job, he will get there before the rest of us. F-!! Who am I f-ing fooling?! The reboot will turn out just as f-ed! Better the endless nothing than for me or anyone else to ever have to experience this puke-stenched piss hole ever again!*

In Flamboyo's eyes, the half-drunk beer set down on the counter before him remained a watery blur.

## Chapter 17

Once the seven primate bulls were brought aboard the Tictoctickian battle saucer, Chef Glork-tek's first order of business was to have them gassed not unconscious, but so tranquilized they could hardly stay awake. They would drift too much in a daze to feel any terror as their fate approached. This was especially important so their stress hormones would not add bitter notes to their taste. If experience with Chonoran flesh was any indication, the head chef had good reason to expect a mild flavor. Such mild flavor, in fact, as to provide the perfect blank canvas for his brush strokes of spice. Perfect, that is, if it were not for his always-present twinge of conscience, however faintly felt.

There were five Marines from Sergeant Frankly's troop, Miguel who had become one of the main producers for the fledgling television station in the settlement on Oomb, and Pedro Perez. They all found themselves groggily sedated, their hands manacled high above their heads. The manacles were linked to chains lowered enough so each human could stand on the rubber floor rather than having to hang in midair. A slowly moving conveyer belt, to which those chains were attached at their top ends, step-by-step pulled and dragged the hapless Earthlings through a maze to slaughter. The maze's twelve-foot walls were lit with soothing lights. Earthling clothes were left on, as previous experience with human-like cattle from Chonora had taught the chefs of Tictoctic that messes for cleanup after slaughter were thereby more easily contained. Towards the end of the maze, each primate bull would pass through a curtain of dangling rubber strips. The next thing each one would know, and the last thing, presumably, would be his head going into a vice, and an aluminum bolt about one inch wide getting hammered with tremendous force and speed through the base of his skull. From this group of seven, the plan was for Pedro to be prepared immediately thereafter for Captain Mat-kek-tek. The captain's feast would consist of one of Chef Glork-tek's gourmet preparations of that particular Earthling's heart and brains. The rest of his body, plus parts of another body, were to subsequently get done up in various ways. Expendable crew members would join their courageous captain in risking their lives to test the cross-genetic safety of this extraterrestrial food source. Chef Glork-tek felt optimistic. The relatively benign after-effects of consuming Chonoran meat only required the smallest genetic modifications. However, one could never be too careful about these matters.

"I don't want to die," Miguel ahead of Pedro twisted his head around to groggily slur in Spanish.

Just then, the deer creatures of Tictoctic amplified the gentle surf ambience they were pumping into the maze. This, in preparation for masking the sound of the first bolt getting hammered through a primate bull's skull.

Pedro struggled with his sedative-induced stupor to conjure something to say to Miguel. However, part of him wished the television producer would just shut up so he could concentrate on memories of Ludi and Alexita. They were always his main source of comfort. In his mind's eye, he could see Alexita dancing with wild abandon to merengue music as Ludi clapped along.

Another part of Pedro felt selfish for wanting to effectively block out the younger man chained up just ahead of him. Miguel would have had so much of his life ahead. Pedro reflected on a story his mama Rotonda had read from the Bible when he was in junior high school. It was about Jesus getting nailed to the cross, with thieves being crucified on either side of him.

POOM! However muted, the first bolt-hammering sent a small vibration through the rubbery floor.

"I don't want to die!" Miguel repeated with more urgency. Desperation cut through his continuing grogginess and slurred speech.

For Pedro, it was like he was also saying to him, *Why haven't you done something about what I am telling you?* He decided to offer a response, however much in vain. "There has to be more to life than we know. We should pray on that, and think about those we love."

POOM!

Miguel's cry of terror got modified by his sedated state into a low bellow, almost more unsettling for Pedro than the second bolt getting hammered. And it was loud enough to draw the attention of the deer creature in charge of supervising this particular slaughter. The next thing Pedro knew, a distinct hiss got mixed in with the recorded surf. It was a hiss not from the foaming and ebbing sea water, but rather from additional sedative getting pumped into the air.

POOM!

Pedro wondered whether it was simply the additional sedative, or his spirit starting to disassociate from his body. Whichever, maybe both, his own terror, however muted by more sedative gas, was still enough for him to think further on that Bible story from his mama. He thought about the part where Jesus asked God why God had forsaken him. There He was, nailed to the cross, trying to assure the thieves on either side of him that there were places in heaven for them as well. And yet God, if there was a God, wasn't exactly making its presence known; it was as if there really was nothing beyond this too-short, too-wretched life but a yawning abyss. *Why hast thou forsaken me?*

It was then that Pedro remembered the wonder of his reawakening on a bed, surrounded by caring people informing him that he and his family were taken aboard a spaceship powered by only the force of light. They were bound for an idyllic planet where they could start a new life, free from the despair and pollution and war of the life they had left. And there was something someone had once said to him, he couldn't recall who or where. "This is not how it happens."

POOM!

Pedro was the fourth to be slaughtered.

"You heard them? Even gassed, they still tried to communicate with one another," observed Kwit-Nik. He, Nekamek and Mik-Fikity were watching the slaughter proceedings from a balcony view overhanging what Chef Glork-tek termed the prologue room. Kwit-Nik was still spooked by what happened when the two tree creatures were chopped up to provide cooking wood. Those creatures didn't try to incapacitate Kwit-Nik and company with silent screams, to make their heads feel like they were going to burst. Rather, they filled the Tictoctickians' minds with gentle exhortations for them to please reconsider what they were doing. They could eat Oombian fruit, hear more of the Oombian music, learn more about playing oof...as the buzz saws went to work, the voices in Kwit-Nik's head grew fainter and fainter until-Kwit-Nik wasn't quite sure whether they faded out altogether, or persisted even unto the present, as part of the background ghost hum always present in one's mind, when one was listening closely enough.

"I heard Chonorans also, back when we were first turning them into so much steak," crisply tongue-clicked

Nekamek. "Did they ever sizzle on the grill! And for that matter, at night on Tictoctic I used to hear little nik-niks rub their hind legs together to make chirping sounds, and then I heard them go squish! when I stepped on them! Baa!"

"Yeah, what are you trying to say, Officer Kwit-Nik?" Mik-Fikity brayed challengingly. Instinctively, he bowed his head crowned by stunted antlers towards Kwit-Nik for the charge. But then he lifted it back up again, thinking better of his behavior as a civilized creature.

"I'm saying I am not sure I can really tell much difference between them and us, and the Chonorans and us for that matter. They wear clothes like we wear clothes, for example."

"Here we go again," baaed Nekamek shaking his head. "So back home on Tictoctic, when the squigglies stitch their cocoons, you think they are wearing clothes also?"

"But they are stitching cocoons so they can metamorphose into flitty-flits! They are doing that by instinct!"

"And these cattle are not making their clothes by instinct?"

"Do they emerge from them looking totally different from their former selves, like the flitty-flits emerge from their cocoons looking totally different from the squigglies?!" Kwit-Nik brayed with mounting frustration.

"I don't know. Has anyone seen them BEFORE they put on their clothes?" Mik-Fikity pounded at the floor with a hind hoof for added emphasis.

Kwit-Nik shook his head. "What about those elaborate homes they built? How are our homes any different?"

"You remember the mud and wood mounds the nik-

nik colonies build on Tictoctic?! Do not the cattle houses resemble more those mounds than our corrugated metal stables?!" Nekamek brayed at higher volume to be heard above the din of bodies getting slapped about on the aluminum cleaning tables as they were skinned, spray-washed and dressed for cooking.

"And what about that laser defense surrounding Oomb? Something that elaborate-"

"Almost like the webs woven by twikky-twiks, you mean?" baaed Nekamek mockingly.

"You can't see the difference from the work of dumb beasts? You can't see how that laser defense had to be no less a product of highly intelligent creatures than anything we have constructed?" Kwit-Nik wondered why he bothered arguing any further.

Nekamek and Mik-Fikity exchanged looks before both turning Kwit-Nik's way and baaing their amusement. Mik-Fikity added, "Officer Kwit-Nik, you are always so entertaining!"

"I will make one last charge at this for now," Kwit-Nik tongue-clicked most tersely. He was having trouble hiding his irritation. "Is it not true we stole our space-flight technology from the Chonorans when we conquered them?"

"'Conquered them'?!?" Nekamek repeated, expressing mocking surprise. "No, we tamed and herded them! And sure, our engineers rooted out inspiration from their instinctively-produced objects. That is precisely how we gathered ideas for flight within the Tictoctic atmosphere. We studied the wings of the flitty-flits. You wouldn't call *that* stealing, would you?"

"But flitty-flits are born with their wings."

"You mean after the squiggly-niks construct their cocoons? Who knows what goes on inside there before the flitty-flits emerge?" Nekamek brayed challengingly.

Kwit-Nik bleated with resignation. "So you don't think that when the cattle are slaughtered, they feel what we would feel were we treated the same way?"

Both deer creatures shook their heads no, and Mik-Fikity brayed on, "So you are among those who believe the animals are no different from us? I think they call that anthropomorphizing, or something. I am with those who trust, those who have faith, in our Creator who brought us our mighty protector, Dek-Fook-Tek."

Even Kwit-Nik felt obliged to join the other two in going down on one knee to honor mention of the Supreme Authority's name, if not chant yet another ritualized praise, especially with Captain Mat-kek-tek not in their presence.

"He provided the animals for our sustenance," Mik-Fikity continued, "and so He made that their nervous systems are not as well developed as ours. Their neurons lack animation from a soul, so that they do not cherish life and suffer the pain of death as we do."

Nekamek nodded his agreement to everything Mik-Fikity baaed.

However, Kwit-Nik decided he wasn't quite finished arguing, after all. He came back with, "What about the final telepathic messages from the tree creatures as they were getting chopped up? When they said eating their fruit and other plant preparations would be more healthful for us than eating meat?, and that playing their game and finding the music we each really enjoy will bring us more happiness than we otherwise would ever know?, except for the even greater happiness we will find spreading all these good things to those less fortunate than us? Baa?"

Mik-Fikity and Nekamek appeared to not be listening.

Rather, they were both raised so high up on their hind legs, with their necks at maximum extension, that their forelegs seemed to Kwit-Nik to dangle down uselessly in front of them. All this, so their busily twitching nostrils could pick up more of what they scented.

"Do you smell what I smell?" Nekamek brayed excitedly to Mik-Fikity.

"To the kitchen! Let's go!"

Nekamek and Mik-Fikity brought down their forelegs to the floor, making loud clicks of their cloven hoof-hands on the metal. They galloped off excitedly, with Kwit-Nik following in a reluctant trot behind.

Once inside the cooking area, Kwit-Nik's fellow officers chattered and baaed eagerly about which body parts they would have eaten, were they among the expendable members of their herd who would be braving first taste of Chef Glork-tek's gourmet preparations to ascertain its safety. This, as they pondered the remains of Pedro and one of the Marines. Those remains were turning ever so slowly as they got roasted over an open pit by the fires from chopped-up Oombians.

Kwit-Nik stood off to one side. He tried to be as unobtrusive as possible, not to call attention to what he was about. He was practicing the swing Mafoosoola had shown him, as though an oof club were actually in his hoof hands. He wondered whether he could repeat the terrific first shot he'd made for the too-brief time he'd gotten to play. The oof ball had arced high through the sky, carrying his spirit soaring…

# Chapter 18

After he unlocked its aluminum gate, Officer Wiklit entered Fred Frankly's pen. He trotted up to Frankly's actual habitation, and he did what was customary when he visited any home dwelling back on Tictoctic, whether that dwelling was surrounded by barbed wire fence, or not. Officer Wiklit turned his back on it, and he kicked at the front door with one of his hind hooves.

Fred opened up to find what more often than not greeted him, ever since he got imprisoned by the extraterrestrial occupation. There stood the armed Tictoctickian soldier who came a-kickin', Oombian Hoogle-Shnoogle to translate telepathically, and someone with whom he was expected to mate, brought to him on a collared leash. This time it was Ciela, who had been helping Pedro's wife Ludi to provide formal schooling to the children of at least kindergarten age.

Officer Wiklit turned over the leash to Sergeant Frankly, and he tersely tongue-clicked what Hoogle-Schnoogle telepathed as, *I will stand guard outside your window, to assure your privacy while you copulate with this cow. When you have concluded, I will return her to her stall.*

*Kripes, I'm glad you've explained this to me for the sixteenth f-n' time,* Frankly thought to himself as he accepted the leash.

Ciela docilely entered, and she stepped softly behind him to get out of sight of the deer creature.

*I'd have forgotten completely had you only told me five or six times!* Frankly continued to rage in his head. "Uh, thanks," he nodded. The tree creature telepathed the translation back to Wiklit while the Marine Corps Sergeant thought further, *You f-n' voyeurs! Like I don't know you're taking a peek, hopin' the blanket slips aside so you can catch some human-on-human action!*

What hurt especially was that, of all the good-looking eligible women in the settlement, Sergeant Frankly considered Ciela special. In a more ideal world, where they weren't going to get f-ed, as he had put it, by these antlered bastards from Tictoctic, Ciela was the one woman he would have wanted to get to know better. She was the one woman with whom he would have wanted to have something more than a mere fluid exchange. What he had told himself "sucked the ultimate" was the first time she'd been brought to him. It had been the look of terror, sheer terror, dread, in her eyes. He and the other "bulls" had only just finished collaborating, with the help of Oombian telepathy. They had discussed how they could handle the situation, isolated from one another in separate mating pens. Originally, they were scheming, wondering whether there wasn't some way to overpower the occupation forces. Enabled by Oombian telepathy, that conversation had even included Officer Leung, who was still hiding out in one of the space shuttles on the dark side of Oomb's irregularly-shaped asteroid moon. Reluctantly, they had concluded the sanest action was no action, sitting tight until the Smoke and Mirrors returned. And so, it had been on to consideration of the awful mating regimen, compulsory irrespective of individual relationships. Sergeant Frankly and company had arrived quickly at a resolution in regard to that regimen. The Oombians had telepathed that resolution to all the women and teenaged girls. However, Ciela had been one of those females who still couldn't believe what was insinuating itself inside her brain.

Fred had suspected as much, from the total dread

that had read clearly across Ciela's face when a deer creature from Tictoctic had brought her to him for the first time, also her first time getting brought to anyone. "Look," he had said most softly, soon as he had gotten her into his bedroom, behind closed door, "I am not going to be doing anything to you. None of the men are. But you have to play along, 'cause we have company keeping an eye on us through that window. We're going to hide under my bed covers, make it look like we're wrestling an alligator under there. That should convince that furry-ass- err, that soldier, that we are doin' the bad nasty."

Ciela had giggled at the alligator wrestling reference. Tears amply demonstrated her relief over what the Marine was telling her.

His heart broken, Sergeant Frankly had nevertheless gone on, "Hoogle-Shnoogle or whatever he calls himself convinced those clothes-wearing fu- err, those deer people that the only way humans mate is undercover. Oh, and one last thing," he had added as they had both crawled under his blanket for their supposed maiden voyage, "We need to make some serious moaning and groaning, as if something were, you know, really happening."

That was days ago.

Presently, Sergeant Frankly and Ciela were finishing their feigned climactic sighs of orgasmic ecstasy whilst roiling Frankly's concealing bed blanket.

This staged mating concluded, Fred was about to draw aside his blanket when Ciela seized his hand to stop him. "Wait," she said.

"You want us to perform again? I think they are probably already on their way back to the front door."

"Is not that," she whispered breathlessly, seeking out his eyes in what little light filtered through the blanket.

Frankly could feel Ciela's warm breath on his face. He had to re-steel himself against an urge to take her into his arms, not so much for actual love-making. Rather, to comfort and protect her from their awful circumstance, how he really actually felt impatient to do.

"Is, I have fear, we all have fear. How long we can play this game before they realize none of us is getting pregnant?"

"Well, hopefully the Smoke and Mirrors will come charging back in like the cavalry before that happens."

"You think so? Please hold me."

Sergeant Frankly hesitantly put his arms around Ciela as she wrapped hers around his broad shoulders and pressed her head to his chest,

And that was when there was a deafening, booming crack of thunder, like lightning had struck Frankly's residence even though the source of this loud noise came nowhere even close. It was laser-cannon fire from the Smoke and Mirrors. The air down through which it pierced got super-heated, thereby sending out concussive sound waves. A bright flash lit up the blanket, bright enough to insinuate itself from thousands of feet away.

***

"We have destroyed their communications center, Officer Leung!" Yoon-hee couldn't help shouting from the command chair on the navigation bridge of the Smoke and Mirrors. "Please tell me the all-is-well transmissions were continued seamlessly!"

"Seamlessly, Captain," verified Buddy Leung. He was monitoring the navigation and control console of the shuttle craft where he was holed up, concealed under layers of Oombian moon dust. Precisely when the laser-cannon fire from the Smoke and Mirrors abruptly broke off alien video transmissions from Oomb to the Tictoctic saucer craft, Buddy's remote recording of prior transmissions took their place, aided by a firefly donut. Not a hint was to be found in any of it that it was pre-recorded. For the time being, at least, the Tictoctic leadership didn't know their conquested territory in the Callaway X Centra system was under attack. All they continued to see was nothing out-of-the-ordinary happening on Oomb. This, accompanied by the voice-over. Bored-sounding baas of ritualized chants praised Dek-Fook-Tek for how well the occupation was going, especially the effective behavior management of the dumb primate cattle.

***

"Hell, yeah! That's gotta be the S and M!" Sergeant Frankly said to himself. Not pausing to explain to Ciela what was happening, he lunged out of bed and through his bedroom window in one, continuous motion. He crisscrossed his arms in front of him to shield himself, minimize the cuts and bruises from shattered glass and splintering window frame. He leapt from a barrel roll along the ground into a running surge forward, whereby he overwhelmed an armed deer creature before that extraterrestrial could finish turning around to see what was happening. Sergeant Frankly kicked his air igniter out of his cloven hoof-hands and shouted at Hoogle-Shnoogle, "Telepath them to lay belly down on the ground with their fore and hind legs splayed far apart! Or I turn them into roasted venison!"

***

Mirrors and various other panels covering the Smoke

and Mirrors were folded back into the starship's hull. Their task was complete for this spacecraft shaped like an asparagus stem, with a rose bloom on the front end and tulip petals on the rear end. Those mirrors and panels had rendered the Smoke and Mirrors seemingly non-existent, whether by visual or by radar detection.

Yoon-hee spoke to Buddy. "What is your ETA, Officer Leung? We've just received a telepath from Hoogle-Shnoogle. The Tictoctic occupation commander is threatening to start torching the women and children if we don't have our bulls, as they term them, lay down the air igniters they've seized! We are given twenty lek-leks, however long that is! Our Oombian friend is trying to mind-read the equivalent for us!"

"I'd have Hoogle-Shnoogle telepath the Marines to do as ordered, Captain! I'm guessing twenty lek-leks last nowhere near the half hour it's going to take for me to deliver the knockout gas! I've just now cleared the moon dust for liftoff!"

As Buddy spoke, the shuttle pod's rocket engine blasted up a mountain's worth of asteroid dust. A minute later, this compact space vehicle was miles from the Oombian moon, and Officer Leung was switching over briefly to light propulsion. Detection instrumentation had confirmed enough dust particles were cleared from the shuttle pod fuselage for safe mirror array deployment.

***

Ludi Perez coughed herself awake in her and Pedro's bed, to where provisional Captain Yoon-hee Park-Smith and Marine Corps Lieutenant Danny Gómez had carried her. She looked up to see Danny handing her a limp Alexita, still asleep from the knockout gas. Captain Park-Smith stood to the Marine's side, and she was just then pulling off her gas mask. Despite Alexita safely in arm, Ludi suddenly anxiously lifted her head off her pillow, to look this way and that. She spotted Louisa Entroper and Hoogle-Shnoogle also in attendance. Hoogle-Shnoogle was stooped forward because the ceiling was too low for his palm frond helicopter assembly, already starting to regenerate atop his trunk. "Is Pedro here? Do you have my husband?"

"No." Yoon-hee couldn't help the pity in her voice. Well did she know what had to be going through this woman's head. That is, Ludi had to be hoping she was experiencing a rerun of the first time she found herself waking up aboard the Smoke and Mirrors. Captain Taylor, husband Chris and the chief medical officer, all three had been looking down at her as though, Ludi recalled thinking, they were her guardian angels. One minute, Pedro's wife had been relieved a random bullet from outside Doña Rotonda's tenement dwelling had not struck Alexita, and she had been despairing over Pedro's deteriorating mental and physical condition, let alone her own. And the next thing she had known, every member of her family was aboard a spacecraft from the future, bound for a distant planet paradise where they could build their lives anew. This, plus assurances Pedro's seemingly irreparable back injury would get taken care of in a matter of days. Was it unreasonable to hope this new, abrupt awakening from a new, abrupt loss of consciousness would bring back Pedro, somehow, from his getting taken away by the deer creatures of Tictoctic aboard their flying saucer?

"What has happened," the provisional captain wanted to sound a hopeful note before she continued about Ludi's husband, "is that we have managed to peacefully disarm the entire occupation force from

Tictoctic with our knockout gas. Apparently none of them thought to bring along gas mask equipment."

"Excuse me, Captain!" Sergeant Frankly rushed into the bedroom before anyone there could react to hearing him enter the log cabin, one of many constructed out of spare branches by the Oombians for the Earthlings, in anticipation of what they were to be about on the second mission of the Smoke and Mirrors. "We have a situation on the oof course! Two deer soldiers are playing with an Oombian. I think the Oombian's name is Toodle-Kaboodle or some other oodle-poodle-what-the-foodle. Anyhow, those soldiers are begging to be allowed to finish their round before we put them in chains! And that Oombian accompanying them is supporting them on this!"

*That is correct, provisional Captain Park-Smith,* Yoon-hee heard Toodle-Kaboodle telepathing in her mind, as she also noted Louisa Entroper out the corner of her eye animately shaking her head. *The two creatures from Tictoctic had set aside their air igniters in the clubhouse to go play, and they are expressing complete willingness to surrender to your authority after they complete their game. Also, I persuaded them to try my fruit, which they have found quite delicious.*

"Oh, well, if they think your fruit is 'quite delicious,' that changes everything!" Sergeant Frankly could not help laying on his sarcasm extra thick. "By all means, let them finish their round, and then let's see if we can secure first-class tickets for them back to Tictoctic aboard a luxury cruise starship!"

Yoon-hee pointedly inhaled and exhaled as Dr. Entroper said, "Captain…" Entroper's voice was meant to convey, by a single word, that Yoon-hee couldn't possibly be considering any other decision than a flat-out NO.

"Where are they in the game?" Yoon-hee asked heedless of her government observer.

*They are on the sixteenth green. Only two more holes to go after that,* Toodle-Kaboodle telepathed for general mental consumption among the Earthlings in Ludi's bedroom, the same as her prior communication.

"Sergeant Frankly, I trust we have an armed marine making sure the Tictoctickians don't suddenly decide to play hide-and-seek instead?"

"Captain Park, he is also making certain they putt out everything."

"What's that?" Yoon-hee's voice cracked girlishly high falsetto. This, over her relief at having successfully overwhelmed the occupation forces from Tictoctic, and from a bit of amusement as well. The deer creatures caught in the laser-cannon attack on their communications center, their fate did weigh on her. Still, she couldn't help herself; she knew exactly what Sergeant Frankly was talking about, regarding putting out everything.

"Nothing worth wasting your time about, Captain. Just a fu-uhhh, a little golf humor." The sergeant was trying not to curse, or f-bomb as it came to be known with him, in Yoon-hee's presence.

"I *have* golfed a few times back on Earth, Sergeant Frankly." Yoon-hee wanted to add, *There ARE some women who know all about the game*. Instead, she went on, with her forehead amply furrowed from her raising her eyebrows at the Marine, "No gimme putts even from six inches, right?"

"You've got it, Captain." Fred swung his head into this answer in a way that conceded nonverbally that he ought to have been ashamed to have assumed any less of her.

"Okay, then make sure they are brought to the holding pen, soon as they roll their last putts," said Yoon-hee. She noticed Entroper jerk from one frozen head direction to another, to and fro between her and the sergeant. Obviously, the government observer meant to convey nonverbally, *You have got to be kidding; you can't be serious!*

"Got it, Captain."

"And one more thing, Sergeant."

"Captain?" Frankly was already out the door; he had to duck his head back in.

"My husband can show them where to go on our artificial intelligence network to compute their handicap."

"Mm-hm," but Fred was thinking, *And I can show them where to go to get their air igniters shoved up their furry little asses!*

Despite Louisa Entroper's wide-eyed, reproving glare, Yoon-hee commented, "Maybe the swords get turned into oof clubs along with the plowshares." Otherwise, the provisional starship captain might have remarked on how Entroper appeared to be trying to outdo the nocturnal regard typically offered by the Fafamans.

"Excuse me, please, Captain." Ludi Perez. She was sitting up and still cradling the recently revived Alexita, who in her dazed state was seeking comfort from an especially vigorous thumb suck. "My husband Pedro, Alexita's papi:-" Ludi nodded down at her daughter. "-Where have the deer that wear uniforms taken him?"

"We're not sure. Officer Leung is going to go look for him and the others, once things settle down here enough for him to shuttle us back to our ship. He has a plan."

"What is the plan?" It was everything Ludi could do to keep from going into hysterics. She reminded herself that coming unglued was no good for her daughter. It didn't matter whether Alexita was recovering from the knockout gas, or had never been exposed to it in the first place. But this was so hard. The Oombians did spare Mrs. Perez a telepathed translation, when those scary, gun-toting deer people sniffed at Pedro and the other men taken aboard the flying saucer. Nevertheless, she could tell they were treating her husband like so much cattle meat.

"It's complicated, Mrs. Perez, but I know Officer Leung's plan has a chance." Yoon-hee had decided the less detail, the less information conveyed to this poor woman, the better, given how potentially horrific…

"Captain Park-Smith," Dr. Entroper finally couldn't help interjecting.

"Dr. Entroper?" Yoon-hee strained to keep her voice innocently quizzical. This, in contrast to the stern weariness she was feeling from the government observer's persistent second-guessing.

"I know we want to do everything we possibly can for Mrs. Perez's husband and the others who were abducted," said Louisa Entroper. "However, the lives of so many more people are at stake. Just imagine, Mrs. Perez, that instead of one saucer invading your small colony, one hundred of them are attacking Earth."

"I understand," Ludi slowly nodded with a lonesome tear running down her cheek.

"So you do understand, don't you? The captain needs to prioritize how her chief science engineer and the two shuttle craft we have out here at the moment are utilized."

"Yes." Ludi's tears were trailing down both cheeks.

"Mami?" Alarmed by her parent's mounting distress, Alexita uncorked her thumb from her mouth.

"Captain, can you and Dr. Entroper-" Ludi pointed at Louisa. "-please leave? I know you have much to worry about is more important..." She hugged Alexita close as she burst into a full sob.

"Nothing is more important than locating your husband, Mrs. Perez. Mr. Perez and the others seized by the deer people, they ARE our top priority." For this last part, Yoon-hee glared at Louisa Entroper. She was unable to contain her fury over how needlessly Louisa had upset this woman. The situation was dire enough, already, without someone callously trying to suggest to Ludi that in some larger scheme of things, her husband didn't matter so much. "THAT is what we now leave to work on," Yoon-hee added with as much definitive firmness in her voice as she could muster.

"Captain Park-Smith?" husband Kevin's voice suddenly crackled in her earpiece as she was halfway out Ludi's bedroom door. "You should get a load of what just folded up its mirrors to decloak beside us! Defense Secretary Spinner is aboard! He's asking permission to shuttle over to us for a conversation with you and Dr. Entroper!"

"Tell him ASAP, Officer Smith."

Louisa sighed relief as Yoon-hee responded.

***

"The American Union Battleship Barack Obama!" Secretary of Defense Michael Spinner compulsively twined together strands of his Santa Claus beard with the thumb and forefinger of his left hand, while with his right hand he proudly gestured, open-palmed, towards the giant spacecraft. The Obama sat in close range on the panoramic view-screen, which occupied nearly an entire wall of the Smoke and Mirrors navigation bridge.

In many ways, Battleship Obama looked just like the Smoke and Mirrors. When deployed, its rear end resembled a green rose in full bloom. Such resemblance resulted from the baffled arrangement of its several paper-thin mirror "petals." Bathed in an electromagnetic field, that array caused the craft to accelerate well past light-speed, a feat formerly thought impossible, and far from fully understood. As the Obama's orbit around Oomb shadowed the Smoke and Mirrors orbit, its rear mirror array was presently folded up into what reasonably enough could have been likened to an amphitheater-sized rose bud, prior to blooming.

The battleship's fore mirror array likewise exactly replicated the Smoke and Mirror's fore mirror array. When retracted, it gave the appearance of a tulip bud on the verge of bloom. At least this much of mirror array physics was understood: the bloomed "tulip petals" funneled all ambient starlight ahead of both starships through their photon shafts, to exit out their rears mysteriously twinkling like fairy dust. By this manner, the inertial friction ahead of both the Smoke and Mirrors and the Barack Obama got effectively reduced to zero. That helped to enable traversing distances in time frames formerly considered impossible without access to a decent-sized wormhole, which might or might not actually exist.

Both starships were also identical in how stabilizer "thorns" adorned their "asparagus stem" hulls, which hulls linked their rosebud rear ends to their tulip-bud front ends.

Then there were the differences. For the Smoke and Mirrors retrofit, weaponry such as the laser cannons, and an additional shuttle bay for additional shuttle pods, had been built into compartments that rotated open. These compartments had been previously meant for additional passenger quarters and on-board gardening. What Yoon-hee first noticed with the Battleship Obama, however, were two significant interruptions, aside from the stabilizer thorns, to the cylindrical, asparagus-stem shape of the hull extending from the fore to the aft mirror assemblies. One interruption was a pronounced bulge just ahead of the rear "rose" mirror array. Yoon-hee found herself thinking, were the body of the Obama a snake, that bulge was to where it had swallowed a cow. A smaller bulge made a ring around the midriff of the craft.

"Let me show you what we brought down the chimney, ho-ho-hoo!" Secretary Spinner boomed. He patted on his heaving belly for added emphasis. Yoon-hee well remembered how the defense secretary had a reputation for studied folksiness, including self-exploitation of his Santa Claus appearance. His affectations had helped him survive his getting caught casually saying especially cruel, insensitive things about poor people that would have sunk the careers of most other public figures. "Okay, so here we have the fighter craft bays," Spinner went on as he worked a remote control device he had extracted from his pants pocket. The Obama's smaller, ring-like bulge opened into eight launch pads, each one occupied by a jet-shaped vehicle. "They're conditioned for outer space. They carry enough air-recycling capacity for them to keep going for two days, plus enough hydrogen nukes for one of them to single-handedly take down the Fafamans' central pyramid, if that was what we were about, ho-ho! And there's another fighter hidden behind each. If we need to, we can send them streaming out like angry hornets from a nest at which someone has thrown a rock! And they all are wired for unmanned drone capability!

"Now let's check out our other bag of goodies." Spinner worked his remote some more. As the fighter launch-pads closed up, the larger bulge in the battleship's rear unfolded and unfolded until Kevin watching said, "Wo!," and others on the bridge made comparable noises indicative of how awestruck they were.

"We call it the peacock display," Secretary Spinner boasted. He savored the aforementioned noises, the "oo"s and "ah"s of people being impressed. "Every 'feather' delivers its own special payload. There's a heat-seeking magnetic resonance device that can literally vibrate a ship the size of ours to pieces after it attaches itself to the hull, like a sucker fish to a shark. There's also the 'tapeworm.' After it burrows through the thickest metal a spacecraft might have, leaking air alone should disable the crew. Just to be certain, though, it then bursts apart with such force, a Smoke and Mirrors would get transformed into ashes and dust, ho-ho-hoo!! And there are any number of other toys we can play with, if we just get the chance!"

"A battleship. So this is built entirely for waging war, Secretary Spinner."

"Well now, I can see why Captain Taylor tapped you for her temporary replacement, while she tries to set things straight doing her peacenik thing on Fafama! Yes, Provisional Captain Park-Smith, you know what those devils from Tictoctic did to your paradise on Oomb, don't you? They've got antlers instead of horns, right? What about pitchforks? The damage they've done, the people they've taken away for a bite to eat, I assume this has welcomed you to the real world. I also assume the rebels taking advantage of Captain Taylor's trusting nature have hopefully given her a new take on the situation there. No?" Spinner noticed Louisa Entroper shrugging her shoulders in reaction to what he said about Helena. "Well, we need to blow up one bridge at a time," he subsequently continued. "What we are also carrying on board are suites of land-, air-, and sea-based missiles.

There's one suite, each, for the defense of Oomb and Fafama. But we can still hold out hope that neither planet ever actually needs to use them."

Yoon-hee got the impression Secretary Spinner thought this was him bending over backwards to meet her concerns.

"Now I'm enough of a realist, myself. Sure, the Fafaman government has clearly indicated they'll welcome any help we give them. And that help will come with the provision it's not to get used on those pesky terrorists, or used beyond set parameters; I'm sure we can work SOMEthing out with them." Spinner raised his voice with extra firmness when he got to the "provision" part.

Louisa Entroper nodded towards Yoon-hee like she wanted to comment, *You see? He's thought of everything; you shouldn't have any problem with his proposals.*

"But as for the tree people of Oomb, we're not deaf to the fact that from their cultural perspective, they are not too keen on defense of ANY sort. They didn't even want the laser shield, gosh darn it! That's why General Warlor and I have flown all the way out here. We will speak face-to-face, face-to-bark, whatever, to help them understand, maybe meet us halfway. Who is the leader who clipped his branches to board your vessel for the second mission to Fafama? Oodles of Noodles?"

"*Her* branches; *she* is Oodle-Noodle." Yoon-hee tried to offer up these corrections in as matter-of-fact a voice as possible, but couldn't help a lecturing tone from creeping in.

"Okay, she is the one we'd like to address. From your reports, she keeps popping up in leadership roles."

***

"Wellll," expansively boomed Secretary Spinner. He and the chair of the military Joint Chiefs of Staff, General Sandy Warlor, were seated directly the other side of a long, wooden table from a comfortably rooted Oodle-Noodle. This, at one end of the cathedral-ceilinged meeting hall for Earthlings and Oombians, the end left undamaged by the flying saucer attack when the deer creatures first arrived. "I'm not sure what takes more getting used to," Spinner went on, "those Oonzy Ootzies, whatever-they're-called, prancing in and out of the surf like they're dancing some Irish jig; your other oodle associates holding us by their arm branches like vines around a lamp post for flying us over here from the beach; or your traditional mid-day butt-baring, to commemorate some prehistoric orgy that first brought together your sweet fruit-bearers with your tuber-bearers! I guess we'd have called them tuber-bearers the savories! Ho-ho!"

"I'm more used to protest signs and people throwing tomatoes at my motorcade," General Warlor nodded, smiling pleasantly.

*Oh, no. There will be no throwing fruit at you from us!* Oodle-Noodle twisted the upper half of her trunk from side to side. She made her leaves rustle as she telepathed, *In fact, I am bearing fruit similar to your tomato, among those you may choose from when you reach across the table to pluck, as befits our welcoming tradition.* She stretched her branches especially far out to her sides to more clearly reveal the choices.

"Well, I feel like I should offer something comparable in return," Secretary Spinner said as he stood up, leaned over the table, and casually plucked something he thought looked like a strawberry the size of an apple.

"Would you like to lop off part of my beard?, ho-ho-ho!" He snuck a glance Sandy Warlor's direction, but thought better of suggesting she offer up one of her breasts if not exactly for plucking, then...When she seemed to notice, he was thankful her mind-reading ability wasn't anything like the Oombians'...at least he hoped.

"Thank you, Oodle-Noodle; something else that takes getting used to, as Secretary Spinner said," spoke General Warlor. "Allow me to express our deep concern over the well-being of your close associates seized by the aliens from Tictoctic. We are going to do everything in our power to rescue them along with our own kind who have been taken."

*I appreciate your concern.*

"Well," Spinner boomed expansively, anew, and he set aside the seemingly over-sized strawberry. Warlor did the same with an apple-looking fruit in the tapered shape of a carrot, while mumbling, "Looks delicious." "So," proceeded Spinner, "you've had quite some trouble with these flame-throwing deer critters and their building-incinerating flying saucer, is that correct?"

*The creatures from Tictoctic are in a lot of mental pain and anguish. For our part, we have been trying to get them to consider healthier plant alternatives to their exclusively carnivorous diet.*

"Well hold on there!" Spinner feigned dissension-inspired gruffness. "You're telepathing to a meat-and-potatoes man here! But go ahead! I know you don't know no better, ho-ho-ho! This is what we call sarcasm."

*I understand. To continue, we were starting to make some progress. We were persuading a few of them to set down their air igniters for our game of oof. One deer creature seemed especially interested in our music, plus our initial delving into Earth music.*

"You know," Secretary Spinner turned to General Warlor, "wouldn't the universe be a wonderful place if it were just full of fun-loving creatures like these Oombians? Getting up foursomes for – they call it oof, we call it golf; to-may-to, to-mah-to? Daily celebrating some prehistoric love fest? Treating all visitors from the cosmos like they could be best friends? Offering the fruit off their branches since they've got no shirts to take off their backs?"

"The universe would be beautiful indeed," Warlor nodded with what Spinner could tell was a strained smile.

*The universe IS beautiful. And as our consciousness evolves, so does our faith in that beauty, including faith there is always a loving way, ultimately, to cope with any problems which may arise.*

"The new spacecraft, fully equipped for battle, on which we flew out here to your neck of the woods, or I guess it's a wood-sy neck in your case, ho-ho-ho!, that battleship is named the Barack Obama. You have picked our brains enough to know who Barack Obama was?" This from Spinner after he and Warlor exchanged we've-got-our-work-cut-out-for-us looks over Oodle-Noodle's gently reproving telepath about how she saw the nature of the universe. In their estimation, the tree creature had offered an exceedingly naïve view born of unusually anomalous limited personal experience on Oomb.

*Barack Obama was the first African-American President of the United States, some years before it got enjoined with Mexico and Canada to form the American Union, what I have mind-read you also sometimes term the United Americas. Yes, we have mind-read with great interest about this most consequential, most kindly and well-meaning political leader.*

"Good! There is an important reason for our naming our new spacecraft in his honor. You maybe have also mind-read about an earlier significant historical figure from India named Mahatma Gandhi."

*We were SO interested in Mr. Gandhi! When we first mind-read about him, we asked permission of Captain Taylor to gain access to historical archives stored in the Smoke and Mirrors computer network.*

To General Warlor's mind, Oodle-Noodle's leaves rustled as though a cool, refreshing breeze were blowing through them.

"Now why doesn't that surprise me?" Spinner directed his question at Warlor, who again presented with her strained smile. "So maybe you also know, that is, um, I realize, Ms. Oodle-Noodle, your mind-reading ability allows you to already be aware of everything we're going to say, excepting how we will respond to whatever you have to telepath in reaction. But, thanks for humoring us just the same with some semblance of what we'd recognize as a conversation." Secretary Spinner winked, and Oodle-Noodle winked in return, albeit sideways since her eyes opened along her tree bark furrows rather than up and down. "So anyway, President Obama used to proclaim himself a big fan of the nonviolent teachings of Gandhi. However, he also understood the limits of those teachings in the real world. Let me quote for you what he said when he received the Nobel Peace Prize back in 2009." Spinner produced a piece of paper he lowered his spectacles to the tip of his nose to read. "'I am living testimony to the moral force of nonviolence. I know there is nothing weak, nothing passive, nothing naïve in the creed and lives of Gandhi and King.' Martin Luther King, of course, was one of our homegrown inspirational figures dedicated to trying to avoid violence. He wanted to overcome, peacefully, discrimination that was used to keep characters such as myself from achieving anything.

Of course, he got shot for his efforts. Back to Obama's Nobel Prize speech: After what he said about nonviolence, he added the big 'but': 'I face the world as it is, and cannot stand idle in the face of threats to the American people. For make no mistake: Evil does exist in the world. A nonviolent movement could not have halted Hitler's armies.' You know all about Hitler and World War 2, I presume."

*Another subject about which we searched the Smoke and Mirrors database with great interest.*

"Well good. So you know all about Adolf Hitler and the Nazis, and the Japanese as well."

*What we learned was that, lacking faith collectively, as a species, too many of you lacked faith individually, in the power of loving conflict resolution. Your species kept closing off possibilities for moving peaceful conflict resolution forward, you kept boxing yourselves into situations where you could see no choice but violence. Then, as today, there was more excitement over getting to use the latest manufactured weapons, than effort to imagine bringing out the best in people.*

"We're talking about Adolf Hitler!" There was no mock-gruffness in Secretary Spinner's exclamation. It was the real, angry thing. "How do you reckon you were going to bring out any good in what some considered evil personified?!?!"

*Adolf Hitler was a troubled, faithless creature, mentally deranged from what we could gather from our research. He was in the wrong place at the wrong time, propelled to power by people's faith-robbing experience of economic deprivation. But there were those around him and his equally troubled cohorts who might have gotten them all removed from power and safely confined for their collective psychiatric illness. That is, if others were not determined to bomb Germany into submission after Hitler's invasion of surrounding countries, although we certainly appreciate how difficult it has to be to respond to such violent, hate-filled aggression with love, to turn the other cheek as one of your more popular religious texts suggested. Anyway, before Hitler's rise to power, German politicians of a far gentler nature might well have prevailed, hadn't there been other politicians determined to keep Germany economically crippled for its key role in World War 1. Fortunately, one lesson did appear to be garnered from that experience. At the conclusion of World War 2, that lesson led to the Marshall Plan. We understand the Marshall Plan was a massive effort to rebuild and demilitarize Germany and Japan, rather than keep them impoverished. Of course, those countries' forced demilitarization opened vast resources for economic development.*

"Unbelievable!" was all Spinner could think to say. He tossed his hands in the air like he might as well have been throwing them away because they'd become useless, Oodle-Noodle got the impression.

"So basically, where World War 2 is concerned, you are blaming the victims for the violence done to them." General Warlor was trying to take a calmer route. "I suppose you believe the six million Jews who were exterminated should also have come up with something different. I mean, please enlighten us, Oodle-Noodle. Are you absolutely certain you're not viewing our history through the rose-colored lens of your society's unique history?, a history perhaps without precedent or parallel anywhere else in the known universe?"

As she twisted her upper trunk in strong denial, like she were winding up to hit an oof ball with her bark-covered butt, Oodle-Noodle's leaves rustled as though a gale force wind were blowing across them. *The Jewish people were blameless victims, yes, of unjust, unfounded demonization, trying to make them the personified cause of other people's mental and physical anguish. And when a person so loses faith in the beneficent workings of the universe that she believes in demons, and in violence as an absolute necessity for dealing with those demons, she also victimizes her own self, she creates her own mental hell, which of course became the fate of Hitler's supporters, both on and off the battlefield. Perhaps one of the most fascinating stories of World War 2 we encountered in our research had to do with Le Chambon.*

"Le Chambon? What the hell was Le Chambon?! I don't recall the battle of Le Chambon. Oh, that's right." Secretary Spinner managed to regain his cool, thinking on the absurdity of this conversation. He resolved that a telepathic tree arrogantly naïve beyond belief wasn't going to get the best of him. "You wouldn't think any of the battles of World War 2, or any battle for that matter, was of much importance compared to someone taking the time to smell the roses, maybe asking Mr. Hitler to paint them a picture or something. So let's hear, let's mind-read about this 'Le Chambon.'"

*Le Chambon is a village in southern France. During World War 2, it had a minister named André Trocme. Father Trocme devoted himself to imagining and inspiring nonviolent ways to resist, to cope with the fear-fueled hatred and violence engulfing everything around them. This approach rubbed off on enough other villagers that as a result, they were able to save several Jews and other persecuted peoples from getting sent off to the Nazi death camps. And most importantly, part of that success was due, apparently, to their making their love and caring contagious, infectious, for certain anonymous occupying Germans and their French collaborators.*

"Let me make sure I've got this straight, Oodle-Noodle." Secretary Spinner held up a hand for the Oombian to pause. "'Certain anonymous occupying Germans and their French collaborators.' So, we're just a little thin on the evidence, are we?"

*Please allow me to explain.*

"Proceed," Spinner bowed his head as he made an "off-you-go" wave of his hand. "But please mark this, and you mark this too, provisional Captain Park-Smith!" Spinner abruptly jerked up his head, and raised his voice on mentioning Yoon-hee. It was as though, if the video monitor didn't transmit adequately to where Yoon-hee was watching back aboard the Smoke and Mirrors, maybe if he spoke loudly enough, his voice could somehow carry all that way unaided by technology. This thought brought a faint grin to Yoon-hee's face, though immediately flat-lined by what Spinner said next, waggling a lecturing forefinger. "Nobody can say we're not giving you a full hearing, am I correct, General Warlor?"

"That is clearly a fair assessment, Secretary Spinner," solemnly nodded Warlor.

Yoon-hee noted Louisa Entroper's likewise approving nod beside her on the bridge of the Smoke and Mirrors. The provisional captain had to strain to keep the sudden chill she felt down her spine from making her tremble visibly. Subsequently, she couldn't bring herself to make eye contact with her husband Kevin, nearby manning her former navigation panel post. Her suspicion was growing, that the three of them - Spinner, Warlor and Entroper - had already decided upon a course of action no matter what anyone else said or telepathed. Perhaps there were even orders from the President himself. For sure, Yoon-hee sensed a palpable sadness in Oodle-Noodle's eyes. Had an extra furrow or two gotten creased into them?

*For a period of days, buses were sent into the town square of Le Chambon, for taking away any Jews that could be rounded up. What happened was that Trocme and his associates were receiving anonymous phone calls. Those calls offered whispered warnings, about which houses the officers and troops would be sweeping in search of hidden peoples. Such warnings provided enough time for the refugees from persecution to get sent into the seclusion of nearby woods until those sweeps were over. The persons anonymously making those calls could only have been German and French collaborators who had access to the most confidential information.*

"Happy to hear, umm," Spinner shook his head, "get telepathed that, Oodle-Noodle. Too bad about six million other Jews, who weren't so successful trying to hide from the bad guys. Look,-" Yoon-hee could tell that Secretary Spinner thought he was striking a most reasonable, conciliatory note. And she wasn't sure he wasn't correct. "-our world would be a much better place, for sure, were it full of more of these Trocme characters you mentioned. Like our saying goes, 'If 'if's and 'but's were candy and nuts, the world would be a better place.' However, for every Trocme or Gandhi or Martin Luther King, for that matter, there are a hundred, a thousand folks set on violence as the only way."

*But how many of that every hundred or thousand are people such as yourselves?, suggesting they wouldn't embrace violent means were it not for so many other people embracing violent means?*

As Warlor's lips puckered, Spinner smiled expansively and shook his head. Yoon-hee wondered whether the secretary of defense was going to take even the briefest moment to reflect on Oodle-Noodle's question, any more than he would consider eating goose droppings for dinner. Or at least that was the folksy way she imagined he would have put it.

"Sad to say, Oodle-Noodle," Spinner went on, "the real world isn't about just winning debate points, especially when the other guy has something to blow your head off, whether you've made your case or not." As he spoke, Spinner found himself glancing over frequently towards the mute General Warlor. The look in Oodle-Noodle's emerald-green eyes was getting increasingly uncomfortable for him to return.

*As far as the real world is concerned, Secretary Spinner, the laser mesh your species insisted on deploying around our planet, despite our objections, does seem to have resulted in more harm than good. We argued before its deployment that it might draw attention here that otherwise would not occur.*

"Okay." Spinner slapped down his hands on the wood table with an air of finality. "We really didn't come here to argue. WE have listened patiently to your perspective, but now...Your childlike faith in everyone's goodness, Oodle-Noodle, it's admirable in children, and it's admirable in you. And just like with children, the adults need to step in here with some inconvenient truths. A child might complain they don't want a vaccination from disease because it hurts so much. 'Why I've got to get a shot, Mommy, when it hurts so much?'" Spinner affected a falsetto voice trying to mimic a young girl. "No responsible parent would ever allow such a complaint to override what she knows is good for her child, and we're not going to allow your complaint, again admirably grounded in your gentle nature, to override what we know is in all our best interests."

Yoon-hee couldn't help gasping at what she regarded as Spinner's breath-taking condescension towards the Oombians. This, while Dr. Entroper standing beside her nodded assertively and said sternly, "He is correct."

"Now you're also correct, Oodle-Noodle, absolutely correct, that the laser mesh wasn't adequate."

Yoon-hee sensed Spinner fancying he was actually bending over backwards to accommodate Oodle-Noodle's perspective.

"What the mesh did do," the secretary of defense continued, "was buy some time for your folks and our folks. Buy some time, that is, had we been allowed to deploy our suite of land-, sea- and air-based missiles to blow that saucer from Tictoctic to Kingdom Come before it ever even landed. Imagine had none of your fellow, um, associates gotten torched, or taken away to heaven-knows-where, most likely to be used for kindling from what the Marines are reporting. And imagine further that your gracious immigrants from Earth had remained with their families intact, instead of the situation we have now. It's a pretty safe bet, you well know, who that kindling is meant for grilling. And please understand: we're not talking about taking the battle back to Tictoctic. We're still only talking about a defensive posture."

*What you deem a defensive posture, the paranoid leadership of Tictoctic will be certain to interpret as preparation for future aggression. It will only sap out the strength even further from more moderate voices in their society, weaken those voices' ability to take root.*

"More moderate voices? What moderate voices? I must not have received the memo!" For this ridiculing remark, Spinner swung his head Warlor's way.

From back aboard the Smoke and Mirrors, Yoon-hee espied through the view-screen monitor Sandy Warlor's faint grin. Yoon-hee wondered which of various possibilities accounted for such a notably reserved reaction. Was the chair of the Joint Chiefs feeling the burden of whatever her role was going to be in the conversation with the Oombians? Or was her first excursion on Oomb proving too much for her? Maybe she was not feeling very well? Or was she embarrassed – could it be? – by Spinner's posing as folksy common sense his casual condescension directed the tree creature's way?

*Weren't there the deserters from Tictoctic?, who fled their society to try to warn outside worlds of their fellow creatures' violent interplanetary plans? Wasn't that some indication of moderation? Yes, you could consider those deserters as two lone mushrooms. Isn't it possible, though, they were hinting at a far more enormous fungus spreading underground?*

Aboard the orbiting starship, Louisa Entroper and Yoon-hee Park-Smith both shook their heads, but for different reasons. For Entroper, it was about regret over the tree creature still not "getting it." For Yoon-hee, it was sympathy for Oodle-Noodle, for how she was yet able to persist with pressing her case, even when she knew the odds were weighted heavily against her prevailing. That wistful sadness in the tree creature's eyes revealed, as much as a telepathed message ever could, that she despaired about the chances of shaking the newly visiting Earthlings from their decided course of action.

"Well I have to say, Oodle-Noodle," said Secretary Spinner, "I don't know about an enormous fungus. I do know that those two deserters, just two of them as you yourself admit, crash-landed their presumably hijacked spacecraft and died from their injuries within hours of our people making their acquaintance. I can't see they accomplished a ding-dong thing, where putting the brakes on their leaders' plans for interplanetary conquest are concerned."

*But isn't getting the word out, as your expression goes, before the first attack from Tictoctic on our planet, isn't that at least "a ding-dong thing"?*

"You know, Oodle-Noodle," Spinner scratched behind his right ear, "I'm going to have to give you that. Score one for your home team. But, umm, can you concede there's a distinct possibility those fatally destined renegades most likely would have applauded, or kicked their hooves together, whatever they do, over our going after their evil-doing fellow antler-bearers with everything we've got?"

*Wasn't one of them quoted as saying on their death bed, "Don't become us"? What do you think THAT meant?*

"Well I sure as hell don't think that meant we should roll over and play dead, then just cross our fingers and hope that what they don't want us to become gets thunderstruck by a strong case of the lovey-doveys!"

Yoon-hee could almost discern Secretary Spinner's jowls shaking with his gruff anger, despite how well they were concealed by his Santa Claus beard.

General Sandy Warlor patted Spinner on the arm. She would have said, *Now, now; you're accomplishing nothing by losing your temper in front of our extraterrestrial guests,* if not for apprehension she might thereby antagonize him all the more. Instead, she said, "This is a very difficult situation for everyone, Oodle-Noodle. I hope you understand that we have nothing but the utmost respect and admiration for your society. I hope you appreciate how upset we are that we did not follow through fully with the information we had at hand, to prevent the terrible suffering inflicted by the unprovoked attack from Tictoctic."

"Totally unprovoked," Spinner butted in on Warlor's smoothing-over preparation for the big announcement she was about to make, "whether you tree people think the laser shield was baiting them or not! Harrumph!"

Again Warlor was gently patting Spinner's arm. She could have said, *You're not making this any easier,* especially for what they had to endure telepathed by Oodle-Noodle next.

*From what we were able to mind-read, the creatures from Tictoctic sincerely believe their attack was fully and justifiably provoked by their need to restore their food supply. And that this attack had to come specifically at the expense of other-world creatures of comparable intelligence, before those creatures could reciprocate with a likewise need. As for yourselves, we much admire your effort to provide some of your less-privileged with a new start, a new chance, on our planet. And we also understand that, like the Tictoctic creatures feel justified, you also feel justified. You also follow a course of logic to a conclusion that has you doing here what you are intent on doing.*

Warlor raised a cautioning hand Spinner's way, signaling, *Let me handle this.* She inhaled and exhaled with a distinct huff before saying, in measured tones she strained to maintain, "I would earnestly hope, Oodle-Noodle, further experience will convince you there is considerable distance between our behavior, and the behavior of the invaders who by now most likely have chopped up and burned to a char some of your associates. Notice, for example, that what we find ourselves compelled to do now involves nothing of imprisonment, nothing of threatening others' lives and well-being."

*At least not on purpose,* but Oodle-Noodle thought better of telepathing this presently.

"We hereby declare that we *will* deploy land-, air-, and sea-based defenses on your planet. Those defenses will provide back-up for a reinforced reconstruction of the laser mesh. Also, we now call to attention provisional Captain Yoon-hee Park-Smith. As you are aware, she has been following this negotiation closely from aboard our starship Smoke and Mirrors. Captain Park-Smith?"

"We are watching and listening from the bridge, General Warlor."

"Captain Park-Smith, President Carey personally extends his thanks and appreciation for the indispensable duties you have performed. You have served with distinction under supremely challenging circumstances, in crew member Helena Taylor's absence."

Yoon-hee felt another icy chill down her back, hearing Captain Taylor referred to as mere "crew member."

"After extensive consultation with Secretary Spinner, me, and the rest of the military chiefs of staff, the president has decided Dr. Louisa Entroper will bring a necessary, fresh perspective to the mission, and that you have a critical role to resume, Officer Park-Smith, as chief navigation officer."

"An especially critical role, Yoon-hee." Entroper patted Officer Yoon-hee Park-Smith encouragingly, if also patronizingly, said officer felt, on her back. Then Entroper left Yoon-hee's side to assume the captain's chair on the navigation bridge of the Smoke and Mirrors. "I'm actually counting on all of you, every single one of you, to guide me as I am guiding you. These are some pretty big shoes I've been so unexpectedly asked to fill. In case you don't know it, I'm in awe of those of you who were around for the first mission of the Smoke and Mirrors."

Kevin Smith-Park wondered at how Dr. Entroper shook her head in the negative as she said she'd need the crew's help, and was "in awe" of crew members aboard for the first mission. Was she unconsciously revealing what she really felt? One more reason Kevin regretted Ali Magabu wasn't there, in this case to give his assessment of what was going through Entroper's mind. And speaking of mind, he wished he could read his wife Yoon-hee's mind to even half the extent the Oombian tree people could read both of theirs if they wanted to. How was she feeling, getting relieved of duty as provisional captain only days after Taylor had appointed her? From the moment the chair of the Joint Chiefs of Staff, Sandy Warlor, turned her full attention on Yoon-hee, Yoon-hee had seemed to be studiously avoiding even a stolen glance his way. Rather, she had trained her eyes on Warlor, then she had jumped them to Entroper. There had been no pause in between, for allowing her sight to wander any other direction.

One thing Second Engineer Kevin Smith-Park WAS certain of, without any mind-reading or consultation: This transfer of power, essentially nullifying Helena Taylor's authority, had to have been in the works for some time, with Entroper in on it. When Warlor made her announcement, Louisa looked about as surprised, Kevin thought, as had she been told a few of the stars in the Oombian night sky were from planets in the same solar system. "So unexpectedly"? *Yeah, right.* If only there were someone he could vent to, instead of having to contain himself.

"General Warlor, Secretary Spinner," went on Entroper, speaking at the view-screen as though that was them standing there on the navigation deck, not just their transmitted images, "this is such an unsurpassed honor you have bestowed upon me, entrusting the remainder of the second mission of the Smoke and Mirrors."

*Yeah, "Captain." No chance YOU'D get taken down a notch before this mission is over, or before the Tictoctickians, whatever you call them, have us all salted and cured for their culinary pleasure.* Kevin continued stifling himself from saying what was on his mind, as what was on his mind continued with, *Although I can understand how the way events have transpired would be making Warlor and Spinner jittery, especially how Captain Taylor – They can name her dog catcher for all I care; she's still the captain. Anyway, I can see how they might think she's playing too much footsie with those hopelessly naïve, too-gentle-for-their-own-good tree critters; sorry, Oodle-Noodle and friends, if you're eavesdropping.*

"Now if everyone will excuse me, I'm going to retire to my quarters to draw up the agenda for our first formal crew-leaders briefing. I'm setting the briefing for 6:30 pm starship time. Officer Park-Smith," she swiveled the captain's chair to look down at Yoon-hee, "please assure that Dr. Cathy James-Leung is in attendance; one of our top items will be corralling that dirty comet for orbit around Fafama. You see?" Captain Entroper looked up from Officer Yoon-hee Park-Smith resuming her navigation duties, and around to as many other faces on the bridge as she could, without swiveling the captain's chair anew. "I *do* want to find a peaceful resolution to the political conflict on Fafama, and a significant addition to their water supply WOULD seem to offer a realistic opportunity. But that's the key: realistic, realism. The same with the threat from Tictoctic. If we could discover a peaceful way out, we would. Of course we would." Entroper shook her white mop-top emphatically, again from side-to-side how someone would usually shake one's head 'no.'

"Captain Entroper," Secretary Spinner said on the conclusion of a relief-exuding exhale, "we are mighty obliged for your finding that exact combination of words which had, up to now, completely eluded the chair of the Joint Chiefs of Staff and myself. Just like you said, we are all about realistic peace agreements. The fact that you're going to try to lasso a comet into planetary orbit, a COMET for goodness sake, speaks to how far we are willing to go for peace if just like you said, it's even at the outer bounds of realistic. Mighty obliged again, Captain. We'll look forward to seeing that meeting agenda."

"We will expect you to eavesdrop on our meeting, Mr. Secretary, and you too, Oodle-Noodle."

All eyes, both on the bridge of the Smoke and Mirrors and at the table in the conference hall on Oomb, turned to Oodle-Noodle. But she did nothing more than blink. Yoon-hee was sure she spotted a golden-amber tear well up in one of her bark-encrusted peepers.

"Well..." General Warlor fidgeted about, as though she were gathering her things together to leave, even though she had nothing to gather together for her departure other than a plucked fruit.

The Oombian leader's absence of any telepathed reaction was grown discomfortingly deafening.

Yoon-hee's heart went out to Oodle-Noodle, although she reflected to herself, however reluctantly, that one might argue the tree creature's nonviolent approach had already been given a fair chance, and look where it had gotten them.

# Chapter 19

Swish! Swish! Swish!

Those swishes were the first sounds to seize Chris Olsen-Taylor's attention. They seized him right in the gut, upon Nanofafo swinging aside the thick entrance doors to one of the Fafamafalafama's many royal chambers scattered throughout the great Fafaman pyramid. Chris recognized the noise from before. He knew it had to be coming from the Fafamafalafama. The Fafaman emperor was making practice battle-moves with his sword, the extra-long one he was always lugging around in an opulently appointed sheath attached to his waist band.

Ever since Chris had been notified the Fafaman ruler desired and therefore ordered a private audience with him, he had several times had to talk himself down off a mental ledge of terror. One of the key points he had made to himself was that the Fafaman ruler wouldn't have insisted he bring along his practice golf club if the plan was to have his head sliced off. Another point had been provided by Ali Magabu who, along with Chris and Helena Taylor, Tanya Petrovsky, and Guy Hanson, was also essentially marooned on Fafama until either the Smoke and Mirrors, or the battle cruiser Barack Obama, could come get them. And who even knew the whereabouts of Marine Corps Sergeant Hanson, assuming he was still alive? Anyhow, Ali had told Chris that the Fafamafalafama wasn't going to risk bringing down upon himself the wrath of a space-faring civilization. Ruler or not, the Fafamafalafama had to know, despite his face-saving bluster, that said civilization was clearly far advanced of his own, and therefore far more potentially destructive if its members felt an outrage had been committed against one of their own. Besides, why would

Chris be a target for elimination by this guy? What was Chris thinking?

Of course, Chris couldn't admit his paranoia to Ali, or to anyone else. That was, his paranoia about maybe the Fafamafalafama having designs on his wife, thereby making his own self an inconvenience that required elimination. Which led to another key point: For a guy with twenty-three wives already, on a ritual path to accumulating an additional spouse a year until his death, would the Fafamafalafama really risk so much, just to add Helena to his box of seductive sweets? Especially since that risk also now included the risk of losing help from the Earthlings if his planet actually did need to defend against an extraterrestrial invasion?

Nevertheless, despite all these key points, Chris was still left with the undeniable evidence this guy was thinking enough about his existence to insist on a private audience with him. Maybe the Fafamafalafama had intuited his fear of this nocturnally wide-eyed man. And so, it had become a matter of amusement, cheap entertainment if cruel sport, for the self-styled emperor of an entire planet to try to scare the crap out of him...or was this merely Chris's desperate notion, to avoid admitting some horrific truth? Namely, that the Fafamafalafama had sensed a spark between Chris and his first wife, the Varalawa. The spark got ignited on her guided tour, when she introduced Chris to the mysteries of the ephemeral dragon that haunted Fafama's largest body of water, the Grand Basin. The way she had described showing Chris around to the Fafamafalafama had only cinched the deal. So now, the Fafamafalafama needed to avenge his jealousy of this puny alien male.

SLAM! How hard Nanofafo pulled the entrance doors shut made Chris visibly flinch. It jolted him out of reflections on the import of past events, out of his futile, final postponement of facing whatever was to be.

There was the Fafamafalafama indeed, as the timing would have it, thrusting his sword directly Chris's direction. A mere ten feet or so closer, and Officer Olsen-Taylor would have been impaled, right through the heart.

The Fafamafalafama's imagined sword fight must have been what had taken him so far off his throne specific to this particular royal chamber. Chris still found himself of enough presence of mind to suppose this.

"Ahhh..." The Fafamafalafama's deep voice echoed without translation from the unobtrusively small yet powerful translator device, courtesy of the Earthlings, strapped to his wide, jewel-encrusted belt. "'Ahffasah Ahlsen-Taylah'," he went on, "he has honored himself by honoring my request for his presence."

Nanofafo tried to draw his supreme master's attention to his own role in bringing there the "Ahthlahn" (Earthling), by making a low sweep of his right hand Chris's way. This, as though to say, *I present to you...* Nanofafo thrilled to the Fafamafalafama's subtle nod of acknowledgement. He got so thrilled, his ridiculously exaggerated handlebar moustache, made up of his twined and waxed-together mouse-y whiskers, uncurled and re-curled multiple times.

Or maybe, Chris thought, it was relief for Nanofafo, over not having to face a consequence for not getting a task done correctly. Whichever, Chris told himself, in a bid to stave off panic: At least the Fafamafalafama's adviser, one of them, was present. He was not going to have to face this intimidating character all by himself. Although, maybe Nanofafo was to serve as witness to the proper execution of the execution.

Yes, maybe it was considerate, even, of the Fafaman

ruler to have had his chambers lit up for this one-on-one audience with a non-nocturnal intelligent being, rather than with the more typical pale-green bioluminescence of a soil-encrusted flounder mouse. But Chris would have far preferred having to wear his night-vision goggles, rather than having to wonder what was the look in the Fafaman ruler's eyes, cloaked by his anti-glare, stars-fade spectacles. Whatever look it was, it was getting accompanied presently by a smile as broad as Chris had ever seen it. Was the "Ahthlahn" to provide court jester amusement? Or did the Fafaman ruler really take that much pleasure in lopping off someone's head? Were the latter to be the case, Chris wasn't noticing any towels, baskets, etc., whatever one would have thought would be necessary to clean up the mess afterwards. Although, Officer Olsen-Taylor speculated ever-more-fearfully, maybe it wasn't that big of a deal for them. Servants armed with buckets of soapy water and mops could burst from side doors on a moment's notice to quickly tidy up, especially off the royal chamber's slippery-smooth, shale-rock floor.

But there was that other key point Chris had noted earlier. His wife Helena didn't appear at all concerned about the Fafamafalafama calling him into his presence. She'd even excused herself from joining him to, as she put it, continue a dialogue with the Fafaman ruler's wives. A dialogue to more fully understand how she'd fit in with his harem after her own husband was sent into the afterlife, if not total oblivion?

The Fafamafalafama swung back his sword from his thrust into an imagined chest, to rest it gently on his left shoulder. Both his hands eased up on their tight grip of its hilt. Chris Olsen-Taylor found himself instinctively taking his golf club, a three-wood, into a slow backswing. From whence he ended up resting it on his own left shoulder, held balanced there by his left hand only. "What's this about?" Officer Olsen-Taylor finally couldn't help blurting out most anxiously.

"Ha! Ha! Ha!" the Fafamafalafama ha-ha-haaed in his cavernously deep voice.

Chris had last heard this identical laugh from him several days earlier. Immediately upon his, Helena, Ali and Tanya's safe return to the two-mile-tall pyramid, they had been brought before the royal presence by the jet pilot who rescued them. This meeting had taken place in a larger chamber than the present one. The Earthlings were to provide a debriefing on what they experienced directly, as opposed to what the Fafamafalafama experienced vicariously through the monitoring "bread crumb" nano-robots. All the sudden, though, Wafalawa had rushed in. His whiskers had uncurled as straight out as his urgent feelings could make them, as he had fa-la-laed, "Supreme Fafamafalafama, it pleasures me to report on the results of your brilliant suggestion for a retaliatory strike! Clouds of dust, recorded by the monitoring nanobot devices before they went dead, are evidence you might have struck a definitive blow against the barbarian leadership!"

"This is wonderful news, isn't it?" the Fafamafalafama had boomed, as he had scanned the faces of his extraterrestrial audience for their reaction.

Chris had felt grateful, for himself and his wife both, as well as for Ali and Tanya, that they had all had to wear their night-vision goggles. The more typical nocturnal setting had been established for this particular audience with the Fafamafalafama. In fact, the one lone flounder mouse/namalumina had glowed so faintly, its attendant, potted-fern-type tree had only partially unfurled.

With the Earthlings' eyes thusly concealed, it had been the Fafamafalafama's turn to guess what accompanied their forced-looking grins.

For Chris's part, he hadn't been sure a bit of mischief wasn't twinkling in the Fafamafalafama's eyes. Chris had wondered whether this ruler wasn't overdoing his joy over the announcement of wrought destruction, to bait what he saw as the aliens' prejudiced notion he was something of a barbarian, himself.

"Supreme Fafamafalafama," Ali Magabu had raised his hand after receiving a nodded approval to proceed from Captain Taylor, "are you concerned about the possibility some innocent children might have been killed?, or at least their homes destroyed?"

Chris had pressed his lips together hard. He had wanted to chime in, *If those hillside collapses were onto family dwellings, the horror, the terror for all those people…*

The Fafamafalafama had lost no time answering, "No one, NO ONE, suffers more than I at the thought of children's pain." A cloud had crossed his face, a cloud full of defiance that narrowed his normally ultra-wide-open nocturnal eyes to a squint.

"His anguish is limitless over the pain inflicted on others," Wafalawa had ritually chanted. He had bowed, and made a low sweep of his left hand towards the Fafamafalafama. Chris had fancied Wafalawa might as well have been introducing the ruler of Fafama for the first time, again.

"However," the Fafamafalafama had gone on, "if enough barbarian leaders were eliminated to finally convince those people living among them of the consequences of their evil, we can hope their surviving children will grow up in authentic innocence."

"I truly believe in what the tree beings of Oomb would say." Ali Magabu had sought to make his own apprehension diplomatically one step removed, by invoking that third party. "It is likely that the surviving children, particularly of the killed resistance leaders, will grow up wanting to avenge their parents' untimely deaths, as violence only begets more violence."

"And how will they grow up, if the fates of my new wife and your brave soldier are allowed to go un-avenged?! Will they grow up believing they can destroy without that destruction ricocheting on them?!"

When the Fafamafalafama had roared in his booming deep voice, Wafalawa had hunched his shoulders and cringed. It had been, Chris had thought, as though Wafalawa were bracing for his ruler's words to clobber him with the force of actual physical blows. Also, Chris would not have been surprised had the Fafamafalafama suddenly unsheathed his sword and swung it back and forth. This, to try irrationally to slice to shreds Ali's words before they could drift anywhere else.

"But listen please." The Fafaman ruler's deep booming had abruptly turned softer, assuming an almost lullaby cadence. "Listen as Wafalawa recites for you our peace proposal." He had paused, to give Chris's wife such a look as though, Chris had felt, he would have bored his eyes deep into Helena's were that physically possible. "Surely, 'Cahptahn Tayhlah,'" he had proceeded with his most mischievous-seeming smile, "surely you don't think I was expecting the survivors of our more-than-justified retaliation to figure out everything without an explicit explanation from us?" The way the Fafaman ruler had totally ignored Ali Magabu, it had been clear he misapprehended that Helena put up Ali to articulate the concerns he articulated. That the Fafaman ruler didn't believe Ali came up with the notion of children avenging their terrorist parents' deaths on his own. Not that Captain Taylor didn't share this worry.

Wafalawa's handlebar moustache had curled and un-curled some more as he had made a subtle bow, with his left hand extended in a low, wide sweep the Fafamafalafama's way. His ensuing fa-la-las had gotten translated as, "To the place from where the terrorists parachuted hungry young 'ahtpah's in amidst our wedding celebration, we have sent a message. It is a message we attached to several parachutes, showered most undeservingly their way." Wafalawa had unfurled a rolled-up, bioluminescently-treated parchment from his right hand, and he had held it up before himself to read. "'Attend well, enemies of the Fafaman kingdom, to the wisdom and kindness of your Fafamafalafama. After tireless research, he has concluded our planet suffers from a water shortage, his loyal subjects as much as his most faithless traitors. Thanks to his brilliant negotiating skills, he has persuaded a space-faring species, creatures who oddly make their home in the void between planets, to implement his plan. The Fafamafalafama's plan is for the space-faring species to seize the largest icy object they can find, and drag it from its meaningless elliptical orbit through worthless emptiness, to establish it into a new, circular orbit around Fafama. There, it will shed gentle rains into our atmosphere, and trail fireworks from its rocky debris which will burn up harmlessly as that debris likewise falls ground-wards. Those fireworks are to be a constant daily reminder of the greatness and wisdom of the Supreme Fafamafalafama! And to think that all you are asked for in return is to surrender to us all your weapons and explosive devices! Or if you choose, you may bury them alongside your victims of the deadly violence you have brought upon yourselves, subject to verification by our inspectors!"

"No! No! No!" Presently, the Fafamafalafama was shaking his head as he stepped up before Chris, who held his three-wood golf club diagonally across his chest. "It is your head you want to defend foremost. You see?" With a swish of his sword, holding its jewel-encrusted hilt by only his left hand, he brought its sharp edge to within a quarter-inch of Chris's Adams Apple. Its tip was prevented from getting any closer to Chris by the Fafamafalafama's protectively-gloved right hand.

Officer Olsen-Taylor strained to gulp, though he had no trouble imagining mischievous glee in the Fafamafalafama's eyes based on his wide, teeth-baring smile.

"But what is the idea with your weapon?" At the same time the Fafaman ruler swung away his sword from so close to Chris, to re-sheathe it, he grabbed at the golf club to examine it more closely. He executed this action faster than Chris could let go, so both Chris's wrists nearly got sprained. "This blunt head on one end," the Fafamafalafama turned it over slowly in the palm of his left hand, "is it for bopping your enemy on the skull? No, that can't be. The way you were making your practice swings in your living quarters, what I saw on the monitors, the idea is to disable your foe with a swift strike to his sperm sack, yes?" This was how his fa-la-las translated. "Maybe you can step back a few paces so I might practice, and see the effect on you! Ho! Ho! Ho!"

The Fafamafalafama's laughter had had this same, booming bass quality when he had toyed with the away team's fears. His toying had taken place during the same, days-ago audience for Wafalawa to read aloud the so-called peace proposal, which was sent into resistance territory attached to a host of parachutes. "There is the question of what you are to do while you await the return of your spacecraft. I was sorry to hear, 'Cahhptahhn,' you were replaced by another officer."

"A provisional captain until it is practical for me to return to duty," had corrected Helena. She had tried to sound nonchalant and non-testy about it.

"'Prahvishanahl cahhptahhn,' of course," the Fafamafalafama had nodded with his teeth-baring smile. He had made a point of repeating the adjective he'd heard next to "captain," rather than allowing for the more accurately pronounced translation of the Fafaman word for "provisional." "And so, about the matter of how your time is to be occupied awaiting the return of your ship with an ice rock in tow, we could make a game of it. For example, for each stars-fade, we could have some tralalafas arranged alongside other plants bearing an astounding likeness to the tralalafa, yet each one deadly in its own special way. The gaddagagga, for example, not only sucks clean its victim's intestinal track, it also sucks out the intestinal track itself, followed by the stomach and various other organs. You each choose a plant for your sleeping arrangement. Each day we host you, should you survive the previous stars-fade, you get to entertain yourself whichever way you see fit, short of bothering my wives!" Here he had swept his goggled eyes Ali and Chris's direction, presumably to glare reprovingly at them. Then silence. He had alternated between looking Wafalawa's way and looking the stunned-speechless Earthlings' way, until finally he had gone, "Hee-hee-heeee!" with all the shrillness of a screeching baboon.

Wafalawa had joined in. Although, he had cut his own hee-hees abruptly short, to fa-la-la to the Earthlings, "The Fafamafalafama's sense of humor is as sharp as the tip of his sword!"

"Yes." The Fafaman ruler had just-as-abruptly broken off

from his own expression of mirth, to return to his severely-booming voice, directed square at Wafalawa. "And I am also certain you find my excrement so divinely inspired, that were it not for the tralalafa, you and Nanofafo would duel to the death over who gets to eat it! Or there would be some ritual chant of wonderment over why everyone else doesn't remain permanently constipated, since the quality of my excrement makes all other excrement not even worth the bother of discharging!" He had latched his left hand onto the hilt of his sheathed sword, working his fingers around about its encrusted jewels to give the impression he was itchy to whip it out, perhaps to take a stab at Wafalawa. Whose rapidly curling and uncurling whiskers had suggested that all joking aside, this ruler guy was "truly," as Ali would have put it, making him nervous.

Chris and company had exchanged astonished looks. Was the Fafamafalafama uncontrollably evidencing that all along, he felt an insulting patronizing by his servants?, singing praises they didn't actually feel? Or...but soon enough the Fafamafalafama's shoulders had been heaving, and he couldn't keep that grim, thin-lined expression on his mouth any longer. Once again, he had shrilly shrieked, "Hee! Hee! Heeee!"

Wafalawa had joined in as rapidly as he had been able to plow under his terror. Or had that terror been faked as well?

"No, no." Back again to the present, Chris was affecting a casualness far from the panic he was trying to keep down like he'd try to keep down acid reflux. He shook his head and waved off the Fafamafalafama from grabbing his club. "We don't use golf clubs to strike our opponents in any location, let alone their sperm-carrying sac." Chris stepped away further from the Fafaman ruler, and he latched on to the grip of his three-wood with both hands. He gave it a few waggles like he was preparing to tee off. "We use our clubs to strike a ball about this big." Chris stood up out of his golf swing posture, and he took his right hand off his club to show with his thumb and forefinger the approximate diameter of a typical golf ball.

"Ahh," the Fafamafalafama nodded knowingly, "and from which sort of animal do you secure testicles of that size?"

Chris couldn't help smiling, no strain to appear amused this time. "We manufacture our golf balls. We don't get them from any animals. Though I will have to admit that when I hit a bad shot, when I hit the ball where I didn't want to hit it, if I could swing my club-head into my own testicles to distract me from that pain with a greater pain, I might be tempted."

"So how do you cause your opponent to hit a bad shot?" The Fafamafalafama took a step closer to Chris as he asked this, with an attendant SWISH! of his sword.

If Chris Olsen-Taylor didn't know better, he would have sworn the ruler's timing was intended to throw off his own practice swing. "You don't cause your opponent to hit a bad shot," Olsen-Taylor finally answered. He backed a step away from the Fafamafalafama as he said this. "You focus on making your own shots as solid as possible. There is no such thing as trying to block a golfer's shot, like there is in other sports on our planet."

"For a successful sword fight, a sword fight you walk away from, 'Offasah Taylah,' it is of vital importance to know your enemy's weakness." SWISH! Again, he took a step closer to Chris.

"In golf, it is of vital importance to know your OWN weaknesses, to play to your strengths." This time instead of backing away, Chris stood his ground from his previous retreat, and he endeavored to take a nice and easy practice swing with his three-wood despite the unnerving behavior of the Fafaman ruler.

"So where is the satisfaction of defeating your enemy in this game you call 'golf'?" SWISH! This sword swing got so close, Chris could feel a breeze, the cold breeze of steel.

"The satisfaction comes in playing better than your opponent, in taking fewer shots to get your ball into a hole in the ground than your opponent takes. In fact, you can even lose to your opponent, but still find happiness in beating yourself."

"Beating yourself?" The Fafamafalafama paused his sword halfway through his latest downswing, and he added with a silly grin and voice as booming deep as ever, "If I were to be defeated in a duel, I would not live long enough to impale myself and think, 'Ah, I was not able to breach my enemy's defenses to drive my weapon into its proper destination, but at least I was able to plunge it deeply into my OWN chest! Ho! Ho! Ho!"

"What I mean is, if your own score is better than any previous score you have made,-"

"Excuse me, Supreme Fafamafalafama." Wafalawa had his left hand cupped over his left ear, and his whiskers in a commotion of curling and uncurling. "We have just received word the Smoke and Mirrors, the alien space vessel from 'Ahth,' has returned. They have successfully ensnared an ice rock, and are about to initiate its descent into water-shedding orbit around Fafama, exactly as you conceived it!"

Fwack! As Wafalawa bowed to his leader after giving him the credit for geologist Cathy James-Leung's idea, the Fafamafalafama neatly sliced through the graphite shaft within a quarter inch of where it was attached to the club-head. This sent the club-head spinning in the air for the briefest moment, before it dropped to the slate floor and tumbled to rest at Chris's feet.

"Now we see who has won our argument, 'Offasah Taylah'! But do not worry about the decapitation of this poor substitute for your own manhood," was how the booming fa-la-las of the Fafamafalafama translated. "I am sure our finest sword engineer can replicate your weapon to far more powerful specifications than you ever imagined! If only the decapitation of the barbarian leadership were this simple! Maybe, we can hope, it already has been with our most recent retaliatory strike!"

# Chapter 20

"We really wish you and the other officers had been here, Helena, for a ringside seat," claimed Captain Louisa Entroper with her tsk-tsk-tsk head shake. "Number one on our lead officer agenda was the issue of whether to try bringing you back on board, before we launch our mountainous cargo into orbit around Fafama. But of course, had you been here, we wouldn't have had to wrestle with that particular issue in the first place."

*And you wouldn't have ended up as captain*, Kevin bit his lower lip to keep from bursting out.

Entroper held up her paper-thin compu-pad, for Officer Geena Murphy-Davis's body cam. This facilitated a close-up of the agenda outline, in case there was any doubt.

Helena and the rest of the away team down on Fafama got to see this, the proof that the newly-instated starship captain was telling the truth, on Chris's porta-screen. The porta-screen was set up on a cleared-off dining table in yet another of the Fafamafalafama's secondary throne rooms. Said away team was stuck, trapped once more deep down inside the city-sized Great Pyramid of Fafama, its apex soaring two miles into the sky.

"We gave careful consideration to the feasibility report by Officer James-Leung. Regretfully, though, I have had to conclude the plan is simply too dangerous. There is significant risk of a tragic accident, were we to attempt to retrieve you before we launch our ice comet payload into Fafaman orbit."

Geena zoomed out the body cam from the meeting agenda. On this wider view, Helena could clearly make out Kevin, behind Entroper and to one side. He was shaking his head to accompany the disgusted look on his face. The former Captain Taylor didn't require an Oombian tree person's mind-reading talents to guess at the source of his disgust. Most likely, Entroper was over-riding Cathy's estimation that the away team could indeed have been safely brought back aboard the Smoke and Mirrors prior to the comet maneuver. Entroper was abusing her newly-appointed power to remind the crew that, whatever their previous allegiances may have been, SHE was in charge now. Also saying to Helena, in so many words, *The priority is that I get privileged seating to view important operations executed by this starship; you may have to settle for less as a crew member under my command.*

"Esteemed Fafamafalafama, if I may address you directly..."

"But of course, 'Cahptahn Ahntropah,'" the Fafaman ruler's fa-la-las translated as he made a low sweep of his left hand. He kept his chin held high, as he didn't want to risk laxing into a posture the starship captain might misconstrue as any slightest hint of a deferential bow.

"Once we are certain the comet has found stable orbit around Fafama, in the hope it will rain down peace on your amazing planet,-"

"Rain down peace," the Fafamafalafama interrupted to repeat the fa-la-las he'd heard translated for that phrase. "Yes," he nodded by way of universal gesture, "you will be pleased to learn that is what we have done to answer the senseless violence which has waylaid your diplomatic team here. That is what we have done, to retaliate for what we can only speculate has happened to my twenty-third wife and one of your soldiers, until we either rescue them or find their remains. And I am pleased to report to you the result of obeisance to my orders for our fighter jets to 'rain down peace' on the noonthrah pit of terrorists. The result is, we have not had one attack since then. What's more, in anticipation of your delivery to us of the final section of this peace puzzle, we have sent a further rain, of parachutes, into the hostile lands. Messages are attached, asking merely that our introduction of a new water source from the larger cosmos be reciprocated by unconditional surrender of any other weapons, and of any other plots for wanton destruction."

Wafalawa made a bow the Fafaman ruler's way as he also made the traditional low sweep of his left hand towards him, and he fa-la-laed, "The wisdom of the Fafamafalafama."

Helena Taylor had to contain herself, to keep from shaking her head in disgust. *It's been only days since the retaliatory strike. Who knows what the resistance might be moved to try in their grief-stoked rage, if indeed those hillsides collapsed on several innocent people?*

Captain Entroper shook her own head, what she almost always did regardless of what she was saying. "That is most encouraging, esteemed Fafamafalafama. And like I was saying," she went on, "once the comet is successfully steered into orbit, the next logical step appears to entail our delivering to you additional lines of defense. You might really need them, should the laser mesh shield surrounding Fafama get compromised."

Helena intuited, to her further irritation, that Louisa's lecturing tone was meant more for her than for the Fafaman ruler.

"It will not be the complete weapons suite," Louisa Entroper continued. "But it will include a complement of land-based missiles for deployment around your central pyramid, plus enough air-based missiles to arm twenty-five to fifty of your fighter jets, depending on whether you install one or two launchers per jet. This contribution to your defenses will also include robotic labor, programmed with tutorials in your language. The entire package will be delivered to your planet as an unmanned vehicle that will automatically separate into three separate containers as it enters Fafaman air space. When on-board sensors detect that those containers have descended to where atmospheric pressure reaches sixty-five per cent, parachutes as well as enveloping bubble cushions will deploy automatically. We recommend a fighter-jet escort as they fall closer to the surface of Fafama. And not to worry; if for some reason, parachute AND bubble cushion, both, were to fail to deploy, the affected container will crash into the ground as harmless rubble. Subsequently, we will send a hazardous materials team to clean up our mess. Again, those packages are only to tide you over, until our defense cruiser can arrive with the full air-, sea-, and land-based suite."

With an approving nod, the Fafamafalafama clapped his hands and rubbed them together. But his eyes could not be read. They were enshrouded by anti-glare goggles made necessary for him by the stars-fade setting of the secondary throne room's lighting, in deference to the away team from Earth. "Those are most adequate plans," the ruler fa-la-laed. "So now, we await the parachuting to us of those three giant drip-drops of peace! Hee! Hee!"

"The sense of humor most magnificent of the Fafamafalafama, he-he-hee!" Once more, Wafalawa bowed and gestured towards his leader as though he were introducing him for the first time.

"Soon as we have gotten wet with that most glorious

weapons shower, 'Cahptahn Ahntropah,' delivery back to you will be in order, of your diplomatic contingent."

This time, Captain Entroper did nod her head, instead of her usual side-to-side shake. Pursuant to which, she carefully slowly said, "Uh, yes. We were thinking, our thinking was indeed that the away team should see the delivery of defense supplies through to safe completion. In that manner, they can be on hand for direct, um, assistance in the unlikely event of any difficulty."

"Also, of course, we will be able to thank your representatives directly for their wise execution of the plans as I envisioned them!" the Fafamafalafama boomed expansively.

Tanya, Ali, Helena and Chris traded significant looks during this awkward exchange. They were all thinking the same thing. Entroper ought to have set the condition that first, the away team would get to return to the Smoke and Mirrors. The weapons delivery would come second. Certainly, Entroper could have made up some excuse. She could have insisted Tanya was needed back aboard the Smoke and Mirrors to help with the safe guidance of the payloads into the Fafaman atmosphere. Therefore, why not have the other three Earthlings accompany her, instead of wasting time and energy on an additional return flight for them? Should the Fafamafalafama have balked at releasing the away team back to the starship before the weapons delivery, that would have confirmed they were getting held hostage. In which case, Helena believed Earthling troops should be deployed to manage the missile launchers. This, instead of leaving said launchers completely in the hands of the Fafamans.

Helena fumed helplessly over Entroper's hesitant response to the ruler's pronouncement, of when would be "the proper time" for the Fafamans to let the Earthlings leave. As far as Helena was concerned, Captain Entroper was acceding to what she well knew was a hostage arrangement. And she was rationalizing that accession, when she spoke of how the away team could "be on hand for direct, um, assistance in the unlikely event of a difficulty."

"Yes, well," Captain Louisa Entroper went on finally, "I think this is where I am going to turn this over to Officer James-Leung. She will narrate what we are seeing. Officer?"

"Thank you, Captain."

Geena shifted her body cam Cathy James-Leung's way. But before she could shift it again, focus it on the view-screen where it was to stay focused for the duration of the operation, Helena jumped in, "Cathy?"

"Yes, Cap- Officer Taylor. Hi!" Cathy nervously waved with an equally nervous, if beaming, smile.

"Yes, is Buddy-"

"*Officer* Buddy Leung!" Entroper grumbled from the background.

"Okay," Helena sighed with weary resignation. "Is Officer Buddy Leung facilitating with you?"

"No; he's hiding out somewhere in the Callaway X Centra System. He's seeing if he can locate the Tictoctic attack vessel. I'm sure he's safe," Cathy nodded, again with the nervous smile though not so beaming.

"Attack vessel? What is this about?" The Fafamafalafama turned from the porta-screen to Helena, then back again to the porta-screen, before he nodded knowingly, "Ahh, yes, of course, what sent the Smoke and Mirrors away from our magnificent realm at a most impulsively inconvenient time. Please continue, woman of 'Ahth.'" He gestured toward Cathy on the porta-screen.

"Geena, I think we're ready," Cathy continued. "You can focus the body cam on the view-screen now? Thank you. Officer Park-Smith, commence left-side camera feed into the view-screen."

What the Smoke and Mirrors's side camera revealed on the view-screen were twinkling, orange-ish sparks, evenly geometrically spaced. This was in place of the usual starry firmament with the Milky Way haze comprised of even more stars in the backdrop. There were sporadic flashes of fine, orange lines connecting the orange-ish sparks, suggestive of a geodesic latticework.

For the Earthlings held captive by the Fafamafalafama, there was only a second-hand look at what showed in the view-screen. This look came by way of Geena's body cam transmission down to Fafama, from up on board the Smoke and Mirrors. Nevertheless, Chris could still sense something enormous. Might as well have been a monster in its cage, he mused.

"You can't actually see the comet itself," explained Cathy. "Only how it's obstructing the star field, so that all you get a look at is the electromagnetic gimmickry with which we have ensnared it. We found this comet heading out of the Alpha Centauri C Oort Cloud back into your solar system on a classic elliptical orbit, with a calculated perihelion of two astronomical units."

"The perihelion is its closest, the closest it gets to your sun on its path in and out of your solar system," Helena asided to the Fafamafalafama. "An astronomical unit is the distance from our sun to our Earth. In the case of your sun and Fafama, in your measurements that unit is about one hundred seventy million labadas."

"Most gracious of you, former 'Cahptahn Taylah,' to spare me from having to explain all of this to Wafalawa."

*And most face-saving egotistical of you, self-proclaimed ruler of your entire planet, to pretend you would have had the slightest idea what "perihelion" referred to if I hadn't elaborated*, Helena thought to herself.

Before Cathy could go on, the Fafamafalafama's adviser, Wafalawa, couldn't leave well enough alone without inserting, "And I appreciate our Supreme Fafamafalafama's even more gracious conviction that anyone should have gotten burdened with having to try to enlighten me, in the first place."

Cathy James-Leung easily, instantly concluded she was better off pretending to be totally oblivious to the two Fafamans' curious interaction. That she was too intent on what she had to share, to pay such interaction any attention, rather than brave adding to it in any least way. So, she simply continued, as though there had been no interruption to her explication, "This comet, which incidentally we have named Varafafafa in honor of your missing twenty-third wife, most esteemed Fafamafalafama..."

The Fafamafalafama pursed his ample lips, and he made an acknowledging nod, too fascinated for the moment to bother over whether he might appear deferential to anyone else.

"This comet, no surprise, is saturated with drinkable water, mostly frozen. There is one molecule of heavy water for every sixteen hundred molecules of the normal stuff. Heavy, of course, means at least one of the two hydrogen atoms within a molecule contains an extra neutron." Cathy hastened to add this definition of heavy water, hoping to pre-empt another awkward interaction back down on Fafama, revolving around the Fafaman ruler's ego. "That's twice the average heavy water content in Fafama's Grand Basin and other large bodies of water. But we believe it's still safely drinkable, still most suitable for shedding into your atmosphere. Our infrared spectroscopic analysis suggests that at sixty-five miles in diameter, or at one hundred thirty-five labadas in diameter, in your Fafaman measurement system, the comet Varafafafa will provide an abundance of this all-important, life-sustaining substance."

"At one hundred thirty-five labadas in diameter, the Varafafafa would have provided far too much abundance for me to get my arms around!" the Fafamafalafama boomed in a voice as deep as it was mischief-laden. "Just as well, that I never got to consummate our marital union!"

"The ahtpah-poison-barbed wit of the Fafamafalafama," Wafalawa ritually spoke with his latest low sweep of his left arm his leader's way. He could have been introducing the Fafaman ruler for the first time, not the umpteenth.

*Sweet. A stupidly crude joke at the expense of his twenty-third wife who, for all he knows, has long since been killed.* On this assessment, Cathy swiftly concluded, like before, she was better off feigning too much absorption in her work to notice anything else. She soldiered on, "Our best estimate from the spectroscopic analysis is that Va-errr, the comet contains between two hundred fifty and three hundred million tons of water. That is approximately four hundred waladas in your measurement system. This is ample, once it is entirely shed, to significantly moisten Fafama beyond its present condition. This might also, perhaps, take the destructive edge off the sunset storm line for the first time in fifty million orbits of your sun." Geophysicist James-Leung caught herself up from repeating the comet's name, lest she give the Fafamafalafama an opening for more of his crude humor.

She needn't have worried.

The planetary ruler's attention was already shifted over entirely to the transmission feed to his view-screen from Geena's body cam, which in turn was focused on a view-screen aboard the Smoke and Mirrors. He was craning his neck forward, as he strained to discern something in the darkness back behind the electrostatic grid displayed on his view-screen. Perhaps, Chris thought, the Fafamafalafama fancied he caught a glimpse of the least shimmer of embedded ice. Chris wasn't sure he didn't catch a glimpse of such a shimmer, himself.

"The first of many tricks," Dr. Cathy James-Leung went on, "was maneuvering the comet out of its elliptical orbit, down closer to Fafama. Simply by the Smoke and Mirrors's slight gravitational pull, we could have set this enormous ice rock on a heading straight into Fafaman orbit. The only problem was, at its former rate of speed, you would not have been seeing it here for another seventy-four solar orbits.

"What we needed to do was get the comet to entrain our spacecraft. Basically, it rode the Smoke and Mirrors to Fafama, so the trip got shortened to three days. Fortunately, we were able to make our ride-hitching rendezvous close to the Oort Cloud, at the outer reaches of your solar system. There, the comet's debris trail was practically non-existent; your sun was too distant for its heat to cause the trail-inducing melting that comets normally undergo closer in to your solar system. And so, it was merely a matter of establishing an electrostatic 'fishnet' around the entirety of the comet. Thereafter, we had to keep the Smoke and Mirrors a safe enough distance away from the comet for our light propulsion system to work, yet close enough for the electrostatic discharge to act as a tractor beam. Before we performed this operation, we had to land myself and two engineers, including Kevin Smith-Park, on the comet's surface, for a preliminary task. We had to strategically embed conventional fuel rockets that would make course corrections, once the comet Varafafafa got sent into orbit some sixteen thousand labadas above the surface of Fafama. The heat shed by those course corrections would also accelerate the comet's shedding of its vast water content. The embedded rockets were specially outfitted with spiral thread drills for their nose cones, to facilitate their penetration steadily deeper into the comet as its size steadily decreases.

"Okay, I think we are just about ready to turn off the electrostatic 'cage.' One other note about that: Say we had been attempting this project even one solar orbit later. The comet Varafafafa would have been flying that much closer to your sun, on its return towards perihelion. Its tail of melted ice and debris would already have gotten so extended, we wouldn't have been able to contain it all electrostatically. What we are doing presently would have proven impossible. By the by, we couldn't max out our speed to arrive any sooner than those three days I mentioned, or the electrostatic 'cling' would have come loose and the comet have gotten away from us.

"There, the electrostatic net is discharged, and Varafafafa is already flaring out, just like that!" Cathy snapped her fingers exultantly. "Its flare extends easily hundreds of labadas behind her. That is some tail!"

Kevin couldn't help mischievously thinking, *That really IS some tail on the Fafamafullofhimselfama's twenty-third wife's namesake!*

The comet, along with its trail of melting ice and rocks, was starting to glow an eerie soft-pale blue, on a heading seemingly into the dawn sky of Fafama. Its increasing distance from the Smoke and Mirrors shrank it steadily smaller in the panoramic view-screen on the navigation bridge.

"Like any satellite getting launched into orbit, our comet is going to assume an elliptical trajectory. Frequent mid-course corrections will be required to adjust it to a more circular path. You're about to see the first embedded rocket flares for that purpose."

No sooner did the geophysicist Cathy James-Leung say this than tiny orange flares erupted on comet Varafafafa. These in turn sent out deep blue plumes of dirt, rock and more melted ice. Chris was reminded of burning natural gas on an antique stovetop.

"The spectacle provided by this comet orbiting Fafama should be plainly visible in the daytime, as well as by night." This was the next installment of Cathy's increasingly spaced-apart bits of narrative. The stunning view of Varafafafa getting corrected into a stable, circular orbit spoke for itself.

"There cannot be a more dramatic daily reminder of how the Fafaman people have kept their end of the agreement!" the Fafamafalafama boomed in a cavernously declarative voice, inspired by the view transmitted back from space. "And now it is up to the terrorists and their collaborators, if there is any trace of decency and civilization to be found in them, to perform their end of the bargain! They must disarm!"

"Officer James-Leung," said Captain Entroper, "can we proceed with launching the defense payloads towards Fafama?"

Helena wondered whether Louisa Entroper was at all conscious of the irony of what she was so urgently about. Here, the Fafamafalafama made this dramatic declaration the resistance should see no other choice than to give up their weaponry, assuming they were possessed of any least bit of propriety. And then, hot on the heels of this call for disarmament, Entroper couldn't wait to ask about delivering military hardware to him.

"One more thing before that, Captain," said Cathy raising a cautionary hand. "We have to insure the laser mesh shield has been properly recalibrated, so it can distinguish between harmless comet debris and intelligently manufactured materials. Otherwise, significant portions of the shed water will get atomized useless."

Pursuant to this warning, Yoon-hee at the navigation panel announced, "Recalibration test is ready to fire, Officer James-Leung."

"Umm, fire!" Cathy hoped she wasn't neglecting some special protocol that would get her chewed out by Captain Entroper.

On the view-screen, the bright, yellow-burning contrail of the test rocket could be easily seen heading for the Fafama-facing underbelly of the enormous comet. Impact was quiet. Clearly, nevertheless, a rock chunk nearly one hundred feet across got chipped off by the dynamite explosion. That chunk's fate was obscured by the comet's ever-lengthening trail. However, ship sensors confirmed that friction from faint traces of upper level atmosphere was tearing it apart. No laser beams were to be blamed. This, while feedback from the laser mesh confirmed the missile fragments were identified and promptly disintegrated by superheated beams exceeding lightning temperature.

***

The blinding-light prowler with Vootoov clasped

securely between its two hind legs yawed to the left, to avoid ensnarement by a free-floating web of the shiny, yellow-striped ahtpah. The yellow-striped ahtpah was working that web like a hang glider. Vootoov's goggle-less, squinting eyes were drawn, nevertheless, to the greater spectacle plainly visible despite mid-day brightness. The least of it was the blown-off comet chunk, flaring out like a shooting star as it fell into the upper stratosphere. More impressive were the fireworks flashes from the signature fine red lines of the triggered laser mesh shield converging on the exploded rocket fragments. But most awe-inspiring, most dramatic of all was the bluish-glowing immensity of comet Varafafafa. Its attendant, lengthening, sparkling tail was already shedding thousands of gallons of H2O towards the Fafaman atmosphere.

*That must be the water-bearing space rock Chief Vituf told us the aliens were promising to send into orbit around our planet, in the naïve hope that would somehow magically bring peace.* Vootoov thought this to himself as he ground his teeth together in a controlled rage of grim determination. *But no matter.* He shot out another vial of blinding-light prowler nest scent from his shoulder-strapped rocket launcher. It burst open so far ahead of them, he couldn't hear its mini-explosion, especially over the loud hum of his prowler's blur-of-motion beetle wings. But it was enough scent, calculated to be enough scent, to assure his six-legged steed would stay on course, headed towards the central pyramid. Three of the ten other soldiers getting transported by this particular blinding-light prowler swarm also launched timed-explosive, nest-scent canisters. Their shed odors were likewise meant to reinforce the illusion a prowler nesting area lay just ahead. To initiate this monster insect attack squadron, the blinding-light prowlers were not fooled into instinctively trusting the soldiers were mates for showering with their fertile seed. Rather, juice collected from a noosanoo grub abdomen had been smeared all over said soldiers. This juice had tricked the swarm into believing they had come across noosanoo grubs newly emerged from multi-year gestation underground. The prowlers were carrying those supposed grubs to what they were lured into expecting would be their nests, as meals for their recently hatched babies.

Vootoov presently found himself isolated, by the beetle wing hum, from hearing or being heard by his fellow suicide mission specialists, even were they all to scream. Alone with his thoughts, he reviewed important aspects of the plan for the umpteenth time. *We have the element of surprise, striking during the glare of stars-fade when so few people are awake. We know it is not untypical for a swarm of blinding light prowlers to innocently, harmlessly buzz the central pyramid, on occasion, out of curiosity. We are camouflaged by outfits stitched together from shed noosanoo grub shell. This includes empty leg exoskeleton sticking out at our chests, and head exoskeleton made to fit over our own heads like helmets. Mirror pieces cover our pants legs, so the glare produced by reflected mid-day sun should be too intense even for the most shaded goggles. A jet squadron of the Fafaman Empire should be able to fly within a hundredth of a labada of us, and their pilots still be unable to tell us apart from real noosanoo grubs.*

*And there are eleven of us. Only one of us has to get through, to assure at least a portion of the Fafamafalafama's wives and one of their nurseries is woken up beyond death, to whatever faces them for their society's cruel, selfish deeds in this life. I have to hope my wife and daughters were actually asleep when the caverns collapsed, that their pain and the terror were next to nothing. Were I to know for sure otherwise, I would want to set off an alarm to awaken the brood and mates of the Fafaman Empire before my impact, so they might experience some of the same pain and terror…Leelee! She was so young, hardly walking, a big generous smile for everyone and anyone, no matter they were family, friend or sworn enemy! She would have tried to pet an ahtpah if her mother had let her!* Vootoov's vision blurred from tears welling up. *If it is God's way, I will soon be rejoining them! I know, I know. The younger recruits anticipate an afterlife where they are fought over by innumerable ardent virgins. But really, they want the same thing I want, only they are too foolish to realize this. I pray the planetary spirit will reward them, nevertheless, for their role as martyrs in the fight against this supreme evil. It is a fight for which we have to trust our inside contacts really did get assigned to pyramid surface-cleaning. And that what's more, in that assignment they have done what is necessary. They have kept re-applying blinding-light prowler pheromone solution to the windows outside royal wife sanctuaries and their attendant nurseries; so much solution, even the sunset storm line cannot wash it all away! For MY family!*

***

"Esteemed Fafamafalafama, I am happy to report to you. All three payloads have been successfully launched with near-zero variance from median expectations. They should be entering your atmosphere within fifty of your nininanas."

"Excellent, 'Cahptahn Ahntropah,' excellent!" The Fafamafalafama descended from his throne, while Tanya

Petrovsky couldn't help thinking, *He probably doesn't know what near-zero variance means, but it sounds good, so…* The Fafaman ruler became a blur of agitated motion. His bioluminescently infused robe fluttered like a super-hero cape behind him, so Chris mused. Menial servants were used to lazily waving tralalafa fronds over their ruler's head, to provide gently refreshing air currents. On this occasion, though, they didn't bother to try keeping up with him. They behaved quite unlike Wafalawa, who well knew he could not afford to NOT keep up with the supreme ruler of Fafama. To Ali Magabu, the adviser appeared pitifully ridiculous, sadly lacking any self-esteem, as he strove to follow no more than two steps behind the Fafamafafalafama's pacing. His handlebar moustache curled and uncurled involuntarily fast.

"Yes!" The Fafamafalafama clenched his fists at his sides and pounded the air with them. "It is the middle of stars-fade, but we must rouse from their tralalafas an elite contingent of witnesses and news media!"

"At once, Supreme Fafamafalafama!" Wafalawa said as he hastily scribbled this directive on a memo pad. He also took mental note that at an opportune time, he must give obeisance for the ruler's kindly sparing of most pyramid citizens. Only a few were to be woken from their intestine-cleansing symbiotic sleep inside Fafaman tralalafas, what Chris had come to think of as monster hybrid crosses between a tumbleweed and a Venus flytrap, especially after his own gross experience inside one of them.

"Wait! There is much more!" With a swirl of his cape, the Fafamafalafama pivoted around and faced Wafalawa. He nearly caused his trusted adviser to run into him, as head-down preoccupied as Wafalawa was with taking notes.

"We must open ALL the bleacher sections! Every last one! When our citizens watch their early evening news, while causing to succumb their first meal of the day, they will appreciate us. They will appreciate how we let them sleep through events of triumphantly historic proportions, yet also were providing more than ample seating for those who did find themselves awoken by the excitement in the air! All to more fully appreciate how the power of my position makes possible a tremendous diminution of our greatest threats!"

It was the opportune time for which Wafalawa was waiting. With yet another low sweep of his left hand towards his leader, he said, "The towering wisdom and mercy of the Fafamafalafama, even though he does not know the condition of the Varafafafa!"

***

"Flight commander Maravala, we have a swarm of eleven blinding-light prowlers on a heading towards the central pyramid that will bring them there within twenty nanas, unless they break off!" Reconnaissance jet pilot Apama reported to headquarters as he flew up alongside the immense beetles, each one the size of a typical Earth helicopter. "They appear to be carrying larvae of some sort by their hind legs! The larvae appear to have something that gives off a blinding glare depending from their underbellies! Please advise!"

"Probably food for their brood, Officer Apama!" was how the fa-la-las of Maravala would have translated. "Just to make sure, maneuver beneath one to get a closer look at the appendage with the blinding glare! It's probably juices squeezed out of the larvae when they were carried off. But with the special public announcement the Fafamafalafama is giving shortly..."

"Really?!"

"Every last bleacher section is ordered to be opened! Whatever THAT is about, we can't be too careful with security!"

"Fifty more wives for the Fafamafalafama!"

"Fifty more wives for the Fafamafalafama! Contact me as soon as you have confirmed you are monitoring a non-hostile situation! Pama!"

"Pama!" With this multi-purpose salutation, Apama clicked off communications. He slowed his jet for an altitude descent behind the swarm. Then, he flew underneath the hindmost blinding-light prowler to look up through his jet's sun roof. "Ahtpah dung!" he cursed, Fafaman style. "Those are human legs!"

***

Veedif whose legs Apama was spotting knew the jet had stayed below him for too long. His glory would have to settle for being the first sacrifice to allow the others to reach the pyramid. With the ritual fa-la-laed declaration, "God shades the just!," he stabbed a short sword into one of his blinding light prowler's bristly legs that had been securely clasping him. The large beetle's reflex reaction to the pain caused it to let go. As the resistance soldier landed atop the jet cockpit, he armed the explosive strapped to his chest so his impact would cause detonation. The resulting explosion engulfed the jet in flame, and charred the lower half of the hapless blinding light prowler so that it fell lifeless out of the sky.

***

As Helena, Chris, Tanya and Ali were taking their seats in the most-honored-guests section of the just-opened bleachers, they espied way up in the sky, despite the mid-day sun, three, pinpoint, moving lights maintaining a triangular formation. Those were the three military payloads. Their respective nosecones had "bloomed" to large enough diameters to act as heat shields, to effectively bear the brunt of entry into the Fafaman atmosphere. The Earthlings noted with satisfaction there were no telltale red lines from the laser mesh shield; the payload encoding had to have been accurate.

What took the Earthlings' attention away from this distant spectacle, as it was fading from view with deceleration reducing the friction flares, was a formation of five Fafaman fighter jets. Seemingly, they zoomed out of nowhere, on an apparent heading towards the Grand Basin. They left sonic booms in their wake. Helena figured they were to be the escort once the payloads descended to parachute-deployment altitude. But she was quickly disabused of this notion once the Fafamafalafama returned from being suddenly called away from their presence.

"Disturbing news, former 'Cahptahn Taylah'!" the Fafamafalafama fa-la-laed in her face, so close she could feel his warm breath nauseously scented by who-knew-what wriggly creature he had last devoured. "One of our reconnaissance jets has been incinerated in the desert not thirty labadas from here! Yes!" To Helena's eyes bugging out of her head, the Fafaman ruler was nodding as in, *There will be no denying this happened!* "And what is more, a blinding-light prowler went down with it, with a scorched underside! That prowler was but one of a swarm, flying this direction!"

The Fafaman ruler turned away from the Earthlings. He ascended the dais podium he would have preferred to have been rising up on from below, what he was used to doing on ceremonial occasions. "THE TERRORISTS MUST

NOT AND WILL NOT RUIN ANOTHER ROYAL OCCASION!! ESPECIALLY THIS ONE!" his shouted fa-la-las got translated as he pounded on the podium with both fists.

Media observers dutifully took notes, and other dignitaries dutifully screeched, "Ee-ee! Ee-ee!" as they vigorously shook their heads. The guards all around joined in.

"YOU SEE, PEOPLE FROM 'AHTH,' THIS IS THE THANKS YOU GET WITH THESE TERRORISTS WHEN YOU TRY TO DO ANYTHING FOR THEM!" Another fist-pound of the podium, as Chris was noticing a faint yet steadily growing hum...like from a swarm of bees back home. "ON FAFAMA, WE CANNOT AND WE MUST NOT BE LED BY NAÏVE NOTIONS OF EVIL BEING AT ALL ABLE TO CHANGE ITS WAYS!!"

The next thing any of them knew, there was the sound of Fafaman fighter jets unleashing their attack on the approaching prowler swarm. BOOM! BOOM! BOOM! BOOM! Of the four booms, only one was indicative of the fired missile having found its mark. Instinctive evasive maneuvers by the other three targeted prowlers resulted in harmless mid-air explosions.

"I wonder what this is about, Captain," Tanya said forgetting Helena's demotion. "They are nowhere near where the payloads are to land."

"I am afraid, my beautiful blessing," Ali gave his wife a consoling shoulder rub, "this will prove to have nothing to do with spoiling the payload delivery. Rather, I fear this will truly turn out to be about 'an eye for an eye and a tooth for a tooth.'"

Three immense parachutes safely brought down the military payloads to where they were surrounded by flatbed trucks. Those trucks were ready to cart off everything to below-ground installations, well before the next sunset storm line could hit. But what transfixed the audience ordered up by the Fafamafalafama was transpiring in a far different direction.

The next jet missile attack, plainly visible to the southeast, proved more successful than the first. Three of the four launches burst apart prowlers so that of the eleven original, only six were left, including the one carrying Vootoov.

Two of the five jets broke off from the pursuit and accelerated over beside the pyramid. There, they converted to helicopter mode. One was sent to hover near the wives' chambers and the royal nursery area, and the other got positioned in between the approaching prowlers and the bleacher area.

Whoosh! BOOM! Whoosh! BOOM! The newest fighter jet attacks missed their marks, as the remaining prowlers got more adept at dodging missiles. Said dodged missiles exploded harmlessly in mid-air, although their concussive effects did cause the remaining prowlers to sway from side to side. Like boats getting pitched about by a turbulent sea, Chris thought.

The six remaining prowlers were buzzing too close to the pyramid for any more fighter jet attacks, without running the risk of a missile accidentally doing the rebel terrorists' work for them. So pilots aboard the other three jets followed the lead of the two converted to helicopter mode. Within nininanas, five aircraft total were hovering where they could fire on the prowlers, should those monstrous beetles head for the ultimate monument to the Fafaman Empire's greatness.

All six remaining prowlers flew right past the bleachers without pausing. Helena held out a faint hope their destination wasn't the pyramid, any part of the pyramid, at all, that they would just keep going. But well she knew this was a hope in vain. It was of a piece with another hope that somehow, the jet incinerated along with a prowler's underbelly could have been somehow due to anything other than a terrorist explosive.

Every last one of those six remaining blinding-light prowlers came to a hovering halt in front of the royal wife and nursery chambers. This, in a clear faceoff with the five Fafaman jets-turned-into-helicopters holding as tight, as close-together of a defensive formation as they safely could. From one of the prowlers hovering especially close and somewhat above one of the Fafaman helicopters, its attendant resistance fighter stabbed at his insect steed's clasping bristly legs. Then he leapt towards the rotary blades atop said copter. He managed to set off the explosive strapped to his own chest before the blades would have sliced him apart. The resultant explosion sent copter and prowler alike crashing sliding down against the pyramid face.

The remaining four copters opened fire on the remaining five prowlers. Three of the immense beetles were shot down, and the resistance fighters they were carrying timed the triggering of their own chest-strapped explosives for just as they were about to hit the side of the pyramid. Glass shards got sent spraying from thick panoramic windows set into the steel walls. This left the remaining two beetles, spotting openings amidst the chaos, to get close to the especially pungent pheromone source that was driving them recklessly mad with desire. Seeking desperately to mate, they slammed themselves against the panoramic windows that looked out from the wives' chambers and royal nursery. Thereby, they also slammed the two remaining resistance fighters against those same windows. Vootoov's last thought before triggering his explosive, which he pushed flat against the window, was, *This life's pain finally ends! And the best hope for recovering my lost family begins!*

The Fafamafalafama had long since unsheathed his sword. He was holding it high before him, ready to impale prowler and attendant resistance fighter both, were they to get anywhere near him. He froze in that aggressive pose, though, as the explosions from the last two suicide bombs got somewhat muffled by blowing inward. It took what seemed to Chris like minutes, what was actually less than thirty seconds, for the Fafaman ruler to realize all the black smoke and bright orange tongues of flame billowing out from the pyramid were coming from wives' chambers and a royal nursery. That is, it took that long for the Fafamafalafama to thaw out of his shell-shock-induced statuesque stance, down from that into a blind rage of unrestrained grief, well beyond anything his people had ever seen from him before. "NOOOOOOOOO!!!!!!!!!" his sustained 'WA' of anguish screamed from Helena's translator. He brought his sword crashing down on the empty review stand chair set before him. He completely, neatly split in half its wooden construction.

All news media cameras were kept focused on the smoke and fire, though with the sound cut off. An explanation went out to the television audience that technical difficulties were getting experienced with the audio.

The Fafamafalafama kept crying out and raging through the slicing, splintering and shattering apart of more review-stand seats and bleachers. His destructive fury brought him steadily closer to where the Earthlings were seated.

"WE BETTER STAND, GET READY TO RUN!!" Ali Magabu shouted in his deepest voice, to be heard above the din of roaring, crackling fire, the Fafaman ruler's fury, random

"Eee!"s of terror, and approaching fire engine sirens.

The other Earthlings took Officer Magabu's advice. They rose up alongside him. This got the Fafamafalafama's attention. Perplexed by how to deal with the extraterrestrials' sudden leave-taking behavior, he temporarily froze his sword halfway into its next swing intended to smash to bits more seating.

"The Varalawa is safe, Supreme Fafamafalafama! She is sleeping in the central chamber, and her guard is under orders not to disturb her with the news yet!" Wafalawa took advantage of the pause in his leader's rampage to shout up to him.

The ruler's lowering shoulders revealed nonverbally to Ali that the Fafamafalafama was at least a little bit relieved, a little bit pulled back from the brink of total insanity, by this news. Then, the Fafamafalafama lifted his eyes to follow where Ali and the rest of the away team were heading. He roared, "GUARDS?!?! Take the 'Ahthlahns' to my central throne room! Bring there the video communications equipment that interfaces with the 'Ahthlahn' spacecraft!" Immediately thereafter, the Fafamafalafama resumed splitting apart and smashing into splinters more chairs and benches. But Ali got the sense, as he and his associates were led away by three armed guards all disciplining themselves not to steal the briefest glance at their ruler's emotional meltdown, that the Fafamafalafama's further destructive onslaught was more perfunctory than heartfelt. He wanted to give the impression, create an illusion, that his raging grief over his personal loss was no less, just because the first wife had been left unaffected.

***

"Esteemed Fafamafalafama,-"

"Do not dare speak to me until I ask you to speak to me!" The Fafamafalafama cut off Captain Entroper with a commanding swirl of his bioluminescently infused cape. His cape's pale-green glow was presently discernible to the Earthlings, what with night-time lighting for the central throne room, despite its being totally glaring stars-fade outside. The Fafamafalafama stormed up before his royal throne and plopped himself down there with such force, the seat cushion squeaked as though, Tanya imagined, he'd just squished some some small, rodent-like creature. "'Cahptahn Ahhntropah,' measure my words most carefully. You must leave, you must take your spacecraft away from where our space station sensors can detect it, which should place you well outside our solar system! You must leave immediately, or I will have to understand your protracted presence as proof you scheme to rescue your former 'cahptahn' and her company from their culpability!"

"Captain Entroper," Ali unclasped his hands to show Louisa watching on the porta-screen he had nothing but stark reality to offer, "I truly believe you must obey without resistance."

"'Ahfahsah Mahgahbah,' that is NOT for you to say!" The Fafaman ruler darted his goggle-freed, nocturnally large, piercing stare Ali's way. His fingers played nervously across the hilt of his sword. "We will hear from your new 'cahptahn' before she receives my reiterated command for her to leave. And believe me, 'Cahptahn Ahntrahpah,' nothing you say is going to modify that command! Nothing! ...Speak!"

Captain Entroper flinched visibly. Yet she still pulled herself together enough to say, with as steady a voice as she could muster, "Esteemed Fafamafalafama, I have NO intent of even thinking about defying your command.

You have to believe me," she added. Entroper wasn't sure whether, through the central throne room darkness, she was discerning the Fafaman ruler's nostrils flaring impatiently. Then she was off to say however much she could get in. For all she knew, this enraged, perhaps murderously enraged, nocturnal being might cut her off as unexpectedly as he had cut off chief counselor Ali Magabu in order to clear the way for her to speak in the first place. "Our monitoring of your public media transmissions has made us aware of the terrible terrorist attack on, um, against the Fafaman Empire. We extend our thoughts and prayers to the victims and their families. And please hear me out on this..."

The Fafamafalafama abruptly grabbed at both arms of his throne to try keeping himself seated, for fear of what he might do to one or more of the Earthlings were he to allow himself to rise to his feet.

"If you are going to accuse Officer Helena Taylor, and maybe to some extent her husband and the other couple who joined them on this away mission...If you are going to complain she is far too trusting, too naïve, about the immediate threat from those monsters who would even dream of doing what they did, let alone actually execute it, I would be the first to agree with you. Personally, I think our fellow beings might have come too much under the sway of those intelligent tree creatures with whom I gather you got to communicate on the previous visit of the Smoke and Mirrors. Believe me, I well understand you must hold some of my officers for interrogation. However, for any of them to have in any way knowingly assisted in the least manner with that horrific attack...! I can assure you, if Officer Taylor had had even the smallest inkling something like this was about to happen,-"

"'Cahhptahhn Ahntropahh,' your allegiance to your crew is nothing less than I would expect! But let us say your crew members here *are* guiltless of having knowingly, as you put it, tried in any way to abet our enemies. If they somehow inadvertently, unknowingly, unwittingly did something on their descent into enemy territory that helped the terrorists with this latest attack, the question becomes what consequences your former 'cahptahn' and company should suffer for their blindness."

*This is bullshit!* Kevin Smith-Park on the navigation bridge of the Smoke and Mirrors thought to himself. He wanted desperately to tear into the Fafamafalafama. But well he knew what he had to say might precipitate a murderous rage from the Fafaman ruler, unable to face the truth, especially under the traumatizing circumstance of a portion of his family getting murdered. So the starship officer settled with thinking to himself, *Sorry to have to tell you, Fafamafullofyourselfama, but your terrorist attacks obviously have been going on long before we were ever even on the scene here! Are you going to blame us for that attack last year, when you rolled out your military might to show off to us? Not that I don't agree that Oodles of Noodles and most of the other Toodlewoodle mind-reading trees are ultra-naïve, with their if-everyone-would-just-pull-down-their-pants-and-shake-their-booty-then-grab-an-oof-club-and-tee-off-and-all-will-be-well routine. There probably is some truth, though, to the notion that when the Fafaman Empire retaliates for a terrorist attack, the incidental killing of innocents, however unintended, provokes a retaliation for the retaliation, on and on, back and forth in an endless eye-for-an-eye cycle. If not for this threat from Tictoctic getting clearer by the minute, we should have followed the prime directive on that old Star Trek series. We should have left you nocturnal-eyed barbarians alone, to keep going at each other until you completely self-destructed! Shit!*

"Esteemed Fafamafalafama," Captain Entroper shook her head again, like she always did to make a point, "I will just emphasize we came here, our people you are holding down there came here, in response to your distress call. We came to help you protect yourselves from what appear to be cruel beasts of another planet, set on making us all part of their food supply. Officer Helena Taylor and company have been on their guard, you can be sure, against inadvertently aiding and abetting terrorists on Fafama, as that would compromise the primary mission. Remember, they have family back on our home world, Earth. They are anxious to protect them above all else."

"Heard and understood. And now you must leave to beyond detectable limits, as fast as your technology can carry you."

"Wait." Entroper held up a forefinger, to further delay the Fafamans cutting off video communications on their end. "About the defense hardware we understand has parachuted down safely to the ground, the robotic tutors for its deployment,-"

"Let me assure you, 'Cahptahn,' a wide security perimeter has been firmly established around those three packages for which we are most grateful, especially under these tragic circumstances so tearing at my heart. However, do not think, 'Cahptahn,' my restraint in speaking to you now means my fury over what has happened is at all diminished, since when I first realized from what region of the pyramid the smoke and fire were pouring out!" With that, the Fafamafalafama rose off his throne, picked it up and hurled it at Entroper's holo-image. Only Wafalawa's quick reaction saved the royal armchair from getting splintered apart against the shale floor.

Helena, Chris, Tanya and Ali traded concerned looks in the dimly, bioluminescently lit simulation of stars-out darkness. *...especially under these tragic circumstances...* They all understood this to mean the distraught Fafaman ruler had given some thought to diverting the gifted military equipment from its intended use as a second line of defense against the extraterrestrial threat. Its new use would be to "deal" with the local terrorist threat. Exactly as Helena had expressly feared. Although, Ali Magabu thought to himself, Captain Entroper would not want to be reminded of that, any more than the Fafamafalafama would have been able to cope rationally with someone suggesting his latest retaliatory strike against the resistance had a causal relationship with the subsequent terrorist attack on the pyramid.

Servants temporarily set aside their breeze-producing tralalafa palm fronds, to relieve Wafalawa of the throne he had rescued from their ruler's royal wrath. They were going to reset it upon the royal dais.

"Rest your mind at ease, 'Cahptahn,'" the Fafamafalafama went on finally. "No number of blinding-light prowlers, nor parachuted ahtpahs, will be able to get anywhere near those precious military equipment packages."

"We are satisfied to hear that, esteemed Fafamafalafama. What I was going to ask, simply a question, is whether you will be wanting our human technical assistance, in case there are any problems with the robotics and the instruction manuals. As a gesture of good faith, of trust your wisdom will lead you to a correct decision regarding our away team, we would be willing to deliver you, unconditionally, a team of one to five specialists before we depart. You decide how many. Our understanding, of course, is that the payloads we have sent down to you are for the express, sole purpose of providing a second line of defense against the Tictoctic menace, should the laser mesh shield get compromised."

"Ahh, 'Cahptahn!'" The Fafamafalafama could not help a smile despite his severe mental turbulence. "This is only your species' latest most generous offer. Unconditional assistance by your specialists with the defense systems deployment here, how very wonderful, indeed! Your civilization's efforts on our behalf, they are not lost on me, whether it is offering us your laser mesh technology, or bringing a water-bearing space rock into orbit around our very special planet, or answering our distress call in the first place. Although, something must be pointed out, however much your pride as a species would keep you from admitting it. There are certain, should we say, deficiencies in your technology when put side-by-side against ours. No time to discuss that now."

*Of course not,* Ali thought to himself. *It is a marvel, truly, how you so obliviously project onto our technology your insecurities you feel about how your own technology compares.*

"You must understand, 'Cahptahn,' the way your technical assistance offer can be construed. It can appear to be a last, pathetic effort to put a plan in motion that might save your crew members down here from my big, bad, evil wrath!" He boomed those final words with mocking anger. "Or worse, if your sympathies as a poorly informed outside observer lie in actuality with the terrorist barbarians!"

*Most interesting how he would suggest a third party might find themselves siding with the resistance to his empire,* Ali shook his head in continuing, fascinated wonder.

"Well..." Captain Entroper shrugged her shoulders to suggest a nonchalant resignation to the inevitable she wasn't feeling. She smacked her lips discernibly loudly, in an impossible effort to re-moisten her panic-dried mouth before she said, "I guess there is nothing else we can do to convince you, um..." She was going to say something about how he was wasting time, energy and irretrievable good will, the way he was treating the away team. Fearful, though, the wrong words could get one or more of the hostages decapitated, she went with, "If only I could convince you, beyond any doubt, that we are here with only the best of intentions! Believe me, we are as appalled and angered as we could be over what those monsters have done! I guess there is nothing else we can do for now to more effectively convey this fact."

"Of course you must say that, 'Cahptahn,' as an urgent truth, or to perpetuate a lie. Too much has wriggled out of my control." The Fafamafalafama took both hands off the hilt of his sword to hold his forehead in them, suggestive he might be experiencing a pounding headache. "I need time to carefully sort through everything, with you and your spacecraft well far away."

"Supreme Fafamafalafama," Wafalawa scurried out of the darker shadows to come between the ruler and Louisa Entroper's holo-image, "Zasafaza says he is reporting to you on your order!"

"Have him enter." Saying this, the Fafamafalafama nodded towards Captain Entroper.

Entroper had a straw in her mouth. She was trying to rehydrate before she would have gone into a coughing spell.

"The Fafamafalafama!" Wafalawa made this introduction with his usual low-swept hand. Zasafaza stepped forward, where he curled into a bow. Like so many others who had entered into the ruler's presence before, he was trying to mimic a furling-up Fafaman fern tree.

The Fafamafalafama stretched his arms wide, also stretching out his cape.

Zasafaza feigned to have been said fern tree unfurled by the cape's embedded pale-green bioluminescence. "Pama, Supreme Fafamafalafama," this technical adviser fa-la-laed.

"You bring me satisfactory news, Zasafaza?"

"Only the undoing of the act of barbarity against the central pyramid would be satisfactory."

"Hmmph," hmmphed the Fafaman ruler approvingly over Zasafaza's successful completion of the ritual phrasing for which the circumstances called.

Zasafaza's two-foot-long goatee was designed by his weaving together, under his chin, never-trimmed whiskers from opposite sides of his face. It curled and uncurled with relief as he continued, "Still, I do bring you the news you so wisely expected. We have been able to re-encode the laser mesh entry circuit so that even 'Ahth' vessels will be unable to safely encroach on our air space, unless we share the new code with them. Also, we have re-encoded the ice rock guidance system."

"As I expected. You see, 'Cahhptahhn Ahhntropahhh,' I was not in any special hurry to conclude our conversation, to end your vain efforts at persuasion. That was, until I could confirm, and have you know, this laser mesh of which you are so boastful, we have now made it our own. One other thing: Should your defense payloads give the slightest indication they have been rigged to not work for us without your approving input, we will have them bombed into obliteration! That is all!"

"But esteemed-"

"I expect our sensors to detect you departing Fafaman orbit within nininanas!" On that note, the Fafamafalafama personally strode over to the holo-projector cube to turn it off.

"Permission to speak, esteemed Fafamafalafama."

"Permission to speak?" The Fafaman ruler repeated the fa-la-laed translation of those words. "Ahh," he tilted back his head, "finally, former 'Cahptahn Taylah,' after all this time. Finally, I learn how superiors must be addressed in your society. Until your demotion, you were not needing to bother over such a detail, were you? Yes, you have my permission to speak," he nodded. "Briefly."

"'Pama.' I only wanted to say, Captain Entroper was probably about to warn you against summarily destroying the entire defense package, for whatever reason, and especially all in the same place. Such destruction would most likely compromise the fissile material containment chambers, thus preventing actual nuclear missile detonation. However, the resultant release of radioactive gases into the Fafaman atmosphere would be so uncontrollably, uncontainably vast as to seriously harm Fafaman ecosystems. And those gases would take several orbits of your sun to finally even begin to settle out of the air."

The Fafamafalafama hesitated a long time before he finally said, "We are aware, 'Offasah Taylah.' But, I have to worry over injured sons and daughters who are about to learn their mothers have been slaughtered. And even worse, I will have to face injured mothers, my wives, who are about to learn, if they haven't learned already, that the products of their joining with me have been murdered! Do you really think, any of you," he swept his glance around to all four Earthlings with a swirl of his cape, "do any of you really think I can be bothered with sparing your new spacecraft 'cahptahn' from worrying so insultingly we might not be any smarter than a flounder mouse?"

When Helena, Chris, Tanya and Ali stole looks to one another, they every one of them knew they were having the same thoughts. They couldn't be sure the Fafamafalafama wasn't bluffing his way out of an admission he was *not* aware of possible environmental consequences until Helena mentioned them.

"Sorry, Most Supreme One, a million sorries." Nanofafo butted open the chamber doors as custom required for such a situation, as opposed to the guards either side swinging them open for him. Down on all fours, he scurried in with the rapidity, Chris marveled, of a rat or some other such rodent seeking shelter. "Someone must reactivate your holo-screen for you, before this sentence is complete!"

Such haste was achieved, thanks to the quick reflexes of the servant to whom the fist-sized cube had been handed over.

"What you see comes from a nanocamera the missing 'Ahthlahn' shed inside the caverns of the terrorists," Nanofafo explained. An approving nod from the Fafamafalafama, including a forefinger-to-mouth gesture for the adviser to say no more, induced Nanofafo's quick rise back up onto his two feet.

The grainy, three-dimensional video revealed three pairs of sandaled feet. Their locations relative to each other suggested their owners were standing in close association.

"Chief Vituf," the fa-la-laed dialect successfully translated for the Earthlings, "as this powerful accomplishment of ultimate justice has succeeded under your wise leadership, it is you who will be best inspired to give the 'mushstrah.'"

'Mushstrah' came through untranslated, for the translator algorithm was unable to locate an acceptable comparable. However, from the context, Helena suspected it meant a toast, of the drinking kind.

"As you wish," someone fa-la-laed, presumably Chief Vituf. Ali and Helena both sensed a certain world-weariness; Vituf could have added, *I don't really want to, but if you insist…* "We with our toes smash these young tapastrahs into nourishment for bigger, stronger tapastrahs, even as our foes are smashed, that from the soil of their carcasses may rise a better, more plentiful world for our people, where the waters run in abundance for the daily cleansing of our spirits and quenching of our thirsts," went Chief Vituf's customary variation on the ritual mushstrah.

"'Papastrafa,'" the other two intoned. Another untranslated word, which Ali took to be comparable to "Amen" or "Shalom" or "Salam 'Aleykum."

Tapastrah caps the size of pancakes were seen dropping down beside the resistance leaders' feet. The next thing the observers on the holo-screen knew, the feet were withdrawn from their sandals, and those caps ceremonially squished between toes.

Unfortunately for the purposes of continuing to eavesdrop, one foot with tapastrah cap substance stuck between its toes came down directly atop the nanocam, and there was darkness, plus a final transmitted sound, "Ouch!," before said cam went completely dead.

"So, former 'Cahptahn,'-"

Helena noticed how often the Fafamafalafama liked to keep saying "former 'cahptahn'" instead of "'Offasah,'" even as she also realized nobody was transmitting to her from the Smoke and Mirrors through her earpiece. Which she considered a wise move, given who knew how irrational the Fafaman ruler was liable to become, if his people were able to somehow break through the noise-scrambling technology to detect such stealthy communication.

"-please if you can explain for me how that 'mushstrah' shows appreciation for our deliverance of the water-bearing rock into Fafaman orbit."

"I can't, supreme Fafamafalafama." The "supreme" part caused as much of an eyebrow rise from the Fafaman ruler as it did from Helena's fellow travelers. "It is beyond disgusting. There are no words for how absolutely reprehensible we find any celebration of bringing hate and destruction to others." Helena left out her sensing Chief Vituf wanted to be anywhere else but where he was, saying that 'mushstrah.' She also left out the first answer that had occurred to her to give: *It is almost as unusual as the way you show your appreciation to us for all we have tried to do for you.*

# Chapter 21

"There is a glow on the western horizon that should not be there," fa-la-laed Yulala, otherwise known as the Varafafafa, the twenty-third wife. She preceded Guy Hanson in reaching the short summit of a craggy sedimentary rock outcropping. Guy and Yulala noticed this geological feature shortly after the passing of the sunset storm line. Stratified, alternating layers of coarse-grain and fine-grain sandstone presented at a dramatic tilt. Guy would have commented to a fellow Earthling that this formation had the feel of a ship's prow frozen in time, in a lurch forward and upward out of a stormy sea, a stormy sea itself also somehow frozen still.

"You are sure that glow is not from sun rays getting refracted over the horizon by the storm line?" Guy asked, after he joined Yulala to get his first look at a peculiar orange-ish light flaring out of the wavy silhouette of Fafaman desert dunes in the far distance. It came from roughly the same direction as the central pyramid. *God help us all if that is some nuclear explosion!* the Marine Corp sergeant couldn't help thinking, though his intuition told him he was favoring needless concern.

"Light refraction? If so, this is the first time I ever notice such a phenomenon. But I am sorry, 'Sahjahnt Hahnsahn.' My exhaustion is too much; it has finally caught up with me. A drink please from your 'coolah,' then I must simply lie down. We are safe here for half of stars-out, at least."

Hanson noticed Yulala lift her nostrils high when he joined her at the shallow-sloped, pebbly summit. She was able to give him such confident assurance, he suspected, because her bloodhound-quality "shnazola" did not detect the faintest hint of ahtpah webbing carrying on the last lingering breezes from the storm line, nor other potential threats of which he was just as happy to be blissfully unaware. "I am feeling what you are feeling, Yula-uhhh, esteemed Varafafafa, believe me. I am right there with you."

"'Yulala' is acceptable," her woozily murmured fa-la-las translated as she handed off the thermos bottle to him for his own swig. Free of that minor encumbrance, she lay back on a patch of ground she'd wiped free of pebbles with a small brush. She draped her left forearm across her forehead in a manner suggestive she might be suffering from a headache.

Sergeant Hanson desired to nestle Yulala in his lap, and draw away sweat-soaked wayward strands of her long, raven-black hair, to tenderly tap his fingertips across her forehead. He had learned this trick some time back. Occasionally it worked, if the headache wasn't too throbbing. Fearful how the twenty-third wife of the Fafamafalafama might react, though, Sergeant Hanson settled with a brief drink from his bottle before giving in to his own, thorough exhaustion. He didn't even bother clearing away any pebbles from where he would be lying down. He even convinced himself of therapeutic massage qualities from the various sharp and rounded small stones pressing against him through his uniform.

As Guy Hanson pondered the plenitude of stars in the Fafaman night sky, his thoughts wandered back over what he and Yulala had experienced earlier that day. He marveled that they were both still alive, let alone perfectly safe and uninjured. Such amazement was not enough to keep him from a steady drift towards sleep, however.

The adventure that turned death-defying had begun about an hour after Guy and who was officially known as the Varafafafa sat inside the cavern network for lunch.

They made quick work of muffin-shaped tapastrah tops, plus a can of string bean rations tucked away in Guy's pants leg compartment as part of his force-of-habit-no-matter-the-circumstances survival gear regimen. And so, their search for an exit had been gotten well underway.

"Good news and bad news," Yulala had fa-la-laed when they rounded a corner and found it lit up well beyond the natural bioluminescence, so much so that Guy removed his night-vision goggles. "Good news, we are approaching an exit to the outside. Bad news, it is also a trap-door ahtpah den. Follow me carefully, mimic as precisely as you can my every move, and we should get out safely. It is doubtful other exits, if there are other exits and they are reachable, will prove any safer. Likely, they are considerably more dangerous. You are accepting?" She had turned her nocturnally large eyes back towards Guy, and she had alighted her right hand to his left. That hand could have been a most beautifully colorfully winged butterfly alighting there, for how Guy was feeling.

"I am accepting," Guy Hanson had nodded. He had wanted to add, *How could I say no to anything you say with those big, entrancingly dark windows into your soul?*

On an issue entirely separate from his growing infatuation, Sergeant Hanson had rued how he'd been forbidden to carry along even the smallest weapon to the meeting with the resistance leadership. He was enough of a trained marksman, he was confident he could have fired shots at the ahtpah's many eyes that would have resulted in several bullets finding their way into its nervous system.

Anyhow, Guy had done as he was told. He had made an awkward step here, ducked his head low there, in exact accordance to Yulala's moves. Sometimes he had noticed a telltale glint from the web strand she was avoiding touching. More often, though, he had not been able to make out what she was seeing, even when in frustration he had re-donned his night-vision goggles. What he had known without asking was that all it would have taken would have been the least jiggle of the shortest web strand. The monster spider would have come charging out, a flurry of hairy legs, from down whatever crevice it had squeezed into for awaiting accomplishment of an ambush. Web strands would have shot anew from its abdomen. Its pincer-lined mouth would have dripped with paralyzing venom. *Better not dwell on that if I'm to keep my cool!*

What had nearly lost Hanson his cool was what he had gotten to see, when both humanoids had reached the stage in their ascent where he could discern sunlight filtering through the dried-out tralalafa leaf that covered over the ahtpah burrow. To Guy and Yulala's side, cramped between two pillar-like stalagmites, was the ahtpah of concern. Its twenty eyes had appeared to glow in the faint light, not more than a yard from where they needed to pass.

"They DO nap with their eyes open," Yulala had whispered by way of assurance,

but then, "Wait." Yulala had grabbed Guy firmly on the wrist to halt his forward movement, just short of the tralalafa frond. "This is the most hazardous part. Pushing against the dessicated tralalafa remnant will awaken the 'ahtpah.' Soon as it is disturbed, we must move fast as we can. You go first." Yulala had carefully crawled aside, making sure not to send the least telltale pebble tumbling back down the jagged incline.

"No," Guy shook his head. "Uhhh, you are already ahead of me, so it does not make sense."

"It makes no sense to argue," was how Yulala's grumble-whispered fa-la-las had translated as she resumed her ascent. She had paused close enough to the bed-comforter-sized tralalafa frond for her to feel her abundant waves of thick, raven-black hair meeting with some resistance. There, she had waited for Hanson to climb closer to her. Once his face had reached her navel level, where he could have encircled her legs with his arms, she had steeled herself with one more deep inhale. Next thing Guy had known, she had been scrambling out of the burrow, trying not to lift up the enormous tralalafa frond any higher than necessary. Guy had followed suit, getting dirt kicked back in his face and up his nostrils by Yulala's moccasins. He had strained not to cough or otherwise give in to reflexive responses to rid his system of the irritating foreign matter. But as he had done so, he had heard a commotion of agitated dirt and rock approaching from behind. That commotion had been getting closer and closer at an alarming speed. Guy had nearly cleared the huge hole in the ground, when he had felt two things grabbing on tight to his right boot. But Yulala had leapt atop the dried-out tralalafa frond, then leapt back off again. It had been as though, Sergeant Hanson thought, she were jumping on and off a trampoline. This had sufficed to make whatever-it-was loosen its grip on Hanson's boot, long enough for him to complete his exit from the trap-door ahtpah burrow, just before something sharp had felt like it was about to pierce through to his foot.

Guy and Yulala had sprinted off, fast as they could. Neither had paused to glance back until they were up a shallow, sandy incline some hundreds of yards away. When finally, they had relented for a look where they had been, they were just in time to notice webbing getting retracted under the trap door. This had been as though, Hanson had thought, the giant spider were a fisherman retrieving his net, after having cast it out. What had also occurred to the Marine Corps Sergeant had concerned the sharpness he sensed penetrating his boot's synthetic leather, just before the Varafafafa's daring leap startled the ahtpah. Were that sharpness to have gotten through to his flesh, Guy had realized he most likely would have gotten injected with paralyzing venom. "You saved my life," he had subsequently been moved to say to Yulala.

She had maintained her profile. Her tousled, soiled hair had clung in wet strands to her mud-and-clay-encrusted cheeks. "Better that I DID go first. You might not have known what to do in my situation. Although, there is something else I am guessing." Yulala's fa-la-las had abruptly softened as she just-as-abruptly had turned to face Guy. Her eyes had been squinted to slits by the, for her, painfully bright sunlight. "There are probably circumstances on your planet where it would be better if YOU went first, 'Sahjahnt Hahnsahn.'"

"Well, most esteemed Varafafafa," Guy had shaken his head with a hearty laugh, "I am not rightly sure there are any circumstances on my planet to quite compare to the danger from these circumstances! Maybe getting charged by an enraged rhinoceros. In that case, however, I would have no better idea than you what to do, except run our tails off, excuse me, run as fast as we can!"

Yulala had bowed her head to don her anti-glare goggles. But if Sergeant Hanson didn't know better, he'd have sworn this action had also conveniently served to conceal her mirth over the fa-la-laed translation of "run our tails off."

"The biggest spider we have," he'd gone on, "you

could still smash it with a rock about this size." He had picked up a chunk of red clay sandstone to illustrate.

By that time, the twenty-third wife had appeared back to all seriousness. How she had lifted her nose high, Guy again would have likened to how a bloodhound lifted its nose, searching for a scent. "We need to find where we will ride out the sunset storm line," she had fa-la-laed. As if by way of exclamation point, the Varafafafa's hair had gotten scattered by a gust of breeze. "Fortunately, we have come out near a drift plant collection area." Yulala had pointed only yards off to where the land sloped into a shallow, saucer-shaped basin amply spotted with greenery.

Guy had found himself reminded of a trip to Spain, when he came hiking across a field of olive trees that grew wild instead of in their usual farm-regimented rows.

On the eastern horizon, the sky's peculiar yellow tint had inspired a far more anxiety-producing recollection, however. The Marine Corps sergeant had associated it with a serious thunderstorm threatening sooner rather than later. That sickly yellow would soon be fading to ominous bluish-gray.

"Yulala, I must defer to your judgment. Please lead us forward."

By then, the couple had already been stepping in amidst plants of varying sizes. Most of them had been with frond-y, open-mouth leaves, like so many pairs of mattress-sized butterfly wings. They were plenty big enough for Guy or even Guy plus Yulala to lie down upon. Some of them had been raised a foot or two off the ground by a stubby trunk rooted in deep. Others of the same ilk hadn't been rooted the least, shallowest bit. Their trunks had lain on their side on the loamy soil, where they had tapered into fully exposed, tightly curled root balls.

Their own, frond-y mouth-leaves had grown atop them, the same as atop the deeply rooted trunks. One leaf of these particular plants had lain flat against said loamy soil, with the other leaf set lifted at roughly forty-five degrees.

Sergeant Hanson had tried not to shudder visibly as he had commented, "Esteemed Varafafafa, these remind me of a plant we have named the Venus Flytrap, only a thousand times larger. So which ones of these are tralalafas, where we can find safe shelter from the storm line?"

"That is even more difficult to establish, 'Hahnsahn,' than determining which tapastrahs are safe to eat. The zahafaza, for example, appears similar to the tralalafa, but it does not stop at cleansing your intestinal tract while you rest. It tries, and usually succeeds, in sucking out the intestinal tract itself, as well as the stomach, the kidneys, and any other organs it can vacuum before the storm line goes through. Then there is the kagarala. Thousands of zla-zlas lie dormant within their tiny pores, until storm line turbulence activates them. At which time they come streaming out of those pores. They engulf whichever creature has taken refuge there. In a matter of thirty nininanas, their high-acid nibbles dissolve the flesh off the bones, or out of an insect's exoskeleton, until all that is left is a creamy mush for the zla-zlas and their host to share."

"I've heard enough." Hanson had held a protesting hand high. "Think I'll trust you to make the calls on where we should hide."

HONNNK!!!

Guy Hanson's eyes had darted side to side as this sudden unanticipated noise had echoed off a distant cliff wall. "What the fried fritter was THAT?!?!"

Yulala's eyes were cloaked in mystery by her anti-glare goggles. But the way she had twisted her head every direction, the sergeant had been able to sense this was not good, not good at all. "The thansama snawyama," she had fa-la-laed finally. "One of the few remaining non-burrowing land mammals of any size, aside from us humans, since the storm line initiated some fifty million solar orbits ago. We need to stand still and hope it is passing far enough distant from us not to notice us. Whatever you do, do not make direct eye contact with it."

No sooner had Yulala warned Guy than he had gotten the impression something was ducking down behind a plant not more than fifty yards away. That plant's trunk had even shivered.

"There," Yulala had pointed to exactly where Guy's attention was drawn.

That's when Sergeant Hanson had realized the creature was far from successful in its stealthy action. Its body had still extended out from behind the enormous, open-mouthed plant where it ducked down. Said body had extended all the way to behind a second such plant further over. What showed of the creature's body in between those two carnivorous flora had reminded Hanson of a dachshund's hot-dog belly, hanging low to the ground. Its reddish-brown fur had had an oily sheen to it, similar to a dachshund's smooth coat.

And it hadn't been finished moving yet.

The hot-dog body had made a waddly motion to the left. This had brought the creature's rear end into view, once more in between the two tralalafa-like plants. Amazingly, where Sergeant Hanson had been concerned, that rear end had born a striking resemblance to the rear end of a dachshund, complete with a rapidly wagging short tail, suggestive of a metronome out of control. The tail wag was so intense, in fact, that again, exactly as with a dachshund, the entire rear end had been sent wagging. Already, the thansama snawyama's long, smooth, yellowish, brown-streaked whatever-it-was had been poking around the other side of the plant to where it had sought to move most stealthily. That whatever-it-was had flared out like the horn end of a cornet. And yet, its poking around had reminded Guy more of a probing elephant trunk. "What *is* that?" he had whispered.

"Truncated nostrils as well as a food vacuum." Yulala had given Guy only her profile, the same as he had given her only his profile when he had asked; both had been with their eyes riveted on the creature. "It performs several functions. The thansama snawyama wraps that trunk around its target's body or neck, and constricts until said target is choked dead. Then, it places the flared out orifice over the target's mouth and nose. It uses mucous secretions to form an airtight seal so it can vacuum out both stomach and sinus contents. In the case of a crushed insect's exoskeleton, the vacuum function of its ultra-flared nostrils is used to pull off the head, and then it sucks out a meal from its torso and skull alike."

Guy had noticed, on the ground just a few feet away from them, the hollow exoskeleton of what looked to have been a beetle the size of an English shepherd dog. Its legs had been twisted skywards, perfectly still. Its pulled-off, drained-out head, lying a few yards away, had somehow reminded the Marine Corp Sergeant of a knight's discarded helmet.

"If an ahtpah or other creature large enough to threaten approaches, it sucks fecal matter out of its own anus and sprays them," Yulala had gone on about the thansama snawyama. "The smell is so bad, if you happen to be anywhere near when it does this, you will need to have all your clothes burned, for you won't be able to get rid of the odor. And one other significant function of its nostrils: rooting itself to cope with the sunset storm line. It seeks an already closed tralalafa, zahafaza, or other, no importance which. Then it waits until the storm line's fury is almost upon it. What happens next is with the flared-out end of its nostrils. That flared-out end seals closed, forming the equivalent of a crowbar. The creature uses this to pry open the selected plant. Then it proceeds to insert most of its trunk. Its body remains outside, coiling up like a beach 'slatha' for handling as much of a beating as any tralalafa, from getting tossed about by the storm line winds. But before descending into a semi-conscious stasis for this daily event, the thansama snawyama's nostrils flare back out, inside the chosen refuge plant. They seek either to compete with the plant's anal evacuator for a passenger's intestinal contents, or to latch onto the evacuator itself to drain the plant of any excrement it hasn't already processed."

*Okay, far from your typical dachshund, but how exactly does that trunk attach to its face? What kind of face does it have- Ahhh; there we are. Wo!*

The head of the thansama snawyama Guy would have compared to that of a pudgy pig, albeit with a trumpet-shaped proboscis. Its ears had been short and fleshy pink. Especially striking had been the triangular shape for the eye sockets, like the eyes on a jack-o-lantern. They had crinkled shut frequently to form two, three-pointed stars. Guy had found those eyes so fascinating, his gaze had remained fixated on them as they had re-opened from a sand-cleansing blink...

...which was when human and beast had made eye contact.

"Oh, no! Esteemed-"

"No time for 'esteemed'! Here I told you to avoid eye contact, and then what-"

HONNNNK!!!! The thansama snawyama's trunk had stiffened into such a shape as to strike Guy Hanson as every bit the monstrously long trumpet it had sounded like. The Marine's last thought before joining Yulala to flee had been of how much he was reminded, again, of a wee little dachshund, a baby dachshund he once needed to watch for a sick friend. It was sniffing here and there on a grassy lawn, wandering ever further from him, when it lifted its head and realized how far from him it was strayed. With a happy wiggy-wag of its entire rear end, it went romping back towards him at great speed, until that rear end caught up to its front end to send it tumbling over on its side.

In full flight right behind Yulala, Guy Hanson had swerved around plant after plant aside from the small ones, which he had trampled over. His panic had been no less, for not having had any idea how the thansama snayama dealt with the awkwardness of lugging around a nasal trunk so disproportionately large compared to the rest of itself.

Immediately upon conclusion of the thansama snawyama's trumpeted declaration of prey to be pursued, autonomic reflexes had flattened out and rolled up its trunk, spiraled tight against its face.

What Guy and Yulala had also missed seeing, in their striving to keep ahead of the beast, was that just like the baby dachshund Guy recalled, its rear legs had caught up with its stubbier forelegs. This had sent it spilling onto its side, trampling over a tralalafa in its path. Unlike anything of which a baby dachshund would have been capable, however, the thansama snawyama had converted this potential setback into a pursuit-enhancing advantage. Immediately upon spilling over onto its side, the creature had rolled up its entire self into an enormous ball, and it had continued faster that way than were it still gallop-waddling. When it seamlessly unwound back up onto its four stubby legs, it had gained so much ground on Yulala and Guy, they could hear its panting tongue. Said tongue had been hanging out to help it keep cool, the same as the tongue of a running dachshund a tiny portion of its size.

"We are not going to be able to stay ahead of it for much longer!" Yulala had shouted her fa-la-las, to carry back behind her to Guy's translator. "And the sunset storm line is impending!"

As though to put special emphasis on Yulala's warning about the harsh weather soon to be upon them, a low-lying cloud, racing ahead of the main squall line, had cast everything in temporary shade as it had crossed in front of the sun. There had been a gusty breeze stronger than the last, and Guy had thought he heard a rumble of distant thunder.

"So this is the plan, unless you have better!: When I spot a safe tralalafa, I will point to it and you will leap onto it!"

"Leap onto it?!?"

"It should close about you quickly enough to confuse the thansama snawyama! Huff! Huff! And by the time that beast has settled on chasing only me, I should already have gotten tucked away inside my own tralalafa! Huff! Huff!"

"Okay! Huff! Huff! Any time now!"

"But one last thing! If you feel the inside getting lumpy!, – Huff! Huff! – that means I accidentally directed you into a zahafaza!"

"Then what?!?"

"Then don't pull down your pants for an intestinal evacuation! And you must fend off the zahafaza – Huff! Huff! – from trying to sneak its vacuum tube down your-There! NOW!!"

Guy had understood clearly which plant Yulala, the Varafafafa, was indicating, and he had gone from his sprint into a running leap atop it. The landing had felt surprisingly cushion-y for how fleshy firm the plant had appeared. A rapid closing had gotten triggered of the butterflied fronds, most snuggly around Guy's body. *This must be,* he had thought with a chill down his spine despite getting all sweaty from running in the dry heat, *what a fly experiences at first when it lands on a Venus flytrap!*

*NO!* Something awful had dawned on Yulala, just as she was about to leap onto her own tralalafa, and also just as Guy was experiencing the inside surfaces of his supposed refuge from the storm line getting all bumpy. *The unevenness of the surface; I DID accidentally send him into a zahafaza! He won't know how to manage, despite what I told him!*

The twenty-third wife of the Fafamafalafama had already started to reverse course, headed back towards the pursuing thansama snawyama.

Which creature, not expecting its prey to come running directly at it, had spilled over on its side again. By the time it had recovered, and unwound its trunk all the better to wrap around Yulala, she had leapt atop the zahafaza to where she had mistakenly guided the Earthling. Also, she had grabbed at the flared-out end of the thansama snawyama's trunk, despite how it had tried to dodge that circumstance. It had writhed about like a cobra looking to strike, at least so Guy might have thought had he been able to get a good look.

Yulala's successful seizure of the trumpet-shaped trunk of the thansama snawyama had coincided with a louder, booming rumble of thunder from the approaching storm line. That rumble had continued rolling and echoing down the valley. Also, Yulala had been able to feel beneath her boots the roiling convolutions of the topside of the zahafaza. Sergeant Hanson within had been struggling frantically to keep the plant's suction tubes from probing under his clothes to latch onto his belly button or some other bodily orifice. Yulala knew he didn't have much time left. And so, she had put every last ounce of her strength and exertion into guiding the flared-out snout end of the infuriated thansama snawyama towards the lip of the carnivorous plant. Indeed, she had found herself riding that snout like a bucking bronco, while she had tried to dig her fingernails into the cactus-y flesh of the zahafaza. Said snout had made an extreme motion like someone cracking a whip. This motion had almost succeeded in throwing off the twenty-third wife, to leave the creature free to suck feces out of its own intestines for its signature putrid expression of rage. But the Varafafafa had managed to hang on. With a well-placed kick into the rib cage of the creature, she had even caused its trunk to go limp for just long enough for her to succeed at bringing the trunk's snout in contact with the zahafaza's giant leafy fronds, which were closed upon one another like some monster Venus flytrap. As the first hail stones had begun to pelt Yulala, one stinging her forehead, autonomic reflexes had taken over for the thansama snawyama; sensing the carnivorous plant's close proximity, its flared-out snout had suddenly sealed up into a thin, sharp wedge. And then the thansama snawyama had used that wedge to effortlessly quickly pry apart the shut zahafaza fronds. Said wedge went exploring for the plant's suction tubes, which in turn had come close to overwhelming Sergeant Hanson's ability to stave them off from fatally latching onto both his navel and his anal cavity.

Yulala had lost no time plunging her right arm in deep, beside the thansama snawyama's crowbar-imitating snout. This, while a close flash of lightning had gotten immediately succeeded by a deafening crash of thunder, and the winds had picked up dramatically. As the zahafaza's roots had retracted from the soil into a root ball for the coming storm-line tumble, Yulala had latched onto Guy's left ankle and began pulling him out. This maneuver had gone easier than she expected, resulting in the Fafaman and the Earthling both rolling backwards on the ground once he was free.

Guy and Yulala had subsequently struggled mightily against the mounting wind to regain their footing. During which, tralalafas, zahafazas and all other manner and size of plants, insects, arthropods and a rare mammal had been getting pushed rolling past them by the front-edge wind gusts from the storm line.

"THAT OBLONG 'MAHLAMA' TUMBLING END OVER END TOWARDS US!! GRAB ON, AND CLAW DEEP!!" That had been all the fa-la-las Yulala could shout above the thunderous, rainy, rolling stampede din, before the indicated silverish-green plant had tumbled up to them. Yulala holding Guy's right hand had helped assure he latched onto the mahlama the same time she did. Their combined weight had temporarily made the mahlama stop tumbling, thus giving Yulala and Guy the opportunity to dig their fingers and boots securely into its fleshiness. Those diggings had caused it to sprout two-foot-long protuberances all over its surface, anywhere not covered by the two clinging bodies.

"Do not worry! I am certain about this one! The only side-effect you will experience is your fingers shriveled and bleeding a little AFTERWARDS!!" Yulala had had to scream that last word at the top of her lungs. Just before, the full fury of the sunset storm line had struck. This had sent the mahlama on its tumbling bouncing way again, to join the other plants and animals in getting chaotically blown across the Fafaman landscape. The mahlama's protuberances had amply protected its passengers from getting scraped and bruised by the ride.

As the worst of the sunset storm line had passed overhead, one by one the bundles of life had rolled, bounced and tumbled to a stop, most of them up the western slope of the saucer-shaped valley. Where Yulala and Guy had come to rest had been not one hundred yards from the rock outcropping they were to ascend.

"Remember, 'Sahjahnt Hahnsahn,' stars-out is when the most dangerous creatures that stalk in the glare of day tend to rest. So it is a good time for us to rest, also. But on an elevation such as that," she had pointed at the outcropping, "provided it is not booby-trapped by ahtpah web."

Despite his trauma from what he'd just experienced, Guy had found himself smiling at how the translation algorithm latched on to "booby-trapped" for something Yulala fa-la-laed.

"'Sahjahnt Hahhnsahhn'! 'Sahjahhnt Hahhnsahhn'!" Yulala was presently startling Guy out of his exhausted, dozing-off reflection on what they'd endured hours earlier. She shook his left shoulder as she fa-la-laed. "What IS that?!?"

The 'sahjahnt' quickly got to his feet, followed by

Yulala. He craned his head back to get a good look at the spectacle crossing the night sky. There was an enormous spherical object, glowing bluish-white and as fuzzy around the edges as a full moon on Earth seen through a fog. It appeared much larger than the largest he'd ever seen Earth's moon from down on Earth, even when magnified by an atmospheric inversion layer. And extending well back behind it was a wispy tail of that same, bluish-white character, only dotted with sparkles as though, Guy fancied, they were thousands of diamond sequins. *What the…?* In a sudden panic, his heart did flip-flops. He feared this might be a comet plunging towards Fafama for an apocalyptic end to Yulala's life, his life, and the lives of everything else on the planet…

…only, he just as suddenly remembered, while Yulala held on to his left shoulder by both hands for dear life, *Good God, they did it! They succeeded!*

"It's okay." Guy put a comforting arm around the Varafafafa's waist, to give her an encouraging hug. "It's not going to crash. Um, here, let me explain." Realizing he had inadvertently made such close contact with the twenty-third wife, he gently pressed her away, including her hands that had been latched onto his shoulder.

"Fwa!" Yulala gasped, bringing her fingertips to her mouth. "You mean, that is the ice rock your starship 'cahptahn' was telling the resistance leaders your people were going to position in orbit around our planet, to bring more water into our atmosphere?"

"There." Guy pointed at it. Yulala stood before him, her mess of hair nearly in his face so she could more directly follow his forefinger. On the underside of the comet, two orange-ish flares flashed on and off. "Those are rockets drilled into the comet. They are fired up periodically to tweak its orbit. As ice and rock is gradually shed, their nose cones will drill deeper into it, until a long time from now, nothing will be left up there. Except, of course, for those rockets. Once their work is done, the plan is for them to get shot off harmlessly into space."

"You mean, on each orbit of Fafama, the ice rock will grow smaller?"

"Very gradually, yes. And unless I miss my guess," by this time the comet was moving directly overhead, "shortly past the end of its tail, over there to the west, we will see what on Earth we call 'shooting stars.' Its shed rock will be burning up harmlessly as meteorites in the atmosphere." As Guy spoke, he was struck by how silently the orbiting comet made its way, given how enormous its presence. Still, he had to discipline himself to stop thinking about wrapping his arms around Yulala, standing so close before him. And nuzzling into her tousled waves of raven-black hair.

"So, you have such an ice rock in orbit around your own planet?"

"No; our shooting stars come directly from deep space." *She keeps standing so close in front of me. Does she wish to sink back into my arms, but her sense of propriety is stopping her? Or she is as fearful how I'd react as I am fearful how she would react if I made my move?* "Uh, but we do have a moon that orbits our planet. However, it's much larger than this comet, and it's orbiting at a far greater distance, so that it appears smaller than this comet when it's visible in our night, uh, during our stars-out. Our moon looks white, with a sharply defined edge. And it crosses our sky much more slowly than this thing is haulin'-errrr, orbiting."

Yulala nodded, "I have read that our astronomers have identified two moons orbiting the next planet out from ours, from our sun."

Guy Hanson nodded. "What I really like is seeing the

full moon at the-"

"Full moon?"

"Oh, that's right. Well, to try to explain, our moon – this comet too for that matter. This comet gets lit up, illuminated, by your sun. This happens, even when your sun is sunk below that horizon, from where you can't see any of its light directly, down here on the surface. Well, as is also the case for this comet, only half our moon can be lit up by our sun at any one time. But that half is not always the half that is facing us when we look up at it. More often, only a quarter or a half of what is facing us is the part reflecting the sunlight. So we speak of quarter moons, half moons, and crescent moons. When the half of the moon facing us is entirely the half of the moon reflecting sunlight, that is our full moon. Did that make any sense?"

"Perfect sense, 'Hahhnsahhn.'"

"Well, that is good, because I'm not sure I even understood what I just said."

"Ee-ee-eee!" Yulala hopped up and down with her amusement. She reminded Hanson of an agitated monkey at the zoo. Yet in her he found this behavior all the more endearing.

"Umm, if you want to call me by my first name... My last name denotes my family, Hanson. My personal name is Guy," the sergeant ventured to explain.

"A name for your family and a name for you. Interesting," Yulala nodded.

Guy was thinking that at some point in their strained-feeling conversation, she might turn to face him. But it was apparent – and he couldn't blame her – she was still transfixed by the spectacle presented by the comet.

"So 'Gah-ee,' you were starting to say something you liked about your full moon when I interrupted."

"Oh, that!" Guy's heart flip-flopped on this evidence that, as absorbed as Yulala might be by the comet, she was closely attending to every last fa-la-laed translation of what he said. Plus, her calling him Guy, "Gah-ee," for the first time. He went on, "What I like is, uhh, walking along a beach on Earth at night, and seeing the full moon reflected off the waters of the ocean, uhh, our larger version of your Grand Basin."

"Do you have to watch out for stepping on roving 'ahtpah' webs, whatever your equivalent for that on your 'Ahth'?"

Guy shook his head and laughed. "No, the closest thing would be getting spit-out chewing gum stuck to the bottom of my bare feet."

"'gahhm'? What is chewing 'gahhm'?"

"That- I am not sure how to describe that; maybe when my spaceship returns, we can tap into the video archive encyclopedia. But, uh, if you were there, at my favorite beach on Earth, at night during a full moon, this is what we would do. There's a path built of wood planks that runs along the beach. It is called a boardwalk. You see, Yulala, on Earth we don't have to deal with a sunset storm line every day, maybe just a couple of lines of thunderstorms over the summer. So people can build stuff right along the water's edge. Although, with global warming raising the sea level, our coastal preservation engineers- Okay, this is getting too complicated; let me back up."

"If you are backing up, 'Gah-ee,' don't back up too much, or you might fall off this summit, ee-ee!" Yulala's shoulders heaved with her bemusement, though her eyes remained transfixed by the comet, at that moment crossing over to the eastern half of the night sky.

"It is just an expression we have for: Let me start

over."

"I suspected as much." Yulala turned her head to her right, and she gave Guy a fleeting regard with her nocturnally large eyes. They seemed to almost glow with the ubiquitous pale-green bioluminescence of the Fafaman night.

"Uh, um, well, yes, on that boardwalk I described, along it are various shops. In one of them, they sell frozen processed milk cream we take from an animal called a cow. They scoop it into something else that is sweet and edible, called a waffle cone."

"A 'wahhfahhl' cone?"

"Yes. Uh, we would, I would get you one, in any flavor you like. Then we would return off the boardwalk, down onto the sand, to eat our ice cream cones while we watched the full moon reflecting off the water."

"And how many of your mates would join us, 'Gah-ee'?"

Sergeant Hanson gently latched his hands onto Yulala's shoulders. He made a motion to have her turn completely around to face him.

She did not resist.

"No other mates," he deliberately shook his head locking his eyes with hers. "Only you."

That is when the Varfafafa's eyes strayed from Hanson's eyes to contemplate his lips, left parted open,

which was all it took for them to collapse into each other's arms. They pressed their lips most desperately together, in a hopeless effort to press through to a place for them far from the madness of their present circumstances...

...so they missed viewing what Guy had predicted, the shower of shooting stars in the wake of the comet's tail. Its enchanted beauty hinted at the couple's deepest wish perhaps being more than just an impossible dream.

# Chapter 22

"Officer Leung? This is Captain Louisa Entroper of the starship Smoke and Mirrors. I am trying to contact you, wherever you are. If you are hearing this, I have an important news update for you. The flying saucer from Tictoctic that brought havoc to Oomb, and abducted tree people and humans alike? Our firefly monitor has confirmed its departure from anywhere near Oomb. Officer Kevin Smith-Park assures me it has completely left the Callaway X Centra system perimeter. It is probably skimming an Oort Cloud in the direction of Cygnitaurus, on the way back home to Tictoctic. So this should be a safe transmission. Even more so, because Officer Yoon-hee Park-Smith has managed to scramble it. For anyone in its receipt other than yourself, it should mimic static from cosmic and background radiation."

A pause and a sigh.

"Okay," continued Entroper, "I don't know whether you are receiving this, so I'll just go ahead."

Pause.

"No," went on Entroper, "I'm not hearing anything either; he might have already jumped a space-time rift if that was his plan. But I didn't think he'd find anything usable, from what you told me, until he got closer to Tictoctic."

Buddy Leung gathered from this part of Entroper's transmission that she was directing her remarks to others on the bridge of the Smoke and Mirrors. Her voice was sounding more distant, fainter. It was what one would have expected from her moving farther away from whatever mouthpiece into which she'd been reaching out to him.

"Or maybe the firefly we leaned on for this

transmission has met an untimely fate. Okay." Entroper's voice resumed its original amplification. "I'll go ahead, Officer Leung. Maybe your response is on its way, and I'm just being overly impatient. Um, well, a lot has happened since Officer Yoon-hee Park-Smith, as provisional captain, um... I understand she sent you to see what you could do with your brilliant hyper-physics applications to somehow thwart the abduction of people and tree persons from Oomb. I'm sure one change is obvious to you already. I've been appointed the new captain of the Smoke and Mirrors. Official order from the President. I received word of this personally from Defense Secretary Spinner. He has arrived to this corner of the galaxy alongside chair of the Joint Chiefs of Staff, Sandy Warlor, on the maiden voyage of the battle cruiser Barack Obama. Again, official order from the President.

"Our first task, with me at the helm, was to drag a comet into orbit around Fafama. That, plus the deployment of a stopgap air- and land-based second line of defense. Later, the Obama will find time to haul the bigger guns into place, hopefully. Anyway, our gifts were supposed to grease the wheels for getting the Fafamans to turn the negotiating team back over to us. The Fafama-what's-his-name is holding them captive until he can digest recent developments. A terrorist plot by Fafaman resistance has led to Sergeant Hanson and the twenty-third wife missing in action, plus one of the Smoke and Mirrors's shuttle pods getting totally destroyed. However, an even bigger, far more horrific terrorist plot resulted in central pyramid damage and, more importantly, fatalities for a number of the ruler's wives and children. We don't know exactly how many, because we were chased out of that region of space if we didn't want to see our negotiating team sentenced to death.

"We are presently descending back down into the orbital plane of Callaway X Centra, on its outskirts just inside its Oort Cloud. We are coming from the direction of Fafama of course. And we are hoping to rendezvous with you ASAP.

"As captain of the Smoke and Mirrors, and you as an officer under my command, First Engineer Buddy Leung, I am ordering you off your rescue mission. Temporarily. If that is another time travel feat you were planning, the past isn't going anywhere. It will always be there. We need you in the here and now, to meet with us so we can all get on the same page, get everyone in alignment on how we are going to deal with every possible contingency related to the threat from Tictoctic. We must also devise a viable scheme to retrieve Officers Helena and Chris Taylor, and Ali Magabu and HIS wife Tanya Petrovsky, from Fafama before, well... We don't want their safety to become another matter of having to undo the fate that already befell them. Officer Leung, we simply cannot afford to spend so much time altering history, trying to alter history, or we risk losing the future.

"The agenda is ready. What we require is your presence." Pause. "We anxiously await your response." Pause. "Well, okay." Click!

*It is most unfortunate, truly, as Ali would say. I have been unable to receive any of your transmission, Captain Entroper,* Buddy Leung thought to himself as he double-checked his shuttle monitor readings. *One of the fireflies must have shot headlong into an asteroid,* he continued to mentally rehearse the alibi, *or one of several other possibilities must have gone wrong. Okay. Time to move out.* With that, Officer Leung ignited the hydrogen-gas, jet-engine thrusters for the shortest possible burn. This, to take the shuttle pod far away from the five-mile-long asteroid, in the shadow of which he had literally been hiding. Far enough away, the pod's photon propulsion technology could accelerate him back to light-speed once again.

The asteroid belonged to an asteroid belt Leung had discovered some forty million miles out past Oomb. It was roughly the same location, relative to Oomb's sun, as the asteroid belt between Mars and Jupiter in Earth's solar system.

*No; this is what I feared.* Buddy shook his head. He was realizing one firefly scout had already identified a small space-time rift. It was less than five astronomical units ahead, well under five hundred million miles. This meant that far distant from any planet, several life forms had met an untimely fate, thus wounding the space-time fabric. At least, that is the explanation which had become the hyper-physics engineer's working hypothesis. The most likely explanation for this particular location was that this was around where the saucer from Tictoctic had been situated, when some if not all the people and trees abducted from Oomb had been slaughtered.

After Buddy programmed the necessary course headings into his navigation panel, he accelerated the shuttle for as many light-speed multiples as he could get it, approaching interface with the rift. Succeeding at which, there was little else left for him to do but to ponder all visible light ahead of the shuttle. That light braided, coiled together, as it got funneled through the mini photon-evacuation chamber set into the underbelly of the shuttle pod. Buddy also worried. Might this particular space-time rift prove too small for him to make it through? If this effort failed, he figured the shuttle pod would skip off what there was of the rift, like a stone skipping across water. In that case, how far away would he end up, nearly instantaneously? Perhaps all the way to Tictoctic, or back to Fafama?

What happened was the same as when the entire Smoke and Mirrors braved a far deeper and larger wound in the fabric of reality, just outside the thin Martian atmosphere at the outset of the second mission. The moment of penetration caused a peculiar tingling sensation, simultaneously stinging cold and burning hot. It was over soon as it started.

To Buddy Leung's immense satisfaction and relief, there before him on the shuttle pod view-screen sat motionless the saucer from Tictoctic. Officer Leung well knew the rift could have sent him back before that saucer had gotten anywhere near Oomb. True, he might have then been able to focus on sabotaging the alien spacecraft, preventing it from ever arriving to Oomb. However, he would have needed to catch up to wherever it was located before the universal quantum field caught up, period. Said quantum field "sensed" Buddy Leung's intrusion on "completed" space-time. It was only a matter of hours, presently, before that field backtracked to the point of Buddy's disruption, to replay history from then onwards. In one of his attempts to explain it to his colleagues, Buddy had likened the universal quantum field to a spider springing into action upon sensing a creature intruding on its past-time web.

Until he boarded the saucer, the hyper-physics engineer still would not know whether he had gotten far enough back in time. He still would not know whether the slaughtering of the abductees had started yet, if not already been completed. And for what he was to accomplish, if he *was* far enough back, Buddy knew, again, that there weren't many hours to spare before the quantum field caught up with him.

Officer Leung nudged the shuttle craft as close to the saucer as he dared. The way the "completed" space-time interacted with his ship reminded him of what he'd seen on an old video of an ice-breaker plowing through the Arctic Sea in mid-winter. Floodlights on that boat had revealed the ice-blanketed water undulating slowly, off into the distance, as a result of its forward motion steadily cracking apart said blanketing. Similarly, the shuttle pod's motion made the starry backdrop undulate. Buddy also imagined a black blanket studded with sequins, hung out to dry in a breeze on an ancient clothesline. Whatever Buddy's comparisons, the Tictoctic saucer got tossed and pitched by those undulations caused by his shuttle pod's intrusion on past space-time.

After Buddy Leung brought the shuttle to a halt, the undulations finally settled out. Buddy soon found himself in his small vehicle's air lock. He had stuffed his backpack full of what he expected to need for the task he'd set, and he suited himself up as though this were just a routine space-walk.

Sergeant Frankly had identified two disembarkation ports on the underbelly of the saucer, when it landed on Oomb. For the short trek over to the port he chose, Officer Leung found he needed to move his arms as though he were wading through water. This resulted in those ripple-effect undulations of the star field again. Buddy Leung had to exercise everything he knew about self-hypnosis to avoid motion sickness.

Buddy used Velcro adaptations to anchor himself beside the aforementioned disembarkation port. Unzipping a small compartment on his backpack, he pulled out a serrated knife for testing the hypothesis crucial to getting everything done in a short enough time.

Buddy breathed a new sigh of relief when, as his

crucial hypothesis predicted, the knife cut through two inches of saucer exterior metal as though it were merely so much corrugated cardboard. Normally, such a knife would hardly have even been able to scratch the surface of such an alloy tempered for hyper-speed space flight. However, the characteristics of matter in past-time suspended animation... The hyper-physics engineer shook his head in wonder as he made short order of cutting a square hole into the saucer's underbelly.

Officer Leung was careful to push gently the cut-out rectangular section of the saucer's exterior through the resulting square hole, into what he hoped to find was an air-lock chamber. That two-inch-thick section floated in vacuum as Buddy carefully climbed feet first through the hole he'd made. He kept reminding himself, any least tear in his spacesuit would prove just as fatal as were this all happening in "real" time.

A flashlight survey confirmed, to his relief, he HAD cut a hole into the air-lock chamber, rather than unwittingly dooming everybody on board with a leak into some main section of the ship. Next step was to find a piece of metal he could glue to the cut-out square section of hull. It would have to be a piece of metal which covered more surface area than the square section. It didn't have to be anywhere near as thick. This, to improvise a new air-lock hatch. The flashlight survey made such metal apparent, immediately. There was a table with a cushion on top. Obviously, the cushion was meant for whichever deer creatures from Tictoctic to recline upon, after their spacewalk, while they waited for air to refill the chamber.

Buddy stripped off the cushion and cut out a square segment of the quarter-inch-thick table top. He cut it larger than the square segment he had cut out of the hull. Then he glued the two segments together. From his backpack, he produced a strip of special putty. He applied that putty strip all around the edge of the cut-out square of hull. The final step in this particular process was to neatly insert the hull section back into where it had been cut out, and press hard to assure the putty was making an airtight seal.

Of course, the flying saucer's air lock contained two hatches. One of them opened to outside the saucer. The other conveyed to a hallway inside the saucer. Buddy had already cut into the hatch that opened to the outside. Next, he had to cut into the hatch that led to the saucer's interior. When he did, the result proved anxiety-lessening because it met his expectation. The oddly dense feeling of vacuum, which had made floating from the shuttle to the saucer feel like he was wading through water, gave way to the far lighter feeling of air everywhere. This was even odder, given how air was surpassingly heavier than so-called "empty space."

Officer Leung still needed to keep on his spacesuit for the entirety of the mission. The best thinking was that trying to inhale "past" air might be like inhaling taffy, the results immediately fatal.

Next on Buddy's agenda was so burned into his brain, he felt no need to write down any of it. He made his way fast as possible to wherever the abductees were being held. He had to hope he wouldn't find any of them already slaughtered. He propelled himself half-floating, half-running, down one hallway after another.

Buddy Leung passed a Tictoctickian deer creature, armed with an air igniter and frozen still in the moment of "completed" space-time to where Buddy had intruded. He thought to himself that what he saw of the creature could just as easily have been a single frame from an old motion picture film. And well did he understand that, once the quantum wave finished backtracking, the film projector would start running again. As an intruder from another location in the space-time continuum, he would no longer be the only one able to move about.

Ever more urgently, Buddy slashed open anywhere he thought he might find Pedro and company, until he came out on a balcony overlooking the slaughterhouse floor.

There they were, Pedro, Miguel and five Marines whose names Buddy hadn't all memorized yet. Their hands were bound and chained together, high over their heads. The one in front, a Marine, had almost reached where a curtain did not allow seeing from ground level what lay beyond. *The chamber where they were to actually be slaughtered*, Buddy thought as he leapt over the railing and grabbed at whatever he could to lower himself down in the weightless environment. He was able to knife through the manacles effortlessly, and just as effortlessly carry the bodies two at a time, leaping back up to the balcony where he'd first entered this large space.

Officer Leung piled the seven humans like they were so much lumber, out in the hallway beside where he had cut a big rectangular hole into the air-lock chamber hatch. After that, he returned to the slaughterhouse area to search for the two tree creatures seized from Oomb. They included Mafoosoola. He found them where he expected the oven area to be. And as with the Earthlings, he also found his time travel had taken him none too far into the past. Mafoosoola was strapped down on a conveyor belt, mere inches short of the giant circular saw obviously intended to split her in half, then most likely to halve her again and again after that to provide- *I suppose their chef was going for that hickory smoke flavor, but what were they doing for ventilation? I don't have time for this,* Buddy reproved himself as he trimmed branches off both Oombians, to make their transport back to the shuttle more manageable.

Officer Leung gradually grew aware of a vague, nonetheless unaccountable mental perturbation. At first, he discounted it as an effect from pushing his body's limits, wading through "past" space-time. But he didn't remember suffering from any such perturbation during the collection of bodies from the Philadelphia neighborhood, at the outset of the Smoke and Mirrors second mission. Besides which, he presently experienced a resolution of the vaguity into mumblings, voices just beyond reach of understanding. *Of course.* He gave Mafoosoola a kind regard, Mafoosoola who he had piled atop the other Oombian like just another log. *They are trying to telepath their appreciation across space-time. But they are having understandable difficulties achieving that. You are more than welcome, wherever and whenever you are attempting such a mental feat!*

Buddy improvised another air-lock seal, this time rectangular. It was the same as he had done for the square hole he had first cut into the outside of the saucer. He used the other half of the resting table platform, glue, and more airtight space-age putty. He set the completed seal aside. Forthwith, he carefully brought the first two humans inside the air-lock chamber, and he put them into airtight specimen bags he unfolded from his backpack. Each bag was big enough to hold a boulder, if need be. Once zip-locked, the original intent had been for whatever contents to be protected from any contamination inside the shuttle that might compromise lab results. The original intent had been for comet analysis; nothing like what Buddy was presently doing had ever been anticipated. But the bags provided plenty of space for the first two humans, two of the Marines. And Buddy had calculated that if there was any sort of respiration going on by those bodies, there would be plenty enough air in the bags to prevent asphyxiation, provided he got them over to the shuttle with all due haste.

It had proven a tedious matter, installing the improvised rectangular air-lock seal, prying open the improvised, square, hull seal to the outside, conveying the bodies over to the shuttle, emptying them out onto the floor of the shuttle pod, then returning to the saucer with the two empty bags to repeat the entire process.

Once all the humans and tree creatures were crowded into the space shuttle, Buddy allowed himself an extra moment to muse over how much easier his rescue would have gone, were he in possession of a transporter like they had in that old *Star Trek* series. He could have simply beamed the abductees off the saucer from Tictoctic. Anyway, it was time for the endgame. The hyper-physics engineer had given some thought to leaving a recorded message. It would have been translated into the series of tongue-clicks by which the deer creatures on their cattle-rustling mission communicated. Something to the effect of: Leave us alone or you'll start disappearing off your spaceship next. But uncertain how they might react, that he might just make matters worse…

…so he went about one final task, to set up a trick. He struggled to maintain his focus, as he got haunted by wistful regret. He had really wanted to poke around the extraterrestrial vehicle, figure out its operation. Very soon, though, a back-tracking quantum wave would be washing over it all, returning it to a substantial, threatening presence!

Back aboard the shuttle pod, the last Marine was strapped in safely to a passenger seat. Buddy focused on putting as much distance between the shuttle and the saucer as possible before the quantum wave could catch up, and the deer creatures would realize what had happened. However, he was also possessed of the thought: *Hopefully, their spaceship isn't going to suffer a vacuum-induced implosion from my hull tampering.*

***

"Captain Mat-kek-tek," brayed Officer Tak-venk-tit, "your brilliant supposition the attack vehicle that disappeared our meat samples would seek refuge inside the asteroid field has been confirmed. I know you have already ascertained this from our data output, but, near-worthless creature that I am, I needed to hear myself uttering such horrendousness aloud!"

The rest of the officers on the bridge of the saucer's navigation deck swelled out their chests the captain's direction, and they baaed, "We are near worthless, most brilliant Captain Mat-kek-tek! All appreciation if you are allowing us to draw our next breath!"

The captain swelled out his chest as well, but as a show of pride in the confirmation of a "brilliant supposition" he hadn't actually made, yet was easily able to imagine he had made, and forgotten, in his haste to sniff out his next "brilliant supposition." This, on the strength of all the past indicators of his genius he'd been given credit for that he could not quite recall, but which seemed upon later reflection to have been well within his range of ability. "Inhale deeply, officers, that you might better enjoy our pursuit and ultimate destruction of the inferior alien craft!, of our baking to a char every last one aboard, so we might better warn the creatures of Oomb to never again even think of such an action, when we return to collect more samples. That is, if any of their youth hope to live to a breedable age!" With these last tongue-clicks, he stamped the floor with his rear hooves.

"Captain Mat-kek-tek," brayed Officer Tak-venk-tit anew, "may it please you to most deservingly be spared wasting your most precious breath, once again. This, by my being who now informs everyone that on your orders, we will fire a magnetic pulse beam at the nearest asteroid! We will make this demonstration not only to evidence how useless will prove any more of their trickery, but also to mount the barbarians' terror, in these final moments before we direct the pulse beam straight-on at their puny spacecraft!"

"Especially since the target rock is of such an impressive size," the captain nodded approvingly. He noted what he presumed to be the asteroid Tak-venk-tit intended to destroy. It came into view on the panoramic navigation bridge view-screen as more than just another star in the distant, distant background.

"The target rock is approximately five gekleks in diameter, for those of you on the bridge who, unlike our most courageous and brilliant captain, cannot view the data output monitor, or are too ignorant to understand what you are looking at...far, far unlike our captain," Tak-venk-tit added, apprehensive Mat-kek-tek might fatally take his "ignorant" remark for the insult it was intended to be. "If any of you wish to express the least disagreement, I shall make it my duty to personally impale you, though such impalement cannot begin to rise to the captain's level of impalement, my sharpest antlers as blunt as they are!" Tak-venk-tit joined the rest of the crew on the bridge, in bowing down on bended fore-knee towards the captain and ritually chanting, "We can be honored with no greater pain than the pain we would know from your impalement, Captain Mat-kek-tek. And we say this only because we know we will never, ever prove deserving of impalement, or even the slightest scratch, by the mighty Dek-Fook-Tek."

With an acknowledging nod, the captain said, "My regret is that we will have to settle with merely destroying the attacking vessel, when I should prefer to personally have you witness my sharpest antlers emerging out the back of their captain!" Mat-kek-tek pointedly worked about his bahvek on the tip of one of his longer antlers. "Officer Tak-venk-tit, can we fire now?"

"Captain, that you precluded my saving you from wasting your breath on such a question speaks volumes to your humility."

"His humility is as vast as the virgin forest," chanted the other officers on the bridge before Tak-venk-tit, with a flick of two switches, tongue-clicked, "It is done!"

A very low-pitched hum throbbed, just once, throughout the flying saucer. It made everyone aboard feel as though they'd experienced a minor electrical shock. From an aperture opened on the spacecraft's underbelly, the magnetic pulse beam was emitted.

On the monitor screen, the deer creatures from Tictoctic were able to see a donut-shaped area of space appear disturbed, as though a donut-shaped magnifying glass were getting moved ever closer to the target asteroid. Quickly, the distorted area, with the stars in it appearing larger and brighter than normal, intersected with the asteroid. Most silently, that mile-wide rock got pulverized. But even more significantly, where Captain Mat-kek-tek and the others were concerned, within moments after that, a second, smaller explosion could be seen happening behind the rapidly dissipating debris field.

"Their attack vessel has been destroyed already!" Captain Mat-kek-tek brayed gleefully.

"A stray rock from the pulverization must have hit them dead center!" interjected Tak-venk-tit.

"Now, let's return to Oomb, and by our pulse-beam demonstration on one of their 'oof' courses, show them just how merciful we were on our first visit! That they ought to have appreciated our kindness so much more than they apparently did! And let us also hope the infesting creatures from another planet bring their finest battleship!, so we might demonstrate once more their futility against our power!"

# Chapter 23

"Ahh! My 'Ahthlahn' guests! Come in! Come in! No!" The Fafamafalafama waved off servants who were going to pull out chairs around the rectangular conference table for Helena, Chris, Ali and Tanya. "This will be MY task!" From his abruptly severe declaration, he just as abruptly turned Chris's way, to give him a toothy smile. Helena's husband found it verging on the ridiculous, for how affected it came off. The Fafaman ruler made a sweeping gesture for Chris to be seated on the chair he pulled out for him.

"The self-abasement of the Fafamafalafama," Nanofafo fa-la-laed with his trademark low sweep towards his leader.

*How truly fascinating,* Ali thought as the Fafamafalafama guided him towards his designated seat. *I would have thought the Fafamafalafama would not approve of the negative connotation of "self-abasement," presuming the translator got it correct. But quite apparently, so long as whatever he does is treated as the most superlative version possible, he accepts that as praise. In other words, he would also most likely have been okay with Nanofafo saying, "The stench of his supreme defecation," so long as he also made that sweeping gesture. Truly fascinating, indeed!*

*The bottle and glasses on the table; I wonder if we're going to get treated to another "up your ass" toast?* Tanya was thinking about an epithet hurled by Officer Kevin Smith-Park on the first mission to Fafama. Fortunately, where diplomacy had been concerned, the Fafamans had misunderstood his intemperate words as a celebratory toast. Which misunderstanding, the Earthlings had decided was better left uncorrected.

"Men and women from 'Ahth,'" the Fafamafalafama

said with a slap of both his hands flat against the table, at the one end where he positioned himself, still standing, "certainly you are perceptive enough to understand I had you separated into four different locations for your own safety and protection, as well as for ours. Those beasts with whom we have to contend, it will prove far more difficult for them, if not impossible, to kill all four of you, secured away thusly. A far different story from if we had allowed you to stay together, which I am sure would have been your preference."

*Also coincidentally making for more difficulty our plotting any sort of escape,* Tanya thought to herself. *How most convenient.*

"It is on this same basis we keep my wives and children in various separate places. I can assure you the terrorists' biggest regret about their most recent attack was that it DID result in the slaughter of 'only' three wives and five children." The Fafaman ruler gripped the table edge, and bowed his head. Clearly, he was struggling to keep himself composed.

During this pause, Chris thought he discerned, even under cover of the pale-green nocturnal lighting, the Fafamafalafama's nostrils flaring angrily, in sync with his noticeably louder breathing.

Captain Taylor, the only one of the Earthlings who thought to bring night-vision goggles, was focused on the two servants behind the Fafamafalafama. They were holding up wood planks between them.

At last, on one of the Fafaman ruler's inhales, he lifted his head and withdrew his sword. With his exhale, he spun around to slash again and again at the wood planks. Each grunt of exertion sounded to Helena like it was infused with a moan of grief.

Halved planks dropped to the slate floor. Somehow,

Chris was reminded of the first chunks of windblown, over-sized hail stones he had heard long ago, hitting the side of his parents' home during an especially fierce thundershower. That had him irrationally anxious there could be a deluge of them. But the Fafaman ruler quickly ran out of wood still long enough for his servants to hold between them. Unless... Ali feared that, until the Fafamafalafama re-sheathed his sword in its jewel-studded scabbard, he just might decide to take a swipe at his servants' body parts...or set his raging sights on his other-world captives.

However, the Fafamafalafama did gradually succeed in calming himself from nearly hyper-ventilating. As he did so, the four Earthlings reflected, each to his or her self, on the unique circumstances in which they had been placed away from one another, purportedly for their own protection.

Helena had been brought to the private quarters of the first wife, the Varalawa. So many puzzles there. For starters, why did the Varalawa ask questions about her husband?, such as what did she, Helena, know about his interests?

And then there were the two pendants the Varalawa was personally etching with the hieroglyphic-appearing lettering of the Fafaman language. When Helena had remarked, "It will be interesting to learn the message you have engraved on them," the first wife had said, "For certain, it should prove most fascinating for both you and your husband, I should hope, at the appropriate time." The appropriate time? When would be the appropriate time? Helena hadn't been able to bring herself to ask this, because what the Varalawa had gone on to say next had had her wondering over something else. Which was, whether this woman had come to think that if a man could have so many wives, so should a woman have so many husbands. Especially the question, "Do women who become captains, or who assume other positions of power on your planet, do they ever take on additional husbands?"

Meantime, Tanya Petrovsky had been sent to work with two women teachers, to help care for the four children who had survived the terrorist attack, but lost their mother. Tanya had guessed the oldest one, Nafana, was six or seven years old. Nafana had just wanted to sit in a corner, telling her stuffed animal faboompa doll she could not assure their protection from "evil ahtpah bombs," but that she would try. This sweet little girl had periodically worked herself into a fury over an imaginary attack, crying at her faboompa doll, "I tried! I tried! But I can't save you! You are going to die like my mother!" Every time she had reached this level of agitation, one of the teachers had gone over and rocked her in her arms, gently fa-la-laing what had gotten translated as, "You are safe, Nafana, and so is your faboompa. Shall we go to the food pit and grab something soft and wiggly, a waspala perhaps? You and your faboompa can share?" This had settled her every time. Nafana had looked most content, sifting through a sandbox in search of a wriggly, worm-like creature to pull out and contentedly chew on. That was, after offering it up to no avail to her stuffed animal faboompa.

The other three children had been mercifully too young, Tanya had thought, to have grasped, to have fully understood, what happened to their mother. Two of them were twin boys, the other a girl. The twins had stagger-walked about with their arms out in front of them for balance as though, Tanya had mused, they were two miniature Frankenstein monsters, Frankensteins in diapers.

The youngest one, the girl, had been barely crawling. What all of them had shared was an instinctive curiosity, puzzlement over the other-worldly creature in their midst. They had loved getting up close to Tanya's face, and exploring her cheeks and ears with their already mouse-y long whiskers. As well, they had kept eyeballing her eyeballs with their beautifully oversized own, which were evolved, adapted for nocturnal viewing. They had sensed there was something different about Tanya's eyes, without realizing exactly what.

Chris and Ali's assigned circumstances had proven not quite so gentle. Chris had been required to join in the grunt work to clear the damaged area of the central pyramid of the heavier pieces of debris left inside the burnt-out wives' and children's chambers. Ali had had to join the cleanup crew outside, down on the ground at the base of the pyramid, to deal with the remains of dead terrorists and blinding-light prowlers. Counselor Magabu had also been ordered to help sweep up piles of shards of outer pyramid glass, at least what remained after individual pieces got turned into deadly flying projectiles by the most recent sunset storm line.

Presently, the Fafamafalafama was finally settled back down enough to continue, "Thankfully, as I commanded, your spacecraft has remained at an undetectable distance from Fafama. This has given me the time I required to mourn, to reflect, to consult with my closest advisers, and finally, to plan. So I have brought you together for an explanation of where we go from here, and even for a minor celebration. But first, and certainly a cause in itself for celebration, Nanofafo?!?" The Fafaman ruler snapped his fingers. "Bring in our honored guests!"

With yet another low hand sweep, and his ridiculously

long (so Chris thought) handlebar moustache all atwirl, Nanofafo fa-la-laed, "I present to you the Varafafafa and 'Sahjahnt Hahnsahn'!"

The Varafafafa, the twenty-third wife of the Fafamafalafama, entered first. She slid forward her right foot, scraping its sandal across the black slate floor, and paused. Then she slid her left foot up beside and past her right foot, and paused. This traditional movement continued, until the Varafafafa arrived over beside the Fafamafalafama. There, she bowed towards her husband until her head was curled into her chest. Ali nodded knowingly; the Varafafafa was mimicking how certain Fafaman fern trees behaved. That was, until the bioluminescence of a surfacing flounder mouse at stars-out caused it to unfurl erect to its full, outspread height. Officer Magabu speculated to himself that the foot-sliding might have had something to do with emulating those same fern trees' root system, as he was aware their roots did extend more laterally than downwards. But he wasn't sure.

In any event, as the Earthlings expected from prior experience, the Fafamafalafama turned towards his twenty-third wife, and he stretched out his arms to fully reveal his cloak's infused bioluminescence.

As he had told Ali previously, Buddy Leung was guessing the Fafamans actually encouraged, actually nurtured a bioluminescent mold to flourish on the royal clothing.

Also as expected, the Varafafafa unfurled back up to her own, full height, still shorter than the Fafaman ruler's. Though Helena, especially, was struck by how the Varafafafa kept her chin tucked into her neck. Modestly, or was it shamefully? The Varafafafa made a motion to take a seat in a chair beside the chair at the head of the table where her husband had yet to rest. But he paused her from that effort. His left forefinger mellifluously yet insistently raised her chin for eye-to-eye contact. Yulala, the Varafafafa, coaxed herself into giving her still-new husband a smile. With that smile's dawning, however meekly and timidly produced, he let her free. By the time he'd reciprocated with his own smile, accompanied by what Helena sensed was an understanding nod, the Varafafafa had already made it down onto her chair.

Meantime, Guy Hanson made a perfunctory bow the Fafaman ruler's way. And he moved as unobtrusively quickly as possible to take his own seat beside Helena Taylor. That put him several chairs removed from Yulala.

"'Sahjahnt Hahnsahn'..."

Helena gave Guy a soothing-intended pat on the wrist; with his hands palms-down flat on the table, he looked to her like he was keeping himself tensely alert, to spring into action at the proverbial drop of a pin. And his startlement at the Fafamafalafama directing attention his way had her giving him a regard where she was wanting to ask, *What the hell is going on? Why so jumpy?*

"...I thank you for your role in the Varafafafa's safe return to the center of my empire! And I expect you will understand the delay of my toast to you, until everything for which we should toast has been revealed. Think of it as the tralalafas waiting to safely release their guests into the safety and comfort of stars-out, until after they have finished hosting them through the harshness of stars-fade."

"The poetic elegance of the Fafamafalafama." Once more, Nanofafo made a low sweep of his left hand the Fafaman ruler's way, as though he were introducing him for the first time, not the umpteenth.

"Beg your pardon, Mr. Fafamafalafama, sir." Guy

rose by his chair, yet he kept his head bowed abjectly low, Ali thought with puzzlement. "I think the toast should actually go to Y-uh, to the Varafafafa. She really knew her way around the more dangerous creatures, life forms, we encountered. Without that knowledge, I'm not sure I would have survived to be here."

Yulala stayed seated as she responded, her head also kept bowed low. "The 'sahjahnt' unjustly undervalues his contribution to our- um, my safety. By having me run ahead of him when we were pursued by the 'thansama snawyama,' that allowed me the necessary moments to plot through our- um, the predicament. And yet..." She forced herself to look up, and seek out the Fafamafalafama's large eyes with her nocturnally-sized own. If he but knew, they were full of plea for mercy and understanding rather than tender affection. "...the real thanks, the real toast, belongs to you, dear beloved Fafamafalafama. It was the inspiration of the examples you always set that lent me the confidence, the courage, to conceive survival." On her way to resuming with her head bowed contritely low, Yulala stole a glance Guy's way,

the same instant he dared lift his head just enough to steal a glance her way.

The Fafamafalafama looked back and forth, from the Marine Corps sergeant to the twenty-third wife. Pursuant to which, he directed his attention at the four other Earthlings besides Guy Hanson, to fa-la-la, "On account of the recent tragic events and momentous circumstances, I have not had sufficient opportunity nor, to be honest, a desire that felt elevated even one sand grain above selfish, to consummate my marriage to the Varafafafa. Perhaps your 'sahjahnt' could relieve me of that burden, ha-ha-haa!"

The Fafaman ruler's deep-throated laugh reminded Helena uncomfortably of when, held captive by him on her first mission to Fafama, she could hear him next door, enjoying the company of one of his wives.

Guy hoped the pale-green nocturnal lighting masked how pale his own face felt like it was turning. He reflected anew on his good fortune, that he had become aware of a faint hum in the air, early enough to separate himself and Yulala from each other's embrace. That was, mere moments before the Fafaman fighter-jet search party had gone helicopter mode, like those antique Ospreys back on Earth. This, for landing beside the rock outcropping from where Guy and Yulala had witnessed the orbiting comet. Guy hadn't known better than to have the impression that just as he had been pushing Yulala away, unlocking his lips from hers, she had been trying to move his left hand up onto her chest.

The four Earthlings aside from Guy Hanson were still with their mouths hanging open in astonishment, while Nanofafo said, "The humor of the Fafamafalafama," with his usual flourish.

"NOOOO!!" the Fafamafalafama suddenly wailed towards the ceiling.

"Oh, no," Ali said under his breath. He was grown fearful that, whether real or imagined, the Fafaman ruler intuited something going on between the Varafafafa and the sergeant. It was what Ali himself had also sensed, however mistakenly he thought he might possibly have been. If so, the Fafaman ruler could have been about to wreak revenge with his over-sized sword coming out swinging.

Guy reflexively jumped to his feet. He was not thinking the Fafaman ruler's outburst had anything to do with him. Rather, he was tensing to deal with who-knew-what out-of-nowhere emergency.

Guards surrounded the Marine Corps sergeant, their

guns drawn in case...

Continuing to address the ceiling, the Fafamafalafama screamed in a high-pitched, sobbing voice, "The 'Kagagara'! The 'Sagarara'! The 'Hafahara'! 'Slava'! 'Tlava'! 'Mrafamafa'! 'Fwafama'! 'Pafafa'!" On this last in a string of mysterious utterances, he buried his face in his hands, and he made "Ee! Ee! Ee!" noises the Earthlings had associated, up until then, more with Fafaman crowd amusement and cheering than with individual Fafaman grieving, though grieving it certainly came off as being on this particular occasion.

"Those are the names of the perished wives and children," Nanofafo went over beside the Earthlings to explain in a quiet voice, while the ruler's lament subsided to a soft whimper.

Said whimper had Tanya, Helena and Chris's hearts going out to the Fafamafalafama.

Ali shook his head in wonderment, thinking to himself, *How curious, truly, that his incredibly crude joke about consummating his latest marriage should get succeeded so immediately by a raging outburst over his personal loss. I would have thought that loss was too recent for him to have conjured such a joke in the first place! If I didn't know better, it would seem to me his outburst was actually an expression of most regretful guilt he doesn't feel more for the deaths in his family than he truly does. And how odd seems the ritual aspect! Shouting aloud those names like pickups at a carryout restaurant!*

"But now," the Fafamafalafama finally raised his head out of his hands, to look down upon his small assembly with drying rivulets of tears striping his face, "now I must share with you my plan, the result of much reflection and consultation.

"'Cahptahn,' former 'Cahptahn Taylah,'" he

directed towards Helena, "I know, I understand the nobility of your efforts to intervene on our behalf, and search for something of worth in the terrorist minds, upon which a peaceful settlement could be built. I can tell that those curious mind-reading tree creatures, unless it was some most clever stunt, even I am not sure…"

"The modesty of the Fafamafalafama."

"I can tell they inspired within you further belief such a miracle was, indeed, achievable. But now you must realize: The things that might be possible in another, better world, we can only dream about them in this world."

Ali wondered whether it was his imagination, or whether he really did discern correctly through the darkness what he thought he discerned. Namely, that the Fafamafalafama shifted his eyes away from Helena, to dart them briefly from the Varafafafa to Guy and then back again to the Varafafafa.

"The real danger is in not making the proper distinction between what can be achieved, and that beast which would destroy us before we could ever drive a sword through its heart. To put this more understandably for you, let me suggest we are dealing with a beast which would destroy us before we could ever befriend it.

"Spaceship officers from 'Ahth,'" the Fafaman ruler clapped his hands together twice, "Wafalawa will now explain to you the plan which, sadly, reality requires us to consider."

"The sensibleness of the Fafamafalafama." Wafalawa was the one this time with the low-sweeping hand and introductory bow the Fafaman ruler's direction. Meantime, an assistant set up an easel with large sheets of paper attached to it. Helena and company hadn't seen such an easel since their first, historic encounter with the Fafamans. "To paraphrase in a manner bound to be inferior to the Fafamafalafama's original utterance," Wafalawa went on as he took the cap off his fluorescent marker, "clearly, we made our best effort possible to bring the terrorists to their reasonable senses. We did this with the very substantial gift of a water-shedding rock mass set into orbit around our planet. We said we would take care of their water shortage issue, and every day, now, they can view the most dramatic evidence possible we were not making idle talk. Every day, now, the great blue comet makes its triumphant trek across the sky."

"Though of course it will take months, at the least, for enough water to shed into the atmosphere to make any substantial difference." Helena directed this caveat at Wafalawa as though the Fafaman ruler were not present. She didn't like where the conversation was going, and she figured her best chance of throwing in a monkey wrench would be to put Wafalawa on the defensive. That way, she could save face for the Fafamafalafama, by giving him a chance to think he was getting bum advice. This, rather than that he was in any way the author of whatever awful scheme had been concocted.

"Former 'Cahptahn,' the terrorists can see most dramatically from where their additional moisture will be issuing." Wafalawa's own whiskers woven into a handlebar moustache curled and uncurled with his strain to keep his indignation under control. "But what has been their response? What has been their response, in the real world as opposed to that fantasy world the Fafamafalafama most eloquently espoused?, wherein we would all wish to live? They have targeted our central pyramid, with the clever intent, successfully executed, of murdering beloved members of the Fafamafalafama's family! This has been their response!"

Helena kept to herself what she couldn't yet find the courage to vocalize. Which was, that most likely the attack on the pyramid constituted retaliation for the Fafaman jet-strike retaliation for the previous terrorist action which resulted in the temporary disappearance of the twenty-third wife of the Fafamafalafama, with the terrorist attack on the twenty-third wedding also doubtless in mind. Which in itself Helena thought safe to assume was in retaliation for some Fafaman government military action that had gone on before. *It wouldn't surprise me if the resistance fighters were lecturing one of their own would-be peace negotiators, on how in the "real world" any reasonable settlement with the Fafaman government was a naively hopeless dream.*

"What we have to conclude, what the data demands we conclude," went on Wafalawa, "is that the terrorists are a pestilence. Like any pestilence, they must be controlled, or eradicated. And what the data has been screaming at us for several orbits of our sun, with the intensity of a flatus emission from an awakening namanacasa, is that controlling the terrorists does not work. Controlling the terrorists has, in fact, failed. The attack on the central pyramid confirms eradication is the only way! Here is how we intend to do it." Wafalawa sketched the comet orbiting Fafama. For illustrative purposes, he depicted it way out of proportion to its actual size. "Let us say that over here, just west of the Grand Basin, is the center of the terrorist infestation." He drew a mountainous ridge on the planet's topside horizon, to one side and below where he had depicted the comet heading. "Now over here," he said as he continued drawing, "we have positioned two of the land-based missile launchers so wisely delivered to us from 'Ahth.'" He paused to respectfully incline his head

Helena's direction. "This is where we would have positioned them anyway, to defend our central pyramid from terrorist as well as extraterrestrial attacks. On the next orbit of the water-bearing rock mass, we will fire two of your nuclear-tipped warheads from this missile system. Our best munitions specialists have most carefully calculated the specific time and target path. An estimated thirty-six 'nanas' following the launching of the warheads, they will detonate against the water-bearing rock mass. Their detonations will steer that rock mass on a new heading, lowering out of its orbit around Fafama. On that new heading, it will gradually descend until it lands plowing into the terrorist homeland. Most adequate 'Ahthlahns'!" Wafalawa held up his hand not occupied with the fluorescent marker, to nonverbally insist they hold off on whatever they might be about to say. He could see their mouths dropping open in astonishment and/or about to speak. "We fully understand the result could very well include the demise of several children who should not be held to blame for the actions of their parents. But this is as with the discovery of a dormant namanacasa. Its destruction and removal before it can poison its surroundings often necessitates the incidental demise of numbers of innocent flounder mice and fern trees that just happened to have taken up residence in the soil above it."

"A loss of flounder mice and fern trees, people from 'Ahth,' which aggrieves us. It aggrieves us so much that, upon the reporting of the successful elimination of a dormant namanacasa, it is insisted everyone everywhere halt what they are doing for a moment of profound silence," affirmingly nodded the Fafamafalafama.

"May I?" Tanya asked Helena. She was grown anxious to have first crack at challenging the stated plan.

"We're all equals now. Remember, Officer Petrovsky?"

"Well, but still..." Ali and Chris nodded heartily in unity with Tanya's sentiment as she went on, "Adviser Wafalawa, so many things can go wrong that would vastly expand the number of innocents who would perish. Have your best munitions specialists taken those possible scenarios into account?"

"'Offasah Pahtrahvskah,' you can rest assured our specialists have carefully considered every contingency." Wafalawa bared his teeth in a manner that reminded Chris of a grinning chimpanzee. For him, the effect was far more unnerving than reassuring.

"Very well," Tanya nodded, trying not to lose her cool yet remain persistent, "can you describe for me one of those contingencies, and what the strategies are for guaranteeing it will not become a problem?"

"Our specialists made a small scale model out in the desert, far to the west of the central pyramid. They launched a conventional warhead at a remote-controlled jet dropped down into the atmosphere by a space station shuttle blade. They studied the dispersal characteristics of the resultant debris field. I can share those results with you if you are really so interested."

"No," Tanya shook her head in disbelief, unable to contain her dismay and astonishment. "There can be little actual comparison between a burst-apart jet and a burst-apart comet! Plus, you should be looking at the consequences of the impact craters! Unless the comet is broken up into small enough fragments, you are looking at enormous amounts of ash and dust getting thrown up into the atmosphere. That ash and dust will block out so much sunlight, plant photosynthesis will get interrupted, and there will result massive animal and plant die-offs!

And, those die-offs will continue for however long it takes for the particulate matter to settle out of the atmosphere!"

Wafalawa's handlebar moustache successively curled and uncurled. This was the only visible indication Wafalawa's steadfast look of being unperturbed by Tanya's outburst was a façade. On Tanya pausing for his response, he made a show of inhaling and exhaling, trying to exude mild exasperation, before he said, "'Offasah Pahtrahvskah,' our best physicists, in collaboration with our best munitions experts, have hypothesized most confidently that, upon their impact, the water freed from the larger rock mass fragments will settle the dust out of the air sooner rather than later. We assume there will be a period of days when no one should want to leave the shelter of the central pyramid. We plan to order everyone in the surrounding developments to either stay indoors, or enter one of the special community centers we will open up inside the central pyramid for this occasion. One of our top medical biologists who we have brought in on this project, he has likened it to our whole-body chemotherapy treatment for cancer. For the cancer to be brought into check, if not eradicated entirely, specially formulated chemicals must temporarily compromise the body's immune system, the same as we must temporarily compromise our planet's ecosystems to rid them of this terrorist cancer."

"Esteemed Fafamafalafama,-" Helena Taylor didn't care whether Wafalawa was finished speaking or not. "-any hypothesis, no matter how confidently it is made, is no more than an educated guess until it has been put to the test at least once. What I am hearing is a plan for gambling you can end your terrorist threat in such a definitive manner, without wreaking planet-wide havoc that could seriously jeopardize the future of your civilization. And incidentally, what we have found on Earth is that there are far safer, more effective ways to eradicate cancer than by the form of chemotherapy you have described. Which therapy, I am sure your medical specialists must have found is often as deadly as the cancer itself."

"Former 'Cahptahn Taylahh,'" the Fafaman ruler's voice boomed with a feel, Helena sensed, of patronizing admonishment, "can it not be said that the terrorist threat to wreak planet-wide havoc, as you term it, has already been put to the test on several occasions in just the short time you 'Ahthlahns' have been here?, with provable, demonstrable results?, as opposed to some idle speculation your crew member makes which might or might not contain some factual basis? What I am also noticing is a continuing, distressing trend by you, former 'Cahptahn.' You brag about your own civilization's seeming accomplishments, as though your scientific advancements were to ours what our central pyramid is to the one built by the first Fafamafalafama. Our psychologists would say you are masking your insecurity, your fear you are perhaps inferior to us."

*And I would guess you are projecting onto "former 'Cahptahn Taylah'" your own insecurity,* Ali Magabu thought to himself as Helena said, "Officer Petrovsky is not making 'idle speculation,' esteemed Fafamafalafama. The 'factual basis' for her concern is the overwhelming evidence we have back on Earth. Sixty-five million orbits of our sun ago, an asteroid far smaller than your orbiting comet caused mass extinctions when it crashed into our planet. It crashed into a watery area, but that made no difference. Geologic records prove that large amounts of matter got propelled into the atmosphere globally, and took several orbits of our sun to settle out, thereby causing a severe cooling-off of our entire planet's climate."

"Ahh, but there you have it!" Wafalawa pointed his forefinger in a randomly chosen direction, as though he had not-so-randomly just spotted whatever "it" was. "Am I correct in gathering that the asteroid of which you speak came hurtling at your planet from deep space? Because its speed would have therefore far surpassed what we will experience from our ice rock descending from such close orbit around Fafama. Its velocity will not begin to approach anywhere near the velocity of your ancient extinction-event mass, correct?" Wafalawa concluded with that chimpanzee-toothy smile again.

"That is most likely the case," Helena nodded impatiently, anxious to make her point before anyone could cut her off. "But bringing down a jet from the upper atmosphere, something the size of a speck in relation to the comet, cannot possibly compare to- What I wish to suggest, esteemed Fafamafalafama, is that you at least hold off on this plan until our Officer Cathy James-Leung can return here to run a computer simulation with the available data. She has gained tremendous expertise in exo-geology and exo-weather from her research on other planets in our solar system. And, um, I am saying this, having full respect and awe for the construction of this central pyramid. It is certainly an architectural achievement, a wonder that dwarfs anything we have attempted back on Earth."

"NO!! Enough of your patronizing condescension!" The Fafamafalafama waved his arms back and forth causing an emphatic swirl of his cloak. "You are seeking a delay!, to see if you can buy time to prevent us from executing our plan! I can tell- Yes, I can tell you think, all of you think,-"

The Earthlings reflexively shook their heads "no" even though they hadn't yet heard what the Fafaman ruler was going to accuse them of thinking.

"-all of you think we are just using the weapons with which you have supplied us for a death-dealing blow to the terrorists!, careless of the threat from 'Tictoctic'! That we are nothing more than ignorant savages! But understand this well, too-proud people from 'Ahth.' The final solution to our terrorist threat will put us in a far stronger position to deal with the extraterrestrial threat! Yes! Remember: Our entire motivation for putting out the distress signal you answered was what we learned from the two extraterrestrials who crashed here!

"But we cannot wait for you to wake up to the real world from your naïve dreams before we act; it could be too late! Guards, have them taken away!, to separate quarters again! We will make arrangements for their return to their spaceship after we have done what we need to do! No up-your-ass toast for any of them! They don't deserve it!"

*How truly ironically true, we don't deserve that particular toast,* Ali thought to himself, as Chris's hand got pulled apart from Helena's by their respective guards dragging them different directions. This, after Helena had made a grab for her husband's hand in the first place. She had sought out his eyes to give him a haunting look he intuited was meant to say, if she could have telepathed like the Oombians, *Things will not be the same if and when we ever meet again; please try to understand.*

Understand what?

# Chapter 24

"C'mon c'mon c'mon. C'mon c'mon c'mon," Buddy Leung urged under his breath. Full of nervous energy, he was rechecking Pedro, Miguel, and every Marine for the umpteenth time, where he'd harnessed them to passenger seats aboard the shuttle craft. He was keen on detecting even the faintest resumption of their respiration, or slightest increase in their feather-light weight. Buddy's worry was growing, over a possibility he fearfully imagined, yet didn't understand. Was the backtracking of the quantum wave not going to revive Pedro and company, this time? Even though it was very clear the flying saucer from Tictoctic had resumed its lethal, pulse-beam-wielding existence? Buddy wished he could coax a more clearly received telepathic transmission from Mafoosoola and the other Oombian whose name he did not know. All he got presently was an unintelligibly faint, static-y garble entering his mind. *Mafoosoola and friend, I can tell you are trying, but I'm still having trouble "hearing" you!* The hyper-physics space engineer had laid down the tree creatures, side by side, in the aisle between the two sets of passenger seats. This made for some very awkward climbing about, to keep checking on everyone's condition.

The shuttle itself was holding stationary drift between two giant rock composites in the asteroid belt to where Buddy had had to flee for refuge from the Tictoctic saucer. His rescue of the fellow Earthlings plus two Oombians "healed" the space-time rift through which he'd sent the shuttle for his heroic effort in the first place. And so, he couldn't return through it.

The Tictoctic saucer in hot pursuit had targeted its magnetic pulse beam on the immense asteroid, behind where Buddy initially fled the shuttle craft. That is when he had fired off, from the shuttle's recent weapons retrofit, a nuclear-tipped missile. That missile had been programmed to detonate a specific number of seconds later, without its having to make impact with anything. The timing had been perfect. Right after the donut-shaped magnetic pulse beam had pulverized the target asteroid, the missile had gone off. The deer creatures from Tictoctic had been left with the impression that the shuttle had suffered catastrophic collateral damage. At least that's what Buddy had been hoping was the case.

The alien saucer had proceeded to depart from near the asteroid belt. It had appeared headed back towards Oomb, rather than continuing on towards the outer perimeter of the Callaway X Centra system. Buddy had thought it was reasonable to assume his deception succeeded; the Tictoctickians weren't able to tell the difference between the shuttle in drift mode and any of the other asteroids.

But presently, Buddy's concern was mounting, that his little back-in-time rescue mission would end up placing far more life forms in peril than he had managed to salvage, if at least the Oombians on board didn't wake up soon. Clearly, the Tictoctickians' magnetic pulse beam would prove easily capable of destroying the Smoke and Mirrors and the battleship Obama as well. If the Oombians didn't revive in another minute or so, for Officer Leung to employ their telepathic powers, he would have to conceive some method for getting out a warning message to Entroper and company. The warning would be that both large starships from Earth needed to zip far away, rather than attempt to engage with the enemy. Tragically, Oomb itself could not be rescued from a calamitously deadly demonstration of the magnetic pulse beam. Buddy figured the Tictoctickians would corral another meteorite swarm into a ring formation, to take incoming from the reactivated laser mesh shield. Thereby would their battle saucer once again successfully descend, undamaged, into the Oombian atmosphere. The question was what exactly the deer creatures would do after that. Would they try to destroy an entire small island? Would they burst into rubble one of the mountain ridges on the Borneo-sized island named Boombeeno? Would they create a massive tidal wave heading out in all directions from an ocean impact? Or, who knew what other terrible plan they might conceive? And who knew what other weaponry they might have in addition to the magnetic pulse beam?

*What you want us to telepath to the visitors from Tictoctic, Officer Leung...anything, anything we can do to stave off more violence.*

Never had Buddy imagined he could be so grateful to see eyes opening between ridges of corrugated bark on a tree trunk, and to hear that trunk's voice echoing in his head.

***

"As of the beginning of this utterance, Captain Mat-kek-tek, we were three hundred twenty-three million lek-leks away from the planet Oomb," crisply tongue-clicked Officer Tak-venk-tit. "On our present deceleration course, we will attain magnetic pulse beam range of the two alien war vessels orbiting Oomb within thirty-one kepektels, starting-"

Officer Kwit-Nik lifted a cloven hoof-hand ceiling-ward, to give Tak-venk-tit the "all-go" signal.

"-now!"

Captain Mat-kek-tek affected the most casual,

nonchalant antler sharpening with his bahvek that he could, given his growing excitement. The prospect was becoming quickly imminent, of making up for the humiliating theft, right under their snouts, of the new extraterrestrial meat sources. Revenge would soon be exacted by downing not one, but rather two alien battleships! Even better, maybe the saucer's asteroid retrieval nets could bag a considerable number of carcasses from the pulverized vessels! The cold of space would flash-freeze them perfectly. And before this happened, some bodies might get roasted through-and-through by incidental explosions of the alien propulsion systems and armaments! If those bodies were overcooked, salt curing might yield some most excellent jerky!, unless they got charred… *Please may the aliens not get overcooked, and please may their biogenetics be compatible with our own!*

"Only because of the calm mood you set, Captain Mat-kek-tek, am I able to perform these calculations anywhere close to your level of efficiency." Kwit-Nik made with this tribute, for all too much time having elapsed since any other officer on the navigation deck had offered anything comparable. But he knew it was a pathetically weak effort; he had to hope the captain was still reveling in his apparently successful effort to destroy the small alien vessel that had somehow abducted the alien carcasses within pektels of their intended slaughter.

"For its most soothing qualities, Captain Mat-kek-tek, your calmness would make a 'myikyik's' breath of the strongest storm winds," the assembled crew on the navigation bridge rose up onto their hind legs to ritually chant. The myikyik referred to a tiny, nat-like bug that was thriving under the current warming climate conditions back home across much of Tictoctic.

"Captain," Kwit-Nik could think of no ritual other thing to say, rather than to launch right into it, "our sensors are detecting a small unidentified flying object approaching us from the direction of the asteroid belt, at one-third light-speed!"

"So we didn't destroy them!" harshly baaed Captain Mat-kek-tek. He carelessly tossed aside his bahvek, and rose off his captain's chair onto his hind legs. "I KNEW it!"

"Of course you knew it," Officer Tak-venk-tit chimed in, shoulders back and chest thrust forward. "Impale me on your longest, sharpest antler for failing to heed your warning the pirate vessel wasn't destroyed yet!"

"Impale us on your longest, sharpest antler, though that be a greater honor than we deserve," other crew chimed in for the ritual litany. This fawning included Kwit-Nik, even though his memory was crystal clear on the matter. At no time did the captain offer, at not time did he express the slightest doubt as to what fate had befallen the alien craft, once the explosion subsidiary to the asteroid pulverization got seen on the panoramic view-screen.

"We ignore them." Captain Mat-kek-tek made a dismissive sweep with his cloven hoof-hand, of both the UFO and the group invite for him to indulge some serious chest-goring. *Kwit-Nik, eventually, but for now...* "They know we are about to destroy their mother warships, and thus maroon them here in this corner of the galaxy. But it is too late for them to stop us! Baa!!"

*Captain Mat-kek-tek, I must warn you.*

The captain's ears perked straight up. Unconcealed panic filled his eyes. His head froze still, as though said eyes had been transfixed by sudden lights. He asked, "Anyone else is hearing in their heads what I am hearing in mine?"

To multiple confirming nods, Kwit-Nik brayed, "We all are, Captain!"

*I do not like what you plan, what I read in your mind you plan, for the future of my fellow Oombians and the creatures from Earth.*

Captain Mat-kek-tek knew this was the same voice they had heard in their heads when the tree creatures and those other bestial aliens were brought aboard the saucer. It was the voice which had been pleading for mercy, for an alternative to their necessary slaughter.

*However, I also do not approve of how the Earthlings intend to respond. The Earthling operating the small space vessel which I am now aboard does not know I am telepathing to you.*

Captain Mat-kek-tek's ears twitched.

"Captain, shall I start the targeting countdown for the large, alien battle vessels?"

"Silence, Officer Tak-venk-tit!" The captain held up a cloven hoof-hand to add emphasis to what he so harshly brayed.

*He is following after you, to make a confirming observation of your vessel's destruction by an explosive device. He planted it on board when he secured our release from, again, what you had several viable alternatives to doing. I wish to see no such violence inflicted on you, any more than I would want to see my own kind suffer. Which is why I am advising you that if there is any way possible, you and your kind should abandon your saucer craft immediately.*

"You can't telepath us how to defuse the explosive?" Kwit-Nik tongue-clicked, and he also tried to thought-project.

*There is insufficient time to read the Earthling officer's mind for that. And even if there was sufficient time, I must be quite honest with you. I would not share such information with you. After you defused the bomb, you would most certainly resume your destructive course of action.*

"He's bluffing!  It's a trick!" Captain Mat-kek-tek kicked out his hind legs to his rear, of course. His hind hooves hit against the captain's chair backrest with such force, he broke the chair's swivel mechanism.

"Captain Mat-kek-tek! Captain Mat-kek-tek! Impale me several times over if you must!" the tongue-clicks erupted over the intercom, flooding the navigation bridge. "This is Chef Glork-tek! What the Oombian is telepathing to us, one of my assistants has discovered an apparatus wired multiply into the underside of one of our stoves! It has a digital countdown display! I don't know how the aliens' time compares to ours, but it reads fourteen, colon, numbers that started descending rapidly from 59. Now it's down to thirteen colon 57! 56!"

"Abandon ship! To the mini-saucers!" Captain Mat-kek-tek baaed as loudly as he could. "Except for us, Officers Tak-venk-tit and Kwit-Nik!" He butted his antlers into the back of Kwit-Nik's chair at the navigation console. "We are going to make the alien pirate into more than just a passive bystander of our saucer's destruction! Rather, he will become an unavoidable participant! Before we depart, I want to see the tractor beam locked onto the pirate craft. And I want the electromagnetic gravitational drag timed to pull it into the saucer when the countdown reaches zero!"

*I implore you not to answer violence with more violence, not to continue on an endless cycle that can only get worse and worse...You can learn of food alternatives, and how to enjoy our game, plus music from multiple planets. You do have your own music, don't you? Tunes you could share with us?*

"OUT OF MY HEAD!!!" Captain Mat-kek-tek covered his ears with his articulated cloven hoof-hands. "Officer Kwit-Nik, produce the loudest possible sustained static noise you can, throughout the ship's intercom system, TO DROWN OUT THAT VOICE!!!"

***

*I want to make sure you understand, Officer Leung. I meant every word I telepathed to the officer aboard the saucer craft about the cycle of violence, its futility on all sides.*

"I understand, Mafoosoola. Believe me, I appreciate the viewpoint you and your fellow Oombians bring to the unprecedented situation we face." Buddy Leung was busy poring over monitor data on his navigation console; he couldn't spare looking up to make eye contact with the trimmed-branchless tree creature standing beside his chair.

The other revived Oombian, Flookle-Dookle, telepathed an update on what was happening for the dazed-yet-rapidly-recovering Earthlings seated behind him.

*And I should also make clear what the only reason was, that I could find it within myself to lie about there being a bomb aboard the saucer. In the time we had available, I could not arrive at a more honest solution to prevent the violence planned by the Tictoctickians.*

"And believe me again, Mafoosoola, none of us are taking your reservations for granted, over what us Earthlings have brought to bear in your neck of the galactic woods."

*It must be reiterated, about the deployment of the laser mesh around Oomb, with its brief but impressive light display it gave off upon its activation. Without that display, the Tictoctickians might never have had their attention drawn here for an invasion.*

"I harbor my own questions about our militarization of space." Buddy sensed he was interrupting Mafoosoola's full completion of her latest telepath with this remark, as he also noted with satisfaction the first two mini-saucers exiting the underbelly of the stationary mother ship. "But at the same time, you have to wonder: Just how ARE we to deal with such an apparently advanced civilization, set on making extraterrestrial intelligences part of its food supply?"

*Without the distraction of the attack on our planet, you would have had more opportunity to explore, to investigate what is driving those creatures to their behavior. Perhaps you could have searched for clues, on one of your excursions through a space-time rift like you used to rescue us.*

"An interesting thought, Mafoosoola," but Buddy's attention was actually more drawn to a faint, yet far-from-illusory, blue light emitting from the giant saucer's underside, and bathing the space shuttle.

*Incidentally, Officer Leung, that blue light you are pondering is a tractor beam. The saucer captain has it timed to draw us inside the saucer at the same time he believes the saucer is going to get blown apart.*

"Okay, that makes sense; we ARE experiencing a tug towards their space craft. I better fire our hydrogen fuel retros to put on the appearance we're anxious to resist getting pulled in. But great; they're making it easier for us to assume control of that intriguing contraption!"

***

"Excellent!" crisply tongue-clicked Captain Mat-kek-tek at the control helm of the mini-saucer into which he'd evacuated from the Third Celestial Breath. Officer Tak-venk-tit seated beside him was the one actually handling the small space vehicle's operation. "You see those blue flares tinged with orange out the back of their ship? They are fighting the pull of the tractor beam, but their effort is proving useless! The only unfortunate thing is that there will be less of the alien fuel left to enhance the alien spacecraft's incineration once the saucer is exploded! Baa!!" he brayed with satisfaction, despite the "unfortunate thing."

"We are blind when compared to your powers of observation, Captain Mat-kek-tek," ritually chanted the officers seated behind the captain and Officer Tak-venk-tit, after they unbuckled their restraints to rise standing onto their hind hooves. Those officers were swept up in their preoccupation with making proper obeisance to the captain, not allowing too much time to elapse before latching onto an excuse to offer more praise. They were so swept up, in fact, they momentarily neglected to attend to the fact they were presently experiencing a weightless environment. Immediately upon completion of their obligatory linking of praise for the captain to their own self-denigration, they became a confusion of klunking-together antlers and other various body-body, body-ceiling and body-chair collisions, as they scrambled to re-fasten their seat restraints.

Captain Mat-kek-tek raised a hoof hand meant to humbly stave off further approbation, for him to tongue-click something else. He was totally oblivious to the fact that the noise continuing to issue from behind him and Officer Tak-venk-tit was zero-gravity-induced chaos rather than a commotion of unbridled enthusiasm over his visual acumen. "Long would we want to linger, to ruminate joyfully over the destruction of the aliens who would destroy us!" Mat-kek-tek brayed to be heard above the noisy ruckus. "We might even desire to pick through their remains, on the chance of collecting some most-tastily-charred morsels of their flesh. However, prudence inspired by the mighty Dek-Fook-Tek guides us to depart this region with all due haste. Yes! We have detected two military spacecraft of the alien forces, in orbit around Oomb. It will be for our full-sized battle saucers, with their magnetic pulse beams, to obliterate them; we are not presently equipped in our evacuation capsules to provide any more than a minor nuisance for those craft. They would succeed in downing us with whatever weapons they have available, even though we can be certain those weapons are inferior and puny, not much better than children's play-things, compared to the mighty armaments of Tictoctic!"

"Your caution makes of us meteors dumbly hurling ourselves burning to cinders, down through the nearest available atmosphere," the other officers all solemnly baaed in unison. Although, they had enough sense this time to keep their seat belts fastened, not to try to stand.

"So, we are returning to Tictoctic?" Officer Tak-venk-tit baaed as quietly as he could to the captain. He didn't want the others to overhear, especially for what he was going to advise if not receiving the answer he was looking for.

"A return to Tictoctic would be suicidal for us," Captain Mat-kek-tek responded just as softly. "An honor to be gored personally on the antlers of Dek-Fook-Tek, once he learns what happened, that is an honor we should want to avoid."

Officer Tak-venk-tit brayed relief. Then, resuming his quiet baas, he said, "So what should I make our course heading? I would initiate more group praise for your wisdom. However, the self-preservation instinct of many of our underlings is about as well-developed as it is for that insect back on our planet that can't tell the difference between a red-hot lava flow, and a bioluminescently red-glowing female in heat. They would be appalled to be made a part of deserting the empire, and would probably even contemplate mutiny to assure we returned for an audience with Dek-Fook-Tek."

"I can hear that my wisdom has infected you well, Officer Tak-venk-tit. That is tribute enough. As for our course heading: Out there, somewhere, until we find a habitable planet not overrun already with a weapon-bearing species. We will make ourselves the new apex predators."

"But mates for propagating…?"

"You haven't noticed Jek-lek, Blik-Lik-Tlik, and Pik-Kil-Nik?, how their uniforms are always kept on in public presence?, even when offering their chests for a wounding impalement should I consider that necessary? I have spied on them in their off-duty stables to confirm the rumors' truth: females have disguised themselves to join the officer ranks. I made certain they evacuated to aboard this pod."

It was all Tak-venk-tit could do to suppress a whinny as he once more baaed under his breath, "I was thinking that being away from home for so long was what made me feel like jumping Pik-Kil-Nik. So, I am not developing an impalement-worthy attraction to our own sex after all! But one other thing: The food provisions aboard this pod would barely suffice to get us back to TicTocTic. Assuming travel to a new habitable world is going to take us that much longer, how are we going to make those provisions last---Ahh, very good, Captain." Officer Tak-venk-tit was gaining a whole new appreciation for his superior.

Captain Mat-kek-tek twisted around his antlered head, to take in the view of a sample officer. When he returned his attention to Tak-venk-tit, he made a production out of licking his chops with his eyes straying back towards said sample officer.

"They don't need to know we're not returning to Tictoctic," explained Captain Mat-kek-tek. "The story will be how each one chosen for the honor we have in mind will be remembered for their sacrifice, in the cause of getting us to Dek-Fook-Tek with vital information about the enemy. For those not chosen, accolades will await them for volunteering to be consumed, even though that ended up not being necessary. And for anyone left once we find a new planet, I am sure they will be happy to start over our society under our direction. We can even share the females once we have had our turn propagating with them."

"Captain, the mini-saucers carrying the others, all appear to be on return course to Tictoctic." Officer Tak-venk-tit's attention was drawn to noticing this on the console monitor.

"Fools; lacking my superior guidance, they know no better than to set a course for their certain doom. No loss, especially where Kwit-Nik is concerned."

*But may our own mini-saucer operate smoothly for long enough for us to get wherever we are going; we should have pulled Kwit-Nik aboard in place of one of the females. He's the only one who really fully understands how these space vessels function, as arrogant and pompous as he can be about it.* This thought, Officer Tak-venk-tit decided, was best kept to himself. Anyhow, he just then realized another thing from the monitor display. "Captain, the detonation device countdown, as best as I can determine, must already have long since gone past zero. Yet we are still picking up a solid object where we abandoned the Third

Celestial Breath."

"It WAS a bluff!" Captain Mat-kek-tek baaed uncontrollably. Even more uncontrollably, he sought to charge his antlers into the navigation monitor console. Only Tak-venk-tit's rapid reflexes, deflecting them with his own albeit more stubby antlers, prevented damage. That damage would have been exactly of the sort that would have taken Kwit-Nik to work around, for restoring the console to full function.

"You knew it was a bluff all along, Captain," Officer Tak-venk-tit was subsequently quick to observe, to give more credit than he well realized was actually due. "You knew, even if we had waited out the bluff, the aliens would have resorted to further trickery. Yes! It would have been further trickery which might even have minimized their accomplishment of putting us into some sort of trance state so they could steal the experimental food supply right out from under our snouts. For all we know, Dek-Fook-Tek is biting off more than he can chew, going after these particular aliens for a renewed food supply. Let him; it is no longer our problem."

"I am gratified you have been able to follow my reasoning, Officer Tak-venk-tit. Again, no better tribute to my brilliance could you have corralled." Captain Mat-kek-tek had been encouraged for a long time, to deceive himself about his own mental prowess. Frequently, he had gotten the credit for the mental work of others. And so, he had no particular problem with Tak-venk-tit's latest flattery, and expressing appreciation to him for it.

***

"Officer Glork-tek," Kwit-Nik brayed at the head chef. Glork-tek was seated beside him, at the navigation panel console aboard the min-saucer into which they'd evacuated from the supposedly bomb-rigged saucer. "Captain Mat-kek-tek's scout craft is heading on a course bound far afield of Tictoctic, and it is ignoring our every effort at communication; the only one to do so."

"No wonder. I doubt the captain and his anus-licking apologist even realize what that flashing light on their console is telling them, Officer Kwit-Nik."

"Our plan is clear, then, Chef Glork-tek," said Kwit-Nik. "It is a plan that would have otherwise guaranteed our impalement, every one of us, upon Dek-Fook-Tek's longest, bahvek-sharpened horns, so far in that they pierced out our backs. But now, it will prove otherwise. We tell the Supreme Authority, we report to him what happened, including screen-shot evidence from this monitor. Then we ask, I ask for command of a saucer to go after the deserters. Doubtless, we will be temporarily detained in a prison slaughterhouse. Doubtless, Dek-Fook-Tek will await the captain's triumphant return for counter-proof no such alleged betrayal took place. The Supreme Authority will expect to be adding us to the food supply, your own career as chef literally grilled away. However, endless days will elapse with no sign of Captain Mat-kek-tek. At the last, advisers will try to convince Dek-Fook-Tek of the truth illustrated by those monitor screen-shots, the truth that the mini-saucer containing Captain Mat-kek-tek took a course heading to come nowhere near ever returning to Tictoctic. Assuming that for their trouble, those advisers won't get their selves gored out in one of Dek-Fook-Tek's demonic rages, we will be called back before his heavily-sedated presence."

"And soon enough, YOU will be made a saucer captain, to lead the development of a coalition which can eventually empower saner leadership at the top, maybe even your own." Chef Glork-tek accurately completed what Officer Kwit-Nik was going to say.

"Baa," Kwit-Nik nodded, though he was thinking, *Would that I would ever be able to return to Oomb, and learn more of how to play 'oof'... If only such a prospect were the least bit actually possible...*

***

"General Warlor, we have put out a translated hail on all available frequencies," reported Captain Entroper from aboard the Smoke and Mirrors. "We specified we are addressing the saucer-shaped UFO holding steady approximately two astronomical units out past Oomb. Of course, we identified Oomb as the fourth planet in this solar system, and also as the name given by its native intelligent species. For our all-frequency hail, we added that the hostilities experienced on Oomb originated from what was described as a giant flying saucer. We emphasized that if the UFO continues to fail to respond, we will have to assume hostile intent, and act accordingly. Still nothing."

For the last half of Entroper's update, Sandy Warlor aboard the Barack Obama waved her hand around in a circle, the nonverbal for "wrap it up." She grew impatient with Captain Entroper's unnecessarily detailed elaboration. "We've done the same, Captain," Sandy jumped in on Entroper's pause to catch her breath. "I suggest we repeat our respective transmissions. If that does not result in any kind of satisfactory response,-"

"You would want us to head out there while the Barack Obama maintains defense watch on the Oombian perimeter?"

Warlor made an exhale of exasperation over Entroper's presumption. "Actually, Captain, the Barack Obama is far better equipped to engage the enemy than the Smoke and Mirrors. And this looks to be as good an initial battlefield test as any, to see what she's made of."

*This is Mafoosoola aboard the saucer-shaped spacecraft from Tictoctic.* The Oombian's telepath suddenly yet gently, tentatively intruded on minds aboard both the Smoke and Mirrors and the Barack Obama. *Officer Buddy Leung and I have managed to trick the creatures from Tictoctic into fleeing their vessel. We are presently endeavoring to understand how to operate it, between Buddy's expertise and my mind-reading of the Tictoctic officers before their distance from us exceeds my telepathic reach.*

"Officer Park-Smith, do we have any firefly donut evidence for smaller UFOs having recently left the unidentified saucer?"

"No we don't, Captain." Yoon-hee double-checked her monitor scan before responding. "But that doesn't necessarily mean anything. We weren't specifically scanning for that, and it was only twenty minutes ago we realized the UFO was out there in the first place. Not to belabor the obvious, Captain, but we WERE just returning from Fafama."

"Yes, I know, Yoon-hee," Entroper reacted gruffly. "We were returning from allowing the Fafamafalafama to kick us out of his neck of the woods…temporarily." She added this qualification for the chair of the Joint Chiefs of Staff to overhear aboard the battleship Obama. "What do you think, Sandy? How can we be sure that foodle-boodle creature is not telepathing under duress?, under threat of getting converted to campfire wood otherwise?"

*Officer Leung thought I better telepath this now instead of waiting for our successfully getting this saucer under our navigational control. He figured, as I am discovering from mind-reading you, that your distrust would mount precipitously the longer we went without any response to your hailing efforts. The simple fact of the matter is that our preoccupation with the saucer's basic operation has distracted us from trying to open any hailing frequencies.*

"Tree creature from Oomb, I'm not even going to attempt to say your name." On the navigation bridge of the Barack Obama, the chair of the Joint Chiefs of Staff, General Sandy Warlor, held up the palm of her left hand facing out. She was fending off any further telepathing from Mafoosoola. "I am stepping in here to observe something. So far, the only evidence we have to go on, to back up your story, is your own telepathic messaging. How are we to know this isn't some kind of trap where you are being coerced to feed us misinformation?"

***

"Officer Leung," Pedro stumbled forward, nearly falling flat on his face from his hurried re-emergence onto the saucer navigation bridge, "I have been following the telepathing of Mafoosoola while I searched for a bathroom. Three things: Thing one, I think those starship captains will have a hard time trusting the thoughts in their heads, trusting that those thoughts come from the tree people of Oomb. They will believe this is a deception somehow produced by the creatures of Tictoctic who were controlling this flying saucer originally. Thing two, some of you Marines could accompany me into the space shuttle, where the tractor beam pulled it up into the belly of the saucer. I have learned how to operate the shuttle's communication console, from a manual I read while the Smoke and Mirrors was transporting me and my family to a new life on Oomb. I could transmit to the starship captains in the more conventional manner, that would include a visual of myself and the Marines who accompany me. And thing three, I will want to use the toilet facilities aboard the shuttle, because I have not been able to understand the bathroom we discovered on this saucer."

"Perez is correct, Officer Leung," chimed in Marine Officer Robertson. "Hell, we're not even sure what we discovered IS a f-in' dump zone!"

"Sorry I went looking without permission, Officer Leung," Pedro added shame-facedly, "but I didn't want to distract you and Mafoosoola. And, and I can wait on the bathroom until I complete the transmission and convince the captains this is no deception."

"I knew there must be a reason I rescued you, Mr. Perez."

***

*Please, if you can be patient for but a few minutes longer, Captain Entroper and General Warlor. Mr. Pedro Perez is an infrastructure engineer who Officer Leung rescued from the Tictoctickians. Mr. Perez is preparing to send you audible and visual assurance of our circumstances here.*

***

"Excuse my speaking before I receive permission from you in your capacity as captain, General Warlor." True to his word, Secretary Spinner did not wait for acknowledgement after he raised his hand. "But, that sounds like the few minutes those bloodthirsty Tictoctic aliens require to charge up who-knows-what infernal contraption they have to vaporize us from one hundred eighty-six million miles away! If ever there was a time to set Dr. Wang loose to try out one of her toys, I respectfully submit that this is it!"

***

"Permission to address General Warlor, Captain." Yoon-hee aboard the Smoke and Mirrors was getting increasingly nervous, seeing on her navigation console that the battleship Barack Obama was swinging around for a conventional rocket boost out of Oombian orbit. She had already gotten plenty jittery enough, thanks to Spinner's remark about Dr. Wang's "toys," in addition to her intuition the situation aboard the saucer was exactly as Mafoosoola was describing it, not a deception.

"Well, Officer Park-Smith, I say we leave that decision up to General Warlor." Captain Entroper raised her voice. "You heard what my navigation officer requested, General? Do you have time for her?" Entroper was talking to Warlor as she appeared in the video feed the Smoke and Mirrors was receiving from the navigation deck of the Barack Obama. That feed was presently filling the panoramic view-screen of the navigation deck aboard the Smoke and Mirrors.

"Speak your peace, Officer." Warlor held a hand Spinner's way, nonverbally insisting on patience.

"General Warlor," Yoon-hee stood up beside her console but held on tightly in the weightless environment of orbit around Oomb, "whatever the Oombian aboard the saucer was telepathing to us, the creatures from Tictoctic could not know it was not what they wanted her to telepath. That is, if the Oombian decided not to share it with them. The Oombians have the power to simultaneously telepath us one thing while they telepath the Tictoctickians something else, pretending that is what they were actually telepathing us. IF the creatures from

Tictoctic were still aboard the saucer of concern, and they were holding our people and some Oombians hostage, I cannot imagine Mafoosoola would not have shared that with us. She would even have telepathed us how to react so the Tictoctickians would mistakenly believe she had followed their orders. And please, only one other thing: Before you commit to any specific action, certainly you can spare an extra minute or two, to see whether we receive a video feed from the infrastructure engineer that Mafoosoola mentioned."

"I'm not sure what this notorious infrastructure engineer's video will prove if the enemy is choreographing his every word from off-camera."

"But General Warlor, you were complaining of only having telepathic-"

"Officer Park-Smith, you are interrupting the chair of the Joint Chiefs of Staff, now provisional captain of the Barack Obama! Sit down!"

"That's alright, Louisa." Warlor's face filled the center of the view-screen aboard the Smoke and Mirrors as she moved closer to the stationary camcorder aboard the Barack Obama. "This unprecedented situation is not exactly bringing out the best in any of us, though you have to understand, Officer Park-Smith is it?" Warlor was cribbing from an identification readout Secretary Spinner caused to appear as a caption under Yoon-hee's face on the video feed from the Smoke and Mirrors.

"Affirmative, General Captain Warlor."

"Good. Well, you have to understand, Officer Park-Smith, nothing will get accomplished by allowing your strong feelings to so own you that you are running haphazardly roughshod over the most basic protocol. Now what I was about to add were two items, actually. The first item is that you might have a point where the telepathing tree creature is concerned, if you have understood its abilities correctly."

Mafoosoola wanted desperately to telepath that Yoon-hee had understood her abilities perfectly correctly. But the Oombian tree creature sensed she would precipitate more talk about "running haphazardly roughshod over the most basic protocol." Worse, such a telepath might lead Warlor to incorrectly wonder whether she, Mafoosoola, had teamed up with the Tictoctickians in the hope of ridding Oomb of both the nuisance Earthlings and the aliens who wanted to eat them.

"Item two: We are fine, waiting the minute or so more for a video feed from the saucer. But certainly, you can understand that while we accede to that request, we are wanting to reposition ourselves. A moving target is usually far more difficult to strike than a stationary one, or a target in a predictable orbit around a planet. And Captain Entroper, I hereby strongly urge you to follow suit with the Smoke and Mirrors."

"Understood, General. You've got that, Officer Kevin Smith-Park?" Entroper swiveled around in her captain's chair to face Kevin directly.

"In five minutes, Captain, we'll be on the far side of Oomb. If the bad guys ARE still commandeering that saucer, they won't have a clear shot at us." As he reported this, Kevin feigned too much preoccupation with maneuver details to look up and make eye contact with Captain Entroper. Otherwise, he feared the temptation might prove too great to burst out, *Seriously?? You're sweating out the possibility of an attack from that far away?! You've got to be friggin' kidding me!* Or at the least, to pun over how appropriate to speak of commandeering with the antlered Tictoctic creatures in the picture.

"Let's hope five minutes will be soon enough,

Officer."

Kevin couldn't help a head shake in disbelief, as his wife Yoon-hee said, "Permission to speak, Captain?"

"That's more like it, Officer Yoon-hee Park-Smith." Entroper nodded most animatedly. "Okay, permission granted."

"So Captain Entroper, General Captain Warlor," said Yoon-hee, "you both really are that concerned the saucer could fire something at us from one hundred eighty-six million miles away?, some kind of ultimate 'spooky action at a distance'?"

"Dr. Wang, would you like to field that question?" General Warlor had weapons specialist Dr. Magdalena "Maggy" Wang step into stationary cam range.

"I would, General Warlor. Officer Park-Smith, my short answer to your question is yes, I really am THAT concerned. Our own technology is now to such a point, thanks to Dr. Leung's pioneering work. We can deliver a small nuclear payload to a destination two hundred million miles away in a minute and twenty seconds, approximately. The problem is targeting across so much space abounding with so many variables such as solar winds, bits of dark matter and hypothesized nascent wormholes, not to mention whatever tiniest micro-millimeter off our aiming mechanism comes to be. The unfortunate consequence is that a destination cannot be specified any more precisely than as somewhere within a seven-hundred-thirty-thousand-mile radius. In other words, were we aiming at an Earth-sized planet at this distance, the odds are excellent we'd miss it. But here's the deal where we can't presume, simply because WE haven't solved the targeting problem yet, nobody else has, either. I've devised an experimental protocol. Not the final solution, even if it pans out, but progress nevertheless. In other words, if we're able to steadily edge closer to that kind of an accomplishment, imagine what a civilization might be able to do that was, for example, a century older than ours. You do know, don't you, the star Tictoctic orbits is millions of years the senior of our-"

"Captain, we're receiving an incoming video transmission off a firefly relay."

"Post it split-screen for us, and forward to the Obama, Officer Park-Smith." Captain Entroper rubbed her hands together. "Let's see what we've got, General Warlor."

"This is Pedro Perez, um, managing infrastructure engineer for the Oombinquen settlement on Oomb. I am transmitting to you from a shuttle vehicle that was pulled into a spaceship from Tictoctic by a tractor beam. Officer Leung is busy working with an Oombian. They are trying to understand how to control the saucer ship. They don't know yet how to use its communications system, so he asked me to transmit from the shuttle to you, because the Oombian mind-read your suspicions and impatience. Um," Pedro shook his head to further clear it, "before I continue, can you confirm you are receiving this transmission on the Smoke and Mirrors? And, um, Mafoosoola is telepathing me there is also a warship?"

Two simultaneous video returns resulted in a split-screen display on the shuttle pod's video monitor, where Pedro was watching. One came from the Barack Obama, the other from the Smoke and Mirrors. The outer space view from the shuttle's present location shrank down to an eighteen-inch screen in the lower right-hand corner. These changes followed the expected half-minute delay. A phenomenally fast turnover time, Pedro had to shake his head in wonderment, even though he was still a little groggy from reanimating in a space-time shift like when he first woke up aboard the Smoke and

Mirrors.

"This is Captain Louisa Entroper of the Smoke and Mirrors, confirming."

"And this is General Sandy Warlor, chair of the Joint Chiefs of Staff, and presently acting captain of the Barack Obama, also confirming. I'm guessing the Obama is what your Oombian termed a 'warship,' what I would term a force for eventual peace. Before you continue, Mr. Perez, there has been a concern expressed. The saucer craft, what you say netted your shuttle pod with a tractor beam, from our perspective we can't be sure it isn't still in hostile hands. This means we must attach low credibility to the accuracy of any message we receive from you and the Oombian."

While Warlor awaited the response, she typed an order on her electronic memo pad for her first navigation officer. She thought maybe she could somehow avoid the Oombian mind-read if she avoided voicing it aloud. What she typed was, *Bloom into one-eighth light-speed on a careening trajectory; the closer we can get...*

"Acting Captain Warlor," at last responded Pedro, "Mafoosoola wants me to say that Officer Park-Smith's point is completely accurate, and speaks directly to your expressed concern. If the deer people of Tictoctic were still in control of this ship, this would not have stopped Mafoosoola from telepathing you an alert. The deer people's psychic powers are no more developed than ours, she assures me. So they would not have been able to intercept that telepath in whatever manner."

"Can I?" One of the Marine Corps officers leaned into view beside Pedro.

"Por favor, please."

"Captain Entroper, acting Captain Warlor, this is Officer Kenny Robertson of the American Union Marine

Corps. I hope you will understand my waiving protocol to save us on the thirty-second delay, as I understand that on your end, you're feeling time is of the essence. Let me make this camcorder my body cam, so we can go anywhere you like aboard the hostile's abandoned warship." Seconds later, Robertson resumed, "See? Nobody outside the gangway into the shuttle. You think they're playing hide-and-seek? Give us a minute and we'll arrive to their navigation bridge. On the way, I just want to make certain you understand something: Officer Leung is a HERO. Got that? A HERO! One moment, we were strung up and drugged out, but still conscious enough to know we were getting dragged along a treadmill like f-in' CATTLE to slaughter! Then the next moment, we're waking up safely strapped into seats aboard the shuttle, and Leung is running this f-in' brilliant plan. He's conning the hostiles into believing we left an explosive device on board, so they all head for their lifeboats and are outta here like that!" Robertson snapped his fingers. "We could even go back to the slaughterhouse where Leung left the decoy; it's probably still harmlessly ticking away in negative post-countdown."

*There was no need to worry over what the traumatized beings from Tictoctic could have done to you from this distance, at any rate.* Mafoosoola telepathed her assurance to Robertson as well as to Entroper and Warlor. *Yes, they do have a magnetic pulse beam capable of impressive destruction when the target is within five thousand miles. And they were discussing coming after you with it before we tricked them into harmlessly abandoning their saucer craft. However, I mind-read no slightest thought of their having even started to develop hyper-speed, long-distance weapons delivery systems, like you have.*

By this time, Robertson's body cam tour had reached the saucer navigation bridge. Buddy Leung was pausing from his labors over the navigation control panel, to look up and wave hello. Mafoosoola was rustling what few leaves had popped back out on her drastically pruned-back branches, to non-telepathically offer greeting. Buddy would have proceeded to tell the Oombian he had just made a breakthrough in understanding the control panel logic. However, he didn't want to be overheard by Entroper or Warlor. So he focused his thoughts as best he could on silently calling Mafoosoola's attention to what he was accomplishing, and to the importance of stalling for more time from the starship captains. Whatever it was that Entroper and Warlor were up to, Buddy felt certain they were up to something.

It worked.

*You sensed correctly, Officer Leung; they are definitely up to something, something of potential peril where we are concerned,* telepathed Mafoosoola. *But I am also mind-reading that provisional Captain Warlor is about to clear the way for someone alongside her to engage me in a dialogue which offers a rich opportunity for delay.*

***

"The Oombian who is so wonderfully adept at telepathy, General Warlor, permission to attempt an understanding with, uh, this being," Dr. Magdalena "Maggy" Wang requested, sure enough.

"Permission GRANTED, Dr. Wang." Warlor was emphatic.

"Oombian, uh, what is your name again?"

*Mafoosoola.*

"Uh, yes, Mafoosoola." Wang had to laugh. "I want

to make sure you understand something. I abhor violence. I hate war. I have seen what it does to friends I made and their families in parts of the, well, they might not mean anything to you, various locations on our planet Earth. I abhor violence so much and my husband does too; he makes sure that when I am not around, our two sons and daughter do not play any violent video games, or download any violent movies for our home movie screen. This is why I do the work I do. People, groups, in this case an extraterrestrial civilization, they develop a bomb, I develop a bigger bomb, so much bigger they will give up war. This magnetic pulse beam of which you telepathed, I am excited to study it so I can develop a more awesome pulse beam than theirs. This is how we will persuade them ultimately to leave alone other creatures on other planets. Then maybe we can, I don't know," she giggled, "turn this battleship into a training facility for people to learn how to play your 'oof,' and for you to learn how to play our 'golf.' But, until that happy day arrives, when we no longer need to worry about threats from space nor groups still set on violence back on Earth... I think it's wonderful how you were able to establish peace all over Oomb so early in your civilization's history, Mafoosoola. But you have to understand how unique that is to your own very special set of circumstances."

Secretary Spinner was nodding emphatically in the background, from what Pedro could see on the shuttle monitor.

"The more pervasive reality," Wang went on, "is what the rest of us have to face. If we don't face it, you got just a small taste of how it is also going to come crashing down on you."

*Dr. Wang, those video games and movies you and*

*your husband don't permit your children to experience, do I understand correctly the violence in them is simulated, and not actually happening? Nor are they records of events which have ever really occurred?*

"Children are very impressionable; they tend to imitate what they see. You have to understand that."

Spinner shook his head; he wondered why Wang bothered wasting her breath trying to explain.

*So, your sons and daughter would not know the violence in video games and movies is not really happening?*

"They're old enough; of course they would know! What's your point?"

*I just consider it odd you find simulations of violence threatening to your family, more threatening than your own development of weapons and weapons delivery systems that, if used, could wreak actual violence on sentient beings within their target range.*

"I'm not planning on using them on my family!" Wang's mouth stayed hung open in uncomprehending disbelief.

*And your progeny are not aware of what you do for a living, so you needn't worry that, as you said, they would tend to imitate?*

Dr. Wang felt herself wanting to bore holes through Mafoosoola's trunk with her eyes. What especially riled her was how she saw the tree creature behaving on the battleship's navigation deck split-screen monitor. She, it, whatever was still remaining turned away from MacKenzie's body cam brought up to the bridge of the hostile's saucer from the tractor-beamed shuttle craft. So, this Oombian was really so preoccupied with helping Officer Leung understand how to fly that thing, it couldn't spare her the minimum courtesy of facing the body cam to insult her to her face? "Out of my head. No more telepathing. Captain Warlor, permission please for me to insist Officer Leung break from what he is doing, to be addressed on the need for our prototype test."

"Dr. Wang, you have my full support. Go for it."

"Excuse me, Captain Warlor," broke in Entroper. "I'm not sure exactly what the protocol is, here..."

"I'm not sure either, as one provisional captain to another, so go ahead."

"What was your name again?, you with the body cam? Robertson?" After seconds went by with no response, Captain Entroper asked Yoon-hee, "Officer Park-Smith, do we have a two-way audio hookup with that body cam?"

"For both the Smoke and Mirrors and the Barack Obama, Captain. I think we've got incoming-"

"Pedro Perez, Captain." Pedro turned the body cam to film himself. "Is there something else we can do for assuring you the creatures of Tictoctic are departed from this spaceship, and Officer Leung is in charge?"

"No." Captain Entroper's voice went up a half octave from the 'N' to the 'o.' "And Officer Leung is NOT in charge." She shook her head vigorously. "*I* am in charge. And I need Officer Leung to pause from his obsession, to talk about that. Officer Leung, if need be, we can tow the hostile's craft into Oombian orbit and put a dozen engineers at your disposal to crack its navigation code. But for now, as your captain, I am commanding you to turn and face the body cam, to show some respect when Dr. Wang aboard the Barack Obama is addressing you."

Buddy Leung was already standing away from the saucer's navigation console, to give Entroper and whoever else his undivided attention. Meanwhile, however, Mafoosoola joined by the other Oombian Leung had rescued from getting turned into so much firewood, Flookle-Dookle, continued to labor over gaining operational control of the Tictoctickian spacecraft. Flookle-Dookle had high hopes they could build on Buddy's progress, to get the alien saucer up and running.

"Believe me, Officer Leung, I am in awe of what you have accomplished for Mr. Perez and the others there. But I need you to hear out Dr. Wang."

"I'm listening, Captain."

"Make that TWO of us in awe of your achievements, Officer Leung." Maggy Wang went down some steps to get closer to the video feed of Buddy Leung. "You are making it possible for us to test the bad guys' warship for vulnerabilities, as well as to test a scheme for projecting our offensive capabilities to previously unheard-of distances in a previously unheard-of short time."

*Attention to me please, Officer Leung. Oodle-Noodle has telepathed me that Helena Taylor, her husband, and three other of your crew members had to be left behind on Fafama. This was due to Fafaman distrust stemming from a terrorist attack in the wake of your fellow officers' diplomatic initiative.*

Buddy Leung struggled to attend to Mafoosoola's telepath at the same time he followed Dr. Wang's continuing address.

"So you can appreciate what we are about to attempt, Officer Leung?"

"Wait a minute." Buddy shook his head as the import of what Wang was proposing sank in fully.

For Kevin watching from aboard the Smoke and Mirrors, the look on Buddy Leung's face had him wondering, *What the hell is going on with Buddy? Is all that time travel turning his brain to mush?*

"You're talking about testing out a light-speed laser cannon delivery system on this saucer while we're still stuck inside it?!" the hyper-physics engineer exclaimed in horrified wonder, finally.

"We're talking about a minimal amplitude burst aimed at the warship's underbelly. From what we know, sifting through the data on the Tictoctickian warship's operational deployment in the Oombian atmosphere, the worst that should happen is its landing gear and airlocks getting compromised. All that you and those you rescued have to do is close off those areas so your life support stays secured. Or, you could take the shuttle a safe distance away from the hostile's craft, and wait out the field test there."

"A no-go on either of those options, Dr. Wang." Buddy closed his eyes as he shook his head. "We have no idea how to secure life support against the exigency you are proposing to inflict, and we have no idea how to have the shuttle leave from the docking bay to where we got tractor-beamed."

"Then you're looking at a calculated risk margin of between four and eleven per cent."

*Officer Leung, Oodle-Noodle telepaths that the Smoke and Mirrors has been ordered not to approach anywhere near the outermost limits of Fafama's location detectable by the Fafamans. The Fafamafalafama has threatened to kill Helena Taylor and the rest of her away team, were the starship to return to even that distance from his planet before he officially tosses us a message in a hi-tech bottle, officially granting his permission. Everything I am telepathing you, Oodle-Noodle had to learn by mindreading Captain Entroper, as my fellow Oombian was not allowed to go on the return voyage to Fafama for launching an ice comet into its orbit.*

*Yet, maybe we COULD approach far closer in this saucer vehicle, and have a better chance at helping out my fellow Earthlings.* Buddy did his best to fill his head with this notion for Mafoosoola's mind-reading pleasure. Buddy also tried simultaneously to attend to Dr. Wang when she went on, "I would think that is an acceptable risk margin for you, Officer Leung, given what the result will contribute to our knowledge of hyper-range defense-projection capability, and given also the unknown risk that another warship from Tictoctic could be on its way to reclaim their hijacked craft. A compromised vessel should prove far more difficult for the hostiles to regain control of, before we can come to your aid, than one with all its systems still completely intact."

"Dr. Wang," responded Buddy Leung, "Mafoosoola managed to mind-read that one of the saucer's mini-saucers is headed for parts unknown. Its crew is searching for a new planet to live out their days. They fear what the Tictoctic leadership might do to them if they return home, for losing one of their premiere spacecraft. The other four mini-saucers are headed up by someone who might try to incite a rebellion. The risk is looking impressively low the Tictoctickian leaders are going to learn what happened before we can get this thing up and running."

*Officer Leung, they are proceeding with their trial hyper-range weapon launch. Shall I take us out of here the instant I've successfully completed execution of your navigation control strategy?*

*They're crazy. Dr. Wang has a toy she can't wait to play with.* These thoughts came effortlessly to Buddy's mind, and he added, *You've got my blessing, Mafoosoola; go for it!, before they get us all killed!*

"Officer Leung, you will understand in the long run why we had to do this. You all need to strap yourselves in while you've still got time."

While Dr. Wang was delivering this stern declaration, the egg-shaped pod containing the hyper-range weapon experimental package was drifting out from behind the shadow cast by the Barack Obama, out into full sunlight. Within seconds, photovoltaic activation caused the four quarters of what Dr. Wang had indeed nicknamed the eggshell to crack open. Those four quarters pushed out from the center on four struts, thus revealing the weapon-bearing rocket. Only, unlike with conventional rockets, the payload was strapped to its side, not packed into its nose cone. And in the place of said nose cone and rocket-fuel exhaust pipes were the rose- and tulip-petal mirror arrays. They were brought to full electromagnetic charge at the same time they were brought to full bloom. The next thing observers aboard the battleship Barack Obama knew, there was a beam of sparkly light running directly through the rocket's photon evacuation tube, and out both ends. That sparkly beam appeared as instantly as had the switch been flipped "on" of a flashlight. And then it was as though the rocket and payload both had vanished, said sparkly beam as well. Although, observers got left with the vague impression the entire package had gone out of sight in a direction opposite from Oomb's sun.

By this time, Buddy Leung was turned away from Pedro. He was rejoining Mafoosoola and Flookle-Dookle in efforts to get the saucer operational, heedless of what Entroper and Warlor wanted. Pedro had already turned off the body cam and clipped it to his shirt pocket; he was anxious to see whether he could be of any assistance understanding the saucer's navigation console.

The five Marines didn't need to be told to strap

themselves in, minimize distraction for the Oombians, Buddy and Pedro. But Officer "Skip" Jones couldn't help harshly whispering, "What the f' with these f-in' seats? I'm already getting a serious wedgie!"

"These SOBs from Tictoctic, their bodies are built differently from ours. Deal with it, Jones!" spat out Robertson. "What I don't like is that we're sittin' ducks unless our miracle workers can spin this Frisbee outta here! Though I suppose it makes some sense if what that Dr. Wang learns, playin' long range whack-a-mole with us, allows them to blow apart the next one of these bad boys that comes a-callin'!"

Vroommmm! A faint yet shrill whir seemed to throb through his whole body, Pedro thought, when Buddy pulled back on a chrome-plated handle on the alien spacecraft's control console. It felt not unlike a minor electrical shock. But then it was gone, as the handle returned to its original position. Buddy tried again. This time, he kept the handle pulled back, with the same result.

"So close," Buddy Leung shook his head, muttering aloud, while only some ten thousand miles away, the rocket carrying the laser cannon piggyback was decelerating out of hyper-speed, engulfed by clouds of twinkling photons that had temporarily "chosen" their physical over their wavelength identity. It was like a flounder kicking up clouds of sand as it lifted off the sea bottom, one of the Earthlings might have thought had the saucer's view-screen been activated. "I think we've got everything else up and running, Mafoosoola," Leung continued. "It's just whatever this thing does electromagnetically to zero out the inertial drag. It would be our luck for it to have broken down!"

"Officer Leung! Let me try!" Pedro's eyes opened

Fafaman-nocturnally wide, so Buddy thought.

"It's all yours, Officer Perez." Leung stepped aside and made a sweeping gesture towards the chrome handle.

Pedro literally jumped forward with his excitement, forgetting they were temporarily dealing with a zero-gravity environment. Only Buddy and Flookle-Dookle's quick reflexes prevented him from bumping his head against the ceiling.

No matter. Soon as Pedro's traction boots latched securely back onto the corrugated navigation deck floor, he eagerly pulled back on the chrome handle again. Only he didn't stop there. He immediately pushed it forward, then pulled it back again, then pushed it forward again, back and forth until it felt to him like it had slipped off a gear and was floating disconnected.

During this time, the laser cannon was fired from where it was attached piggyback to the hyper-speed rocket. A fiery red ball was sent hurtling towards the saucer.

"Of course!" Buddy slapped his hand against his forehead as a distinct throb coursing through his body became disconnected, became removed to a distant-sounding hum. "This is like cranking up an ancient Model T!"

"Then what is happening now?"

"No time to explain, Pedro." Buddy Leung was playing his fingers across the console keyboard with the rapidity of a concert pianist, so Pedro Perez thought. Finally, Buddy froze. He had his right forefinger crooked poised, ready to pounce, hovering above a square green button somewhat larger than the rest, and engraved with lettering from a Tictoctic language. His eyes hopped anxiously back and forth between two different screen displays. "Now," he said as at last, he pressed down firmly on said green button, and maintained pressure until it caught hold, stayed down on its own. With a slight, unexpected jolt,

"Does that mean we're on our way?" Robertson asked as he moved about uncomfortably in his seat designed more to suit the rear ends of the deer-like creatures of Tictoctic.

"I think so," said Buddy, back to playing his fingers across the navigation console. "We seem to be acquiring what I'm guesstimating is at least one quarter of Earth gravitational pull. And we haven't gotten rocked by a laser cannon burst unless that jolt was a glancing blow, though I don't think so. We'll know for sure once we get the view-screen and other monitoring systems online."

What the Earthlings and Oombians could not know was that Buddy had the saucer spinning off and away at the last possible second, before the laser cannon would have burst to catastrophic effect against its upper half. The fiery red laser ball could not make a sharp enough nor fast enough turn to keep pursuing the intended target. It ended up homing in on a one-mile-wide asteroid along the outer fringe of the asteroid belt where Buddy had hidden out in the shuttle earlier. It blew off boulder-sized chunks with a silent, yellowish-orange flash.

"There we go!" Buddy exclaimed excitedly as the view-screen finally lit up, thanks to Flookle-Dookle's efforts. "Wow!"

Back when Buddy was aboard the Smoke and Mirrors as it achieved light-speed multiples, he was used to the view-screen revealing all starlight ahead of the spaceship blending, converging together into a single, mysteriously twinkling light stream headed into and through the photon exhaust chamber. Presently, however, the saucer's view-screen revealed a quite different spectacle. Multiple convergencies were tapering into irregular, jagged light beams like lightning bolts. Those lightning bolt likenesses were wiggling, dancing constantly from side to side. Buddy Leung presumed their tips were somehow interacting with the saucer. Of course, such interaction proved unobservable through the video monitor, any more than the photon stream could be viewed actually entering into the photon exhaust chamber from the Smoke and Mirrors monitor. Buddy fancied that if the saucer could be viewed by an observer flying parallel, those lightning bolt semblances interacting with it would have looked not unlike electrical discharges emanating from a Van de Graff generator. *The same basic principle as for the Smoke and Mirrors: Light is used to push the saucer along, but applied to have this spacecraft's outer shell spin like a top! Wow!*

The saucer experienced a far more significant jolt, which knocked Buddy off his feet, and caused Mafoosoola to collide with Flookle-Dookle with a loud klunk! Bark chips sprayed off from both tree creatures.

*Officer Leung, if I am understanding this readout correctly, whatever we just experienced has sent this craft traversing a light year in less than a minute,* telepathed Mafoosoola. *We've already departed what you have named the Callaway X Centra system out the far end, in the direction of the Fafaman star system. I suggest we make the steepest ascent possible off the orbital plane before we can meet with a most horrendous fate by plowing into an asteroid or some such.*

"A wise precaution. I'm adjusting our trajectory now, Mafoosoola. However, at the speeds the outer shell is likely spinning, I'm not certain this contraption wouldn't buzz-saw through anything in its path like a hot knife through warm butter. But I repeat, Wow!" Buddy couldn't help chuckling over his amazement. "If I'm not mistaken, what caused that big bump in the road we just experienced was this saucer careening off some space-time irregularity, maybe even a wormhole. It was like a stone skipping across a pond, only we basically skipped across a solar system! This is beyond impressive what these determined carnivores from Tictoctic have invented. Though I suppose if they've been around a century or more longer than us, who knows what other marvels they might have engineered?"

*There was something I found especially curious when I rooted about the Tictoctickian minds for important information,* Mafoosoola telepathed to all the humans as Flookle-Dookle nodded along most knowingly. *The sense I intuited from their most experienced flight and navigation engineers was that they were not among those who originated this technology.*

"That IS curious, Mafoosoola, but we've got something to contend with maybe even curiouser. Look! Thar she blows!" Buddy pointed towards a circular, lavender-glowing object clearly visible in the center of the view-screen. It appeared motionless. Besides which, it was the only source of radiance that did not have a thin line of light extending from it, like an umbilical cord, to converge with one of the three, dancing lightning bolts.

"That object must be going at our speed. Aye Dios!" Pedro exclaimed as the UFO suddenly sped out of sight.

"Hmm," was Buddy's meager reaction. He recalled tracking a UFO early on in the maiden voyage of the Smoke and Mirrors.

***

"So the hostile's saucer craft simply vanished? Then

what did the laser cannon hit?"

"Captain, as best our long-range monitors can determine, the impact zone was an asteroid, probably a tag-along of the asteroid belt. Wait, we're picking up on a UFO nearly out the far side of the Callaway X Centra system!" Yoon-hee couldn't contain her gleeful relief. "It has the same spectrographic signature profile as the saucer craft!"

"Officer Park-Smith," Captain Entroper's tone of voice went lecturingly severe, "I'm sure that you, many of the crew here, are happy your Officer Leung and the people he rescued came out safe from Dr. Wang's hyper-distance missile-launch experiment." The several exhalations were not lost on the captain, however muted, suppressed, they were. "But you DO understand, don't you," Entroper went on huffily, "that Leung's actions to avoid possible injury constitute a clear act of insubordination? And that as a result of his going to such lengths to spare the saucer craft from any damage, we may have lost information crucial to our future efforts to defend ourselves from the Tictoctic threat? Not to mention how whatever he's up to now is delaying our opportunity to study the hostile's weapons capabilities?"

"Captain, if I might speak freely." Yoon-hee pushed herself to standing up from her navigation console. She tried to keep her focus on Entroper even though she could sense, on the half of the panoramic view-screen not displaying outer space, provisional Captain Warlor as well as Dr. Wang looking on most attentively. "I did not like the idea of targeting the saucer craft under these circumstances. Certainly a follow-up analysis of the laser cannon's asteroid impact will yield most of what you were after."

"Except for how the hostile's craft would have been

affected, Officer Park-Smith," Dr. Wang broke in. "If one or more other hostile saucers appear in Callaway X Centra space before we can have a closer look at the one presumably under our control, there will be critical uncertainty how to deal with them."

"Thank you, Dr. Wang," Entroper nodded approvingly, then back to Yoon-hee, "So Officer Park-Smith, you're saying you would have done the same thing as Officer Leung, in his shoes?"

"Umm, I'm more inclined to just follow orders. All I'm saying is that I understand why he did what he did."

"'just' follow orders." For once, Captain Entroper nodded rather than her usual side-to-side head shake. "Officer Park-Smith, you would be well advised to remain 'more inclined to just follow orders,' if you wish to avoid whatever consequences will unfortunately need to be meted out to Officer Leung."

The deafening silence that descended on the navigation bridge satisfied Entroper she'd gotten her message across. At the same time, though, she was left feeling that now that she'd laid down the law, she needed to backpedal a bit so she didn't lose her crew's support. Chief Medical Officer Davis-Murphy WAS nodding approvingly, but as for the rest... "Um, so Kevin, you think Officer Leung is headed back to Fafama?"

"He's got two Oombians on board, Captain. Maybe one of them mind-read why we got chased away from there. And now, Buddy is thinking he can get closer to the situation than we can, perhaps even pose as another extraterrestrial civilization answering their distress call on the late end." Kevin really, really wanted to tear into Captain Entroper, for her testy exchange with his wife, Yoon-hee. However, he stifled himself. And as for Buddy Leung, Kevin wasn't sure that he shouldn't come in for some criticism. They were essentially on a wartime footing, for a most unfortunately ground-breaking interplanetary war. Earth civilization might have been better prepared, were it not for all the starry-eyed dreaming that Buddy had seemed to buy into, about what to expect from space-faring civilizations. The Oombian philosophies weren't helping either, though with their telepathic powers, Kevin couldn't help adding, "Captain, would it make sense to bring along Oodle-Noodle for some added insight?"

"I appreciate the question, Officer Smith." Entroper was back to shaking her head in seeming negation, "but there are many things Oodle-Noodle does not appreciate."

"Understood, Captain," Kevin nodded most heartily.

"Yoon-hee Park-Smith, please set a course for the Alpha Centauri C star system, above the orbital and Oort Cloud planes."

"Aye, Captain."

"Captain Warlor, I trust you'll be patrolling the Callaway X Centra system and its environs for any further hostile activity. And I'm leaving you in charge of ground operations on Oomb."

"Got that, Captain. And good luck resolving matters with Officer Leung and the hostages on Fafama. We need a close look at that magnetic pulse beam weapon."

Dr. Wang could be seen nodding eagerly behind Warlor.

## Chapter 25

"Ahh, 'Cahhptahhn,' former 'Cahhptahhn,' you have reconsidered? Ahh," the Fafamafalafama nodded knowingly. "Guards! Away with you! The 'Ahthlahn' has been rendered harmlessly unarmed, and she has remained that way for several stormlines already! And, I have my sword! I think I can fend for myself! Be gone!"

"The courage of the Fafamafalafama," the three guards ritually chanted. They made sweeping hand gestures towards their leader as he slammed the heavy wooden door in their faces with a thud. A thud of finality, Helena thought grimly to herself. This, as in a necessary sealing of her fate.

"Courage, pah!" the Fafamafalafama spat upon the cold slate floor. "They must fear you capable of shooting daggers from your eyes. Anyhow, I shall now insist on saying 'Cahptahn,' and leave off the 'former' qualifier. Though in their defense," his left hand rested clasped comfortably loosely round the hilt of his sheathed sword, as he held up his right forefinger for the point he was about to make, "one cannot be too sure, in the harsh glare of these terrible days, from where a barbaric attack might issue next. But back to you, 'Cahhptahhn,'" a mischievous gleam in the ruler's eyes accompanied his drawn-out "ahh"s, "you don't need to answer my question. I can see it in your look. Of course you have not reconsidered. And I know you know better than to have requested this audience to try to persuade *me* to reconsider. That is, to reconsider what I am off to officially preside over, once we are done here. And so, I am curious what this is about. Do you appreciate how I have ordered the lighting in here suspended between stars-out and stars-fade?"

"Yes, I do," Helena nodded demurely. She took a seat along the edge of the spread-open tralalafa planted near the wall opposite from the thudded-shut entrance.

The Fafamafalafama tilted his head quizzically. He found himself struck by several details. Was it accidental, or was this 'Ahthlahn' intentionally sitting where she left plenty of room for him to sit beside her, if he so decided? And her uniform; it was customarily buttoned-up, uncomfortable-looking, to just under her chin. Yet this time, she had it so far unbuttoned, he could espy the swell of her breasts. Was she not feeling well? How she lifted her chin, to run her hand down the front of her throat to across her bosom, as though she were somehow overheated...

The Fafaman ruler took one hesitant step forward, towards her. "Ahh," he forced himself to affect nodding nonchalantly, "you wouldn't know of the amusing incident with your 'Sahjahnt Hahnsahn'?"

"No." Helena looked up, concerned.

"Completely amusing, 'Cahhptahhn.'" The Fafamafalafama calmly lifted a hand, to assure Helena there was nothing to worry over. "It was reported to me that 'Hahnsahn' was suffering from the peculiar bacterial effects we experienced when you first arrived to our planet. This was reported just after I received word the Varafafafa was enduring the same symptoms. So, I made a point of visiting him, to advise him of my twenty-third wife's discomfort. Ee-ee-ee! How his face turned more greenish-pale than a surfacing flounder mouse! I could tell exactly what was going on! 'Hahnsahn' was thinking I was certain the only way they both could have been having these same symptoms was if they had indulged intimate contact! Ee-ee-ee! You should have been there when I unsheathed my sword, and said I was going to take care of it for him! I thought he might die from fright as I pulled the full secretion from his nostrils and slashed it into tiny pieces! Ee-ee-ee! And the way he struggled to compose himself to thank me in our language. 'P – P – P – P – Pama,' he sounded like one of our antique mobile transport engines struggling to turn over! Ee-ee-ee!"

Helena forced a faint smile as she self-consciously primmed her hair. Her nerves were set way too far on edge, over what she came to do, for dwelling on the question of whether the Fafamafalafama suspected what she suspected, about some chemistry having developed between Guy Hanson and the twenty-third wife. It seemed he did suspect, and moreover that he was getting perverse enjoyment from baiting her about the situation.

Whether or not this was the case, for the ensuing awkward silence, the Fafamafalafama tilted his head from one side to the other and back again, pondering former 'Cahptahn Taylah.' Meekly, she was patting the area of tralalafa beside her, clearly indicative she wanted him to have a seat beside her.

"I must say, 'Cahhptahhn,'" his new fa-la-las in a booming voice translated, "as odd as I always find the behavior of 'Ahthlahns,' to be expected of course since they are from another planet," he made a deferential bow to this fact, "I find your present comportment even odder than usual."

"I was thinking about how little I actually share in common with Officer Olsen-Taylor."

"Your husband." The Fafamafalafama ventured a step closer.

"Yes." Helena nodded grimly. She was continuing to avoid eye contact with the Fafaman ruler, for at least the time-being, as she struggled to keep her nerve. "It- It has never been fair to him, but, what I really want to say," she steeled herself to look into the Fafamafalafama's eyes, "even though you and I, we come from two separate worlds, very different worlds, there are important things we understand about one another. I know the loneliness of making decisions that affect many lives. I know, I can feel, that what you do, you don't do lightly." Helena's eyes were watering up,

and the Fafamafalafama's heart was going out to her. He couldn't help finally taking up her understated invite for him to sit down on the open tralalafa beside her. Though he misunderstood her welling tears as the toll from the courage it was requiring of her to bare her soul. He had no idea she was grieving over what she was sacrificing for a larger cause, whatever degree of truth there might have been in her statements. Again, for the greater good, she was stretching that truth to false extremes.

Nervously, Helena sought to rest her hands gently upon the Fafamafalafama's hand which was not ever-clasping on the hilt of his sword. Thereupon, she looked away from him, and she brought herself to lie, "When I was here with you before, I- I wish I hadn't pushed you away."

With this, the Fafamafalafama leapt to his feet. He unsheathed his sword, and he swung it back and forth at such speed, Helena could hear its swish! through the air to accompany the grunts of his furied effort. The former starship captain couldn't help crying out, "What?! What?!" in her startlement. That second "What?!" melted into a tearful sob,

which brought the Fafamafalafama sitting back down beside her, comfortingly encircling her shoulder-heaving frame with his right arm. He left off from clasping his unsheathed sword, he let it fall to the slate floor with a loud clang, to gently caress Helena's cheek instead. He realized that clearly, whatever she had been about, she was not now about to somehow try to assassinate him. There was something else.

Helena resteeled herself, calmed down despite a somber realization. She was on the verge of crossing a boundary, back from which, whether she accomplished her goal or not, she was unlikely to ever be able to return, especially for the memory of what she had done. She lifted her head, and she gave the Fafamafalafama a searching look as she said, "Your wives cannot know what I know, of the burden always upon you, even if one of them were to truly care for you, um, like you should be cared for." Helena couldn't quite bring herself to say, *like I care for you,* despite what she was imminently willing to do. Which included what she then proceeded with, while keeping her eyes searching his. She latched onto the hand that was caressing her cheek, and she slowly pulled it in a descent, down onto her chest.

"'Halanah' is your first name, yes? A beautiful name." He allowed his hand to stay cupping her breast to where she had delivered it. "'Halanah,' I don't know that any of my wives, even the one- that any of them feel for me what-" Abruptly, he removed his hand, stood up and turned away. "I want to go on, but I have to supervise the missile launch for taking down the comet."

"NO!!" Helena blurted out as she likewise arose. She sped over between the Fafamafalafama and the door, where she climbed her hands up his broad shoulders, to latch them together around behind the nape of his neck. "Let's see how this crazy world looks," she spoke intimately softly, "after we- You want me, don't you?" As the Fafamafalafama surrendered to at least smiling into her eyes, Helena unlatched her right hand, to stroke at his chin as she said in a softer voice still, "You can tell them to wait?"

"NOOOO!!!!" The Fafaman ruler's eyes lit up blazing with his dawning realization. He seized Helena's wrists and shook them violently as he roared, "You are stalling for time! Hoping it's long enough for your friends with their hi-tech magic tricks to stop me, and rescue you!"

Helena shook her head, more over dread of what was coming next than trying to deny the truth of his accusations, as the Fafamafalafama hurled her sprawled back onto the tralalafa. "You would sacrifice your own marriage...! I cannot believe that after one husband for so long...! You want me?! Then I will have you! In my own time! Again and again! And your husband can watch! And then he can join in the fatal misfortune that will befall all of you! It will be better for your fellow 'Ahthlahns' as they wage war against the extraterrestrial menace! One less needless distraction! Maybe those tree creatures crazed you! Only 'Hahnsahn' will be spared!"

"But you- Your people might be irreclaimably wrecking this beautiful planet if they bring down the comet!" Helena's voice grew faint with her horror.

"If the terrorists aren't stopped from multiplying like flounder mice, even as their senseless, unprovoked attacks multiply, THEY will be the ones who destroy Fafama!"

"But you must know it's more complicated than that." Continuing in her faint voice, Helena instinctively, imploringly stretched out her hands towards the Fafamafalafama, as useless as they would have proven were he to wield his sword to slice them off. "There is nothing, no damage the terrorists can do that could compare to bringing such an enormous mass to- to crash against the surface of Fafama."

"To believe that, again it is former 'Cahptahn Taylah,' you must think I am even more powerful than I see myself! I cannot even get one woman to REALLY love me! May you rot before I return!"

SLAM!

# Chapter 26

"The Fafamafalafama." With this hand-sweeping introduction, Nanofafo unobtrusively swept himself right back out the door through which the Fafaman ruler had just entered on dramatic swirls of his bioluminescently lit cape.

A waiting family made the traditional pretense, of ferns unfurling in the pale-green bioluminescence supplied by flounder mice surfacing from underground at night. Only, the light was courtesy of the cape held outstretched like bat wings by the Fafaman ruler.

"Most esteemed, supreme Fafamafalafama," the father's fa-la-las would have translated, "they said you were coming for an audience with us. But, with all you have to attend to in these harshly lit days, how were we to believe that you could possibly spare any time for such pathetic creatures as us?"

The Fafamafalafama welcomed father, mother, uncle and grandmother into his royal grieving embrace. He tried to enfold every last one of them by his cape. "The Hafahara, your Falulu, she was my most treasured wife. However, you cannot share this with anyone else."

"No, of course not." The family shook their heads frantically in agreement.

"No! No! No!" Falulu's mother continued shaking her head. Her own agreement was transforming rapidly into additional grieving over the loss of her beloved daughter, the eighteenth wife of the Fafamafalafama.

"Of course this cannot be a fact known by anyone else," added the father, striving not to get overwhelmed anew by his own profound sorrow. "How would that make the other wives and their families feel?"

"And daughter Mrafamafa, how she got taken away

from us," the Fafaman ruler shook his head. "It leaves a hole in my heart, never to get refilled."

Those fa-la-las sent Falulu's mother, also Mrafamafa's grandmother, of course, sobbing even more inconsolably than initially.

"Most esteemed, supreme Fafamafalafama, we are depending on you to avenge the death of the eighteenth wife!" The father made a fist and he punched it high.

"Yes!" the mother chimed in through her tears. She lifted her own fist even higher than her husband's.

"And that is why you have all been brought to this room." The Fafamafalafama delicately backed out of the group hug, it already having begun to come unglued with the fist pumps. On yet another dramatic cape swirl, he directed the family's attention to the television monitor. "Here you can watch the launching of the missiles supplied by the extraterrestrials. They are the missiles that will bring down the ice-laden rock you have seen crossing the sky at stars-out. They will bring it down on the very center of terrorist activity!" This last part was fa-la-laed in his most booming voice. "The people from the planet 'Ahth' are a strange, naïve species. They wanted to believe there was some sort of redemption possible for the terrorists, by increasing the available water supply. Yet fortunately, they also had the good sense to provide us with the weaponry we would need to turn that gift against those monsters, were they not to appreciate it!"

"Go! Do not let us hold you up on your far more important task!" The father waved away the Fafamafalafama, though immediately thereafter he thought better of speaking thusly to his supreme ruler. And so, he fell to his knees to add, "If that is your will. It is not for me, a most wretched yet loyal miner, to say."

The Fafamafalafama nodded his approving acknowledgement with a faint grin. "There is no more important task than consoling the family of one of my prematurely deceased wives for their loss, AND AVENGING THAT LOSS!" he concluded with a booming shout to accompany his dramatic exit, slamming the door shut behind him. *Good. I have finished with the last family. Now I must quiz the experts one final time before I give my final go-ahead. The sooner we are over with this, and the former "Cahptahn" sees it does not mean the end of the world, the better!*

***

"The Varalawa."

Helena's attention got drawn immediately to the first wife's long, curved, sheathed knife. It was strapped by a wide belt to her dark-green tunic woven out of tralalafa fibers. Was she there to gore her? Helena could hear her sending away the guards. So there would be no one to overhear? Maybe they even knew what she was there about, and they were more than willing accomplices in avoiding any witnesses?, any evidence?

The Varalawa gave Helena a puzzled, quizzical look with her over-sized, nocturnal eyes.

*Is she sensing my apprehensive thoughts?*

"My- The Fafamafalafama is under a lot of stress, far more than usual," the first wife said at last. "The loss of wives and children...he is consoling their families, and through it all he needs to make momentous decisions."

"The stress can make any of us do things we realize too late are ill-considered."

"Yes," the Varalawa fa-la-laed haltingly. Clearly, and perhaps mercifully where Helena was concerned, the first wife seemed a bit mystified by her remark. "The engraving of the pendant for you is nearly completed. And I have gathered the others," meaning the Earthlings, Helena divined, "in my chambers. We ought to hurry."

"But I- We don't want to get you in trouble." Helena said this, even as she nevertheless allowed the Varalawa to lead her out the door.

"That makes no difference to me at this point." The first wife looked back at Helena to smile grimly.

"You- More important than attending to our circumstances, you need to convince the Fafamafalafama not to launch the attack! So many variables, so much could go wrong that would jeopardize your entire planet!"

The Varalawa froze. In the dim, bioluminescently lit darkness, she said, without turning around to directly face Helena's plea, "If you could not get the Fafamafalafama to reconsider, how do you expect I could?"

Silence.

Helena heard the first wife's question echoing off through the labyrinth catacombs of the part of the central pyramid to where they had reached.

Finally, the Varalawa did turn her head to add, "Your one and only husband is waiting for you, whether this is as you wished, or not." The first wife was about to take off again, pulling on Helena's hand in tow. First, though, she added in a softer, gentler tone, "Can we realistically hope your people back in space will find a way to rescue you?, and stop the plot to destroy the terrorists?"

***

"So what's the plan, Buddy? You keep keepin' us in suspense!" Marine Corps Officer Kenny Robertson was peering over Officer Leung's shoulder. He knew full well it was hopeless trying to decipher this "friggin' genius's" furiously wrought scribbles. But he'd long since gotten too uncomfortable, his tail bone especially, from trying to find a tolerable way to stay seated in any of the chairs on the saucer's navigation bridge. "You're going to tell the Fafamawhozywhatzama to hand over our people, or we use that magnetic pulse blaster to play target practice on their pyramid city?"

"Actually, Kenny," Buddy kept up his mad-dash scribbles, including several lines of function equations, while he spoke, "this looks like it's going to work. We're going to un-threaten them by asking for their help."

"Damn."

Just then, Pedro and Mafoosoola had gotten the saucer to decelerate a shade under light-speed. The alien spacecraft was on its descent past the Oort Cloud, down into the outer fringes of the orbital plane for the Alpha Centauri C System. Converging star lines were shrinking back into distinct, lavender-hued streaks on the panoramic view-screen. Buddy paused from his calculations to look up, take in the cosmic scenery. What he saw did not diverge all that much from how antique science fiction movies depicted outer space appearing when whichever spacecraft flew hyper-speed.

"Officer Leung, we're receiving a message via firefly donut link," Pedro suddenly reported. "Audio only."

"Let's have it on the intercom, Pedro."

"Sí."

The next thing Buddy Leung knew, it was clearly Captain Entroper's voice, albeit somewhat broken up by the long distances the firefly had had to convey the transmission. "This is Captain Louisa Entroper aboard the Smoke and Mirrors. I am calling out to Officer Buddy Leung. Officer Leung, I have no idea what you are planning. Maybe this message is finding you too late, already in the middle of executing heaven-only-knows-what fantastic scheme. Whether that is the case or not, I'm guessing the gesture is futile, to threaten to court-martial you. Besides which, I really don't have the stomach for that. - - - - - - - - - - - - - - - - I don't know why I paused to await some confirmation you're receiving this. Any response from you is going to take at least seven minutes. But I don't need to tell you that, do I? Force of habit on my part, I suppose. Okay, so here's the rest of it.

"All along, Officer Leung, my plain and simple thought had been that, if before your bold actions – and I understand you felt the need for bold action. Nevertheless, if we could have just sat down and discussed the possibilities... I suspect you don't like agendas any more than Helena Taylor, but for example, your rescue mission into the near past. Yes, it was brilliant! Brilliant! Still, the past wasn't going anywhere. If you could have just taken the time to run your plan by us… I'll be the first to concede your ingenuity. With a little more input from us mere mortals, though, we might have been better able to coordinate. You thereby might not have had to have been sitting ducks inside that saucer until you understood its operation. You really were lucky, you know, the hostiles weren't ready with another warship, to tow you back to Tictoctic, put the people you rescued back onto their menu, and add you there as well. We still can't know for sure some distress beacon didn't go out from the saucer automatically, alerting those particular ETs, so that heaven-only-knows what they have coming our way any time now. Which brings me to another reason we wish you had been better able to exercise self-restraint, where your sense of urgency to help out your kindred spirits was concerned. It's another reason we wish you had reigned in your emotions until we had better assessed the situation out this end. This reason is, Dr. Wang told me that even a cursory examination of the saucer's weaponry would almost certainly have helped our preparations, in case there is an attack imminent.

"I know. That's water under the bridge," Entroper's message went on as Buddy shook his head and exhaled with his frustration. "We have to deal with what we have to deal with now. You have made your choice, and as far as I can determine, our best option is to get your end pronto, where we will offer whatever support we can. We only ask that in return, we be able afterwards to confiscate the hostile's saucer. So if you could, I would really, deeply appreciate if you would just hang around the outer perimeter of the Alpha Centauri C System, near the Oort Cloud boundary. Just wait long enough for the Smoke and Mirrors to catch up with you. We can quickly vet your scheme, whatever it may be; I'm sure your colleagues Kevin and Yoon-hee here would be eager to provide useful input. And then I pledge to you, I am crossing my heart as I am recording this for you, I will personally recommend you continue on at your post aboard the Smoke and Mirrors."

"Oh yeah? What about Helena Taylor?" Buddy said as though Entroper could respond directly, instantaneously.

"Well, I guess that's it. This is Captain Louisa Entroper. We are anxiously awaiting your response, and we are cruising your brainchild at the maximum safe light-speed multiple to catch up to you. Over."

Buddy sat back in his chair, however uncomfortable the deer-creature-friendly seating had proven for him, as much as for his fellow travelers. This, after having leaned forward, on edge, to carefully take in Entroper's every word. He thought to himself, *Actually, it wouldn't be a bad idea if I could bounce this plan off Yoon-hee and Kevin. Hmmm….* "Pedro," he said finally.

Pedro lifted his head. He had been bent over, for sifting through reams of calculations. He had also been intent on loading additional programming into what was become the easily decipherable and manipulable navigation console of the Tictoctic saucer. But none of this was actually happening. His attention had long since been diverted, instead, to concentration on Captain Entroper's pleading communication.

"Pedro, let's decel to a mid-space hover."

*Officer Leung, I am so sorry to have to impinge on your cognitive processes before you have completed your directive to Pedro. However, what I have just gleaned from a few Fafaman mental horizons, which seem to include the Fafamafalafama's, really can't wait. I suspect a crucial impact will result for your plans.*

"I'm all neurons, Mafoosoola."

*A missile launch is imminent on Fafama, to try to bring the orbiting comet crashing down on the rebel stronghold.*

"How much time do we have?"

*At most, a few hours.*

"Pedro and Mafoosoola, bring this saucer to the maximum speed possible that will still allow enough deceleration for an arrival to Fafama, not an overshoot of the planet! And what do you think, Mafoosoola? The pulse beam could be enough to safely disintegrate the comet?"

*Unfortunately, given the comet's size, Officer, the magnetic pulse beam would only serve to push it on a collision course down towards the Fafaman surface.*

At a blur of speed, Buddy typed out a response to

Captain Entroper's entreaty. He urged her to get the Smoke and Mirrors to Fafama ASAP, with laser cannons ready to attempt comet disintegration, presuming calculations by Smoke and Mirrors officers gave that plan a reasonable prospect for success. Although realistically, there was no way they could possibly arrive on time. "Mafoosoola," he said as something occurred to him in the midst of his furiously paced finger-pecking, "Can you-

*No indication I can discern from the Fafaman mental landscape as to where the missile silo is housed. Everyone involved or in-the-know with the launch execution is too focused on the launch itself, or embedded too deeply inside the pyramid for my mental powers to reach.*

"Maybe some of the technicians involved with the robotic training programming have some idea." Buddy was practically mumbling this to himself as he added a request for such information to his text message for Entroper, despite his strong suspicion that would prove a fruitless line of inquiry. Also, he kept turning a plan over and over again in his mind, worried he might be forgetting or missing some crucial element. But he couldn't keep doing this indefinitely.

He had to begin preparations to abandon the saucer.

***

"Naratama, I am asking you to explain for my sake, one last time, how the objective will be achieved." The Fafamafalafama spoke in the deepest, gravest voice he could summon. He was looming over the diminutive launch control engineer.

The launch control engineer feigned total preoccupation with data output from the missile launch control console, even though it was all he could do to keep from quivering in his moccasins.

"I ask this," went on the Fafamafalafama, "not because I am having even the least difficulty understanding the process, but because I want you to review it one last time, both for yourself and for your colleagues here assembled. I want you to make absolutely certain you are not overlooking anything. Even the tiniest detail could mean disaster if not properly addressed!"

"Most esteemed Fafamafalafama, were your wisdom a pyramid, a sunset storm line one hundred times more powerful than the Fafaman storm line could not hope to deface it with even the most inconsequential striation."

Naratama's remark got met over-the-top enthusiastically by other Fafamans. Woven-together handlebar moustache whiskers curled and uncurled with the happy gusto of a dog wagging its tail. This, accompanied by he-he-hees which crescendoed to such a loud shrill, they nearly drowned out the final la-la-las of Naratama's praise, because he was as soft-spoken as he was effusive.

"The calculations have been repeated to exhaustion, loading in every possible variable," Launch Control Engineer Naratama continued once the ruckus died down, to the Fafamafalafama's approving nod. "On its journey, the comet will reach this precise coordinate in its orbit, on the far side of the planet from us." Naratama paused to direct the Fafaman ruler's attention to an animation loop on one of the launch console screens. "When this happens, we will fire two of the 'Ahth' missiles tipped with hydrogen-bomb nuclear explosives. Those two missiles will catch up to the comet at exactly this juncture." Naratama skipped the simulation video ahead to another loop that showed the missiles as two pinpoints of light, overtaking the comet a few hundred labadas west of the central pyramid. "Their precisely timed detonations, one of them five point seven nininanas after the other, will send the comet on a shallow downward descent that will both accelerate and become steeper as it approaches the barbarian stronghold. Impact will utterly destroy their underground network of tunnels and caves. Moreover, the water content of the comet combined with the passing-through of the sunset storm line a mere twenty nanas after impact should tamp down the particulate matter, minimize how much of it gets hurled into the upper atmosphere. Thereby, any long-term atmospheric cooling should also be minimized. At worst, the one- to two-degree cooling-off of the planet's climate is not liable to last more than two full orbits of the sun. Of course, these particular calculations cannot be performed with anything approaching the scientific exactitude of our collision formulas."

"Your honesty on that count is appreciated, Naratama," the Fafaman ruler nodded approvingly yet again.

The launch control engineer would have liked to have raised his head, crane it around to take in his leader's confirming nonverbal. He continued to worry, though, over the least perception he was other than fully preoccupied with the task at hand.

"However, please pardon my redundancy on this issue, if I have raised the matter before," the Fafamafalafama went on. "You have been able to precisely calculate the decay rate of the comet as it continues to shed dirt and water?, and what effect that will have on its trajectory once the missiles detonate?"

"Precisely, Fafamafafalafama; all of that and more,

including the friction factor posed by trace atmospherics found even at orbital heights above Fafama." As Naratama was fa-la-la-ing this, he was also mentally revisiting for the umpteenth time the long list of variables he and his missile-control crew, trained by the "Ahth" robotics, had run through ad nauseum. He couldn't yet quite fully suppress a creeping anxiety over the possibility he was overlooking something, something insurmountably important. *Surely, this is just the paranoia of the ultra-conscientious!! A minor temporary climate change, that is the worst to be expected from this final solution to the terrorist threat...a small enough price to pay to finally rid ourselves once and for all of that senselessly violent vermin!*

***

*Fafamafalafama, this distress telepath goes out both to you and to all your loyal subjects. We are under attack by a saucer vehicle from Tictoctic. We are attempting every evasive maneuver conceivable in our small shuttle craft. Chief Officer Leung would be signaling you directly, but he is too consumed by the evasive maneuvers; he cannot afford even the briefest distraction from them without leaving us deadly vulnerable to the saucer's pulse beam, by far the most destructive weapon known to Earth creatures. Also, we could not realistically hope for his communication to arrive your end with anything approaching the immediacy of my telepath.*

Naratama and the Fafamafalafama exchanged significant looks, and both noticed out the corners of their eyes whisker-curling perplexity written all over the faces of their fellow Fafamans there assembled.

So, the Fafamafalafama thought to himself, *one of the tree creatures sends mind messages anew, and not just to me. Rather, it shares its messages with everyone around me.* The Fafamafalafama found himself in an oddly reflective mood, given the momentousness of the missile launch he was about to order, and with such momentousness getting interrupted by the telepathed distress call. *This tree creature, perhaps the "Ahthlahns" also, they do not respect my supreme position. Just as well. Suppose I were the only one privileged with this telepathic communication? Potential enemies, who knows?, maybe even another barbarian infiltrator in our midst, they would certainly like nothing better than to poison susceptible minds, with the suggestion I was crazily alone among my people, hearing voices in my head.* "We are sorry for your imperilment from the other-world threat," the Fafamafalafama fa-la-laed unabashedly aloud for his fellow Fafamans to clearly hear. "But what exactly is it you think we can do to help? Or are you alerting us with low expectation in mind? Are you anticipating no more than that we will pass along these details to the other people of 'Ahth' still here on our planet? The idea being, they can brace for the possibility your evasive maneuvers will not cope successfully with this enemy of us all?"

*Esteemed Fafamafalafama, we are getting chased into your solar system, even as I telepath you. We have barely dodged another pulse-beam attack. We hope to buy ourselves a little time by hiding behind a giant asteroid.*

"Esteemed-" Naratama was going to relay a message he received over his earpiece from the Fafaman space station. However, he cut himself off from continuing; he could see his supreme ruler was lost in concentration on what he had to assume were further mind messages for the Fafamafalafama only.

However, Mafoosoola continued to telepath, *this is an untenable solution for the long term. What Officer Leung proposes is to make a sudden run for Fafama that would get us there in fifty-three nanas. Before our arrival, your space station crew would relay to us the pass code for safely breaching the laser mesh defense shield. Once we are through that shield without triggering any response, the Tictoctickians will likely follow right behind us. They will have no reason to suspect they are flying into a trap, until too late. Their saucer will get utterly destroyed, one less tool for their conquest. By way of a backup, a second line of defense... I mind-read the plan for your imminent missile launch against your rebels. We earnestly believe those missiles would be better reconfigured to deal with the saucer. This, on the off chance the laser mesh does not function as it is supposed to, when a breaching object fails to provide the pass code for keeping the circuit flow intact. That would also give us time to review your plans to bring down the orbiting comet. All the potential unexpected apocalyptic consequences could be checked and re-checked, especially those that your technicians' best calculations may have somehow overlooked.*

On receipt of this last telepathed item, the Fafamafalafama could not help a grin stretching most broadly from ear to ear, accompanied by a deep-voiced, "Hmmm." From which he abruptly swung his head Naratama's direction to fa-la-la, "You were about to say, Naratama?"

"Only, esteemed Fafamafalafama," he bowed deeply his gratitude for such recognition, "that we are in receipt of a transmission from the space station. It is something to the effect of their having detected two UFOs at the outer limits of our solar system. Those UFOs' trajectories do suggest one is following the other. This would appear consistent with the distress message we received mentally from their tree entity."

"Yes." The Fafamafalafama made a perfunctory nod. He was already preoccupied, distracted with his response for Mafoosoola. "Tree creature in association with the beings from 'Ahth,'" the Fafaman ruler fa-la-laed anew in his unabashedly booming voice, head held high. His attention was directed towards a being not in his immediate physical presence. "I commend you, I commend all of you, for desiring a solution to our people's struggle against the forces of blinding-white harshness, a solution that would not require so much violence, so much death and destruction. But, you simply do not understand, you do not grasp, the full extent of what we are up against. Your generous seizure of a giant ice rock into orbit around Fafama, to shed more water for the replenishment of the barbarian stronghold: What has been the result? What do we have to show for it? Ask the parents of my wives who were recently murdered, along with their children! Ask them what reciprocal generosity has been demonstrated by the bloodthirsty beasts!"

*Hearts cannot be softened overnight. But that is not our present focus. We are just trying to survive. Wait- Ah, at least this: Officer Leung was able to make it appear the pulse beam destroyed our shuttle craft. In actuality, it has just disintegrated a small asteroid between us and the saucer! This should purchase us a little extra time to flee closer to your planet before the Tictoctic creatures realize they have been tricked. Still, it's no guarantee we will make it to Fafama before they find their mark! Okay, don't reconfigure the missiles, even though we persist in believing that is the best choice. Please, though, at least have passed along to us the code for safe entry through your laser mesh. And have the mesh itself double-checked, to assure it will expend all its fire power on the saucer!*

"Excuse me again, if I am interrupting additional mind transfers, supreme Fafamafalafama. There is new word from our space station; a flare-out has been detected in the proximity of the previously detected UFOs. The craft from 'Ahth,' perhaps it met its fate at the hands of the enemy force from Tictoctic? No! Wait!" Naratama held out a restraining hand. "Two UFOs remain. They are both approaching Fafama at velocities that should arrive them here about the same time our two missiles reach the far longitude, on their course heading for the orbiting ice rock. This is presuming, of course, the missile launch is to go off as planned, within the next several nininanas."

"That continues to be consistent with what the tree creature is relaying. Telepathic associate of the creatures from 'Ahth,'" the Fafamafalafama resumed directing his communication out towards who he could not see, had to settle with only "hearing" inside his head, "as you approach us ever closer, I will do the following. I will command one of our officers aboard our space station to transfer to you the necessary security code to safely cross our laser mesh threshold! Be well advised, however: This has nothing to do with, will have nothing to do with, our defensive missile launch."

*You appear to be seeking to obliterate the rebels, not merely to defend against them. You pursue this faithless goal at the risk of wreaking significant havoc on your planet's delicate life-sustaining balance. This, the very possible consequence of plunging a large comet into its surface.* Mafoosoola gave this telepath virtually unrestricted access beyond the Fafamafalafama, including everyone aboard the Fafaman space station.

The Fafaman ruler was not so mesmerized by the Oombian's thought projections echoing in his own head that he did not notice something else most significant. Namely, everybody around him was suddenly giving one another those same quizzical looks they had shared when they were previously in receipt of a telepathic message. "Three points, tree person!" For many reasons, there was testiness in the Fafamafalafama's voice. "One: When all that the barabarians seem to know how to engage in are deadly terrorist acts, their obliteration is the only conceivable defense! Would that their children could somehow be delivered away from the poisonous indoctrination by their parents!, that their collateral elimination could be avoided! Two: My launch command engineer here, Naratama, has accounted for every possible variable in his calculations! He gives us his assurance we face no such 'significant havoc'!" The Fafamafalafama looked Naratama's way as he fa-la-laed this in booming tones, but Naratama avoided reassuring eye contact by feigning continued absorption in calculations and data displayed on the missile launch control console. "Point three!" the Fafamafalafama boomed even louder. He was trying to drown out a sickening tremor of doubt that rumbled uncontrollably through his head, like the rumble of a Fafaman snail tank emerging from its underground lair. "I am ordering initiation of the final launch sequence, effective NOW!"

Within nininanas, a missile silo slid open, two labadas north of the central pyramid. A thunderous roar ensued that woke local residents and sent them rushing out of their mini-pyramids squinting in "blazing-light." Two nuclear-tipped missiles lifted slowly out of the ground. They rapidly gained speed as they rocketed into the western sky's hazy glare, trailing billowing plumes of light-gray smoke.

***

"I do realize the priority the defense secretary places on securing the saucer. We might have been able to hang around the outskirts here, await your direct input, to collectively develop an alternate plan to free Helena and the rest of her away team. But the imminent threat the Fafaman government, in the person of the Fafamafalafama, is going to use the missiles we provided to knock the comet out of orbit...you're not going to be able to get here on time." Click!

The final noise from Buddy's transmission reminded Yoon-hee of someone hanging up the phone, on some century-old movie she'd indulged recently.

"Damn it! Damn it! Damn it!" With each utterance of this curse, Captain Entroper's fists pounded the arms of the captain's chair on the navigation bridge of the Smoke and Mirrors. Her raging frustration thusly spent, she rubbed her forehead against stretched-wide thumb and forefinger. "Uhh, Officer Smith-Park, Kevin," she said finally, "there is no way we can get this contraption to become a skipping stone across the space-time lake, like the saucer apparently was able to do for leaving the Callaway X Centra System?"

"Sorry, Captain, but no. There is no way. Maybe there is a way Buddy, um, Officer Leung could have jury-rigged, but I'm stuck on the overall design issue. The Tictoctic saucer is ideally shaped. It's comparable to the sort of flat stone you'd want for lake skipping."

Again Entroper pounded the chair arms, albeit this time with no accompanying curse. "We can have a firefly donut relay reach them once more before they execute their plan?" She labored to keep her voice level, restrained.

"Most likely, Captain. Ready if you are."

Captain Entroper sat up taller in her chair, and she raised her voice just shy of a shout to say, "Officer Leung, I insist you wait on carrying out any action involving potential harm to the saucer craft until our arrival your end. Destruction of the saucer will be considered an act of extreme insubordination, subject to your full prosecution before a military tribunal!" Head subsequently bowed into her left hand, Entroper silently motioned with her right hand for message transmittal.

***

"Are you getting what I'm getting, Pedro?"

"Sí, Officer Leung," Pedro Perez nodded grimly. Where Robertson was concerned, Pedro's complexion looked far paler than normal in the light of the navigation console, despite days-old unshaven stubble. "Appears they have launched both missiles."

*You might need to know this, Buddy.* Mafoosoola was again intruding on all minds aboard the shuttle craft. *The Fafamafalafama is wrestling with doubt about the picture you are painting for him, of this pod getting pursued by the Tictoctic saucer craft. The possible consequence…*

"Buddy, um, Officer Leung," said Pedro, "maybe we need to pre-empt the Fafamafalafama communicating his doubt to us, by doing something dramatic." Pedro struggled to keep his eyes from welling up so much that the overflow would send a tear streaking down his cheek. He was suddenly overtaken, nearly overwhelmed, with a longing to be back in Ludi's arms, enjoying some silliness of Alexita, such as her advising them she was about to fart as she pointed her little butt towards a nearby bush...and also nearly overwhelmed with a wave of fear, like a wave of nausea. He might never see Ludi nor Alexita, ever again, whether due to his own fate, or theirs at the hands, hooves, of the Tictoctic creatures should they attack Oomb anew with unthwartable force. But just as he had fought down nausea from threatened space sickness, he fought down fear and longing both, to re-engage with the task at hand. "We could, um, could we safely permit an attack beam from the saucer to inflict minor damage on our shuttle pod?, and hope the Fafamans can detect this from their space station to confirm what we report about it?"

"Great minds think alike, Officer Perez." Buddy was already busily typing away, loading new programming into his console. "No, wait." He abruptly stopped, flopped back in his shuttle pod swivel chair, so much more comfortable than the saucer seats designed in consideration of Tictoctic deer creature anatomy. "What if we actually admitted to the Fafamafalafama we were pretending the saucer was chasing us, but then we noticed the missile firing, and we calculated the missiles were headed on a trajectory- We'd be making this up, of course, our certainty the missiles were going to hit the orbiting comet in a way that was going to send it crashing into their central pyramid..."

*If I may interject, Officer Leung, I did detect lingering concern on the Fafamafalafama's part; he would be susceptible to such an assertion.*

"Yes!" Buddy pounded the air with his suddenly clenched fist. "So then hopefully, the Fafamafalafama would relievedly grant us the laser mesh security code, with his blessing to subsequently safely sail the saucer in close enough to blow those missiles out of the sky! The skipping stone function should facilitate our arrival there in plenty of time for this!"

"Officer Leung," Pedro couldn't help this time a tearfulness choking up his voice, "a fantastic idea with one stupendous problem: the skipping stone acceleration. We won't be able to decelerate in time even if we shift to deceleration a split second after we skip. We'll overshoot Fafama by millions of miles at a minimum."

"Wait! You're right. Wait!" Buddy spread out both his arms, fingers all splayed. He gave Pedro the impression he was trying to keep his balance after getting struck by a dizzy spell. In truth, Officer Leung was staving off hyperventilation, wrought of panic and anxiety not helped by his recent lack of sleep. "We can still- The plan might not have been workable anyway if the Fafamafalafama feared we were under the control of the Tictotoctickians, and were getting coerced to try to sucker-punch him into allowing the saucer through the laser mesh for a Trojan Horse attack. And-And he might..." Buddy paused to focus on his breathing, force himself to slow down his inhale, exhale.

"Officer Leung?"

"I was just- Well anyway, the Fafamafalafama might- Even if we stick to our original story, it might occur to him that giving us the code for safely passing through the laser mesh, he will have to trust we won't hand it over to the saucer aliens as well. He could intentionally have his people transmit to us the wrong code, to assure our destruction. You're right, Pedro, we need to stage an attack on our shuttle pod, successful-looking without being crippling."

***

"This is what I don't understand." Captain Entroper

lifted her forehead out of her hand after what seemed to Kevin and Yoon-hee the longest time. "On your first mission, and even on this mission for Buddy making a past-time detour to rescue the Marines and two civilians, there was always, always some rabbit you could pull out of your hat, something to avoid disaster. Officer Petrovksy hauled to safety your companions who were hanging on by a monster spider web. Chris Olsen-Taylor used that invisible dragon, or whatever weird natural phenomenon that was, to burn an ice rock out of the photon evacuation chamber. Reading through your debriefing was almost like experiencing an antique *Star Trek* adventure. But now you're saying that hurrying us over to Fafama by the same time as Officer Leung with the shuttle pod and saucer... It just doesn't seem all that much more outrageous than what you folks already have been able to accomplish. Part of me feels like I should pull a Captain Kirk on you, and just order, 'Get it done! No excuses!'"

"I- No..." Yoon-hee practically popped out of her chair, but then she slumped back down into it again, deflated.

"What?" Entroper didn't want to let go of whatever had just occurred to Yoon-hee, even if Yoon-hee already had.

"I was just thinking, time travel might facilitate our return to Fafama, plenty soon enough. But we'd require a wound in the space-time fabric sufficiently far away from any celestial object, and the closest such wound of which I'm aware is located back in Callaway X Cen- No," Yoon-hee shook her head, "not even that; it would be healed from Buddy's rescue effort. Maybe we could find one near Fafama, but not too near Fafama. But we don't know of any outer space calamity there. We'd have to be lucky enough to get the Smoke and Mirrors haunted so I'd be able to focus in on where to pick up the time rift signature..."

Captain Entroper turned her head aside and tossed her hands in the air in resignation.

"Look, Captain, here's the thing." Kevin tried to keep any tone of frustration out of his voice. "That *Buck Rogers, Star Trek, Star Wars* stuff, that was all sci-fi bull dooky. In the real world, there are limits to what you can do. Yes, sometimes you can get away with some amazing shit like we did on the first mission. But that doesn't mean you can always get away with amazing shit, no matter what. That's not an excuse. That is reality. It doesn't mean we've given up trying to brainstorm some way to cheat an additional light year or two, and I'd guess Buddy hasn't given up on a way to save the day without sacrificing the saucer. It's just..."

***

BOOM!!

If Buddy, Pedro and company could have gotten an exterior view of their shuttle pod, they would have seen the laser cannon strafing from the Tictoctic saucer appear to splatter like red paint, albeit silently, across its right stabilizer solar panel wing. Both wings had been electrostatically deployed after the egg-shaped vehicle dropped below twenty percent light-speed.

"Ay, Officer Leung, I hope my hit wasn't too direct," Pedro Perez groaned dizzily. He wondered at how the panoramic screen-view of the Callaway X Centra sun conveyed a feeling the universe was spinning around when in reality, it was the shuttle pod that was spiraling about most wildly. This, thanks to the calculatedly ineffectual "attack" from the alien saucer in faux, remote-controlled pursuit.

"Your hit was damn near perfect, Officer Perez," Buddy shook his head as he worked furiously hard to stabilize the pod, and his imagination worked furiously hard to conceive a plan regarding the missiles already launched from the surface of Fafama. "Mafoosoola, I trust you're reading my mind on communicating a certain urgency-"

*That you're going to need a little lead time for loading in the code before we reach the laser mesh shield. Of course, Officer Leung. Consider your certain urgency having already been communicated to the Fafamans.*

***

The two nuclear-tipped missiles were whining through the Fafama sub-stratosphere, beneath a starry night sky. They were passing over salt flats that millions of years earlier hosted a shallow sea nearly as vast as the Grand Basin. What Naratama had failed to calculate, what he could not have known, was that well before the missiles approached this region, a magma chamber miles underneath had found significant crust weaknesses. In just the previous twenty days, said chamber had sent molten rock tendrils close enough to the surface to heat the ground-level air sufficiently for creating more than the normal updraft. And this updraft was resulting in a slight, but ultimately significant, shifting of the missiles to an inches-higher altitude.

***

"Esteemed Fafamafalafama, we are receiving confirmation from the space station of what the mind reader has telepathed us: The spacecraft from 'Ahth' has sustained another attack by the spacecraft from Tictoctic that may have crippled it."

"Very well. Have the security code- Someone stare at the security code, and meditate upon it intently, rather than transmitting it. This way, we avoid the Tictoctic creatures intercepting a communication. If 'Mahfoosoolahhh' can telepath over such an expanse, it can also mind-read."

*Indeed I can, esteemed Fafamafalafama. We appreciate your thinking of this.*

The Fafaman ruler grinned with untempered satisfaction over such an instantaneous affirmation of his wisdom. He was oblivious to the fact that launch engineer Naratama's whiskered visage was paling even more than the faint bioluminescence already made it to appear.

***

*Officer Leung, I am now in mind-read receipt of the laser mesh code, but I am sensing sudden, extreme distress on the part of the Fafaman missile launch officer. He's thinking about a slight course alteration due to an unknown variable. He's convinced that alteration will cause both missiles to make impact with the comet higher up its face than originally intended.*

"Shit, Mafoosoola, I'm no mind-reader, but I'm afraid I know where you're going with this."

*You do. The missile launcher is thinking about how the new impact coordinates might lead to a steeper descent trajectory for the comet, directly towards their central pyramid. Even if it misses, and touches down just before or just after the pyramid, or to one side, the results will still be cataclysmic. He is torn between two choices. He could try the missile-abort protocol first, then apprise the*

*Fafamafalafama of the situation. Or he could apprise him first, then suggest they try for the abort.*

"Well isn't that a blessing in disguise? Either way, doesn't the comet get left alone? We needn't worry they're going to lay waste to the planet just to avenge a terrorist attack?"

*That would be the case, if only. Naratama, the missile launcher, he is thinking about how he left the redundancy for missile abort un-installed. He didn't even bother to test the main system. Should he be so afraid the abort won't work? Or, should I telepath him, to assure him…*

"Oh, no." Buddy shook his head. "From what I know about those systems, there is almost always a glitch that has to be corrected. Of course back on Earth, we fortunately never had to actually fire one under real circumstances. And here they are dealing with a slightly lower gravitational pull, slightly different atmospheric component ratios…With what we know about their home-grown capabilities, we're going to have to figure out whether there is anything we can telepath them to try, in the highly likely case they don't pull a miraculous untested first-abort out of their hat!"

***

"Esteemed Fafamafalafama, from whose radiance I deserve not the tiniest photon, nor the faintest shade," Naratama fell to his knees before the supreme Fafaman ruler and bowed his head so far down, his forehead was pushing against the cold slate floor, "should you decide you must lop off my head, I do not deserve even the mercy of a swift blow. Rather, I expect the pain of a slow sawing off."

"Enough!" The Fafamafalafama kicked him over on his side. Drawing a sword on Naratama was the furthest thing from the supreme ruler's mind; he felt a sickening dread seeming to turn his blood to lead, similar to how he felt after drinking too much fermented tralalafa juice. "What is this about?! Quickly!!"

"The-The missiles have experienced- We ran analyses on every conceivable variable, but this-"

"No more words than the information requires!" The Fafamafalafama kicked him again.

"The missiles have inexplicably departed from their original plotted trajectory. Now, where they will strike the ice satellite will send it on a collision course at or just to one side of the central pyramid!!"

"And the contingency to deal with an errant flight path?!?! What is the contingency?!?!"

"There- There is an abort function-"

"So what are you doing cowering like a navanasalala before a full-grown ahtpah? Implement the abort function!!" The Fafaman ruler made to crouch down, to personally pull Naratama back up on his feet. But two security guards rushed to forestall what they regarded as an effort unworthy of, undignified for the Fafamafalafama to undertake, as much as such intent underlined for them his supreme nobility.

"This is how you honor your Fafamafalafama giving you an order instead of justifiably terminating your existence?!" angrily fa-la-laed one of the guards as he yanked on Naratama's tunic collar to inflict a choking sensation. "The sloth of a 'tapastrah' slug?!"

"Enough!" boomed the Fafaman ruler. "No time for this!"

The security guard shoved the missile launch engineer towards his control console with as much hostile force as he thought he could get away with, and not bring further reprimand upon himself. Instantly pursuant to which, he backed down into a most deferential bow.

"Your reason rules your passion how we can only admire as helplessly as we admire the brutal force of the sunset storm line, Supreme Fafamafalafama."

***

"Officer Leung, could we target the missiles with two advance guard fireflies? At top speed they would arrive early enough..."

"So many incalculable atmospheric variables, Officer Perez, most likely including whatever threw off both missile trajectories. I'd put the odds of achieving even one of the two targets at less than one in a thousand. Which means that, in all likelihood, the two advance guard fireflies are left to penetrate deep into the Fafaman surface, possibly down to its mantel, at the light-speed fractions we're talking. We still know next to nothing about Fafaman geology; my wife was just starting to gather data. So we have no idea whether the firefly impacts, despite their relatively small size, wouldn't prove even more catastrophic than what Fafama can expect from the comet. At least the comet will be coming in relatively slowly, at a relatively shallow angle. And how big was that iron-nickel asteroid that produced Meteor Crater in Arizona? One hundred fifty feet across?"

"I wouldn't know." MacKenzie shrugged his shoulders.

"Yeah, it was about that," Buddy nodded as he gained confidence his memory retrieval was accurate. "And true, that made it enormous compared to our fireflies. But it entered Earth's atmosphere at twenty-some thousand miles per hour, while our fireflies would be going more than that per SECOND, with deflector shields preventing significant burn-up before impact. And let's say one or both fireflies DID cross paths with the comet.

They are so small, they would merely break apart the comet into large, icy chunks. And those chunks would land with enough force to cause considerable damage over an even broader area. I'm not sure the subsequent disastrous climate-cooling projection of particulates into the atmosphere would be any less. It might even be more.

"But please..." Buddy gave Pedro and the Marines alike a most earnest, respectful regard. "...don't stop trying to imagine a solution. No matter how outrageous it might sound initially. For myself, for now, I'm going to have to keep my attention on retrieving our away team, and maybe even some Fafamans into the bargain."

*Two of each kind for the ark,* Pedro found himself haunted with remembering from his childhood days, when his mama had made him attend church school.

"We will have little enough time for rescues before comet impact; the window is that small," Buddy offered by way of explanation for where he would be keeping his attention.

Mafoosoola was well aware from her remote mind-reading that Naratama was trying to execute the missile abort function. However, she refrained from telepathing this, for fear of inspiring hope just in time for it to get cruelly dashed. Especially given what she had intuited of Naratama's anxiety, stemming from his having neglected to have the abort system field-tested. And also keeping in mind Buddy Leung had communicated to her that he expected failure.

***

"I have orders, directly from my husband, to keep this 'Ahthlahn' here under guard alongside the other detained 'Ahthlahns.'" The Varalawa nudged the butt of her rifle into Helena Taylor's back as she attempted her pronunciation of "Earthling."

Helena feigned with an affected wince that the Varalawa, the first wife, gave her a painfully hard nudge.

"They all must be kept deep enough inside our central pyramid to assure that even the mind-reading of their telepathic alien friends cannot penetrate through."

"I understand all of that," nodded the security guard in a darkness tempered only by scattered splotches of bioluminescent moss cultivated on the periodically moistened, adobe-plastered walls. "But why the wives' quarters? I have been trying to contact the Fafamafalafama about this ever since the twenty-third wife arrived with the others under her own armed escort. Sources have told me he is too preoccupied at the moment with a matter of the most urgent priority."

The first wife knew, from the security guard's nocturnally wide-eyed, frozen-still, whiskered regard, that this was a test of her nerve. This was a test to see whether she might give the slightest hint, unavoidable due to her shame, that what she was about was an offense to, a betrayal of, the Fafaman Empire. She was ready. "What more faithful, more loyal subjects could OUR supreme ruler hope to find, for the most delicate task of keeping a watchful eye on our extraterrestrial visitors, without agitating them any further than was necessary...Who better for this task, at no more than the task requires, than his own wives?" The Varalawa gave the guard an unflinching, what he regarded as a defiantly imperious staredown, for the duration of this question. Which did not let up as she continued, "But do continue laboring to take the Fafamafalafama's attention away from that most urgent priority, if you must. I hope it works out for you."

The guard at-the-last lowered his rifle. Ultimately, he got intimidated, bowled over, by the first wife's steely regard. It didn't help that he found her unnervingly beautiful, the dark silhouettes of her curves set off by the soft-green bioluminescence instinctively causing his nocturnal eyes to open even wider still. He bowed his head most abjectly deferentially as he meekly fa-la-laed, "Revered Varalawa, I have behaved with an impudence that would deservedly see me fired from my post, or worse."

"Nonsense," the first wife shook her head dismissively. "You have behaved with a caution, in these uncertain times, worthy of the most trusted protectors of our kingdom. And I will be sure to relay this to the Fafamafalafama at the first opportune time."

"You are kinder than I deserve." The guard backed away still bowing as he spoke.

"No. Not kind. I am as just as you have earned. Pama."

"Pama." With that, the guard hurried off, fearful he'd stupidly gone out of his way to irritate the Varalawa.

For her first time inside what the first wife told her was a general reception area for the royal family and its guests, Helena found herself most curiously reminded of an indoor play area for children. Years ago, she had found herself wandering through part of a shopping mall during the early morning hours before the stores opened. Way back then on Earth, with only the sparsest lighting, it took her eyesight a few moments to resolve the mysteriously shadowy forms into composite material slides, tunnels, and climbable monster mushrooms that could have been mistaken for real-life tapastrahs by the rebels. Presently in the wives' reception area, what those new shadowy forms resolved themselves into were tralalafas, scattered about. They were planted into circular holes cut into the floor for soil wells.

The relieved-from-duty starship captain also noted a trio of small, refrigerator-appearing appliances positioned side by side along one wall. There were noises of commotion coming from them, as though their contents were trying to escape. The middle one was even wobbling a bit, bumping against the others.

"Those are food repositories quaking full of only the feistiest delicacies," the Varalawa's fa-la-las translated. "But I am assuming your appetite is not tempted."

"The same as I'm guessing you would not find our finest delicacies errr, feisty enough." Helena grinned wanly. "Umm, you're putting on your sun shades."

"They are for the next chamber, where we have left on the blazing-light simulation especially for your fellow 'Ahthlahns.' You should be able to remove your night-vision spectacles. But before I roll back this veil..." She grabbed Helena by the wrist, but not roughly, not harshly. Rather what got conveyed to the former Captain Taylor was an urgency tempered by caring. "You do understand my plan? Yulala is the only other one in there who knows. She has not had the opportunity to communicate with your fellow 'Ahthlahns' alone, out of the presence of the Farasarala, the eleventh wife. So they will not be acting if they appear terrified, anxious, alarmed, whatever negative emotion, upon hearing the plan as it will be described for the Farasarala's consumption. Were the eleventh wife really joyful, not so bitter, were she to understand her own self better, she would not begrudge your soldier 'Hahnsahn' and Yulala their love for one another in complete disregard for the royal custom."

Helena couldn't help a gasp.

"I love the Fafamafalafama," continued the Varalawa as though the former starship captain's reaction were nothing. "I know my own self, so I can only feel delight over what has clearly uncurled between a Fafaman and an 'Ahthlahn,' doubtless during stars-out on their desert trial. Ready?"

"Ready."

The Varalawa, the first wife, pushed a faintly glowing button beside the veil. Said veil rolled aside like a carpet being rolled up, Helena thought. Clearly, inspiration was drawn from what Fafaman fern trees did at each dawn of blazing light. No surprise for Helena, more curiosities got revealed. In the place of tralalafas, there were cactus-like plants growing from the randomly-situated soil wells, plus an occasional curled-up fern tree of some shorter species extant across Fafama. Laid out in the central area were stitched-together tralalafa leaves. Stuffed with what Helena could not have known were dried-out, chopped-up ferns, the appearance was given of an enormous, seaweed-green comforter. Four of her fellow Earthlings sat cross-legged on it, beside one another. They faced three of the Fafamafalafama's wives also sitting cross-legged, facing them in return. It looked like a meditation competition, Helena found herself unexpectedly musing. Soon as Chris saw her, he said, "Captain, I mean-" Before he could correct himself to address his wife more personally, Helena was over to his side, down on her knees. All protocol forgotten, an arm around Chris's shoulders pulling his head below her chin nearly into her bosom, she murmured, "Chris, you're okay. You're all okay," she looked up to direct this expanded message at Ali, Tanya and Sergeant Hanson.

"Your favoritism is most truly understandable, CAPTAIN Taylor." Where his calling her "Captain" was concerned, Ali would not brook any dissent from Helena.

The Farasarala, the eleventh wife, had already sprung to her feet and taken three long strides to the first wife's side. Whereupon, she made a pivot to point an accusatory finger Yulala's way. "Beloved first wife of our dearest Fafamafalafama, it is my most wretched duty to report to you, in case you have not noticed, what the Narafasala and I could not help observing and sensing like the pincer of an 'ahtpah' through our skulls! Yulala doesn't deserve to be mentioned by her name as the twenty-third wife! Yulala has betrayed our husband with her yearning regard of the 'Ahthlahn' named 'Hahnsahn'!" The Farasarala's fa-la-las seemed to Helena to rise in pitch to a tearful falsetto.

Yulala shamefully bowed her head. She cast her line of sight down towards the tralalafa comforter on which she sat cross-legged.

Ali and Tanya's mouths dropped open.

Clearly, Helena apprehended, married Officers Magabu and Petrovsky had not the slightest idea this angry outburst was anywhere in the offing.

Guy Hanson noticed Yulala's reaction out the corner of his eyes. He strained not to mimic it as he was instinctively inclined to. He well knew such behavior on his part would prove only that much more incriminating. Instead, he followed Ali and Tanya's gaping mouth example.

"I was well aware of it, most beloved Farasarala. I can only wonder at why you and the Narafasala have not been keeping the lot of them under gunpoint during my absence to secure 'Cahptahn Taylah.'" For emphasis, the first wife abruptly raised her rifle to train it on Chris and Helena.

Whereupon the nineteenth wife, the Narafasala,

scrambled to her feet to retrieve two rifles where they'd been left leaning against a cactus. She hastily handed one over to the Farasarala.

"Yulala," the Varalawa motioned towards her with her rifle, "over beside the 'Ahthlahns,' and all of you up on your feet."

"Can you ever forgive me, most beloved Varalawa, for doubting for even a nininana your powers of perception?" The eleventh wife made a deferential bow the first wife's way, even as she kept her rifle trained on Yulala.

"There is nothing to forgive, eleventh wife. I have special directions from our Fafamafalafama. We are to bring them, all of them including the FORMER twenty-third wife, to the northwest corner of the central pyramid, to leave them sacrificed to the skull-crushing pincers of the kamakala!"

"The wisdom of our loving Fafamafalafama," the Narafasala and the Farasarala both solemnly bowed as they intoned this ritual litany.

***

"Ah-" Naratama clipped short an expression of relief over the flashing of the abort signal, once he concluded punching in the security code sequence for that particular function. His heart beating out-of-control fast, he tried to remember: Was the flashing light a good thing? Were the nuclear missiles safely boosted onto an outer space trajectory so they would both explode harmlessly in the black void? Or, was the abort signal supposed to stabilize into a persisting orange glow, once the on-board missile computer confirmed the command was successfully carried out?

"That flashing light: Does it tell you the task is getting

completed?" The Fafamafalafama could not help his fa-la-las thundering with a sense of urgency, as imperiously detached and in control of his own emotions as he wanted to make them. He hovered over Naratama's left shoulder with his cape halfway open. The missile launch engineer was reminded of a picnic, when he was about to bring a delectably writhing slathafass to his mouth. He could sense one of Fafama's owl-sized beetle-ish creatures alighting on a fern up behind him. Its wings were also halfway open, as it weighed the safety of attempting to snatch the worm-like morsel away from an animal large enough and strong enough to seize it and pull its legs apart from its body.

What neither the Fafaman ruler nor his loyal subject could have known was what was happening while they both pondered the abort light. Thousands of miles away, to the west, on-board missile computers had indeed received the new flight trajectory commands...and then those computers had frozen. They were unable to proceed any further, without a specific troubleshooting diagnostic for which Naratama would have had to have read deep into the Fafaman translation of the instruction manual left behind by the "Ahthlahns."

Naratama noted no change in the original flight-path trajectory the two missiles were transmitting back to his tracking screen. At the least, he knew the abort wasn't happening. "We will soon find out," he nevertheless lied to the Fafamafalafama's anxious query, as he retyped the abort function code, hoping desperately to somehow jolt the system into action.

"I actually understand very little of what you are about with your control panel, Naratama. Yet I understand enough to know there is panic to how you are pounding at those keys!"

Naratama bowed even further, down over his control

panel. This, with the idea it would not be the worst thing in the world if the Fafamafalafama were to take advantage of this opportunity to most swiftly, mercifully sever his head from his torso. "I wish," he mumbled his fa-la-las most despairingly, "I wish I could personally place myself in the path of both missiles, to have them detonate harmlessly against my otherwise worthless-"

"BUT YOU CAN'T!!!!" The Fafamafalafama roared his fa-la-las with unbridled contempt. With a swirl of his bioluminescently lit cape, he stepped away from Naratama to better address everyone there assembled. "So save us at least from your idle dream of undeserved martyrdom!, especially since you can save us from nothing else!! And rest assured, you will remain here to perish, as you most deservedly are meant to, if nothing can be done to thwart the disastrous scenario you say has been stupidly, stupidly unleashed!! Guards!! Chain him to his post!!" Then directly at Naratama again, "I can only hope you come up with something, or that you are simply incorrect in your projections so that ultimately, we are safe by virtue of your incompetence!

"Nanofafo! Order an immediate evacuation of the central pyramid to the eastern suburbs! Dwellings there are to each take in as many citizens as possible!"

"Excellent, oh wise Fafamafalafama." Nanofafo paused on his way towards an arched exit, to make a deferential bow. "From what we gather, the effects of the ice rock descending towards our blessed pyramid from the west ought to be somewhat counteracted by the sunset storm line approaching from-"

"Time spent celebrating a wise decision itself becomes the worst possible decision, if the result is too little time for full implementation! Be gone!"

"Of course." Nanofafo rose out of his bow, to scurry

for the exit. His whiskers curled and uncurled in maximum agitation.

"Wafalawa, alert the air force to deploy every available jet! Their mission is to fire everything they've got at the ice rock!, to pulverize it as much as possible before it reaches the central pyramid! And alert the space station commander to deploy an armed shuttle blade down into the Fafaman atmosphere, to chip away at the ice rock from above!, with everything *they've* got!"

"Begging a pardon I certainly do not deserve." Again, Naratama bowed low, half hoping to feel cold steel slice swiftly all the way through his neck. "Our jets are unable to fly safely to altitudes where they can reasonably expect to successfully deliver the payload on a direct hit against the ice rock. At best, success may require a suicide mission."

"Suppose one or more loyal pilots DO succeed, and such success results in their untimely demise. And then, suppose you should survive the subsequent impact of lesser ice fragments. In that case, your new mission, Naratama, will be as exclusive servant to the families of those heroic martyrs, for the remainder of your wretched days! No more for that task than that task requires, and your full-time obligation will be all that will be required!"

***

The first evacuees streamed out ground-level exits from the east-facing flank of the central pyramid. Initially, they constituted a commotion of fa-la-las sprinkled with he-he-hees expressive of their general apprehension. But within the briefest while, metallic creaking issuing from overhead fell them silent. They looked skywards to see a half-mile-long slit growing steadily wider, some five stories up the pyramid's side. The creaking stopped as the air hangar shield finished sliding open. For a moment, many of the first Fafamans exited from the pyramid held their breath, and paused from their forward trek on foot. The only significant sound was a booming, female, intercom voice. It was intended to be calming, soothing, fa-la-laing. It called on evacuees to NOT crowd one another, rather to form orderly lines marching at a steady pace for the mini-pyramids of the eastern suburbs. There, they would get greeted by suburb dwellers with unfurling arms and comforting, most shadow-y capes to ease the discomfort of moving around outside in the middle of blazing-light.

Soon enough, however, high-pitched whines could be heard from within the hangar. They revved up one right after the other, until there was a droning chorus of them that produced an echoing thunder. One by one, Fafaman jets shot out into a blue sky blemished with too few cirrus wisps to temper its blinding brilliance.

The last part of the intercom recording, before it replayed, got entirely drowned out by the continuing exit of the Fafaman jet squadron. It was the part about the evacuation constituting a precautionary exercise, nothing to worry about.

The initial jets to leave the hangar all banked right, to circle round to the rear of the pyramid from where the evacuation was getting directed. They were on a course heading for rendezvous with the ice comet. During which, a single Fafaman voice howled his fa-la-las as shriekingly loud as possible, to get heard above the collective din of revving jet engines and intercom recording. "Is the entire Fafaman air force also getting evacuated?!?!, to not be there when the terrorists blow up the pyramid?!?!"

By the time this questioning got spread back inside the ground level of the pyramid, it didn't take long for it to mutate into panic-filled statements to the effect the pyramid was about to get blown up. That was why all the jets were emptying out. Quickly thereafter, the Fafaman exodus at ground level swelled into a chaotic stampede, easily overwhelming the stationed guards' efforts to maintain even the least semblance of orderly, if not at all calm, fleeing for presumably safer locales. Those guards quickly realized that firing warning shots, not to mention firing into the crowd, would only ramp up the frenzy. And further, that they best join this human storm line lest they get trampled underfoot by it, as was already happening to several Fafamans of all ages.

The first of the mob were already reaching the four-family pyramid duplexes. They were pounding so furiously on the garage-door-like entrances, the inhabitants were too frightened to open them.

It also didn't help that overhead, as well as on the southwest horizon, swarms of giant insects flew collectively one direction, then the other, then circled back again. They appeared unable to decide which way to go. Earthlings would have been reminded of flocks of birds preparing to migrate during late fall.

Lost in all of this were thousands of miseries that would never make it into any historical accounts of what was transpiring. For the sufferers, though, they would mark a most crushingly cruel end to a world where space had gotten carved out for them, in the comfort of a cherished item, to feel safe and secure.

Here, a little girl's stuffed animal version of a flounder mouse got trampled nearly as deep down into the gravelly soil as its living counterpart. It was hopelessly lost to her moments after terrifying shoving and pushing wrested it from her tiny grasp, while it was all her parents could do to keep her from getting trampled underfoot along with it.

There, a limping elderly man clutched a pocket-sized framed portrait of his beloved deceased wife close to his heart. That was, until someone pushing him from behind caused him to drop it, as he reflexively extended his hands forward to try keeping his balance, not fall flat on his face. His very next staggered step was smack down atop it. He crushed it so that the shards of the shattered glass frame ripped apart said portrait.

The girl and the man were among the luckier ones who didn't expire, either suffocating or getting their necks broken underfoot by the panic-y stampede. Though once they realized the fate in store for them, who knew that they would not have thought those first victims more mercifully delivered, for what they were not going to have to so fearfully experience?

Something might have given the stampede survivors hope, however cruelly false, besides learning the jets were to try to disintegrate the orbiting comet. That something would have been viewing the shuttle blade descending into the Fafaman atmosphere, at just the right angle to avoid either burning up or bouncing off uncontrollably into space, and then learning it was on a mission to join the jets with its own special fire power.

None of which would have concerned a certain ahtpah on the night side of Fafama. It was responding excitedly to the tremors of something big, just gotten caught in its web. That something big, the appearance of a praying mantis the size of a two-seater sports car, struggled frantically with its two front claws to sever the bottom-most parts of its six comb-like feet, where they were stuck to wire-thick silken strands. Meal time for the cow-sized spider. However, its twenty eyes noticed two distant flashes of light. Those flashes stood out in stark relief against a background of streaming sparkles. The ahtpah instinctively mistook them for the eyes of a dangerous beast, perhaps a thief wanting to make off with its fresh prey. And so, it turned to face the mistakenly perceived threat. It arched its bulbous rear like a scorpion, over the top of its head. It was readying an attack rather than bracing for defense. Which thereby gave the monster mantis, down to just one appendage still stuck on the web, plenty of time to engineer its escape. The lift generated by the mantis's wings at full, panicky buzz grew so powerfully strong, it succeeded in detaching its body from its stuck leg, leaving that leg behind on its flight to freedom.

What the hapless ahtpah could not have known was that those two eyes were really the two explosions from where the two nuclear-tipped missiles made impact with the orbiting ice comet.

***

Naratama clenched his left, chained hand into a fist, and then he slowly unfurled it like a Fafaman fern experiencing flounder mouse glow at stars-out. This was a customary expression of personal triumph in the Fafaman kingdom. But he made this gesture stealthily, under cover of the impenetrable shadows beneath his control console. No sense encouraging the other personnel still assembled there, personnel who were trusted, unlike him, to remain suicidally at their posts despite the approaching ice comet. No sense in revealing to them the least hope, until he could be sure what had just occurred to him would really save the day.

It was so simple: He could kill his dinner before eating, for not having had it occur to him earlier. It was something, unlike those missile fail-safes, that had been tried and tested by the "Ahthlahns" early on when they were fine-tuning the ice comet's Fafaman orbit. It had been in use ever since, to keep readjusting the orbit as more asteroid and ice debris got shed across the planet. It had to do with the multiple, automatic-adjustment booster rockets embedded into the comet's rear. The calculations were easy. He'd already done them in his head, soon as this solution occurred to him. With manual control override, he would steer the ice-laden asteroid's trajectory away from Fafaman orbit, quite harmlessly out into space. In fact, Naratama realized that if they hadn't all gotten so carried away with the idea of employing alien jet-fired missiles to bring down the ice rock on the terrorists' territory, they could have accomplished the same goal, simply by using the embedded rockets to steer the ice rock steadily downwards instead of continuing on its previous orbit.

Naratama tried to make it appear as though he were just aimlessly gathering more data from the console, hoping for inspiration to strike to save them. As nonchalantly as he could affect, he punched in a radically new flight path for the comet.

***

*Officer Leung, Naratama has implemented a new tactic he has hope will work.*

"Let's ALL hear it, Mafoosoola. I mean, umm, please dump it into all our minds." Buddy Leung looked up from his calculations for this too-brief moment of blessed whimsy.

*Of course, this telepath is for all here assembled. I knew what you meant. Anyway, it has occurred to Naratama to readjust the rocket fire from the boosters embedded in the comet, to put its trajectory on an outer space heading. He exudes optimism over this plan, because the booster program over-ride has been tested and retested.*

"Well that's better news than we've gotten in a while. Might not have to tickle the comet's underbelly with the saucer after all. Ha!"

"But if that still becomes necessary, Buddy..." Pedro kept his eyes scanning his console information readout to recheck his handiwork. He would not allow himself to relax enough to look up, until he made double-certain. "Appears we now have a direct line for implanting the laser mesh code within the saucer's circuitry, after we have programmed it into ours."

"Captain Entroper will be thrilled if we manage to save the saucer, Pedro, so muchas gracias, señor. I must say, are you sure you aren't from our time, and you just accidentally woke up one day sixty years ago? Ha!"

"Wait, man," Pedro held up a cautioning hand. "There is still much I don't understand about your technology, starting with your mirror array!"

"You and me both, Pedro. Yes, I invented it, but I still don't get it. Why do you think we brought along another hyper-physics guy to try figuring it out? Ha! Listen..." Buddy abruptly shook his head; this mental break was fine, but he knew they all needed to refocus. "What I also don't understand, Mafoosoola,- No, I do understand, but it's frustrating that you can't mentally access even one away team member. And, I can't figure out how to jury-rig a communication pathway to one of their devices through extant metals and ores in the pyramid's construction. Meanwhile, though, you've had no problem picking Naratama's brain. I know. I know from our first mission to Fafama. You don't need to telepath me a reminder. The pyramid core is carved out of so many blocks of granite, where they'd first kept Captain Taylor. Most likely, that's where they are keeping her and the others now."

*I wish it were mere reiteration I had to offer you now, Officer Leung. There is something else, as unfortunate as it is new. The recalibration of the comet boosters apparently hasn't worked. Naratama is reasonably certain, to his utter horror, that the missile detonations against the comet's upper quadrant have so jolted the booster rocket guidance systems, those systems have experienced significant damage. They are so damaged, they can no longer take in new guidance for recalibration. Now, Naratama is praying to the planet spirit who some of them worship. He is praying the jet and shuttle blade deployments will work.*

Buddy shook his head. "Again, Pedro, good job assuring that once we receive the laser mesh code, IF we receive the laser mesh code, we can load it into the saucer's circuitry. Looks like it's going to be essential to save the alien saucer craft, after all, so we can use it to take a whack at disintegrating the comet before it can crash into Fafama. Too bad those jets and shuttle blade are on a fools' errand, but we can't hope to arrive there before they try whatever they are going to unsuccessfully try."

*From what I've mind read, the "fool's errand" will also prove suicidal, Officer Leung. But you're right; neither my telepath, anything I could telepath, nor your electronic communication, is going to dissuade them. They are under direct orders from the Fafamafalafama, and he is yet another person occluded from my telepathic reach, were there any hope of convincing him to call off their attack.*

***

"Forgive in advance my impudence, esteemed Varalawa," the security guard bowed low with the traditional Fafaman diagonal downward arm sweep across his torso. "You all appear headed, with what look to be your prisoners, in a direction opposite to the ordered evacuation flow. Assuming this is the case, I have to ask how it would come to pass that the first and eleventh wives of the Fafamafalafama should need demean themselves playing armed guards to these creatures from 'Ahth.' And how it also comes to pass that the newest wife should be getting treated like just one more prisoner. Again, forgive my impudence." Another low bow.

"Are you finished, Guard?!" The Varalawa spoke in as imperious a tone as she could bluster.

"Yes. I did not mean to-"

"Enough!" translated the Varalawa's fa-la-las on Helena's ear implant translator. "This is all you need to know: She is no longer the twenty-third wife. Rather, she returns to her former name of Yulala." The Varalawa pointed her pistol Yulala's direction. She affected an arm shiver as though she were struggling mightily to keep her self-control, not pull the trigger. "The shame she has committed has been sanctioned and abetted by the 'Ahthlahns,' who have already done damage enough with their ill-placed trust in the terrorists. And so, our supreme Fafamafalafama-"

"His mercy tolerating cave mold such as myself goes more profoundly deep than the Grand Basin," the guard ritually chanted.

"Exactly so! He has commanded we take them into a kamakala tunnel, and set off a cave-in to imprison them to their fate there! And if we were to happen across a guard such as yourself, we were to honor you with accompanying us to complete this task before we rejoin that precautionary evacuation!"

"The beneficence of the Fafamafalafama." The unnamed guard swept his left hand open to his side as though, Ali Magabu mused, the Fafaman ruler's beneficence were presenting itself there like a royal poodle or some such.

***

"The ice rock is much larger than I expected," would have translated the fa-la-las of Tha-tha-la, commander of the shuttle blade deployed from the Fafaman space station. The sword-shaped spacecraft was making its shallow descent just far enough behind the orbiting comet to stay out of reach of the shimmery, sparkling trail of debris it was shedding to comprise its considerable wake. Said wake was become even more considerable than before, thanks to the comet starting its descent into the Fafaman troposphere, and thanks also to the impact of the two nuclear-tipped missiles which brought about that descent. Tropospheric air friction and pulverizing missile impact both were accelerating the immense celestial object's disintegration. "No," Commander Tha-tha-la shook his head, already regretting his remark. "I knew its proportions precisely. What I meant was that, seeing it this close, it is going to be a lot to pulverize, yes?, Officer Safama?"

Weapons Officer Safama looked up from his missile control console, like he hadn't been paying attention until his name got called. But instead of fa-la-laing, *What was that?*, he fa-la-laed, with his handlebar whiskers all a-twirl, "Commander, it will be like chiseling down granite into smaller and smaller chunks. But we have the fire power to accomplish the objective, and I am ready on your orders to launch the first battery!"

"Beg your pardon, Commander Tha-tha-la," intervened Flight Engineer Parthahaha, "but what concerns me are two perils. One peril concerns the heat friction stress our shuttle blade is presently experiencing. That stress lies well within tolerance parameters, but it is going on for a far longer time frame than has been previously tested. Peril two involves how closely we are chasing the ice rock for our purposes. You know, of course, that when you drop a plate on the floor,-"

"Your concerns are duly noted, Officer Parthahaha," broke in the commander, "but we don't have time to worry like old women over every little concern!"

"But they aren't little concerns!"

"Launch those missiles, Officer Safama! Officer Parthahaha, cut the engines to glide mode for twenty nininanas! That should have us fall further behind the ice rock, as well as temporarily lower the friction quotient."

"Aye, Commander."

Six mini-missiles whooshed quietly from the undercarriage of the shuttle blade, headed for six equidistant targets on the comet. Two of them got detonated by the shimmering debris stream before they ever reached their programmed destination. They exploded with only the faintest concussive boom, in an upper tropospheric layer littered with only the scantest number of air molecules. They reminded Safama of a fireworks display, albeit ghostly quiet. Soon thereafter, the other four missiles found their respective marks. Each one dislodged a significant amount of rock bound together by copious ice permeations. Although clearly, so much more of the comet was left to go before the Fafamans made a serious dent in its destructively large potential. Each explosion appeared vanishingly small on the shuttle blade's view screen, up against the full immensity of the comet. Commander Tha-tha-la feared those impacts taken all together might prove as inconsequential as spatterings of desert sand by precious few rain drops. What was not immediately apparent was that one of several big blown-off chunks was blown off directly towards the shuttle blade. Impact was over before the crew knew what hit them. Said chunk's metal-shearing crash into the "hilt" of the "blade" sent the entire craft into a fire-y tailspin, made so much more quickly engulfing by growing hull weaknesses. Those weaknesses were caused by the longevity of exposure to air friction at a speed of fifteen thousand miles an hour. They had already been well underway towards ruining the spacecraft's structural integrity.

What Officer Parthahaha had been cut off from remarking about was how, when you dropped a plate on the floor, there was always a particularly large fragment that shot out way far away from the rest.

***

*Officer Leung, tragic news with regard to the three Fafamans aboard their shuttle blade craft, who I was mind-reading to follow their efforts to partially disintegrate the comet. They've gotten themselves killed and their craft completely destroyed by an outlier incidental shrapnel from their missile attack.*

"And how did you determine they're dead, Mafoosoola?" Robertson couldn't help inserting himself. "Sorry, Officer Leung, I'm just curious."

Buddy nodded his okay for the soldier to continue.

"Did their thoughts suddenly stop? Or is their intelligence continuing beyond the grave?"

*Always an interesting question, Officer Robertson. What I can telepath you is that unto the moment when clearly their lives ended in sudden horror and unfathomable pain, none of them knew what happened. Although, the flight engineer did evidence a fleeting suspicion. It was after presumably their spacecraft turned into a fireball that I sensed an awareness, from an indeterminate source, of how this occurred. We have experienced similar with our deceased loved ones on Oomb. Anyway, all too soon, also similar to our experience with our own loved ones, a veil came down. We still sense something, but it is at what can only be described to you as a low hum, occasionally static-y. It blends with the mysterious more general background hum from whence new intelligence seems to emerge whenever a new Oombian takes root on our planet.*

"Okay, that's fascinating. Really, Mafoosoola." To the tree creature's wistful-looking eyes peering out from between corrugations of tree bark, Buddy Leung gave his most sincere regard. "But we are fast approaching the laser mesh shield of Fafama, and I need to make certain whoever has remained aboard their space station doesn't hesitate on the mesh code transmittal."

"One final 'attack' by the saucer, Officer Leung?"

"Pedro Perez, it is as though you read my mind." Buddy gave Mafoosoola a wink that was reciprocated. "We're prepared when you are, yes?"

"All strapped down here!" shouted Robertson.

The shuttle pod was already executing variable zigzag maneuvers. This, to fool the Fafamans remaining aboard the space station into thinking it was successfully staving off the Tictoctic saucer from being able to home in on its target. Mafoosoola's mind-reading of those Fafamans gave no indication they were anything less than fully credulous, believing of the picture getting painted for them. However, Buddy and Pedro both feared said credulity could turn a quick corner to suspicion, mere seconds before they otherwise would have transmitted the laser mesh code. That was, without another piece of reinforcing evidence. Wherefore the "one final attack," as Fafama filled up close to a quarter of the shuttle's view-screen, with the sunset storm line from that distance in space looking like a cottony-brown line dramatically separating the day side from the night side. As Buddy and Pedro both saw it, those remaining Fafaman space station crew would be anticipating a certain sort of behavior by the saucer occupants. Said crew would be supposing the alien saucer was incapable of safe flight down into an atmosphere. Soon, therefore, the saucer's occupants would have to break off their pursuit. And so, the Fafamans still aboard the space station would be expecting one last shot fired from the flying saucer at the shuttle pod, before either vehicle got too much closer to the upper troposphere.

Operated remotely by Pedro, a laser beam shot out from the saucer. That beam harmlessly strafed one of the shuttle pod's electrostatically bound micron-layer stabilizer fins. The small craft wobbled dramatically, but again, minute damage actually got inflicted.

"Laser mesh code incoming from Mafoosoola's mind-reading, Officer Leung!" Pedro reported excitedly, his fingers a flurry of tapping on his console keyboard. "And now it's also loaded into the saucer!"

"Let's beeline it to the mesh, pronto!"

Within seconds, the shuttle pod's trajectory had flattened out on its path headed for the mid-afternoon sky east of the central pyramid. Buddy made a slight adjustment to assure they wouldn't accidentally collide with one of the laser mesh satellites. These satellites were scattered in latticework stationary orbits around Fafama.

Buddy would have likened them to acupuncture stress points.

"We're through?!" Pedro burst out half-questioning, half-exclaiming. He could hardly believe it, even though he felt the planetary gravity pull him deep down into his seat cushion with ever-increasing force.

"We are through! Ha!" relievedly confirmed Buddy. He had to shout to get heard above the whoosh-y din of increasing air density outside the shuttle pod.

Growing friction made the shuttle pod appear like an orange flare for any Fafaman happening to peer into the eastern, pastel-blue firmament. But actually, most Fafamans had their full attention focused on the more-gradually-descending comet further west, despite their fleeing eastward.

"I've switched our screen to rear view to see that the saucer- NO!"

Soon as the flying saucer breached the laser mesh threshold, a latticework of red lines lit up. Several of them converged on this immense alien spaceship, while a few made an octagonal circumvention of it. Said spaceship stalled out, and went into a hovering wobble. As ball lightning, generated by the laser mesh satellites, rode the laser beams to approach the disabled craft, Pedro was reminded of a spinning top slowed so much that it was about to careen over on its side. Successive collisions of the ball lightning with the flying saucer caused it to burst apart in explosion after explosion. For Pedro, it could have been a 4th-of-July fireworks finale, albeit totally quiet.

"Crap!" swore Buddy Leung with his dawning realization. "I don't know whether this was intentional, but instead of feeding us the code algorithm, the Fafamans must have only fed us the latest entry code!"

"What the f- are you talkin' about?" cursed

Robertson.

"After each space vessel descends through the mesh, the code is automatically reconfigured to prevent a mass invasion from hostiles who might manage to steal it!"

***

"This is rear left guard to squadron leader!" would have translated the fa-la-las transmitted by a co-pilot of the Fafaman fighter jet in the rear-most left side of the 'V' formation, on a heading west of the central pyramid.

"This is squadron leader Fasafa! If this is about a successfully thwarted attempt by a large, saucer-shaped spacecraft to breach the laser mesh, preceded by the entry into Fafaman air space of a small, tear-shaped spacecraft, we already know! I have a report from the space station that a space vehicle of unknown alien origin was chasing a shuttle craft from 'Ahth' through our solar system! Unfortunately, we also have a report the shuttle blade has experienced catastrophic structural failure after mounting a pulverization attack on the ice rock! Unless the 'Ahthlahns' have a plan, and I don't think they can in such a puny vehicle located so far behind us!, then we are it! We are the last line of defense between that rock and our pyramid kingdom!! So, with the power granted me by the Fafamafalafama, listen carefully, all squadron pilots and co-pilots! We have calculated the ice rock hurtles through our atmosphere most rapidly! In fact, it hurtles too rapidly, for us to be able to circle around behind it and yet still keep up with it for a rear-guard pulverization effort! By the time we finished circling around, the ice rock would have outdistanced us by far too far! By the time we caught up with it, it would have already reached impact! And so, to our greater honor, to save the future of the Fafaman Empire, we must fly directly towards the ice rock! We must expend all our firepower at varying levels and from side to side!, across the ice rock's length and width! We must break it apart as much as possible to minimize its impact on the central pyramid! And you must understand that even if we succeed, it is very likely that every one of us will fatally collide with one or more of the broken rock fragments! I have transmitted this plan to the Fafamafalafama himself, and he has responded that his prayers fly with us! TO THE GLORY OF THE FAFAMAN EMPIRE!!!"

"TO THE GLORY OF THE FAFAMAN EMPIRE!!!" erupted fa-la-las in chorus through the squadron leader's cockpit intercom, from every squadron pilot and co-pilot.

***

*Lots of important information I need to telepath you.* Mafoosoola made this communication generally available to all aboard the shuttle pod on gradual descent into the Fafaman atmosphere, rather than only to Buddy Leung. *First, a squadron of jets-*

"That we're detecting down below, about a thousand miles ahead of us, towards the comet?"

*The same, Officer Perez. Their squadron leader has just concluded essentially a suicide pact with all the pilots and co-pilots. They will approach the comet head-on, guns blazing, as it lowers to a level they can manage. They hope to break it apart enough before they crash into it.*

"Officer Leung," Pedro Perez redirected his attention, "is there any realistic chance that strategy will work?"

"No." Buddy shook his head tentatively, then with mounting conviction as he finished re-crunching the relevant, best-case-scenario numbers. "If you have ever gone after a clay rock formation with a pick ax to get at an embedded fossil, like I've done with Cathy, errr, my wife, it's the same thing. As much as has gotten shorn away by the friction from atmospheric descent, and by the nuclear-tipped missiles that have been fired into its rear, we are still looking at something tens of miles across. Sure, more missiles fired into it head-on will burst off more shards of it, like a pick ax bursting off chunks of clay. But by the time the comet reaches the pyramid, it will still be several miles wide."

*Another related factor, Officer Leung: I have mind-read that at least some of the pilots and co-pilots affirmed their solidarity with the squadron leader's plan in words only. They intend on either breaking out of the attack formation before it is too late, or breaking out of formation after they fire their first few missiles if they are not sensing the desired result.*

*More pertinent to our humble-sized mission: I am now finally reading the mental horizons of former Captain Taylor and the others. They are nearing the northwest corner of the central pyramid under armed guard, with an escape plan in the works.*

"Beg all yours pardon," interrupted Robertson, a tentative tone to his voice. "About those rocket boosters the Naratama guy tried unsuccessfully to redirect, that seem to have gotten stuck or something: Any reason we can't fly around back of the comet, have one of us space-walk over to unstick them? I know that would be dangerous..."

Buddy shook his head most regretfully. "The comet is already down in too much air and gravitational pull for a space-walk, and anyway the debris it's shedding would fatally compromise the toughest space-walk suit we've got. No, we're going to have to settle with seeing if we can get the away team off the planet, along with maybe a few cooperative Fafamans. But keep trying to think of something, Officer Robertson."

*I will telepath a useful assurance to the away team.*

***

The away team plus Yulala continued under armed guard by a security officer plus the Fafamafalafama's first and eleventh wives. They had long since left behind the general exodus towards the east-facing side of the central pyramid. Minutes earlier, they encountered two more security officers. Those officers were making a final sweep of the lower northwest corner of the pyramid. They were looking for anyone who might have somehow wandered astray, or not gotten the word about the evacuation orders. They asked the Varalawa whether she and the Farasarala wouldn't like them to take their place so they could rejoin the evacuation.

"No. The Fafamafalafama requires my direct confirmation these terrorist sympathizers from another world, including Yulala for her personal betrayal, have been sealed away in a kamakala chamber. I must personally assure they will meet their fate by skull-crushing mandibles rather than by bullets." The first wife feared that, left to their own devices, those guards were likely to just shoot Yulala and the Earthlings. And then they would toss the corpses into the structural weakness. After they detonated the area closed, who would ever know exactly what happened?

From the shuttle pod, Mafoosoola was telepathing Ali, Tanya, Guy and Chris an assurance which Helena and Yulala had not had the opportunity to share with them. That is, not without that vengeful eleventh wife and presently the assisting security guard easily overhearing. Mafoosoola's comforting messaging pertained to the escape plan. This messaging went on as guard, wives, Yulala and captive Earthlings alike approached an area cordoned off by rope. Signs hanging from that rope read in Fafaman hieroglyphics: ***Danger: construction area and kamakala nesting site***. With their night-vision goggles the Earthlings saw that beyond the rope, the ground sloped steeply down a bowl-shaped, gravelly incline to a black pit devoid of the usual bioluminescent moss.

"Tossing us in there, to whatever beast awaits us, is going to accomplish nothing," were Helena's words before her translator spit out the associated fa-la-las. She had already sensed some suspicion by the eleventh wife and the guard. It was suspicion regarding how docilely the Earthlings and Yulala behaved, given that they were getting led to their doom. So, she figured she'd better put up some sort of token resistance, at least.

To this same end, Yulala affected a grieving whimper.

"Proceed to comfort her, 'Ahthlahn' soldier," fa-la-laed the Farasarala as she nudged her gun barrel into Sergeant Hanson's rib cage. "Let us see how the former twenty-third wife betrays the Fafamafalafama by her welcome of your tenderness!"

"Farasarala: No more for the task than the task requires! And the task does not require whatever you call what you are doing!"

The eleventh wife looked up from her attempted provocation of the extraterrestrial from "Ahth," to find the first wife giving her a most glowering, reprimanding stare. At first, the eleventh wife was tempted to stare her back in challenging fashion. Maybe she could have even added something spiteful, about how she wasn't thinking she was the real problem there, she who had always remained dedicated faithful to the Fafamafalafama. But then the Farasarala thought better of it. She resigned herself for the umpteenth time to the grim truth that she could never hope to ever usurp the authority of the first wife, no matter how many lapses of judgment that human ahtpah, so she considered her, demonstrated!

"Are any of you going to answer me?" went on Helena. "Do you really think you can do this without bringing down the wrath of our people? Soon, their battle cruiser will return full of new armaments for you to protect yourselves from our mutual threat from Tictoctic!"

"Yes, what are you doing here? Truly, it makes no sense." Ali was able to make himself sound especially sincere because, prior to Mafoosoola's comforting telepath, those were exactly the words he had planned on saying to support fellow Earthlings' protests.

"This is about the honor of the Fafaman Empire!" fiercely responded the Varalawa. "This is about the fact that, whatever you thought you were doing with the enemy, it resulted in the deaths of wives and children of the Fafamafalafama!, and now possibly the imperilment of our centuries-old pyramid civilization! The final insult is one of your own wooing the twenty-third wife! If you were not setting out to betray our trust, you might as well have been!, because that has been the sum effect!"

*Wow, the first wife is really lathering it on,* Ali thought to himself. *Most likely, she is trying to assure the eleventh wife of her allegiance to their shared circumstance, as the tension between them has been shining far more brightly than the bioluminescent moss.*

"Well," former Captain Taylor hemmed as she made a subtle, eye-contact nod of *Ready to go* to Tanya, Yulala, Ali and Guy.

Just like that, Yulala and the Earthlings were diving for the wives' and guard's legs, to throw them off balance.

They dodged serious hurt from guns getting brought down to beat them, in a way that intentionally sent themselves rolling under the rope and avalanching, barreling down the gravelly slope into the black pit below.

Soon as the last one, Ali, got lost from view, consumed by the total darkness, the guard uncorked an egg-shaped device strapped to his chest, and he lobbed it in after the "Ahthlahn." The grenade-like device bounced end over end down the slope. After it, too, vanished into the black pit, there was a concussive blast which sent sparks, flames, and pebbles spewing from there. The appearance was given of an active fumarole on the flank of a volcanic crater.

"Esteemed Farasarala, their fate will be what it should be."

After a nininana's worth of reflection on what had just transpired, the eleventh wife made an approving nod. *No wonder the Varalawa is the Varalawa; I need to give thanks for my own station in the life of this mighty empire.*

***

To Pedro, Mafoosoola seemingly floated on her hundreds of stunted, knobby roots down the exit ramp from the landed shuttle pod. She arrived, safely balanced, on Fafaman soil held firm against the daily ravages of the sunset storm line by zoysia-like intertwining grass. The Oombian tree creature probed two of her larger roots deep below the surface, until they found moisture. Whereupon Mafoosoola spread out her branches, which she had trimmed back dramatically so she could fit comfortably aboard any spacecraft. She shook them to give her dark-green leaves a healthy, carbon-dioxide-absorbing rustle. *Ahhh, fresh air,* she telepathed the Earthlings in her presence.

"Very good, Mafoosoola," said Buddy Leung, trying to stifle his anxious impatience. "But can you tell us what you have been able to mind-read, of how our friends are going to escape out this corner of the pyramid? Anything we can do to help? Look back there at how quickly the comet is approaching; I'm not sure we have more than a half hour, forty minutes left before we're going to have to lift off from here."

Air friction was causing the gradually descending comet to shed meteoric fragments like so many falling stars, from all across its surface. Buddy and Pedro both were lent the most unsettling, misleading impression the entire, formerly celestial object had become molten rock through and through.

*What is making manageable your fellow officers' escape-in-progress is a weakness in the pyramid foundation. Pyramid engineers have been dealing with that for the past two decades, since its latest base area expansion. Goat-sized, ant-like creatures they call the kamakala have been stubbornly rebuilding their tunnel network at this corner of the foundation. Soon as new cement is laid, they burrow through it. The architectural engineers tried gassing them out, when a namanacasa was located nearby that needed to be removed. But new ones kept coming in to replace the deceased.*

Officer Leung was about to tell Mafoosoola, *Enough with the history lesson; manageable or not, how's the escape actually going?* Glancing towards the comet again, though, he noticed small but pronounced flashes, on and off like firefly lights. "Look!" he said, pointing. "I think that must be the Fafaman fighter jets on their suicide mission!"

Just as Buddy said this, there were between ten and twenty larger flashes. These included a few closer to the comet's outer perimeter. Officer Leung figured the fighter jet pilots tried too late to peel off from their uselessly ineffectual missile barrage, to avoid crashing into the comet. Clearly, there would be no survivors.

***

Ali felt himself getting jostled out of his daze by his wife Tanya, and found himself on his back. He was lying against a mix of the hard and the jagged with the soft and the moist. Gritty dirt clung all over his arms and face. For that first moment coming to, his entire body tensed instinctively. He feared what he was going to discover about his condition once he allowed himself to relax into his present state of being. Could bones be broken? That moistness underneath him, was that blood? Would his first, tentative movements produce excruciating pain?

"You're okay, Ali?" Tanya worriedly craned her face down close to her husband's.

"We will soon find out, truly. How is everyone else? Phew!" Dr. Magabu couldn't help this exhalation of relief. He discovered that, slowly lifting up on his elbows to a seated position, the worst for him consisted of perhaps no more than a few minor scrapes and bruises.

"Everyone is in about your same condition. Many of us have ringing in our ears from that grenade-type device they lobbed in after us."

"So Yulala," Ali unexpectedly, where his wife was concerned, turned his attention to their accompanying Fafaman woman who had led them this far, "I understand, courtesy of our tree-telepathing friend from the planet Oomb, that you are to provide our salvation." The counselor was going to add something about their good fortune Sergeant Hanson had formed a bond with her. But he thought better of it.

"I wish we had time to talk more, to…explain more." The former twenty-third wife cast a sheepish look Guy's way while her fa-la-las got automatically translated. Then she proceeded, "We have little enough time for our task now than the time our task will require. Every one of us must lie down in this ground water mud. We must roll ourselves around in it until it is adhering all over, as I am demonstrating. We must act quickly. The kamakala will be entering here soon."

Yulala paused. The Earthlings who so depended on her could indeed hear scraping and clicking noises getting incrementally louder, however faint they still were, for the time being.

"After we roll around in the mud," Yulala proceeded, "we must bunch ourselves together, and slap as much more mud upon ourselves as we can. Then we must lie down on our sides, and curl into fetal positions."

"And then what?" asked Helena, although she was already rolling over onto her belly in the mud.

"And then we wait for the kamakala to carry us out of here, on their mission to reopen their latest burrowed exit to get blasted shut."

***

After leaving the "Ahthlahns" plus Yulala to their fate, the first wife, the Varalawa, told the guard and the eleventh wife they could go ahead to join the general evacuation. She'd catch up with them after she secured what she would only say were special items from her private quarters. The Farasarala insisted she had special items to secure from *her* private quarters, especially if the entire pyramid was in danger. And of course, under these apocalyptically dire circumstances, the royal security guard wasn't going to leave behind two royal wives, unattended.

When this small contingent re-entered the outer reception area of the wives' quarters, the Farasarala wasn't really any more surprised than the Varalawa to find the Fafamafalafama waiting there, three security guards in tow. The eleventh wife had suspected the first wife was concealing her real reason for returning to her quarters. It had only been a matter of who it was she planned to meet there, whether an illicit lover or, far more likely, the supreme ruler himself.

On the first wife causing the entrance veil to roll into a thick cylinder to one side, her nocturnal eyes snatched the final split-nininana of the Fafamafalafama dashing into a recline on the nearest tralalafa. Clearly, he wanted to pretend to a certain nonchalance awaiting her return, as opposed to the restless impatient pacing she could be certain he had been about.

"Ahh, there you are," the Fafamafalafama's fa-la-las would have translated. He affected to casually, lazily sit up, and to get back on his feet in a comparably leisurely manner. He even stretched out his arms. Everything short of a yawn, while his guards averted their eyes from any least contemplation of his two wives at the same time as they saluted them. All three guards knew well the story of a colleague whose eyes had lingered a bit too lustfully long on the fair face of a royal wife. This had happened several years ago, when the Fafamafalafama was a lot younger, of course. Upon his noticing how entranced, how bewitched the reckless guard had become, the Fafamafalafama had ordered him bound to a fern beside an ahtpah web. The hapless man's eyes were taped open so that as they got painfully stinging dry, they also could not help but watch as the enormous spider came at him to paralyze him and then suck out his entrails.

"Esteemed Fafamafalafama," the security guard for the wives bowed low as he made the traditional downward diagonal arm sweep across his chest, "the Varalawa and the Farasarala had me accompany them to successfully complete the task you asked of the Varalawa. She can now give you her personal assurance she witnessed its completion."

"Pama." The Fafamafalafama faked his approving acknowledgment of the guard's explanation for his presence, as he had no idea what said guard was talking about. What task? He set his wide-eyed, nocturnal sight on the first wife and fa-la-laed, "This is as the guard says?"

The Varalawa disciplined herself not to give a side glance, to how the Farasarala was sizing up the situation, as she responded, "The guard is most exacting, no more for the report than the report requires, my dear Fafamafalafama."

"Excellent." Again, the Fafaman supreme ruler faked an all-knowing approving nod.

"Beg your pardon for our unworthy impertinence, esteemed Fafamafalafama," one of the supreme ruler's three guards made so bold as to interject with the ritual sweeping bow. "Will you now be wanting us to escort all of you from the pyramid to the safest possible location?"

"Hmmm," the Fafamafalafama hmmed, "would that there really were a safest possible location. No. What you guards will do, for the 'nininana,' is await my further orders outside this ante-chamber. Now!"

"Your patience with us is only exceeded by your wisdom," all four guards said in unison as they backed bowingly out the entrance and caused it to unroll shut.

"You desire details about the task's execution, my

dearest?" fa-la-laed the Farasarala. She stepped in between the Varalawa and the Fafamafalafama, to affectionately as well as possessively plant the palms of her hands upon the Fafamafalafama's upper chest, and look searchingly into his eyes.

"I desire both of you," he responded as he encircled the eleventh wife's waist to pull her over to his right side, and drew the first wife to his left side, the side where his sword lay unsheathed. "Both of you I desire to sit down atop this tralalafa beside me, for what I have to say."

Both women complied without the least resistance. The Varalawa kept her head bowed demurely while the Farasarala pouted her lips and searchingly continued to try to draw the supreme ruler's eyes into hers.

"There. I am afraid that a terrible-"

"I cannot allow you to lie like that, my dearest!" fa-la-laed the Farasarala, rearing back from him and slapping him on his shoulder. "You are NEVER afraid!"

The Fafamafalafama pulled his eleventh wife so close, she could feel his breath in her face. It was pungent from minute strands of his last squirming meal caught between his unbrushed teeth. "Understand this, dear Farasarala: For myself, I fear nothing. But for you, I fear everything! The giant ice rock the people of 'Ahth' reined into orbit around Fafama is sinking out of its orbit into a collision path with the central pyramid. It appears unlikely anything or anyone is going to stop it!"

"That is what the evacuation is about!" the eleventh wife gasped. In her subsequent distress, she worked her knuckles into her mouth.

"That is what the evacuation is about," the Fafaman ruler nodded. "But it will be for neither me nor the first wife, unless the Varalawa prefers a different path. We both must retire down inside the original pyramid at the central core, from where if we are meant to survive, we will lead the rebuilding of the Fafaman center of power."

"I must stay here with you! If you are the only ones to survive while the rest perish, you will require more than one soil to plant your seed, for growing the rebirth of our people! And if you do perish, it is only fitting that your most devoted wives should perish with you, and quite obviously-"

The Fafamafalafama gently yet firmly pressed his forefinger against the Farasarala's lips. This caused the Farasarala to think better of speaking ill of the wives not present. Such talk might have turned him to fury, given how she'd seen him behave on other occasions, and also based on the stories she'd heard about him.

"Most devoted first wife," the eleventh wife leaned forward to look across the Fafamafalafama to the Varalawa seated on his other side, "should you prefer that different path, I could remain here in your stead. It would be the deepest honor I could imagine."

The Varalawa reached her hand across the Fafamafalafama's lap to grasp the Farasarala's hand, also gently yet firmly. Then the first wife looked steadily, unwaveringly into the eleventh wife's eyes to sternly, definitively fa-la-la, "I do not prefer a different path."

"Very well! But, do not duty and honor dictate I remain down here beside you both, to share your fate?" She squeezed the Varalawa's hand imploringly. And she looked pleadingly into the Fafamafalafama's eyes, which were giving her a most wistful regard.

The Fafamafalafama gently shook his head, and he spoke so softly, his deep voice was just above a cavernous whisper, "No more for the task than the task requires. This task requires only the Varalawa. What is required of you..." He paused to lean against the first wife so he could reach down into his zippered pocket on the Farasarala's side. Whatever it was he withdrew, he kept it clutched in a concealing fist as he went on, "Assume we should perish, and you should survive, dear Farasarala. In that circumstance, I entrust you to choose my successor, the next Fafamafalafama."

The eleventh wife's eyes watered as much as they lit up. With a hand to her chest as she labored to catch her breath, she poutingly fa-la-laed, "Of all your other wives, certainly it cannot come down to me...!" She found herself at a loss for any further words. She just shook her head, mouth hanging open.

"But you are not all of my other wives!" The bass boom was returning to the Fafamafalafama's voice as he gave the Farasarala a sly grin. The first wife, off to his other side, demurely folded together her hands in her lap, and she looked down at them, exuding patient self-discipline.

"Yes, but how are others to know? What is to keep another wife from claiming you have entrusted HER to select the next Fafamafalafama? How will anyone be able to tell who really holds the power?"

"Ahh, that you have so immediately perceived this issue is no small part of why it is you who has earned this sacred trust." The supreme Fafaman ruler held towards the Farasarala his fist. Whereupon he unclenched it to reveal in the palm of his hand a gold-plated signet ring. "The signet is engraved with the sacred seal of the Fafamafalafama. Go ahead; pick it up and adorn your left pinkie finger."

Before placing the ring where she was directed to, the eleventh wife took a few nininanas to study and admire its engravings. A pyramid had wispy lines to its right, representing the sunset storm line. The pyramid's center was taken up with the phallic sword hieroglyph, an exacting replica of the Fafamafalafama's signature.

"Anyone who challenges your authority, you need only show them this ring to definitively settle the matter." What the Fafaman ruler was leaving out was that she was the fifth wife to receive such a ring. In the event more than one wife survived the ice rock collision with Fafama – though he doubted anyone would survive at all – he had confided to most of his advisers that only one of the rings was forged of gold through and through. The wife who presented with that solid gold artifact, she would be anointed the new first wife, in charge of selecting the new Fafamafalafama. Any of his advisers in the know who survived, it would be their duty to explain this. They would have to assure the wives they were the Fafamafalafama's top picks. He had had to entrust more than one wife, to increase the odds of continuity. Also, the ring that was gold through and through was not known to him. This was intentional, so he would not know to whom he was actually giving it. And in the event the owner of the solid gold signet did not survive, it would be for the wife who scraped all the gold plating off her ring first to assume the new Varalawa position.

Not suspecting any of this, the Farasarala stood up and fa-la-laed, "I wish it were in my power to convince you both to leave, try to save yourselves while I took your place inside the core pyramid. That would be my clear choice."

"And another clear reason to entrust you!" inserted the Fafamafalafama with his fa-la-las back to full boom.

"But I clearly cannot. So I leave you now, with the assurance that as desperately as I pray for your safety to the planetary spirit, I will just as desperately strive to survive the ice rock collision. If I am to get buried beneath rock, so be it. However, I hereby swear to you both that I will nevertheless continue to live long enough to get unearthed, and then to select your successor, even if that be on my last, dying breath!"

The Fafaman ruler nodded his approving acknowledgement, but his only additional words were, "You must leave now, with no further delay. I command it! Have the guards escort you to wherever they judge that safety might be found!"

Unnerved by a hint of impatient ferocity in the Fafamafalafama's command, the Farasarala did not even pause to make one last bow with the diagonal arm sweep down. Rather, she pivoted on her moccasin-wearing feet, and she raced for the exit, which had been left rolled open.

Soon as she was gone, the Fafamafalafama and the Varalawa made tentative motions to hold lightly one another's hands. They did not yet dare allow themselves to look one another's way. There was still the possibility the eleventh wife might return bursting back into the reception area on whichever pretext. But, so soon as the sets of departing footsteps stopped at the nearest subway car, and that car could be heard pulling off into the echoing distance, not only did the Fafaman ruler and the first wife turn to one another. They virtually collapsed, melted into one another's arms.

***

*A telepath of comfort while you are enduring what has to be a most unsettling circumstance: Officer Leung has brought the shuttle pod in for a landing near the corner of the pyramid where the kamakala will be carrying you out.*

*Thank you, Mafoosoola,* was the thought with which Helena initially filled her head, so the Oombian could easily mind-read her heartfelt appreciation. And then she went *on, Mafoosoola, can you confirm for me that the kamakala have picked up all of us?, that we are all now in transport? Nobody left behind?*

*I can indeed, Helena Taylor. From what I can glean of your thoughts, Officer Magabu was the last one to receive a lift, so to telepath.*

*It is truly amazing, as though this dialogue with you at its hub, Mafoosoola, were not amazing enough,* Ali Magabu focused on thinking. *How amazing, a creature the size of a goat could so easily pick up one of us by its pincers and so rapidly proceed uphill carrying that person. Though I would guess this is of a piece with the ants on our planet, far more miniscule. They have no difficulty carrying objects several times their own weight.*

*Officer Olsen-Taylor confirms that is a most cogent comparison,* telepathed Mafoosoola. *Incidentally, he feels like griping over the cloth you all had to paper-maché over your night-vision goggles. However, he well understands this additional discomfort is well worth it, to avoid the kamakala detecting any slightest eye-lens reflection of ambient bioluminescent glow. Such detection, of course, would have sent them into a murderous, stinging fury.*

*Mafoosoola,* thought Sergeant Hanson with great intention, *please telepath Yulala I want to ask her: Is this what she used to do for diversion in her youth?*

*I have so telepathed, Sergeant.*

*What is unnerving for me,* Tanya focused on thinking, *is how this clayey matter with which we covered ourselves, how quickly it seems to be drying, and contracting as it dries.*

*Mafoosoola, please advise Officer Petrovsky that truly, the contracting of the drying clay about her being will be as nothing compared to how tightly I intend to hug her, once we are safely aboard the shuttle pod!*

*That, Officer Magabu, and I am also sharing what Yulala has made mind-readable,* responded Mafoosoola. *For many solar orbits, construction crew members have been trying to fill the corner weakness of the pyramid with a cement-like material. Combined with the ground water, a clay-cement slurry mix has been produced, with the contracting-when-drying property you described. Fortunately, Yulala has found there is no real danger of, for example, rib-breaking suffocation.*

*Always good to know, Mafoosoola,* Chris thought for mind-reading purposes.

*The comet, Mafoosoola: Has Buddy Leung or anyone on Fafama been able to make progress stopping it?*

*No, Officer Taylor. We were going to try with a Tictoctic saucer craft Officer Leung hijacked, but the laser mesh destroyed it.*

*Will the evacuation of the pyramid do any good?, save any lives?*

*Based on Officer Leung's calculations, impact of the comet with Oomb is likely to precipitate an extinction event wherein only some of the smaller insect species will survive.*

*Once we're aboard the shuttle pod* – It was Sergeant Hanson thought-transmitting with what Mafoosoola easily sensed was desperate urgency – *we can try rescuing other Fafamans? Ferry them to the space station until the Smoke and Mirrors arrives? For starters, maybe we can find- you can mind-read the location of Yulala's relatives?*

*I wish I could telepath otherwise, Sergeant, but there will hardly be time to ferry yourselves before impact. Whether we can go after anyone else, post-impact, will depend on the planet's tectonic stability, and what happens to the planet's orbital path.*

*What happens to the planet's orbital path…My God,*

what have we done? Helena couldn't help asking herself.

*Yulala is most upset. Nevertheless, she wants you to focus on the directions I now telepath you. She appreciates she doesn't have to try whispering these reminders, since the kamakala possess extraordinary hearing ability. First, she says that upon the kamakala depositing you on the ground outside the pyramid, await her signal, by way of my telepath. This signal will indicate the kamakala have returned underground, to excavate new pieces of clay from where an opening was bombed closed again. Once I have telepathed Yulala's "all clear" sign, you will want to kick out the bottom of your clay shell. You will need to unbend your legs, more and more, until they have broken through. Then, you should maneuver about until any two of you can bump together to loosen up the dried slurry about your arms. Those of you who can get on your feet, mostly uninhibited by the cement, you should work as rapidly as possible to free up the others. Okay, this was none too soon. Yulala telepaths that you can start kicking. Good luck! Several minutes ago, we landed the shuttle close to where we expected you would be carried out of the ground by the kamakala. But we had to take off again, to lure an ahtpah far away from there. We should be landing a second time within minutes.*

Helena Taylor found, after her first couple of leg flexes, it was not too difficult to break out her feet and fully unbend. However, the same as her companions were experiencing, she noticed a distant crackling. It was comparable to a forest firestorm as could be heard on a television news report. Initially, she attempted to reconcile, understand that crackling as the gravelly sound of the dried clay-cement slurry continuing to crumble off her soiled-gray, light-blue uniform and her just-freed arms. However, looking into the western dusk, Helena soon realized from whence horrifically issued said crackling. This realization was made possible, of course, by her facilely managing to tear the de facto paper mache cloth off her night-vision goggles, and removing the goggles themselves. It was the descending comet, become a fireball curiously framed by a rainbow halo due to all the water vapor getting shed. It still remained far distant from impact. But the Earthlings and one Fafaman could not have been more upset, for how much of the sky it already filled, noticeably enlarging to take up more and more as it approached.

"Oh!" Helena gulped, though she realized instantly the dark silhouette that dove past was not another monster insect, after all. It was the shuttle pod coming in for a second landing. The former captain spun around to make sure everyone else was on their feet, enough free and clear of the dried slurry to be on their feet. She saw that all of them, the same as she was, were transfixed by the awful spectacle of the collision-course comet.

Suddenly, there was a shrill whistle, plus a stiff breeze from the shuttle pod landing anew. That breeze kicked up a cloud of dried clay particles. The cloud quickly thickened so much, the humans and Fafaman experienced difficulty keeping one another in view. They instinctively bunched themselves together. Tanya and Ali out-and-out embraced, though with the bulk of their attention remaining directed towards the steadily descending, steadily approaching comet. It remained clearly visible, despite all the dirt the shuttle pod's descent was continuing to stir up into billowing brown clouds. Sergeant Hanson protectively tried to enfold Yulala in his arms, as she disciplined herself to ignore him despite her own strong desire to simply melt into his comforting care. Well did she know she needed to keep fiercely focused on looking, smelling and listening around about for danger signs. Helena Taylor latched onto Chris's upper left arm. He wasn't sure how much of that was simply about Helena trying to maintain her balance despite the debris-laden wind gusts from the shuttle pod, and how much was about seeking his loving protection. Regardless, Officer Olsen-Taylor noticed something else most disturbing. Yulala also noticed. It was one of those danger signs for which Yulala had her senses on the alert. Namely, there was a commotion of disturbed clay and gravel from something other than the shuttle pod.

*Yulala is thinking you all must remain perfectly still, while several kamakala are emerging from other holes in the ground to make for the shuttle pod. A leg or a shell might brush against you, but you must not react, or you will make yourself a target of their attention.*

No sooner did Helena think to herself, *This can't be good*, than a shell did indeed graze her leg, and a sharp edge on it rip her uniform pants, nearly cutting into her.

Mafoosoola added, *We have another problem: The kamakala are crawling all over the shuttle pod. They think it is a large flying insect they can overwhelm before it takes off again. Some of them are already dinging the hull with a stinger on their abdomens. They are probing for a soft spot in the articulation between segments of a presumed exoskeleton, to inject a paralyzing fluid. And Yulala is thinking the situation has grown even worse. At least two ahtpah have arrived on the scene. Yulala can hear them hissing. They are looking to cast out some webbing, like fishing nets, to pull in a few stray kamakala. She is thinking you had all better crouch down on the ground, and try digging your feet and hands into the soil to brace yourselves to resist the tug of any sticky strands which might get incidentally sprayed your way.*

*Mafoosoola,* thought Helena for the tree creature's mind-reading benefit, *please telepath to Officer Leung that unless he has a specific plan other than hope and prayer, he is not to linger to try to rescue us. If he does linger, he will only get you, himself, and everyone else accompanying you killed by the crashing comet before you can successfully depart. If he can somehow shake off the added weight from the swarming kamakala, you should probably leave now. Then you can pray all you want, for us to figure out something.*

***

The Fafamafalafama and the Varalawa continued in silent embrace upon the open tralalafa in the wives' reception area, otherwise devoid of any activity. They were not unlike Ali Magabu after he revived from the explosion-induced cave-in. Only, instead of fear over what physical injury their first tentative movement out of each other's arms might reveal, they dreaded the spiritual torment to come once they spoke to one another.

The Fafamafalafama made the initial move. He softly fa-la-laed into the first wife's ear as he gently entwined ringlets of her ahtpah-shell-shiny black hair around his fingers, "My Varalawa..."

That's as far as he got before she recoiled. She pushed against his chest, to look sternly deep into his extra-large nocturnal eyes and say, "I wanted to dream my dream for just a few nininanas more before you spoiled it, telling me what you tell the others, including trying to assure me that in my case, you really mean it."

"But I will be ordering you away also," the Fafaman ruler practically whimpered, far from his customary booming voice. "I wanted you to hear-"

"Wanted me to hear I am actually the one you are sending away to find the next Fafamafalafama?" The first wife had drawn completely apart from the supreme Fafaman ruler. "That what you said to the rest was just to salve their egos, while I am the real intended? Then you're retreating to the original pyramid?, where some of your more recent marital conquests are waiting for an orgy while the rest of the world ends?, so you can re-emerge as the sole father of the post-doom Fafaman civilization?, to be immortalized in memory like the very first Fafamafalafama?!"

The Fafamafalafama opened his palms for the Varalawa's viewing. It was the universal nonverbal sign he had nothing to hide. He thereupon fa-la-laed with uncharacteristic meekness, "I deserve all of that and more. But here is the truth: I could not bring myself to tell the others what I am about to tell you, which is that to the best of my knowledge and judgment, it is most unlikely any Fafaman anywhere is going to survive the impact of the orbiting ice rock. Not in any suburban mini-pyramid. Not at the bottom center of this central pyramid. Not anywhere."

"Except possibly for Yulala who I sent off with the 'Ahthlahns,' telling security this was your order."

"Ahh," the Fafamafalafama nodded, at long last starting to comprehend what the eleventh wife had been referring to earlier.

"The cover story for security was that the 'Ahthlahns' and Yulala alike would meet their doom in the mandibles of the kamakala. But the actual plan was for your twenty-third wife to help the 'Ahthlahns' to escape through a weakness in the pyramid's northwest corner base. She is supposed to have accomplished this feat after we left them all for dead in a kamakala burrow, having blown it closed with an explosive. Once outside the pyramid, they are expecting an

'Ahth' space craft to return to rescue them. Whether that rescue mission is actually going to happen, and whether the 'Ahth' rescuers have any plan for minimizing the threat from the descending ice rock, these things are not known."

"The interest of Yulala in 'Sahjahnt Hahnsahn,' and the 'Sahjahnt's' interest in her, were not lost on me." The Fafamafalafama winced like he were experiencing physical pain fa-la-laing this.

The Varalawa felt moved to shuffle a little nearer him again upon the tralalafa. She got close enough to gently, comfortingly place a hand on his cape-covered left knee.

"I hope they are all able to escape safely," the Fafamafalafama went on, "and I hope my former twenty-third wife will find the happiness with that 'Ahthlahn' she could never have realistically hoped to have had with me, given my own true feelings. Not to mention the pain it has been slowly occurring to me, that I have slowly been bringing myself to admit, the pain which I have made the burden of so many women, yourself included. I fear it is a pain from having to share the same man, no matter whether that man were the supreme ruler of the entire known universe!" While the Varalawa rubbed his knee with seeming mounting urgency to comfort him – at an emotional distance – the Fafamafalafama added, "And probably it is too much to hope for something else, from those 'Ahthlahns' returning to Fafama in welcome defiance of my previous command to stay away until we conveyed to them the message that we could trust them to return. It is doubtless too much to hope they could undo the recent redirection of the ice rock's path, especially with so little time left."

The Varalawa asked, "Is there nothing our scientists or military can concoct? No plan they can implement?"

"The booster rockets implanted in the ice rock's crust

are not responding to missile-launcher Naratama's efforts to reprogram their firing." The Fafamafalafama looked down between his legs, and he fa-la-laed further, "I don't know what a good answer would have been to the continuing terrorist threat; all I know now is that my decisions about how to use the 'Ahth' technology are going to get us all killed, almost certainly. I do not deserve the slightest consoling from you." He paused again, to brush the first wife's hand away from his knee, before continuing, "I don't know if there is any possible way you can survive, by your evacuation of this, what is certain to become my tomb, perhaps the biggest tomb for anyone the universe has ever known. But if there is, I specifically do NOT want you to choose the next Fafamafalafama."

The first wife blinked her eyes in disbelief; this was the last remark she expected to hear uttered by the Fafamafalafama.

"No; find someone more worthy of your loving intention than I. That should not prove difficult."

The Varalawa furiously shook her head so that the supreme ruler wasn't sure whether she was indicating strong disagreement, or more amazement at the fa-la-las issuing from him.

"Once you find someone more worthy of your love, both of you must steal away to some place safe, perhaps with other surviving couples. You must begin life anew, free from the imprisonment of ultimately cruel conventions. If those 'Ahth' people could deliver you to their planet, perhaps that would be all to the better. The 'Ahthlahns' have told me that many-legged creatures such as our 'ahtpah' cannot grow on 'Ahth' to more than the size of something that could fit into the palm of your hand."

"It is not a matter of who may or may not be worthy

of me," the Varalawa shook her head some more as she stood up purposefully. "It is a matter of who I care for, who has made my heart feel as though the sunset storm line were raging through it, every time I leave his presence, ever since the first time I met him. It is a matter of who has made it all the more painful for me that his seed has never been able to grow a child within me. What my caring HAS grown is a pendant I would hope to share with him. But if it is another with whom he would share it, then so be that."

The Fafamafalafama watched with furrowed-brow puzzlement as the Varalawa worked a wall safe to unlock it. She withdrew two pendants, actually. "The one is for you, while the other was intended for 'Cahptahn Taylah.' In all the tumult, I was not afforded the necessary last moments with the 'cahptahn,' away from the prying scrutiny of the eleventh wife."

The Fafamafalafama welcomed the golden, cylindrical jewelry into his hands as though, the Varalawa thought wistfully, he was receiving one of his newborn children to hold for the first time. He studied carefully the Fafaman hieroglyphics with which the Varalawa had engraved it. When he was through, he fa-la-laed tearfully, shaking his head, "I do not deserve this."

"There is no living thing on Fafama who does not deserve this." On a sudden impulse, the Varalawa skooched close to the Fafamafalafama. She planted her palms on his chest, and she tried to anchor her nocturnal vision deep into his eyes as she fa-la-laed further, "YOU are the one I deserve; YOU are the one with whom I would joyfully steal away to protective shelter from the ice rock's impact, if that is still possible! We can go off by ourselves; no one needs to know we have renounced how we were unfurled into this life!" She shook her head eagerly. "There," she cherishingly rubbed both his dimples with her forefingers. "You can allow your whiskers to grow out for your new identity, and I will garishly smear fungal bioluminescence all over my face for MY new identity! No one needs to know!" she repeated.

"But I am the Fafamafalafama! *I* will know!" He forcefully stood away from her, up off the tralalafa. The Varalawa sensed futility if she latched onto his shoulders, to try keeping him down close to her. That he would not have been at all inhibited from his move to separation from her, by the possibility of inadvertently hurting her.

The confessions from them both made the Varalawa feel as though they had gotten more naked to one another than they had ever gotten physically. But now, it was as though the eye-burning sun was rising into the sky again to blind her to his true self...

...which stirred her, raged her irrationally, into wanting to blind him to *her* true self. "And I am the first wife, the Varalawa," she fa-la-laed imperiously, in her deepest voice, as she got to her feet, "and I must join you in the original pyramid!"

"What if I command you not to?" He settled his left hand, itchy fingers, on the hilt of his sword.

"What if I reject your command, on the basis of the blasphemous lack of respect you have admitted for your unfurlment into this royal existence?"

The Fafamafalafama backed away from the Varalawa. He inched towards the entrance to the wives' quarters, as he unsheathed his sword and held it up before him by both hands on its hilt. He was ready to bring it swinging, slashing down, whichever direction. "I do not deserve to have you perish by my side, and you deserve better than to perish by my side!"

"So you would sooner lop off my head to have me

perish before you, rather than at your side?" How much the first wife cared for him inspired her to speak fearlessly, practically mocking him.

Far from further enraging him, the Fafamafalafama couldn't help her observation disarming him to the edge of amusement, albeit bitter. He even allowed a grin to flash across his face before he silently spun around to give the first wife his back. He re-sheathed his sword, then caused the entrance woven of fern-frond fibers to unfurl open.

"No living thing on Fafama deserves to die from what the ice rock will do!!" the Varalawa fa-la-laed after the Fafamafalafama. She chased him out the entrance to the wives' antechambers. "Not even the terrorists! There!"

On this last remark, the Fafaman ruler paused in his flight away from her. From his back she could tell he was considering, pausing to ponder, what to do next. Should he fulfill what he'd already resolved unwaveringly ought to happen? Or, should he totally change course, make himself open for advice?

"Now do I deserve to die by your side? Yes, you have already earned death, for your decisions having led to the imminent ice rock catastrophe. But now, haven't I earned that same fate?, for the mercy I would show to those who murdered your wives and children?"

"There cannot be too much mercy!! That mind-reading tree they found on another planet: Maybe she was correct! So you do still deserve to survive, but I do not!" With this said, the Fafamafalafama resumed his trek down towards the original pyramid, at the umbilical core of a city-sized construction. It was the humble foundation upon which a civilization had been built.

"If I deserve to live, help me to find the means to survive, if it is possible, that I might not achieve by myself!"

The Varalawa had long since determined to follow her beloved to his end, not desist from trying to change his heart. She would strive to be the surfacing flounder mouse that would cause his attitude to unfurl wide open into better more hopeful possibilities, until the walls caved in around them.

"If I accede to your demand, I survive as well, which I do not deserve!" complained the Fafamafalafama. "Anyhow, I doubt there is any plan I could conceive that you are not shadow-y enough to conceive yourself!"

"Then survive undeservedly to assure I live!, whoever conceives the plan!" The Varalawa was panting as she strove to keep up with him at the same time she strove to unfurl him. "Your shame living with yourself can be the mental anguish you have to live with for the rest of your life!, if a fitting punishment is what you require!"

"You have offered me an impossible choice!" The Fafamafalafama was panting, himself, the Varalawa could tell, from the exertion of his haste to remain well ahead of her. Lugging around that big sword couldn't be helping, she figured. "I meet my deserved fate, and you are thereby intent on meeting your undeserved fate. But I join you,-"

"I know!" Her fa-la-las echoed off granite brick walls as they were nearing the original pyramid. For the Fafamafalafama, it felt like her tender beautiful voice was engulfing him. "After you assure my survival, you can head for the nearest 'ahtpah' web, or seek any other of a number of ways a person can doom themselves on Fafama!"

"Perhaps- Perhaps it is to be agony enough for me, in my final nininanas, knowing my demise has led to yours! Of course, my most perverse consolation would be to learn that every Fafaman on the planet was doomed no matter their efforts to survive!" These remarks were met with panting silence the first wife's end. The self-dethroning Fafaman supreme ruler seized on what he perceived as a moment of vulnerable doubt to further press his case: "Why will you not try to save yourself?, given the hopelessness of in any way reasoning me out of my resolve?"

"If you understood, you would join me!"

The Fafamafalafama could hear tearfulness in her fa-la-las. He responded, "Why would you join me in certain death when you know I will not join you in an uncertain effort to survive?" He couldn't keep his own booming voice from cracking, especially as he thought on how imminent the ice rock impact must surely be.

"If you understood how to forgive yourself, you would join me!" Raging frustration colored her grief, especially as she thought on how there might not be enough time left for them to evacuate, even were her beloved to experience a last-nininana change of heart. "If I were to just give up on you,-"

THOOM! The Fafamafalafama pulled shut what he intended to be his tomb. The noise reverberated throughout multiple surrounding corridors.

"-I would never be able to forgive MYSELF!" The Varalawa craned her head ceiling-ward to wail this final fa-la-la, even as she collapsed down onto her knees, scraping them and tearing holes into her skirt.

***

"So let me get this straight, Pedro my man." Officer Robertson had already sat down as instructed. "When you're ready, we've all got to lift our magnetoboots off the floor, like this." He lifted his knees so high, they nearly touched his chin. "Then you're gonna send a strong current through the entire shuttle pod hull. It will be like some damn electrified fence, which hopefully will put an end to that f-in' racket from those f-in' ant monsters! They're pokin' away like they were livin' can openers tryin' to punch a hole in this thing so's they could chug our blood in the place of beer!"

"Something like that," nodded Officer Perez as he continued to bounce back and forth between the pod's navigation console, and what Robertson would have termed a spaghetti dish's worth of wires hanging in colorful bunches from where a panel had been unscrewed from the ceiling. "And we have to hope enough of the kamakala and the ahtpah are stunned, and stunned for a long enough time, for our friends on Fafama to safely make their way over to us!" Pedro found himself shouting that last part, as the poking of so many kamakala pincers against the shuttle pod's hull suddenly intensified. It was as though, he couldn't help fearing, the kamakala knew what he was attempting, so they were grown that much more determined to break through, thereby thwarting him.

***

*When I telepath you that Officer Perez's electrocution scheme has succeeded,* Mafoosoola was coincidentally telepathing to Helena Taylor and company, *you should make haste to reach the shuttle-pod entrance ramp. If you happen to notice the kamakala and ahtpah frenzy becoming dispersed before I can alert you, don't wait for my confirmation, of course!*

*And if we don't make it to the shuttle pod, make sure, please, that our fellow Earthlings leave, that they do not delay for any longer, to attempt something heroic. They will only wind up getting you all crushed in the descending comet's impact!* Just as Helena completed focusing on this thought intended for Mafoosoola's mind-read, she found herself suddenly, most unexpectedly engulfed in a refreshingly cool breeze. Clouds of grimy, gritty dirt kicked up by the ahtpah-kamakala tumult got blown away faster than those monster bugs could keep producing it. The result being, she got the clearest view yet of the comet bearing down on them all, a slow-turning fireball that somehow reminded her of a slow-moving bowling ball. So much of the sky got filled with this spectacle, she had to wonder whether it wasn't too late already for the shuttle pod to escape, even if lift-off was achieved right then and there.

As though matters weren't bad enough, there was an added, most horrible consequence of those aforementioned dirt clouds getting scoured out, thanks to air displaced by the descending comet. Earthlings and Fafaman alike got left completely, most vulnerably exposed. Not a one of the monster bugs could have asked for a much clearer look at the six humanoids. It made no difference whether it was the additional kamakala clamoring to join the other kamakala already swarming the shuttle pod, or an especially large ahtpah Chris reckoned to be the size of a large elephant. They took no time to shift their attention to the two-legged, clothed creatures suddenly revealed in their midst. Although, the especially monstrous ahtpah got distracted, shooting out web filaments to randomly snag several of the goat-sized kamakala.

All five Earthlings crouched low to the ground, while Yulala actually stood higher, on her tippy toes. The same as previously, Guy Hanson was reminded of a dog lifting its snout to detect a particular scent. Upon Yulala's return to flat-footed, she fa-la-laed at the top of her lungs, to get heard above the deafening din of the crackling fireball comet and the monster bug tumult, "I AM AFRAID THERE IS YET ANOTHER PROBLEM!"

Guy, Helena and Ali had their translators turned all the way up so what they could understand also came out shouted.

"THE KAMAKALA THAT WENT BACK INTO THE TUNNEL TO REMOVE MORE CAVE-IN DEBRIS: THEY ARE RETURNING!!"

No sooner did the translation of Yulala finish than Tanya and Ali shifted their attention back towards where they had emerged from under the northwest corner of the pyramid, carried partially entombed in semi-hardened clay by the kamakala. They noticed a large, boulder-shaped portion of said clay seeming to rise of its own volition from the kamakala tunnel, but with the huge pincers which supported it becoming soon enough apparent.

"HELP!!" Chris suddenly shouted. One of the sticky, randomly-sprayed-out web filaments had caught him on his right shoulder. From one moment to the next, he found himself getting dragged towards the elephant-sized ahtpah. Three kamakala were also stuck on the dragnet web, in between him and a pincer-filled maw already actively crushing a giant ant exoskeleton.

"CHRIS!!" Helena screamed. She lunged forward to catch her husband's legs, but she came up just short.

ZZZZZTTT!!!

The crackly noise burst from the hull of the shuttle pod. Due to the pod's electrification, several kamakala that had swarmed it suddenly froze like they had been paralyzed. They fell off the hybrid air-and-space vehicle onto their backs. One of the ahtpah also received a jolt through webbing it had cast onto those kamakala. It froze electrocuted into place, still standing on its eight legs.

And yet still there were unaffected kamakala. Heedless of what happened to their fellow insects, they were continuing their steady approach, unlike the others that were getting netted away like Chris. Those were in addition to the clay-burdened kamakala continuing to emerge from the tunnel behind them.

*It's hopeless for us!* With all her mental might, Helena focused on this thought for Mafoosoola to mind-read. *Leave while you can!*

That is precisely when the humans heard a WHOOF!, like an abruptly lit torch, or a gas grill, Sergeant Hanson imagined. Ahead of them, a ball of fire seemingly emanated out of thin air. This fire quickly carbonized to frail ash a segment of the ahtpah web filament in between Chris and the frantically flailing kamakala also stuck to it.

"EFFY!" shouted Chris, as the seeming monstrously proportioned blowtorch got re-directed to blazing a trail, safe passage, for Yulala and her Earthling companions. Which trail led straight towards the lowering entrance ramp from the shuttle pod.

The humanoids made maximum haste up the ramp. Chris, a short strand of web filament still stuck to his shoulder, noted with deep satisfaction and relief the familiar coolness of Effy, the ephemeral dragon, sliding past him on its own way back safely into the shuttle pod.

Buddy Leung activated the magnetic impulse drive, seconds ahead of the ramp's full retraction. "We're not out of here yet," he cautioned lest anyone think of making the least celebratory remark. As though to prove a point, there were more tinny ding-ding-dings from the kamakala. A new group of them had clambered over their electrocuted kin to once again treat the shuttle pod as though it were some other large bug that had made the mistake of landing amidst their colony.

"Sorry, Officer Leung," Pedro said in a low, abject voice. He felt miserable with having gotten this far, only to have to face what he feared could be an ultimately dooming reality. "We cannot charge up the hull a second time without burning out the magnetic impulse drive!"

"Don't write our obituary yet!" Buddy was gritting his teeth as he fought the console system to beg, borrow and steal as much electricity as he could from any onboard systems unrelated to life support. "If we can just get enough... There!"

With a lurch, the shuttle pod lifted vertically, but was tipped over to one side.

"Officer Leung!" Pedro couldn't keep the alarm out of his voice. "The rear monitor is showing an ahtpah swinging from a web strand that must be attached to the hull! Must be why we are careening so much!"

"Obviously we can't try for any more altitude yet without stalling into a crash, Officer Perez!"

"Um, are you heading us on a direct course for the comet, Buddy?" Helena also couldn't keep alarm from creeping into her voice. "Buddy?"

"I think I know what Buddy is trying to do, Captain Taylor." Again, Tanya feigned to forget it was FORMER Captain Taylor. "Yikes! I hope everyone is strapped in tight!"

*Officer Leung has to stay too focused to afford the least distraction, trying to explain to any of you what he is about.*

As the shuttle pod got closer to the underbelly of the ever-descending comet, the ahtpah along for the ride sent out additional web filaments. It was trying to net some of the kamakala still poking away at the flying vehicle's hull. With the result being further imbalance, especially as it succeeded in dragging two of the giant ants nearer and nearer to its deadly embrace. The shuttle pod got completely tipped over, upside down.

Whoosh!

"That flaming debris from the comet almost sideswiped us!" Ali couldn't help blurting this out after what they saw on the view-screen.

"And with any luck at all," Buddy said with his eyes as glued to the monitor as his fingers were glued to particular console keys, "we'll get even closer to that next one approaching! Hang on!"

Officer Leung depressed some of the aforementioned console keys, sending the shuttle pod into a dizzying, wobbly spin. The view-screen filled with fire. Its flaming roar could be heard coming from just outside the hull. But the next thing the others on board knew, Buddy was shouting, "We're free!" as he sent the shuttle into a steep ascent.

Amidst all this discombobulation, it suddenly occurred to Helena, most relievedly, that the pincer-pinging from the kamakala had ceased.

*Officer Leung torched the large bugs off the shuttle pod's hull with a sideswipe of a meteoric fragment burst flaming off the descending comet,* Mafoosoola telepathed everyone else aboard, thus saving Buddy the bother, so he could continue to focus on an escape trajectory. *Would that we were living in a world where we could co-exist with bugs in peace.*

In minutes, the shuttle pod was flying well above the descending comet. Nevertheless, severe turbulence rippling out from the ever-expanding debris trail wrested it totally out of Buddy's control, sent the vehicle pitching variously end over end and side to side.

But then, the shuttle pod's occupants heard a dull, sickening loud, thunderous THUD! A pressure wave from the comet at last impacting the surface of Fafama hurled the pod well out beyond the planet's stratosphere.

***

Not too many minutes had elapsed since the Fafamafalafama sealed himself off from the rest of his world, inside the pyramid at the bottom center of the central pyramid. It was the pyramid that tradition had was the very first pyramid ever constructed on Fafama, pieced together by the very first Fafamafalafama. The present Fafamafalafama found himself meditating upon the demonstration the "Ahthlahn" husband of the "Ahthlahn" starship captain had given him, of how to swing a most curious stick for a most curious game. The objective was to hit a very small ball, marked by more than three hundred dimples, across vast fields. Said small ball had to dodge trees, bushes, and lakes, to ultimately get rolled into a small hole in the ground. He was surprised at himself, for how he could be dedicating focus to this extraterrestrial game on the threshold of the likely end of the world as he had known it. Nevertheless, the supreme Fafaman ruler unsheathed his emblem sword in the pyramid darkness, amply lit for his nocturnal vision by the bioluminescent moss covering the cold, damp stone walls, and he pretended it was a golf club. As Chris Olsen-Taylor had tried to get him to do, he took a few swings. He imagined he was striking a golf ball. *So silly, and yet, so intriguing.*

As per Chris's advice, the Fafamafalafama told himself he would concentrate on keeping his head down. He would visualize not taking his eye off the ball...and if by some miracle they survived – he and whoever – his solemn most determined pact with himself was to gather up as many swords as he could, and have them melted down to produce multitudes of special sticks for this game. Of course, there was also the important matter of how to manufacture the balls. Actually, there was a certain, peculiar fern found closer to Fafama's north pole. Explorers had told him it bled a white, smooth, elastic tree sap when you chopped into its especially thick trunk. Couldn't the balls...and what if what that tree alien had telepathed to him one time were correct? Suppose that plentiful balls and ball-hitting sticks were supplied to his loyal subjects as well as to the terrorists, along with playing fields for all, with the holes cut into them. Would that really provide so much intrigue, the resolution to a quarrel that had endured for generations would get arrived at in less than ten sunset storm lines, just so everyone could turn more attention...?

The rumble from the descending comet's impact with the Fafaman surface, just short of the central pyramid, like nothing the Fafamafalafama had ever experienced before, woke him from his intentionally distracting thoughts as assuredly, as disorientingly, as had it woken him from a deep sleep. Yes, he had successfully, however temporarily, avoided dwelling on what he cared about the most, not to mention the sheer terror of his own imminent demise. Presently, though, he found himself helplessly giving in to unbearable grief over the fate certain to overwhelm his Sasamara...the name she never should have had to give up to be called the Varalawa instead.

If it were true that for some, their entire lives pass before their eyes during their final living moments, for the Fafamafalafama, it was regret over the emphases he had placed, thinking they were the practical priorities to have. The comet's approaching devastation created a deafening hum, together with land tremors of earthquake intensity. As this happened, the supreme Fafaman ruler realized he'd lived way too much of his life based on fear of whatever situation working out badly, rather than a life based on hopeful embrace of, for example, a love life devoted singularly to Sasamara.

If he could have known twenty-three orbits ago what he knew presently, of Sasamara's feelings for him as she had engraved- where was that pendant? The rapidly growing intensity of the ice-rock impact – he could already hear granite getting crushed to bits; it would be only a matter of nininanas before the original pyramid caved in, imploded on itself, crushing him. The intensity amplified his panic over not at least having secured this token of his first wife's true sentiment, over having misplaced it so he could not embrace it for his burial. Any thoughts he had subversively permitted himself, all those Fafaman years ago, of confiding to her what he felt, he had easily squelched. He had always assumed she would have let the whole world know he was trying to betray the Fafaman Empire by running away with the first wife. That he would have been accused of an abdication devoid of formality, of his rightful earned supreme role. And thereby, would he have abruptly plunged the Fafaman Empire into a profound crisis of faith, at a time when the terrorists were first starting to make their presence known on a whole new level from what their forebears had been doing for generations.

But what had he accomplished? It had turned out the first wife was feeling what he was feeling for all those solar orbits. However, he had made it impossible for her to believe such a thing, by his acceptance of an additional wife every year. This, while he had continued to feel a profound emptiness that filling no number of women with his seed could lessen.

"Pama," rather than worrying about the hazards, he would have been better off focusing on his dreams. And as for the recently discovered, other-worldly threat which had led to contact with the extraterrestrials from "Ahth"? Let them and those mind-reading tree creatures deal with it!

Finally allowing his heart full sway to lead him, the Fafamafalafama let fall his sword to the cement floor, and he lurched for the rock slab he would need to push aside to exit the original pyramid. By then, so deafening was the growing wave of destruction from the comet impact, he could not even hear his ceremonial weapon clanging on the ground. Nor did he care. All his effort was devoted to seeing what lay beyond the stone veil he had brought down between himself and the rest of the world only nininanas earlier. It was a task so much more difficult with the very ground beneath him in constant tremor, like an earthquake of impossibly long duration. He struggled mightily, in fact, just to keep from toppling over, even having shed his sword.

Yet at the last, this lone Fafaman did manage to push the slab far enough aside for the glimpse he desired selfishly, but which selflessly he would have made impossible, had that been within his power.

It was only a glimpse, before the torrent of falling rubble got so heavy, it was lost entirely from view, mere moments before the final veil came down over the Fafamafalafama's consciousness in that particular existence. But what he saw was unmistakable.

Sasamara was seated cross-legged there on the floor. The look in her overly large nocturnal eyes was as patient as it was wistful. Instead of leaving, instead of seeking evacuation, she'd waited for him, as perhaps she had done all those evenings he had spent with his other wives. He could not tell whether she noticed what he had done, as he lurched forward and fa-la-laed most desperately yearningly lovingly his final word, "Sasamara!!"

***

Despite comet impact shock waves that carried well beyond the Fafaman atmosphere, Buddy Leung quickly succeeded at steadying the shuttle pod into a geosynchronous orbit. He flew it upside down so he and everyone aboard could get a better view, through the vehicle's wide-screen cockpit window, of what was happening to the semi-arid planet. The great Fafaman pyramid was already shrouded from view by billowing brown clouds of debris that dwarfed the sunset storm line. In fact, those debris clouds appeared to be racing eastward to merge with if not totally overwhelm the storm line. And the same as the storm line, they were laced by flashes of lightning and lightning bolts. Yulala could only endure witnessing so much of this awful spectacle before she sought to bury her face in the shoulder of Sergeant Hanson, strapped down beside her.

Just as well, Chris thought, so she would need not be haunted by the next, most ominous events. There was the long, thin tower, of the appearance of a radio tower, atop the pyramid. It had served as a lighthouse to assure there was no collision danger for the few Fafaman space vehicles that trafficked between the space station and the ground. Lights were still winking on and off, up and down what still remained visible of it above the roiling fog of destruction down below. But not for much longer.

After having persisted erect for so many minutes despite the rest of the pyramid getting obscured from view, after having lasted just long enough to provide false hope for observers aboard the shuttle pod, it finally started to topple over. Mere seconds later, it too was lost from view, in additional brown clouds which were billowing up almost beyond the Fafaman stratosphere. There could be only one explanation, Helena and the others well knew, for what had happened to the home of so many million Fafamans, the pyramid that had accreted so many layers over the centuries, it had become the size of a large city on Earth. This supreme tribute of the Fafaman people to their ability to construct ample space for their civilization to safely flourish, despite the daily ravages of the sunset storm line, had been brought crumbling down.

*Mafoosoola, if you're paying attention to my mental horizon or whatever you term it,* Chris worked on telepathing, *then maybe you can make sense for me of what I have been thinking. I don't dare to verbalize for my fellow Earthlings, for fear of their taking great offense I am not sure wouldn't be entirely justified. But, the oddest thing occurred to me. The way the pyramid's lighthouse tower toppled over, I got reminded of a flag pin on an oof course or a golf course, how it topples over after it has been uprooted from its hole in the ground, and let go. That is, if it isn't lowered gently to the ground. From that impression, I went on to regard the fallen comet as an enormous golf ball having crashed into a hazard instead of safely greening the planet with its gently shed water. I view this tragedy and I want to scream NO-NO-NO-NO-NO! for all the suffering and death and destruction it is causing. And that reaction somehow seems to be of a kind with what I feel when my golf ball or oof ball flies hopelessly lost into a hazard, even though a lost golf ball means less than nothing by comparison.*

*How can I be so callous?*

*In my estimation, Officer Olsen-Taylor, your sense of a connection between the triviality of your mishit oof shot and this most profound of tragedies, where I fear we bear witness to the end of a world, is not at all untoward. At the root source of both of them is too much attention to avoiding a hazard, and not nearly enough attention to achieving a positive goal. And I telepath positive goal, because the original goal, of bringing down the orbiting comet on the center of a rebellion, was more about eliminating a hazard, not the least about producing anything positive.*

"Captain!? Helena?! Tanya?! Anyone?! Did you see the lateral lightning?!" Buddy would have lifted clear out of his seat with his agitation, were he not tightly strapped down.

"Something about that particular cloud-to-cloud lightning display did strike me as truly odd, Officer Leung," Ali Magabu said in his usual, measured tones. "It seemed to be acting as a sort of barrier or boundary, beyond which the debris clouds billowing up from below it could not pass. Or those clouds were somehow passing behind it, because truly, they did not appear deflected by it."

"Or they were passing THROUGH it; I don't know." Buddy shook his head.

What neither Buddy nor Ali could have possibly known was that they got a good glimpse of a tear in the fabric of space-time. And that it was the same tear through which the second pendant engraved by the first wife of the Fafamafalafama had been drawn, only to fall out of the sky onto the roof of a tenement building in north Philadelphia, some sixty years earlier.

By then, Yulala had gently pressed herself away from Sergeant Hanson. She was studying most intently the view-screen, seeking some hint of what the Earthlings were discussing even though it was long past, having transpired in less than five seconds.

"We could have a play-back of the last few minutes," Helena suggested. This suggestion was not only for herself, having totally missed out on whatever it was, in her focus on how the debris cloud was merging with the sunset storm line. It was also for Yulala, as Helena noticed the former twenty-third wife's curiosity distracted her from her grief and horror, at least temporarily.

*Officer Taylor, I think we first need to address the remainder of the Fafaman space station crew. They left in the other shuttle blade, to return to the surface of Fafama.* Mafoosoola discreetly restricted this telepath's audience to Helena, for fear of further upsetting Yulala. *May I suggest I communicate to that crew the urgency of their aborting their descent, and returning to their space station to await our deliverance?*

Helena Taylor focused her thoughts on her approval of Mafoosoola's proposal. She hoped Yulala was not noticing the referred-to shuttle blade showing up as a thin glint of light rising from the lower right-hand corner of the panoramic view-screen. Or that if she did notice it, she would dismiss it as some meaningless reflection image, some refractory phenomena off their shuttle pod.

No such luck.

"What are they doing?!" Yulala's fa-la-las translated as she pointed at that thin glint descending ever closer to the roiling waves of debris clouds. "Can we tell them to turn around?!? Can you put me through to them?!?!" She gave Guy Hanson her most beseeching, wide-eyed nocturnal look.

*I have been telepathing them, but they are ignoring me.*

"Patch us through, Buddy!" Helena joined her science officer at his console to see if she could help expedite the process,

No sooner doing that than Officer Leung said, "Go ahead from where you're seated, Yulala; they should hear you loud and clear!"

Yulala fa-la-laed in most urgent tones, her words left un-translated; Buddy had made an on-the-fly judgment the extraterrestrials could better concentrate on the former twenty-third wife's desperate entreaty if they didn't have to also hear the English translation.

To no avail. As the fa-la-laed response in firm, no-uncertain tones crackled over the shuttle pod loudspeakers, Yulala slumped into Hanson's side. She nearly fainted from her despair.

The Marine Corps sergeant quietly tried to comfort her. He gently dabbed his fingertips across her forehead, without a word, as much as he wanted to ask her about her fellow extraterrestrials' response. She offered up that response anyway. The Earthlings got to hear it translated, because Buddy reactivated that function. "They said they have to rescue their families, or see that their families were safe. And when, sniff!, when I told them nobody could possibly be safe down there now, that they could not possibly hope to save anyone, they said the Fafamafalafama together with the planetary spirit would assure all who did what the task required WOULD survive! I wish I could believe that!!" With this last remark, she burst into a sustained sob into Hanson's shoulder. Her own shoulders heaved with her utter despair.

*At least she is realistic,* Ali Magabu thought as his heart went out to her, *but thank goodness her tears are preventing her from seeing what is happening next!*

What Ali was referring to became quickly evident to

the others. At first, Helena thought she was witnessing some peculiar lightning bolts of a reddish-orange hue. But then she realized their coming and going had to do with the varying thickness of the still-billowing debris clouds. That fire-y hue had to be from lava flows, massive lava flows, on the Fafaman surface. *Mafoosoola,* she focused on thinking, *please alert Buddy to assure he's putting us on an orbit far enough away to guarantee we're not impacted.*

There was a tiny but pronounced flash of light, about where the second shuttle blade had descended into the debris cloud carrying the remainder of the crew from the Fafaman space station. The Earthlings knew that had to be said shuttle bursting apart, most likely from a hull breach caused by a boulder-sized chunk of the disintegrated comet.

*My God,* Helena thought to herself as the lava flows became ever more evident, *the comet's impact must have ripped open the planet's crust!*

*Officer Leung informs me of what he is sure you have already most easily surmised,* Mafoosoola telepathed. The Oombian tree creature was acting as a silent go-between for the Earthlings, to spare Yulala from having to overhear talk, albeit translated talk, about the demise of her home planet. *Any rescue mission in present time, once the Smoke and Mirrors arrives, would prove impossibly dangerous. And as for such a mission into past time, Officer Leung also communicates he has already given thought to once again making use of a space-time rift, to see if we might not save Fafama into an alternate universe scenario. For now, however, some major problems with that are all too evident, Officer Leung thinks. "For starters," as he puts it, the available rifts are too close to the surface of Fafama. There is significant danger that out their other ends, the crew could find themselves buried several hundred miles down into the planet, unable to escape. And even if the crew successfully navigated that issue, there would remain the most significant other issue of timing. How can we arrive within the hours-long window when the two launched missiles were on their heading for the comet, to pluck them out of their trajectory and have them explode harmlessly in outer space, which is clearly the most logical plan to pursue? Based on his quite literally past experience, Officer Leung thinks he would be as likely to travel through the rift to twenty years ago as to hit the sweet spot three hours ago. He is also afraid that for something on this large a scale, there might be quantum inertia, for want of a better term, powerfully resisting human efforts to redirect the planet's history. He hasn't given up on the idea by any means, but for now he would consider any such attempt most foolishly and fatally reckless.*

*As would I,* Helena thought grimly to herself when suddenly the intercom erupted with Captain Entroper's scratchy voice. "Officer Leung, Officer anybody who might be hearing me, we have descended past the Alpha Centauri C Oort Cloud onto the orbital plane, and are approximately two hours out from Fafama! Mafoosoola has telepathed us what has transpired." Pause. "No words from me, certainly, can begin to describe my sorrow for the people of Fafama! We hope parts of the planet, at least, will still prove habitable. But in the meantime, Officer Leung, were you able to secure the safety of the Tictoctic spacecraft?"

Shaking-head disbelief spread throughout the shuttle pod until finally, Helena Taylor said, "Captain Entroper, we are too overwhelmed by what we are dealing with here presently." Helena made a nod towards grieving Yulala, even though she knew Louisa didn't have a video monitor window into the small spacecraft presently. "There will be a better time to discuss that specific concern." It was all Helena could do, not to launch into a curse-laden rant. What helped in this regard was a promise she made to herself, not to pull any punches once she was back in Entroper's presence, her own future with the space program be damned.

"I get that completely, Officer Taylor!"

If Helena did not know better, it sounded like the new Smoke and Mirrors captain was acknowledging there was some understandable rage being felt.

"For my part," Captain Entroper went on, "I was hoping against hope our flight engineers here could have come up with something to return us to Fafama a little faster! Maybe if we'd had Officer Leung along...but I guess you're saying the saucer vehicle was lost."

Helena Taylor gritted her teeth; she knew she could plausibly pretend Entroper's last message wasn't received. She decided on some intentional ambiguity, after a suitable pause. "Whatever you said, Captain Entroper, we didn't get."

Ali Magabu grinned and nodded grimly. Truly appropriate, he thought.

"Ah!" Yulala gasped abruptly. She had lifted her head anew from Hanson's reassuring warmth to brave, on an intuition, another contemplation of the dust-cloud-enshrouded destruction of Fafama. "There!" her fa-la-las translated as she pointed towards the panoramic view-screen. "The planet's spirit ascends! It ascends!"

Ali Magabu figured it was Yulala's watery eyes making her imagine she was seeing something phantasmal. He wasn't sure he hadn't noticed something strange himself, but well he knew how much his own eyes were watering. Still, he didn't have the heart to say anything. *If it provides a bit of comfort, let her believe…*

"Did you see that?!" whispered Tanya beside Ali. She nudged his upper arm with her elbow.

"What?"

"It was like, for a moment, the constellations changed. Suddenly, there were more stars in them, then a blurry transition back to what they had been."

"Yeah, I thought I saw something like that too," Chris added.

"Damn!" went Kenny Robertson, with a "Huh" from Ali.

Yulala nodded emphatically. "That is the spirit of Fafama, of the entire planet! Sniff!"

"Dear Yulala," said Ali, "if that is truly the case, then I for one hope it shall always accompany us and never leave us!"

"I second that motion!" Hanson sobbed as he raised a hand like he was waiting to get called upon inside a schoolhouse classroom, Chris Olsen-Taylor fancied. Chris promptly joined everyone else to raise his hand, as well, with Mafoosoola lifting her longest branch.

And Pedro wondered where he had heard, who had said, what started to haunt him: "This is not how it happens."

## Chapter 27

Knuckles to nostrils, Captain Louisa Entroper struck what appeared to Chris Olsen-Taylor a most statuesque pose. She sat perfectly motionless in the captain's chair on the navigation bridge aboard the Smoke and Mirrors. She was pondering the planetary devastation playing out on the panoramic view-screen. She made an occasional "mmph," but that was it.

The away team, along with Yulala, were safely secured on the huge starship. The shuttle pod was tucked back snuggly into its berth. And enough debris from the apocalyptic crash-landing of a comet into the surface of Fafama had settled out of the atmosphere for observers from space to get fleeting looks at the mountainous piles of resultant rubble. Fleeting looks, because thick smoke from the multiple plumes of supervolcanoes was spreading and merging together. All too soon, the surface of Fafama would get totally obscured from view.

As compelling in the most awful way as this rapidly worsening spectacle became, Chris Olsen-Taylor found his attention more focused elsewhere. There were other little tableaus, besides Captain Entroper's, playing out around him on the bridge. In the first public display of affection he ever remembered the couple allowing themselves, Cathy James-Leung had welcomed her husband Buddy Leung-James onto the navigation bridge with a most relieved embrace and kiss. Minutes later, they yet remained in one another's arms, to share their grim fascination with Fafama's planet-wide extinction event. Although, Chris Olsen-Taylor did espy a certain aloofness to Buddy's regard. Chris didn't need to be an Oombian mind-reader to tell Officer Leung's thoughts were far distant, on how one might time travel to revert the course of this planet's history away from such ultimate catastrophe.

There was no aloofness in the expression on either Yoon-hee's face or Kevin's face. The way they clung to one another deepened Chris's impression they were trying to provide co-anchor, keep from getting swept away by their mutually felt horror.

Officer Chris Olsen-Taylor could only dream Helena depended on him in such a manner. And that he could likewise depend on her. With her arms folded across her abdomen, Helena's own attention was focused entirely on the despondent Louisa Entroper. Chris didn't need a mind-reader to tell that his wife was gearing herself up to get brutally frank with Entroper.

As for the Oombian named Mafoosoola, for all Chris knew she was plumbing telepathic depths to try to touch mental base across the light-years with her beloved Schnoodle-Coodle left behind on Oomb. But what he saw was her slow blinking at the panoramic view-screen. Thick, maple-syrupy-looking sap trickled down her corrugated bark-cheeks as it welled from the corners of her eyes.

No tears for Yulala; perhaps her tear ducts had long since gotten emptied dry by her immense grief. Moreover, while billowing clouds brought down a black curtain over Fafama, her attention seemed drawn to the celestial firmament. Was she in search of that so-called planetary spirit she claimed to have seen? Arm-in-arm with her, Sergeant Hanson was devotedly scanning outer space for what he wasn't clear he was supposed to be looking for. Chris could read that in his face.

As for Counselor Ali Magabu, he was the one other entity on the navigation bridge, besides Buddy and Chris, taking a detached perspective. Albeit, he was still holding hands with wife Tanya, the same as Buddy was remaining arm-in-arm with Cathy. Chris knew for his own self why Dr. Ali Magabu was seeking aloofness. He feared the circumstances swallowing him up in despair. But well did he understand that Dr. Magabu, ever-faithful to his counseling duties, was trying to figure out how to move matters along from the obvious tension born of equally obvious reasons. To that end, shortly after Chris settled upon this contemplation of him, Ali Magabu made a gearing-himself-up inhale and exhale. Following which, he gently disentwined his hand from Tanya's, though with an affectionately reassuring pat. He approached Louisa Entroper. "Please pardon my intrusion, Captain Entroper," he said. "I truly respect your need for ample time to process what is unfolding. However, as the ship's counselor, I know the toll this extreme situation is exacting on all of us. So I feel duty-bound to pry into your current thoughts you would be willing to share. I understand full well that those thoughts are liable to change dramatically as you ponder where we proceed from here." With hunched shoulders Ali spread his open palms wide.

For Louisa Entroper's lack of reaction, Chris thought, Ali might as well have been addressing her armchair.

On the view-screen, the entire sunlit portion of Fafama continued getting engulfed by billowing black clouds, set in ghastly relief by lightning flashes variously blue, green and white.

When Ali determined a reasonable number of minutes had elapsed for awaiting a response, he added in a tentatively quizzical tone, careful not to suggest the least impatience, "Captain?"

An additional thirty seconds of total non-responsiveness elapsed, following which Entroper suddenly swiveled in her chair to face Helena Taylor. Ignoring Officer Magabu, the captain abruptly erupted with, "Officer Taylor, the decision to ensnare the comet-" She pointed at the view-screen. "-on some ultra-naïve notion a group of murderous, heartless thugs might suddenly seek redemption if there is more rain, that decision has cost an entire planet!"

"You're blaming what the Fafamafalafama ordered on our placing the comet into orbit?!?"

"If the comet wasn't there to begin with, what the Fafamafalafama ordered would not have been possible!" Entroper shook her head adamantly.

"If Fafama had not been armed by us, they wouldn't have had anywhere near the capability with their own weapons to bring down that comet, Captain!" Helena was to the point she didn't care what the consequence for her speaking her peace. To hell with trying to walk on eggshells after what had happened. "Armed by us, by the way, on the ultra-naïve assumption, talk about being ultra-naïve!, or PRETENDING to be ultra-naïve!, the assumption the Fafaman government would resist the temptation to use their new, destructive toys on their enemies!"

Captain Entroper's mouth dropped open as assuredly as it would have had Helena Taylor slapped her in the face, Tanya thought. And then Entroper leaned forward. She looked ready to charge like an enraged bull, Kevin fancied. She rebutted, "Helena Taylor, Officer!, we did not come here to settle an extraterrestrial political dispute! We came here to protect our interests against a clear and present danger posed by Tictoctic! That is all!! And you would do well to understand something, Officer Leung!" Entroper swiveled her chair anew to this time be more directly facing Buddy Leung, still in his wife's comfort-seeking arms. "I understand, and indeed admire, your dedication to your former captain and associates, where you were willing to sacrifice anything to save them, even the critical knowledge we could have gained from studying the Tictoctic saucer craft you hijacked. Nevertheless, sometimes great sacrifices need to be made for the greater good! I thought we *all* understood that!" Entroper swiveled about some more as she grew cognizant of Yoon-hee, Tanya, and others' shock over her remarks. "I'm not saying your water plan for Fafama was not arrived at with the very best intentions!, the same, again, Officer Leung, as your desire to rescue these people!" She made a general hand sweep. "I'm saying that none of that will matter, NONE OF THAT WILL MATTER!-" Her voice broke with her agitation. "-IF THOSE MONSTERS FROM TICTOCTIC ARE ABLE TO HERD US TO SLAUGHTER LIKE SO MUCH CATTLE!!!!!"

"And so, just what will matter, where stopping the Tictoctic, um, creatures is concerned,-" Helena couldn't quite bring herself to term them monsters. "-if we just throw away all of our values, everything we believe in, and everyone we care for, to do that?!"

*I must object. The Tictoctic creatures are not monsters. They have gotten themselves into a desperate situation which compels them to do monstrous things. They are led by someone suffering from a severe mental illness, someone who has attracted likewise mentally ill creatures to join him in his faithless work. And as for the plan to moisten the Fafaman atmosphere: Given enough time to succeed, and without the weapons you supplied in the meantime, which had the impact of lit matches thrown on dry tinder, political tensions were likely to have been eased most dramatically.*

"I never said they wouldn't have been eased."

Entroper shook her head as she kept it bowed low to concentrate on Mafoosoola's telepathed admonishment.

*But that is not the extent of the potential results, Captain Entroper. A dramatic reduction in political and military tensions would also most likely have left the Fafaman government better able to assist us in addressing the threat posed by the Tictoctic civilization, to help us brainstorm more constructive strategies.*

"Do you mean getting the Fafamans to buy into your peace-y love-y, they'll-leave-us-alone-if-we-offer-them-flowers?"

"If I may, Captain Entroper, permission to speak freely."

"You have that, Sergeant Hanson, although you're the only one to even bother asking."

"Captain, no offense, but I am not sure, without getting into how impractical it might prove, I am not sure you are offering a fair characterization of how our friends from Oomb would have us deal with Tictoctic."

"I see. So..." Entroper darted looks around at every single other person assembled on the navigation bridge. "Is this how it is? Because this Mafoosoola can telepath, she automatically, her message automatically carries more weight with all of you?"

"That's not what I am saying, Captain."

"You all think the planet was destroyed to save it?, and now you'd far prefer if Officer Taylor here resumed command of the Smoke and Mirrors?"

"Captain Entroper, truly-"

"Stifle it, Officer Magabu! President Carey and General Warlor might want to weigh in with different directives. For now, though, I am hereby relieving myself of the captain's position. As my last official action before I do so, I am ordering Helena Taylor to resume her original post. Captain," with which bitterly intoned naming, Louisa rose from the captain's armchair and gestured towards it for Helena.

Yoon-hee and others contained what would have been exhalations of relief, while Ali thought to himself that what Entroper's bluster really amounted to was a feeling of too much guilt to carry on in her position. It was a feeling of guilt she could not admit to herself without going suicidally insane.

*Louisa Entroper, this telepath is for you only: That is a heavy burden you carry, the heaviest of burdens, when you insist on believing in the necessity of violence to answer violence. You should see how far the exploration of lifting that burden might carry you.*

*That burden is only as heavy as goes the unwillingness of well-meaning, yet ultimately blindly naïve creatures such as yourself to acknowledge its necessity. No thank you, Mafoosoola; I will keep this burden.* Then to Helena, the newly re-anointed Captain Taylor, "So, Captain, your orders? Is it back to Oomb, see what you can do to- Sorry." She held up a warding-off hand.

*My God,* Helena nevertheless found herself thinking, *was that woman going to suggest I will see what I can do to get Oomb destroyed as well?!*

Yoon-hee and Tanya gasped each other's way, and Ali Magabu shook his head. Ali believed Entroper was projecting onto Taylor what she feared applied to herself.

Helena was tempted to say, *Don't worry; I don't plan on trying to arm them with nuclear missiles.* "Buddy?" the newly-reinstated Captain Taylor went on instead, leaning her head towards the dark spectacle continuing to play out on the view-screen.

"It will take some time, if it's at all possible. I mean, it will take some time, no matter what..."

"Understood, Officer Leung." Helena Taylor held up her hand in the place of saying to Buddy, *Enough already*. "Then back to Oomb it is. To put it mildly, I suspect some Oombians and people there will want to see that some Oombians and people here are safe. Yulala..."

"There is nothing you can say, 'Cahptahn.'" Yulala pointedly pushed away from her comfort-seeking by Hanson's side. "But I am thankful. If I can have a dark room to myself for a while..." She reached back to squeeze Hanson's hand, but with his other hand he gestured as he nodded most understandingly, "It's okay."

# Chapter 28

When the prison guards brayed they were blindfolding him and Chef Glork-tek, Kwit-Nik knew they were both getting taken for an audience with Dek-Fook-Tek, the mighty ruler of the planet Tictoctic. There had been much puzzlement among his fellow starship engineers about where exactly Dek-Fook-Tek held court. Some of them had been honored by prior audiences with the Supreme Authority, way back before the food-sampling mission to Fafama got sidetracked to Oomb. Every one of those meetings, though, had surreptitiously involved blindfolded transport. The scorched-land locations where Kwit-Nik and the others had found themselves, once their blindfolds were removed, could have been anywhere within a one-thousand-lek-lek-wide band around either the northern or southern mid-latitudes of the planet. But this time, the blindfolded transport proved far different. This time, Chef Glork-tek and Kwit-Nik had to have been brought to one of only three possible locations. They could plainly see this, as they trotted on all fours down the disembarkation ramp from a vehicle much like an Earth passenger jet.

Right off, Kwit-Nik's probe-wriggling nostrils enjoyed an inhale of refreshingly cool air. It was pleasantly scented by towering wik-wik-lik trees, not unlike the fragrance of eucalyptus trees on Earth. There grew an entire forest of them, set well back from the government airport runway. Moreover, green mountain slopes stretched for several hundred square lek-leks even further back. Kwit-Nik well knew there were only three such forests rumored to be remaining on the entire planet. Two of them could be found, legend had it, in the sub-arctic northern hemisphere, the other one in the sub-antarctic southern hemisphere. With it being late summer in the northern hemisphere, this particular woodland region must have been located in the sub-arctic.

Events had been transpiring on the more unnerving end of what Kwit-Nik and Chef Glork-tek had anticipated. Originally, Dek-Fook-Tek was going to have them, plus all the others back from the interplanetary food-gathering debacle, summarily executed. They were not even going to be allowed the traditionally final, traditionally useless, statement in their own defense. Fortunately for them, however, soon as the Supreme Authority brayed their collective death sentence, he went into an out-of-control rage. He kicked a hole through his throne chair, as he stood up from it to vent his fury and frustration at the closed-circuit television he used to address Kwit-Nik and the rest, who were being held imprisoned aboard the Tictoctic space station. This violent tantrum gave Dek-Fook-Tek's servile handlers the perfect opportunity to reroute what would transpire for Kwit-Nik and his fellow officers. Those handlers seized the moment to cut off the transmission. Pursuant to which, they sedated Dek-Fook-Tek. They praised him for his restraint, in what they lied was only a rehearsal. It was only a rehearsal, they claimed, for actually addressing the cowards who turned tail instead of triumphing against all odds over what was hoped to be a safely deliciously consumable enemy. Most delicately, the servile handlers also preemptively praised the Supreme Authority for the undeserved mercy they knew he was going to show. This show of mercy would involve the traditional offering of a last chance for the cowards, the unworthy cowards, to verbally defend themselves, however lame such a defense was certain to turn out.

Guards for the space station holding cell were well

experienced in the routine. They had waited patiently, quietly, their guns trained steadily on the saucer craft crew, for the transmission to continue. This, instead of already dragging the prisoners off to their deaths.

Dek-Fook-Tek had finally rebooted the token trial, without the faintest clue that that was what he got led to do.

So there it had been, Kwit-Nik and Chef Glork-tek's last chance to save themselves.

Dek-Fook-Tek had taken in Kwit-Nik's allegations, of Captain Mat-kek-tek having ordered the saucer evacuation, then having fled for parts unknown with his fellow deserters, rather than staying to rally a fight. For once, the Supreme Authority's reaction to purported bad news had not been violent. Rather, said purported news had given him pause, with a quizzical, confused-looking head tilt. His antler handlers had had to strain to the maximum, to assure his out-of-proportion cranial growths didn't tip over all the way, thus breaking his neck. The maneuver had proven a most delicate one. The whole idea had been to allow Dek-Fook-Tek to continue to delude himself his neck was strong enough to accomplish this antler-balancing feat with no help.

Very soon, Dek-Fook-Tek had lifted his head back up to its full, erect height. He had been none the wiser of the effort his servants needed to make with his antlers to fool him into thinking he did this all by himself. He had softly tongue-clicked, "Officer Rikky-tik?" This had been the space station commander present for the trial. "Can you confirm or deny that Captain Mat-kek-tek has neither returned, nor has he communicated to you the imminence of his return? Is it possible Officer Kwit-Nik lies? Is it possible that in reality, Captain Mat-kek-tek, with a brave skeleton crew, is still aboard the saucer, fulfilling my glory by battling to obtain a new food source for my people?"

Chef Glork-tek as well as Kwit-nik knew that any chance for their scheme to continue had come down to Rikky-tik's response. All the space station commander would have needed to say, to result in those two Tictoctickians promptly getting transformed into so much ground meat, was what Dek-Fook-Tek suggested was indeed possible. Period. Instead, and knocking together his two cloven hand-hooves as he did so, Officer Rikky-tik had tongue-clicked, "That *would* have been possible, as you so perceptively have charged galloping into, oh Supreme Dek-Fook-Tek. Only, as I am sure you were already about to say, Captain Mat-kek-tek would have alerted us there were these cowardly deserters fleeing somewhere, if not necessarily so brazenly our way. The despicable fact is, we have received not the slightest contact from the captain. Also, if these returning officers committed a mutiny, certainly at least one of them would have broken their ranks of silence to alert us to the traitorous actions of the rest."

"Of course, such a courageous informant would have been guaranteed a most extreme honor," Dek-Fook-Tek had nodded. Obviously, where Kwit-Nik was concerned, the Supreme Authority had been baiting his comrades for at least one of them to become that particular, courageous person. "Very well," Dek-Fook-Tek, the Supreme Authority, had continued after his remark was met with ruminating silence. "Officer Rikky-tik, you will have them transported down to the surface. They are to be kept in a holding cell the necessary number of planetary rotations for us to rest assured Captain Mat-kek-tek will not be returning with a sufficient explanation for his lack of communication. And then, assuming such is still the case, we will proceed from there."

Over the ensuing days, one Tictoctickian soldier had "confessed" mutiny to one of the prison guards. As the other deer creatures in the holding cells were apprised afterwards, that soldier had been ordered brought for a personal appearance before Dek-Fook-Tek. Dek-fook-Tek had proceeded to explain to him that he never ought to have participated in the alleged mutiny in the first place, and that if it turned out there was not such a mutiny, said soldier was betraying the empire with his lie. Either way, despicable. Which judgment earned him a personal goring by Dek-Fook-Tek, a goring he assured him the rest of the prisoners would also suffer if it turned out he was telling the truth. One of the soldier's roasted thighs had gotten served that same day, as the main course at the royal dinner. That was the most extreme honor to which Dek-Fook-Tek was referring.

Thinking back on these events, witnessed by or described to Kwit-Nik, ceased for him as he and Chef Glork-tek were presently brought up before what had to be Dek-Fook-Tek's far-northern stronghold. The two-story-tall concrete square base measured about one hundred feet on a side (in Earthling terms). Seated atop that base and extending out a couple hundred feet in opposite directions was another two-story construction. It appeared to be made of some lighter material like vinyl. Nevertheless, Kwit-nik rested himself assured it was securely built around a latticework of steel beams. The two furthest ends each sported a three-story tower. Two more such towers were erected equidistant from each other in between. The entire effect, for Chef Glork-ek, was of some angularly stark, austere, imposing-looking evocation of antlers. Lego antlers writ epic large, were Chris Olsen-Taylor there to see. An artsy tribute to Dek-Fook-Tek's antlers.

Kwit-Nik and Chef Glork-tek had to wait under continuing armed guard outside the throne room, in the central hall with its mural ceiling some three stories above their knobby-antlered heads. They got to see servants exiting the royal reception area, pushing a wheeled trash bin between them. That bin was full to the brim with broken-apart, jagged-edged wood paneling, chalky drywall fragments, blood-stained clothing torn to shreds, and what looked to be the splintered wreckage of an immense, elaborately carved armchair. Moreover, from past the one-story-tall double doors to the throne room, Officer Kwit-Nik and Chef Glork-tek could hear a commotion of hammering, sawing, and painting. Kwit-Nik could not help but be impressed, in a bad way, with the lengths to which the Tictoctic ruler's handlers went to repair, to cover over, the extreme ravages of his daily rages.

Just before Kwit-Nik and Glork-tek were finally ushered into Dek-Fook-Tek's royal presence, one television camera with a shattered lens was wheeled out at a galloping pace.

At last, the two Tictoctickians from the expeditionary saucer craft lost to the Earthlings came to face the newly-installed, summer-palace throne. Whereupon they were instructed to lower their hand-hooves to the slate-tiled floor, down on all fours.

A side door was opened by a servant, who was also down on all fours. Another servant clip-clopped in. Naked save for a dark brown blanket engraved with the orange antler emblem of the Tictoctic Empire draped across his back, he brayed, "All bow to Dek-Fook-Tek!"

"His sharpest antlers through our chests would be a blessing we don't deserve," everyone there assembled ritually tongue-clicked. They bent their leggy forearms down flat against the floor, in a genuflection that brought them into an even lower bow than they had already been achieving.

As they waited there silent and still, Dek-Fook-Tek swaggered in. His out-sized antlers got turned slowly from side to side in rhythm with his hips. He assumed his seat on the royal throne, thereupon braying, "All rise to savor my countenance!"

Everyone took a deep inhale and exhale, the traditional savoring-his-countenance part, as they variously got back up on their hind legs or, in the case of Kwit-Nik and Chef Glork-tek, stayed down on all fours.

It was with a great deal of self-control that Glork-tek kept himself from leaving his mouth parted open in minor shock. Unlike on other occasions, no servants got pushed along on wheeled ramps by Dek-Fook-Tek's side, laboring to keep his ridiculously overgrown antlers level. But Glork-tek soon realized said antlers were attached to hair-thin, transparent wires that ran straight up into the ceiling. If you weren't looking closely, or your vision were less than excellent, the chef surmised, you would never notice they were there. And of course if you valued your life, you weren't going to mention them, even if you did notice them.

Chef Glork-tek darted the swiftest possible glance his companion's way, to confirm he was noticing the strings as well. Kwit-Nik was just-then realizing it was an optical illusion, that those antler-supporting wires ran up into an unbroken ceiling. It was an optical illusion wrought by a most clever positioning of long, narrow mirrors. The flight engineer concluded there were servants concealed overhead. They were manipulating the antlers like those bony growths were marionette puppets. One good thing about this arrangement at least, Kwit-Nik told himself.

Where the slits in the ceiling had to have been cut, for running the antler-supporting wires, it would be most difficult for Dek-Fook-Tek to come over to gore his or Glork-tek's chest. Although Kwit-Nik supposed the Tictoctic ruler could always have servants who were down inside the throne room help out. He could have them latch onto both ends of his antlers, to safely lower that unnaturally overgrown headgear for the fatal or severely wounding impalement. This, depending on how deeply the Supreme Authority felt offended.

Dek-Fook-Tek gave the two subjects he'd ordered brought before him his flared-nostril regard, meant to communicate right away his dissatisfaction. What he crisply tongue-clicked next would have translated, "What do you two have to bray for yourselves?"

Kwit-Nik and Glork-tek both, still down on all fours, reared back their shoulders as far as possible, to swell their chests forward. Kwit-Nik as spokesman baaed, "Supreme Authority whose name we don't even deserve to bray, we congratulate you on your portion of the mission. It has proved a tremendous success worthy of celebration ever after...and we condemn ourselves for our miserable failure in our part of the scheme. That failure left us no choice but to hurry home for the punishment we know we deserve."

Dek-Fook-Tek's righteous-anger-fueled exhalation involved air so moisture-laden, two puffs of steam were seen to issue from his still-flared nostrils. He pounded a cloven hoof against the slate floor, and he brayed shrilly, "As you smell it, what exactly is this 'tremendous success' with which you credit me?!" He told himself he was too consumed by attention to future necessary decisions to be bothered recalling every last one of what he assured himself were his several prior strokes of brilliance. But he also wanted to assure he wasn't being patronized, that this subject wasn't saying just anything to save his own sorry, miserable, stubby antlers.

To Glork-tek's carefully cloaked relief, Kwit-Nik was ready to answer with specifics. "It is indeed a success worthy of recounting any number of times," he nodded heartily as he tongue-clicked. "Clearly, your conceptualization of our mission's details left us vulnerable, intentionally, so the loyalty of your most critical advance scouts could be put to the ultimate test. Thanks to that test, we learned of the cowardly ways of Captain Mat-kek-tek, and those who would desert you to follow him. Where we failed came after flushing such cowardice out into the open. It was our abject inability to regain control of your saucer craft to complete the mission."

Dek-Fook-Tek nodded with satisfaction. His self-fancied intuitive gift to arrange situations just as they should be arranged had him ever more impressed with his own self. Leave it for lesser minds to determine and savor the particulars of how those situations worked out, ultimately. "Back onto your hind legs," he tongue-clicked finally. "You aren't worthy of impalement upon my antlers, on account of the loyalty you have demonstrated. Yet neither are you deserving of royal scarring across your chests, on account of your own failure as you have so accurately described. Captain Mat-kek-tek has also proven himself unworthy of impalement upon my antlers, but for a different reason. Had he been merely disloyal, yet achieved an act of courage, however traitorous, he would have earned the honor of my impalement. But now, should he ever be captured, let a thick tree branch be sharpened into a stake, and let that stake be driven from his mouth through his anus, for him to be slowly roasted over an open spit, that at least his cooked flesh serve some valuable purpose."

"His mercy is boundless," everyone else there assembled went down on one elbow to ritually bray.

Kwit-Nik was the first back up on his hind limbs. He crisply tongue-clicked, "Dek-Fook-Tek, my Supreme Authority, may I make so bold as to ask you how, now, we can best serve you?, meaning I, and Chef Glork-tek, and the remainder of the saucer crew who loyally, if disgracefully failingly, chose to return to Tictoctic?"

"Officer Kwit-Nik, if I was not so urgently needed for matters of governance under the extreme food shortages here on the home world, I would be heading up the necessary mission back into deep space, personally. But I am aware you are one of the few others, besides my own self, who fully grasps the interstellar technology."

"Which is only to be expected, my Supreme Authority, as your fearless inspiration led to its origin," Kwit-Nik made even bolder to interrupt Dek-Fook-Tek's stream of thought to humbly baa. Over and over, Kwit-Nik reminded himself that, as revolting as he found them, he had to keep reiterating these commonly accepted lies, to avoid the Tictoctic dictator's slightest whiff of a scent of disloyalty. He had to keep masking, with this sickly sweet musk odor of deception, a crystal clear understanding. The only thing Dek-Fook-Tek inspired, and indeed led, was the bloodthirsty co-opting of the spaceship know-how and equipment from a superior, if equally warmongering, civilization.

Dek-Fook-Tek nodded appreciative acceptance of Kwit-nik's praise before he continued, "My core sense of judgment is as sharp as any antler sharpened by the finest bahvek. It tells me, Officer Kwit-Nik, that you have brought to bear on your experience of the other-worldly threat an adequately strong perceptiveness. It is the same perceptiveness you have brought to understanding and articulating clearly my critical role in the development of a space program that will ultimately carry us to our proper role in the affairs of multiple star systems. Therefore, I am encharging you with the solemn duty to head up the strike force we will use to overwhelm the imperial colonists of 'Koombk.' When all has been ruminated and regurgitated, you will have prosecuted the defensive conquest of their planet, as well as of the original target destination they named 'Kakamak.' Commander Kwit-Nik, please attend to the view-screen on my right, for a first look at the total force you will send galloping to the 'Koombk' world."

With that, on the wall perpendicular to the wall before which Dek-Fook-Tek sat upon his throne, the wall to his right, a six-hundred-square-foot segment slid to one side. Thus revealed was a theatre-sized blank screen. Soon thereafter, a camera view from the Tictoctic space station filled that screen with a spectacle; Kwit-Nik counted seven saucer-shaped spacecraft, every bit the size of the saucer that was lost to the aliens. For the time being, they were hovering at random coordinates.

"Every spacecraft is fully outfitted with magnetic pulse emitters. Under the careful guidance of my personal dietician, they have also been provided with just enough dried meat to sustain your forces until your arrival back to 'Koombk.' Thereafter, you and your forces will be expected to survive on, and in fact justifiably savor as a part of your reward for your mission's success, some of the fresh meat you gather. You, Chef Glork-tek, will apply the principles of my culinary genius to its preparation. And one other thing you should know before you are ferried out to the lead saucer..."

As Glork-tek made an accepting nod regarding his orders, Kwit-Nik caught himself from making even the slightest "baa" with another question before Dek-Fook-Tek finished his speech. Kwit-Nik, the newly-anointed saucer fleet commander, figured a second interruption had a good chance of not going as well as the earlier one had, especially given the concern he would have wished to have raised.

"...I call your attention to the television screen again."

The view of the seven saucers awaiting deployment got replaced by a view of a large room filled with rows of naked Tictoctickians. They were down on all fours, except for the few who guards were dragging off braying in terror-filled protest.

"Heroes of Tictoctic!" most severely crisply tongue-clicked the Tictoctic dictator, "do you hear your Dek-Fook-Tek?!"

"We hear, we delight in, and we wallow in the soothing quality of your voice as from the gently flowing waters of a mountain stream. We nestle in its warmth as from a bed of fallen pine needles in the forest," is how the ritual response tongue-clicks, sounded in near-perfect if monotonously toned unison, would have translated. A lone frantic bray seemed to Kwit-nik increasingly distant, remote.

On a nod of approving acknowledgement, Dek-Fook-Tek continued, "Look up at your television screen, and you will see Officer Kwit-Nik, newly commissioned by me as Commander Kwit-Nik. He will lead our triumphant mission into deep space, to herd from there the barbarian civilizations as the final solution to our food supply problems! Never again will our children starve!

Never again will we live in fear of aggression from a hostile planet!

"Now, Commander Kwit-Nik's mission, as you can understand, is of the highest priority. But so is yours! Yes, your sacrifice will be the final sacrifice, the very last time that Tictoctickian will be cruelly forced to eat Tictoctickian for the greater survival of all! Your tender meat will be the final span of the bridge that carries us over from a food-deprived hell to a food-abundant paradise!"

Everyone seen on the TV screen bent down on a forelimb knee to ritually baa, "We are not deserving of your most beneficent guidance." With Kwit-Nik thinking to himself, *Yes, we are not deserving, but not in this sense.*

"To honor your ultimate sacrifice, words are not enough!!" Dek-Fook-Tek bellowed with fury in his voice. "The least that can be done is what I am offering, if you look closely at my antlers, from here and from here." He pointed with cloven hoof-hand to both the left and right sides of his oversized complex of horny growths. A television camera Kwit-Nik hadn't noticed until then put them in close-up for the rows of Tictoctickians assembled in the large room at some other location. "On my command, two of my antler tips have been sawed off. Pursuant to which, a most trusted aid has used a 'bahvek,' my personal 'bahvek,' to arrive them to a sharpness that would tear a hole in time, were that possible. As a small token of my gratitude all Tictoctickians everywhere must feel for your highest level of sacrifice, you will each personally, most swiftly be impaled on one or the other of those horns, in the initial stage of your processing into our food supply bridge!"

"We are so undeserving of that honor, may you forgive us for accepting it," the chorus of baas ritually responded in unison while guards hauled away, kicking and panic-filled bleating, a few more hapless Tictoctickians.

As the television screen went blank for those in Dek-Fook-Tek's throne room, he said to Kwit-Nik, "So you must fully appreciate now the responsibility with which I have entrusted you."

Kwit-Nik was going to seize this particular moment to get into what he'd stifled himself from baaing, just before Dek-Fook-Tek introduced his sacrificial lambs, so to speak, on the big-screen TV. However, Chef Glork-tek beat him to the punch. The chef figured it was better coming from his own self, what he was sure his partner was going to ask. That, rather than risk any second thoughts by the Supreme Authority over who he was placing in charge of the invasion force. "A profound responsibility indeed," Chef Glork-tek tongue-clicked by way of agreeably, ingratiatingly easing himself into what he had to say. "Excuse my insertion into this momentous conversation, my leader. However, given the impressive record of your insights all along, into this extraterrestrial threat we are facing, I wish to ruminate on your every word regarding the safety of other-world meat. Our taste testers, many of whom fled with the traitor, never did have the opportunity to sample the meat in question."

"Baa, that!" Dek-Fook-Tek stuck out his thick, fleshy tongue derisively. "So many preliminaries, and what did we get for them? A stolen warship, and zero samples!"

"And flushing into the open who could not be relied upon, as assuredly as a forest fire flushes its hidden meat sources out into the open." Kwit-Nik went down on his right forelimb, upon this bold correction of the Tictoctic dictator's bleak assessment of the first mission.

Dek-Fook-Tek regarded Kwit-Nik with the most

penetrating stare he could conjure. When he was satisfied he had finally unsettled his subject, he at last tongue-clicked, "There are many reasons I am commissioning you to command the second mission into deep space, Commander Kwit-Nik. You have just impressively demonstrated one of them. Fulfill my expectations, and you may yet earn an honorary scarring across your chest.

"As for the food safety concern,-" Dek-Fook-Tek so abruptly turned his head back Chef Glork-tek's way, his antler handlers had to scramble to keep up. One of them pulled a forelimb muscle as he yanked on the particular wire for which he was responsible, to help keep the antlers from tipping over to one side or the other.

"-meat is meat! If you wish someone to sample your first culinary creation with the extraterrestrial flesh, before others join in, I leave that for your commander here to decide!"

Kwit-Nik nodded slowly, steadily to this responsibility thrust upon him, as he thought to his own self, *There is really no need for his "bridge sacrifice"; enough dried meat is left for another full orbit of the sun, at least! Including from the sister planet whose civilization we destroyed, as much as their hostilities earned it! No, the "bridge sacrifice" Tictoctickians are probably an assemblage of those who make Dek-Fook-Tek feel the most threatened. They've likely been tortured so much, many of them look forward to their "honorable sacrifice" as finally putting an end to their suffering. What will be my real responsibility will be to pause the invasion forces just outside our solar system. There, I must convince them our food gathering back to "Koombk" should focus on dumb creatures of the land and sea, rather than on clothes-wearing intelligences arguably as enlightened as ours, if not moreso! When fellow officers see we can reason with the extraterrestrials instead of going to war with them, then maybe they will at last understand we don't need a crazed egomaniac to lead us. We can put him and his closest associates away in an insane asylum where they belong, and embark on the environmental reconstruction of Tictoctic. Perhaps we will be aided in that task by those mind-reading tree creatures of "Koombk." Who knows? Eventually, maybe we will grow enough grasslands to afford to investigate the intriguing curiosity of continually launching and pushing along small, highly bounceable little spheres until they find their way dropping down into little holes in the ground…*

***

*The problem is this, Captain Taylor,* Mafoosoola telepathed on the navigation bridge of the Smoke and Mirrors. Nearly a quarter of that bridge's panoramic view-screen got filled with the turquoise crescent light of Oomb. *Pedro's family, relatives of you through your husband Chris, they have reasons for celebrating your return. Those reasons extend well beyond the more obvious ones of, for example, Pedro reuniting with his wife and daughter. Clearly, the pall of the destruction of Fafama cannot be indefinitely forestalled from getting cast across their land. Soon, the chair of the Joint Chiefs of Staff, General Sandy Warlor, plans to inform all the Earthling soldiers of exactly what happened. It is unreasonable to expect such sharing not to get leaked to the Oombinquen community. So many good relationships, so many strong bonds, have formed between that community and the soldiers. Not to mention their collective intuitive sense, however poorly developed as of yet, that something of tremendous import is being kept from them. Plus, I cannot guarantee that a fellow Oombian will not ignore all our leadership's strongly telepathed advice, not to intervene in any significant way in your affairs. That such an Oombian will not take it upon his or her self to do a mass telepath of the unsurpassably tragic news.*

"Well," Captain Taylor slapped her hands with *that's it* finality against both arms of her centrally-positioned chair. "Umm, Mafoosoola, I trust you have been sharing your telepath with others aboard the Smoke and Mirrors?"

*I have now, Captain.*

"Very good. So," Captain Taylor rose from her chair to address the other humanoids on the navigation bridge, "you should all understand when I say it would behoove us to make our immediate descent to the Oombian surface. Hopefully, we can get to enjoy a momentary reprieve, anyway, from what we've been having to deal with. Beyond the no small thing of loved ones' reunions, that reprieve looks to include whatever those other reasons are, for our settlers raptured here from Earth wanting to celebrate our return. Hopefully, they will get to share out before inevitably they must learn the fate of Fafama. Are you okay with that, Officer Perez?"

"I am okay with that, Captain." Pedro's joy over soon returning to Ludi's arms was leavened by the unfathomable horror of what had happened to Fafama. The untold number of couples, not to mention- It was too much for Señor Perez to dwell on. Captain Taylor could see it in his strained, wincing look even as he smiled.

Helena Taylor swiveled around to face who might have been the lone surviving member of Fafama's most intelligent species. The captain was ever-fascinated by how this nocturnal-eyed extraterrestrial had wanted to remain on the bridge, with Hanson at her side, for the flight back to Oomb. That was, after her initial self-imposed isolation in a specially-prepared darkroom. "Yulala, I can well appreciate that you, and you also, Sergeant Hanson, might wish to remain aboard..."

"No." Yulala shook her head in the universal negation expression, before Helena's remark finished emitting, translated into fa-la-las, from her waist-belted translator. "With your approval, 'Cahptahn Taylah,' I should like to see the world of 'Mahfoosoolah,' and meet 'Ahffahsah Pahrahz's' only wife and their daughter. And I admit a curiosity over what could be those special other reasons for celebrating which the people down there want to share."

"Yulala, that is wonderful." Helena could feel her own eyes water as she spoke. "I am certain many of those people, and tree people, would like to get to know you."

"Starting with Ludi," Pedro nodded emphatically. "To spread the local gossip, I'm sure she wouldn't mind sitting in the darkest room with you!"

"He-hee!" Yulala couldn't help the squeal-y laugh of her species, the same time her eyes watered, too. She gave an extra tight hug to Sergeant Hanson seated beside her.

"Helena Taylor," the intercom suddenly crackled as General Warlor's severe countenance appeared on the left half of the panoramic view-screen. The crescent Oomb vista got shrunk over to the right half, while Secretary Spinner at Warlor's side looked to Chris like he was posing with a can't-get-these-hemorrhoids-to-stop-hurting pained expression on his face for a family portrait. "We welcome you back to the Callaway X Centra system, and thank you for temporarily re-assuming your former duties, since Officer Entroper decided for understandable reasons to de-commission herself.

Reasons which, may I add, reflect poorly on both you and certain other of your officers. So poorly, in fact, we cannot guarantee your reassumed office will not be temporary."

*Interesting how she has avoided saying the word, Captain,* Helena was not the only one on the bridge to note. She also wondered whether Louisa Entroper was having this transmission made available to her in her quarters where she had kept to herself for most of the return flight.

"We don't know what your present plans were intended to be," Warlor went on, "but they are pre-empted by the debriefing protocols critical for planning where we go from here. Those protocols include what is to be your role, and the role of your colleagues, if any."

Captain Taylor did not hesitate to firmly shake her head 'no.' "General Warlor, Secretary Spinner, for the past days of our return flight, we have done little else than self-debriefings, until we are sick of them." Helena wasn't ready yet to launch into a verbal attack on the result of the extraterrestrial militarization of Fafama. "We have tens of hours of video, plus hundreds of pages of transcripts of those debriefings. I can transmit them immediately, for you to pore over while we take a break to attend to other pressing business. And for your information, that other pressing business has to do with family reunification, and what Mafoosoola here telepathed us is something significant that people want to share with us down on Oomb's surface."

"Forget about that, Helena." Secretary Spinner made a sweep of his left arm, like he was clearing away what Captain Taylor mentioned as though it were so much worthless underbrush he was pushing aside for their forward progress. "You noticed we didn't get on your case for returning at something less than a maximum pace, especially with your hyper-space whizz kid Officer Leung on board? That we gave you some room to decompress?"

"Did you understand what I just said, Secretary Spinner?! We were flying away from the destruction of a planet's entire ecology! We couldn't decompress! We were too haunted to do anything other than replay the events over and over in our heads, and to each other! I'm not sure that whatever the Oombians and our Earth settlement have to share, that it will succeed in distracting us from our lingering collective nightmare for any time at all. But even Yulala, here, who is the only known Fafaman survivor..." Helena wasn't about to bring up the ephemeral dragon. "...even Yulala wants to give that distraction a chance!"

"Truly, Secretary Spinner and Chief Warlor," Ali stood for his offering, "we know that getting away from an urgent situation, a breathing space if you will," he untwined his hands and splayed his fingers far apart for emphasis, "can allow people to return back to its consideration with a refreshed view, more helpful insights than we might ever have gained otherwise."

"Sure," Secretary Spinner nodded. He cleared his throat with a noisier production than Ali thought should have been required. It was as though, the counselor suspected, said production added weight to that with which he proceeded. "Of course. And while you are taking the time to just get away from it all, Oomb is attacked by four Tictoctickian battle saucers, suddenly de-cloaking. BOOM! A second planet lost!" His shaking jowls would have been evident, Helena knew, if not for his Santa's beard.

*So what if, Secretary Spinner,* Mafoosoola made no

apology for intruding on the heated discussion, *the insight to be gleaned that would help regarding your hypothesized saucer invasion can only come from a certain someone? What if such insight can only come from a certain someone fully acquainted with all the known facets of what you are dealing with, AND who has, his or her self, taken the necessary time off, a period of relative tranquility, to more clearly consider the matter? For all you know, what my fellow Oombians, and your fellow Earthlings who have settled on Oomb, have to share will be just the things to lead to such clarity.*

"Not to want to spoil the surprise for you, but I happen to know from our ground troops there is some pride in what tree critters and human critters alike have done down there while you were away. It includes what one soldier told me was by far the strangest mix of music he has ever heard. I am sure, Helena Taylor,-"

Again, Helena found it remarkable how Spinner could not bring himself to utter the word, Captain.

"-some weird music and perhaps a round or two of 'oof' into the bargain will prove the missing keys to figuring out how to stop the Tictoctic invasion."

*Secretary Spinner,-*

So soon as Mafoosoola intruded anew, General Warlor shook her head into the palms of her hands.

*-it might seem Captain Taylor's intended visit down to Oomb's surface, with its family reunions and whatever they have to share down there, is, as the captain put it, "getting us mentally away" from what comprises our major concern. But everything is ultimately interconnected, I would argue. Using an Earth metaphor I mind-read during the Smoke and Mirrors's first arrival to Oomb, what we will be doing is stepping back from an unproductively long and isolated contemplation of a*

*single tree, to try to see the entire forest. This is perhaps an especially apt metaphor in my case. Anyhow, it stands to reason that-*

"Captain Taylor," General Warlor erupted heedless of Mafoosoola's telepath having not been completed, while Ali recalled the Shakespeare line, *by indirection find direction out*, "are you refusing to comply with my order, to present yourself and certain other of your crew, immediately, aboard the Barack Obama for a debriefing? Incidentally, there are likely to be questions we will want to ask, not covered in your self-debriefing."

"General Warlor, I am announcing my intended delay of compliance with your order."

"Which is the same as refusing to comply. Are you sure you want to do this, Helena? You might find yourself out of a commission and in fact unable to return to the Smoke and Mirrors in any capacity after your little vacation. That is the same for all of you."

"Yulala as well? You're going to de-commission her?"

"Be reasonable, Helena. I do not want to have to do any of what I am going to have to do if you do not establish that there will be prompt compliance with my orders! You have a choice!"

"And YOU have a choice!"

When Captain Taylor pointed at the camera, Warlor and Spinner both stepped back, shocked, not unlike they would have reacted had she been actually standing before them, whipping out a gun instead of a forefinger.

"I have three firefly donuts ready to launch with the press of a button on this console," Taylor went on. "That launch will send them flying to within transmission range of the firefly communications linkage network back to Earth. All three of them carry the same information, about how your additional militarization of Fafama has resulted in its civilization's destruction."

"Then you are blackmailing us."

"I am saying that if you are not going to be reasonable, after instituting a policy which has so obviously failed on an apocalyptic level, then I am not going to trust you to give the people at home a full and accurate picture of what has happened thus far!"

"Then forget about Tictoctic," said Secretary Spinner. "We are the real enemy."

"If that is what you conclude I'm saying, then you need a break from all this, to see the whole forest, even more than we do! Yoon-hee, end the communications link!"

"Got that, Captain."

"Captain," added Engineer Kevin Smith-Park, "Yoon-hee and I will hold down the fort while the rest of you are gone. If they send anyone to assume control, the fireflies will be sent on their way."

"What I expected to hear, Kevin."

***

Tens of flying trees filled the air with swish-swish-swishes from their rapidly spinning, super-thick and bamboo-strong helicopter-blade palm fronds. Those trees were escorting the shuttle pod from the Smoke and Mirrors on its final descent to the landing beach of choice on Oomb's largest, Borneo-sized land mass. Sergeant Guy Hanson grinned appreciatively to see his beloved Yulala, goggles protecting her nocturnally adapted eyes, with her button nose pressed smudging against a porthole. She was sighing variously "Oooo" and "Ahhh" over the otherworldly spectacle, like a little girl seeing dolphins leaping from the sea for the first time. At least that was the memory that struck Guy, from a glass bottom boat ride some ten years earlier. Said little girl had turned her parents' way, to assure they were sharing in what she was beholding. Similarly, Yulala did not get so caught up in the flying tree spectacle that she did not also turn Guy's way. She cared for him that much.

Oonzy Ootzies happened to make their presence known at the beach where the welcome-home celebration took place. On their first, dancing-seeming emergence from the sea, they got suddenly joined by two little boys. Those boys aped the creatures' behavior as a woman, Ciela, called after them, "You two both come here this minute!" They weren't listening. Rather, they were busy backing their way into the gentle surf, up to their necks alongside ten-foot-tall Oonzy Ootzies to either side of them. Said Oonzy Ootzies moved their round mouths fishlike, an apprehensive Tanya thought, as they noted their alien company.

"I'm going in after them," Tanya announced, with the boys and Ootzies alike re-emerging completely back onshore. But it turned out she didn't need to bother. Each Oonzy Ootzy was carrying, by a dexterous four-clawed flipper, a fish the size and silver-shiny appearance of a yellow-fin tuna. With which fish, they heartily slapped both boys by the seat of their swimming trunks so powerfully hard, they sent those two mischief-makers flying squealingly yet safely up the beach.

Ciela and Ali grabbed them before they could run down the shore to experience it all over again.

By then, Mafoosoola and Schnoodle-Coodle were well into their reunified embrace. How they managed to coil their lower trunks around one another fascinated Yulala no end.

Just as fascinating, the former twenty-third wife of the Fafamafalafama found, was how the other Oombian tree creature who Buddy Leung had rescued rejoined his loved one. Flookle-Dookle had gone into a protective hibernation stasis aboard the shuttle pod, continued aboard the Smoke and Mirrors, for his return home. His leaves and fruit had all fallen off well before Buddy had reached Fafama. No matter to his significant other. She embraced him how he was too weak to lift his own branches to reciprocate. Then, they both strove to inconspicuously blend themselves back in with the mix of permanently-rooted and semi-rooted kinfolk, where they both felt the most comfortable.

Meantime, the reunification of Pedro with his family proved anything but inconspicuous. The Marines who had worked most closely with Sergeant Hanson disciplined themselves to maintain their standing-at-attention cool decorum, not swarm him and Yulala for a group hug. However, the instant Pedro appeared at the top of the shuttle pod exit ramp to descend down onto the beach, Ludi shouted, "Pedro!! Cariño!!" and Alexita shouted, "Papi!! Papi!!," and they both broke into a sprint to greet him with holding-on-for-dear-life hugs. They attained this goal soon as Pedro's first magnetoboot touched the pink-hued sand consisting of ground-up seashell. Following right behind mother and daughter were Doña Rotonda and Don Placido arm-in-arm, Don Típico and Doña Norma arm-in-arm, and Gloria and Jerri cradling their sons Espacio and Galaxio.

The officiating Oombian tree creature, Snooky-Watooky, gave up on her formally-planned, welcome-back telepath. Several other settlers taken from their northern Philadelphia tenement homes of sixty years earlier were boisterously hopping up and down, sharing the excitement.

"Now come, you have to come." Ludi unwrapped

herself from Pedro to grab his one hand as with his other hand, he supported Alexita leaping into his arms.

"How Pedro and his family are moving off there for sharing whatever-it-is with him, the way they're staying crowded around him, it's almost like they are a single living organism, ha!"

To Helena Taylor, Buddy Leung seemed to be thinking out loud, talking to himself...and entertaining himself besides, regardless of Cathy's presence beside him.

"If their daughter and those other babies aren't careful," Chris nevertheless responded, "they could turn into that organism's mitochondria!" He tried to screw up the courage to succeed his words with an affectedly casual affectionate grabbing of Helena's hand. But he chickened out.

"I must say, Captain Taylor," Ali gave Tanya's hand a squeeze, as he reached for words to paraphrase, *Let's all be thankful,* "I feel truly privileged to have listened in on this exchange between your husband and Cathy's husband. I could not realistically hope to overhear it coming from anyone else, anywhere!"

"Don't you mean you realistically hope NOT to overhear it coming from anyone else?" Tanya playfully pinched Ali's arm.

"Go on, Oodle-Noodle; your telepaths." Helena feigned resignation in her voice. "I don't need to mind-read to tell that you are itching – or however you put it – to telepath something. Remember: We are all friends here. I know you're admirably sensitive to not wanting to intrude on our most private thoughts. Nevertheless, please feel free to rustle your leaves, rustle OUR leaves, whenever the spirit moves you."

*Thank you, Captain Taylor, and how appropriate*

*your imagery is for what I have to communicate. It is regarding that unique "exchange" between Officer Olsen-Taylor and Officer Leung. Your great yoga masters have always said that at their deepest meditative state, they experience a unity where seeming boundaries and separations are proven illusory. What we have experienced as well, informing our profound dread over the course your military is taking, in dealing with Tictoctic…I'm sorry, Captain; you all DO need a rest. That is as it should be.*

***

"Samantha Perez-Olsen! This is an unexpected honor!" President Carey welcomed the diminutive, mousey-haired woman into the oval office with the same fluid gestures with which he also waved off the two Secret Service agents who accompanied her. Thereby, did the president and Ms. Perez-Olsen end up alone behind closed doors.

Straight off, President Carey was struck by how well-postured Samantha was for her age, with her head held high.

After a hearty handshake, Samantha accepted, by subtle nod, his invitation for her to join him on the sofa.

"Thank you, Mr. President," Chris Olsen-Taylor's mother said after settling herself in comfortably. "I do have to admit to you, um, I was half-expecting what I want to share with you would set off the security sensors. I did receive an assurance that would not happen, and yet, um, well, it has to be conceded the assurance was obviously well-founded."

"Oh, and so what is it exactly you wanted to share, Ms. Perez-Olsen?" President Carey tried to sound as nonchalant as he could feign. His heart was racing, though not out of any fear over whatever mysterious thing to which Samantha might be alluding. In fact, if Secret Service were to come barging in, worried over what this woman was talking about, he had not the least doubt he was going to chase them right back out again. No, what had Carey struggling in order to maintain a veneer of calm, steady consideration was something else altogether. It was the occurrence which led to him working this woman's requested private audience into his over-extended schedule in the first place.

Six nights earlier, he had suddenly, inexplicably sprung awake, not for his usual, frequent need to pee. Or was it one of those dreams where you think you have woken up, but you're still dreaming? Whichever, his wife was snoring soundly, unaffected. What had happened next, had happened at the foot of his bed. Swirling mists had suddenly materialized as from a block of dry ice. Initially, Carey was inclined to dismissively blame some hitherto unknown plumbing issue below the second floor. Whatever that issue was, it had to have led to an unusual condensation effect. Before Mr. President could go further, though, to mentally sort out the situation in a reassuringly conventional manner, those mists had coagulated into the shape of a woman, another diminutively statured woman similar to Samantha, yet thinner, more gaunt. She'd spoken. Carey had heard her say as clearly as had she been Samantha sitting there presently before him, "The mother of a crew member of the Smoke and Mirrors is going to ask for a private audience with you. She will be seeking the fulfillment of an intention begun a vastly long way from here. That fulfillment will prove exceedingly crucial, for life and love are at stake, not to get too redundant about it. I wish I could (garbled) longer to-" The rest was garbled also, as the woman's image dissolved back down into those swirling mists again, which had rapidly proceeded to dissipate entirely. All that Carey had heard afterwards was a loud snort from his wife as she rolled over to face him, still fast asleep.

Two days had passed since this seeming ghostly visitation, with no follow-up incident. The American Union President had grown increasingly confident it was just a most peculiar nightmare. Perhaps the mushrooms in the lasagna earlier that same evening had done their work. But then a staffer had mentioned, in casual passing, there was a holo-message purportedly from the mother of Captain Taylor's husband. She asked to speak with President Carey alone. Said staffer had presumed such an audience was completely out of the question, what with everything else on Carey's platter.

"Mr. President," Samantha was going on presently, "I hate to take you away from all your pressing business for this, but, um, I was assured you were the person I needed to go to for my most extraordinary request. I only hope you won't find it too unreasonable."

*Dare I ask her who did this assuring? It can't be that same phantasm I must have been- Did she have a related dream or vision?* President Carey's mind raced with these thoughts that welled out from his spirit's certain knowledge of the truth. "Mrs. Olsen-Taylor, how could I refuse an audience with the mother of one of the first people to so courageously voyage outside our solar system?" This, instead of the question about who assured her. Carey knew what would be the dreaded answer to said question. However, so long as the matter didn't get voiced aloud, he could continue to pretend his own, comparable experience was not real.

"Thank you, Mr. President." Samantha self-consciously busied her hands, nervously trying to smooth out her skirt. After reaching for the brim of her security blanket San Francisco Giants baseball hat in vain, she recalled that out of deference for the office of the president, she had left it at home. "My extraordinary request is this: If you have another spacecraft scheduled to join the Smoke and Mirrors, um, out there…" She swirled around one arm in the general direction of the bay window. "Um, I should like to be on that flight, to see my son, Christopher. I have something special to share with him."

President Carey couldn't help sitting back on the sofa with his startlement. "How did you know about another spacecraft?" Soon as these words left his mouth, he wanted to retract them. He really didn't want to find out. Although at the same time, he couldn't bring himself to say, *You don't have to answer that.*

"I didn't know. I was speculating." As much as Carey didn't want to ask how she knew, Samantha didn't want to share with him the phantasmal visitations SHE had been experiencing. Of course, if he asked about the origin of the pendant…

"So, what special thing do you have to share with your son, Mrs. Perez-Olsen?"

Samantha unslung a shoulder bag and unzipped it. With her nervously trembling hands, she extracted a neatly folded handkerchief. She unfolded the hanky on her lap with methodical care, thereby revealing the pendant with the mysterious engraved lettering bearing somewhat the appearance of Egyptian hieroglyphics.

President Carey was on his guard, to not let his amazement show. He well knew those were the same hieroglyphics, the very same hieroglyphic writing he had seen in a debriefing. They made up the prevailing writing system on the planet Fafama. And yet, as desperately as he wanted to ask this little old lady how she had come into this, again he wasn't ready to hear the answer. He used the time he took, slowly turning this golden object around in the palm of his hand, to formulate a most careful, guarded reaction. During which, he also mused nostalgically to himself about long ago, when he was a contestant on the television show, *Survivor.* Samantha's mysterious pendant could have been the hidden immunity idol he'd been searching for.

When he sensed he couldn't delay any longer, President Carey rewrapped the pendant in the handkerchief, as carefully as Samantha had unveiled it for him, and he said, "So you want us to provide interstellar transport to see your son?" He intentionally neglected to betray any curiosity as to the reason why. "Well I would say, Mrs. Perez-Olsen, it is the least we can do for the mother of the husband behind the captain for the successful first mission of the Smoke and Mirrors. And a successful second mission also, let's hope!"

"Um...thank you. Yes, let's hope." Samantha found herself suddenly hastening to return the wrapped-up pendant to her shoulder bag, and zipping that bag shut, protectively. What puzzled her was why the president seemed unwilling to put her on the spot about how she got the pendant, and why she needed to share it with her son. If she didn't know better, her intuition was telling her he was avoiding those questions.

"I will have the transport cargo ship captain, himself, contact you with the details."

"That's...Thank you, Mr. President. Um, I have just one more request. I hope you will agree it is very minor, compared to the enormous favor you have just granted me."

"Yes, Ms. Perez-Olsen?" President Carey could think of many questions he could have asked, to try to forestall Samantha wanting to make her proposed journey, such as: Are you sure you are prepared, at your age, for the rigors of your getting from this planet's surface up to the space station launch dock? However, any risk of having to hear her voice aloud...

"I do not wish my son to be alerted to my coming. Especially should he and his crew be in the middle of whatever task...I don't in any way want to create the slightest impediment to, the slightest distraction from, that task's completion."

"Understood." Understood without question.

***

"RUN!!! Don't dance!!! RUN!!!" was how Norma's imploring shouts at her husband, Don Típico, would have translated from her Spanish. She jumped up and down with what Pedro would have characterized as his grandma-in-law's wild abandon behind the home plate backstop.

Don Típico had just hit a grounder between the first base Oombian and the second baseman, the softball having been pitched by Don Placido. His wife's advice appeared to Pedro and Ludi, both, to have made a difference. Subsequent to that advice, from a most curious sidestep punctuated by hip swivels, Ludi's grandpa accelerated into a full-out sprint. He slid into second before he could be tagged out.

Captain Taylor shook her head in total disbelief, and Ali Magabu nodded most approvingly. Pedro shouted in Ludi's ear, to be heard above the raucous din of players and softball fans alike, "I thought tu abuelo (*your grandfather*) and my Placido were set on watching fifty years of missed baseball seasons on the big holo-screen televisions!"

"They like that too!" Ludi shouted back. "But there is so much peace and quiet here!, especially after the scare from Tictoctic! I think they reacted like me! They finally appreciated all the trouble our descendants went to, to give us this new life on a paradise planet! And they knew how much you wanted this for us!, mi cariño! (*my love*, said with her arm tightening around his waist), but they could not know whether you were going to survive!"

Pedro wasn't sure how much came from Ludi's sweat streaming down her face, due to the heat of one of Oomb's occasional days with twenty-plus hours of sunlight, and how much was her tearfulness.

"I think it was that under this circumstance," Ludi went on, "we were finally hearing a voice from inside our souls, about what gave us true joy! And the telepathy from the Oombians was helping to guide us there!!"

"I..." Pedro knew without a doubt, the streams down his own cheeks were tears. He shook his head and, unsure how to express the joy flooding his own heart, he ended up crying, "I never realized how big a fan was Doña Norma of baseball!"

"Not simply a fan! She's the next-up at bat! But after we see her hit, I have to take you to hear what your sisters are doing!"

"What?!" Pedro laughed and cried as he noticed an Oombian on Típico and Norma's team, next on deck, swinging his tree-trunk butt. Obviously, the tree creature intended to hit the softball in that manner, if he got to be batter-up after Norma.

By the time Ludi and Pedro slunk off to experience what his sisters were about, Sergeant Hanson was animatedly explaining to Yulala how softball was played. She was only half-attentive, as she continued to take in what were for her mesmerizingly exotic vistas all around, so different from the desert-like Fafaman landscape. She felt especially soothed by the caressing warmth of Oombian telepathy ebbing and flowing on the outer reaches of her mental landscape. It was an ebb and flow that over the weeks had helped to produce the wondrous character transformations to which Pedro was getting introduced.

"I remembered what you said, Pedro mi hermano (*my brother*), about what would I want to do with myself if I had no worries, no problems." Gloria was seated beside Jerri on a reclining Oombian tree creature. Said creature appeared preoccupied with casually pruning its own dead branches and a few rotting fruits, while both women were each balancing a small Puerto Rican guitar called a cuatro on their knees. "Of course, much of our day is typically eaten up by care for our dear sons, Espacio and Galaxio, and also by time with our boyfriends who are playing softball at the moment, I think."

"And also by OUR share of the responsibilities for constructing Oombinquen," added Jerri.

"Sí, Jerri is right," Gloria nodded. "But this question of what we would want to do, if we had all the time in the world: We were listening to the 'estrange' music coming from a 'treebaro' standing alone in the middle of the 'oof' course."

"'Treebaro'!" Jerri giggled, "That's what we call them!"

Pedro grinned from ear to ear. He remembered well the word, jibaro, for legendary country folk of Puerto Rico.

"Yes, and we were thinking how amazing the treebaro's music would sound, mixed with a plena or something from Puerto Rico."

"A new type of salsa." Jerri strummed her cuatro in a manner suggestive to Pedro and Ludi she was getting ready to play something.

"That treebaro, his name is Fafooble-winky-woodle, he explained this spooky thing," said Gloria. "From a fifth-dimensional view, he says he is seeing the oof balls, the paths they fly, as so many strings he can pluck like guitar strings."

*I am Fafooble-winky-woodle,* telepathed a nearby Oombian who the newly-returned Earthlings hadn't noticed previously.

Meantime, the Oombian acting as a bench for Gloria and Jerri paused from his pruning to close his eyes. Pedro gathered that the tree person was entering into blissful anticipation of what was about to transpire.

For Pedro, Ludi, Helena and the others who had gathered around out of curiosity, it appeared that Fafooble-Winky-Woodle was strumming empty air with his branch tips. But a haunting tune seemed to emanate from everywhere, clearly in perfect sync with the air-plucking. Gloria and Jerri gave most impassioned, finger-plucking attention to their cuatros. The women coaxed from their stringed instruments a complex of rhythms and melodies common to Puerto Rican folk music. They blended perfectly with what sounded to Pedro like a harp modulating in and out of a bagpipe tone. Gloria repeated that Fafooble-winky-woodle was strumming oof-ball flight paths from a fifth-dimensional awareness, as though those flight paths were guitar strings. Supplementing this extraordinary performance, the Oombian providing bench space started rhythmic rubbing-together of his branches. The percussion section.

More tears welled in Pedro's eyes over finding his sisters thusly occupied, as Ludi whispered in his ear, "I didn't know they could play the cuatro."

"They couldn't," Pedro shook his head. It was all he

could do to get these words out, he was so choked up. "They must have listened to their deeper selves."

"And you know what I heard when I listened to my own deeper self, cariño?"

"Mama oof!" interceded Alexita jumping up and down, before Pedro could pull himself back together enough to venture an answer, or to say he had no idea.

"You?! Oof?!" Pedro couldn't believe his ears.

"Cariño, it's your kingdom, *our* kingdom, beyond the stars! Let's go grab some clubs!"

"Captain, have you had enough shore leave yet for that refreshed perspective on things you were searching for? Can you return up to orbit now, for our conversation on where we go from here?" It was Sandy Warlor's voice suddenly crackling in Helena's earpiece. From her tone, Helena could tell the chair of the Joint Chiefs of Staff was straining to be diplomatic about it. *Perhaps,* Captain Taylor started to think, *or is it too much to hope for?, that how the unfathomably massive disaster unfolded on Fafama with our introducing weapons into the picture, perhaps Warlor and the others are feeling a little chastened?*

"Thank you, General Warlor. I'm going to need just a little more time. Then I should be ready for our talk." Helena Taylor concluded this with a wink Oodle-Noodle's way. She wanted to "hear" from this particular tree creature first.

***

The hijacked cargo ship, *Philadelphia Freedom*, sat anchored a few miles off the southeast coast of the island of Las Palmas in the Canary Islands. Flamboyo Sanchez, at the lower deck railing, began to dwell on how he would have liked to have gotten something a bit better than a late-sunset view. But he stopped himself. Yes, the gentle sea air was uncontaminated by the stench of human-produced pollutants that nauseated him on the way out of harbor near Philadelphia. That tangy ocean fragrance could be intoxicating, together with the gentle lapping of the calm waters against the hull of the vessel. Flamboyo could get lulled close to a thought about the Earth not being such a bad place after all. He reminded himself, however, of what he kept reminding himself whenever he started to feel affected by the beauty of nature, or by a stray remembrance of Shelly Taylor's naïve faith in the possibility for a better humanity. Which was, that what was best about the world really wasn't going to get lost in what Dr. Engeling had planned. Yes, having the moon slammed into the Earth would dramatically reshape things. The transformation would prove as dramatic as when an enormous asteroid collided with the Earth over four billion years earlier, and led to the creation of the moon in the first place. However, there would be new beautiful vistas, none of that would get lost. Only a temporary setback. Most importantly, the human pestilence, an endless chain of people hurting one another and their habitat, would be eradicated, permanently.

With his binoculars, Flamboyo spotted towering canary pines. They were set in silhouette relief along the Las Palmas crater ridge by the fading yellow sky behind them. Many of them had branches that stretched out like spindly arms attempting some exercise pose. And one of them, the soil at its base had gotten so eroded, its thick roots exposed there looked to be three legs on which it was standing. Maybe in the new, post-collision world, these ancient trees would survive to evolve into intelligent, mobile plant creatures. Reports suggested that such creatures most peacefully and nurturingly presided over the ecology of the planet Oomb. Thinking of which, reminded Flamboyo there were humans wandering around, trillions of miles away, Shelly's mother among them. But he knew nothing of the battleship, Barack Obama, and the couple hundred people resettled on Oomb from sixty years earlier. And so, he believed it was not too much to hope, that the members of his species would remain too few out there in the cosmos to inflict much harm, once he and the rest of the humans back on Earth were exterminated.

Suddenly, abruptly taking Flamboyo out of his grim reverie, he heard from down on the surface of the Atlantic Ocean a series of sharp, staccato clicks punctuated by high-pitched squeaks. He feared United Nations law enforcement had already seen through the cargo ship's camouflage, and sonar-signal-masking device. That they were about to board, unless they could be shot or otherwise disposed of. However, as a beacon light was directed shining towards the source of these noises, he realized they came from dolphins surfacing close to the vessel.

Flamboyo suppressed an unsettling feeling there was an urgent, pleading tenor to the sea mammals' sounds. This suppression made it possible for him to nod to himself that, if enough of those dolphins could survive the moon impact, maybe they could become the new, better, apex intelligent species on Earth. *Of course their tone would feel urgent and pleading*, Flamboyo realized in a quick reconsideration of what he'd been trying initially to suppress. *They're not mind-reading about Engeling's plan; more immediately they're asking that people stop poisoning their world! They might welcome what we're about, if they were to understand it!*

The growing Whup! Whup! Whup! coming from the helicopter pad reminded Señor Sanchez that a critical piece of Engeling's plan was close to execution.

Of the copter itself, only its rapidly accelerating blades spinning atop it were visible. The rest, including a payload being hauled underneath it, were cloaked in a ballooned-out, metallic yet paper-thin, one-way-transparent, buckey-ball-strong material. Copter lights made the immense cloak glow, with the intended purpose of convincing any observers they were seeing a classic UFO, flying saucer, or whatever else they wanted to call it. The cloak was engineered for radar to fail to pick up on it, as it went to sit for some hours at night on a remote ridge along the dead Cumbre Vieja crater. No one would want to make the effort to check it out up close. As well, few if any would want to report it, for fear of getting labeled crazy, perhaps unworthy of remaining outside the quarantine zones.

The helicopter cloaked to be confused for a flying saucer lifted off into a sky where more and more stars were becoming visible with the rapidly suffusing night.

Flamboyo pondered anew this crucial stage of the plan, if only to stave off a reconsideration of the several dolphins who, with their persisting clicks and squeaks, had obviously decided to linger around the cargo ship.

Dr. Morel Engeling had explained to him there was actually no geological evidence for a super tsunami ever having resulted from one of the landslides into the sea from the old crater. The best guess was that those landslides had occurred in small segments, rather than as an entire massive area all at once. However, Engeling and loyal crew members were going to strategically burrow nuclear-tipped explosives into the crater. The idea was that those explosives' simultaneous detonation would at last precipitate the otherwise unlikely apocalyptic scenario of a thirty-mile-wide portion of crater wall avalanching into the Atlantic Ocean all at once. A monster tsunami would thereby get triggered, heading towards the Atlantic seaboard of the east coast of the American Union, and specifically targeting Florida.

For those loyal to Flamboyo, that would be enough. They would think that was all there was to it. Most of Florida, non-quarantine and quarantine zones alike, would go underwater. People living outside the no-zones, attending theme parks with their children, would learn something. They would learn that, so long as any people have to live like caged animals in wretched fenced-off areas, nobody is really safe, nobody can confidently presume to live at ease.

But this was only the first phase of the plan. Phase two would begin with the hijacking of a shuttle craft at the Kennedy Space Center. At least, Flamboyo kept reassuring a part of himself that seemed continually to teeter on the edge of panic, at least that phase involved him boarding said craft, right alongside the mad genius. There was still...

***

"For all practical purposes, Captain Helena Taylor, we are suspended upside down here, in relation to Oomb. I am imagining the blood flowing one way only, into my brain. Otherwise, I would have wanted to stand for this meeting, magnetoboots be damned, as we contemplate that world bejeweled with Hawai'i's, far as I can reckon." Strapped into his chair at an oval conference table aboard the Barack Obama starship battle cruiser, Secretary of Defense Spinner motioned towards the panoramic window view set into the ceiling.

The weapons-loaded starship was in geosynchronous orbit above Oomb's largest archipelago. This archipelago included the planet's largest, Borneo-shaped land mass, named Boombeeno. The Earthling settlement was located along its eastern shore. A cloud deck enshrouded Boombeeno's tallest peaks. Scattered cumulus freckled, with pinpoint shadows, the planet-enrobing sea otherwise hued variously indigo-blue, turquoise and emerald. *This is a global paradise,* Helena thought to herself. *"Truly," as Ali would say, I must do everything within my power to keep us, the Tictoctickians, and anyone else from ruining it!*

"Excuse me, Madame Oodle-Noodle. I realize this isn't going to be exactly one of the first things you would have expected to hear from me after what I just said." Secretary Spinner strained to keep up his folksy repartee without bursting out laughing over having to deal with a mobile, intelligently communicating tree, and with such a ridiculous name. "Are you sure you're comfortable standing there? We could have you gently lowered down on your back side; I promise none of us will mistake you for a bench! Sorry about that; I have a history of stuff just slipping out of my mouth. But you're probably already well aware of that, if you've been mind-reading this garbage heap up here." Spinner pointed at his forehead as General Warlor gave him try-to-control-yourself pats on his hand.

*Secretary Spinner, thank you. I am adequately comfortable here, remaining upright, as I spend most of my life, with rare exception. What is helping, especially in these weightless circumstances, is the Velcro floor material to which my roots and cilia instinctively cling.*

"So Helena Taylor," General Warlor had no trouble plunging into the matter at hand, rather than making the slightest reference to Oodle-Noodle's telepathed response, "what are your thoughts, your input, you would wish to make on the orders you are to receive as the newly reinstated captain of the Smoke and Mirrors?"

*So they're keeping me in charge after all.* Helena allowed herself a centering, calming inhale and exhale, focused on her lower abdomen, before saying, "Secretary Spinner, General Warlor, I have, um, had communicated to me a compelling case for an exploratory reconnaissance probe to Tictoctic. It would be done covertly, of course, to gain a deeper understanding of the Tictoctickians, so we will be better able to know what to do about them."

"Advance scouts to detect their weaknesses, perhaps, and discover more fully what we're up against where their strengths are concerned, so victory will be closer to our reach," Secretary Spinner nodded with an approving frown. Then he went on to Oodle-Noodle, "I assume you or another of your kind telepathed that compelling case to the captain. A little chastened, are we, by the courtesy call to your planet from Tictoctic? It has maybe occurred to you those antlered critters aren't so amenable to your peace and love tactics?"

Captain Taylor bowed her head as she fended off the strong urge to burst out, *Where is YOUR chastening from the destruction of Fafama? What did YOU learn about the real world impracticality of planned violence?* Helena kept reminding herself the goal here was to gain approval for the mission without revealing what-all the mission would entail. Not to win an argument. And anyhow she well knew the shape Spinner's folksily-invoked rebuttal would take. There'd be something for sure about how a substantial Earthling military presence should have been maintained on Fafama. That presence could have flexed its muscles, so to speak, when the Fafaman government went about playing with their new toys rather than saving them for use in the event of a Tictoctic invasion.

Oodle-Noodle, though, proved not so reticent about a response, however diplomatically she couched her still-most-firm telepath. *On Oomb, we harbor no illusions about the immensity of the challenge facing us. The same as we can be sure our great ancestors harbored no illusions about what they were risking when they literally bared all for love. It was no easy task to change our own psychology away from that of enemy fighting sworn enemy. No one on or off our planet should naively romanticize about our life's evolution, in its earlier stages, having been any less harsh or cruel than what we have mind-read has transpired on Earth. As regards Captain Taylor's proposed mission, should this meet with your approval, I would only hope you would grant enough time for its completion.*

"Time." Warlor pointedly repeated that one word only. "Well," she sighed, "I must admit, Captain, your reconnaissance probe is not far afield from our own thinking. But what- Time for what is Oodle-Noodle telepathing about? Time to perform a miracle?"

"I'm not sure what our friend here has in mind exactly, beyond what it sounds like you and the secretary and I are thinking." Helena's weasel word to satisfy her own self she wasn't lying was "exactly." Yes, she didn't understand "exactly" what Oodle-Noodle had in mind, the details. She well knew, though, the broad outlines, and how mention of those outlines could get the mission scuttled, if not herself relieved from duty again. "I am guessing it is safe to say that in the end, we all want the same thing."

Everyone nodded, even Oodle-Noodle.

Helena braced for the expected response from General Warlor or the secretary, which they surprised her by not initiating. What she expected was some comment about how Oodle-Noodle could clear up any ambiguity, simply by telepathing to them what she had in mind when she asked for enough time.

Still, Helena fretted over the silence after her diplomatically conceived remark. If it continued for much longer, she wasn't certain it wouldn't act as a vacuum, and finally suck said expected response out into the open. So with no further additional delay, she went on, "All I would ask for, besides sufficient time of course, would be a certain degree of flexibility in what personnel and resources I am allowed to carry along on the mission."

"I understand how you operate, Captain." General Warlor spoke in tones as much full of frustration as they were with resignation. "Any less than complete autonomy for you, and you will pick up all your marbles and leave, thereby effectively scrapping the service of Officer Leung and others who refuse to serve without you. So very well; short of draining the Barack Obama of all its troops or some such, you have your flexibility. But understand this: We expect a full report in no later than three weeks. And if, at any moment before your report, forces from Tictoctic take aggressive action again, or we obtain credible evidence such action is imminent, we are not waiting a second longer to launch an all-out defense. Ideally, we wait for the results of your reconnaissance mission, because an additional starship equipped comparably to the Obama should be arriving by then.

"Again, Officer Leung, it is regrettable you were unable to secure safely the enemy saucer craft for us to more fully benefit from study of its military assets."

Buddy Leung nodded with a stiff upper lip.

Captain Helena Taylor was determined not to take the bait. She wasn't going to argue with the chair of the Joint Chiefs of Staff on any of her points. Instead, Helena merely said, also with a deferential nod, "Thank you."

"Well," said Spinner, as he exchanged looks with Warlor which suggested to Taylor they were expecting some pushback that obviously wasn't to be forthcoming, "the clock is tic-toc-ticking. I suppose we shouldn't be holding you up any longer."

On the shuttle pod back to the Smoke and Mirrors, Helena said, in the hope of receiving some mind-read illumination from Oodle-Noodle, "I am amazed they left matters as they left them, not pushing any further to learn what you or I have got in mind, Oodle-Noodle."

*It is two things, Captain,* Oodle-Noodle telepathed, proceeding not to disappoint Helena. *In a way they can't yet admit to themselves, they ARE disturbed, if not outright ashamed, by what the logic of their violence-embracing initiatives has led to on Fafama. Secondly, more significantly for now, they are planning to have the Smoke and Mirrors covertly shadowed by a cloaked pod craft. Its crew will be focused solely on obtaining information of military value. A complication for us, but one I believe we can steer around successfully.*

***

"I have to say, Professor Skepticus, I've never seen you in that particular pair of pants before." On their way to the navigation bridge of the Smoke and Mirrors, Helena Taylor and Buddy Leung happened upon both Dr. Aquinas and Dr. Skepticus. The starship captain couldn't help commenting; Skepticus's pants had a gray plastic sheen to them. It reminded her of how extraterrestrial clothing was portrayed in century-old, black-and-white science fiction movies. Anyway, she felt she needed some entry point for gently reminding these two curious creatures, who it seemed argued as much as they hung out together, that they should likewise be headed towards the bridge.

"There is a most specific reason you are seeing me thusly attired, Captain Taylor. Oh yes!! What you cannot observe is a pocket sewn onto the side of these specially made pants, wherein I have concealed one of your husband's most delicious chocolate chip cookies. My theory is-"

Helena nodded with a strained grin. She was trying hard to conceal her impatience given everything else on her platter; why didn't she keep her mouth shut about his pants?

"-the gaseous coherence from Fafama – that's what I have named it – "

"You mean, Dr. Skepticus, the ephemeral dragon," corrected Dr. Aquinas in his most imperious voice.

"You say po-tay-to, I sat po-tah-to. But you say dragon, I say GAS!" Dr. Skepticus wagged an admonishing forefinger in Aquinas's face. "The kind of gas that might as well be a random cloud in the sky you are mistaking for a rabbit! My theory is that the gaseous coherence precipitates a fiery reaction after being chemically attracted to the components of said cookie! My resultant hypothesis is this: If you place the correct barrier between that coherence and said cookie, the reaction will be prevented from happening!"

"Or the ephemeral dragon will be prevented from smelling 'said cookie,' thereby proving absolutely nothing. Captain," Aquinas didn't skip a beat, nor pause for breath, to emphasize his dismissiveness of his colleague's ideas, as he went on, "I know we are required to join you now on the bridge..."

"I was about to remind you of that."

"Yes, of course. However, I wanted to let you know I have made, I think I've made some progress in determining how, why the mirror array system successfully, most safely, cheats the speed of light, as it were."

"Oh?" There was a laugh in Buddy Leung's voice.

"Yes, Officer Leung, and it involves you. That progress consists in the realization we are looking at a quantum process on the *macro*scopic level. As surely as the act of observation, measurement impacts the otherwise indeterminate location of an electron in an electron shell, the fundamental workings of the mirror array would seem to be most profoundly influenced by its founding observer, which is namely YOU, Officer Leung!"

"Wait; so while you ridicule me for concealing a chocolate chip cookie inside my specially formulated pants, you are essentially arguing that the mirror array works because Officer Leung WISHES it to work??! Absurd!!"

"Not absurd! Are you familiar with the slit light experiment?"

"No, but I'm rather suspecting there is a slit brain here among us!"

Aquinas nodded, blithely oblivious to Skepticus's insult, and he continued, "The good news is, Officer Leung, I don't believe we will have to kill you to test my realization."

"So I won't have to go on a guilt trip about not allowing you to murder me? I can live with that!"

"YEOW!!" Dr. Skepticus suddenly wailed as he leapt off the floor clutching at the seat of his pants.

Buddy Leung thought he caught out the corner of his

eye a torch-like flame. It seemed to flare out of seemingly nothing more than thin air, in the vicinity of Skepticus's shiny gray pants.

"I hope it works out for him," Helena commented as Skepticus hurried into a nearby restroom. "Dr. Aquinas, you can bring your colleague up to speed on whatever he misses. We really have to get going to the navigation bridge. And Effy, you're welcome there as well." Helena glanced about for some telltale other sign of the creature.

Aquinas nodded, "There you go," with a chest-thumping sense of self-satisfaction.

Captain Taylor and Buddy Leung got welcomed back onto the navigation bridge with a standing ovation. In the case of Oodle-Noodle and Wafoodle-boodle, it would have been standing no matter what, with noisy leaf rustles in the place of applause.

Louisa Entroper felt peer pressure after glancing around. And so, she stood and clapped as slowly as she thought she could get away with clapping, and not be found impolite.

The applause soon died down. Perhaps, Chris mused, this was hastened by Aquinas's entrance after his wife and Buddy. The professor waved his hand as though the hero's reception were meant for him. Whatever the reason, Helena Taylor took a moment to survey and reflect on everyone there in attendance.

With Oomb steadily shrinking in the panoramic view-screen behind them, Helena first settled her gaze on Oodle-Noodle and Wafoodle-boodle. Their branches were intertwined in a loving embrace. If the plan succeeds, Helena thought to herself, they will be the ones deserving of the applause.

Then there was Deborah, the lead medical

technician, arm-in-arm with her wife, Officer Geena Murphy-Davis. They had both made a point of coming to Helena's office to assure her that if she wanted them on this mission, they would be there despite past disagreements. They appreciated how positively their relationship was accepted, and also the fact that, so far as they could gather, the captain had not in neither obvious nor subtle ways retaliated for their past support for her removal from the helm, including when Entroper was made captain. Helena had explained that, while she did not appreciate what they had done, and strongly disagreed with them on several issues, she also didn't want to always surround herself with yes-people. Besides, she did recognize that when it came to medicine in Deb's case and engineering in Geena's case, they were among the best. A group hug had ensued. What Helena did not share was how Oodle-Noodle's gentle telepathic prodding had guided her away from sending them both back home to Earth. *If I'm going to accept Oombian counsel, I may as well accept it all the way…until such time as I'm convinced they haven't figured out matters any better than any intelligent non-tree characters.*

*Certainly, Tanya with her matter-of-fact fearlessness in the face of extreme danger, and Ali with his always-gentle counsel, "truly," probably figured as much as anyone in my predisposition to give the Oombian perspective as much of a hearing as I have; look at them standing there hand-in-hand like two young lovers!*

*And then there are my two odd lovers, Buddy and Cathy. They are looking at what to do with their hands like two kids out on a first date.* Helena had previously thanked Cathy for agreeing to go along, despite thereby getting threatened with spending more time close to Buddy than she was used to in a typical year. Cathy's climate-engineering expertise would prove especially critical.

As for Pedro and Ludi, they had both been fully prepared to beg their way on board. But Helena was already sold, after what Buddy told her Pedro had contributed to the Fafama rescue mission. And Ludi was going to get tapped, anyway, for her phenomenal cooking and agricultural skills. About their insisting on bringing along their two-year-old daughter Alexita, at first Helena had resisted. Ali helped her to realize, however, that if their plan didn't succeed, none of the children would be safe from winding up on the Tictoctic menu, whether they remained back on Oomb, or they accompanied the adults all the way into, as it were, the belly of the beast.

Which also dovetailed conveniently, if ever more spinning-out-of-control complicatedly, with Ciela bringing along those homeless seven-year-old fraternal twins, Tomás and Jorge. And why was Ciela leaving her teaching job on Oomb?

"Sergeant Hanson, Sergeant Frankly, I understand some congratulations are in order."

"You betcha, Captain!" Fred Frankly stepped forward on the bridge, pulling Ciela by the hand alongside him. "I popped the question to Señorita Bacalao here, and she didn't know well enough about me to not say yes. We're engaged!" He held up Ciela's hand ceilingward to show off the engagement ring. Chris was reminded of a presidential or gubernatorial candidate holding up the running mate's hand at a political convention.

Ciela's mischievous adopted twins were not there to see this, as they were bedded down for a nap with Alexita under the watchful eyes of Rotonda and Placido:

more complication.

"And Sergeant Hanson, isn't it going to be a double wedding?" Helena prodded, smiling to see Guy's ears turn bright red.

"Yes, Captain, Yulala here-"

The last known surviving Fafaman leaned into his shoulder.

"-has done me the honor of also agreeing to holy matrimony."

"I'll be available for all the tips you need, good buddy, 'cause the matrimony won't be all that holy for me, except-"

Guy cupped his hand over Fred Frankly's mouth, which didn't stop Fred from winking. Dressed in full Marine Corps Honor Guard gear didn't seem to make the slightest difference where Sergeant Frankly was concerned.

As the rest assembled laughed and applauded, Helena made the easy call, not to embarrass Sergeant Hanson any further by mentioning Dr. Davis-Murphy's DNA work to try to give Guy and Yulala's interspecies baby production a realistic chance.

"Ahh hahve tahned ahff mah trahnslahtah, becahse Ah wahnt tah tahlk tah youah ahn Ahnglahsh." *(I have turned off my translator, because I want to talk to you in English.)* As Yulala stepped forward from her fiancé to speak, she caught Helena and everyone else off guard, except for Guy. He nodded proudly, if still red-earedly. "Cahptahn, Ah wahnted tah goah with Gahy ahn youah mishahn, naht ahnly becahse Ah lahve him, whahch is stahll ahlaht." *(Captain, I wanted to go with Guy on your mission, not only because I love him, which is still a lot.)* Yulala turned to give Guy a most affectionate regard he felt to his core, despite protective goggles hiding her nocturnal eyes. "But

Ah ahlso wahnt to do whaht Ah cahn doah. Ah know, Cahptahn Taylah, you would hahve rescuahed more thahn yah did, if yah could hahve. Yah shahld naht cahrry ahny guilaht fah the ahcshuhns of mah peopahl with thah weapahns with thaht youahr peopahl entrahstahd thahm. Ahlsoah, whaht smahll pahht ahf thah Oomb plahn Ah knowah, Ah lahike!" *(But I also want to do what I can do. I know, Captain Taylor, you would have rescued more than you did, if you could have. You should not carry any guilt for the actions of my people with the weapons with that your people entrusted them. Also, what small part of the Oomb plan I know, I like!)* As Yulala at this point, tears streaming down her cheeks, thrust an affirmative fist skyward, Guy gathered her into his arms with an unabashedly unembarrassed embrace. "To thah glory ahf Fafama!!" she shouted through her tears.

"TO THE GLORY OF FAFAMA!!!!!" everyone on the bridge answered in perfect unison.

As the resultant deafening applause subsided, Helena said in a faux-strict voice that brought on chuckles, "Officer Christopher Olsen-Taylor?"

"Yes, Captain?"

"I trust you have stocked up on plenty of chocolate chips plus the requisite other ingredients?"

"Ay, sí!" Ludi jumped in. "Made from ground-up, cocoa-like beans found on Oomb, the first chocolate chips of extraterrestrial origin! You have to try them, Yulala! They're delicious! This invisible dragon, he keeps burning that guy's pants to get at them!"

"Excuse me, Captain," said Yoon-hee with her eyes returned most intently to focus on her navigation console.

*Ah, Yoon-hee and Kevin, as solid in their care of the Smoke and Mirrors operation in my and Buddy's absence,* Helena took the time to reflect before responding, *as they are in their marriage*. "Yes, Officer Park-Smith? We've achieved the safe distance coordinates above the orbital plane for, uhh, what has to happen next?"

The look Louisa Entroper got at that point, Kevin thought, were she a rabbit, her ears would have been sticking straight up.

"We're there and parked, Captain."

"Excuse me, Captain," Entroper couldn't contain herself any further, "so what is it exactly that 'has to happen next'?"

"You need to know, all of you need to know, before we go any further, an important component of what we are going to be about."

"A reconnaissance mission, right?" Entroper was getting nervous.

"A reconnaissance mission, yes," Captain Taylor slowly nodded, "where we are not going to be carrying any weapons. We are going to eliminate our weapons capacity, entirely. You all have the right to know this, and I understand completely if this is intolerable for any of you. We can arrange for a shuttle pod delivery of you back to Oomb sooner rather than later. And this also applies to any other crew members throughout the Smoke and Mirrors, listening in on the intercom."

"Captain," Entroper couldn't contain herself any longer, "I understand that weapons wouldn't be expected to come into play. But, but flying into the heart of Tictoctic territory, is it really that wise to presume you won't need to resort to at least a minimum amount of their use? Besides which, the Smoke and Mirrors is retrofitted with them. They are there, whether they come in handy or not."

"They're actually going to come in handy right now, though not in a way you would imagine."

"Not in a way I would imagine?! What are you talking about?!"

"If I might, Captain," intervened Buddy Leung. "Dr. Entroper, I was involved in the retrofit design to assure that if we needed to, we could disengage the weapons package in one fell swoop."

"In 'one fell swoop'?!? Why would you need to do that?!"

"In this case, we need to do that," said Taylor in an as-matter-of-fact a voice as she could muster, "so we can set them off, detonate them, a safe distance away from anyone."

"Oh, I get it," Entroper nodded her head sarcastically, pretending she understood. "You detonate all your firepower out here above the planetary orbital plane. They detect this on Tictoctic, and they deduce we're that much more vulnerable to their next attack! Makes perfect sense, doesn't it, everyone?!?!" She made a sweeping look of everyone else assembled there. She was looking for someone, anyone, to chime in. Perhaps Dr. Murphy-Davis. But whether from shock or from too much tension, nobody else offered to speak. "Okay," she added at last, "so the plan is to waste all of those weapons. You received Warlor and Spinner's permission for this?"

"Not specifically."

"'Not specifically,' Captain?!"

*If I might add, Captain Taylor,* Oodle-Noodle intervened, *the harmless detonation of the weapons will not be a waste, if that sends a love message to Tictoctic prior to our arrival their end. Yes, I would actually hope they do detect exactly what we've done.*

"'A love message'?!?!? 'A LOVE MESSAGE'?!?!?!?! Captain?!?! Why don't you turn over command of the

Smoke and Mirrors to these, these bizarre creatures while you're at it?!?!"

"Like I said before, you, any of you, you have the option to leave if you're uncomfortable with what we're doing."

"Oh, I'm leaving. You don't have to ask me twice. I'm leaving." Entroper started making her way, stumbling a bit, towards the entrance onto the bridge.

"Hey, Captain," Fred Frankly spoke up, "do I still get to keep my AK-51? It's like my credit card back on Earth; don't like to leave home without it."

"No AK-51, Sergeant Frankly," said Taylor in her steadiest firmest voice. She was thinking about the black cloud that enveloped Fafama, with only the fire-y colors of out-of-control volcanic activity breaking through sporadically. "You will have to turn that over to us."

"Damn."

"So, no AK-51," Entroper paused to say. Clearly, where Ali was concerned, she was hoping against hope this would prove the deal-breaker, that this no-AK-51 business would precipitate an exodus off the bridge headed for the shuttle pod bay.

But no such exodus was forthcoming, so Louisa Entroper paused longer, this time to say, chest heaving with her anger, "Captain, you dishonor the sacrifice, you dishonor the memory, of every American Union soldier who has ever given their life for their country, for the freedom from evil tyranny the American Union represents."

"Captain Taylor, please, I have to," said Sergeant Hanson. "Officer Entroper, I disagree with you most profoundly. Every soldier who has ever fought in a war, every victim of war, will tell you war is hell. Any good alternatives found to war, their implementation would constitute the best way to honor those whose lives have been wrecked by war. As I see it, Captain Taylor, the extent to which every single soldier's sacrifice, every single war victim's fate, inspires humanity, of course including out-of-this-world humanity, plus other intelligent beings, to seek the workable alternatives to hate that the great religious and inspirational figures have dreamed of, none of those deaths and cripplings were in vain. Every single one of those deaths and cripplings will be honored in the most ultimate way. Not that I am yet fully convinced, to be bluntly honest, such workable alternatives actually exist for certain scenarios, this one included. To quote that old John Lennon song, though, I want to give peace a chance."

"You're all being seduced by the ability of these creatures." Entroper waved her hand in the general direction of Oodle-Noodle and Wafoodle-boodle. "Their mental telepathy, it's making you forget one basic fact also spoken of by all those religious figures: There IS evil in the world!"

*But is evil a presence, or an absence? Does hate have substance, or is it merely a deep abyss, empty of any loving faith? It sucks all who come near it down into a whirling vortex of ignorance and fear, like the suction effect from a vacuum?*

Oodle-Noodle's telepath earned him a parting scowl from Entroper.

***

"Helena, excuse me for saying so, but, it really does feel like you chased Dr. Entroper off the ship. That she had no alternative but to leave."

Deborah Davis-Murphy came up behind Captain Helena Taylor. Helena had walked up close to the navigation bridge's view-screen, to follow the flight of the shuttle pod carrying Entroper back to the battle cruiser in orbit around Oomb. That was, until it got lost amidst the haze of stars of the Milky Way Galaxy.

"Well, Deborah," Taylor turned to face the chief medical officer with a stiff upper lip, "we're just going to have to agree to disagree. You know, my greatest fear now is that there ARE no good solutions to be had to this situation, as Sergeant Hanson hinted. That every one of them, including doing nothing, leads to disaster. That ultimately, those futurists from decades ago will be proven correct. No civilization that continues to embrace violence can survive very far into its space age. I am unsure whether it is already too late for our civilization to evolve away from keeping war in its tool kit. But one thing I AM sure of: The militarization of Fafama resulted in its utter destruction."

"And you don't think Tictoctic will continue to thrive well into its space age were we to roll over and play dead, Captain? Which I'm not clear isn't what we're doing here."

"And you think they are thriving now?, having to seek food from other planets, Deb? You really think we're going to find all's well on their home world?"

"Excuse me, Captain; the shuttle pod is safely out of range, and the weapons retrofit is prepared for final disengagement from the Smoke and Mirrors."

"Very well, Officer Leung. Disengage!"

The panoramic view was shifted to showing the Smoke and Mirrors from the perspective of a nearby firefly donut. That particular surveillance object always ran on a parallel path, spiraling around the starship. It kept a constant check on hull integrity and other potential maintenance issues.

With Buddy Leung's depression of two green buttons simultaneously on the navigation control console, clunky sounds echoed throughout the navigation bridge. For Chris, they were reminiscent of a jet lowering its landing gear. What everyone noticed on the panoramic view-screen, next, was what those little mechanical pushes did to the retrofitted weaponry-encasing that received them. Disconnected, detached thereby from the ship's hull, one end of said encasing fell back away from the Smoke and Mirrors, ever so slowly.

Captain Taylor recalled where she had seen something like this, indeed had experienced something like this, before. It had been Dr. Entroper's team-building exercise, shortly before they arrived to Oomb for the second time. It was allowing yourself to fall backwards, and trusting someone behind you would not let you fall. It was having complete faith in the power of love and caring.

The weaponry-encasing separated entirely. It went spinning slowly, end over end, far from the Smoke and Mirrors. The panoramic view-screen got shifted, to follow that encasing until it got too far away to see with the unaided eye.

"Detonate, Captain?"

"Detonate, Buddy."

The next thing they knew, off in the star-studded distance to where the encasing had shrunk out of sight, there was a small flash of light, then a bigger one, and a bigger one still. At the last, there were multiple colorful silent bursts of light. As this light show continued, growing ever more spectacular from a chain reaction getting set off, Captain Helena Taylor thought to herself: Will this become the real meaning of fireworks displays?, how awe-inspiring explosions have gone from manifestations of war to celebrations of how war has forever gotten left behind?

As the final bursts of light faded away, Oodle-Noodle telepathed not only for everyone aboard the Smoke and Mirrors, but as well for all to whom she could extend herself on Oomb and in orbit around it, *Your Dr. Martin Luther King Jr. said, "Darkness cannot drive out darkness; only light can do that. Hate cannot drive out hate; only love can do that."*

"Advance guard fireflies are deployed. They are already one-half light-year ahead, smooth sailing all four quadrants, Captain."

"Ready with electromagnetic impulses, Yoon-hee?"

"Ready, Captain."

Helena Taylor returned to the captain's centrally located armchair. She backed away from the view-screen so she needn't take her eyes from it in the process. "Let's bloom the mirror arrays and head on out, full steam ahead, all the appropriate clichés."

"All the appropriate clichés, Captain!"

The ever-mysterious, ever-enigmatically beautiful stream of sparkling light particles developed flowing into the Smoke and Mirrors's photon evacuation tube, funneled there by the tulip mirror-array bloom.

Captain Helena Taylor thought to herself, *I remember the conclusion to the first movie produced in that antique Star Wars series. Luke Skywalker pushed aside all the guidance equipment, to aim unaided for the destruction of the Death Star as a voice told him, "May the Force be with you." The Oombians would have that we have done something incomparably better, pushing aside all weaponry to aim for a creative, non-destructive solution to the Tictoctic problem. And they would have that voice, their voice, whispering to me, "May the Force be with you...and may that force be love." I have to wonder what the English novelist I quoted at the outset of our first mission, Charles Dickens, would have thought. Would he have found this is a better thing, a far better thing we do, than we have ever done before...or a descent into an ever-deepening madness?*

# Appendix: Relativity

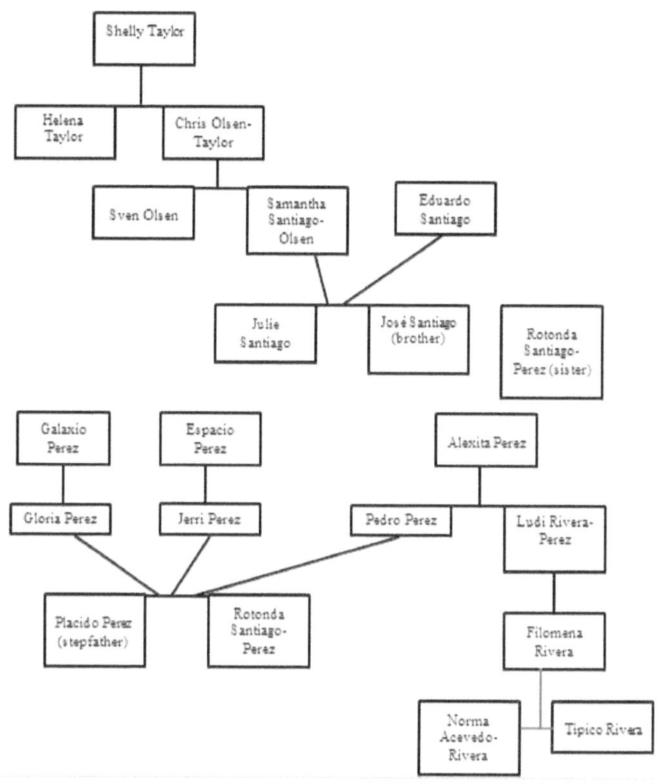

www.ingramcontent.com/pod-product-compliance
Lightning Source LLC
Chambersburg PA
CBHW031956060726
47497CB00015B/1

* 9 7 8 1 6 2 1 3 7 9 9 7 3 *